THE LINCOLN HIGHWAY

ALSO BY AMOR TOWLES

A Gentleman in Moscow
Rules of Civility

THE

LINCOLN HIGHWAY

—.—

Amor Towles

VIKING

VIKING
An imprint of Penguin Random House LLC
penguinrandomhouse.com

CREDITS
Pages viii–ix: Map based on an original design by Alex Coulter.
Page 268: Photo by Edward Hausner/The New York Times/Redux.

LIBRARY OF CONGRESS CATALOGING-IN-PUBLICATION DATA
Names: Towles, Amor, author.
Title: The Lincoln highway / Amor Towles.
Description: [New York] : Viking, [2021]
Identifiers: LCCN 2021024465 (print) | LCCN 2021024466 (ebook) |
ISBN 9780735222359 (hardcover) | ISBN 9780735222373 (ebook) |
ISBN 9780593489338 (international edition)
Classification: LCC PS3620.O945 L56 2021 (print) |
LCC PS3620.O945 (ebook) | DDC 813/.6—dc23
LC record available at https://lccn.loc.gov/2021024465
LC ebook record available at https://lccn.loc.gov/2021024466

Printed in the United States of America
1st Printing

Designed by Amanda Dewey

For
My brother Stokley
And
My sister Kimbrough

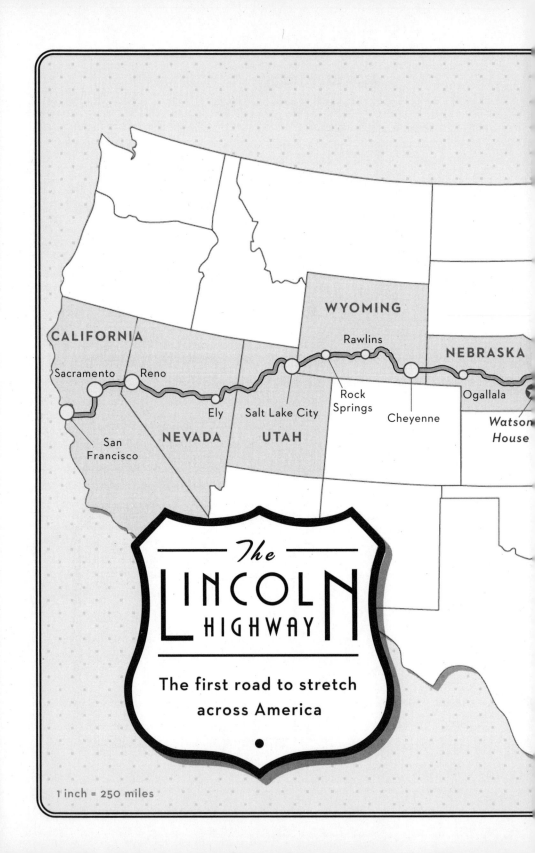

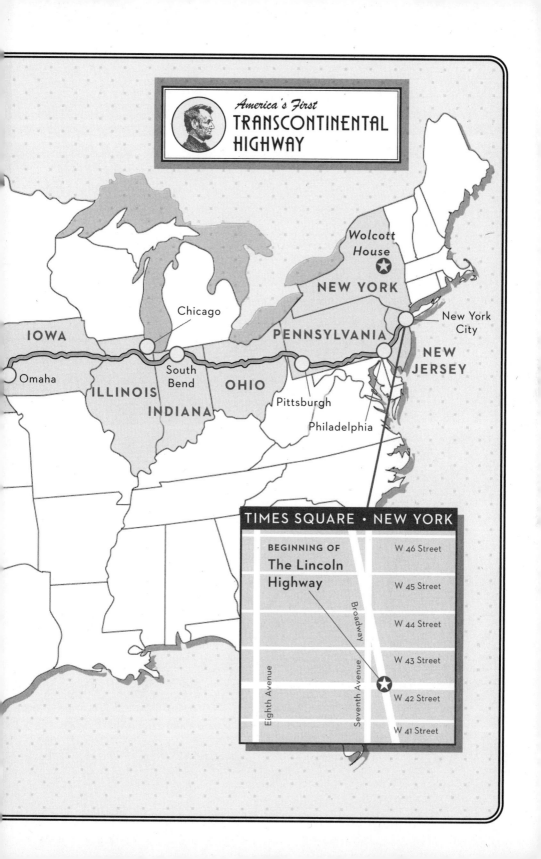

Evening and the flat land,
Rich and somber and always silent;
The miles of fresh-plowed soil,
Heavy and black, full of strength and harshness;
The growing wheat, the growing weeds,
The toiling horses, the tired men;
The long empty roads,
Sullen fires of sunset, fading,
The eternal, unresponsive sky.
Against all this, Youth . . .

—O *Pioneers!*, Willa Cather

TEN

—.—

Emmett

JUNE 12, 1954—The drive from Salina to Morgen was three hours, and for much of it, Emmett hadn't said a word. For the first sixty miles or so, Warden Williams had made an effort at friendly conversation. He had told a few stories about his childhood back East and asked a few questions about Emmett's on the farm. But this was the last they'd be together, and Emmett didn't see much sense in going into all of that now. So when they crossed the border from Kansas into Nebraska and the warden turned on the radio, Emmett stared out the window at the prairie, keeping his thoughts to himself.

When they were five miles south of town, Emmett pointed through the windshield.

—You take that next right. It'll be the white house about four miles down the road.

The warden slowed his car and took the turn. They drove past the McKusker place, then the Andersens' with its matching pair of large red barns. A few minutes later they could see Emmett's house standing beside a small grove of oak trees about thirty yards from the road.

To Emmett, all the houses in this part of the country looked like they'd been dropped from the sky. The Watson house just looked like it'd had a rougher landing. The roof line sagged on either side of the chimney and the window frames were slanted just enough that half the windows wouldn't quite open and the other half wouldn't quite shut. In another moment, they'd be able to see how the paint had been shaken right off the clapboard. But when they got within a hundred feet of the driveway, the warden pulled to the side of the road.

—Emmett, he said, with his hands on the wheel, before we drive in there's something I'd like to say.

That Warden Williams had something to say didn't come as much of a surprise. When Emmett had first arrived at Salina, the warden was a Hoosier named Ackerly, who wasn't inclined to put into words a piece of advice that could be delivered more efficiently with a stick. But Warden Williams was a modern man with a master's degree and good intentions and a framed photograph of Franklin D. Roosevelt hanging behind his desk. He had notions that he'd gathered from books and experience, and he had plenty of words at his disposal to turn them into counsel.

—For some of the young men who come to Salina, he began, whatever series of events has brought them under our sphere of influence is just the beginning of a long journey through a life of trouble. They're boys who were never given much sense of right or wrong as children and who see little reason for learning it now. Whatever values or ambitions we try to instill in them will, in all likelihood, be cast aside the moment they walk out from under our gaze. Sadly, for these boys it is only a matter of time before they find themselves in the correctional facility at Topeka, or worse.

The warden turned to Emmett.

—What I'm getting at, Emmett, is that you are not one of them. We haven't known each other long, but from my time with you I can tell that that boy's death weighs heavily on your conscience. No one imagines what happened that night reflects either the spirit of malice or an expression of your character. It was the ugly side of chance. But as a civilized society, we ask that even those who have had an unintended hand in the misfortune of others pay some retribution. Of course, the payment of the retribution is in part to satisfy those who've suffered the brunt of the misfortune—like this boy's family. But we also require that it be paid for the benefit of the young man who was the *agent* of misfortune. So that by having the opportunity to pay his debt, he too can find some solace, some sense of atonement, and thus begin the process of renewal. Do you understand me, Emmett?

—I do, sir.

—I'm glad to hear it. I know you've got your brother to care for now and the immediate future may seem daunting; but you're a bright young man and you've got your whole life ahead of you. Having paid your debt in full, I just hope you'll make the most of your liberty.

—That's what I intend to do, Warden.

And in that moment, Emmett meant it. Because he agreed with most of what the warden said. He knew in the strongest of terms that his whole life was ahead of him and he knew that he needed to care for his brother. He knew too that he had been an agent of misfortune rather than its author. But he didn't agree that his debt had been paid in full. For no matter how much chance has played a role, when by your hands you have brought another man's time on earth to its end, to prove to the Almighty that you are worthy of his mercy, that shouldn't take any less than the rest of your life.

The warden put the car in gear and turned into the Watsons'. In the clearing by the front porch were two cars—a sedan and a pickup. The warden parked beside the pickup. When he and Emmett got out of the car, a tall man with a cowboy hat in his hand came out the front door and off the porch.

—Hey there, Emmett.

—Hey, Mr. Ransom.

The warden extended his hand to the rancher.

—I'm Warden Williams. It was nice of you to take the trouble to meet us.

—It was no trouble, Warden.

—I gather you've known Emmett a long time.

—Since the day he was born.

The warden put a hand on Emmett's shoulder.

—Then I don't need to explain to you what a fine young man he is. I was just telling him in the car that having paid his debt to society, he's got his whole life ahead of him.

—He does at that, agreed Mr. Ransom.

The three men stood without speaking.

The warden had lived in the Midwest for less than a year now, but he knew from standing at the foot of other farmhouse porches that at this point in a conversation you were likely to be invited inside and offered something cool to drink; and when you received the invitation, you should be ready to accept because it would be taken as rude if you were to decline, even if you did have a three-hour drive ahead of you. But neither Emmett nor Mr. Ransom made any indication of asking the warden in.

—Well, he said after a moment, I guess I should be heading back.

Emmett and Mr. Ransom offered a final thanks to the warden, shook his hand, then watched as he climbed in his car and drove away. The warden was a quarter mile down the road when Emmett nodded toward the sedan.

—Mr. Obermeyer's?

—He's waiting in the kitchen.

—And Billy?

—I told Sally to bring him over a little later, so you and Tom can get your business done.

Emmett nodded.

—You ready to go in? asked Mr. Ransom.

—The sooner the better, said Emmett.

They found Tom Obermeyer seated at the small kitchen table. He was wearing a white shirt with short sleeves and a tie. If he was also wearing a suit coat, he must have left it in his car because it wasn't hanging on the back of the chair.

When Emmett and Mr. Ransom came through the door, they seemed to catch the banker off his guard, because he abruptly scraped back the chair, stood up, and stuck out his hand all in a single motion.

—Well, hey now, Emmett. It's good to see you.

Emmett shook the banker's hand without a reply.

Taking a look around, Emmett noted that the floor was swept, the counter clear, the sink empty, the cabinets closed. The kitchen looked cleaner than at any point in Emmett's memory.

—Here, Mr. Obermeyer said, gesturing to the table. Why don't we all sit down.

Emmett took the chair opposite the banker. Mr. Ransom remained standing, leaning his shoulder against the doorframe. On the table was a brown folder thick with papers. It was sitting just out of the banker's reach, as if it had been left there by somebody else. Mr. Obermeyer cleared his throat.

—First of all, Emmett, let me say how sorry I am about your father. He was a fine man and too young to be taken by illness.

—Thank you.

—I gather when you came for the funeral that Walter Eberstadt had a chance to sit down with you and discuss your father's estate.

—He did, said Emmett.

The banker nodded with a look of sympathetic understanding.

—Then I suspect Walter explained that three years ago your father took out a new loan on top of the old mortgage. At the time, he said it was to upgrade his equipment. In actuality, I suspect a good portion of that loan went to pay some older debts since the only new piece of farm equipment we could find on the property was the John Deere in the barn. Though I suppose that's neither here nor there.

Emmett and Mr. Ransom seemed to agree that this was neither here nor there because neither made any effort to respond. The banker cleared his throat again.

—The point I'm getting to is that in the last few years the harvest wasn't what your father had hoped; and this year, what with your father's passing, there isn't going to be a harvest at all. So we had no choice but to call in the loan. It's an unpleasant bit of business, I know, Emmett, but I want you to understand that it was not an easy decision for the bank to make.

—I should think it would be a pretty easy decision for you to make by now, said Mr. Ransom, given how much practice you get at making it.

The banker looked to the rancher.

—Now, Ed, you know that's not fair. No bank makes a loan in hopes of foreclosing.

The banker turned back to Emmett.

—The nature of a loan is that it requires the repayment of interest and principal on a timely basis. Even so, when a client in good standing falls behind, we do what we can to make concessions. To extend terms and defer collections. Your father is a perfect example. When he began falling behind, we gave him some extra time. And when he got sick, we gave him some more. But sometimes a man's bad luck becomes too great to surmount, no matter how much time you give him.

The banker reached out his arm to lay a hand on the brown folder, finally claiming it as his own.

—We could have cleared out the property and put it up for sale a month ago, Emmett. It was well within our rights to do so. But we didn't. We waited so that you could complete your term at Salina and come home to sleep in your own bed. We wanted you to have a chance to go through the house with your brother in an unhurried fashion, to organize your personal effects. Hell, we even had the power company leave on the gas and electricity at our own expense.

—That was right kind of you, said Emmett.

Mr. Ransom grunted.

—But now that you are home, continued the banker, it's probably best for everyone involved if we see this process through to its conclusion. As the executor of your father's estate, we'll need you to sign a few papers. And within a few weeks, I'm sorry to say, we'll need you to make arrangements for you and your brother to move out.

—If you've got something that needs signing, let's sign it.

Mr. Obermeyer took a few documents from the folder. He turned them around so that they were facing Emmett and peeled back pages, explaining the purpose of individual sections and subsections, translating the terminology, pointing to where the documents should be signed and where initialed.

—You got a pen?

Mr. Obermeyer handed Emmett his pen. Emmett signed and initialed the papers without consideration, then slid them back across the table.

—That it?

—There is one other thing, said the banker, after returning the documents safely to their folder. The car in the barn. When we did the routine inventory of the house, we couldn't find the registration or the keys.

—What do you need them for?

—The second loan your father took out wasn't for specific pieces of agricultural machinery. It was against any new piece of capital equipment purchased for the farm, and I'm afraid that extends to personal vehicles.

—Not to that car it doesn't.

—Now, Emmett . . .

—It doesn't because that piece of capital equipment isn't my father's. It's mine.

Mr. Obermeyer looked to Emmett with a mixture of skepticism and sympathy—two emotions that in Emmett's view had no business being on the same face at the same time. Emmett took his wallet from his pocket, withdrew the registration, and put it on the table.

The banker picked it up and reviewed it.

—I see that the car is in your name, Emmett, but I'm afraid that if it was purchased by your father on your behalf . . .

—It was not.

The banker looked to Mr. Ransom for support. Finding none, he turned back to Emmett.

—For two summers, said Emmett, I worked for Mr. Schulte to earn the money to buy that car. I framed houses. Shingled roofs. Repaired porches. As a matter of fact, I even helped install those new cabinets in your kitchen. If you don't believe me, you're welcome to go ask Mr. Schulte. But either way, you're not touching that car.

Mr. Obermeyer frowned. But when Emmett held out his hand for the registration, the banker returned it without protest. And when he left with his folder, he wasn't particularly surprised that neither Emmett nor Mr. Ransom bothered seeing him to the door.

When the banker was gone, Mr. Ransom went outside to wait for Sally and Billy, leaving Emmett to walk the house on his own.

Like the kitchen, Emmett found the front room tidier than usual—with the pillows propped in the corners of the couch, the magazines in a neat little stack on the coffee table, and the top of his father's desk rolled down. Upstairs in Billy's room, the bed was made, the collections of bottle caps and bird feathers were neatly arranged on their shelves, and one of the windows had been opened to let in some air. A window must have been opened on the other side of the hall too because there was enough of a draft to stir the fighter planes hanging over Billy's bed: replicas of a Spitfire, a Warhawk, and a Thunderbolt.

Emmett smiled softly to see them.

He had built those planes when he was about Billy's age. His mother had given him the kits back in 1943 when all Emmett or his friends could talk about were the battles unfolding in the European and Pacific theaters, about Patton at the head of the Seventh Army storming the beaches of Sicily, and Pappy Boyington's Black Sheep Squadron taunting the enemy over the Solomon Sea. Emmett had assembled the models on the kitchen table with all the precision of an engineer. He had painted the insignias and serial numbers on the fuselages with four tiny bottles of enamel paint and a fine-haired brush. When they were done, Emmett had lined them up on his bureau in a diagonal row just like they would have been on the deck of a carrier.

From the age of four, Billy had admired them. Sometimes when Emmett would come home from school, he would find Billy standing on a chair beside the bureau talking to himself in the language of a fighter pilot. So when Billy turned six, Emmett and his father hung the planes from the ceiling over Billy's bed as a birthday surprise.

Emmett continued down the hall to his father's room, where he found the same evidence of tidiness: the bed made, the photographs on the bureau dusted, the curtains tied back with a bow. Emmett approached one of the windows and looked out across his father's land. After being plowed and planted for twenty years, the fields had been left untended for just one season and you could already see the tireless advance of nature—the sagebrush and ragwort and ironweed establishing themselves among the prairie grasses. If left untended for another few years, you wouldn't be able to tell that anyone had ever farmed these acres at all.

Emmett shook his head.

Bad luck . . .

That's what Mr. Obermeyer had called it. A bad luck that was too great to surmount. And the banker was right, up to a point. When it came to bad luck, Emmett's father always had plenty to spare. But Emmett knew that wasn't the extent of the matter. For when it came to bad judgment, Charlie Watson had plenty of that to spare too.

Emmett's father had come to Nebraska from Boston in 1933 with his new wife and a dream of working the land. Over the next two decades, he had tried to grow wheat, corn, soy, even alfalfa, and had been thwarted at every turn. If the crop he chose to grow one year needed plenty of water, there were two years of drought. When he switched to a crop that needed plenty of sun, thunderclouds gathered in the west. Nature is merciless, you might counter. It's indifferent and unpredictable. But a farmer who changes the crop he's growing every two or three years? Even as a boy, Emmett knew that was a sign of a man who didn't know what he was doing.

Out behind the barn was a special piece of equipment imported from Germany for the harvesting of sorghum. At one point deemed essential, it was soon unnecessary, and now no longer of use—because his father hadn't had the good sense to resell it once he'd stopped growing sorghum. He just let it sit in the clearing behind the barn exposed to the rain and snow. When Emmett was Billy's age and his friends would come over from the neighboring farms to play—boys who, at the height of the war, were eager to climb on any piece of machinery and pretend it was a tank—they wouldn't even set foot on the harvester, sensing instinctively that it was some kind of ill omen, that within its rusting hulk was a legacy of failure that one should steer clear of whether from politeness or self-preservation.

So one evening when Emmett was fifteen and the school year nearly over, he had ridden his bike into town, knocked on Mr. Schulte's door, and asked for a job. Mr. Schulte was so bemused by Emmett's request that he sat him down at the dinner table and had him brought a slice of pie. Then he asked Emmett why on earth a boy who was raised on a farm would want to spend his summer pounding nails.

It wasn't because Emmett knew Mr. Schulte to be a friendly man, or because he lived in one of the nicest houses in town. Emmett went to Mr. Schulte because he figured that no matter what happened, a carpenter would always have work. No matter how well you build them, houses run down. Hinges loosen, floorboards wear, roof seams separate. All you had to do was stroll through the Watson house to witness the myriad ways in which time can take its toll on a homestead.

In the months of summer, there were nights marked by the roll of thunder or the whistle of an arid wind on which Emmett could hear his father stirring in the next room, unable to sleep—and not without reason. Because a farmer with a mortgage was like a man walking on the railing of a bridge with his arms outstretched and his eyes closed. It was a way of life in which the difference between abundance and ruin could be measured by a few inches of rain or a few nights of frost.

But a carpenter didn't lie awake at night worrying about the weather. He *welcomed* the extremes of nature. He welcomed the blizzards and downpours and tornadoes. He welcomed the onset of mold and the onslaughts of insects. These were the natural forces that slowly but inevitably undermined the integrity of a house, weakening its foundations, rotting its beams, and wilting its plaster.

Emmett didn't say all of this when Mr. Schulte asked his question. Putting his fork down, he simply replied:

—The way I figure it, Mr. Schulte, it was Job who had the oxen, and Noah who had the hammer.

Mr. Schulte gave a laugh and hired Emmett on the spot.

For most of the farmers in the county, if their eldest came home one night with news that he'd taken a job with a carpenter, they would have given him a talking-to he wouldn't soon forget. Then, for good measure, they would have driven over to the carpenter's house and given him a few words—a few words to remember the next time he had the inclination to interfere with the upbringing of another man's son.

But the night Emmett came home and told his father he had secured a job with Mr. Schulte, his father hadn't grown angry. He had listened carefully. After a moment of reflection, he said that Mr. Schulte was a good man and carpentry a useful skill. And on the first day of summer, he made Emmett a hearty breakfast and packed him a lunch, then sent him off with his blessing to another man's trade.

And maybe that was a sign of bad judgment too.

—·—

When Emmett came back downstairs, he found Mr. Ransom sitting on the porch steps with his forearms on his knees and his hat still in his hand. Emmett sat beside him and they both looked out across the unplanted fields. Half a mile in the distance, you could just make out the fence that marked the beginning of the older man's ranch. By Emmett's last accounting, Mr. Ransom had over nine hundred head of cattle and eight men in his employ.

—I want to thank you for taking in Billy, Emmett said.

—Taking in Billy was the least we could do. Besides, you can imagine how much it pleased Sally. She's about had it with keeping house for me, but caring for your brother's another matter. We've *all* been eating better since Billy arrived.

Emmett smiled.

—Just the same. It made a big difference to Billy; and it was a comfort to me knowing that he was in your home.

Mr. Ransom nodded, accepting the younger man's expression of gratitude.

—Warden Williams seems like a good man, he said after a moment.

—He is a good man.

—Doesn't seem like a Kansan. . . .

—No. He grew up in Philadelphia.

Mr. Ransom turned his hat in his hand. Emmett could tell that something was on his neighbor's mind. He was trying to decide how to say it, or whether to say it. Or maybe he was just trying to pick the right moment to say it. But sometimes the moment is picked for you, as when a cloud of dust a mile up the road signaled his daughter's approach.

—Emmett, he began, Warden Williams was right to say that you've paid your debt—as far as society is concerned. But this here's a small town, a lot smaller than Philadelphia, and not everyone in Morgen is going to see it the way the warden does.

—You're talking about the Snyders.

—I am talking about the Snyders, Emmett, but not just the Snyders. They've got cousins in this county. They've got neighbors and old family friends. They've got people they do business with and members of their congregation. We all know that whatever trouble Jimmy Snyder happened to find himself in was generally of Jimmy's own making. In his seventeen years, he was the engineer of a lifetime of shit piles. But that don't make any difference to his brothers. Especially after they lost Joe, Jr., in the war. If they were none too pleased that you got just eighteen months in Salina, they were in a state of righteous fury when they learned you'd be let out a few months early because of your father's passing. They're likely to make you feel the brunt of that fury as much and as often as they can. So while you do have your whole life in front of you, or rather, because you have your whole life in front of you, you may want to consider starting it somewhere other than here.

—You've no need to worry about that, said Emmett. Forty-eight hours from now, I don't expect Billy and me to be in Nebraska.

Mr. Ransom nodded.

—Since your father didn't leave much behind, I'd like to give you two a little something to help you get started.

—I couldn't take your money, Mr. Ransom. You've done enough for us already.

—Then consider it a loan. You can pay it back once you get yourself situated.

—For the time being, observed Emmett, I think the Watsons have had their fill of loans.

Mr. Ransom smiled and nodded. Then he stood and put his hat on his head as the old pickup they called Betty roared into the driveway with Sally behind the wheel and Billy in the passenger seat. Before she had skidded to a stop with a backfire out of the exhaust, Billy was opening the door and jumping to the ground. Wearing a canvas backpack that reached from his shoulders to the seat of his pants, he ran right past Mr. Ransom and wrapped his arms around Emmett's waist.

Emmett got down on his haunches so he could hug his little brother back.

Sally was approaching now in a brightly colored Sunday dress with a baking dish in her hands and a smile on her face.

Mr. Ransom took in the dress and the smile, philosophically.

—Well now, she said, look who's here. Don't you squeeze the life out of him, Billy Watson.

Emmett stood and put a hand on his brother's head.

—Hello, Sally.

As was her habit when nervous, Sally got right down to business.

—The house has been swept and all the beds have been made and there's fresh soap in the bathroom, and butter, milk, and eggs in the icebox.

—Thank you, said Emmett.

—I suggested the two of you should join us for supper, but Billy insisted you have your first meal at home. But seeing as you're just back, I made the two of you a casserole.

—You didn't have to go to all that trouble, Sally.

—Trouble or not, here it is. All you have to do is put it in the oven at 350° for forty-five minutes.

As Emmett took the casserole in hand, Sally shook her head.

—I should have written that down.

—I think Emmett will be able to remember the instructions, said Mr. Ransom. And if he doesn't, Billy surely will.

—You put it in the oven at 350° for forty-five minutes, said Billy.

Mr. Ransom turned to his daughter.

—I'm sure these boys are eager to catch up, and we've got some things to see to at home.

—I'll just go in for a minute to make sure that everything—

—Sally, Mr. Ransom said in a manner that broached no dissent.

Sally pointed at Billy and smiled.

—You be good, little one.

Emmett and Billy watched as the Ransoms climbed into their trucks and drove back up the road. Then Billy turned to Emmett and hugged him again.

—I'm glad you're home, Emmett.

—I'm glad to be home, Billy.

—You don't have to go back to Salina this time, do you?

—No. I never have to go back to Salina. Come on.

Billy released Emmett, and the brothers went into the house. In the kitchen, Emmett opened the icebox and slid the casserole onto a lower shelf. On the top shelf were the promised milk and eggs and butter. There was also a jar of homemade applesauce and another of peaches in syrup.

—You want something to eat?

—No, thank you, Emmett. Sally made me a peanut butter sandwich just before we came over.

—How about some milk?

—Sure.

As Emmett brought the glasses of milk to the table, Billy took off his backpack and set it on an empty chair. Unbuckling the uppermost flap, he carefully removed and unfolded a little package wrapped in aluminum foil. It was a stack of eight cookies. He put two on the table, one for Emmett and one for himself. Then he closed the foil, put the rest of the cookies back in his backpack, rebuckled the flap, and returned to his seat.

—That's quite a pack, Emmett said.

—It's a genuine US Army backpack, said Billy. Although it's what they call an army surplus backpack because it never actually made it to the war. I bought it at Mr. Gunderson's store. I also got a surplus flashlight and a surplus compass and this surplus watch.

Billy held out his arm to show the watch hanging loosely on his wrist.

—It even has a second hand.

After expressing his admiration for the watch, Emmett took a bite of the cookie.

—Good one. Chocolate chip?

—Yep. Sally made them.

—You help?

—I cleaned the bowl.

—I bet you did.

—Sally actually made us a whole batch, but Mr. Ransom said she was overdoing it, so she told him that she would just give us four, but secretly she gave us eight.

—Lucky for us.

—Luckier than just getting four. But not as lucky as getting the whole batch.

As Emmett smiled and took a sip of milk, he sized up his brother over the rim of the glass. He was about an inch taller and his hair was shorter, as it would be in the Ransom house, but otherwise he seemed the same in body and spirit. For Emmett, leaving Billy had been the hardest part of going to Salina, so he was happy to find him so little changed. He was happy to be sitting with him at the old kitchen table. He could tell that Billy was happy to be sitting there too.

—School year end all right? Emmett asked, setting down his glass.

Billy nodded.

—I got a hundred and five percent on my geography test.

—A hundred and five percent!

—Usually, there's no such thing as a hundred and five percent, Billy explained. Usually, one hundred percent of anything is as much as you can get.

—So how'd you wrangle another five percent out of Mrs. Cooper?

—There was an extra-credit question.

—What was the question?

Billy quoted from memory.

—*What is the tallest building in the world.*

—And you knew the answer?

—I did.

. . .

—Aren't you going to tell me?

Billy shook his head.

—That would be cheating. You have to learn it for yourself.

—Fair enough.

After a moment of silence, Emmett realized that he was staring into his milk. He was the one now with something on his mind. He was the one trying to decide how, or whether, or when to say it.

—Billy, he began, I don't know what Mr. Ransom's told you, but we're not going to be able to live here anymore.

—I know, said Billy. Because we're foreclosed.

—That's right. Do you understand what that means?

—It means the Savings and Loan owns our house now.

—That's right. Even though they're taking the house, we could stay in Morgen. We could live with the Ransoms for a while, I could go back to work for Mr. Schulte, come fall you could go back to school, and eventually we could afford to get a place of our own. But I've been thinking that this might be a good time for you and me to try something new . . .

Emmett had thought a lot about how he would put this, because he was worried that Billy would be disconcerted by the notion of leaving Morgen, especially so soon after their father's death. But Billy wasn't disconcerted at all.

—I was thinking the same thing, Emmett.

—You were?

Billy nodded with a hint of eagerness.

—With Daddy gone and the house foreclosed, there's no need for us to stay in Morgen. We can pack up our things and drive to California.

—I guess we're in agreement, said Emmett with a smile. The only difference is that I think we should be moving to Texas.

—Oh, we can't be moving to Texas, said Billy, shaking his head.

—Why's that?

—Because we've got to be moving to California.

Emmett started to speak, but Billy had already gotten up from his chair and gone to his backpack. This time, he opened the front pocket, removed a small manila envelope, and returned to his seat. As he carefully unwound the red thread that sealed the envelope's flap, he began to explain.

—After Daddy's funeral, when you went back to Salina, Mr. Ransom sent Sally and me over to the house to look for important papers. In the bottom drawer of Daddy's bureau, we found a metal box. It wasn't locked, but it was the kind of box you *could* lock if you wanted to. Inside it were important papers, just as Mr. Ransom had said there'd be—like our birth certificates and Mom and Dad's marriage license. But at the bottom of the box, at the very bottom, I found these.

Billy tipped the envelope over the table and out slid nine postcards.

Emmett could tell from the condition of the cards that they weren't exactly old and weren't exactly new. Some of them were photographs and some were illustrations, but all were in color. The one on top was a picture of the Welsh Motor Court in Ogallala, Nebraska—a modern-looking lodge with white cabanas and roadside plantings and a flagpole flying the American flag.

—They're postcards, Billy said. To you and me. From Mom.

Emmett was taken aback. Nearly eight years had passed since their mother had tucked the two of them in bed, kissed them goodnight, and walked out the door—and they hadn't heard a word from her since. No phone calls. No letters. No neatly wrapped packages arriving just in time for Christmas. Not even a bit of gossip from someone who'd happened to hear something from somebody else. At least, that's what Emmett had understood to be the case, until now.

Emmett picked up the card of the Welsh Motor Court and turned it over. Just as Billy had said, it was addressed to the two of them in their mother's elegant script. In the manner of postcards, the text was limited to a few lines. Together, the sentences expressed how much she already missed them despite having only been gone for a day. Emmett picked up another card from the pile. In the upper left-hand corner was a cowboy on the back of a horse. The lariat that he was spinning extended into the foreground and spelled out *Greetings from Rawlins, Wyoming—the Metropolis of the Plains*. Emmett turned the card over. In six sentences, including one that wrapped around the lower right-hand corner, their mother wrote that while she had yet to see a cowpoke with a lasso in Rawlins, she had seen plenty of cows. She concluded by expressing once again how much she loved and missed them both.

Emmett scanned the other cards on the table, taking in the names of the various towns, the motels and restaurants, sights and landmarks, noting that all but one of the pictures promised a bright blue sky.

Conscious that his brother was watching him, Emmett maintained an unchanged expression. But what he was feeling was the sting of resentment—resentment toward their father. He must have intercepted the cards and hidden them away. No matter how angry he had been with his wife, he had no right to keep them from his sons, certainly not from Emmett, who had been old enough to read them for himself. But Emmett felt the sting for no more than a moment. Because he knew that his father had done the only sensible thing. After all, what good could come from the occasional reception of a few sentences written on the back of a three-by-five card by a woman who had willfully abandoned her own children?

Emmett put the postcard from Rawlins back on the table.

—You remember how Mom left us on the fifth of July? asked Billy.

—I remember.

—She wrote us a postcard every day for the next nine days.

Emmett picked up the card from Ogallala again and looked just above the spot where their mother had written *Dearest Emmett and Billy*, but there was no date.

—Mom didn't write down the dates, Billy said. But you can tell from the postmarks.

Taking the Ogallala card from Emmett's hand, Billy turned all the cards over, spread them on the table, and pointed from postmark to postmark.

—July fifth. July sixth. There was no July seventh, but there are two July eighths. That's because in 1946, July seventh was on a Sunday and the post office is closed on Sunday, so she had to mail two of the cards on Monday. But look at this.

Billy went back to the front pocket of his backpack and took out something that looked like a pamphlet. When he unfolded it on the table, Emmett could see it was a road map of the United States from a Phillips 66. Cutting all the way across the middle of the map was a roadway that had been scored by Billy in black ink. In the western half of the country, the names of nine towns along the route had been circled.

—This is the Lincoln Highway, explained Billy, pointing to the long black line. It was invented in 1912 and was named for Abraham Lincoln and was the very first road to stretch from one end of America to the other.

Starting on the Atlantic Seaboard, Billy began following the highway with his fingertip.

—It starts in Times Square in New York City and it ends three thousand three hundred and ninety miles away in Lincoln Park in

San Francisco. And it passes right through Central City, just twenty-five miles from our house.

Billy paused to move his finger from Central City to the little black star that he had drawn on the map to represent their home.

—When Mom left us on the fifth of July, this is the way she went . . .

Taking up the postcards, Billy turned them over and began laying them across the lower half of the map in a westward progression, placing each card under its corresponding town.

Ogallala.

Cheyenne.

Rawlins.

Rock Springs.

Salt Lake City.

Ely.

Reno.

Sacramento.

Until the last card, which showed a large, classical building rising above a fountain in a park in San Francisco.

Billy gave an exhale of satisfaction to have the cards laid out in order on the table. But the whole collection made Emmett uneasy, like the two of them were looking at someone else's private correspondence—something they had no business seeing.

—Billy, he said, I'm not sure that we should be going to California. . . .

—We have to go to California, Emmett. Don't you see? That's why she sent us the postcards. So that we could follow her.

—But she hasn't sent a postcard in eight years.

—Because July thirteenth was when she stopped moving. All we have to do is take the Lincoln Highway to San Francisco and that's where we'll find her.

Emmett's immediate instinct was to say something to his brother that was sensible and dissuasive. Something about how their mother didn't necessarily stop in San Francisco; how she could easily have continued on, and most likely had; and that while she might have been thinking of her sons on those first nine nights, all evidence suggested that she hadn't been thinking of them since. In the end, he settled for pointing out that even if she were in San Francisco, it would be virtually impossible for them to find her.

Billy nodded with the expression of one who had already considered this dilemma.

—Remember how you told me that Mom loved fireworks so much, she took us all the way to Seward on the Fourth of July just so we could see the big display?

Emmett did not remember telling this to his brother, and all things considered, he couldn't imagine having ever had the inclination to do so. But he couldn't deny it was true.

Billy reached for the last postcard, the one with the classical building and the fountain. Turning it over, he ran his finger along their mother's script.

—*This is the Palace of the Legion of Honor in San Francisco's Lincoln Park and every year on the Fourth of July it has one of the biggest fireworks displays in all of California!*

Billy looked up at his brother.

—That's where she'll be, Emmett. At the fireworks display at the Palace of the Legion of Honor on the Fourth of July.

—Billy . . . , Emmett began.

But Billy, who could already hear the skepticism in his brother's voice, began shaking his head, vigorously. Then looking back down at the map on the table, he ran his finger along their mother's route.

—Ogallala to Cheyenne, Cheyenne to Rawlins, Rawlins to Rock Springs, Rock Springs to Salt Lake City, Salt Lake City to Ely, Ely to Reno, Reno to Sacramento, and Sacramento to San Francisco. That's the way we go.

Emmett sat back in his chair and considered.

He had not chosen Texas at random. He had thought about the question of where he and his brother should go, carefully and systematically. He had spent hours in the little library at Salina turning through the pages of the almanac and the volumes of the encyclopedia until the question of where they should go had become perfectly clear. But Billy had been pursuing his own line of thinking just as carefully, just as systematically, and he could see his own answer to the question with just as much clarity.

—All right, Billy, I'll tell you what. Why don't you put those back in their envelope and let me take a little time to think about what you've said.

Billy began nodding now.

—That's a good idea, Emmett. That's a good idea.

Gathering the postcards together in their east-to-west order, Billy slipped them into their envelope, spun the red thread until they were securely sealed, and returned them to his pack.

—You take a little time to think about it, Emmett. You'll see.

— · —

Upstairs, while Billy occupied himself in his room, Emmett took a long, hot shower. When he was done, he picked his clothes off the floor—the clothes that he'd worn both to and from Salina—removed the pack of cigarettes from the shirt pocket, and threw the heap in the trash. After a moment, he threw the cigarettes away too, being sure to tuck them under the clothes.

In his room he dressed in a fresh pair of jeans and denim shirt along with his favorite belt and boots. Then he reached into his top bureau drawer and took out a pair of socks tucked into a ball. Unfolding the socks, he gave one of them a shake until out came the keys to his car. Then he crossed the hall and stuck his head into his brother's room.

Billy was sitting on the floor beside his backpack. In his lap was the old blue tobacco tin with the portrait of George Washington on it, while on the rug were all his silver dollars laid out in columns and rows.

—Looks like you found a few more while I was away, said Emmett.

—Three, Billy answered while carefully putting one of the dollars in its place.

—How many more to go?

With his index finger Billy poked at the empty spots in the grid.

—1881. 1894. 1895. 1899. 1903.

—You're getting pretty close.

Billy nodded in agreement.

—But 1894 and 1895 will be very hard to find. I was lucky to find 1893.

Billy looked up at his brother.

—Have you been thinking about California, Emmett?

—I have been thinking about it, but I need to think about it a little bit more.

—That's okay.

As Billy turned his attention back to the silver dollars, Emmett looked around his brother's room for the second time that day, once again taking in the collections that were neatly arranged on their shelves and the planes that hung over the bed.

—Billy . . .

Billy looked up again.

—Whether we end up going to Texas or California, I think it may be best if we plan to travel light. Since we'll be making something of a fresh start.

—I was thinking the same thing, Emmett.

—You were?

—Professor Abernathe says that the intrepid traveler often sets out with what little he can fit in a kit bag. That's why I bought my backpack at Mr. Gunderson's store. So that I'd be ready to leave as soon as you got home. It already has everything in it that I need.

—Everything?

—Everything.

Emmett smiled.

—I'm headed out to the barn to check on the car. You want to come?

—Now? asked Billy in surprise. Hold on! Wait a second! Don't go without me!

Having carefully laid out the silver dollars in chronological order, Billy now swept them up and began pouring them back into the tobacco tin as quickly as he could. Closing the lid, he put the tin back in his backpack and the backpack back on his back. Then he led the way downstairs and out the door.

As they crossed the yard, Billy looked over his shoulder to report that Mr. Obermeyer had put a padlock on the barn doors, but Sally had broken it off with the crowbar she kept in the back of her truck.

Sure enough, at the barn door they found the bracket—with the padlock still secured to it—hanging loosely on its screws. Inside, the air was warm and familiar, smelling of cattle though there hadn't been cattle on the farm since Emmett was a boy.

Emmett paused to let his eyes adjust. Before him was the new John Deere and behind that a battered old combine. Proceeding to the back of the barn, Emmett stopped before a large, sloping object draped with canvas.

—Mr. Obermeyer took off the cover, said Billy, but Sally and I put it back.

Gripping the canvas by the corner, Emmett pulled with both hands until it was piled at his feet, and there, waiting just where he'd left it fifteen months ago, was a powder-blue, four-door hardtop—his 1948 Studebaker Land Cruiser.

After running his palm along the surface of the hood, Emmett opened the driver's door and climbed inside. For a moment, he sat with his hands on the steering wheel. When he'd bought her, she already had 80,000 miles on the odometer, dents in the hood, and cigarette burns in the seat covers, but she ran smoothly enough. Inserting and turning the key, he pushed the starter, ready for the soothing rumble of the engine—but there was silence.

Billy, who had been keeping his distance, approached, tentatively.

—Is it broken?

—No, Billy. The battery must be dead. It happens when you leave a car idle for too long. But it's an easy thing to fix.

Looking relieved, Billy sat down on a hay bale and took off his backpack.

—You want another cookie, Emmett?

—I'm fine. But you go right ahead.

As Billy opened his backpack, Emmett climbed out of the car, stepped to the rear, and opened the trunk. Satisfied that the upright lid blocked his brother's view, Emmett pulled back the felt that covered the recess in which the spare tire rested and gently ran his hand around its outer curve. At the top, he found the envelope with his name on it, right where his father had said it would be. Inside was a note in his father's script.

Another handwritten missive from another ghost, thought Emmett.

Dear Son,

By the time you read this, I imagine the farm will be in the hands of the bank. You may be angry or disappointed with me as a result, and I wouldn't blame you for being so.

It would shock you to know how much my father left me when he died, how much my grandfather left my father, and how much my great-grandfather left him. Not simply stocks and bonds, but houses and paintings. Furniture and tableware. Memberships in clubs and societies. All three of those men were

*devoted to the Puritan tradition of finding favor in the eyes of
the Lord by leaving more to their children than had been
left to them.*

*In this envelope, you will find all that I have to leave
you—two legacies, one great, one small, both a form of sacrilege.*

*As I write this, it shames me some to know that in leading
my life as I have, I have broken the virtuous cycle of thrift
established by my forebears. But at the same time, it fills me with
pride to know that you will undoubtedly achieve more with this
small remembrance than I could have achieved with a fortune.*

With love and admiration,

Your father, Charles William Watson

Attached to the letter by a paper clip was the first of the two
legacies—a single page torn from an old book.

Emmett's father wasn't one to lash out at his children in anger even
when they deserved it. In fact, the only time Emmett could remember
his father expressing unmitigated ire toward him was when he was sent
home from school for defacing a textbook. As his father made painfully
clear that night, to deface the pages of a book was to adopt the manner
of a Visigoth. It was to strike a blow against that most sacred and noble
of man's achievements—the ability to set down his finest ideas and
sentiments so that they might be shared through the ages.

For his father to tear a page from any book was a sacrilege. What
was even more shocking was that the page was torn from Ralph Waldo
Emerson's *Essays*—that book which his father held in greater esteem
than any other. Near the bottom, his father had carefully underlined
two sentences in red ink.

There is a time in every man's education when he
arrives at the conviction that envy is ignorance; that
imitation is suicide; that he must take himself for better,
for worse, as his portion; that though the wide universe

is full of good, no kernel of nourishing corn can come to him but through his toil bestowed on that plot of ground which is given to him to till. The power which resides in him is new in nature, and none but he knows what that is which he can do, nor does he know until he has tried.

Emmett recognized immediately that this passage from Emerson represented two things at once. First, it was an excuse. It was an explication of why, against all good sense, his father had left behind the houses and paintings, the memberships in clubs and societies in order to come to Nebraska and till the soil. Emmett's father offered this page from Emerson as evidence—as if it were a divine decree—that he had had no choice.

But if, on the one hand, it was an excuse, on the other, it was an exhortation—an exhortation for Emmett that he should feel no remorse, no guilt, no hesitation in turning his back on the three hundred acres to which his father had dedicated half his life, as long as he abandoned them in order to pursue without envy or imitation his own portion, and in so doing discover that which he alone was capable of.

Tucked in the envelope behind the page of Emerson was the second legacy, a stack of brand-new twenty-dollar bills. Running his thumb over the crisp, clean edges, Emmett figured there were about 150 in all, amounting to some three thousand dollars.

If Emmett could understand why his father considered the torn page a sacrilege of sorts, he couldn't accept that the bills were. Presumably, his father characterized the money as a sacrilege because he was bestowing it behind the backs of his creditors. In so doing, he had gone against both his legal obligation and his own sense of what was right and wrong. But after meeting the interest payments on his mortgage for twenty years, Emmett's father had paid for the farm two times over. He had paid for it again with hard labor and disappointment, with his marriage, and finally with his life. So, no, the setting aside of three thousand dollars was not a sacrilege in Emmett's eyes. As far as he was concerned, his father had earned every penny.

Taking one of the bills for his pocket, Emmett returned the envelope to its spot above the tire and laid the felt back in place.

—Emmett . . . , said Billy.

Emmett closed the trunk and looked to Billy, but Billy wasn't looking at him. He was looking at the two figures in the doorway of the barn. With the late afternoon light behind them, Emmett couldn't tell who they were. At least not until the wiry one on the left stretched out his arms and said:

—Ta-da!

Duchess

Y OU SHOULD HAVE SEEN the look on Emmett's face when he realized who was standing in the door. From his expression, you would've thought we'd popped out of thin air.

Back in the early forties, there was an escape artist who went by the name of Kazantikis. Some of the wisecrackers on the circuit liked to call him the half-wit Houdini from Hackensack, but that wasn't totally fair. While the front half of his act was a little shaky, the finale was a gem. Right before your eyes, he'd get bound up in chains, locked in a trunk, and sunk to the bottom of a big glass tank. A good-looking blonde would wheel out a giant clock as the emcee reminded the audience that the average human being can only hold his breath for two minutes, that deprived of oxygen most grow dizzy after four and unconscious after six. Two officers of the Pinkerton Detective Agency were present to ensure that the padlock on the trunk was secure, and a priest from the Greek Orthodox Church—complete with a long black cassock and long white beard—was on hand should it prove necessary to administer the last rites. Down into the water the trunk would go and the blonde would start the clock. At two minutes, the members of the audience would whistle and jeer. At five minutes, they would ooh and aah. But at eight minutes, the Pinkertons would exchange worried glances. At ten, the priest would cross himself and recite an indecipherable prayer. At the twelfth minute, as the blonde burst into tears, two stagehands would rush from behind the curtains to help the Pinkertons hoist the trunk from the tank. It would be dropped to the stage with a thump as water gushed across the footlights and into the orchestra pit. When one of the Pinkertons fumbled with his keys, the other would brush him aside, draw his pistol, and shoot off the lock. He would rip open the lid and tip over the trunk, only to discover . . . it was empty. At which point, the orthodox priest would pluck off his beard revealing that he was none other than Kazantikis, his hair still wet, as every single member of the audience looked on in holy amazement. That's how Emmett Watson looked when he realized who was standing in the door. Of all the people in the world, he just couldn't believe it was us.

—Duchess?

—In the flesh. And Woolly too.

He still looked dumbfounded.

—But how . . . ?

I laughed.

—That's the question, right?

I put a hand to the side of my mouth and lowered my voice.

—We hitched a ride with the warden. While he was signing you out, we slipped into the trunk of his car.

—You can't be serious.

—I know. It's not what you'd call first-class travel. What with it being a hundred degrees in there and Woolly complaining every ten minutes about having to go to the bathroom. And when we crossed into Nebraska? I thought I was going to get a concussion from the divots in the road. Someone should write a letter to the governor!

—Hey, Emmett, said Woolly, like he'd just joined the party.

You've got to love that about Woolly. He's always running about five minutes late, showing up on the wrong platform with the wrong luggage just as the conversation is pulling out of the station. Some might find the trait a little exasperating, but I'd take a guy who runs five minutes late over a guy who runs five minutes early, any day of the week.

Out of the corner of my eye I had been watching as the kid, who'd been sitting on a hay bale, began edging his way in our direction. When I pointed, he froze like a squirrel on the grass.

—Billy, right? Your brother says you're as sharp as a tack. Is that true?

The kid smiled and edged a little closer until he was standing at Emmett's side. He looked up at his brother.

—Are these your friends, Emmett?

—Of course we're his friends!

—They're from Salina, Emmett explained.

I was about to elaborate when I noticed the car. I'd been so focused on the charms of the reunion that I hadn't seen it hiding behind the heavy equipment.

—Is that the Studebaker, Emmett? What do they call that? Baby blue?

Objectively speaking, it looked a little like a car that your dentist's wife would drive to bingo, but I gave it a whistle anyway. Then I turned to Billy.

—Some of the boys in Salina would pin a picture of their girl back home on the bottom of the upper bunk so they could stare at it before lights out. Some of them had a photo of Elizabeth Taylor or Marilyn Monroe. But your brother, he pinned up an advertisement torn from an old magazine with a full-color picture of his car. I'll be honest with you, Billy. We gave your brother a lot of grief about that. Getting all moon-eyed over an automobile. But now that I see her up close . . .

I shook my head in a show of appreciation.

—Hey, I said, turning to Emmett. Can we take her for a spin?

Emmett didn't answer because he was looking at Woolly—who was looking at a spider web without a spider.

—How are you doing, Woolly? he asked.

Turning, Woolly thought about it for a moment.

—I'm all right, Emmett.

—When was the last time you had something to eat?

—Oh, I don't know. I guess it was before we got in the warden's car. Isn't that right, Duchess?

Emmett turned to his brother.

—Billy, you remember what Sally said about supper?

—She said to cook it at 350° for forty-five minutes.

—Why don't you take Woolly back to the house, put the dish in the oven, and set the table. I need to show Duchess something, but we'll be right behind you.

—Okay, Emmett.

As we were watching Billy and Woolly walk back toward the house, I wondered what Emmett wanted to show me. But when he turned in my direction, he didn't look himself. As a matter of fact, he seemed out of sorts. I guess some people are like that when it comes to surprises. Me, I love surprises. I love it when life pulls a rabbit out of a hat. Like when the blue-plate special is turkey and stuffing in the middle of May. But some people just don't like being caught off guard—even by good news.

—Duchess, what are you doing here?

Now it was me who looked surprised.

—What are we doing here? Why, we've come to see you, Emmett. And the farm. You know how it is. You hear enough stories from a buddy about his life back home and eventually you want to see it for yourself.

To make my point, I gestured toward the tractor and the hay bale and the great American prairie that was waiting right outside the door, trying its best to convince us that the world was flat, after all.

Emmett followed my gaze, then turned back.

—I'll tell you what, he said. Let's go have something to eat, I'll give you and Woolly a quick tour, we'll get a good night's sleep, then in the morning, I'll drive you back to Salina.

I gave a wave of my hand.

—You don't need to drive us back to Salina, Emmett. You just got home yourself. Besides, I don't think we're going back. At least not yet.

Emmett closed his eyes for a moment.

—How many months do you have left on your sentences? Five or six? You're both practically out.

—That's true, I agreed. That's perfectly true. But when Warden Williams took over for Ackerly, he fired that nurse from New Orleans. The one who used to help Woolly get his medicine. Now he's down to his last few bottles, and you know how bluesy he gets without his medicine. . . .

—It's not his medicine.

I shook my head in agreement.

—One man's toxin is another man's tonic, right?

—Duchess, I shouldn't have to spell this out for you, of all people. But the longer you two are AWOL and the farther you get from Salina, the worse the consequences are going to be. And you both turned eighteen this winter. So if they catch you across state lines, they may not send you back to Salina. They may send you to Topeka.

Let's face it: Most people need a ladder and a telescope to make sense of two plus two. That's why it's usually more trouble than it's worth to explain yourself. But not Emmett Watson. He's the type of guy who can see the whole picture right from the word go—the grander scheme and all the little details. I put up both of my hands in surrender.

—I'm with you one hundred percent, Emmett. In fact, I tried to tell Woolly the very same thing in the very same words. But he wouldn't listen. He was dead set on jumping the fence. He had a whole plan. He was going to split on a Saturday night, hightail it into town, and steal a car. He even pilfered a knife when he was on kitchen duty. Not a paring knife, Emmett. I'm talking about a butcher knife. Not that Woolly would ever hurt a soul. You and I know that. But the cops don't know it. They see a fidgety stranger with a drifty look in his eye and a butcher knife in his hand, and they'll put him down like a dog. So I told him if he put the knife back where he'd found it, I'd help him get out of Salina safe and sound. He put back the knife, we slipped into the trunk, presto chango, here we are.

And all of this was true.

Except the part about the knife.

That's what you'd call an embellishment—a harmless little exaggeration in the service of emphasis. Sort of like the giant clock in Kazantikis's act, or the shooting of the padlock by the Pinkerton. Those little elements that on the surface seem unnecessary but that somehow bring the whole performance home.

—Look, Emmett, you know me. I could have done my stretch and then done Woolly's. Five months or five years, what's the difference. But given Woolly's state of mind, I don't think he could have done five more days.

Emmett looked off in the direction that Woolly had walked.

We both knew that his problem was one of plenty. Raised in one of those doorman buildings on the Upper East Side, Woolly had a house in the country, a driver in the car, and a cook in the kitchen. His grandfather was friends with Teddy *and* Franklin Roosevelt, and his father was a hero in the Second World War. But there's something about all that good fortune that can become too much. There's a tender sort of soul who, in the face of such abundance, feels a sense of looming trepidation, like the whole pile of houses and cars and Roosevelts is going to come tumbling down on top of him. The very thought of it starts to spoil his appetite and unsettle his nerves. It becomes hard for him to concentrate, which affects his reading, writing, and arithmetic. Having been asked to leave one boarding school, he gets sent to another. Then maybe another. Eventually, a guy like that is going to need *something* to hold the world at bay. And who can blame him? I'd be the first to tell you that rich people don't deserve two minutes of your sympathy. But a bighearted guy like Woolly? That's a different story altogether.

I could see from Emmett's expression that he was going through a similar sort of calculus, thinking about Woolly's sensitive nature and wondering if we should send him back to Salina or help him safely on his way. As a quandary it was pretty hard to parse. But then I guess that's why they call it a quandary.

—It's been a long day, I said, putting a hand on Emmett's shoulder. What say we go back to the house and break bread? Once we've had something to eat, we'll all be in a better frame of mind to weigh the whys and wherefores.

—·—

Country cooking . . .

You hear a lot about it back East. It's one of those things that people revere even when they've never had any firsthand experience with it. Like justice and Jesus. But unlike most things that people admire from afar, country cooking deserves the admiration. It's twice as tasty as anything you'd find at Delmonico's and without all the folderol. Maybe it's because they're using the recipes their great-great-grandmas perfected on the wagon trail. Or maybe it's all those hours they've spent in the company of pigs and potatoes. Whatever the reason, I didn't push back my plate until after the third helping.

—That was some meal.

I turned to the kid—whose head wasn't too far over the tabletop.

—What's the name of that pretty brunette, Billy? The one in the flowery dress and work boots whom we have to thank for this delectable dish?

—Sally Ransom, he said. It's a chicken casserole. Made from one of her own chickens.

—One of her own chickens! Hey, Emmett, what's that folksy saying? The one about the fastest way to a young man's heart?

—She's a neighbor, said Emmett.

—Maybe so, I conceded. But I've had a lifetime supply of neighbors, and I've never had one who brought me a casserole. How about you, Woolly?

Woolly was making a spiral in his gravy with the tines of his fork.

—What's that?

—Have you ever had a neighbor bring you a casserole? I asked a little louder.

He thought about it for a second.

—I've never had a casserole.

I smiled and raised my eyebrows at the kid. He smiled and raised his eyebrows back.

Casserole or no casserole, Woolly suddenly looked up like he'd had a timely thought.

—Hey, Duchess. Did you get a chance to ask Emmett about the escapade?

—The escapade? asked Billy, poking his head a little higher over the table.

—That's the other reason we came here, Billy. We're about to set off on a little escapade and we were hoping your brother would come along.

—An escapade . . . , said Emmett.

—We've been calling it that for lack of a better word, I said. But it's a good deed, really. A sort of mitzvah. In fact, it's the fulfillment of a dying man's wish.

As I began to explain, I looked from Emmett to Billy and back again since the two seemed equally intrigued.

—When Woolly's grandfather died, he left some money for Woolly in what they call a trust fund. Isn't that right, Woolly?

Woolly nodded.

—Now, a trust fund is a special investment account that's set up for the benefit of a minor with a trustee who makes all the decisions until the minor comes of age, at which point the minor can do with the money as he sees fit. But when Woolly turned eighteen, thanks to a little bit of fancy jurisprudence, the trustee—who happens to be Woolly's brother-in-law—had Woolly declared temperamentally unfit. Wasn't that the term, Woolly?

—Temperamentally unfit, Woolly confirmed with an apologetic smile.

—And in so doing, his brother-in-law extended his authority over the trust until such a time as Woolly should improve his temperament, or in perpetuity, whichever comes first.

I shook my head.

—And they call that a *trust* fund?

—That sounds like Woolly's business, Duchess. What does it have to do with you?

—With us, Emmett. What does it have to do with us.

I pulled my chair a little closer to the table.

—Woolly and his family have a house in upstate New York—

—A camp, said Woolly.

—A camp, I amended, where the family gathers from time to time. Well, during the Depression, when the banks began failing, Woolly's great-grandfather decided he could never entirely trust the American banking system again. So, just in case, he put a hundred and fifty thousand dollars in cash in a wall safe at the camp. But what's particularly interesting here—even fateful, you might say—is that the value of Woolly's trust today is almost exactly a hundred and fifty thousand dollars.

I paused to let that sink in. Then I looked at Emmett directly.

—And because Woolly's a man who's big of heart and modest of needs, he has proposed that if you and I accompany him to the Adirondacks to help him claim what is rightfully his, he will divvy up the proceeds in three equal parts.

—One hundred and fifty thousand dollars divided by three is fifty thousand dollars, said Billy.

—Exactly, I said.

—All for one and one for all, said Woolly.

As I leaned back in my chair, Emmett stared at me for a moment. Then he turned to Woolly.

—This was your idea?

—It was my idea, Woolly acknowledged.

—And you're not going back to Salina?

Woolly put his hands in his lap and shook his head.

—No, Emmett. I'm not going back to Salina.

Emmett gave Woolly a searching look, as if he were trying to formulate one more question. But Woolly, who was naturally disinclined to the answering of questions and who'd had plenty of practice in avoiding them, began clearing the plates.

In a state of hesitation, Emmett drew a hand across his mouth. I leaned across the table.

—The one hitch is that the camp always gets opened up for the last weekend in June, which doesn't give us a lot of time. I've got to make a quick stop in New York to see my old man, but then we're heading straight for the Adirondacks. We should have you back in Morgen by Friday—a little road weary, maybe, but on the sunny side of fifty grand. Think about that for a second, Emmett. . . . I mean, what could you do with fifty grand? What *would* you do with fifty grand?

There is nothing so enigmatic as the human will—or so the head-shrinkers would have you believe. According to them, the motivations of a man are a castle without a key. They form a multilayered labyrinth from which individual actions often emerge without a readily discernible rhyme or reason. But it's really not so complicated. If you want to understand a man's motivations, all you have to do is ask him: *What would you do with fifty thousand dollars?*

When you ask most people this question, they need a few minutes to think about it, to sort through the possibilities and consider their options. And that tells you everything you need to know about them. But when you pose the question to a man of substance, a man who merits your consideration, he will answer in a heartbeat—and with specifics. Because he's already thought about what he would do with fifty grand. He's thought about it while he's been digging ditches, or pushing paper, or slinging hash. He's thought about it while listening to his wife, or tucking in the kids, or staring at the ceiling in the middle of the night. In a way, he's been thinking about it all his life.

When I put the question to Emmett, he didn't respond, but that wasn't because he didn't have an answer. I could see from the expression on his face that he knew *exactly* what he'd do with fifty thousand dollars, nickel for nickel and dime for dime.

As we sat there silently, Billy looked from me to his brother and back again; but Emmett, he looked straight across the table like he and I were suddenly the only people in the room.

—Maybe this was Woolly's idea and maybe it wasn't, Duchess. Either way, I don't want any part of it. Not the stop in the city, not the trip to the Adirondacks, not the fifty thousand dollars. Tomorrow, I need to take care of a few things in town. But on Monday morning, first thing, Billy and I are going to drive you and Woolly to the Greyhound station in Omaha. From there you can catch a bus to Manhattan or the Adirondacks or anywhere you like. Then Billy and I will get back in the Studebaker and go on about our business.

Emmett was serious as he delivered this little speech. In fact, I've never seen a guy so serious. He didn't raise his voice, and he didn't take his eyes off me once—not even to glance at Billy, who was listening to every word with a look of wide-eyed wonder.

And that's when it hit me. The blunder I'd made. I had laid out all the specifics right in front of the kid.

Like I said before, Emmett Watson understands the whole picture better than most. He understands that a man can be patient, but only up to a point; that it's occasionally necessary for him to toss a monkey wrench in the workings of the world in order to get his God-given due. But Billy? At the age of eight, he probably hadn't set foot out of the state of Nebraska. So you couldn't expect him to understand all the intricacies of modern life, all the subtleties of what was and wasn't fair. In fact, you wouldn't *want* him to understand it. And as the kid's older brother, as his guardian and sole protector, it was Emmett's job to spare Billy from such vicissitudes for as long as he possibly could.

I leaned back in my chair and gave the nod of common understanding.

—Say no more, Emmett. I read you loud and clear.

After supper, Emmett announced that he was walking over to the Ransoms to see if his neighbor would come jump his car. As the house was a mile away, I offered to keep him company, but he thought it best that Woolly and I stay out of sight. So I remained at the kitchen table, chatting with Billy while Woolly did the dishes.

Given what I've already told you about Woolly, you'd probably think he wasn't cut out for doing dishes—that his eyes would glaze over and his mind would wander and he'd generally go about the business in a slipshod fashion. But Woolly, he washed those dishes like his life depended on it. With his head bent at a forty-five-degree angle and the tip of his tongue poking between his teeth, he circled the sponge over the surface of the plates with a tireless intention, removing some spots that had been there for years and others that weren't there at all.

It was a wonder to observe. But like I said, I love surprises.

When I turned my attention back to Billy, he was unwrapping a little package of tinfoil that he'd taken from his knapsack. From inside the tinfoil he carefully withdrew four cookies and put them on the table—one cookie in front of each chair.

—Well, well, well, I said. What do we have here?

—Chocolate chip cookies, said Billy. Sally made them.

While we chewed in silence, I noticed that Billy was staring rather shyly at the top of the table, as if he had something he wanted to ask.

—What's on your mind, Billy?

—All for one and one for all, he said a little tentatively. That's from *The Three Musketeers*, isn't it?

—Exactly, *mon ami*.

Having successfully identified the source of the quotation, you might have imagined the kid would be pleased as punch, but he looked despondent. Positively despondent. And that's despite the fact that the mere mention of *The Three Musketeers* usually puts a smile on a young boy's face. So Billy's disappointment rather mystified me. That is until I was about to take another bite, and I recalled the all-for-one-and-one-for-all arrangement of the cookies on the table.

I put my cookie down.

—Have you seen *The Three Musketeers*, Billy?

—No, he admitted, with a hint of the same despondency. But I have read it.

—Then you should know better than most just how misleading a title can be.

Billy looked up from the table.

—Why is that, Duchess?

—Because, in point of fact, *The Three Musketeers* is a story about *four* musketeers. Yes, it opens with the delightful camaraderie of Orthos and Pathos and Artemis.

—Athos, Porthos, and Aramis?

—Exactly. But the central *business* of the tale is the means by which the young adventurer . . .

—D'Artagnan.

— . . . by which D'Artagnan joins the ranks of the swashbuckling threesome. And by saving the honor of the queen, no less.

—That's true, said Billy, sitting up in his chair. In point of fact, it is a story about four musketeers.

In honor of a job well done, I popped the rest of my cookie in my mouth and brushed the crumbs from my fingers. But Billy was staring at me with a new intensity.

—I sense that something else is on your mind, young William.

He leaned as far forward as the table would allow and spoke a little under his breath.

—Do you want to hear what I would do with fifty thousand dollars?

I leaned forward and spoke under my breath too.

—I wouldn't miss it for the world.

—I would build a house in San Francisco, California. It would be a white house just like this one with a little porch and a kitchen and a front room. And upstairs, there would be three bedrooms. Only instead of a barn for the tractor, there would be a garage for Emmett's car.

—I love it, Billy. But why San Francisco?

—Because that's where our mother is.

I sat back in my chair.

—You don't say.

Back at Salina, whenever Emmett mentioned his mother—which wasn't very often, to be sure—he invariably used the past tense. But he didn't use it in a manner suggesting that his mother had gone to California. He used it in a manner suggesting that she had gone to the great beyond.

—We're leaving right after we take you and Woolly to the bus station, added Billy.

—Just like that, you're going to pack up the house and move to California.

—No. We're not going to pack up the house, Duchess. We're going to take what little we can fit in a kit bag.

—Why would you do that?

—Because Emmett and Professor Abernathe agree that's the best way to make a fresh start. We're going to drive to San Francisco on the Lincoln Highway, and once we get there, we'll find our mother and build our house.

I didn't have the heart to tell the kid that if his mother didn't want to live in a little white house in Nebraska, she wasn't going to want to live in a little white house in California. But setting the vagaries of motherhood aside, I figured the kid's dream was about forty thousand dollars under budget.

—I love your plan, Billy. It's got the sort of specificity that a heartfelt scheme deserves. But are you sure you're dreaming big enough? I mean, with fifty thousand dollars you could go a hell of a lot further. You could have a pool and a butler. You could have a four-car garage.

Billy shook his head with a serious look on his face.

—No, he said. I don't think we will need a pool and a butler, Duchess.

I was about to gently suggest that the kid shouldn't jump to conclusions, that pools and butlers weren't so easy to come by, and those who came by them were generally loath to give them up, when suddenly Woolly was standing at the table with a plate in one hand and a sponge in the other.

—No one needs a pool or a butler, Billy.

You never know what's going to catch Woolly's attention. It could be a bird that settles on a branch. Or the shape of a footprint in the snow. Or something someone said on the previous afternoon. But whatever gets Woolly thinking, it's always worth the wait. So as he took the seat next to Billy, I quickly went to the sink, turned off the water, and returned to my chair, all ears.

—No one needs a four-car garage, Woolly continued. But I think what you will need is a few more bedrooms.

—Why is that, Woolly?

—So that friends and family can come visit for the holidays.

Billy nodded in acknowledgment of Woolly's good sense, so Woolly continued making suggestions, warming to his subject as he went along.

—You should have a porch with an overhanging roof so that you can sit under it on rainy afternoons, or lie on top of it on warm summer nights. And downstairs there should be a study, and a great room with a fireplace big enough so that everyone can gather around it when it snows. And you should have a secret hiding place under the staircase, and a special spot in the corner for the Christmas tree.

There was no stopping Woolly now. Asking for paper and pencil, he swung his chair around next to Billy's and began drawing a floor plan in perfect detail. And this wasn't some back-of-the-napkin sort of sketch. As it turned out, Woolly drew floor plans like he washed dishes. The rooms were rendered to scale with walls that were parallel and corners at perfect right angles. It gave you a zing just to see it.

Setting aside the merits of a covered porch versus a four-car garage, you had to give Woolly credit on the dreaming front. The place he imagined on Billy's behalf was three times the size of the one the kid had imagined on his own, and it must have struck a chord. Because when Woolly was done with the picture, Billy asked him to add an arrow pointing north and a big red star to mark the spot where the Christmas tree should go. And when Woolly had done that, the kid carefully folded the floor plan and stowed it away in his pack.

Woolly looked satisfied too. Although, when Billy had cinched the straps nice and tight and returned to his chair, Woolly gave him his sad sort of smile.

—I wish I didn't know where my mother is, he said.

—Why is that, Woolly?

—So that I could go and look for her just like you.

—·—

Once the dishes were clean and Billy had taken Woolly upstairs to show him where he could shower, I did some poking around.

It was no secret that Emmett's old man had gone bust. But all you had to take was one look around the place to know it wasn't from drinking. When the man of the house is a drunk, you can tell. You can tell from the look of the furniture and the look of the front yard. You can tell from the look on the faces of the kids. But even if Emmett's old man was a teetotaler, I figured there had to be a drink of something somewhere—like maybe a bottle of apple brandy or peppermint schnapps tucked away for special occasions. In this part of the country, there usually was.

I started with the kitchen cabinets. In the first, I found the plates and bowls. In the second, the glasses and mugs. In the third, I found the usual assortment of foodstuffs, but no sign of a bottle, not even hiding behind the ten-year-old jar of molasses.

There wasn't any hooch in the hutch either. But in the lower compartment was a jumble of fine china covered in a thin layer of dust. Not just dinner plates, you understand. There were soup bowls, salad plates, dessert plates, and teetering towers of coffee cups. I counted twenty settings in all—in a house without a dining-room table.

I seemed to remember Emmett telling me his parents had been raised in Boston. Well, if they were raised in Boston, it must have been on the top of Beacon Hill. This was the sort of stuff that is given to a Brahmin bride with every expectation it will be handed down from one generation to the next. But the whole collection could barely fit in the cupboard, so it certainly wasn't going to fit in a kit bag. Which sort of made you wonder . . .

In the front room, the only place to stow a bottle was in the big old desk in the corner. I sat in the chair and rolled up the top. The writing surface had the normal accessories—scissors, a letter opener, a pad and pencil—but the drawers were cluttered with all sorts of things that had no business being there, like an old alarm clock, a half a deck of cards, and a scattering of nickels and dimes.

After scraping up the loose change (waste not, want not), I opened the bottom drawer with my fingers crossed, knowing it to be a classic stowing spot. But there was no room for a bottle in there, because the drawer was filled to the brim with mail.

It didn't take more than a glance to know what this mess was all about: unpaid bills. Bills from the power company and the phone company, and whoever else had been foolish enough to extend Mr. Watson credit. At the very bottom would be the original notices, then the reminders, while here at the top, the cancellations and threats of legal action. Some of those envelopes hadn't even been opened.

I couldn't help but smile.

There was something sort of sweet in how Mr. Watson kept this assortment in the bottom drawer—not a foot away from the trash can. It had taken him just as much effort to stuff the bills inside his desk as it would have to consign them to oblivion. Maybe he just couldn't bring himself to admit that he was never going to pay them.

My old man certainly wouldn't have gone to the trouble. As far as he was concerned, an unpaid bill couldn't find its way into the garbage fast enough. In fact, he was so allergic to the very paper on which bills were printed, he would go to some lengths to ensure that they never caught up with him in the first place. That's why the incomparable Harrison Hewett, who was something of a stickler when it came to the English language, was occasionally known to misspell his own address.

But waging a war with the US Postal Service is no small affair. They have entire fleets of trucks at their disposal, and an army of foot soldiers whose sole purpose in life is to make sure that an envelope with your name on it finds its way into your mitts. Which is why the Hewetts were occasionally known to arrive by the lobby and depart by the fire escape, usually at five in the morning.

Ah, my father would say, pausing between the fourth and third floors and gesturing toward the east. *Rosy-fingered dawn! Count yourself lucky to be of its acquaintance, my boy. There are kings who never laid eyes upon it!*

Outside, I heard the wheels of Mr. Ransom's pickup turning into the Watsons' drive. The headlights briefly swept the room from right to left as the truck passed the house and headed toward the barn. I closed the bottom drawer of the desk so that the whole pile of notices could remain safe and sound until the final accounting.

Upstairs, I stuck my head into Billy's room, where Woolly was already stretched out on the bed. He was humming softly and staring at the airplanes hanging from the ceiling. He was probably thinking about his father in the cockpit of his fighter plane at ten thousand feet. That's where Woolly's father would always be for Woolly: somewhere between the flight deck of his carrier and the bottom of the South China Sea.

I found Billy in his father's room, sitting Indian style on the bedcovers with his knapsack at his side and a big red book in his lap.

—Hey there, gunslinger. What're you reading?

—*Professor Abacus Abernathe's* Compendium of Heroes, Adventurers, *and Other Intrepid Travelers.*

I whistled.

—Sounds impressive. Is it any good?

—Oh, I've read it twenty-four times.

—Then *good* may not be big enough a word.

Entering the room, I took a little stroll from corner to corner as the kid turned the page. On top of the bureau were two framed photographs.

The first was of a standing husband and seated wife in turn-of-the-century garb. The Watsons of Beacon Hill, no doubt. The other was of Emmett and Billy from just a few years back. They were sitting on the same porch that Emmett and his neighbor had sat on earlier that day. There was no picture of Billy and Emmett's mother.

—Hey, Billy, I said, putting the photograph of the brothers back on the bureau. Can I ask you a question?

—Okay, Duchess.

—When exactly did your mother go to California?

—On the fifth of July 1946.

—That's pretty exactly. So she just up and left, huh? Never to be heard from again?

—No, said Billy, turning another page. She was heard from again. She sent us nine postcards. That's how we know that she's in San Francisco.

For the first time since I'd entered the room, he looked up from his book.

—Can I ask you a question, Duchess?

—Fair's fair, Billy.

—How come they call you that?

—Because I was born in Dutchess County.

—Where is Dutchess County?

—About fifty miles north of New York.

Billy sat up straight.

—You mean the city of New York?

—None other.

—Have you ever been to the city of New York?

—I've been to hundreds of cities, Billy, but I've been to the city of New York more than I've been to anywhere else.

—That's where Professor Abernathe is. Here, look.

Turning to one of the first pages, he offered up his book.

—Small print gives me a headache, Billy. Why don't you do the honors.

Looking down, he began reading with the help of a fingertip.

—*Dearest Reader, I write to you today from my humble office on the fifty-fifth floor of the Empire State Building at the junction of Thirty-Fourth Street and Fifth Avenue on the isle of Manhattan in the city of New York at the northeastern edge of our great nation—the United States of America.*

Billy looked up with a certain level of expectation. I responded with a look of inquiry.

—Have you ever met Professor Abernathe? he asked.

I smiled.

—I've met a lot of people in our great nation and many of them from the isle of Manhattan, but to the best of my knowledge, I have never had the pleasure of meeting your professor.

—Oh, said Billy.

He was quiet for a moment, then his little brow furrowed.

—Something else? I asked.

—Why have you been to hundreds of cities, Duchess?

—My father was a thespian. Although we were generally based in New York, we spent a good part of the year traveling from town to town. We'd be in Buffalo one week and Pittsburgh the next. Then Cleveland or Kansas City. I've even spent some time in Nebraska, believe it or not. When I was about your age, I lived for a stretch on the outskirts of a little city called Lewis.

—I know Lewis, said Billy. It's on the Lincoln Highway. Halfway between here and Omaha.

—No kidding.

Billy set his book aside and reached for his knapsack.

—I have a map. Would you like to see?

—I'll take your word for it.

Billy let go of the knapsack. Then his brow furrowed again.

—When you were moving from town to town, how did you go to school?

—Not all worth knowing can be found between the covers of compendiums, my boy. Let's simply say that my academy was the thoroughfare, my primer experience, and my instructor the fickle finger of fate.

Billy seemed to consider this for a moment, apparently unsure of whether he should be willing to accept the principle as an article of faith. Then, after nodding twice to himself, he looked up with a touch of embarrassment.

—Can I ask you something else, Duchess?

—Shoot.

—What is a thespian?

I laughed.

—A thespian is a man of the stage, Billy. An actor.

Extending a hand, I looked into the distance and intoned:

> She should have died hereafter.
> There would have been a time for such a word.
> Tomorrow, and tomorrow, and tomorrow
> Creeps in this petty pace from day to day
> To the last syllable of recorded time;
> And all our yesterdays have lighted fools
> The way to dusty death. . . .

It was a pretty good delivery, if I do say so myself. Sure, the pose was a little hackneyed, but I put a world of weariness into the *tomorrows*, and I hit that old *dusty death* with an ominous flare.

Billy gave me his patented wide-eyed look.

—William Shakespeare from the Scottish play, I said. Act five, scene five.

—Was your father a Shakespearean actor?

—Very Shakespearean.

—Was he famous?

—Oh, he was known by name in every saloon from Petaluma to Poughkeepsie.

Billy looked impressed. But then his brow furrowed once again.

—I have learned a little about William Shakespeare, he said. Professor Abernathe calls him the greatest adventurer to have never set sail on the seas. But he never mentions the Scottish play. . . .

—Not surprisingly. You see, the Scottish play is how theater folk refer to *Macbeth*. Some centuries ago, it was determined that the play was cursed, and that to speak of it by name can only bring misfortune upon the heads of those who dare perform it.

—What sorts of misfortune?

—The worst sorts. At the very first production of the play back in the sixteen hundreds, the young actor cast as Lady Macbeth died right before going onstage. About a hundred years ago, the two greatest Shakespearean actors in the world were an American named Forrest and a Brit named Macready. Naturally, the American audience was partial to the talents of Mr. Forrest. So when Macready was cast in the role of Macbeth at the Astor Place Opera House—on the isle of Manhattan—a riot broke out in which ten thousand clashed and many were killed.

Needless to say, Billy was enthralled.

—But why is it cursed?

—Why is it cursed! Have you never heard the tale of Macbeth? The black-hearted Thane of Glamis? What? No? Well then, my boy, make some room, and I shall bring you into the fraternity!

Professor Applenathe's *Compendium* was set aside. And as Billy got under the covers, I switched off the light—just as my father would have when he was about to tell a dark and grisly tale.

Naturally enough, I began on the fen with the three witches bubbling, bubbling, toil and troubling. I told the kid how, spurred by the ambitions of the Missus, Macbeth honored the visit of his king with a dagger through the heart; and how this cold-blooded act of murder begot another, which in turn begot a third. I told him how Macbeth became tormented by ghostly visions, and his wife began sleepwalking the halls of Cawdor while wiping the specter of blood from her hands. Oh, I stuck the courage to the sticking place, all right!

And once the trees of Birnam Wood had climbed the hill of Dunsinane, and Macduff, that man of no woman born, had left the regicide slain upon the fields, I tucked Billy in with a wish of pleasant dreams. And as I retreated down the hall, I took a bow with a gentle flourish when I noted that young Billy had gotten out of bed to switch the light back on.

———•———

Sitting on the edge of Emmett's bed, what struck me immediately about his room was all that wasn't in it. While there was a chip in the plaster where a nail had once been lodged, there were no pictures hanging, no posters or pennants. There was no radio or record player. And while there was a curtain rod above the window, there were no curtains. If there had been a cross on the wall, it could well have been the cell of a monk.

I suppose he could have cleared it out right before going to Salina. Putting his childish ways behind him, and what have you, by dumping all his comic books and baseball cards in the trash. Maybe. But something told me this was the room of someone who had been preparing to walk out of his house with nothing but a kit bag for a long, long time.

The beams from Mr. Ransom's headlights swept across the wall again, this time from left to right as the truck passed the house on its way to the road. After the screen door slammed, I heard Emmett turn off the lights in the kitchen, then the lights in the front room. When he climbed the stairs, I was waiting in the hall.

—Up and running? I asked.

—Thankfully.

He looked genuinely relieved, but a little worn out too.

—I feel terrible putting you out of your room. Why don't you take your bed and I'll sleep downstairs on the couch. It may be a little short, but it's bound to be more comfortable than the mattresses at Salina.

In saying this, I didn't expect Emmett to take me up on the offer. He wasn't the type. But I could tell he appreciated the gesture. He gave me a smile and even put a hand on my shoulder.

—That's all right, Duchess. You stay put and I'll join Billy. I think we could all use a good night's sleep.

Emmett continued down the hall a few steps, then stopped and turned back.

—You and Woolly should switch out of those clothes. He can find something in my father's closet. They were about the same size. I've already packed things for Billy and me, so you can take what you want from mine. There's also a pair of old book bags in there that you two can use.

—Thanks, Emmett.

As he continued down the hall, I went back into his room. From behind the closed door, I could hear him washing up, then going to join his brother.

Lying down on his bed, I stared at the ceiling. Over my head were no model airplanes. All I had was a crack in the plaster that turned a lazy curve around the ceiling lamp. But at the end of a long day, maybe a crack in the plaster is all you need to trigger fanciful thoughts. Because the way that little imperfection curved around the fixture was suddenly very reminiscent of how the Platte River bends around Omaha.

Oh, Omaha, I remember thee well.

It was in August of 1944, just six months after my eighth birthday. That summer, my father was part of a traveling revue claiming to raise money for the war effort. Though the show was billed as *The Greats of Vaudeville*, it might just as well have been called *The Cavalcade of Has-Beens*. It opened with a junkie juggler who'd get the shakes in the second half of his act, followed by an eighty-year-old comedian who could never remember which jokes he had already told. My father's bit was to perform a medley of Shakespeare's greatest monologues—or, as he put it: *A lifetime supply of wisdom in twenty-two minutes.* Wearing the beard of a Bolshevik and a dagger in his belt, he would lift his gaze slowly from the footlights in search of that realm of sublime ideas located somewhere in the upper right-hand corner of the balcony, and thence wouldst commence: *But soft, what light through yonder window breaks* . . . and *Once more unto the breach, dear friends* . . . and *O reason not the need!* . . .

From Romeo to Henry to Lear. A tailor-made progression from the moonstruck youth, to the nascent hero, to the doddering old fool.

As I recall, that tour began at the Majestic Theatre in glamorous Trenton, New Jersey. From there, we headed west, hitting all the bright lights of the interior from Pittsburgh to Peoria.

The last stop was a one-week residence at the Odeon in Omaha. Tucked somewhere between the railway station and the red-light district, it was a grand old Deco spot that hadn't had the good sense to turn itself into a movie theater when it still had the chance. Most of the time while we were on the road, we stayed with the other performers in the hotels that were suited to our kind—the ones frequented by fugitives and Bible salesmen. But whenever we reached the final stop on a tour—that stop from which there would be no forwarding address—my father would check us into the fanciest hotel in town. Sporting the walking stick of Winston Churchill and the voice of John Barrymore, he would saunter up to the front desk and ask to be shown to his room. Discovering that the hotel was fully booked and had no record of his reservation, he would express the outrage appropriate to a man of his station. *What's that! No reservation! Why, it was none other than Lionel Pendergast, the general manager of the Waldorf Astoria (and a close personal friend), who, having assured me that there was no other place in Omaha to spend the night, called your offices in order to book my room!* When the management would eventually admit that the presidential suite was available, Pops would concede that, though he was a man of simple needs, the presidential suite would do very nicely, thank you.

Once ensconced, this man of simple needs would take full advantage of the hotel's amenities. Every stitch of our clothing would be sent to the laundry. Manicurists and masseuses would be summoned to our rooms. Bell boys would be sent out for flowers. And in the lobby bar every night at six, drinks would be ordered all round.

It was on a Sunday in August, the morning after his last performance, that my father proposed an excursion. Having been hired for a run at the Palladium in Denver, he suggested we celebrate by having a picnic on the bank of a meandering river.

As we carried our luggage down the hotel's back stairs, my father wondered whether perhaps we should augment our festivities by bringing along a representative of the gentler sex. Say, Miss Maples, that delightful young lady whom Mephisto, the cross-eyed magician, had been sawing in half every night in the second act. And who should we find standing in the alley with her suitcase in hand, but the buxom blonde we'd just been discussing.

—Tallyho! said my father.

Ah, what a delightful day that turned out to be.

With me in the rumble seat and Miss Maples up front, we drove to a large municipal park on the edge of the Platte River, where the grass was lush, the trees were tall, and the sunshine glistened on the surface of the water. The night before, my father had ordered a picnic of fried chicken and cold corn on the cob. He had even stolen a tablecloth right out from under our breakfast plates (try that one, Mephisto!).

Miss Maples, who couldn't have been more than twenty-five,

seemed to delight in my old man's company. She laughed at all his jokes and warmly expressed her gratitude whenever he refilled her glass with wine. She even blushed at some of the compliments he had stolen from the Bard.

She had brought along a portable record player, and I was put in charge of picking the records and cuing the needle as the two of them danced uncertainly on the grass.

It has been observed that that which comforts the stomach dullens the wits. And surely, no truer words have ever been said. For after we had tossed the wine bottles into the river, packed the phonograph into the trunk, and put the car in gear, when my father mentioned that we needed to make a quick stop in a nearby town, I thought nothing of it. And when we pulled up to an old stone building on top of a hill and he asked me to wait with a young nun in one room while he spoke to an older nun in another, I still thought nothing of that. In fact, it was only when I happened to glance through the window and spied my father speeding down the driveway with Miss Maples's head on his shoulder that I realized I'd been had.

NINE

—.—

Emmett

EMMETT WOKE TO THE smell of bacon frying in a pan. He couldn't remember the last time he'd woken to the smell of bacon. For over a year, he'd been waking to the complaint of a bugle and the stirring of forty boys at six fifteen in the morning. Rain or shine they had forty minutes to shower, dress, make their beds, eat their breakfast, and line up for duty. To wake on a real mattress under clean cotton sheets with the smell of bacon in the air had become so unfamiliar, so unexpected, it took Emmett a moment to wonder where the bacon had come from and who was cooking it.

He turned over and saw that Billy was gone and the clock on the bedside table read 9:45. Swearing softly, he climbed out of bed and dressed. He had hoped to get in and out of town before church let out.

In the kitchen, he found Billy and Duchess sitting across from each other—and Sally at the stove. In front of the boys were plates of bacon and eggs, in the middle of the table a basket of biscuits and a jar of strawberry preserves.

—Boy are you in for a treat, said Duchess when he saw Emmett.

Pulling up a chair, Emmett looked toward Sally, who was picking up the percolator.

—You didn't have to make breakfast for us, Sally.

By way of reply, she set down a mug on the table in front of him.

—Here's your coffee. Your eggs will be ready in a minute.

Then she turned on her heels and went back to the stove.

Duchess, who had just taken a second bite from a biscuit, was shaking his head in appreciation.

—I've traveled all around America, Sally, but I've never had anything like these biscuits. What's your secret recipe?

—There's nothing secret about my recipe, Duchess.

—If there isn't, there should be. And Billy tells me you made the jelly too.

—Those are preserves, not jelly. But yes, I make them every July.

—It takes her a whole day, said Billy. You should see her kitchen. There are baskets of berries on every counter and a five-pound bag of sugar and four different pots simmering on the stove.

Duchess whistled and shook his head again.

—It may be an old-fashioned endeavor, but from where I sit, it's worth the effort.

Sally turned from the stove and thanked Duchess, with a touch of ceremony. Then she looked at Emmett.

—You ready yet?

Without waiting for an answer, she brought over his serving.

—You really didn't have to go to all this trouble, Emmett said. We could have seen to our own breakfast, and there was plenty of jam in the cabinet.

—I'll be sure to keep that in mind, Sally said, setting down his plate.

Then she went to the sink and began scrubbing the skillet.

Emmett was staring at her back when Billy addressed him.

—Did you ever go to the Imperial, Emmett?

Emmett turned to his brother.

—What's that, Billy? The Imperial?

—The movie theater in Salina.

Emmett directed a frown at Duchess, who quickly set the record straight.

—Your brother never went to the Imperial, Billy. That was just me and a few of the other boys.

Billy nodded, looking like he was thinking something over.

—Did you have to get special permission to go to the movies?

—You didn't need permission, so much as . . . initiative.

—But how did you get out?

—Ah! A reasonable question under the circumstances. Salina wasn't exactly like a prison, Billy, with guard towers and searchlights. It was more like boot camp in the army—a compound in the middle of nowhere with a bunch of barracks and a mess hall and some older guys in uniform who yelled at you for moving too fast when they weren't yelling at you for moving too slow. But the guys in uniform—our sergeants, if you will—didn't sleep with us. They had their own barracks, with a pool table, and a radio, and a cooler full of beer. So after lights-out on Saturday, while they were drinking and shooting pool, a few of us would slip out the bathroom window and make our way into town.

—Was it far?

—Not too far. If you jogged across the potato fields, in about twenty minutes you'd come to a river. Most of the time, the river was only a few feet deep, so you could wade across in your skivvies and make it downtown in time for the ten o'clock show. You could have a bag of popcorn and a bottle of pop, watch the feature from the balcony, and be back in bed by one in the morning, leaving no one the wiser.

—Leaving no one the wiser, repeated Billy, with a hint of awe. But how did you pay for the movies?

—Why don't we change the subject, suggested Emmett.

—Why not! said Duchess.

Sally, who had been drying the skillet, set it down on the stovetop with a bang.

—I'll go make the beds, she said.

—You don't have to make the beds, said Emmett.

—They won't make themselves.

Sally left the kitchen and they could hear her marching up the stairs.

Duchess looked at Billy and raised his eyebrows.

—Excuse me, said Emmett, pushing back his chair.

As he headed upstairs, Emmett could hear Duchess and his brother launching into a conversation about the Count of Monte Cristo and his miraculous escape from an island prison—the promised change of subject.

When Emmett got to his father's room, Sally was already making the bed with quick, precise movements.

—You didn't mention that you were having company, she said, without looking up.

—I didn't know I was having company.

Sally fluffed the pillows by giving them a punch on either end, then set them against the headboard.

—Excuse me, she said, squeezing past Emmett in the doorway as she went across the hall to his room.

When Emmett followed, he found her staring at the bed—because Duchess had already made it. Emmett was a little impressed by Duchess's effort, but Sally wasn't. She pulled back the quilt and sheet and began tucking them back in with the same precise movements. When she turned her attention to the punching of pillows, Emmett glanced at the bedside clock. It was almost ten fifteen. He really didn't have time for this, whatever this was.

—If something's on your mind, Sally . . .

Sally stopped abruptly and looked him in the eye for the first time that morning.

—What would be on my mind?

—I'm sure I don't know.

—That sounds about right.

She straightened her dress and made a move toward the door, but he was standing in her way.

—I'm sorry if I didn't seem grateful in the kitchen. All I was trying to say was—

—I know what you were trying to say because you said it. That I didn't need to go to the trouble of skipping church so that I could make you breakfast this morning; just like I didn't need to go to the trouble of making you dinner last night. Which is fine and dandy. But for your information, telling someone they didn't have to go to the trouble of doing something is not the same as showing gratitude for it. Not by a long shot. No matter how much store-bought jam you have in the cabinet.

—Is that what this is about? The jam in the cabinet? Sally, I did not mean to slight your preserves. Of course they're better than the jam in the cabinet. But I know how much effort it takes for you to make them, and I didn't want you to feel you had to waste a jar on us. It's not like it's a special occasion.

—It may interest you to know, Emmett Watson, that I am quite happy to have my preserves eaten by friends and family when there is no occasion to speak of. But maybe, just maybe, I thought you and Billy might like to enjoy one last jar before you packed up and moved to California without saying so much as a word.

Emmett closed his eyes.

—Come to think of it, she continued, I guess I should thank my lucky stars that your friend Duchess had the presence of mind to inform me of your intentions. Otherwise, I might have come over tomorrow morning and made pancakes and sausage only to find there was no one here to eat them.

—I'm sorry I haven't had the chance to mention that to you, Sally. But it wasn't like I was trying to hide it. I talked about it with your father yesterday afternoon. In fact, he was the one who brought it up—saying it might be best if Billy and I were to pull up stakes and make a fresh start somewhere else.

Sally looked at Emmett.

—My father said that. That you should pull up stakes and make a fresh start.

—In so many words . . .

—Well, doesn't that just sound delightful.

Pushing past Emmett, Sally continued into Billy's room, where Woolly was lying on his back and blowing at the ceiling, trying to stir the airplanes.

Sally put her hands on her hips.

—And who might you be?

Woolly looked up in shock.

—I'm Woolly.

—Are you Catholic, Woolly?

—No, I'm Episcopalian.

—Then what are you still doing in bed?

—I'm not sure, admitted Woolly.

—It's after ten in the morning and I've got plenty to do. So at the count of five, I'm going to make that bed, whether you're in it or not.

Woolly jumped out from under the covers in his boxer shorts and watched in a state of amazement as Sally went about the business of making the bed. While scratching the top of his head, he noticed Emmett on the threshold.

—Hey, Emmett!

—Hey, Woolly.

Woolly squinted at Emmett for a moment, then his face lit up.

—Is that bacon?

—Ha! said Sally.

And Emmett, he headed down the stairs and out the door.

—·—

It was a relief for Emmett to be alone behind the wheel of the Stude-baker.

Since leaving Salina, he'd barely had a moment to himself. First there was the drive with the warden, then Mr. Obermeyer in the kitchen and Mr. Ransom on the porch, then Duchess and Woolly, and now Sally. All Emmett wanted, all he needed, was a chance to clear his head so that, wherever he and Billy decided to go, whether to Texas or California or someplace else altogether, he could set out in the right frame of mind. But as he turned onto Route 14, what Emmett found himself dwelling on was not where he and Billy might go, it was his exchange with Sally.

I'm sure I don't know.

That's how he'd replied when she had asked him what might be on her mind. And in the strictest sense, he hadn't known.

But he could have made a pretty good guess.

He understood well enough what Sally had come to expect. At one time, he may even have given her cause for expecting it. That's the sort of thing young people do: fan the flames of each other's expectations—until the necessities of life begin to make themselves known. But Emmett hadn't given her much cause for expectations since he went to Salina. When she had sent him those packages—with the homemade cookies and hometown news—he had not replied with a word of thanks. Not on the phone and not in a note. And in advance of coming home, he had not sent her word of his pending arrival or asked her to tidy the house. He hadn't asked her to sweep or make beds or put soap in the bathroom or eggs in the icebox. He hadn't asked her to do a thing.

Was he grateful to discover that she had chosen to do these things on his and Billy's behalf? Of course he was. But being grateful was one thing, and being beholden, that was another thing altogether.

As Emmett drove, he saw the intersection with Route 7 approaching. Emmett knew that if he took a right and circled back on 22D, he could reach town without having to pass the fairgrounds. But what would be the point of that? The fairgrounds would still be there whether he passed them or not. They'd still be there whether he went to Texas or California or someplace else altogether.

No, taking the long route wouldn't change a thing. Except maybe letting one imagine for a moment that what had happened already hadn't happened at all. So not only did Emmett continue straight through the intersection, he slowed the car to twenty miles an hour as he approached the fairgrounds, then pulled over on the opposite shoulder where he had no choice but to give it a good hard look.

For fifty-one weeks of the year, the fairgrounds were exactly like they were right now—four empty acres scattered with hay to hold down the dust. But in the first week of October, they would be anything but empty. They would be filled with music and people and lights. There would be a carousel and bumper cars and colorful booths where one could try one's hand at pitching or riflery. There would be a great striped tent where, with an appropriate sense of ceremony, judges would convene, confer, and bestow blue ribbons for the largest pumpkin and the tastiest lemon meringue pie. And there would be a corral with bleachers where they would hold the tractor pull and calf roping, and where more ribbons would be awarded by more judges. And back there, just beyond the food concessions, would be a spot-lit stage for the fiddling contest.

It was right by the cotton-candy vendor, of all places, on the last night of the fair that Jimmy Snyder had chosen to pick his fight.

When Jimmy called out his first remark, Emmett thought he must be talking to someone else—because he barely knew Jimmy. A year younger, Emmett wasn't in any of Jimmy's classes and didn't play on any of his teams, so he had little reason to interact with him.

But Jimmy Snyder didn't have to know you. He liked running people down whether he knew them or not. And it didn't matter for what. It could have been for the clothes you were wearing, or the food you were eating, or the way your sister crossed the street. Yes, sir, it could have been about anything, as long as it was something that got under your skin.

Stylistically speaking, Jimmy was one for framing his insults as inquiries. Looking curious and mild, he'd ask his first question to no one in particular. And if that didn't hit a sore spot, he'd answer the first question himself, then ask another, circling ever inward.

Isn't that cute? was the question he'd posed when he'd seen Emmett holding Billy's hand. *I mean, isn't that the cutest thing you ever saw?*

When Emmett realized that Jimmy was referring to him, he brushed it off. What did he care if he was seen holding his younger brother's hand at the county fair. Who wouldn't be holding the hand of a six-year-old boy in the middle of a large crowd at eight in the evening?

So Jimmy tried again. Shifting gears, as it were, he wondered out loud whether the reason Emmett's father hadn't fought in the war was because he'd been 3-C, the Selective Service classification that allowed farmers to defer. This struck Emmett as an odd taunt given how many men in Nebraska had received the 3-C designation. It struck him as so odd that he couldn't help but stop and turn around—which was his first mistake.

Now that Jimmy had Emmett's attention, he answered the query himself.

No, he said, *Charlie Watson wouldn't have been 3-C. 'Cause he couldn't grow grass in the Garden of Eden. He must have been 4-F.*

Here, Jimmy turned a finger around his ear to imply Charlie Watson's incapacity to reason.

Granted, these were juvenile taunts, but they had begun to make Emmett grit his teeth. He could feel the old heat rising to the surface of his skin. But he could also feel that Billy was tugging at his hand—maybe for the simple reason that the fiddling contest was about to begin, or maybe because, even at the age of six, Billy understood that no good could come from engaging with the likes of Jimmy Snyder. But before Billy could tug Emmett away, Jimmy took one more crack at it.

No, he said, *it couldn't have been because he was 4-F. He's too simple*

to be crazy. I suppose if he didn't fight, it must have been because he was
4-E. What they call a conscientious—

Before Jimmy could say the word *objector*, Emmett had hit him. He had hit him without even letting go of his brother's hand, extending his fist from his shoulder in one clean jab, breaking Jimmy's nose.

It wasn't the broken nose that killed him, of course. It was the fall. Jimmy was so used to speaking with impunity that he wasn't prepared for the punch. It sent him stumbling backward, arms flailing. When his heel caught on a braid of cables, Jimmy fell straight back, hitting his head on a cinderblock that was bracing the stake of a tent.

According to the medical examiner, Jimmy landed with such force that the corner of the cinderblock dug a triangular hole an inch deep into the back of his skull. It put him in a coma that left him breathing, but that was slowly sapping his strength. After sixty-two days, it finally drained the life out of him altogether, as his family sat at his bedside in their fruitless vigil.

Like the warden said: *The ugly side of chance.*

Sheriff Petersen was the one who brought the news of Jimmy's death to the Watsons' doorstep. He had held off on pressing charges, waiting to see how Jimmy would fare. In the meantime, Emmett had maintained his silence, seeing no virtue in rehashing the events while Jimmy was fighting for his life.

But Jimmy's pals did not maintain their silence. They talked about the fight often and at length. They talked about it in the schoolhouse, at the soda fountain, and in the Snyders' living room. They told of how the four of them had been on their way to the cotton-candy stand when Jimmy bumped into Emmett by mistake; and how before Jimmy even got the chance to apologize, Emmett had punched him in the face.

Mr. Streeter, Emmett's attorney, had encouraged him to take the stand and tell his own version of events. But whatever version prevailed, Jimmy Snyder was still going to be dead and buried. So Emmett told Mr. Streeter that he didn't need a trial. And on March 1, 1953, at a hearing before Judge Schomer in the county courthouse, after freely admitting his guilt, Emmett was sentenced to eighteen months at a special juvenile reform program on a farm in Salina, Kansas.

In another ten weeks, the fairgrounds wouldn't be empty, thought Emmett. The tent would be raised and the stage rebuilt and the people would gather once again in anticipation of the contests and food and music. As Emmett put the Studebaker in gear, he took little comfort from the fact that when the festivities commenced he and Billy would be more than a thousand miles away.

—·—

Emmett parked along the lawn at the side of the courthouse. As it was Sunday, only a few stores were open. He made quick stops at Gunderson's and the five-and-dime, where he spent the twenty dollars from his father's envelope on sundries for the journey west. Then after putting his bags in the car, he walked up Jefferson to the public library.

At the front of the central room, a middle-aged librarian sat at a V-shaped desk. When Emmett asked where he could find the almanacs and encyclopedias, she led him to the reference section and pointed to various volumes. As she was doing so, Emmett could tell that she was scrutinizing him through her glasses, giving him a second look, as if maybe she recognized him. Emmett hadn't been in the library since he was a boy, but she could have recognized him for any number of reasons, not least of which was that his picture had been on the front page of the town paper more than once. Initially, it was his school portrait set alongside Jimmy's. Then it was Emmett Watson being taken into the station house to be formally charged, and Emmett Watson descending the courthouse steps in the minutes after his hearing. The girl at Mr. Gunderson's had given him a similar look.

—Can I help you find anything in particular? the librarian asked after a moment.

—No, ma'am. I'm all set.

When she retreated to her desk, Emmett pulled the volumes he needed, brought them to one of the tables, and took a seat.

For much of 1952, Emmett's father had been wrestling with one illness or another. But it was a flu he couldn't shake in the spring of '53 that prompted Doc Winslow to send him to Omaha for some tests. In the letter Emmett's father sent to Salina a few months later, he assured his son that he was *back on his feet* and *well on the road to recovery*. Nonetheless, he had agreed to make a second trip to Omaha so that the specialists could do a few more tests, *as specialists are wont to do*.

Reading the letter, Emmett wasn't fooled by his father's folksy assurances or his wry remark on the penchants of medical professionals. His father had been using mollifying words for as long as Emmett could remember. Mollifying words to describe how the planting had gone, how the harvest was coming, and why their mother was suddenly nowhere to be found. Besides, Emmett was old enough to know that the road to recovery was rarely lined with repeat visits to specialists.

Any doubts as to Mr. Watson's prognosis were swept aside one morning in August when he stood up from the breakfast table and fainted right before Billy's eyes, prompting a third trip to Omaha, this one in the back of an ambulance.

That night—after Emmett had received the call from Doc Winslow in the warden's office—a plan began to take shape. Or to be more accurate, it was a plan that Emmett had been toying with for months in the back of his mind, but now it was in the forefront, presenting itself in a series of variations that differed in timing and scope, but which always took place somewhere other than Nebraska. As his father's condition deteriorated over the fall, the plan became sharper; and when he died that April, it was clear as could be—as if Emmett's father had surrendered his own vitality to ensure the vitality of Emmett's intentions.

The plan was simple enough.

As soon as Emmett was out of Salina, he and Billy were going to pack their things and head to some metropolitan area—somewhere without silos or harvesters or fairgrounds—where they could use what little remained of their father's legacy to buy a house.

It didn't have to be a grand house. It could be a three- or four-bedroom with one or two baths. It could be colonial or Victorian, clapboard or shingled. What it had to be was in disrepair.

Because they wouldn't be buying this house to fill it with furniture and tableware and art, or with memories, for that matter. They'd be buying the house to fix it up and sell it. To make ends meet, Emmett would get a job with a local builder, but in the evenings while Billy was doing his schoolwork, Emmett would be setting the house right, inch by inch. First, he'd do whatever work was needed on the roof and windows to ensure the house was weather tight. Then he'd shift his attention to the walls, doors, and flooring. Then the moldings and banisters and cabinets. Once the house was in prime condition, once the windows opened and closed and the staircase didn't creak and the radiators didn't rattle, once every corner looked finished and fine, then and only then would they sell.

If he played his cards right, if he picked the right house in the right neighborhood and did the right amount of work, Emmett figured he could double his money on the first sale—allowing him to invest the proceeds in two more run-down houses, where he could start the process over again. Only this time, when the two houses were finished, he would sell one and rent out the other. If Emmett maintained his focus, within a few years he figured he'd have enough money to quit his job and hire a man or two. Then he'd be renovating two houses and collecting rent from four. But at no time, under any circumstances, would he ever borrow a dime.

Other than his own hard work, Emmett figured there was only one thing essential to his success, and that was to pursue his plan in a metropolitan area that was big and getting bigger. With that in mind, he had visited the little library at Salina, and with volume eighteen of the *Encyclopedia Britannica* open on the table, he had written down the following:

Population of Texas

1920	4,700,000
1930	5,800,000
1940	6,400,000
1950	7,800,000
1960E	9,600,000

When Emmett had the Texas entry in front of him, he hadn't even bothered to read the opening paragraphs—the ones that summarized the state's history, its commerce, culture, and climate. When he saw that between 1920 and 1960 the population would more than double, that was all he needed to know.

But by the same logic, he should be open to considering any large growing state in the Union.

As he sat in the Morgen library, Emmett removed the scrap of paper from his wallet and set it on the table. Then he opened volume three of the encyclopedia and added a second column.

Population of Texas		Population of California	
1920	4,700,000	1920	3,400,000
1930	5,800,000	1930	5,700,000
1940	6,400,000	1940	6,900,000
1950	7,800,000	1950	10,600,000
1960E	9,600,000	1960E	15,700,000

Emmett was so surprised by California's growth that this time he read the opening paragraphs. What he learned was that its economy was expanding on multiple fronts. Long an agricultural giant, the war had turned the state into a leading builder of ships and airplanes; Hollywood had become the manufacturer of dreams for the world; and taken together, the ports of San Diego, Los Angeles, and San Francisco amounted to the single largest gateway for trade into the US of A. In the 1950s alone, California was projected to grow by more than five million citizens, at a rate of close to fifty percent.

The notion that he and his brother would find their mother seemed as crazy as it had the day before, if not crazier, given the growth of the state's population. But if Emmett's intention was to renovate and sell houses, the case for California was indisputable.

Emmett returned the scrap to his wallet and the encyclopedia to its shelf. But having slid the third volume back in its slot, Emmett removed the twelfth. Without sitting down, he turned to the entry on Nebraska and scanned the page. With a touch of grim satisfaction, Emmett noted that from 1920 to 1950 its population had hovered around 1.3 million people, and that in the current decade it wasn't expected to increase by a soul.

Emmett replaced the volume and headed for the door.

—Did you find what you were looking for?

Having passed the reference desk, Emmett turned to face the librarian. With her eyeglasses now resting on her head, Emmett saw that he had been wrong about her age. She was probably no older than thirty-five.

—I did, he said. Thank you.

—You're Billy's brother, aren't you?

—I am, he said, a little surprised.

She smiled and nodded.

—I'm Ellie Matthiessen. I could tell because you look so much like him.

—Do you know my brother well?

—Oh, he's spent a lot of time here. At least, since you've been away. Your brother loves a good story.

—He does at that, agreed Emmett with a smile.

Although as he went out the door, he couldn't help but add to himself: *for better or worse.*

—.—

There were three of them standing by the Studebaker when Emmett returned from the library. He didn't recognize the tall one on the right in the cowboy hat, but the one on the left was Jenny Andersen's older brother, Eddie, and the one in the middle was Jacob Snyder. From the way that Eddie was kicking at the pavement, Emmett could tell that he didn't want to be there. Seeing Emmett approach, the tall stranger nudged Jake in the side. When Jake looked up, Emmett could tell that he didn't want to be there either.

Emmett stopped a few feet away with his keys in his hand and nodded to the two men he knew.

—Jake. Eddie.

Neither replied.

Emmett considered offering Jake an apology, but Jake wasn't there for an apology. Emmett had already apologized to Jake and the rest of the Snyders. He'd apologized in the hours after the fight, then at the station house, and finally on the courthouse steps. His apologies hadn't done the Snyders any good then, and they weren't going to do them any good now.

—I don't want any trouble, said Emmett. I just want to get in my car and go home.

—I can't let you do that, said Jake.

And he was probably right. Though Emmett and Jake had only been talking for a minute, there were already people gathering around. There were a few farmhands, the Westerly widows, and two boys who had been biding their time on the courthouse lawn. If the Pentecostal or Congregational church let out, the crowd would only grow. Whatever happened next was sure to get back to old man Snyder, and that meant there was only one way that Jake could let the encounter come to its conclusion.

Emmett put his keys in his pocket, leaving his hands at his side.

It was the stranger who spoke up first. Leaning against the door of the Studebaker, he tilted back his hat and smiled.

—Seems like Jake here's got some unfinished business with you, Watson.

Emmett met the gaze of the stranger, then turned back to Jake.

—If we've got unfinished business, Jake, let's finish it.

Jake looked like he was struggling with how to begin, like the anger that he'd expected to feel—that he was *supposed* to feel—after all these months was suddenly eluding him. Taking a page from his brother's book, he started with a question.

—You think of yourself as quite a fighter, don't you, Watson?

Emmett didn't reply.

—And maybe you are something of a fighter—as long as you get to hit a man unprovoked.

—It wasn't unprovoked, Jake.

Jake took half a step forward, feeling something closer to anger now.

—Are you saying Jimmy tried to hit you first?

—No. He didn't try to hit me.

Jake nodded with his jaw clenched, then took another half step.

—Seeing as you like to take the first swing so much, why don't you take the first swing at me?

—I'm not going to take a swing at you, Jake.

Jake stared at Emmett for a moment, then looked away. He didn't look at his two friends. He didn't look at the townspeople who had gathered behind him. He turned his gaze in order to look at nothing in particular. And when he turned back, he hit Emmett with a right cross.

Given that Jake hadn't been looking at Emmett when he went into motion, his fist glanced off the top of Emmett's cheek rather than hitting him squarely in the jaw. But he made enough contact that Emmett stumbled to his right.

Everyone took a step forward now. Eddie and the stranger, the onlookers, even the woman with the stroller who had just joined the crowd. Everyone, that is, but Jake. He remained where he was standing, watching Emmett.

Emmett returned to the spot where he'd been the moment before, his hands back at his side.

Jake was red in the face with some combination of exertion and anger and maybe a hint of embarrassment too.

—Put up your fists, he said.

Emmett didn't move.

—Put up your goddamn fists!

Emmett raised his fists high enough to be in the stance of a fighter, but not so high as to defend himself effectively.

This time, Jake hit him in the mouth. Emmett stumbled three steps back, tasting blood on his lips. He regained his footing and advanced the three steps that would bring him back within Jake's reach. As he heard the stranger egging Jake on, Emmett halfway raised his fists and Jake knocked him to the ground.

Suddenly, the world was out of kilter, sloping away at a thirty-degree angle. To get onto his knees, Emmett had to support himself with both hands on the pavement. As he pushed himself upward, he could feel the heat of the day rising up from the concrete through his palms.

On all fours, Emmett waited for his head to clear, then he began to stand.

Jake took a step forward.

—Don't you get up again, he said, his voice thick with emotion. Don't you get up again, Emmett Watson.

When Emmett reached his full height, he started to raise his fists, but he hadn't been ready to stand, after all. The earth reeled and angled upward, and Emmett landed back on the pavement with a grunt.

—That's enough, someone called out. That's enough, Jake.

It was Sheriff Petersen pushing through the onlookers.

The sheriff instructed one of his deputies to pull Jake aside and the other to disperse the crowd. Then he got down on his haunches to assess Emmett's condition. He even reached out and turned Emmett's head so he could get a better look at the left side of his face.

—Doesn't seem like anything's broken. You gonna be all right, Emmett?

—I'm gonna be all right.

Sheriff Petersen stayed on his haunches.

—You gonna want to press charges?

—For what.

The sheriff signaled to a deputy that he could let Jake go, then turned back to Emmett, who was sitting on the pavement now, wiping the blood from his lip.

—How long have you been back?

—Since yesterday.

—Didn't take long for Jake to find you.

—No, sir, it didn't.

—Well, I can't say as I'm surprised.

The sheriff was quiet for a moment.

—You staying out at your place?

—Yes, sir.

—All right then. Let's get you cleaned up before we send you home.

The sheriff took Emmett's hand in order to help him off the ground. But as he did so, he took the opportunity to look at Emmett's knuckles.

The sheriff and Emmett were driving through town in the Studebaker with Emmett in the passenger seat and the sheriff behind the wheel, moving at a nice easy pace. Emmett was checking his teeth with the tip of his tongue when the sheriff, who had been whistling a Hank Williams song, interrupted himself.

—Not a bad car. How fast can she go?

—About eighty without shaking.

—No kidding.

But the sheriff kept driving at his easy pace, taking wide lazy turns as he whistled his tune. When he drove past the turnoff to the station house, Emmett gave him a quizzical glance.

—I thought I'd take you to our place, the sheriff explained. Let Mary have a look at you.

Emmett didn't protest. He had appreciated the chance to get cleaned up before heading home, but he had no desire to revisit the station house.

After they'd come to a stop in the Petersens' driveway, Emmett was about to open the passenger-side door when he noted that the sheriff wasn't making a move. He was sitting there with his hands on the wheel—just like the warden had the day before.

As Emmett waited for the sheriff to say whatever was on his mind, he looked out the windshield at the tire swing hanging from the oak tree in the yard. Though Emmett didn't know the sheriff's children, he knew they were grown, and he found himself wondering whether the swing was a vestige of their youth, or the sheriff had hung it for the benefit of his grandchildren. Who knows, thought Emmett; maybe it had been hanging there since before the Petersens owned the place.

—I only arrived at the tail end of your little skirmish, the sheriff began, but from the look of your hand and Jake's face, I'd have to surmise you didn't put up much of a fight.

Emmett didn't respond.

—Well, maybe you thought you had it coming to you, continued the sheriff in a tone of reflection. Or maybe, having been through what you've been through, you've decided that your fighting days are behind you.

The sheriff looked at Emmett as if he were expecting Emmett to say something, but Emmett remained silent, staring through the windshield at the swing.

—You mind if I smoke in your car? the sheriff asked after a moment. Mary doesn't let me smoke in the house anymore.

—I don't mind.

Sheriff Petersen took a pack from his pocket and tapped two cigarettes out of the opening, offering one to Emmett. When Emmett accepted, the sheriff lit both cigarettes with his lighter. Then out of respect for Emmett's car, he rolled down the window.

—The war's been over almost ten years now, he said after taking a drag and exhaling. But some of the boys who came back act like they're still fighting it. You take Danny Hoagland. Not a month goes by without me getting a call on his account. One week he's at the roadhouse in a brawl of his own making, a few weeks later he's in the aisle of the supermarket giving the back of his hand to that pretty young wife of his.

The sheriff shook his head as if mystified by what the pretty young woman saw in Danny Hoagland in the first place.

—And last Tuesday? I got hauled out of bed at two in the morning because Danny was standing in front of the Iversons with a pistol in his hand, shouting about some old grievance. The Iversons' didn't know what he was talking about. Because, as it turned out, Danny's grievance wasn't with the Iversons. It was with the Barkers. He just wasn't standing in front of the right house. Come to think of it, he wasn't on the right block.

Emmett smiled in spite of himself.

—Now at the other end of the spectrum, said the sheriff, pointing his cigarette at some unknown audience, were those boys who came back from the war swearing that they would never again lay a hand on their fellow men. And I have a lot of respect for their position. They've certainly earned the right to have it. The thing of it is, when it comes to drinking whiskey, those boys make Danny Hoagland look like a deacon of the church. I never get called out of bed on their account. Because they're not out in front of the Iversons' or the Barkers' or anybody else's at two in the morning. At that hour, they're sitting in their living room working their way to the bottom of a bottle in the dark. All I'm saying, Emmett, is I'm not sure either of these approaches works that well. You can't keep fighting the war, but you can't lay down your manhood either. Sure, you can let yourself get beat up a time or two. That's your prerogative. But eventually, you're going to have to stand up for yourself like you used to.

The sheriff looked at Emmett now.

—You understand me, Emmett?

—Yes, sir, I do.

—I gather from Ed Ransom you might be leaving town. . . .

—We're headed out tomorrow.

—All right then. After we get you cleaned up, I'll take a ride over to the Snyders' and make sure they keep out of your way in the interim. While I'm at it, are there any other people who've been giving you trouble?

Emmett rolled down his window and tossed out the cigarette.

—Mostly, he said, what people have been giving me is advice.

Duchess

WHENEVER I COME TO a new town, I like to get my bearings. I want to understand the layout of the streets and the layout of the people. In some cities this can take you days to accomplish. In Boston, it can take you weeks. In New York, years. The great thing about Morgen, Nebraska, is it only took a few minutes.

The town was laid out in a geometric grid with the courthouse right in the middle. According to the mechanic who'd given me a lift in his tow truck, back in the 1880s the town elders spent a whole week deliberating how best to christen the streets before deciding—with an eye to the future—that the east-west streets would be named for presidents and the north-south streets for trees. As it turned out, they could have settled on seasons and suits because seventy-five years later the town was still only four blocks square.

—Howdy, I said to the two ladies coming in the opposite direction, neither of whom said howdy back.

Now, don't get me wrong. There's a certain charm to a town like this. And there's a certain kind of person who would rather live here than anywhere else—even in the twentieth century. Like a person who wants to make some sense of the world. Living in the big city, rushing around amid all that hammering and clamoring, the events of life can begin to seem random. But in a town this size, when a piano falls out of a window and lands on a fellow's head, there's a good chance you'll know why he deserved it.

At any rate, Morgen was the sort of town where when something out of the ordinary happens, a crowd is likely to gather. And sure enough, when I came around the courthouse, there was a semicircle of citizens ready to prove the point. From fifty feet away I could tell they were a representative sample of the local electorate. There were hayseeds in hats, dowagers with handbags, and lads in dungarees. Fast approaching was even a mother with a stroller and a toddler at her side.

Tossing the rest of my ice cream cone in the trash, I walked over to get a closer look. And who did I find at center stage? None other than Emmett Watson—being taunted by some corn-fed kid with a corn-fed grievance.

The people who had gathered to watch seemed excited, at least in a midwestern sort of way. They weren't shouting or grinning, but they were glad to have happened along at just the right moment. It would be something they could talk about in the barbershop and hair salon for weeks to come.

For his part, Emmett looked fantastic. He was standing with his eyes open and his arms at his sides, neither eager to be there nor in a hurry to leave. It was the taunter who looked anxious. He was shifting back and forth and sweating through his shirt, despite the fact that he'd brought along two cronies to back him up.

—Jake, I don't want any trouble, Emmett was saying. I just want to get in my car and go home.

—I can't let you do that, replied Jake, though it looked like that's exactly what he wanted Emmett to do.

Then one of the wingmen—the tall one in the cowboy hat—tossed in his two cents.

—Seems like Jake here's got some unfinished business with you, Watson.

I had never seen this cowboy before, but from the tilt of his hat and the smile on his face, I knew exactly who he was. He was the guy who's started a thousand fights without ever throwing a punch.

So what did Emmett do? Did he let the cowboy unsettle him? Did he tell him to shut up and mind his own business? He didn't even deign to respond. He just turned to Jake and said:

—If we've got unfinished business, let's finish it.

Pow!

If we've got unfinished business, let's finish it.

You could wait your whole life to say a sentence like that and not have the presence of mind to say it when the time comes. That sort of level-headedness isn't the product of upbringing or practice. You're either born with it or you're not. And mostly, you're not.

But here comes the best part.

It turned out that this Jake was the brother of the Snyder kid whom Emmett put out of commission back in 1952. I could tell because he started talking some nonsense about how Jimmy had been sucker-punched, as if Emmett Watson would ever stoop to hitting a man with his guard down.

When the prodding didn't work, Mr. Fair Fight here looked off in the distance as if he were lost in thought, then, without any warning, hit Emmett in the face. After stumbling to his right, Emmett shook off the blow, straightened up, and started moving back in Jake's direction.

Here we go is what everybody in the crowd was thinking. Because Emmett could clearly beat this guy to a pulp, even if he was ten pounds lighter and two inches shorter. But much to the crowd's dismay, Emmett didn't keep coming. He stopped on the very spot where he'd been standing the moment before.

Which really got to Jake. His face turned as red as his union suit, and he started yelling that Emmett should raise his fists. So Emmett raised them, more or less, and Jake took another crack at it. This time, he hit Emmett right in the kisser. Emmett stumbled again, but didn't topple. Bleeding from the lip, he regained his footing and came back for another helping.

Meanwhile, the cowboy—who was still leaning dismissively on the door of Emmett's car—shouted, *You show him, Jake*, as if Jake were about to teach Emmett a lesson. But the cowboy had it upside down. It was Emmett who was teaching the lesson.

Alan Ladd in *Shane*.

Frank Sinatra in *From Here to Eternity*.

Lee Marvin in *The Wild One*.

You know what these three have in common? They all took a beating. I don't mean getting a pop in the nose or having the wind knocked out of them. I mean a *beating*. Where their ears rang, and their eyes watered, and they could taste the blood on their teeth. Ladd took his at Grafton's Saloon from Ryker's boys. Sinatra took his in the stockade from Sergeant Fatso. And Marvin, he took his at the hands of Marlon Brando in the street of a little American town just like this one, with another crowd of honest citizens gathered around to watch.

The willingness to take a beating: That's how you can tell you're dealing with a man of substance. A man like that doesn't linger on the sidelines throwing gasoline on someone else's fire; and he doesn't go home unscathed. He presents himself front and center, undaunted, prepared to stand his ground until he can't stand at all.

It was Emmett who was teaching the lesson, all right. And he wasn't just teaching it to Jake. He was teaching it to the whole goddamn town.

Not that they understood what they were looking at. You could tell by the expressions on their faces that the whole point of the instruction was going right over their heads.

Jake, who was beginning to tremble, was probably thinking that he couldn't keep it up much longer. So this time, he tried to make it count. Finally getting his aim and his anger into alignment, he let one loose that knocked Emmett clear off his feet.

The whole crowd gave a little gasp, Jake breathed a sigh of relief, and the cowboy let out a snicker of satisfaction, like he was the one who'd thrown the punch. Then Emmett started getting up again.

Man, I wish I'd had a camera. I could've taken a picture and sent it to *Life* magazine. They would've put it on the cover.

It was beautiful, I tell you. But it was too much for Jake. Looking like he might burst into tears, he stepped forward and began shouting at Emmett that he should not get up. That he should not get up, so help him God.

I don't know if Emmett even heard him, given that his senses were probably rattled. Though whether he heard Jake or not didn't make much difference. He was going to do the same thing either way. Stepping a little uncertainly, he moved back within range, stood to his full height, and raised his fists. Then the blood must have rushed from his head because he staggered and fell to the ground.

Seeing Emmett on his knees was an unwelcome sight, but it didn't worry me. He just needed a moment to gather his wits so he could get up and return to the hitting spot. That he would do so was as certain as sunrise. But before he got the chance, the sheriff spoiled the show.

—That's enough, he said, pushing his way through the gawkers. That's enough.

At the sheriff's instruction, a deputy began dispersing the crowd, waving his arms and telling everyone it was time to move along. But there was no need for the deputy to disperse the cowboy. Because the cowboy had dispersed himself. The second the authorities appeared on the scene, he had lowered the brim of his hat and started ambling around the courthouse like he was headed to the hardware store for a can of paint.

I ambled after him.

When the cowboy reached the other side of the building, he crossed one of the presidents and headed up a tree. So eager was he to put some distance between himself and his handiwork, he walked right past an old lady with a cane who was trying to put a grocery bag in the back of her Model T.

—Here you go, ma'am, I said.

—Thank you, young man.

By the time granny was climbing behind the wheel, the cowboy was half a block ahead of me. When he took a right down the alley beyond the movie theater, I actually had to run to catch up, despite the fact that running is something I generally avoid on principle.

Now, before I tell you what happened next, I think I should give you a little context by taking you back to when I was about nine and living in Lewis.

When my old man dropped me off at St. Nicholas's Home for Boys, the nun in charge was a woman of certain opinions and uncertain age named Sister Agnes. It stands to reason that a strong-minded woman who finds herself in an evangelical profession with a captive audience would be likely to avail herself of every opportunity to share her point of view. But not Sister Agnes. Like a seasoned performer, she knew how to choose her moments. She could make an unobtrusive entrance, remain at the back of the stage, wait until everyone had delivered their lines, then steal the show with five minutes in the spotlight.

Her favorite time to impart her wisdom was just before bed. Coming into the dormitory, she would quietly watch as the other sisters scurried about in their habits instructing one kid to fold his clothes, another to wash his face, and everyone to say their prayers. Then when we had all climbed under the covers, Sister Agnes would pull up a chair and deliver her lesson. As you might imagine, Sister Agnes was partial to a biblical grammar, but she spoke with such a sympathetic inflection that her words would silence the intermittent chatter and linger in our ears long after the lights were out.

One of her favorite lessons was something she referred to as the

Chains of Wrongdoing. *Boys,* she would begin in her motherly way, *in your time you shall do wrong unto others and others shall do wrong unto you. And these opposing wrongs will become your chains. The wrongs you have done unto others will be bound to you in the form of guilt, and the wrongs that others have done unto you in the form of indignation. The teachings of Jesus Christ Our Savior are there to free you from both. To free you from your guilt through atonement and from your indignation through forgiveness. Only once you have freed yourself from both of these chains may you begin to live your life with love in your heart and serenity in your step.*

At the time, I didn't understand what she was talking about. I didn't understand how your movements could be hampered by a little wrong-doing, since in my experience those who were prone to wrongdoing were always the first ones out the door. I didn't understand why when someone had done wrong unto you, you had to carry a burden on their behalf. And I certainly didn't understand what it meant to have seren-ity in your step. But as Sister Agnes also liked to say: *What wisdom the Lord does not see fit to endow us with at birth, He provides through the gift of experience.* And sure enough, as I grew older, experience began to make some sense of Sister Agnes's sermon.

Like when I first arrived at Salina.

It was the month of August, when the air was warm, the days were long, and the first crop of potatoes had to be dug from the earth. Old Testament Ackerly would have us working from dawn till dusk, such that when dinner was over, the only thing we wanted was a good night's sleep. And yet, once the lights were out, I would often find myself stewing over how I'd come to be at Salina in the first place, reviewing every bitter detail until the rooster crowed. On other nights, I would imagine being called to the warden's office, where he would solemnly deliver the news of a car crash or a hotel fire in which my old man had lost his life. And while such visions would appease for the moment, they would badger me for the rest of the night with a sense of shameful remorse. So there they were: indignation and guilt. Two contradictory forces so sure to confound, I resigned myself to the possibility I might never sleep soundly again.

But when Warden Williams took over for Ackerly and initiated his era of reform, he instituted a program of afternoon classes designed to prepare us for lives of upright citizenship. To that end, he had a civics teacher come talk about the three branches of government. He had a selectman instruct us on the scourge of Communism and the importance of every man's vote. Pretty soon, we were all wishing we could get back to the potato fields.

Then a few months ago, he arranged to have a certified public accountant explain the basics of personal finance. After describing the interplay between assets and liabilities, this CPA approached the chalkboard and in a few quick strokes demonstrated the balancing of accounts. And right then, while sitting in the back row of that hot little classroom, I finally understood what Sister Agnes had been talking about.

In the course of our lives, she had said, we may do wrong unto others and others may do wrong unto us, resulting in the aforementioned chains. But another way to express the same idea was that through our misdeeds we put ourselves in another person's debt, just as through their misdeeds they put themselves in ours. And since it's these debts—those we've incurred and those we're owed—that keep us stirring and stewing in the early hours, the only way to get a good night's sleep is to balance the accounts.

Emmett wasn't much better than me at listening in class, but he didn't need to pay heed to this particular lesson. He had learned it long before coming to Salina. He had learned it firsthand by growing up under the shadow of his father's failure. That's why he signed those foreclosure papers without a second thought. That's why he wouldn't accept the loan from Mr. Ransom or the china from the bottom of the cabinet. And that's why he was perfectly happy to take the beating.

Just like the cowboy said, Jake and Emmett had some unfinished business. Regardless of who had been provoked by who, or whom by whom, when Emmett hit the Snyder kid at the county fair, he took on a debt just as surely as his father had when he had mortgaged the family farm. And from that day forward, it hung over Emmett's head—keeping *him* up at night—until he satisfied the debt at the hands of his creditor and before the eyes of his fellow men.

But if Emmett had a debt to repay to Jake Snyder, he didn't owe a goddamn thing to the cowboy. Not a shekel, not a drachma, not one red cent.

—Hey, Tex, I called as I jogged after him. Hold up!

The cowboy turned and looked me over.

—Do I know you?

—You know me not, sir.

—Then what do you want?

I held up my hand to catch my breath before I replied.

—Back there at the courthouse, you suggested that your friend Jake had some unfinished business with my friend Emmett. For what it's worth, I think I could just as easily argue that it was Emmett who had unfinished business with Jake. But either way, whether Jake had the business with Emmett or Emmett had the business with Jake, I think we can both agree it was no business of yours.

—Buddy, I don't know what you're talking about.

I tried to be more clear.

—What I'm saying is that even though Jake may have had good reason to give Emmett a beating, and Emmett may have had good reason to take one, you had no cause for all that goading and gloating. Given time, I suspect you'll come to regret the role you played in today's events, and you'll find yourself wishing you could make amends—for your own peace of mind. But since Emmett's leaving town tomorrow, by then it'll be too late.

—You know what I suspect, said the cowboy. I suspect you can go fuck yourself.

Then he turned and began walking away. Just like that. Without even saying goodbye.

I admit, I felt a little deflated. I mean, here I was trying to help a stranger understand a burden of his own making, and he gives me the back of his shirt. It's the sort of reception that could turn you off charitable acts forever. But another of Sister Agnes's lessons was that when one is doing the work of the Lord, one should be willing to have patience. For just as surely as the righteous will meet setbacks on the road to justice, the Lord will provide them the means to prevail.

And lo and behold, what suddenly appeareth before me but the movie theater's dumpster filled to the brim with the previous night's trash. And poking out from among the Coca-Cola bottles and popcorn boxes was a two-foot length of two-by-four.

—Hey! I called once more while skipping down the alley. Hold on a second!

The cowboy turned on his heels and from the look on his face I could tell that he had something priceless to say, something that was likely to bring smiles to the faces of all the boys at the bar. But I guess we'll never know, because I hit him before he could speak.

The blow was a good crack along the left side of his head. His hat, which went lofting in the air, did a somersault before alighting on the other side of the alley. He dropped right where he'd been standing like a marionette whose strings have been cut.

Now, I had never hit anybody in my life. And to be perfectly honest, my first impression was how much it hurt. Shifting the two-by-four to my left hand, I looked at my right palm, where two bright-red lines had been left behind by the edges of the wood. Tossing it on the ground, I rubbed my palms together to take out the sting. Then I leaned over the cowboy to get a better look. His legs were folded under him and his left ear was split down the middle, but he was still conscious. Or conscious enough.

—Can you hear me, Tex? I asked.

Then I spoke a little louder to make sure he could.

—Consider your debt repaid in full.

As he looked back at me, his eyelashes fluttered for a moment. But then he gave a little smile, and I could tell from the way his eyelids closed that he was going to sleep like a baby.

Walking out of the alley, I became conscious not simply of a welling sense of moral satisfaction, but that my footfall felt a little lighter and my stride a little jauntier.

Well, what do you know, I thought to myself with a smile. There's serenity in my step!

And it must have showed. Because when I emerged from the alley and said howdy to the two old men passing by, they both said howdy back. And though on the way into town, ten cars had passed me before the mechanic picked me up, on the way back to the Watsons', the first car that came along pulled over to offer me a ride.

Woolly

THE FUNNY THING ABOUT A STORY, thought Woolly—while Emmett was in town, and Duchess was on a walk, and Billy was reading aloud from his big red book—the funny thing about a story is that it can be told in all sorts of lengths.

The first time Woolly heard *The Count of Monte Cristo*, he must have been younger than Billy. His family was spending the summer at the camp in the Adirondacks, and every night his sister Sarah would read him a chapter before he went to bed. But what his sister was reading from was the original book by Alexander Dumas, which was a thousand pages long.

The thing about hearing a story like *The Count of Monte Cristo* from the one-thousand-page version is that whenever you sense an exciting part is coming, you have to wait and wait and wait for it to actually arrive. In fact, sometimes you have to wait so long for it to arrive you forget that it's coming altogether and let yourself drift off to sleep. But in Billy's big red book, Professor Abernathe had chosen to tell the entire story over the course of eight pages. So in his version, when you sensed an exciting part was coming, it arrived lickety-split.

Like the part that Billy was reading now—the part when Edmond Dantès, convicted of a crime he didn't commit, is carted off to spend the rest of his life in the dreaded Château d'If. Even as he is being led in chains through the prison's formidable gates, you just know that Dantès is bound to escape. But in Mr. Dumas's telling, before he regains his freedom you have to listen to so many sentences spread across so many chapters that it begins to feel like *you* are the one who is in the Château d'If! Not so with Professor Abernathe. In his telling, the hero's arrival at the prison, his eight years of solitude, his friendship with the Abbé Faria, and his miraculous escape all occur on the very same page.

Woolly pointed at the solitary cloud that was passing overhead.

—That's what I imagine the Château d'If looked like.

Carefully marking his place with his finger, Billy looked up to where Woolly was pointing and readily agreed.

—With its straight rock walls.

—And the watchtower in the middle.

Woolly and Billy both smiled to see it, but then Billy's expression grew rather more serious.

—Can I ask you a question, Woolly?

—Of course, of course.

—Was it hard to be at Salina?

As Woolly considered the question, far overhead the Château d'If transformed itself into an ocean liner—with a giant smokestack where the watchtower once had been.

—No, said Woolly, it wasn't so hard, Billy. Certainly not like the Château d'If was for Edmond Dantès. It's just that . . . It's just that every day at Salina was an every-day day.

—What's an every-day day, Woolly?

Woolly took another moment to consider.

—When we were at Salina, every day we would get up at the same time and get dressed in the same clothes. Every day we had breakfast at the same table with the same people. And every day we did the same work in the same fields before going to sleep at the same hour in the same beds.

Though Billy was just a boy, or maybe because he was just a boy, he seemed to understand that while there is nothing wrong with waking up or getting dressed or having breakfast, per se, there is something fundamentally disconcerting about doing these things in the exact same fashion day in and day out, especially in the one-thousand-page version of one's own life.

After nodding, Billy found his place and began to read again.

What Woolly did not have the heart to tell Billy was that while this was unquestionably the way of life at Salina, it was also the way of life in many other places. It was certainly the way of life at boarding school. And not simply at St. George's, where Woolly had most recently been enrolled. At all three boarding schools that Woolly had attended, every day they would wake up at the same time, get dressed in the same clothes, and have breakfast at the same table with the same people before heading off to attend the same classes in the same classrooms.

Woolly had often wondered about that. Why did the heads of boarding schools choose to make every day an every-day day? After some reflection, he came to suspect that they did so because it made things easier to manage. By turning every day into an every-day day, the cook would always know when to cook breakfast, the history teacher when to teach history, and the hall monitor when to monitor the halls.

But then Woolly had an epiphany.

It was in the first semester of his second junior year (the one at St. Mark's). On his way from physics down to the gymnasium, he happened to notice the dean of students getting out of a taxi in front of the schoolhouse. As soon as he saw the taxi, it occurred to Woolly what a pleasant surprise it would be were he to pay a visit to his sister, who had recently bought a big white house in Hastings-on-Hudson. So, jumping in the back of the cab, Woolly gave the address.

You mean in New York? the driver asked in surprise.

I mean in New York! Woolly confirmed, and off they went.

When he arrived a few hours later, Woolly found his sister in the kitchen on the verge of peeling a potato.

Hallo, Sis!

Were Woolly to pay a surprise visit to any other member of his family, they would probably have greeted him with an absolute slew of whos, whys, and whats (especially when he needed 150 dollars for the taxi driver, who was waiting outside). But after paying the driver, Sarah just put the kettle on the stove, some cookies on a plate, and the two of them had a grand old time—sitting at her table and discussing all the various topics that happened to pop into their heads.

But after an hour or so, Woolly's brother-in-law, "Dennis," walked through the kitchen door. Woolly's sister was seven years older than Woolly, and "Dennis" was seven years older than Sarah, so mathematically speaking "Dennis" had been thirty-two at the time. But "Dennis" was also seven years older than himself, which made him almost forty in spirit. That is why, no doubt, he was already a vice president at J.P. Morgan & Sons & Co.

When "Dennis" discovered Woolly at the kitchen table, he was a little upset on the grounds that Woolly was supposed to be someplace else. But he was even more upset when he discovered the half-peeled potato on the counter.

When is dinner? he asked Sarah.

I'm afraid I haven't started preparing it yet.

But it's half past seven.

Oh, for heaven's sake, Dennis.

For a moment, "Dennis" looked at Sarah in disbelief, then he turned to Woolly and asked if he could speak to Sarah in private.

In Woolly's experience, when someone asks if they can speak to someone else in private, it is difficult to know what to do with yourself. For one thing, they generally don't tell you how long they're going to be, so it's hard to know how deeply you should involve yourself in some new endeavor. Should you take the opportunity to visit the washroom? Or start a jigsaw puzzle that depicts a sailboat race with fifty spinnakers? And how *far* should you go? You certainly need to go far enough so that you can't hear them talking. That was the whole point of their asking you to leave in the first place. But it often sounds like they may want you to come back a bit later, so you need to be close enough to hear them when they call.

Doing his best to split the hair down the muddle, Woolly went into the living room, where he discovered an unplayed piano and some unread books and an unwound grandfather clock—which, come to think of it, was very aptly named since it once had belonged to their grandfather! But as it turned out, given how upset "Dennis" had become, the living room wasn't far enough away, because Woolly could hear every word.

You were the one who wanted to move out of the city, "Dennis" *was saying. But I'm the one who has to get up at the crack of dawn in order to catch the 6:42 so that I can be at the bank in time for the investment committee meeting at 8:00. For most of the next ten hours, while you're here doing God knows what, I am working like a dog. Then, if I run to Grand Central and I'm lucky enough to catch the 6:14, I just might make it home by half past seven. After a day like that, is it really so much to ask that you have dinner waiting on the table?*

That's the moment the epiphany came. Standing there before his grandfather's clock listening to his brother-in-law, it suddenly occurred to Woolly that maybe, just maybe, St. George's and St. Mark's and St. Paul's organized every day to be an every-day day not because it made things easier to manage, but because it was the best possible means by which to prepare the fine young men in their care to catch the 6:42 so that they would always be on time for their meetings at 8:00.

At the very moment that Woolly concluded the recollection of his epiphany, Billy reached the point in the story when Edmond Dantès, having successfully escaped from prison, was standing in the secret cave on the isle of Monte Cristo before a magnificent pile of diamonds, pearls, rubies, and gold.

—You know what would be magnificent, Billy? You know what would be absotively magnificent?

Marking his place, Billy looked up from his book.

—What, Woolly? What would be absotively magnificent?

—A one-of-a-kind kind of day.

Sally

A T LAST WEEK'S SUNDAY SERVICE, Reverend Pike read a parable from the Gospels in which Jesus and His disciples, having arrived in a village, are invited by a woman into her home. Having made them all comfortable, this woman, Martha, retreats into her kitchen to fix them something to eat. And all the while she's cooking and generally seeing to everyone's needs by filling empty glasses and getting second helpings, her sister, Mary, is sitting at Jesus's feet.

Eventually, Martha has had enough and she lets her feelings be known. *Lord,* she says, *can't you see that my idler of a sister has left me to do all the work? Why don't you tell her to lend me a hand?* Or something to that effect. And Jesus, He replies: *Martha, you are troubled by too many things when only one thing is needful. And it is Mary who has chosen the better way.*

Well, I'm sorry. But if ever you needed proof that the Bible was written by a man, there you have it.

I am a good Christian. I believe in God, the Father almighty, creator of heaven and earth. I believe that Jesus Christ, His only begotten Son, was born of the Virgin Mary and suffered under Pontius Pilate, was crucified, died, was buried, and on the third day rose again. I believe that having ascended to heaven, He will come again to judge the quick and the dead. I believe that Noah built an ark and herded every manner of living thing up the gangplank two by two before it rained for forty days and forty nights. I am even willing to believe that Moses was spoken to by a burning bush. But I am *not* willing to believe that Jesus

Christ Our Savior—who at the drop of a hat would heal a leper or restore sight to the blind—would turn his back on a woman who was taking care of a household.

So I don't blame Him.

Whom I blame is Matthew, Mark, Luke, and John, and every other man who's served as priest or preacher since.

From a man's point of view, the one thing that's *needful* is that you sit at his feet and listen to what he has to say, no matter how long it takes for him to say it, or how often he's said it before. By his figuring, you have plenty of time for sitting and listening because a meal is something that makes itself. The manna, it falls from heaven, and with a snap of the fingers, the water can be turned into wine. Any woman who's gone to the trouble of baking an apple pie can tell you that's how a man sees the world.

To bake an apple pie, you've first got to make the dough. You've got to cut the butter into the flour, gather it with a beaten egg and a few tablespoons of ice water, let it bind overnight. The next day, you've got to peel and core the apples, cut them into wedges, and toss them with cinnamon sugar. You've got to roll out the crust and assemble the pie. Then you bake it at 425° for fifteen minutes and 350° for another forty-five. Finally, when supper's over, you carefully plate a slice and set it on the table where, in midsentence, a man will fork half of it into his mouth and swallow without chewing, so that he can get right back to saying what he was saying without the chance of being interrupted.

And strawberry preserves? Don't you get me started on strawberry preserves!

As young Billy pointed out so rightly, making preserves is a *time-consuming* venture. Just picking the berries takes you half a day. Then you have to wash and stem the fruit. You have to sterilize the lids and jars. Once you combine the ingredients, you have to set them on simmer and watch them like a hawk, never letting yourself stray more than a few feet from the stove to make sure they don't overcook. When they're ready, you pour the preserves, seal the jars, and lug them into the pantry one tray at a time. Only then can you start the process of cleaning up, which is a job in itself.

And yes, as Duchess pointed out, the canning of preserves is a little *old-fashioned*, hearkening back to the era of root cellars and wagon trains. I suppose the very word *preserves* is bygone when compared to the blunt precision of *jam*.

And as Emmett pointed out, it is, above all else, *unnecessary*. Thanks to Mr. Smucker, at the grocery there are fifteen varieties of jam selling for nineteen cents a jar, season in and season out. In fact, jam has become so readily available, you can practically buy it at the hardware store.

So yes, the making of strawberry preserves is time-consuming, old-fashioned, and unnecessary.

Then why, you might ask, do I bother to do it?

I do it *because* it's time-consuming.

Whoever said that something worthwhile shouldn't take time? It took months for the Pilgrims to sail to Plymouth Rock. It took years for George Washington to win the Revolutionary War. And it took decades for the pioneers to conquer the West.

Time is that which God uses to separate the idle from the industrious. For time is a mountain and upon seeing its steep incline, the idle will lie down among the lilies of the field and hope that someone passes by with a pitcher of lemonade. What the worthy endeavor requires is planning, effort, attentiveness, and the willingness to clean up.

I do it *because* it's old-fashioned.

Just because something's new doesn't mean it's better; and often enough, it means it's worse.

Saying *please* and *thank you* is plenty old-fashioned. Getting married and raising children is old-fashioned. Traditions, the very means by which we come to know who we are, are nothing if not old-fashioned.

I make preserves in the manner that was taught to me by my mother, God rest her soul. She made preserves in the manner that was taught to her by her mother, and Grandma made preserves in the manner that was taught to her by hers. And so on, and so forth, back through the ages all the way to Eve. Or, at least as far as Martha.

And I do it *because* it's unnecessary.

For what is kindness but the performance of an act that is both beneficial to another and unrequired? There is no kindness in paying a bill. There is no kindness in getting up at dawn to slop the pigs, or milk the cows, or gather the eggs from the henhouse. For that matter, there is no kindness in making dinner, or in cleaning the kitchen after your father heads upstairs without so much as a word of thanks.

There is no kindness in latching the doors and turning out the lights, or in picking up the clothes from the bathroom floor in order to put them in the hamper. There is no kindness in taking care of a household because your only sister had the good sense to get herself married and move to Pensacola.

Nope, I said to myself while climbing into bed and switching off the light, there is no kindness in any of that.

For kindness begins where necessity ends.

Duchess

HAVING COME UPSTAIRS AFTER SUPPER, I was about to flop down on Emmett's bed when I noticed the smoothness of the covers. After freezing in place for a moment, I leaned over the mattress to get a closer look.

There was no question about it. She had remade it.

I thought I'd done a pretty good job, if I do say so myself. But Sally had done a better one. There wasn't a ripple on the surface. And where the sheet gets folded at the top of the blanket, there was a four-inch-high rectangle of white running from one edge of the bed to the other as if she had measured it with a ruler. While at the base, she had tucked in the covers so tightly that you could see the corners of the mattress through the surface of the blanket, the way you can see Jane Russell through the surface of her sweater.

It was such a thing of beauty, I didn't want to disturb it until I was ready to go to bed. So I sat on the floor, leaned against the wall, and gave some thought to the Watson brothers, as I waited for everyone else to fall asleep.

Earlier that day when I had gotten back to the house, Woolly and Billy were still lying out on the grass.

—How was your walk? asked Woolly.

—Rejuvenating, I replied. What have you two been up to?

—Billy has been reading me some of the stories from Professor Abernathe's book.

—Sorry I missed that. Which ones?

Billy was in the middle of running down the list when Emmett pulled into the drive.

Speaking of stories, I thought to myself . . .

In another moment, Emmett was going to emerge from his car a little worse for wear. He was certainly going to have a fat lip and some bruises; he might even have the beginnings of a shiner. The question was how was he going to explain them? Did he trip on a crack in the sidewalk? Did he tumble down a set of stairs?

In my experience, the best explanations make use of the unexpected. Like: *I was crossing the lawn of the courthouse admiring the sight of a whippoor-will perched on the branch of a tree when a football hit me in the face.* With an explanation like that, your listener is so focused on the whippoor-will up in the tree, they never see the football coming.

But when Emmett walked over and a wide-eyed Billy asked what had happened, Emmett said that he'd run into Jake Snyder while in town, and Jake had hit him. Just like that.

I turned to Billy, expecting an expression of shock or maybe outrage, but he was nodding his head and looking thoughtful.

—Did you hit him back? he asked after a moment.

—No, said Emmett. Instead, I counted to ten.

Then Billy smiled at Emmett, and Emmett smiled right back.

Truly, Horatio, there are more things in heaven and Earth, than are dreamt of in your philosophy.

—·—

Shortly after midnight, I poked my head into Woolly's room. From the sound of his breathing, I could tell that he was lost in his dreams. I crossed my fingers that he hadn't taken too much of his medicine before going to bed since I was going to have to roust him soon enough.

The Watson brothers were sound asleep too, Emmett flat on his back and Billy curled on his side. In the moonlight I could see the kid's book on the foot of the bed. If he happened to stretch his legs, it might drop to the floor, so I moved it to the spot on the bureau where his mother's picture should have been.

I found Emmett's pants hanging over the back of a chair—with all of its pockets empty. Tiptoeing around the bed, I squatted at the bedside table. The drawer wasn't more than a foot from Emmett's face, so I had to ease it open inch by inch. But the keys weren't there either.

—Harrumph, I said to myself.

I had already looked for them in the car and in the kitchen before coming upstairs. Where in the hell could he have put them?

As I was mulling this over, the beam from a set of headlights swept across the room as a vehicle pulled into the Watsons' drive and rolled to a stop.

Quietly, I headed down the hall and paused at the top of the stairs. Outside I heard the door of the vehicle open. After a moment, there were footsteps on and off the porch, then the door closed and the vehicle drove away.

When I was sure that no one had woken, I went down into the kitchen, opened the screen door, and stepped out onto the porch. In the distance I could see the lights of the vehicle headed back up the road. It took me a moment to notice the shoebox at my feet with big black letters scrawled across the top.

I may be no scholar, but I know my own name when I see it, even by the light of the moon. Getting down on my haunches, I gently lifted the lid, wondering what in God's name could be inside.

—Well, I'll be damned.

EIGHT

—.—

Emmett

WHEN THEY PULLED OUT of the driveway at five thirty in the morning, Emmett was in good spirits. The night before, with the help of Billy's map, he had laid out an itinerary. The route from Morgen to San Francisco was a little over fifteen hundred miles. If they averaged forty miles an hour for ten hours a day—leaving time enough to eat and sleep—they could make the trip in four days.

Of course there was plenty to see between Morgen and San Francisco. As their mother's postcards attested, there were motor courts and monuments, rodeos and parks. If you were willing to drive out of your way, there were Mount Rushmore, Old Faithful, and the Grand Canyon. But Emmett didn't want to waste time or money on the journey west. The sooner they got to California, the sooner he could get to work; and the more money they had in hand when they got there, the better a house they would be able to buy. If they began frittering away what little they had while in transit, they'd have to settle for buying a marginally worse house in a marginally worse neighborhood, which, when the time came to sell, would result in a marginally worse profit. As far as Emmett was concerned, the faster they crossed the country the better.

Emmett's primary worry when he'd gone to bed had been that he wouldn't be able to rouse the others, that he'd waste the first hours of daylight getting them up and out the door. But he needn't have worried. When he rose at five, Duchess was already in the shower and he could hear Woolly humming down the hall. Billy had gone so far as to sleep in his clothes so he wouldn't have to get dressed when he woke. By the time Emmett took his place behind the wheel and retrieved his keys from above the visor, Duchess was already in the passenger seat and Billy was sitting beside Woolly in the back with his map in his lap. And when, shortly before dawn, they turned out of the driveway, not one of them cast a backward glance.

Maybe they all had reasons for wanting to make an early start, thought Emmett. Maybe they all were ready to be someplace else.

As Duchess was sitting in front, Billy asked if he wanted to hold the map. When Duchess declined on the grounds that reading in cars made him queasy, Emmett felt a little relieved, recognizing that Duchess didn't always pay the closest attention to details, while Billy was practically born to navigate. Not only did he have his compass and pencils at the ready, he had a ruler so he could calculate mileage off the one-inch scale. But when Emmett signaled a right-hand turn onto Route 34, he found himself wishing that Duchess had taken on the job, after all.

—You don't need to switch on your signal yet, said Billy. We need to go straight for a little longer.

—I'm turning onto Route 34, Emmett explained, because that's the fastest way to Omaha.

—But the Lincoln Highway goes to Omaha.

Emmett pulled onto the shoulder and looked back at his brother.

—It does, Billy. But it takes us a little out of the way.

—A little out of the way of what? asked Duchess with a smile.

—A little out of the way of where we're going, said Emmett.

Duchess looked into the back seat.

—Just how far is it to the Lincoln Highway, Billy?

Billy, who already had his ruler on the map, said it was seventeen and a half miles.

Woolly, who had been quietly looking at the scenery, turned to Billy with an awakened curiosity.

—What's the Lincoln Highway, Billy? Is it a special highway?

—It was the first highway to cross America.

—The first highway to cross America, repeated Woolly in awe.

—Come on, Emmett, prodded Duchess. What's seventeen and a half miles?

It's seventeen and a half miles, Emmett wanted to reply, on top of the hundred and thirty that we're already going out of our way in order to take you to Omaha. But at the same time, Emmett knew that Duchess was right. The added distance wasn't much to speak of, especially given how disappointed Billy would be if he insisted on taking Route 34.

—All right, he said. We'll go by way of the Lincoln Highway.

As he pulled back onto the road, he could almost hear his brother nodding in affirmation that this was a good idea.

For the next seventeen and a half miles, no one said a word. But when Emmett took the right at Central City, Billy looked up from his map in excitement.

—This is it, he said. This is the Lincoln Highway.

Billy began leaning forward to see what was coming, then looking over his shoulder to see what they'd passed. Central City may only have been a city in name, but having dreamed for months about the journey to California, Billy was taking satisfaction from the handful of restaurants and motels, pleased to find they were not unlike the ones on their mother's postcards. That he was headed in the wrong direction didn't seem to make much difference.

Woolly was sharing in Billy's excitement, looking at the roadside services with new appreciation.

—So this road stretches from coast to coast?

—It stretches almost from coast to coast, corrected Billy. It goes from New York City to San Francisco.

—That sounds pretty coast-to-coast, said Duchess.

—Except that the Lincoln Highway doesn't begin or end at the water. It begins in Times Square and ends at the Palace of the Legion of Honor.

—Is it named for *Abraham* Lincoln? Woolly asked.

—It is, said Billy. And there are statues of him all along the way.

—All along the way?

—Boy Scout troops raised money to commission them.

—There's a bust of Abraham Lincoln on my great-grandfather's desk, said Woolly with a smile. He was a great admirer of President Lincoln.

—How long has this highway been around? asked Duchess.

—It was invented by Mr. Carl G. Fisher in 1912.

—Invented?

—Yes, said Billy. Invented. He believed the American people should be able to drive from one end of the country to the other. He built the first sections in 1913, with the help of donations.

—People *gave* him money to build it? asked Duchess in disbelief.

Billy nodded in earnest.

—Including Thomas Edison and Teddy Roosevelt.

—Teddy Roosevelt! exclaimed Duchess.

—Bully, said Woolly.

As they made their way eastward—with Billy dutifully naming every town they passed—Emmett took satisfaction that at least they were making good time.

Yes, the trip to Omaha was going to take them out of their way, but having gotten an early start, Emmett figured they could drop Duchess and Woolly at the bus station, turn the car around, and easily make Ogallala before dark. Maybe they'd even make it as far as Cheyenne. After all, at this point in June they would have eighteen hours of light. As a matter of fact, thought Emmett, if they were willing to drive twelve hours a day and averaged fifty miles an hour, they could make the whole trip in under three days.

But that's when Billy pointed to a water tower in the distance with the name Lewis painted across it.

—Look, Duchess. It's Lewis. Isn't that the city where you lived?

—You lived in Nebraska? Emmett asked, looking at Duchess.

—For a couple of years when I was a kid, Duchess confirmed.

Then he sat up a little in his seat and began looking around with heightened interest.

—Hey, he said to Emmett after a moment. Can we swing by? I'd love to get a look at the place. You know, for old times' sake.

—Duchess . . .

—Oh, come on. Please? I know you said you wanted to be in Omaha by eight, but it seems like we've been making pretty good time.

—We're twelve minutes ahead of schedule, said Billy after looking at his surplus watch.

—There. See?

—All right, said Emmett. We can swing by. But just for a look.

—That's all I'm asking.

When they reached the edge of the city, Duchess took over the navigation, nodding at the passing landmarks.

—Yes. Yes. Yes. There! Take that left by the fire station.

Emmett took the left, which led into a residential neighborhood with fine houses on nicely groomed lots. After a few miles, they passed a high-steepled church and a park.

—You take that next right, said Duchess.

The right led them onto a wide, curving road interspersed with trees.

—Pull over up there.

Emmett pulled over.

They were at the bottom of a grassy hill on the top of which was a large stone building. Three stories high with turrets on either end, it looked like a manor.

—Was this your house? asked Billy.

—No, said Duchess with a laugh. It's a school of sorts.

—A boarding school? asked Woolly.

—More or less.

For a moment they all admired its grandeur, then Duchess turned to Emmett.

—Can I go in?

—For what?

—To say hi.

—Duchess, it's six thirty in the morning.

—If no one's up, I'll leave a note. They'll get a kick out of it.

—A note for your teachers? asked Billy.

—Exactly. A note for my teachers. What do you say, Emmett. It'll only take a few minutes. Five minutes tops.

Emmett glanced at the clock in the dash.

—All right, he said. Five minutes.

Grabbing the book bag at his feet, Duchess climbed out of the car and jogged up the hill toward the building.

In the back seat, Billy began explaining to Woolly why he and Emmett needed to be in San Francisco by the Fourth of July.

Turning off the engine, Emmett stared through the windshield, wishing he had a cigarette.

Duchess's five minutes came and went.

Then another five.

Shaking his head, Emmett chastised himself for letting Duchess go into the building. No one drops in anywhere for five minutes, whatever the time of day. Certainly no one who liked to talk as much as Duchess.

Emmett got out of the car and walked around to the passenger side. Leaning against the door, he looked up at the school, noting that it was made from the same red limestone that they had used to build the courthouse in Morgen. The stone probably came from one of the quarries in Cass County. In the late 1800s, it had been used to build city halls, libraries, and courthouses in every town for two hundred miles. Some of the buildings were so similar in appearance that when you went from one town to the next it felt like you hadn't gone anywhere at all.

Even so, there was something that didn't seem quite right about this building. It took Emmett a few minutes to realize that what was odd was that there wasn't a prominent entrance. Whether it had originally been designed as a manor house or school, a building this grand would have had a fitting approach. There would have been a tree-lined drive leading up to an impressive front door.

It occurred to Emmett that they must be parked at the back of the building. But why hadn't Duchess directed them to drive up to the front?

And why had he taken the book bag?

—I'll be right back, he said to Billy and Woolly.

—Okay, they replied, without looking up from Billy's map.

Climbing the hill, Emmett made his way toward a door that was in the center of the building. As he walked, he was feeling a growing sense of irritation, almost looking forward to the dressing down he would be giving Duchess once he found him. Telling him, in no uncertain terms, that they didn't have time for this sort of nonsense. That his uninvited appearance was already an imposition and that the trip to Omaha was taking them two and a half hours out of their way. Five hours when you accounted for there and back. But these thoughts went out of Emmett's head as soon as he saw the broken pane—the one closest to the doorknob. Easing the door open, Emmett stepped inside, shards of glass crunching under the soles of his boots.

Emmett found himself in a large kitchen with two metal sinks, a ten-burner stove, and a walk-in refrigerator. Like most institutional kitchens, it had been put in order the night before—its counters cleared, its cabinets closed, and all of its pots hung on their hooks.

The only sign of disorder, other than the broken glass, was in a pantry area at the other side of the kitchen, where several drawers had been pulled open and spoons were scattered on the floor.

Passing through a swinging door Emmett entered a paneled dining room with six long tables like you'd expect to find in a monastery. Adding to the religious aura was a large stained-glass window that was casting patterns of yellow, red, and blue on the opposite wall. The window depicted the moment that Jesus, risen from the dead, displayed the wounds in His hands—only, in this depiction, the amazed disciples were accompanied by children.

Exiting the dining room's main doors, Emmett stepped into a grand entrance hall. To his left was the impressive front door that he'd expected, while to his right was a staircase made of the same polished oak. Under different circumstances, Emmett would have liked to linger in order to study the carvings on the door panels and the balusters of the staircase, but even as he was noting the quality of the workmanship, he heard sounds of commotion coming from somewhere overhead.

Taking the steps two at a time, Emmett passed over an additional scattering of spoons. On the second-floor landing, hallways led in opposite directions, but from the one on the right came the unmistakable sound of children in turmoil. So that's the way he went.

The first door Emmett came to opened on a dormitory. While the beds were arranged in two perfect rows, their linens were in disarray and they were empty. The next door led to a second dormitory with two more rows of beds and more linens in disarray. But in this room, sixty boys in blue pajamas were clustered in six raucous groups at the center of each of which was a jar of strawberry preserves.

In some of the groups, the boys were dutifully taking turns, while in others they were fighting for access, stabbing their spoons into the jam and transferring the contents into their mouths as quickly as possible, so they could get another crack at the jar before it was empty.

For the first time, it occurred to Emmett that this wasn't a boarding school. It was an orphanage.

As Emmett was taking in the disorder, a ten-year-old boy with glasses who had noticed him, tugged at the sleeve of one of the older boys. Looking up at Emmett, the older boy signaled a peer. Without exchanging a word, the two advanced shoulder to shoulder in order to place themselves between Emmett and the others.

Emmett raised both of his hands in peace.

—I'm not here to bother you. I'm just looking for my friend. The one who brought the jam.

The two older boys stared at Emmett in silence, but the boy with the glasses pointed in the direction of the hallway.

—He went the way he came.

Emmett left the room and doubled back to the landing. He was about to head down the stairs when from the opposite hallway he heard the muted sound of a woman shouting, followed by the pounding of a fist on wood. Emmett paused, then proceeded to the hallway, where he found two doors with tilted chairs tucked under the knobs. The shouting and pounding were coming from behind the first one.

—Open this door right this minute!

When Emmett removed the chair and opened the door, a woman in her forties wearing a long white nightgown nearly fell into the hallway. Behind her, Emmett could see another woman sitting on a bed weeping.

—How dare you! the pounder shouted, once she had regained her footing.

Emmett ignored her and went to the second door to remove the second chair. Inside this room was a third woman kneeling beside her bed in prayer and an older woman sitting peacefully in a high-back chair smoking a cigarette.

—Ah! she said when she saw Emmett. How good of you to open the door. Come in, come in.

As the older woman tamped out her cigarette in the ashtray that was in her lap, Emmett took a step forward uncertainly. But even as he did so, the sister from the first room came in behind him.

—How dare you! she shouted again.

—Sister Berenice, said the older woman. Why are you raising your voice at this young man? Can't you see that he is our liberator?

The weeping sister now came into the room still in tears, and the older woman turned to address the one who was kneeling.

—Compassion before prayers, Sister Ellen.

—Yes, Sister Agnes.

Sister Ellen rose from her place beside the bed and took the weeping sister in her arms, saying, *Hush hush hush*, while Sister Agnes turned her attention back to Emmett.

—What is your name, young man?

—Emmett Watson.

—Well, Emmett Watson, perhaps you can illuminate us as to what has been transpiring here at St. Nicholas's this morning.

Emmett felt a strong inclination to turn and walk out the door, but his inclination to answer Sister Agnes was stronger.

—I was driving a friend to the bus station in Omaha and he asked me to stop. He said he used to live here. . . .

All four sisters were looking at Emmett keenly now, the crying sister no longer crying and the hushing sister no longer hushing. The shouting sister was no longer shouting, but she took a threatening step toward Emmett.

—*Who* used to live here?

—His name is Duchess. . . .

—Ha! she exclaimed, turning to Sister Agnes. Didn't I tell you we hadn't seen the last of him! Didn't I say that he would return some day to perpetrate some final act of mischief!

Ignoring Sister Berenice, Sister Agnes looked toward Emmett with an expression of gentle curiosity.

—But tell me, Emmett, why did Daniel lock us in our rooms? To what end?

Emmett hesitated.

—Well?! demanded Sister Berenice.

Shaking his head, Emmett gestured in the direction of the dormitories.

—As best as I can tell, he got me to stop so that he could bring the boys some jars of strawberry jam.

Sister Agnes let out a sigh of satisfaction.

—There. You see, Sister Berenice? What our little Daniel has returned to perpetrate is an act of charity.

Whatever Duchess was perpetrating, thought Emmett, this little diversion had already set them back thirty minutes; and he sensed that if he hesitated now, they might be stuck here for hours.

—Well then, he said as he backed toward the door, if everything's all right . . .

—No, wait, said Sister Agnes, extending her hand.

Once in the hallway, Emmett moved quickly to the landing. With the voices of the sisters rising behind him, he dashed down the staircase, back through the dining room, and out the kitchen door, feeling a general sense of relief.

He was halfway down the hillside before he noticed that Billy was sitting on the grass with his backpack at his side and his big red book in his lap—while Duchess, Woolly, and the Studebaker were nowhere to be seen.

—Where's the car? Emmett said breathlessly, when he reached his brother.

Billy looked up from his book.

—Duchess and Woolly borrowed it. But they're going to bring it back.

—Bring it back after what?

—After they go to New York.

For a moment Emmett stared at his brother, at once dumbfounded and irate.

Sensing that something was wrong, Billy offered his assurance.

—Don't worry, he said. Duchess promised they'd be back by the eighteenth of June, leaving us plenty of time to get to San Francisco by the Fourth of July.

Before Emmett could respond, Billy was pointing at something behind him.

—Look, he said.

Turning, Emmett saw the figure of Sister Agnes descending the hill, the hem of her long black habit billowing behind her as if she were floating on air.

———•———

—You mean the Studebaker?

Emmett was standing alone in Sister Agnes's office talking to Sally on the phone.

—Yes, he said. The Studebaker.

—And Duchess took it?

—Yes.

There was silence on the other end of the line.

—I don't understand, she said. Took it where?

—To New York.

—New York, New York?

—Yes. New York, New York.

. . .

—And you're in Lewis.

—Nearly.

—I thought you were going to California. Why are you nearly in Lewis? And why is Duchess on his way to New York?

Emmett was beginning to regret having called Sally. But what choice had he had?

—Look, Sally, none of that matters right now. What matters is that I've got to get my car back. I called the depot in Lewis and apparently an eastbound train stops there later today. If I catch it, I can beat Duchess to New York, retrieve the car, and be back in Nebraska by Friday. The reason I'm calling is that in the meantime I need someone to take care of Billy.

—Then why didn't you say so.

After giving Sally directions and hanging up Sister Agnes's phone, Emmett looked out the window and found himself thinking of the day that he'd been sentenced.

Before heading into the courthouse with his father, Emmett had taken his brother aside to explain that he had waived his right to a trial. He explained that while he had intended Jimmy no serious harm, he had let his anger get the best of him, and he was ready to accept the consequences for his actions.

While Emmett was explaining this, Billy didn't shake his head in disagreement or argue that Emmett was making a mistake. He seemed to understand that what Emmett was doing was the right thing to do. But if Emmett was going to plead guilty without a hearing, then Billy wanted him to promise one thing.

—What's that, Billy?

—Promise me that whenever you feel like hitting someone in anger, first you'll count to ten.

And not only had Emmett promised to do so, they had shaken on it.

Nonetheless, Emmett suspected that if Duchess were there right now, ten might not be a high-enough number to do the trick.

———·———

By the time Emmett entered the dining hall, it was filled with the clamor of sixty boys talking all at once. Any dining hall crowded with boys was likely to be loud, but Emmett guessed this one was louder than usual as they relived the events of the morning: the sudden appearance of a mysterious confederate who delivered jars of jam after locking the sisters in their rooms. From his time in Salina, Emmett knew that the boys weren't simply reliving the events in service of their excitement. They were reliving the events in order to establish them in lore—to settle upon all the key particulars of this story that was sure to be told in the halls of the orphanage for decades to come.

Emmett found Billy and Sister Agnes sitting beside each other in the middle of one of the long monastic tables. A half-eaten plate of French toast had been pushed aside to make room for Billy's big red book.

—I should have thought, Sister Agnes was saying as she laid a finger on a page, that your Professor Abernathe would have included Jesus in place of Jason. For surely He was one of the most intrepid travelers of all. Don't you agree, William? Ah! Here is your brother!

Emmett took the chair opposite Sister Agnes since the chair opposite Billy was occupied by his backpack.

—Can we offer you some French toast, Emmett? Or perhaps some coffee and eggs?

—No, thank you, sister. I'm fine.

She gestured to the backpack.

—I don't think you've had the opportunity to tell me where you two were headed when you chanced into our company.

Chanced into our company, thought Emmett with a frown.

—We were just taking Duchess—or Daniel—and another friend to the bus station in Omaha.

—Ah, yes, said Sister Agnes. I think you did mention that.

—But the trip to the station was just a detour, said Billy. We are actually on our way to California.

—California! exclaimed Sister Agnes, looking at Billy. How exciting. And why are you headed to California?

So Billy explained to Sister Agnes about their mother leaving home when they were young, and their father dying of cancer, and the post-cards in the box in the bureau—the ones their mother had mailed from nine different stops along the Lincoln Highway on her way to San Francisco.

—And that's where we're going to find her, concluded Billy.

—Well, said Sister Agnes with a smile, that does sound like an adventure.

—I don't know about an adventure, said Emmett. The reality is that the bank foreclosed on the farm. We needed to make a fresh start and it seemed sensible to do so in a place where I can find work.

—Yes, of course, said Sister Agnes in a more measured manner.

She studied Emmett for a moment, then looked at Billy.

—Are you finished with your breakfast, Billy? Why don't you clear your things. The kitchen is right over there.

Sister Agnes and Emmett watched as Billy placed his silverware and glass on his plate and carried them carefully away. Then she turned her attention back to Emmett.

—Is something wrong?

Emmett was a little surprised by the question.

—What do you mean?

—A moment ago, you seemed a little put out when I echoed your brother's enthusiasm over your journey west.

—I suppose I'd rather you hadn't encouraged him.

—And why is that?

—We haven't heard from our mother in eight years and have no idea where she is. As you've probably sensed, my brother has a strong imagination. So when possible, I try to help him steer clear of disappointments—rather than heap on cause for more.

As Sister Agnes studied Emmett, he could feel himself shifting in his chair.

Emmett had never liked ministry. Half the time it seemed like a preacher was trying to sell you something you didn't need; and the other half he was selling you something you already had. But when it came to people of the cloth, Sister Agnes unnerved him more than most.

—Did you happen to notice the window behind me? she asked finally.

—I did.

She nodded, then gently closed Billy's book.

—When I first came to St. Nicholas's in 1942, I found that window to have a rather mysterious effect on me. There was something about it that captured my attention, but in a manner I couldn't quite pin down. Some afternoons, when things were quiet, I would sit with a cup of coffee—about where you're sitting now—and stare at it, simply to take it in. Then one day, I realized what it was that had been affecting me so. It was the difference between the expressions on the faces of the disciples and the faces of the children.

Sister Agnes turned a little in her chair so that she could look up at the window. Almost reluctantly, Emmett followed her gaze.

—If you look at the faces of the disciples, you can tell that they remain quite skeptical about what they have just seen. *Surely*, they are thinking to themselves, *this must be some kind of hoax or vision, for with our own eyes we witnessed His death on the Cross, and with our own hands we carried His body into the tomb.* But if you look at the faces of the children, there isn't a hint of skepticism. They look upon this miracle with awe and wonder, yes, but without disbelief.

Emmett knew that Sister Agnes was well intentioned. And given that she was a woman in her sixties who had devoted her life not only in service to the Church, but in service to orphans, Emmett knew when she began her story that she deserved his full attention. But as she spoke, Emmett couldn't help noting that the yellow, red, and blue patterns from the very window she was describing had moved from the wall to the surface of the table, marking the progress of the sun and the loss of another hour.

—.—

— . . . Then he went up the hill with Emmett's book bag and broke the window to the kitchen door!

Like one of the boys in the orphanage, Billy was recounting the morning's events in a state of excitement as Sally maneuvered Betty through traffic.

—He broke the window?

—Because the door was locked! And then he went into the kitchen and got a fistful of spoons and carried them upstairs to the dormitories.

—What did he want with a fistful of spoons?

—He wanted the spoons because he was bringing them your strawberry preserves!

Sally looked over at Billy with an expression of shock.

—He gave them a jar of my strawberry preserves?

—No, said Billy. He gave them six. Isn't that what you said, Emmett?

Both Billy and Sally turned to Emmett, who was looking out the passenger-side window.

—That sounds about right, he replied without looking back.

—I don't understand, said Sally, almost to herself.

Leaning forward over the steering wheel, she accelerated in order to pull around a sedan.

—I only *gave* him six jars. They might have lasted him from now until Christmas. Why on earth would he hand over the whole batch to a bunch of strangers?

—Because they are orphans, explained Billy.

Sally considered this.

—Yes, of course, Billy. You're absolutely right. Because they are orphans.

As Sally nodded her head in acknowledgment of Billy's reasoning and Duchess's charity, Emmett couldn't help but note that she'd been plenty more indignant about the fate of her jam than she had been about the fate of his car.

—There, said Emmett pointing to the station.

In order to make the turn, Sally cut in front of a Chevy. When she skidded to a stop, the three of them climbed from the cab. But as Emmett was glancing at the entrance of the station, Billy went to the bed of the truck, grabbed his backpack, and began swinging it onto his back.

Seeing this, Sally exhibited a moment of surprise, then she looked toward Emmett with the narrowed eyes of castigation.

—You haven't told him? she asked under her breath. Well, don't expect me to!

Emmett took his brother aside.

—Billy, he began, you don't need to put your backpack on right now.

—It's okay, Billy said, while tightening the shoulder straps. I can take it off when we get on the train.

Emmett got down on his haunches.

—You're not coming on the train, Billy.

—What do you mean, Emmett? Why aren't I coming on the train?

—It makes more sense for you to go with Sally while I get the car. But as soon as I've got it, I'm coming right back to Morgen to pick you up. It shouldn't take me more than a few days.

But even as Emmett was explaining this, Billy was shaking his head.

—No, he said. No. I can't go back with Sally, Emmett. We have already left Morgen and we are on our way to San Francisco.

—That's true, Billy. We are on our way to San Francisco. But right now, the car is on its way to New York. . . .

When Emmett said this, Billy's eyes opened wide with revelation.

—New York is where the Lincoln Highway begins, he said. After we take the train and find the Studebaker, we can drive to Times Square and start our journey from there.

Emmett looked to Sally for support.

She took a step forward and put a hand on Billy's shoulder.

—Billy, she said in her no-nonsense tone, you are absolutely right.

Emmett closed his eyes.

Now it was Sally he was taking aside.

—Sally . . . , he began, but she cut him off.

—Emmett, you know that there is nothing I would rather do than keep Billy at my side for another three days. As God is my witness, I would be happy to keep him for another three years. But he has already spent fifteen months waiting for you to return from Salina. And in the meanwhile, he's lost his father and his home. At this juncture, Billy's place is at your side, and he knows it. And I imagine, by now, he thinks that you should know it too.

What Emmett actually knew was that he needed to get to New York and find Duchess as quickly as possible, and that having Billy along wasn't going to make the job any easier.

But in one important respect, Billy had been right: They had already left Morgen. Having buried their father and packed their bags, they had put that part of their lives behind them. It would be something of a comfort for both of them to know that whatever happened next, they wouldn't have to go back.

Emmett turned to his brother.

—All right, Billy. We'll go to New York together.

Billy nodded in acknowledgment that this was the sensible thing to do.

After waiting for Billy to retighten the straps on his pack, Sally gave him a hug, reminding him to mind his manners and his brother. Then without giving a hug to Emmett, she climbed in her truck. But once she had turned the ignition, she beckoned him to her window.

—There's one more thing, she said.

—What's that?

—If you want to chase your car to New York that's your own

business. But I have no intention of spending the next few weeks waking up in the middle of the night in a state of worry. So a few days from now, you need to give me a call and let me know that you're safe.

Emmett began to express the impracticality of Sally's request—that once in New York, their focus would be on finding the car, that he didn't know where they'd be staying, or whether they'd have access to a phone . . .

—You didn't seem to have any trouble finding the means to call me at seven this morning so I could drop whatever I was doing and drive all the way to Lewis. I have no doubt that in a city as big as New York, you'll be able to find another telephone and the time to use it.

—Okay, said Emmett. I'll call.

—Good, said Sally. When?

—When what?

—When will you call?

—Sally, I don't even—

—Friday then. You can call me on Friday at two thirty.

Before Emmett could respond, Sally put the truck in gear and pulled to the depot's exit, where she idled, waiting for a break in the traffic.

Earlier that morning when they had been preparing to leave the orphanage, Sister Agnes had bestowed on Billy a pendant on a chain saying it was the medallion of Christopher, the patron saint of travelers. When she turned to Emmett, he worried that she was about to bestow a medallion on him too. Instead, she said there was something she wanted to ask him, but before doing so, she had another story to tell: the story of how Duchess had come into her care.

One afternoon in the summer of 1944, she said, a man of about fifty had appeared at the orphanage door with a scrawny little eight-year-old at his side. Once the man was alone with Sister Agnes in her office, he explained that his brother and sister-in-law had died in a car crash, and that he was the boy's only surviving relative. Of course, he wanted nothing more than to care for his nephew, especially at such an impressionable age; but as an officer in the armed forces, he was due to ship out for France at the end of the week, and he didn't know when he would return from the war or, for that matter, if he would return at all. . . .

—Now, I didn't believe a word this man had to say. Never mind that his unkempt hair was hardly befitting an officer in the armed forces and that he had a lovely young girl waiting in the passenger seat of his convertible car. It was plain enough that he was the boy's father. But it is not my calling to concern myself with the duplicity of unscrupulous men. It is my calling to concern myself with the welfare of forsaken boys. And let there be no doubt about it, Emmett, young Daniel was forsaken. Yes, his father reappeared two years later to reclaim Daniel, when it suited him to do so, but Daniel didn't know to expect that. Most of the boys who come into our care are truly orphans. We have boys whose parents died together of influenza or in fires, whose mothers died in childbirth and fathers died at Normandy. And it is a terrible trial for these children who must come of age without the love of their parents. But imagine becoming an orphan not by calamity, but by your father's preference—by his determination that you have become an inconvenience.

Sister Agnes let that sink in for a moment.

—I have no doubt that you are angry with Daniel for taking liberties with your car. But we both know that there is goodness in him, a goodness that has been there from the beginning, but which has never had the chance to fully flourish. At this critical time in his life, what he needs more than anything else is a friend who will stand reliably at his side; a friend who can steer him clear of folly and help him find the way to fulfilling his Christian purpose.

—Sister, you said you were going to ask me something. You didn't say you were going to ask something of me.

The nun studied Emmett for a second, then smiled.

—You are absolutely right, Emmett. I am not asking you this. I'm asking it of you.

—I have someone to watch over already. Someone who is my own flesh and blood and who is an orphan in his own right.

She looked at Billy with an affectionate smile, but then turned back to Emmett with undiminished intent.

—Do you count yourself a Christian, Emmett?

—I'm not the churchgoing sort.

—But do you count yourself a Christian?

—I was raised to be one.

—Then I imagine you know the parable of the Good Samaritan.

—Yes, sister, I know the parable. And I know that a good Christian helps a man in need.

—Yes, Emmett. A good Christian shows compassion toward those who are in difficulty. And that is an important part of the parable's meaning. But an equally important point that Jesus is making is that we do not always get to *choose* to whom we should show our charity.

When Emmett had come to the end of his driveway shortly before dawn, he had turned onto the road knowing that he and Billy were unencumbered—free of any debts or obligations as they began their life anew. And now, having traveled just sixty miles from home headed in the wrong direction, he had made two promises in as many hours.

Once the traffic finally subsided and Sally took a left out of the station, Emmett expected her to turn and wave. But leaning forward over her wheel, Sally punched the gas, Betty backfired, and they both headed west without a glance in his direction.

Only as they sped out of sight did Emmett realize he didn't have any money.

Duchess

WHAT A DAY, WHAT A DAY, what a day! Emmett's car may not have been the fastest one on the road, but the sun was high, the skies were blue, and everyone we passed had a smile on their face.

After leaving Lewis, for the first one hundred and fifty miles we had seen more grain elevators than human beings. And most of the towns we passed through seemed to be limited to one of everything by local decree: one movie theater and one restaurant; one cemetery and one savings and loan; in all likelihood, one sense of right and wrong.

But for most people, it doesn't matter where they live. When they get up in the morning, they're not looking to change the world. They want to have a cup of coffee and a piece of toast, put in their eight hours, and wrap up the day with a bottle of beer in front of the TV set. More or less, it's what they'd be doing whether they lived in Atlanta, Georgia, or Nome, Alaska. And if it doesn't matter for most people where they live, it certainly doesn't matter where they're going.

That's what gave the Lincoln Highway its charm.

When you see the highway on a map, it looks like that Fisher guy Billy was talking about took a ruler and drew a line straight across the country, mountains and rivers be damned. In so doing, he must have imagined it would provide a timely conduit for the movement of goods and ideas from sea to shining sea, in a final fulfillment of manifest destiny. But everyone we passed just seemed to have a satisfied sense of their own lack of purpose. *Let the road rise up to meet you*, say the Irish, and that's what was happening to the intrepid travelers on the Lincoln Highway. It was rising up to meet each and every one of them, whether they were headed east, headed west, or going around in circles.

—It was awfully nice of Emmett to loan us his car, said Woolly.

—It was at that.

He smiled for a moment, then his brow furrowed just like Billy's.

—Do you think they had any trouble getting home?

—No, said I. I'll bet you Sally came racing over in that pickup of hers, and the three of them are already back in her kitchen eating biscuits and jelly.

—You mean biscuits and preserves.

—Exactly.

I did feel a little bad about Emmett having to make the journey to Lewis and back. If I'd known he kept his keys above the visor, I could have saved him the trip.

The irony is that when we set out from Emmett's house, I had no intention of borrowing the car. By then I was looking forward to taking the Greyhound. And why not? On the bus you get to sit back and relax. You can take a nap, or make a little conversation with the shoe-leather salesman across the aisle. But just as we were about to make the turn toward Omaha, Billy piped up about the Lincoln Highway, and next thing you know, we were on the outskirts of Lewis. Then when I came out of St. Nick's, there was the Studebaker sitting by the curb with the key in its slot and the driver's seat empty. It was as if Emmett and Billy had planned the whole thing. Or the Good Lord. Either way, destiny seemed to be announcing itself pretty loud and clear—even if Emmett had to make the round trip.

—The good news, I said to Woolly, is that if we keep up this pace, we should be in New York by Wednesday morning. We can see my old man, zip out to the camp, and be back with Emmett's share before he misses us. And given the size of the house that you and Billy cooked up, I think Emmett's going to be glad to have a little extra cabbage when he lands in San Francisco.

Woolly smiled at the mention of Billy's house.

—Speaking of our pace, I said, how long until we get to Chicago?

The smile left Woolly's face.

In Billy's absence, I had given him the job of navigating. Since Billy wouldn't let us borrow his map, we had to get one of our own (from a Phillips 66, of course). And just like Billy, Woolly had carefully marked our route with a black line that followed the Lincoln Highway all the way to New York. But once we were under way, he acted like he couldn't get that map into the glove compartment fast enough.

—You want me to calculate the distance? he asked with an unmistakable sense of foreboding.

—I'll tell you what, Woolly: Why don't you forget about Chicago and find us a little something to listen to on the radio.

And just like that, the smile was back.

Presumably, the dial was normally set to Emmett's favorite station, but we had left that signal somewhere back in Nebraska. So when Woolly turned on the radio, all that came through the speaker was static.

For a few seconds, Woolly gave it his full attention, as if he wanted to identify exactly what kind of static it was. But as soon as he began to turn the tuner, I could tell that here was another of Woolly's hidden talents—like the dishes and the floor plan. Because Woolly didn't just spin the dial and hope for the best. He turned it like a safecracker. With his eyes narrowed and his tongue between his teeth, he moved that little orange needle slowly across the spectrum until he could hear the faintest hint of a signal. Then slowing even further, he would let the signal gain in strength and clarity until he suddenly came to a stop at the incidence of perfect reception.

The first signal Woolly landed on was a country music station. It was playing a number about a cowboy on the range who'd either lost his woman or his horse. Before I could figure out which, Woolly had turned the dial. Next up was a crop report coming live to us all the way from Iowa City, then the fiery sermon of a Baptist preacher, then a bit of Beethoven with all the edges sanded down. When he didn't even stop for *Sh-boom, sh-boom,* I began to wonder if anything on the radio was going to be good enough. But when he tuned into 1540, a commercial for a breakfast cereal was just beginning. Letting go of the knob, Woolly stared at the radio, giving the advertisement the sort of attention that one would normally reserve for a physician or fortune-teller. And so it began.

Oh, how this kid loved a commercial. Over the next hundred miles, we must have listened to fifty. And they could have been for anything. For a Coupe DeVille or the new Playtex bra. It didn't seem to matter. Because Woolly wasn't looking to buy anything. What captivated him was the drama.

At the beginning of a commercial, Woolly would listen gravely as the actor or actress articulated their particular dilemma. Like the tepid flavor of their menthol cigarettes or the grass stains on their children's pants. From Woolly's expression, you could see that he not only shared in their distress, he had a looming suspicion that *all* quests for happiness were doomed to disappointment. But as soon as these beleaguered souls decided to try the new brand of this or that, Woolly's expression would brighten, and when they discovered that the product in question had not only removed the lumps from their mashed potatoes but the lumps from their life, Woolly would break into a smile, looking uplifted and reassured.

A few miles west of Ames, Iowa, the commercial that Woolly happened upon introduced us to a mother who has just learned—to her utter dismay—that each of her three sons has arrived for supper with a guest. At the revelation of this setback, Woolly let out an audible gasp. But suddenly we heard the twinkling of a magic wand and who should appear but Chef Boy-Ar-Dee with his big puffy hat and even puffier accent. With another wave of the wand, six cans of his Spaghetti Sauce with Meat appeared lined up on the counter ready to save the day.

—Doesn't that sound delicious, Woolly sighed, as the boys on the radio dug into their dinner.

—Delicious! I exclaimed in horror. It comes out of a can, Woolly.

—I know. Isn't that amazing?

—Whether it's amazing or not, that is no way to eat an Italian dinner.

Woolly turned to me with a look of genuine curiosity.

—What is the way to eat an Italian dinner, Duchess?

Oh, where to begin.

—Have you ever heard of Leonello's? I asked. Up in East Harlem?

—I don't think so.

—Then you'd better pull up a chair.

Woolly made a good faith effort to do so.

—Leonello's, I began, is a little Italian place with ten booths, ten tables, and a bar. The booths are lined with red leather, the tables are draped with red and white cloths, and Sinatra's playing on the jukebox, just like you'd expect. The only hitch is that if you walked in off the street on a Thursday night and asked for a table, they wouldn't let you sit down for supper—even if the place was empty.

As one who always loves a conundrum, Woolly's expression brightened up.

—Why won't they let you sit down for supper, Duchess?

—The reason they won't let you sit down, Woolly, is because all the tables are taken.

—But you just said the whole place was empty.

—And so it is.

—Then taken by whom?

—Ay, my friend, there's the rub. You see, the way that Leonello's works is that every table in the place is reserved in perpetuity. If you're one of Leonello's customers, you might have the table for four by the jukebox on Saturdays at eight. And you pay for that table every Saturday night, whether you show up or not, so no one else can use it.

I looked over at Woolly.

—You with me so far?

—I'm with you, he said.

And I could tell he was.

—Let's say you're not a customer of Leonello's, but you're lucky enough to have a friend who is, and this friend has given you the use of his table when he's out of town. When Saturday night rolls around, you put on your best duds and head up to Harlem with your three closest friends.

—Like you and Billy and Emmett.

—Exactly. Like me and Billy and Emmett. But once we're all settled and we've ordered a drink, don't bother asking for menus.

—Why not?

—Because at Leonello's, they don't have them.

I really had Woolly with that one. I mean, he let out a bigger gasp than he had during the Chef Boy-Ar-Dee commercial.

—How can you order dinner without a menu, Duchess?

—At Leonello's, I explained, once you've taken your seat and ordered your drinks, the waiter will drag a chair over to your table, spin it around, and sit with his arms on its back so that he can tell you exactly what they're serving that night. *Welcome to Leonello's,* he'll say. *Tonight for starters we got stuffed artichokes, mussels marinara, clams oreganata, and calamari fritti. For the first course we got linguine with clams, spaghetti carbonara, and penne Bolognese. And for the main course, chicken cacciatore, veal scallopini, veal Milanese, and osso buco.*

I took a quick glance at my copilot.

—I can see from your expression that you're a little daunted by all this variety, Woolly, but worry not. Because the only dish that you have to order at Leonello's is the one the waiter hasn't mentioned:

Fettuccine Mio Amore, the specialty of the house. A fresh-made pasta that's tossed in a sauce of tomatoes, bacon, caramelized onions, and pepper flakes.

—But why doesn't the waiter mention it, if it's the specialty of the house?

—He doesn't mention it *because* it's the specialty of the house. That's the way it goes with *Fettuccine Mio Amore*. Either you know enough to order it, or you don't deserve to eat it.

I could tell from the smile on Woolly's face that he was enjoying his night at Leonello's.

—Did your father have a table at Leonello's? he asked.

I laughed.

—No, Woolly. My old man didn't have a table anywhere. But for six glorious months, he was the maître d', and I was allowed to hang out in the kitchen, as long as I didn't get in the way.

I was about to tell Woolly about Lou, the chef, when a truck driver came barreling around us with a shake of the fist.

Normally, I would have replied with a bite of the thumb, but when I looked up to do so, I realized I had gotten so wrapped up in the telling of my tale, I had let our speed drop to thirty miles an hour. No wonder the trucker was out of joint.

But when I punched the accelerator, the little orange needle in the speedometer dropped from twenty-five to twenty. When I pushed the pedal to the floor, we slowed to fifteen, and when I pulled onto the shoulder, we rolled to a stop.

Turning the key off and on, I counted to three and pushed the starter to no effect.

Fucking Studebaker, I muttered to myself. It's probably the battery again. But even as I thought this, I realized the radio was still playing, so it couldn't be the battery. Maybe it had something to do with the spark plug . . . ?

—Are we out of gas? asked Woolly.

After looking at Woolly for a second, I looked at the fuel gauge. It too had a thin orange needle, and sure enough, the needle was sitting on the bottom.

—So it would seem, Woolly. So it would seem.

As luck would have it, we were still in the Ames city limits, and not far up the road I could see the flying red horse of a Mobil station. Putting my hands in my pockets, I withdrew what change was left from Mr. Watson's desk drawer. After accounting for the hamburger and ice cream cone I'd purchased back in Morgen, it amounted to seven cents.

—Woolly, you wouldn't happen to have any money on you?

—Money? he replied.

Why is it, I wondered, that people born with money are always the ones who say the word like it's in a foreign language?

Getting out of the car, I looked up and down the road. Across the street was a diner beginning to get busy with the lunch crowd. Next was a laundromat with two cars in the lot. But farther up the way was a liquor store that didn't look like it had opened yet.

In New York City, no liquor store owner worth his salt would leave cash on the premises overnight. But we weren't in New York City. We were in the heartland, where most of the people who read *In God We Trust* on a dollar bill took the words literally. But on the off chance there wasn't any money sitting in the till, I figured I could grab a case of whiskey and offer a few bottles to the gas station attendant in exchange for filling the tank.

The only problem was how to get in.

—Hand me the keys, would you?

Leaning over, Woolly removed the keys from the ignition and passed them through the window.

—Thanks, I said, turning toward the trunk.

—Duchess?

—Yeah, Woolly?

—Do you think it's possible . . . ? Do you think I might . . . ?

Generally, I don't like to tinker with another man's habits. If he wants to get up early and go to mass, let him get up early and go to mass; and if he wants to sleep until noon wearing last night's clothes, let him sleep until noon wearing last night's clothes. But given that Woolly was down to his last few bottles of medicine and I needed help with the navigation, I had asked him to forgo his midmorning dose.

I took another glance at the liquor store. I had no idea how long it was going to take for me to get in and out. So in the meantime, it was probably just as well if Woolly was lost in his thoughts.

—All right, I said. But why don't you keep it to a drop or two.

He was already reaching for the glove compartment as I headed to the back of the car.

When I opened the trunk, I had to smile. Because when Billy had said that he and Emmett were heading for California with what little they could fit in a kit bag, I figured he was speaking figuratively. But there was nothing figurative about it. It was a kit bag, all right. Setting it aside, I folded back the felt that covered the spare. Nesting beside the tire, I found the jack and handle. The handle was about the width of a candy cane, but if it was strong enough to crank up a Studebaker, I figured it would be strong enough to open a country door.

Picking up the handle with my left hand, I went to fold the felt back in place with my right. And that's when I saw it: a little corner of paper sticking up from behind the black of the tire, looking as white as an angel's wing.

Emmett

IT TOOK EMMETT HALF AN HOUR to find his way to the gates of the freight yard. While the passenger and freight lines were adjacent, they had their backs to each other. So even though their respective terminals were just a few hundred yards apart, to get from the entrance of one to the entrance of the other, you had to walk a circumventing mile. The route initially took Emmett along a well-groomed thoroughfare of shops, but then over the tracks and into a zone of foundries, scrapyards, and garages.

As he followed the wire fence that bordered the rail yard, Emmett began to sense the enormity of the task before him. For while the passenger terminal was just large enough to accommodate the few hundred travelers who arrived or departed from this midsized city in a day—the freight yard sprawled. Fanning out over five acres, it encompassed a receiving yard, a switching yard, wheelhouses, offices, and maintenance areas, but most of all, boxcars. Hundreds of them. Rectilinear and rust-colored, they were lined end to end and row by row for almost as far as the eye could see. And whether they were slotted to head east or west, north or south, laden or empty, they were exactly as common sense should have told him they would be: anonymous and interchangeable.

The entrance to the yard was on a wide street lined with warehouses. As Emmett approached, the only person in sight was a middle-aged man in a wheelchair positioned near the gates. Even from a distance, Emmett could see that both of his legs had been cut off above the knee—a casualty of the war, no doubt. If the veteran's intention was to profit from the kindness of strangers, thought Emmett, he would have been better off in front of the passenger terminal.

In order to assess the situation, Emmett took up a position across the street from the gates, in the doorway of a shuttered building. Not far behind the fencing he could see a two-story brick building in relatively good repair. That's where the command center would be—the room with the manifests and timetables. Naively, Emmett had imagined that he would be able to slip into the building sight unseen and cull the information he needed from a schedule posted on a wall. But just beyond the gates was a small building that looked very much like a guardhouse.

Sure enough, as Emmett was studying it, a truck pulled into the entrance and a man in uniform emerged from the house with a clipboard in order to clear the truck for admission. There wasn't going to be any slipping or culling, thought Emmett. He would have to wait for the information to come to him.

Emmett glanced at the dial of the army surplus watch, which Billy had loaned him. It was quarter past eleven. Figuring he would get his chance when the lunch hour came, Emmett leaned back in the shadows of the doorway and bided his time, his thoughts returning to his brother.

When Emmett and Billy had entered the passenger terminal, Billy was all eyes, taking in the high ceilings and ticket windows, the coffee shop and shoe shine and newsstand.

—I've never been in a train station before, he said.

—Is it different than you expected?

—It's just as I expected.

—Come on, said Emmett with a smile. Let's sit over here.

Emmett led his brother through the main waiting area to a quiet corner with an empty bench.

Removing his backpack, Billy sat down and slid over to make room for Emmett, but Emmett didn't sit.

—I need to go find out about the trains to New York, Billy. But it might take a little while. Until I get back, I want you to promise you'll stay put.

—Okay, Emmett.

—And keep in mind, this isn't Morgen. There's going to be plenty of people coming and going, all of them strangers. It's probably for the best if you keep to yourself.

—I understand.

—Good.

—But if you want to find out about the trains to New York, why don't you ask at the information window? It's right there under the clock.

When Billy pointed, Emmett looked back toward the information window, then he joined his brother on the bench.

—Billy, we're not going to be taking one of the passenger trains.

—Why not, Emmett?

—Because all of our money is in the Studebaker.

Billy thought about this, then reached for his backpack.

—We can use my silver dollars.

With a smile, Emmett stayed his brother's hand.

—We can't do that. You've been collecting those for years. And you only have a few more to go, right?

—Then what are we going to do, Emmett?

—We're going to hitch a ride on one of the freight trains.

For most people, Emmett figured, rules were a necessary evil. They were an inconvenience to be abided for having the privilege of living in an orderly world. And that's why most people, when left to their own devices, were willing to stretch the boundaries of a rule. To speed on an empty road or liberate an apple from an untended orchard. But when it came to rules, Billy wasn't simply an abider. He was a stickler. He made his bed and brushed his teeth without needing to be asked. He insisted that he be at school fifteen minutes before the first bell, and he always raised his hand in class before speaking. As a result, Emmett had thought a lot about how he was going to put this, eventually settling on the phrase *hitch a ride* in the hope it might diminish any qualms his brother was sure to have. From Billy's expression, Emmett could see that he had chosen well.

—Like stowaways, Billy said, a little wide-eyed.

—That's right. Like stowaways.

Patting his brother on the knee, Emmett rose from the bench and turned to go.

—Like Duchess and Woolly in the warden's car.

Emmett paused and turned back.

—How do you know about that, Billy?

—Duchess told me. Yesterday after breakfast. We were talking about *The Count of Monte Cristo* and how Edmond Dantès, imprisoned unjustly, escaped from the Château d'If by stitching himself into the sack that was meant for the body of Abbé Faria, so that the unwitting guards would carry him out of the prison gates. Duchess explained how he and Woolly had done almost the exact same thing. How, unjustly imprisoned, they had hidden in the trunk of the warden's car and the warden had unwittingly driven them right through the gates. Only Duchess and Woolly weren't tossed in the sea.

As Billy related this, he spoke with the same excitement that he had shown when describing for Sally the incident at the orphanage—with the broken window and fistful of spoons.

Emmett sat down again.

—Billy, you seem to like Duchess.

Billy looked back in perplexity.

—Don't you like Duchess, Emmett?

—I do. But just because I like someone doesn't mean I like everything they happen to do.

—Like when he gave away Sally's preserves?

Emmett laughed.

—No. I'm all right with that one. I meant other things. . . .

As Billy continued to stare back at him, Emmett searched for an appropriate example.

—You remember Duchess's story about going to see the movies?

—You mean when he would sneak out the bathroom window and jog across the potato fields.

—Right. Well, there's a little more to that story than Duchess related. He wasn't just a participant when it came to sneaking into town, he was the instigator. He's the one who came up with the idea and who would rally a few of the others whenever he wanted to see a movie. And for the most part, it was like he said. If they slipped out on a Saturday night around nine, they could be back by one in the morning, leaving no one the wiser. But one night, Duchess was eager to see some new western with John Wayne. Since it had been raining all week and it looked as if it might rain some more, the only one he could convince to go was my bunkmate, Townhouse. They weren't halfway across the fields when it started to pour. Though they were getting drenched and their boots were getting stuck in the mud, they pushed on. But when they finally got to the river, which was riding high because of the rain, Duchess just sat down and quit. He said he was too cold, too wet, too tired to go farther. Townhouse figured he'd come that far, he wasn't turning back. So he swam across, leaving Duchess behind.

Billy was nodding as Emmett spoke, his brow furrowed in concentration.

—All of this would have been fine, continued Emmett, but after Townhouse left, Duchess decided he was too wet, too cold, and too tired to walk all the way back to the barracks. So he went to the nearest road, flagged down a passing pickup, and asked if he could get a lift to a diner up the way. The only problem was that the driver of the pickup was an off-duty cop. Instead of taking Duchess to the diner, he took him to the warden. And when Townhouse returned at one in the morning, the guards were waiting.

—Was Townhouse punished?

—He was, Billy. And pretty severely, at that.

What Emmett didn't tell his brother was that Warden Ackerly had two simple rules when it came to *willful infractions*. The first rule was that you could pay the piper in weeks or strokes. You get in a fight in the mess hall and that's either three weeks tacked onto your sentence or three lashes on your back. His second rule was that since Negro boys were only half as suited to learning as white boys, their lessons had to be twice as long. So while Duchess took four extra weeks tacked onto his sentence, Townhouse received eight strokes from the switch—right there in front of the mess hall with everyone lined up to watch.

—The point is, Billy, that Duchess is full of energy and enthusiasm and good intentions too. But sometimes, his energy and enthusiasm get in the way of his good intentions, and when that happens the consequences often fall on someone else.

Emmett had hoped this recollection would be a little sobering for Billy, and from Billy's expression it seemed to have hit the mark.

—That is a sad story, he said.

—It is, said Emmett.

—It makes me feel sorry for Duchess.

Emmett looked at his brother in surprise.

—Why for Duchess, Billy? He's the one who got Townhouse in trouble.

—That only happened because Duchess wouldn't cross the river when it was riding high.

—That's true. But why would that make you feel sorry for him?

—Because he must not know how to swim, Emmett. And he was too ashamed to admit it.

—.—

Just as Emmett anticipated, shortly after noon some of the railyard's employees began walking through the gates on their way to get lunch. As he watched, Emmett noted that he couldn't have been more wrong about where the vet positioned himself. Nearly every man who exited had something for him—be it a nickel, a dime, or a friendly word.

Emmett understood that the men who emerged from the administrative building were most likely to have the information he needed. Responsible for scheduling and dispatching, they would know which boxcars were to be attached to which trains at which times and where they would be headed. But Emmett didn't approach them. Instead, he waited for the others: the brakemen and loaders and mechanics—the men who worked with their hands and were paid by the hour. Instinctively, Emmett knew that these men would be more likely to see in him a version of themselves and, if not exactly overcome with sympathy, at least reasonably indifferent to whether the railroad collected another fare. But if instinct told Emmett that these were the men he should approach, reason told him that he should wait for a straggler, because even though a working man might be open to bending the rules on behalf of a stranger, he'd be less likely to do so in the company of others.

Emmett had to wait almost half an hour for his first opportunity— a lone workman in jeans and a black tee shirt who looked no more than twenty-five. As the young man paused to light a cigarette, Emmett crossed the street.

—Excuse me, he said.

Waving out his match, the young man gave Emmett a once-over but didn't reply. Emmett forged ahead with the story he had fashioned, explaining that he had an uncle from Kansas City who was an engineer, who was scheduled to stop in Lewis sometime that afternoon on a freight train headed for New York, but Emmett couldn't remember which train it was, or when it would arrive.

When Emmett had first seen this young man, he'd imagined their proximity in ages would play to his advantage. But as soon as he began speaking, he realized he'd been wrong about that too. The young man's expression was as dismissive of Emmett as only a young man's expression can be.

—No kidding, he said with a slanted smile. An uncle from Kansas City. Imagine that.

The young man took a drag and flicked his unfinished cigarette into the street.

—Why don't you do yourself a favor, kid, and head on home. Your momma's wondering where you've gotten to.

As the young man sauntered away, Emmett made eye contact with the panhandler, who had watched the entire exchange. Emmett shifted his gaze to the guardhouse to see if the guard had been watching too, but he was leaning back in his chair reading a newspaper.

An older man in a jumpsuit came through the gates now and stopped to exchange a few friendly words with the panhandler. The man had a cap pushed so far back on his head, it made you wonder why he wore it at all. When he began walking away, Emmett approached.

If proximity in age had proven a liability with the first man, Emmett decided he'd make the most of the difference in age with the second.

—Excuse me, sir, he said, with deference.

Turning, the man looked at Emmett with a friendly smile.

—Hey there, son. What can I do you for?

As Emmett repeated the story about his uncle, the man in the jumpsuit listened with interest, even leaning a little forward as if he didn't want to miss a word. But once Emmett finished, he shook his head.

—I'd love to help ya, fella, but I just fix 'em. I don't ask where they're headed.

As the mechanic continued down the street, Emmett began to accept that he needed a whole new plan of action.

—Hey there, someone called.

Emmett turned to find it was the panhandler.

—I'm sorry, Emmett said, drawing the pockets out of his pants. I've got nothing for you.

—You're misunderstandin', friend. It's me who's got somethin' for you.

As Emmett hesitated, the panhandler wheeled himself closer.

—You're lookin' to hop a freight train headed for New York. That about it?

Emmett exhibited a little surprise.

—I lost my legs, not my ears! But listen: If you're tryin' to hop a train, you're askin' the wrong guys. Jackson wouldn't stomp on your foot if your toes were on fire. And like Arnie says, he just fixes 'em. Which is no small matter, mind you, but it's got everythin' to do with how a train is runnin', and nothin' to do with where it's goin'. So there's no point in askin' Jackson or Arnie. No, sirree. If you want to know how to hop a train to New York, the guy you should be talkin' to is me.

Emmett must have betrayed incredulity, because the panhandler grinned and pointed a thumb to his chest.

—I worked for the railroads for twenty-five years. Fifteen as a brakeman and ten in the switchin' yard right here in Lewis. How do you think I lost my legs?

He pointed to his lap with another smile. Then he looked Emmett over, though in a more generous manner than the young workman had.

—What are you—eighteen?

—That's right, said Emmett.

—Believe it or not, I started ridin' the rails when I was a few years younger than you. Back in the day, they'd take you on if you was sixteen; maybe fifteen, if you was tall for your age.

The panhandler shook his head with a nostalgic smile, then he leaned back like an old man who was sitting in his favorite living room chair, making himself comfortable.

—I got my start on the Union Pacific lines and worked the southwest corridor for seven years. I spent another eight workin' for the Pennsylvania Railroad—the largest in the nation. In those days, I spent more time in motion than I spent standin' still. It got so when I was home, when I'd get out of bed in the mornin' it would feel like the whole house was rollin' under my feet. I'd have to hold on to the furniture just to make my way to the bathroom.

The panhandler laughed and shook his head again.

—Yep. The Pennsylvania. The Burlington. The Union Pacific and Great Northern. I know all the lines.

Then he was quiet.

—You were talking about a train to New York, Emmett prompted gently.

—Righto, he replied. The Big Apple! But are you sure about New York? The thing about a freight yard is you can get to anywhere you've thought of, and plenty of places you haven't. Florida. Texas. California. How about Santa Fe? You been there? Now that's a town. This time of year, it's warm durin' the day and cool at night, and it's got some of the friendliest *señoritas* you'll ever meet.

As the panhandler began laughing, Emmett worried he was losing the thread of their conversation again.

—I'd love to go to Santa Fe at some point, Emmett said, but for the time being, I need to go to New York.

The panhandler stopped laughing and adopted a more serious expression.

—Well, that's life in a nutshell, ain't it. Lovin' to go to one place and havin' to go to another.

The panhandler looked left and right, then he wheeled a little closer.

—I know you were askin' Jackson about an afternoon train to New York. Now that would be the Empire Special, which leaves at one fifty-five, and she's a beauty. Runnin' at ninety miles an hour and stoppin' only six times, she can make it to the city in under twenty hours. But if you want to *get* to New York, then you don't want to ride the Empire Special. 'Cause when she reaches Chicago, she takes on a carload of bearer bonds headed for Wall Street. She never has fewer than four armed guards, and when they decide to remove you from the train, they don't wait for it to come into a station.

The panhandler looked up in the air.

—Now, the West Coast Perishables, she comes through Lewis at six o'clock. And she ain't a bad ride. But this time of year, she'll be filled to the brim and you'd have to board her in broad daylight. So you don't want the Perishables neither. What you want is the Sunset East, which will be comin' through Lewis shortly after midnight. And I can tell you exactly how to board her, but before I do, you'll have to answer me a question.

—Go ahead, said Emmett.

The panhandler grinned.

—What's the difference between a ton of flour and a ton of crackers?

———— • ————

When Emmett returned to the passenger terminal, he was relieved to find Billy just where he'd left him—sitting on the bench with his backpack at his side and his big red book in his lap.

When Emmett joined him, Billy looked up with some excitement.

—Did you figure out which train we're going to hitch a ride on, Emmett?

—I did, Billy. But it doesn't go until shortly after midnight.

Billy nodded to express his approval, as if shortly after midnight was exactly when it should go.

—Here, said Emmett, taking off his brother's watch.

—No, said Billy. You wear it for now. You need to keep track of the time.

While strapping the watch back on, Emmett saw that it was nearly two.

—I'm starving, he said. Maybe I'll take a look around and see if I can scrounge up something for us to eat.

—You don't have to scrounge up something, Emmett. I have our lunch.

Billy reached into his backpack and took out his canteen, two paper napkins, and two sandwiches wrapped in wax paper with tight creases and sharp corners. Emmett smiled, noting that Sally wrapped her sandwiches as neatly as she made her beds.

—One is roast beef and one is ham, Billy said. I couldn't remember if you liked roast beef more than ham, or ham more than roast beef, so we decided on one of each. They both have cheese, but only the roast beef has mayonnaise.

—I'll take the roast beef, said Emmett.

The brothers unwrapped their sandwiches and both took healthy bites.

—God bless, Sally.

Billy looked up in agreement with Emmett's sentiment, but apparently curious as to the timing of the remark. By way of explanation, Emmett held his sandwich in the air.

—Oh, said Billy. These aren't from Sally.

—They're not?

—They're from Mrs. Simpson.

Emmett froze for a moment with his sandwich in the air, while Billy took another bite.

—Who is Mrs. Simpson, Billy?

—The nice lady who sat beside me.

—Sat beside you here?

Emmett pointed to the spot on the bench where he was sitting.

—No, said Billy pointing to the empty spot on his right. Sat beside me here.

—She made these sandwiches?

—She bought them in the coffee shop, then brought them back because I told her I had to stay put.

Emmett set his sandwich down.

—You shouldn't be accepting sandwiches from strangers, Billy.

—But I didn't accept the sandwiches when we were strangers, Emmett. I accepted them when we were friends.

Emmett closed his eyes for a moment.

—Billy, he said as gently as he could, you can't become friends with someone just by talking to them in a train station. Even if you spent an hour together sitting on a bench, you would hardly know anything about them.

—I know a lot about Mrs. Simpson, Billy corrected. I know that she was raised outside Ottumwa, Iowa, on a farm just like ours, although they only grew corn and it never got foreclosed. And she has two daughters, one who lives in St. Louis and one who lives in Chicago. And the one who lives in Chicago, whose name is Mary, is about to have a baby. Her first. And that's why Mrs. Simpson was here in the station. In order to take the Empire Special to Chicago so that she could help Mary with the care of the baby. Mr. Simpson couldn't go because he's the president of the Lions Club and is presiding over a dinner on Thursday night.

Emmett held up his hands.

—All right, Billy. I can see that you've learned a lot about Mrs. Simpson. So the two of you may not be strangers, exactly. You've been getting acquainted with each other. But that still doesn't make you friends. To become friends doesn't take just an hour or two. It takes a bit longer. Okay?

—Okay.

Emmett picked up his sandwich and took another bite.

—How much? asked Billy.

Emmett swallowed.

—How much?

—How much longer do you need to talk to a stranger before they become your friend?

For a moment, Emmett considered wading into the intricacies of how relationships evolve over time. Instead, he said:

—Ten days.

Billy thought about this for a moment, then shook his head.

—Ten days seems like a very long time to have to wait to become a friend, Emmett.

—Six days? suggested Emmett.

Billy took a bite and chewed as he considered, then nodded his head with satisfaction.

—Three days, he said.

—All right, said Emmett. We'll agree that it takes at least three days for someone to become a friend. But before that we'll think of them as strangers.

—Or acquaintances, said Billy.

—Or acquaintances.

The brothers went back to eating.

Emmett gestured with his head toward the big red book, which Billy had set down in the spot where Mrs. Simpson had been.

—What is this book you've been reading?

—*Professor Abacus Abernathe's Compendium of Heroes, Adventurers, and Other Intrepid Travelers.*

—Sounds compelling. Can I take a look?

With a touch of concern, Billy looked from the book to his brother's hands and back again.

Setting his sandwich down on the bench, Emmett carefully wiped his hands on his napkin. Then Billy passed him the book.

Knowing his brother as he did, Emmett did not simply open the book to some random page. He began at the beginning—the *very* beginning—by opening to the endpapers. And it was a good thing he had. For while the book's cover was solid red with a golden title, the endpapers were illustrated with a detailed map of the world criss-crossed by an array of dotted lines. Each of the different lines was identified by a letter of the alphabet and presumably indicated the route of a different adventurer.

Billy, who had put down his sandwich and wiped his hands on his own napkin, moved a little closer to Emmett so that they could study the book together—just as he had when he was younger and Emmett would read to him from a picture book. And just as in those days, Emmett looked to Billy to see if he was ready to continue. At Billy's nod, Emmett turned to the title page, where he was surprised to find an inscription.

> *To the Intrepid Billy Watson,*
> *With wishes for all manner of travels and adventures,*
> *Ellie Matthiessen*

Though the name seemed vaguely familiar, Emmett couldn't re-member who Ellie Matthiessen was. Billy must have sensed his broth-er's curiosity, because he gently put a finger on her signature.

—The librarian.

Of course, thought Emmett. The one with the glasses who had spoken so fondly of Billy.

Turning the page, Emmett came to the table of contents.

Achilles
Boone
Caesar
Dantès
Edison
Fogg

Galileo
Hercules
Ishmael
Jason
King Arthur
Lincoln
Magellan
Napoleon
Orpheus
Polo
Quixote
Robin Hood
Sinbad
Theseus
Ulysses
da Vinci
Washington
Xenos
You
Zorro

—They're in alphabetical order, said Billy.

After a moment, Emmett turned back to the endpapers to compare the heroes' names with the letters attached to the various dotted lines. Yes, he thought, there was Magellan sailing from Spain to the East Indies, and Napoleon marching into Russia, and Daniel Boone exploring the wilds of Kentucky.

Having glanced briefly at the introduction, Emmett began turning through the book's twenty-six chapters, each of which was eight pages long. While each offered a glimpse of the hero's boyhood, the primary focus was on his exploits, achievements, and legacy. Emmett could understand why his brother could return to this book again and again, because each chapter had an array of maps and illustrations designed to fascinate: like the blueprint of da Vinci's flying machine and the plan of the labyrinth in which Theseus fought the Minotaur.

As he neared the end of the book, Emmett came to a stop on two pages that were blank.

—Looks like they forgot to print a chapter.

—You missed a page.

Reaching over, Billy turned the page back. Here again the leaves were blank except that at the top of the left-hand page was the chapter title: **You**.

Billy touched the empty page with a hint of reverence.

—This is where Professor Abernathe invites you to set down the story of your own adventure.

—I guess you haven't had your adventure yet, said Emmett with a smile.

—I think we're on it now, said Billy.

—Maybe you can make a start of setting it down while we're waiting for the train.

Billy shook his head. Then he turned all the way back to the very first chapter and read the opening sentence:

—*It is fitting that we begin our adventures with the story of Swift-Footed Achilles, whose ancient exploits were forever immortalized by Homer in his epic poem* The Iliad.

Billy looked up from his book to explain.

—The causes of the Trojan War began with the Judgment of Paris. Angered that she was not invited to a banquet on Olympus, the goddess of discord threw a golden apple on the table with the inscription *For the Fairest*. When Athena, Hera, and Aphrodite each claimed the apple as their own, Zeus sent them to earth, where Paris, a Trojan prince, was chosen to resolve the dispute.

Billy pointed to an illustration of three loosely clad women gathered around a young man sitting under a tree.

—To influence Paris, Athena offered him wisdom, Hera offered him power, and Aphrodite offered him the most beautiful woman in the world, Helen of Sparta, the wife of King Menelaus. When Paris chose Aphrodite, she helped him spirit Helen away, resulting in Menelaus's outrage and the declaration of war. But Homer didn't begin his story at the beginning.

Billy moved his finger to the third paragraph and pointed to a three-word phrase in Latin.

—Homer began his story *in medias res,* which means *in the middle of the thing.* He began in the ninth year of the war with the hero, Achilles, nursing his anger in his tent. And ever since then, this is the way that many of the greatest adventure stories have been told.

Billy looked up at his brother.

—I am pretty sure that we are on our adventure, Emmett. But I won't be able to make a start of setting it down until I know where the middle of it is.

Duchess

WOOLLY AND I WERE lying on our beds in a HoJo's about fifty miles west of Chicago. When we had passed the first one, right after crossing the Mississippi into Illinois, Woolly had admired the orange roof and blue steeple. When we passed the second one, he did a double take—like he was worried that he was seeing things, or that I had somehow lost my bearings.

—No need to fret, I said. It's just a Howard Johnson's.

—A Howard Who's?

—It's a restaurant and motor lodge, Woolly. They're everywhere you go, and they always look like that.

—All of them?

—All of them.

By the time Woolly was sixteen, he had been to Europe at least five times. He'd been to London and Paris and Vienna, where he'd wandered the halls of museums and attended the opera and climbed to the top of the Eiffel Tower. But while on his native soil, Woolly had spent most of his time shuttling between an apartment on Park Avenue, the house in the Adirondacks, and the campuses of three New England prep schools. What Woolly didn't know about America would fill the Grand Canyon.

Woolly looked back over his shoulder as we passed the entrance to the restaurant.

—Twenty-eight flavors of ice cream, he quoted in some amazement.

So when it was growing late and we were tired and hungry and Woolly saw a bright blue steeple rising above the horizon, there was just no escaping it.

Woolly had spent plenty of nights in hotels, but never in one like a Howard Johnson's. When we came into the room, he examined it like a private detective from another planet. He opened the closets, startled to find an ironing board and iron. He opened the bedside drawer, startled to find a Bible. And when he went into the bathroom, he came right back out holding up two little bars of soap.

—They're individually wrapped!

Once we had settled in, Woolly turned on the television. When the signal came up, there was the Lone Ranger, wearing a hat even bigger and whiter than Chef Boy-Ar-Dee's. He was talking to a young gunslinger, giving him a lecture on truth, justice, and the American way. You could tell the gunslinger was losing his patience, but just when he was about to reach for his six-shooter, Woolly turned the channel.

Now it was Sergeant Joe Friday in a suit and fedora giving the exact same speech to a delinquent working on his motorcycle. The delinquent was losing his patience too. But just when it looked like he was going to hurl his ratchet at Sergeant Friday's head, Woolly turned the channel.

Here we go again, I thought.

Sure enough, Woolly kept switching the channel until he found a commercial. Then after lowering the volume all the way, he propped his pillows and made himself comfortable.

Wasn't that classic Woolly? In the car he was mesmerized by the sound of advertisements without their pictures. Now he wanted to watch the pictures of advertisements without their sounds. When the commercial break was over, Woolly turned off his light and slid down so he could lie with his hands behind his head and stare at the ceiling.

Woolly had taken a few more drops of medicine after dinner and I figured they'd be working their magic right about now. So I was a little surprised when he addressed me.

—Hey, Duchess, he said, still looking at the ceiling.

—Yeah, Woolly?

—On the Saturday night at eight when you and me and Emmett and Billy are sitting at the table by the jukebox, who else will be there?

Lying back, I looked up at the ceiling too.

—At Leonello's? Let's see. On a Saturday night you'd have a few of the top dogs from city hall. A boxer and some mobsters. Maybe Joe DiMaggio and Marilyn Monroe, if they happen to be in town.

—They would all be at Leonello's on the same night?

—That's the way it goes, Woolly. You open a place that no one can get into, and everybody wants to be there.

Woolly thought about this for a minute.

—Where are they sitting?

I pointed to a spot on the ceiling.

—The gangsters are in the booth next to the mayor. The boxer is over by the bar eating oysters with some chantoosie. And the DiMaggios are at the table next to ours. But here's the most important part, Woolly. Over there in the booth by the kitchen door is a small balding man in a pinstripe suit sitting all by himself.

—I see him, said Woolly. Who is he?

—Leonello Brandolini.

. . .

—You mean the owner?

—None other.

—And he sits by himself?

—Exactly. At least, in the early part of the evening. Usually, he settles in around six o'clock before anyone else is in the place. He'll have a little something to eat and a glass of Chianti. He'll go over the books and maybe take a call on one of those phones with the long cord that they can bring right to your table. But then around eight, when the place is starting to hum, he'll polish off a double espresso and make his way from table to table. *How is everybody tonight?* he'll say, while patting a customer's shoulder. *It's good to see you again. You hungry? I hope so. 'Cause there's gonna be plenty to eat.* After giving the ladies a few compliments, he'll signal the bartender. *Hey, Rocko. Another round over here for my friends.* Then he'll move on to the next table, where there'll be more shoulder patting, more compliments for the ladies, and another round of drinks. Or maybe this time, it's a plate of cala-mari, or some tiramisu. Either way, it's on the house. And when Leonello's finished making his rounds, everybody in the place—and I mean everybody from the mayor to Marilyn Monroe—will feel like tonight is something special.

Woolly was silent, giving the moment its due. Then I told him something I had never told anyone before.

—That's what I would do, Woolly. That's what I would do, if I had fifty grand.

I could hear him roll over on his side so he could look at me.

—You'd get a table at Leonello's?

I laughed.

—No, Woolly. I'd open *my own* Leonello's. A little Italian place with red leather booths and Sinatra on the box. A place where there are no menus and every table is spoken for. In the booth by the kitchen, I'd have a little dinner and take some calls. Then around eight, after a double espresso, I'd go from table to table greeting the customers and telling the bartender to send them another round of drinks—on the house.

I could tell that Woolly liked my idea almost as much as he liked Billy's, because after he rolled on his back he was smiling at the ceiling, imagining what the whole scene would look like almost as clearly as I could. Maybe even more so.

Tomorrow, I thought, I'll get him to draw me a floor plan.

—Where would it be? he asked after a moment.

—I don't know yet, Woolly. But once I've decided, you'll be the first to know.

And he smiled at that too.

A few minutes later, he was in Slumberland. I could tell because when his arm slipped off the edge of the bed, he left it hanging there with his fingers grazing the carpet.

Getting up, I returned his arm to his side and covered him with the blanket from the bottom of the bed. Then I filled a glass with water and placed it on the nightstand. Though Woolly's medicine always left him thirsty in the morning, he never seemed to remember to put a glass of water within reach before drifting off to sleep.

When I had turned off the TV, undressed, and climbed under my own covers, what I found myself wondering was *Where would it be?*

From the beginning, I had always imagined that when I had my own place it would be in the city—probably down in the Village on MacDougal or Sullivan Street, in one of those little spots around the corner from the jazz clubs and cafés. But maybe I was on the wrong track. Maybe what I should be doing is opening in a state where they don't have a Leonello's yet. A state like . . . California.

Sure, I thought. California.

After we had picked up Woolly's trust and driven back to Nebraska, we wouldn't even have to get out of the car. It would be just like this morning with Woolly and Billy in the back seat, and me and Emmett up front, only now the arrow on Billy's compass would be pointed west.

The problem was that I wasn't so sure about San Francisco.

Don't get me wrong. Frisco's a town with plenty of atmosphere— what with the fog drifting along the wharf, and the winos drifting through the Tenderloin, and the giant paper dragons drifting down the streets of Chinatown. That's why in the movies someone's always getting murdered there. And yet, despite all its atmosphere, San Francisco didn't seem to warrant a spot like Leonello's. It just didn't have the panache.

But Los Angeles?

The city of Los Angeles has so much panache it could bottle it and sell it overseas. It's where the movie stars have lived since the beginning of movie stars. More recently, it's where the boxers and mobsters were setting up shop. Even Sinatra had made the move. And if Ol' Blue Eyes could trade in the Big Apple for Tinseltown, so could we.

Los Angeles, I thought to myself, where it's summer all winter long, every waitress is a starlet in the making, and the street names have long since run out of presidents and trees.

Now that's what I call a fresh start!

But Emmett was right about the kit bag. Making a fresh start isn't just a matter of having a new address in a new town. It isn't a matter of having a new job, or a new phone number, or even a new name. A fresh start requires the cleaning of the slate. And that means paying off all that you owe, and collecting all that you're due.

By letting go of the farm and taking his beating in the public square, Emmett had already balanced his accounts. If we were going to head out west together, then maybe it was time for me to balance mine.

It didn't take me long to do the math. I'd spent more than enough nights in my bunk at Salina thinking about my unsettled debts, so the big ones rose right to the surface, three of them in all: One I would have to make good on, and two I would have to collect.

Emmett

EMMETT AND BILLY MOVED quickly through the scrub at the base of the embankment, headed west. It would have been easier going were they to walk on the tracks, but the notion of doing so struck Emmett as reckless even in the moonlight. Stopping, he looked back at Billy, who was doing his best to keep up.

—Are you sure you don't want me to carry your backpack?

—I've got it, Emmett.

As Emmett resumed his pace, he glanced at Billy's watch and saw that it was quarter to twelve. They had left the station at quarter past eleven. Though the walking had been harder than Emmett had anticipated, it seemed like they should have been at the pine grove by now, so he breathed a sigh of relief when he finally saw the pointed silhouettes of evergreens up ahead. Reaching the grove, they took a few steps into its shadows and waited in silence, listening to the owls overhead and smelling the scent of the pine needles underfoot.

Glancing again at Billy's watch, Emmett saw that it was now eleven fifty-five.

—Wait here, he said.

Climbing the embankment, Emmett looked down the tracks. In the distance he could see the pinpoint of light that emanated from the front of the locomotive. As Emmett rejoined his brother in the shadows, he was glad they hadn't walked on the tracks. For even though to Emmett's eye the locomotive had seemed a mile away, by the time he reached his brother, the long chain of boxcars was already flashing past.

Whether from excitement or anxiety, Billy took Emmett's hand.

Emmett guessed that fifty cars raced by before the train began to slow. When it finally rolled to a stop, the last ten cars were right in front of where Emmett and Billy were standing, just as the panhandler had said they would be.

So far, everything had happened as the panhandler had said it would.

What's the difference between a ton of flour and a ton of crackers? That's what the panhandler had asked Emmett back at the freight yard. Then with a wink he had answered his own riddle: *About a hundred cubic feet.*

A company that has freight traveling back and forth along the same route—he went on to explain in his good-natured way—was generally better off if they had their own capacity so they weren't exposed to fluctuations in price. Since Nabisco's facility in Manhattan received weekly deliveries of flour from the Midwest and sent weekly deliveries of finished goods back to the region, it was sensible for them to own their own cars. The only problem was that there are few things more dense than a bag of flour, and few things less so than a box of crackers. So while all of the company's cars were full when they headed west, on the way back to New York there were always five or six that were empty and that no one bothered to secure.

From the free-rider's perspective, the panhandler pointed out, the fact that the empty cars were hitched at the back of the train was particularly fortuitous, because when the engine of the Sunset East arrived in Lewis a few minutes after twelve, its caboose would still be a mile from the station.

Once the train had stopped, Emmett quickly scaled the embankment and tried the doors of the closest cars, finding the third one unlocked. After beckoning Billy and giving him a boost, Emmett climbed inside and pulled the door shut with a loud clack—throwing the car into darkness.

The panhandler had said that they could leave the hatch in the roof open for light and air—as long as they were sure to close it when they were approaching Chicago, where an open hatch was unlikely to go unnoticed. But Emmett hadn't thought to open the hatch before he closed the boxcar's door, or even to make note of where it was. Reaching out his hands, he felt for the latch so that he could open the door again, but the train jolted forward, sending him stumbling back against the opposite wall.

In the darkness he could hear his brother moving.

—Stay put, Billy, he cautioned, while I find the hatch.

But suddenly there was a beam of light shining in his direction.

—Do you want to use my flashlight?

Emmett smiled.

—Yes, Billy, I would. Or better yet, why don't you train the beam on that ladder in the corner.

Climbing the ladder, Emmett threw the hatch open, letting in moonlight and a welcome rush of air. Having been exposed to the sun all day, the boxcar's interior must have been eighty degrees.

—Why don't we stretch out over here, Emmett said, leading Billy to the other end of the car, where they wouldn't be so easily seen were someone to look through the hatch.

Taking two shirts from his backpack, Billy handed one to Emmett, explaining that if they folded them over, they could use them as pillows, just like soldiers. Then having refastened the straps, Billy lay down with his head on his folded shirt and was soon sound asleep.

Though Emmett was almost as exhausted as his brother, he knew that he wouldn't be able to fall asleep so quickly. He was too keyed up from the day's events. What he really wanted was a cigarette. He would have to settle for a drink of water.

Quietly picking up Billy's backpack, Emmett carried it to a spot beneath the hatch, where the air was a little cooler, and sat with his back to the wall. Unfastening the backpack's straps, he removed Billy's canteen, twisted off the cap, and took a drink. Emmett was so thirsty he could easily have emptied it, but they might not have a chance to get more water until they arrived in New York, so he took a second swallow, returned the canteen to the pack, and securely refastened the straps just as his brother would. Emmett was about to set the backpack down when he noticed the outer pocket. Glancing at Billy, he undid the flap and removed the manila envelope.

For a moment Emmett sat with the envelope in his hands as if he were trying to weigh it. After taking a second glance at his brother, he unwound the red thread and poured his mother's postcards into his lap.

As a boy, Emmett would never have described his mother as un-happy. Not to another person and not to himself. But at some point, at an unspoken level he had come to know that she was. He had come to know it not by tears or open laments, but by the sight of unfinished tasks in the early afternoon. Coming downstairs into the kitchen, he might find a dozen carrots lying on the cutting board beside the chop-ping knife, six of them sliced and six of them whole. Or returning from the barn, he might find half of the laundry flapping on the line and the other half damp in a basket. Looking for where his mother had gotten to, he would often find her sitting on the front steps with her elbows on her knees. When quietly, almost tentatively, Emmett would say, *Mom?*, she would look up as if pleasantly surprised. Making room for him on the step, she would put her arm over his shoulder or tussle his hair, then go back to looking at whatever it was that she had been looking at before—something somewhere between the front porch steps and the horizon.

Because young children don't know how things are supposed to be done, they will come to imagine that the habits of their household are the habits of the world. If a child grows up in a family where angry words are exchanged over supper, he will assume that angry words are exchanged at every kitchen table; while if a child grows up in a family where no words are exchanged over supper at all, he will assume that all families eat in silence. And yet, despite the prevalence of this truth, the young Emmett knew that chores left half done in the early afternoon were a sign of something amiss—just as he would come to know a few years later that the shifting of crops from one season to the next was the sign of a farmer who's at a loss what to do.

Holding the postcards up to the moonlight, Emmett revisited them one by one in their westward order—Ogallala, Cheyenne, Rawlins, Rock Springs, Salt Lake City, Ely, Reno, Sacramento, San Francisco—scanning the pictures from corner to corner and reading the messages word for word, as if he were an intelligence officer looking for a coded communication from an agent in the field. But if tonight he studied the cards more closely than he had at the kitchen table, he studied none more closely than he studied the last.

This is the Palace of the Legion of Honor in San Francisco's Lincoln Park, it read, *and every year on the Fourth of July it has one of the biggest fireworks displays in all of California.*

Emmett had no recollection of telling Billy about their mother's love of fireworks, but it was uncontestably so. When she was growing up in Boston, his mother would spend her summers in a little town on Cape Cod. While she hadn't spoken much about her time there, she had described with an old excitement how the volunteer fire department would sponsor a fireworks display over the harbor every Fourth of July. When she was a child, she and her family would watch from the end of their pier. But once she got older, she was allowed to row out among the sailboats that were swinging on their moorings so she could watch the pyrotechnics while lying alone in the bottom of her boat.

When Emmett was eight, his mother learned from Mr. Cartwright at the hardware store that the town of Seward—a little more than an hour from Morgen—had quite a little celebration on the Fourth of July, with a parade in the afternoon and fireworks after dark. Emmett's mother wasn't interested in the parade. So after an early supper, Emmett and his parents got in their truck and made the journey.

When Mr. Cartwright had said it was *quite a little celebration*, Emmett's mother had imagined it would be like any other small-town festivity, with banners made by the schoolchildren and refreshments sold off folding tables by the women of the parish. But when they arrived, she was stunned to discover that the Fourth of July in Seward put to shame any Fourth of July that she had ever seen. It was a celebration that the township prepared for all year and to which people came from as far away as Des Moines. By the time the Watsons arrived, the only parking was a mile from the center of town, and when they finally walked into Plum Creek Park, where the fireworks display was to take place, every square inch of lawn had been claimed by families on blankets eating their picnic dinners.

The following year, his mother had no intention of making the same mistake. At breakfast on the Fourth, she announced they would be leaving for Seward right after lunch. But once she had prepared their picnic dinner and opened the cutlery drawer to take out some forks and knives, she stopped and stared. Then turning around, she walked out of the kitchen and up the stairs with Emmett close on her heels. Moving a chair from her bedroom, she climbed up on it and reached for a short length of string that was hanging from the ceiling. When she pulled the string, a hatch dropped down with a sliding ladder that led to an attic.

Wide-eyed, Emmett was prepared for his mother to tell him that he should wait right there, but she was so intent upon her purpose she mounted the ladder without pausing to deliver a cautionary remark. And when he climbed up the narrow steps after her, she was so engaged in moving boxes she didn't bother to send him back down.

As his mother went about her search, Emmett surveyed the attic's strange inventory: an old wireless that was almost as tall as he was, a broken rocking chair, a black typewriter, and two large trunks covered in colorful stickers.

—Here we are, his mother said.

Giving Emmett a smile, she held up what looked like a small suitcase. Only instead of leather, it was made of wicker.

Back in the kitchen, his mother put the suitcase on the table.

Emmett could see that she was perspiring from the warmth of the attic, and when she wiped her brow with the back of her hand, she left a streak of dust on her skin. After throwing the clasps on the case, she smiled at Emmett again, then opened the lid.

Emmett knew well enough that a suitcase stored in an attic was likely to be empty, so he was startled to find that not only was this one packed, it was packed to perfection. Neatly arranged inside was everything you could possibly need to have a picnic. Under one strap there was a stack of six red plates, while under another, a tower of six red cups. There were long narrow troughs holding forks, knives, and spoons, and a shorter one for a wine opener. There were even two specially shaped indentations for salt and pepper shakers. And in the recess of the lid, there was a red-and-white-checkered tablecloth held in place by two leather straps.

In all his life, Emmett had never seen anything so ingeniously put together—with nothing missing, nothing extra, and everything in its place. He wouldn't see anything quite like it again, until at the age of fifteen, when he saw the worktable in Mr. Schulte's shed with its orderly arrangement of slots, pegs, and hooks to hold his various tools.

—Golly, Emmett had said, and his mother had laughed.

—It was from your great aunt Edna.

Then she shook her head.

—I don't think I've opened it since the day we were married. But we're going to put it to use tonight!

That year they arrived in Seward at two in the afternoon and found a spot right in the center of the lawn to spread out their checkered cloth. Emmett's father, who had expressed some reluctance about going so early in the day, showed no signs of impatience once they were there. In fact, as something of a surprise, he produced a bottle of wine from his bag. And as Emmett's parents drank, Emmett's father told stories about his penny-pinching aunt Sadie and his absent-minded uncle Dave and all his other crazy relatives back East, making Emmett's mother laugh in a way she rarely laughed.

As the hours passed, the lawn filled with more blankets and baskets, with more laughter and good feelings. When night had finally fallen, and the Watsons lay on their checkered cloth with Emmett in the middle, and the first of the fireworks whistled and popped, his mother had said: *I wouldn't have missed this for the world.* And driving home that night, it had seemed to Emmett that the three of them would be attending Seward's Fourth of July celebration for the rest of their lives.

But the following February—in the weeks after Billy was born—his mother was suddenly not herself. Some days she was so tired she couldn't even start the chores that she used to leave half done. Other days she didn't get out of bed.

When Billy was three weeks old, Mrs. Ebbers—whose children had children of their own—began to come every day to help keep house and see to Billy's needs while Emmett's mother tried to regain her strength. By April, Mrs. Ebbers was coming just in the mornings, and by June, she wasn't coming at all. But over dinner on the first of July, when Emmett's father asked with some enthusiasm what time they should head out for Seward, Emmett's mother said she wasn't sure she wanted to go.

Looking across the table, Emmett didn't think he had ever seen his father so heartbroken. But as was his way, Emmett's father pushed ahead, buoyed by a confidence that wasn't overly inclined to learn from experience. On the morning of the Fourth, Emmett's father made the picnic dinner. He pulled down the hatch and climbed the narrow ladder in order to retrieve the basket from the attic. He put Billy in the basinet and brought the truck around to the front door. And when at one o'clock he came inside and called, *Come on, everybody! We don't want to lose our favorite spot!* Emmett's mother agreed to go.

Or rather, she acquiesced.

She climbed in the truck and didn't say a word.

None of them said a word.

But once they arrived in Seward and had made their way to the center of the park and his father had billowed out the checkered cloth and begun to take the forks and knives from their troughs, Emmett's mother said:

—Here, let me help.

And in that moment, it was as if a great weight had been lifted from them all.

After putting out the red plastic cups, she laid out the sandwiches that her husband had made. She fed Billy the apple sauce that her husband had thought to pack, and rocked Billy's basinet back and forth until he fell asleep. As they drank the wine that her husband had remembered to bring, she asked him to tell some of those stories about his crazy uncles and aunts. And when, shortly after nightfall, the first salvo exploded over the park in a great distending spray of colored sparks, she reached out in order to squeeze her husband's hand, and gave him a tender smile as tears ran down her face. And when Emmett and his father saw her tears, they smiled in return, for they could tell that these were tears of gratitude—gratitude that rather than relenting to her initial lack of enthusiasm, her husband had persisted so that the four of them could share in this grand exhibition on this warm summer night.

When the Watsons got home, as Emmett's father brought in the basinet and the picnic basket, Emmett's mother led him upstairs by the hand, tucked him tightly under his covers, and gave him a kiss on the forehead, before going down the hallway to do the same for Billy.

That night Emmett slept as soundly as any night in his life. And when he woke in the morning, his mother was gone.

With a final look at the Palace of the Legion of Honor, Emmett returned the postcards to their envelope. He spun the thin red thread to seal them inside, and stowed them in Billy's backpack, being sure to tightly cinch the straps.

That first year had been a hard one for Charlie Watson, Emmett remembered as he took his place beside his brother. The trials of weather continued unabated. Financial difficulties loomed. And the people of the town, they gossiped freely about Mrs. Watson's sudden departure. But what weighed on his father the most—what weighed on them both—was the realization that when Emmett's mother had gripped her husband's hand as the fireworks began, it hadn't been in gratitude for his persistence, for his fealty and support, it had been in gratitude that by gently coaxing her from her malaise in order to witness this magical display, he had reminded her of what joy could be, if only she were willing to leave her daily life behind.

SEVEN

—.—

Duchess

IT'S A MAP! exclaimed Woolly in surprise.

—So it is.

We were sitting in a booth at the HoJo's waiting for our breakfast. In front of each of us was a paper place mat that was also a simplified map of the state of Illinois showing major roads and towns along with some out-of-scale illustrations of regional landmarks. In addition, there were sixteen Howard Johnson's, each with its little orange roof and little blue steeple.

—This is where we are, Woolly said, pointing to one of them.

—I'll take your word for it.

—And here's the Lincoln Highway. And look at this!

Before I could look over to see what *this* was, our waitress—who couldn't have been more than seventeen—set our plates down on top of our place mats.

Woolly frowned. After watching her retreat, he nudged his plate to the right so that he could continue studying the map while he pretended to eat.

It was ironic to see how little attention Woolly paid to his breakfast, given how much attention he had paid to ordering it. When our waitress had handed him the menu, he looked a little unnerved by its size. Taking a breath, he set about reading the descriptions of every single item out loud. Then, to make sure he hadn't missed anything, he went back to the beginning and read them again. When our waitress returned to take our order, he reported with self-assurance that he was going to have waffles—or make that scrambled eggs—only to switch to the hotcakes when she was turning to go. But when his hotcakes arrived, having decorated them with an elaborate spiral of syrup, Woolly ignored them at his bacon's expense. I, on the other hand, who hadn't even bothered to glance at the menu, made quick business of my corned beef hash and sunny-side ups.

Having cleaned my plate, I sat back and took a look around, thinking if Woolly wanted to get a sense of what my restaurant was going to be like, he need look no further than a Howard Johnson's. Because in every respect it was going to be the opposite.

From the standpoint of ambience, the good people at Howard Johnson's had decided to carry the colors of their well-known rooftop into the restaurant by dressing the booths in bright orange and the waitresses in bright blue—despite the fact that the combination of orange and blue hasn't been known to stimulate an appetite since the beginning of time. The definitive architectural element of the space was an uninterrupted chain of picture windows, which gave everyone an unimpeded view of the parking lot. The cuisine was a gussied-up version of what you'd find in a diner, and the defining characteristic of the clientele was that with a single glance you could tell more about them than you wanted to know.

Take the red-faced fellow in the next booth who was wiping up his yolk with a corner of whole wheat toast. A traveling salesman, if ever I saw one—and I've seen a lifetime supply. On the family tree of unmemorable middle-aged men, traveling salesmen are the first cousins of the has-been performers. They go to the same towns in the same cars and stay at the same hotels. In fact, the only way you can tell them apart is that the salesmen wear more sensible shoes.

As if I needed any proof, after watching him use his command of percentages to tally his waitress's tip, I saw him annotate the receipt, fold it in two, and stow it in his wallet for the boys back in accounting.

As the salesman stood to go, I noticed from the clock on the wall that it was already half past seven.

—Woolly, I said, the whole point of getting up early is to get an early start. So why don't you tackle some of those hotcakes while I go to the john. Then we can pay the bill and hit the road.

—Sure thing, said Woolly, while pushing his plate another few inches to the right.

Before going to the men's room, I got some change from the cashier and slipped into a phone booth. I knew that Ackerly had retired to Indiana, I just didn't know where. So I had the operator look up the number for Salina and put me through. Given the hour, it rang eight times before someone finally answered. I think it was Lucinda, the brunette with the pink glasses who guarded the warden's door. Taking a page from my father's book, I gave her the old King Lear. That's what my father would use whenever he needed a little help from someone on the other end of the line. Naturally, it entailed a British accent, but with a touch of befuddlement.

Explaining that I was Ackerly's uncle from England, I told her that I wanted to send him a card on Independence Day in order to assure him there were no hard feelings, but I seemed to have misplaced my address book. Was there any way that she could see to helping a forgetful old soul? A minute later, she returned with the answer: 132 Rhododendron Road in South Bend.

With a whistle on my lips, I traveled from the phone booth to the men's room, and who should I find standing at the urinals but the red-faced fellow from the neighboring booth. When I finished doing my business and joined him at the sinks, I gave him a quick smile in the mirror.

—You, sir, strike me as a salesman.

A little impressed, he looked back at me in the reflection.

—I am in sales.

I nodded my head.

—You've got that friendly man-of-the-world look about you.

—Why, thanks.

—Door-to-door?

—No, he said, a little offended. I'm an account man.

—Of course you are. In what line, if you don't mind me asking.

—Kitchen appliances.

—Like refrigerators and dishwashers?

He winced a little, as if I'd hit a sore spot.

—We specialize in the smaller electric conveniences. Like blenders and hand mixers.

—Small but essential, I pointed out.

—Oh, yes, indeed.

—So tell me, how do you do it? When you go into an account, I mean, how do you make a sale? Of your blender, for instance?

—Our blender sells itself.

From the way he delivered the line, I could tell that he had done so ten thousand times before.

—You're too modest, I'm sure. But seriously, when you speak of your blender versus the competitions', how do you . . . differentiate it?

At the word *differentiate*, he grew rather grave and confidential. Never mind that he was talking to an eighteen-year-old kid in the bathroom of a Howard Johnson's. He was gearing up for the pitch now and couldn't stop himself even if he wanted to.

—I was only half kidding, he began, when I remarked that our blender sells itself. Because, you see, it wasn't so long ago that all the leading blenders came with three settings: low, medium, and high. Our company was the first to differentiate its blender buttons by the *type* of blending: mix, beat, and whip.

—Ingenious. You must have the market to yourself.

—For a time, we did, he admitted. But soon enough our competitors were following suit.

—So you've got to keep one step ahead.

—Precisely. That's why this year, I'm proud to say, we became the first blender manufacturer in America to introduce a fourth stage of blending.

—A fourth stage? After mix, beat, and whip?

The suspense was killing me.

—Puree.

—Bravo, I said.

And in a way, I meant it.

I gave him another once-over, this one in admiration. Then I asked him if he had fought in the war.

—I didn't have the honor of doing so, he said, also for the ten thousandth time.

I shook my head in sympathy.

—What a hoopla when the boys came home. Fireworks and parades. Mayors pinning medals on lapels. And all the good-looking dames lining up to kiss any putz in a uniform. But you know what I think? I think the American people should pay a little more homage to the traveling salesmen.

He couldn't tell if I was having him on or not. So I put a hint of emotion into my voice.

—My father was a traveling salesman. Oh, the miles he logged. The doorbells he rang. The nights he spent far from the comforts of home. I say to you that traveling salesmen are not simply hardworking men, they are the foot soldiers of capitalism!

I think he actually blushed at that one. Though it was hard to tell given his complexion.

—It's an honor to meet you, sir, I said, and I stuck out my hand even though I hadn't dried it yet.

. . .

When I came out of the bathroom, I saw our waitress and flagged her down.

—Do you need something else? she asked.

—Just the check, I replied. We've got places to go and people to see.

At the phrase *places to go*, she looked a little wistful. I do believe if I had told her we were headed for New York and offered her a ride, she would have hopped into the back seat without taking the time to change out of her uniform—if for no other reason than to see what happens when you drive off the edge of the place mat.

—I'll bring it right over, she said.

As I headed to our booth, I regretted making fun of our neighbor for his attention to receipts. Because it suddenly occurred to me that we should be doing something similar on Emmett's behalf. Since we were using the money from his envelope to cover our expenses, he had every right to expect a full accounting upon our return—so that he could be reimbursed before we divvied up the trust.

The night before, I'd left Woolly to pay the dinner bill while I checked into the hotel. I was going to ask him how much it ended up costing, but when I got to our booth, there was no Woolly.

Where could he have gotten to, I wondered, with a roll of the eyes. He couldn't be in the bathroom, since that's where I had just come from. Knowing him to be an admirer of shiny and colorful things, I looked over at the ice cream counter, but there were just two little kids pressing their noses against the glass, wishing it wasn't so early in the morning. With a growing sense of foreboding, I turned to the plate-glass windows.

Out I looked into the parking lot, moving my gaze across the shimmering sea of glass and chrome to the very spot in which I had parked the Studebaker, and in which the Studebaker was no longer. Taking a step to my right—in order to see around a pair of beehive hairdos—I looked toward the parking lot's entrance just in time to see Emmett's car taking a right onto the Lincoln Highway.

—Jesus fucking shitting Christ.

Our waitress, who happened to arrive with the check at that very moment, turned pale.

—Excuse my French, I said.

Then glancing at the check, I gave her a twenty from the envelope.

As she hurried off for the change, I slumped down in my seat and stared across the table to where Woolly should have been. On his plate, which was back where it had started, the bacon was gone, along with a narrow wedge of hotcakes.

As I was admiring the precision with which Woolly had removed such a slender little slice from the stack, I noticed that under the white ceramic of his plate was the Formica surface of the table. Which is to say, the place mat was gone.

Shoving my plate aside, I picked up my own place mat. As I said before, it was a map of Illinois, with major roads and towns. But in the lower right-hand corner there was an inset with a map of the local downtown area, at the center of which was a little green square, and rising from the middle of that little green square, looking as large as life, was a statue of Abraham Lincoln.

Woolly

Hum de-dum de-dum, Woolly hummed as he took another look at the map in his lap. *Performance is sweeter, nothing can beat her, life is completer* . . . Oh, hum de-dum de-dum.

—Get out of the road! someone yelled as they passed the Studebaker with a triple honk of the horn.

—Apologies, apologies, apologies! replied Woolly in reciprocal triplicate, with a friendly wave of the hand.

As he angled back into his lane, Woolly acknowledged that it probably wasn't advisable to drive with a map in your lap, what with all the looking up and looking down. So keeping the steering wheel in his left hand, he held the map up in his right. That way he could look at the map out of one eye and the road out of the other.

The day before, when Duchess had secured the Phillips 66 Road Map of America at the Phillips 66 gas station, he handed it to Woolly, saying that since he was driving, Woolly would have to navigate. Woolly had accepted this responsibility with a touch of unease. When a gas station map is handed to you, it's almost the perfect size—like a playbill at the theater. But in order to read a gas station map, you have to unfold and unfold and unfold it until the Pacific Ocean is up against the gear shift and the Atlantic Ocean is lapping at the passenger-side door.

Once a gas station map is open all the way, just the sight of it is likely to make you woozy, because it is positutely crisscrossed from top to bottom and side to side by highways and byways and a thousand little roads, each of which is marked with a tiny little name or tiny little number. It reminded Woolly of the textbook for a biology class that he had taken while at St. Paul's. Or was it St. Mark's? Either way, early in this volume, on a left-hand page was a picture of a human skeleton. After looking carefully at this skeleton with all of the various bones in their proper places, when you turned to the next page fully expecting the skeleton to disappear, the skeleton was still there—because the next page was made of see-through paper! It was made of see-through paper so that you could study the nervous system right on top of the skeleton. And when you turned the page after that, you could study the skeleton, the nervous system, *and* the circulatory system with all of its little blue and red lines.

Woolly knew that this multilayered illustration was meant to make things perfectly clear, but he found it very unnerving. Was it a picture of a man or a woman, for instance? Old or young? Black or white? And how did all the blood cells and nerve impulses that were traveling along these complicated networks know where they were supposed to go? And once they got there, how did they find their way home? That's what the Phillips 66 road map was like: an illustration with hundreds of arteries, veins, and capillaries branching ever outward until no one traveling along any one of them could possibly know where they were going.

But this was hardly the case with the place-mat map from Howard Johnson's! It didn't have to be unfolded at all. And it wasn't covered with a confusion of highways and byways. It had exactly the right amount of roads. And those that were named were named clearly, while those that weren't named clearly weren't named at all.

The other highly commendable characteristic of the Howard Johnson's map was the illustrations. Most mapmakers are particularly good at shrinking things. The states, the towns, the rivers, the roads, every single one of them is shrunk to a smaller dimension. But on the

Howard Johnson's place mat, after reducing the towns, rivers, and roads, the mapmaker added back a selection of illustrations that were *bigger* than they were supposed to be. Like a big scarecrow in the lower left-hand corner that showed you where the cornfields were. Or the big tiger in the upper right-hand corner that showed you the Lincoln Park Zoo.

It was just the way the pirates used to draw their treasure maps. They shrunk down the ocean and the islands until they were very small and simple, but then they added back a big ship off the coast, and a big palm tree on the beach, and a big rock formation on a hill that was in the shape of a skull and was exactly fifteen paces from the X that marked the spot.

In the box that was in the lower right-hand corner of the place mat, there was a map within the map, which showed the center of town. According to this map, if you took a right on Second Street and drove an inch and a half, you would arrive at Liberty Park, in the middle of which would be a great big statue of Abraham Lincoln.

Suddenly, out of his left eye, Woolly saw the sign for Second Street. Without a moment to spare, he took a sharp right turn to the tune of another honking horn.

—Apologies, he called.

Leaning toward the windshield, he caught a glimpse of greenery.

—Here we go, he said. Here we go.

A minute later he was there.

Pulling to the curb, he opened his door and it was nearly taken off by a passing sedan.

—Whoops!

Closing the door, Woolly skootched over the seat, climbed out the passenger side, waited for a break in traffic, and dashed across the street.

In the park, it was a bright and sunny day. The trees were in leaf, the bushes in bloom, and the daisies sprouting up on both sides of the path.

—Here we go, he said again as he went zipping along.

But suddenly the daisy-lined path was intersected by another path, presenting Woolly with three different options: go left, go right, or go straight ahead. Wishing he'd thought to bring the place-mat map, Woolly looked in each direction. To his left were trees and shrubs and dark-green benches. To his right were more trees, shrubs, and benches, as well as a man in a baggy suit and floppy hat who looked vaguely familiar. But straight ahead, if Woolly squinted, he could just make out a fountain.

—Aha! he shouted.

For in Woolly's experience, statues were often found in the vicinity of fountains. Like the statue of Garibaldi that was near the fountain in Washington Square Park, or the statue of the angel on top of that big fountain in Central Park.

With heightened confidence, Woolly ran to the lip of the fountain and paused in the refreshing mist to get his bearings. What he discovered from a quick survey was that the fountain was an epicenter from which eight different paths emanated (if you included the one that he'd just come zipping along). Fending off discouragement, Woolly slowly began working his way clockwise around the fountain's circumference, peering down each of the individual paths with a hand over his eyes like a captain at sea. And there, at the end of the sixth path, was Honest Abe himself.

Rather than zip down this path, out of respect for the statue Woolly walked in long Lincolnian strides until he came to a stop a few feet away.

What a wonderful likeness, thought Woolly. Not only did it capture the president's stature, it seemed to suggest his moral courage. While for the most part, this Lincoln was depicted as one might expect, with his Shenandoah beard and his long black coat, the sculptor had made one unusual choice: In his right hand, the president was holding his hat lightly by the brim, as if he had just removed it upon meeting an acquaintance in the street.

Taking a seat on a bench in front of the statue, Woolly turned his thoughts to the day before, when Billy was explaining the history of the Lincoln Highway in the back of Emmett's car. Billy had mentioned that when it was first being constructed (in nineteen something-something), enthusiasts had painted red, white, and blue stripes on barns and fenceposts all along the route. Woolly could picture this perfectly, because it reminded him of how on the Fourth of July his family would hang red, white, and blue streamers from the rafters of the great room and the rails of the porch.

Oh, how his great-grandfather had loved the Fourth of July.

On Thanksgiving, Christmas, and Easter, Woolly's great-grandfather hadn't cared whether his children chose to celebrate the holiday with him or went off to celebrate with somebody else. But when it came to Independence Day, he did not abide absenteeism. He made it perfectly clear that every child, grandchild, and great-grandchild was expected in the Adirondacks no matter how far they had to travel.

And gather they did!

On the first of July, family members would start to pull up in the driveway, or arrive at the train station, or land at the little airstrip that was twenty miles away. By the afternoon of the second, every sleeping spot in the house was taken—with the grandparents, uncles, and aunts in the bedrooms, the younger cousins on the sleeping porch, and all the cousins who were lucky enough to be older than twelve in the tents among the pines.

When the Fourth arrived, there was a picnic lunch on the lawn, followed by canoe races, swim races, the riflery and archery contests, and a great big game of capture the flag. At six o'clock on the dot there were cocktails on the porch. At half past seven the bell would be rung and everyone would make their way inside for a supper of fried chicken, corn on the cob, and Dorothy's famous blueberry muffins. Then at ten, Uncle Bob and Uncle Randy would row out to the raft in the middle of the lake in order to launch the fireworks that they had bought in Pennsylvania.

How Billy would have loved it, thought Woolly with a smile. He would have loved the streamers on the fence rail and the tents among the trees and the baskets of blueberry muffins. But most of all, he would have loved the fireworks, which always started with whistles and pops, but would grow bigger and bigger until they seemed to fill the sky.

But even as Woolly was having this wonderful memory, his expression grew somber, for he had almost forgotten what his mother would refer to as *The Reason We're All Here*: the recitations. Every year on the Fourth of July, once all the food had been set out, in lieu of grace, the youngest child older than sixteen would take his or her place at the head of the table and recite from the Declaration of Independence.

When in the course of human events, and *We hold these truths to be self-evident*, and so forth.

But, as Woolly's great-grandfather liked to observe, if Messrs. Washington, Jefferson, and Adams had the vision to found the Republic, it was Mr. Lincoln who had the courage to perfect it. So, when the cousin who had recited from the Declaration had resumed his or her seat, the youngest child older than ten would take his or her place at the head of the table in order to recite the Gettysburg Address in its entirety.

When that was completed, the speaker would take a bow and the room would erupt into an ovation that was almost as loud as the one that followed the finale of the fireworks. Then the platters and baskets would go zipping around the table to the sound of laughter and good cheer. It was a moment that Woolly always looked forward to.

Looked forward to, that is, until the sixteenth of March 1944, the day that he turned ten.

Right after his mother and sisters had sung Happy Birthday on his behalf, his oldest sister, Kaitlin, had felt it necessary to note that come the Fourth of July, it would be Woolly's turn to stand at the head of the table. Woolly was so unnerved by this bit of news that he could barely finish his piece of chocolate cake. Because if Woolly knew anything by the age of ten, it was that he wasn't any good at rememorizing.

Sensing Woolly's concern, his sister Sarah—who seven years before had given a flawless recitation—offered to serve as his coach.

—Memorizing the Address is well within your grasp, she said to Woolly with a smile. After all, it's only ten sentences.

Initially, this assurance heartened Woolly. But when his sister showed him the actual text of the speech, Woolly discovered that while at first glance it might *seem* to be only ten sentences, the very last sentence was actually three different sentences disguised as one.

—For all intents and porpoises (as Woolly used to say), there are twelve sentences, not ten.

—Even so, Sarah replied.

But just to be sure, she suggested they start their preparations well in advance. In the first week of April, Woolly would learn to recite the first sentence word for word. Then in the second week of April, he would learn the first and second sentences. Then in the third week, the first three sentences, and so on, until twelve weeks later, just as the month of June was drawing to a close, Woolly would be able to recite the entire speech without a hitch.

And that's exactly how they prepared. Week by week, Woolly learned one sentence after another until he could recite the speech in its entirety. In fact, by the first of July he had recited it from beginning to end, not only in front of Sarah, but by himself in front of the mirror, at the kitchen sink while helping Dorothy do the dishes, and once in a canoe in the middle of the lake. So when the fateful day arrived, Woolly was ready.

After his cousin Edward had recited from the Declaration of

Independence and received a friendly round of applause, Woolly assumed the privileged spot.

But just as he was about to begin, he discovered the first problem with his sister's plan: the people. For while Woolly had recited the Address many times in front of his sister and often by himself, he had never recited it in front of anybody else. And this wasn't even anybody else. It was thirty of his closest relatives lined up on opposite sides of a table in two attentive rows, with none other than his great-grandfather seated at the opposite end.

Casting a glance at Sarah, Woolly received a nod of encouragement, which bolstered his confidence. But just as he was about to begin, Woolly discovered the second problem with his sister's plan: the attire. For while Woolly had previously recited the Address in his corduroys, his pajamas, and his bathing suit, not once had he recited it in an itchy blue blazer with a red-and-white tie gripping at his throat.

As Woolly pulled at his collar with a crooked finger, some of his younger cousins began to giggle.

—Shh, said his grandmother.

Woolly looked back to Sarah, who gave him another friendly nod.

—Go ahead, she said.

Just as she had taught, Woolly stood up straight, took two deep breaths, and began:

—*Four score and seven years*, he said. *Four score and seven years ago.*

There was more sniggering from the younger cousins, followed by another shush from his grandmother.

Remembering that Sarah had said if he got nervous he should look over the heads of the family, Woolly raised his eyes to the moose head on the wall. But finding the gaze of the moose unsympathetic, he tried looking instead at his shoes.

—*Four score and seven years ago* . . . , he began again.

—*Our fathers brought forth*, Sarah softly prompted.

—*Our fathers brought forth*, Woolly said looking up at his sister. *Our fathers brought forth on this countenance.*

—*On this continent . . .*

—*On this continent a new nation. A new nation . . .*

— *. . . Conceived in Liberty*, said a friendly voice.

Only it wasn't Sarah's voice. It was the voice of cousin James, who had graduated from Princeton a few weeks before. And this time, when Woolly renewed his recital, Sarah and James joined in.

—*Conceived in Liberty*, the three of them said together, *and dedicated to the proposition that all men are created equal.*

Then other relatives who in their time had been tasked with reciting Mr. Lincoln's Address added their voices. Then joining the chorus were members of the family who had never been required to recite the Address, but who had heard it so many times before that they too knew it by heart. Soon, everyone at the table—including Great-grandpa—was reciting; and when all together they said those grand and hopeful words that the *government of the people, by the people, for the people, shall not perish from the earth*, the family burst into a round of cheering like the room had never heard.

Surely, this was the way that Abraham Lincoln had meant his Address to be recited. Not as a little boy standing alone at the head of a table in an itchy coat, but as four generations of a family speaking together in unison.

Oh, if only his father could have been there, thought Woolly, wiping a tear from his cheek with the flat of his hand. If only his father could be here now.

—.—

After Woolly had battled away the blues and finished paying his respects to the president, he went back the way he'd come. This time, when he reached the fountain, he was careful to walk *counterclockwise* around its circumference until he reached the sixth path.

No path looks quite the same in both directions, so as Woolly progressed, he began to wonder if he'd made a mistake. Perhaps he had miscounted the number of paths when he had counterclockwised the fountain. But just as he was considering retracing his steps, he saw the man in the floppy hat.

When Woolly gave him the smile of recognition, the man gave him the smile of recognition back. But when Woolly gave him a little wave, the man didn't return it. Instead, he reached into the baggy pockets of his baggy jacket. Then he formed a circle with his arms by placing the fist of his right hand on his left shoulder and the fist of his left hand on his right shoulder. Intrigued, Woolly watched as the man began moving his hands down the length of the opposing arms leaving little white objects at every consecutive inch.

—It's popcorn, Woolly said in amazement.

Once the pieces of popcorn extended from the top of his shoulders to the top of his wrists, ever so slowly the man began to open his arms until they were stretching out at his sides like . . . like . . .

Like a scarecrow! Woolly realized. That's why the man in the floppy hat had seemed so familiar. Because he looked exactly like the scarecrow in the bottom left-hand corner of the place-mat map.

Only, this man wasn't a scarecrow. He was the opposite of a scarecrow. For once his arms were fully extended, all the little sparrows which had been milling about began to flutter in the air and hover near his arms.

As the sparrows pecked at the popcorn, two squirrels that had been hiding under a bench scurried to the gentleman's feet. His eyes wide, Woolly thought for a moment that they were going to climb him like a tree. But the squirrels, who knew their business, waited for the sparrows to knock the occasional piece of popcorn from the gentleman's arms to the ground.

I must remember to tell Duchess all about this, thought Woolly as he hurried along.

For the Birdman of Liberty Park seemed just like one of those old vaudevillians that Duchess liked to tell them about.

But as Woolly emerged onto the street, the joyful image of the Birdman standing with his arms outstretched was replaced by the much less joyful image of a police officer standing behind Emmett's car with a ticket book in hand.

Emmett

EMMETT WOKE WITH A vague awareness that the train was no longer moving. Glancing at Billy's watch, he could see it was shortly after eight. They must have already reached Cedar Rapids.

Quietly, so as not to wake his brother, Emmett rose, climbed the ladder, and stuck his head through the hatch in the roof. Looking back, he could see that the train, which was now on a siding, had been lengthened by at least twenty cars.

Standing on the ladder, his face exposed to the cool morning air, Emmett was no longer stirred by thoughts of the past. What stirred him now was hunger. All he had eaten since leaving Morgen was the sandwich his brother had given him in the station. Billy, at least, had had the good sense to eat breakfast at the orphanage when it was offered to him. By Emmett's estimation, they still had another thirty hours before reaching New York, and all they had in Billy's backpack was a canteen of water and the last of Sally's cookies.

But when the panhandler had told Emmett that they would stop for a few hours on a private siding outside of Cedar Rapids, he'd said it was so that General Mills could hitch some of their cars to the back of the train—cars stacked from floor to ceiling with boxes of cereal.

Emmett went down the ladder and gently woke his brother.

—The train's going to be stopped here for a bit, Billy. I'm going to see if I can find us something to eat.

—Okay, Emmett.

As Billy went back to sleep, Emmett climbed up the ladder and out the hatch. Seeing no signs of life up or down the line, he began working his way to the rear of the train. As the General Mills cars were laden, Emmett knew that they were likely to be locked. He simply had to hope that one of the hatches had been left unsecured inadvertently. Figuring he had less than an hour before they were under way, he moved as quickly as he could, leaping from the top of one boxcar to the next.

But when he reached the last of the empty Nabisco cars, he came to a stop. While he could see the flat rectangular tops of the General Mills cars stretching into the distance, the two that were immediately in front of him had the curved rooftops of passenger cars.

After a moment's hesitation, Emmett climbed down onto the narrow platform and peered through the small window in the door. Most of the interior was obscured by the curtains that bordered the inside of the window, but what little Emmett could see was promising. It appeared to be the sitting room of a well-appointed private car after a night of festivities. Beyond a pair of high-back chairs with their backs to him, Emmett could see a coffee table covered with empty glasses, a champagne bottle upside down in an ice bucket, and a small buffet on which were the remnants of a meal. The passengers were presumably in the sleeping compartments of the adjacent car.

Opening the door, Emmett quietly stepped inside. As he took his bearings, he could see that what festivities there had been had left the room in disarray. Strewn across the floor were feathers from a busted pillow along with bread rolls and grapes, as if they'd been used as ammunition in a fight. The glass front of a grandfather clock was open, the hands missing from its face. And sound asleep on a couch by the buffet was a man in his midtwenties wearing a soiled tuxedo and the bright red stripes of an Apache on his cheeks.

Emmett considered backing out of the car and continuing over the roof, but he wasn't going to get a better chance than this. Keeping his eyes on the sleeping figure, Emmett passed between the high-back chairs and advanced cautiously. On the buffet were a bowl of fruit, loaves of bread, hunks of cheese, and a half-eaten ham. There was also an overturned jar of ketchup, no doubt the source of the war paint. At his feet, Emmett found the case of the busted pillow. Loading it quickly with enough food for two days, he spun it around by the neck to cinch it. Then he took one last look at the sleeper and turned toward the door.

—Oh, steward . . .

Slumped in one of the high-back chairs was a second man in a tuxedo.

With his attention trained on the sleeper, Emmett had walked right by this one without noticing him—which was all the more surprising given his size. He must have been nearly six feet tall and two hundred pounds. He wasn't wearing war paint, but he had a slice of ham sticking neatly out of his breast pocket, as if it were a handkerchief.

With his eyes half open, the reveler raised a hand and slowly unfolded a finger in order to point at something on the floor.

—If you would be so kind. . . .

Looking in the indicated direction, Emmett saw a half-empty bottle of gin lying on its side. Setting down the pillowcase, Emmett retrieved the gin and handed it to the reveler, who received it with a sigh.

—For the better part of an hour, I have had my eye on this bottle, sorting through the various stratagems by which it might be delivered into my possession. One by one, I had to discard them as ill conceived, ill advised, or defying the laws of gravity. Eventually, I turned to the last recourse of a man who wants something done and who has exhausted every option short of doing it himself—which is to say, I prayed. I prayed to Ferdinand and Bartholomew, the patron saints of Pullman cars and toppled bottles. And an angel of mercy hath descended upon me.

Looking to Emmett with a grateful smile, he suddenly expressed surprise.

—You aren't the steward!

—I'm one of the brakemen, said Emmett.

—My thanks all the same.

Turning to his left, the reveler picked up a martini glass that was on a small round table and began carefully filling it with gin. As he did so, Emmett noted that the olive in the bottom of the glass had been speared with the minute hand of the clock.

Having filled the glass, the reveler looked to Emmett.

—Could I interest you . . . ?

—No, thank you.

—On duty, I suppose.

Raising his drink briefly toward Emmett, he emptied the glass at a toss, then considered it, ruefully.

—You were wise to decline. This gin is unnaturally tepid. Criminally so, you might say. Nonetheless . . .

Refilling the glass, he raised it once again to his lips, but this time stopped short with a look of concern.

—You wouldn't happen to know where we are?

—Outside Cedar Rapids.

—Iowa?

—Yes.

—And the time?

—About half past eight.

—In the morning?

—Yes, said Emmett. In the morning.

The reveler began to tilt his glass, but stopped again.

—Not *Thursday* morning?

—No, said Emmett trying to contain his impatience. It's Tuesday.

The reveler exhaled in relief, then leaned toward the man who was sleeping on the couch.

—Did you hear that, Mr. Packer?

When Packer didn't respond, the reveler set down his glass, took a bread roll from a jacket pocket, and threw it at Packer's head, accurately.

—I say: Did you hear that?

—Hear what, Mr. Parker?

—It's not Thursday yet.

Rolling onto his side, Packer faced the wall.

—Wednesday's child is full of woe, but Thursday's child has far to go.

Parker stared at his companion thoughtfully, then leaned toward Emmett.

—Between us, Mr. Packer is also unnaturally tepid.

—I heard that, said Packer to the wall.

Parker ignored him and continued confiding in Emmett.

—Normally, I am not one to fret over such things as the days of the week. But Mr. Packer and I are bound by a sacred trust. For sound asleep in the next cabin is none other than Alexander Cunningham the Third, the beloved grandson of the owner of this delightful car. And we have vowed that we will have Mr. Cunningham back in Chicago at the doors of the Racquet Club (that's racquet with a *q*, mind you), by Thursday night at six, so that we can deliver him safely—

—Into the hands of his captors, said Packer.

—Into the hands of his bride-to-be, corrected Parker. Which is a duty not to be taken lightly, Mr. Brakeman. For Mr. Cunningham's grandfather is the largest operator of refrigerated boxcars in America and the bride's grandfather is the largest producer of sausage links. So I think you can see the importance of our getting Mr. Cunningham to Chicago on time.

—The future of breakfast in America depends upon it, said Packer.

—Indeed, it does, agreed Parker. Indeed, it does.

Emmett was raised to hold no man in disdain. To hold another man in disdain, his father would say, presumed that you knew so much about his lot, so much about his intentions, about his actions both public and private that you could rank his character against your own without fear of misjudgment. But as he watched the one called Parker empty another glass of tepid gin and then draw the olive off the minute hand with his teeth, Emmett couldn't help but measure the man and find him wanting.

Back in Salina, one of the stories that Duchess liked to tell—when they were working in the fields or biding time in the barracks—was about a performer who called himself Professor Heinrich Schweitzer, Master of Telekinesis.

When the curtain rose on the professor, he would be sitting in the middle of the stage at a small table with a white tablecloth, a single dinner setting, and an unlit candle. From offstage a waiter would appear, serve the professor a steak, pour a glass of wine, and light the candle. When the waiter left, in an unhurried manner the professor would eat some of the steak, drink some of the wine, and stick his fork upright in the meat—all without saying a word. After wiping his lips with his napkin, he would hold a parted thumb and finger in the air. As he slowly closed them together, the flame of the candle would sputter, then expire, leaving a thin trail of smoke. Next, the professor would stare at his wine until it boiled over the rim. When he turned his attention to his plate, the top half of the fork would bend until it was at a ninety-degree angle. At this point, the audience, which had been warned to maintain a perfect silence, was rumbling with expressions of amazement or disbelief. With a raised hand, the professor would quiet the house. Closing his eyes, he would point his palms toward the table. As he concentrated, the table would begin to tremble to such a degree that you could hear its legs knocking against the surface of the stage. Then reopening his eyes, the professor would suddenly swipe his hands to the right, and the tablecloth would shoot into the air, leaving the dinner plate, wine glass, and candle undisturbed.

The whole act was a hoax, of course. An elaborate illusion achieved through the use of invisible wires, electricity, and jets of air. And

Professor Schweitzer? According to Duchess, he was a Pole from Pough-keepsie who hadn't enough mastery over telekinesis to drop a hammer on his own foot.

No, thought Emmett with a touch of bitterness, the Schweitzers of this world were in no position to move objects with a glance or a wave of the hand. That power was reserved for the Parkers.

In all probability, no one had ever told Parker that he had the power of telekinesis; but they hadn't needed to. He had learned it through experience, starting from the days of his childhood, when he would demand a toy that was in the window of a shop or an ice cream from a vendor in the park. Experience had taught him that if he wanted something badly enough, it would eventually be delivered into his hands, even if in defiance of the laws of gravity. With what but disdain can one look upon a man who in possession of this extraordinary power uses it to retrieve the remnants of a bottle of gin from across a room without having to get up from his chair?

But even as Emmett was having this thought, there was a delicate whirring and the handless clock began to chime. Glancing at Billy's watch, Emmett saw with a flash of anxiety that it was already nine. He had completely underestimated how much time had passed. The train could be under way at any moment.

As Emmett reached for the pillowcase at his feet, Parker shifted his gaze.

—You're not leaving?

—I need to get back to the engine.

—But we were just getting to know one another. Surely there's no rush. Here, have a seat.

Reaching over, Parker pulled the empty armchair closer to his own, effectively blocking Emmett's path to the door.

In the distance Emmett heard a hiss of steam as the brakes were released and the train began to move. Shoving the empty chair aside, Emmett took a step toward the door.

—Wait! Parker shouted.

Placing his hands on the arms of his chair, he hoisted himself up. Once Parker was standing, Emmett realized he was even larger than he'd seemed. With his head nearly hitting the ceiling of the car, he swayed in place for a moment, then lurched forward with his hands extended, as if he intended to grab Emmett by the shirt.

Emmett felt a surge of adrenaline and the sickening sensation that time was replaying itself for ill. A few feet behind Parker was the coffee table with the empty glasses and the overturned champagne bottle. Given the unsteadiness of Parker's stance, Emmett knew without even thinking that if he gave Parker a single push in the sternum, he could topple him like a tree. It was another opportunity presented by chance for Emmett to upend all of his plans for the future with the action of an instant.

But with surprising agility, Parker suddenly slipped a folded five-dollar bill into the pocket of Emmett's shirt. Then he stepped back and fell into his chair.

—With the utmost gratitude, Parker called, as Emmett went out the door.

Gripping the pillowcase in one hand, Emmett scaled the ladder, moved quickly across the length of the boxcar's roof, and leapt over the gap to the next car—just as he had earlier that morning.

Only now the train was moving, lurching lightly left and right, and it was gaining speed. Emmett guessed it was traveling at only twenty miles an hour, but he had felt the force of the oncoming air when he'd made the jump between the cars. If the train reached thirty miles an hour, he would need to be moving pretty fast to clear the gap; and if it reached forty, he wasn't sure he would be able to clear the gap at all.

Emmett began to run.

He couldn't remember how many boxcars he had crossed earlier that morning before reaching the Pullman. With a growing sense of urgency, he looked up to see if he could pinpoint the car with the open hatch. What he saw instead was that half a mile ahead, the train was curving over a bend in the tracks.

While it was the bend in the tracks that was fixed and the train that was moving, from Emmett's vantage point it seemed like it was the bend that was in motion, making its way rapidly down the chain of boxcars, heading toward him inexorably, the way that slack moves along a length of a rope when one end has been whipped.

Emmett began to sprint as fast as he could in the hope of making it to the next boxcar before the curve arrived. But the curve came faster than he anticipated, passing under his feet just as he made the leap. With the boxcar swaying, Emmett landed unevenly and went hurtling forward such that a moment later he was splayed across the roof with one foot hanging off its edge.

Intent on not letting go of the pillowcase, Emmett scrambled to grab something, anything, with his free hand. Blindly, he caught hold of a metal lip and pulled himself toward the middle of the roof.

Without standing, Emmett eased his way backward toward the gap that he'd just leapt across. Finding the ladder with his feet, he slid farther back, climbed down, and collapsed on the narrow platform, heaving from the exertion and burning with self-recrimination.

What had he been thinking? Jumping from car to car at a sprint. He could easily have been thrown from the train. Then what would have happened to Billy?

The train was moving at least fifty miles an hour now. At some point in the coming hour it was sure to slow, then he would be able to make his way safely back to their car. Emmett looked down at his brother's watch to log the time, only to find that the crystal was broken and the second hand frozen in place.

Pastor John

WHEN PASTOR JOHN SAW that there was somebody asleep in the boxcar, he nearly moved along. When one has far to go, there is much to be said for companionship. The journey in a boxcar is long in hours and short in common comforts, and every man, however vagabond, has a story that may edify or entertain. But ever since Adam last saw Eden, sin has been lodged in the hearts of men such that even those predisposed to be meek and kind may of a sudden become covetous and cruel. So, when a weary traveler has in his possession a half-pint of whiskey and eighteen dollars that he has earned by the sweat of his own brow, prudency counsels that he forgo the benefits of fellowship and pass the hours in the safety of his own solicitude.

This is what Pastor John was thinking when he saw the stranger sit up, switch on a flashlight, and direct its narrow beam upon the pages of an oversize book—revealing that he was no more than a boy.

A runaway, thought Pastor John with a smile.

No doubt he'd gotten in a tiff with his parents and slipped away with his rucksack over his shoulder, setting out in the manner of Tom Sawyer—little reader that he was. By the time he reached New York, the boy would welcome the moment of his discovery, so that he could be returned by the authorities to his father's stern reproach and his mother's warm embrace.

But New York was still a day's journey, and though boys may be impetuous, inexperienced, and naïve, they are not without a certain practical intelligence. For while a grown man who storms off in the heat of anger is likely to do so with only the shirt upon his back, a boy who runs away will always have the foresight to pack a sandwich. Perhaps even a bit of his mother's fried chicken left over from the night before. And then there was the flashlight to consider. How often in the last year alone would Pastor John have found it providential to have a flashlight near at hand? More times than he could count.

—Well, hello there!

Without waiting for a response, Pastor John climbed down the ladder and brushed the dust from his knees, noting that while the boy had looked up in some surprise, he had the good manners not to train the beam of his light on a newcomer's face.

—For the foot soldiers of the Lord, began Pastor John, the hours are long and the comforts few. So I, for one, would welcome a little company. Do you mind if I join you by your fire?

—My fire? asked the boy.

Pastor John pointed to the flashlight.

—Forgive me. I was speaking in the poetical sense. It is an occupational hazard for men of the cloth. Pastor John, at your service.

When John offered his hand, the boy rose and shook it like a little gentleman.

—My name is Billy Watson.

—A pleasure to meet you, William.

Though suspicion is as old as sin, the boy didn't betray a hint of it. But he did exhibit a reasonable curiosity.

—Are you a real pastor?

Pastor John smiled.

—I do not have a steeple or bells under my command, my boy. Rather, like my namesake, John the Baptist, my church is the open road and my congregation the common man. But yes, I am as real a pastor as you are likely to meet.

—You are the second person of the cloth that I have met in two days, said the boy.

—Do tell.

—Yesterday, I met Sister Agnes at St. Nicholas's in Lewis. Do you know her?

—I have *known* many a sister in my time, the pastor said with an inward wink. But I don't believe I have had the pleasure of knowing one named Agnes.

Pastor John smiled down at the boy, then took the liberty of sitting. When the boy joined him, John expressed his admiration for the flashlight and wondered if he might take a closer look. Without a moment's hesitation, the boy handed it over.

—It's an army surplus flashlight, he explained. From the Second World War.

As if to marvel at the flashlight's beam, Pastor John used it to survey the rest of the boxcar, noting with pleasant surprise that the boy's rucksack was bigger than it first had seemed.

—The Lord's first creation, Pastor John observed in appreciation while returning the flashlight to its owner.

Once again, the boy looked at him with curiosity. By way of explanation, Pastor John quoted the verse.

—*And the Lord said*, Let there be light, *and there was light*.

—But in the very beginning, God created the heavens and the earth, said the boy. Wouldn't light be His third creation?

Pastor John cleared his throat.

—You're perfectly right, William. At least, in the technical sense. Either way, I think we can assume that the Lord takes great satisfaction from the fact that having witnessed his *third* creation be harnessed for the benefit of men at war, the device has found a second life in the service of a boy's edification.

With this satisfactory observation the boy was silenced, and Pastor John found himself glancing rather longingly at his bag.

The day before, Pastor John had been preaching the Word of the Lord at the edge of a traveling Christian revival meeting on the out-skirts of Cedar Rapids. Although the pastor was not *officially* a part of the meeting, so taken were the attendees with his own special brand of fire and brimstone that he had preached from dawn till dusk with-out even taking time for a brief repast. In the evening, when the crew had begun to roll up the tents, Pastor John had planned to retire to a nearby tavern, where a lovely young member of a Methodist choir had agreed to join him for supper and, perhaps, a glass of wine. But it so happened that the girl's choirmaster was also her father, and one thing leading to another, Pastor John was forced to make a hastier departure than he'd intended. So when he'd taken his seat with the boy, he was quite eager to skip along to the moment when they would break bread.

But there is as much call for etiquette in an empty boxcar as there is at the table of a bishop. And what the etiquette of the road demanded was that one traveler should come to know another before expecting to share in his food. To that end, Pastor John took the initiative.

—Tell me, young man: What is that you're reading?

—*Professor Abacus Abernathe's Compendium of Heroes, Adventurers, and Other Intrepid Travelers.*

—How appropriate! May I?

Again the boy handed over one of his possessions without the slight-est hesitation. A Christian through and through, thought Pastor John, while opening the book. Reaching the table of contents, John saw that it was in fact a compendium of heroes, more or less.

—No doubt, you are headed off on an adventure of your own, prompted John.

In response, the boy nodded energetically.

—Don't tell me. Let me guess.

Glancing down, Pastor John ran his finger along the list.

—Hmm. Let me see. Yes, yes.

With a smile he tapped the book, then looked up at the boy.

—I suspect you are off to circumnavigate the globe in eighty days—in the manner of Phileas Fogg!

—No, said the boy. I am not off to circumnavigate the globe.

Pastor John glanced back at the table of contents.

—You plan to sail the Seven Seas like Sinbad . . . ?

The boy shook his head again.

In the earnest silence that followed, Pastor John was reminded of how quickly one becomes bored with children's games.

—You have me, William. I give up. Why don't you tell me where your adventure is taking you.

—To California.

Pastor John raised his eyebrows. Should he tell the lad that of all the possible directions in which he might travel, he had chosen the one least likely to get him to California? The news would undoubtedly prove valuable to the boy, but it also might disconcert him. And what was to be gained by that?

—California, you say? An excellent destination. I imagine you are headed there in hopes of finding gold.

The pastor smiled encouragingly.

—No, the boy replied in his parrotlike manner, I am not headed to California in hopes of finding gold.

Pastor John waited for the boy to elaborate, but elaboration did not appear to be in his nature. At any rate, thought Pastor John, that seemed conversation enough.

—Wherever we happen to be traveling and for whatever the reasons, I count it a stroke of good fortune to find myself in the company of a young man with knowledge of Scripture and a love of adventure. Why, the only thing missing to make our journey more perfect . . .

As the pastor paused, the boy looked at him expectantly.

— . . . Would be a little something to nibble upon as we pass the time in conversation.

Pastor John gave a wistful smile. Then it was his turn to look expectantly.

But the boy didn't blink.

Hmm, thought Pastor John. Was it possible that young William was being cagey?

No. He wasn't the sort. Guileless as he was, he would share a sandwich if he had one. Unfortunately, whatever sandwich he'd had the good sense to pack had probably been eaten. For if runaway boys had the unusual foresight to pack some food, what they lacked was the self-discipline to ration it out.

Pastor John frowned.

What charity the Good Lord bestows upon the presumptuous, He does so in the form of disappointment. This was a lesson that John had taught many times under many tents to many souls and to great effect. And yet, whenever proof of the lesson emerged in the course of his own interactions, it always seemed such an unpleasant surprise.

—You should probably turn off your light, said Pastor John a little sourly. So that you don't waste the batteries.

Seeing the wisdom in the suggestion, the boy picked up his flashlight and clicked it off. But when he reached for his rucksack in order to stow it away, a delicate sound emanated from the bag.

Upon hearing it, Pastor John sat a little more upright and the frown disappeared from his face.

Was it a sound that he recognized? Why, it was a sound so familiar, so unexpected, and so welcome that it stimulated every fiber of his being—in the manner that the rustle of a field mouse in the autumn leaves will stimulate a cat. For what had emanated from the rucksack was the unmistakable jangle of coins.

As the boy tucked the flashlight away, Pastor John could see the top of a tobacco tin and hear the currency shifting musically inside it. Not pennies and nickels, mind you, which announce themselves with an appropriate poverty of sound. These were almost certainly half- or silver dollars.

Under the circumstances, Pastor John felt the urge to grin, to laugh, even to sing. But he was, above all else, a man of experience. So instead, he offered the boy the teasing smile of an old familiar.

—What's that you have there, young William? Is that tobacco I see? Don't tell me you indulge in the smoking of cigarettes?

—No, Pastor. I don't smoke cigarettes.

—Thank goodness. But why, pray tell, are you lugging about such a tin?

—It's where I keep my collection.

—A collection, you say! Oh, how I love a collection. May I see it?

The boy took the tin from his bag, but despite having been so ready to share his flashlight and book, he was visibly reluctant to exhibit his collection.

Once again, the pastor found himself wondering if young William was not quite as naïve as he pretended to be. But following the boy's gaze to the boxcar's rough and dusty floor, Pastor John realized that if the boy hesitated, it was because he didn't feel the surface a worthy one.

It was perfectly natural, conceded John, for a collector of fine china or rare manuscripts to be finicky about the surfaces on which his prized possessions were laid. But when it comes to metal currencies, surely one surface was as good as the next. After all, within its lifetime a typical coin is likely to journey from the coffers of a magnate to the palm of a beggar and back again many times over. It has found itself on poker tables and in offering plates. It has been carried into battle in the boot of a patriot and lost among the velvety cushions of a young lady's boudoir. Why, the typical coin has circumnavigated the globe *and* sailed the Seven Seas.

There was hardly any call for such finickiness. The coins would be as ready to fulfill their purpose after being spread across the floor of a boxcar as they were on the day they were struck at the mint. All the boy needed was a little encouragement.

—Here, said Pastor John, let me help.

But when Pastor John reached out, the boy—who still had his hands on his tin and his eye on the floor—pulled back.

Reflexes being what they are, the boy's sudden backward motion prompted the pastor to lurch forward.

Now they both had their hands on the tin.

The boy showed an almost admirable determination as he pulled it toward his chest, but the strength of a child is no match for that of a grown man, and a moment later the tin was in the pastor's possession. Holding it off to the side with his right hand, John held his left against the boy's chest in order to keep him at bay.

—Mind yourself, William, he cautioned.

But as it turned out, he needn't have. For the boy was no longer trying to reclaim the tin or its contents. Like one who has been taken with the Spirit of the Lord, the boy was now shaking his head and uttering incoherent phrases, seemingly unaware of his surroundings. With his rucksack pulled tightly into his lap, he was clearly agitated, but also contained.

—Now, said a satisfied Pastor John, let us see what's inside.

Opening the lid, he spilled out the contents. While the jostling of the tin had resulted in a lovely little jangle, the spilling of the contents onto the hard wooden floor recalled the sound of a Liberty Bell machine paying off. With the tips of his fingers, Pastor John gently spread the coins across the floor. There were at least forty of them and they were all silver dollars.

—Praise the Lord, said Pastor John.

For surely it was divine providence that had delivered this bounty into his hands.

Glancing quickly at William, he was pleased to find him still in his state of self-containment. It allowed John to turn his full attention upon the windfall. Picking up one of the dollars, he angled it toward the morning light that was beginning to shine through the hatch.

—Eighteen eighty-six, the pastor whispered.

Quickly, he took another from the pile. Then another, and another. 1898. 1905. 1909. 1912. 1882!

Pastor John looked at the boy with an expression of fresh appreciation, for he had not spoken lightly when he called the contents of his tin a collection. Here was not simply a country boy's savings. It was a patiently gathered sampling of American silver dollars minted in different years—some of which were likely to be valued at more than a dollar. Perhaps *much* more than a dollar.

Who knew what this little pile was worth?

Pastor John didn't, that's for sure. But once he was in New York, he would be able to find out easily enough. The Jews on Forty-Seventh Street would certainly know their worth and would probably be willing to buy them. But they could hardly be trusted to give him a fair price. Perhaps there was literature somewhere on the value of the coins. Yes, that was it. There was always literature on the value of items that collectors liked to collect. And as luck would have it, the main branch of the New York Public Library was right around the corner from where the Jews plied their trade.

The boy, who had been quietly repeating the same word over and over, was beginning to raise his voice.

—Easy now, said Pastor John, in admonition.

But when he looked at the boy—rocking in place with his rucksack in his lap, far away from home, hungry and headed in the wrong direction—Pastor John was struck by a pang of Christian sympathy. In a moment of exhilaration, he had imagined that God had sent the boy to him. But what if it was the other way around? What if God had sent *him to the boy?* Not the God of Abraham, who would sooner strike down a sinner than call him by name, but the God of Christ. Or even Christ Himself, the One who assured us that no matter how often we have strayed, we can find forgiveness and even redemption by redirecting our steps toward the path of virtue.

Perhaps he was meant to help the boy sell his collection. To bring him safely into the city and to negotiate with the Jews on his behalf to ensure that he wasn't taken advantage of. Then John would bring him to Pennsylvania Station, where he would put him on the train to California. And in exchange, all he would ask for was a nominal offering. A tithe, perhaps. But under the lofty ceiling of the station, surrounded by fellow travelers, the boy would insist they split their windfall down the middle!

Pastor John smiled at the thought of it.

But what if the boy had a change of heart . . . ?

What if in one of the shops on Forty-Seventh Street, he suddenly objected to his collection's sale. What if he were to hold the tin to his chest as tightly as he held his rucksack now, proclaiming to any who would listen that the coins were *his.* Oh, how the Jews would enjoy that! How they would relish the chance to call the police, point their fingers at a pastor, and have him carted away.

No. If the Good Lord had intervened, it was to bring the boy to him, and not the other way around.

He looked to William with an almost sympathetic shake of his head.

But as he did so, Pastor John couldn't help but take note of just how tightly the boy gripped his rucksack. Pulling it against his chest, he had wrapped both arms around it, tucked up his knees, and lowered his chin as if to make it invisible to the naked eye.

—Tell me, William. What else do you have in that bag of yours . . . ?

Without rising, the boy began to slide back across the boxcar's rough and dusty floor without letting up on his grip.

Yes, remarked the pastor. Look how he holds it to his chest even as he edges away. There is something else in that bag, and so help me, I shall know what it is.

As Pastor John rose to his feet, he heard the squeak of metal wheels as the train began to move.

Perfect, he thought. He would liberate the bag from the boy and the boy from the boxcar. Then he could travel to New York in the safety of his own solicitude with a hundred dollars or more.

With his hands extended, Pastor John took a small step forward as the boy came up against the wall. When the pastor took another step, the boy began to slide to his right, only to find himself wedged in the corner with nowhere to go.

Pastor John softened his tone from one of accusation to one of explanation.

—I can see that you do not wish me to look in your bag, William. But it is the Lord's will that I should do so.

The boy, who was still shaking his head, now closed his eyes in the manner of one who acknowledges the approach of the inevitable but who wishes not to witness its arrival.

Gently, John reached down, took hold of the rucksack, and began to lift it away. But the boy's grip was fast. So fast that when John began to lift, he found he was lifting the bag and the boy together.

Pastor John let out a little laugh at the comedy of the situation. It was something that might have occurred in one of the films of Buster Keaton.

But the more Pastor John tried to lift the bag away, the tighter the boy held on; and the tighter he held on, the more clear it became that something of value was hidden within.

—Come now, said John, in a tone that betrayed a reasonable loss of patience.

But shaking his head with his eyes tightly closed, the boy simply repeated his incantation more loudly and clearly.

—Emmett, Emmett, Emmett.

—There is no Emmett here, said John in a soothing voice, but the boy showed no signs of slackening his hold.

Having no choice, Pastor John struck him.

Yes, he struck the boy. But he struck him as a schoolmarm might strike a student, to correct his behavior and ensure his attention.

Some tears began to progress down the boy's cheeks, but he still wouldn't open his eyes or loosen his grip.

With something of a sigh, Pastor John held the rucksack tightly with his right hand and drew back his left. This time, he would strike the boy as his own father had struck him—firmly across the face with the back of the hand. Sometimes, as his father liked to say, to make an impression on a child, one must leave an impression on a child. But before Pastor John could set his hand in motion, there was a loud thump behind him.

Without letting go of the boy, John looked over his shoulder.

Standing at the other end of the boxcar, having dropped through the hatch, was a Negro six feet tall.

—Ulysses! exclaimed the pastor.

For a moment, Ulysses neither moved nor spoke. The scene before him may well have been obscured by his sudden transition from daylight into shadow. But his eyes adjusted soon enough.

—Let go of the boy, he said in his unhurried way.

But Pastor John did not have his hands on the boy. He had his hands on the bag. Without letting go, he began explaining the situation as quickly as he could.

—This little thief snuck into the car while I was sound asleep. Luckily, I woke just as he was going through my bag. In the struggle that followed, my savings spilled to the floor.

—Let go of the boy, Pastor. I won't tell you again.

Pastor John looked at Ulysses, then slowly released his grip.

—You're perfectly right. There's no need to admonish him further.

At this point, he has surely learned his lesson. I will just gather up my dollars and return them to my bag.

Fortuitously, the boy did not object.

But somewhat to Pastor John's surprise, this was not out of fear. Quite to the contrary, the boy, who was no longer shaking his head with his eyes closed, was staring at Ulysses with an expression of amazement.

Why, he has never seen a Negro, thought Pastor John.

Which was just as well. For before the boy regained his senses, Pastor John could gather up the collection. To that end he fell to his knees and began sweeping up the coins.

—Leave them be, said Ulysses.

With his hands still hovering a few inches above the windfall, Pastor John looked back at Ulysses and spoke with a hint of indignation.

—I was just going to reclaim what is rightfully—

—Not a one, said Ulysses.

The pastor shifted his tone to reason.

—I am not a greedy man, Ulysses. Though I have earned these dollars through the sweat of my own brow, may I suggest that we follow the counsel of Solomon and split the money in half?

Even as he made this suggestion, Pastor John realized with some dismay that he had gotten the lesson upside down. All the more reason to press onward.

—We could split it three ways, if you'd prefer. An equal share for you, me, *and* the boy.

But while Pastor John was making this proposal, Ulysses had turned to the boxcar's door, thrown the latch, and slid it rumbling open.

—This is where you get off, said Ulysses.

When Pastor John had first taken the boy's bag in hand, the train had been barely moving, but in the interim it had gained considerable speed. Outside, the branches of trees were flashing by in what amounted to a blur.

—Here? he replied in shock. Now?

—I ride alone, Pastor. You know that.

—Yes, I remember that to be your preference. But the journey in a boxcar is long in hours and short in common comforts; surely a little Christian fellowship—

—For more than eight years, I have been riding alone without the benefit of Christian fellowship. If for some reason I suddenly found myself in need of it, I certainly wouldn't be in need of yours.

Pastor John looked to the boy in an appeal to his sense of charity and in the hope that he might come to his defense, but the boy was still staring at the Negro in amazement.

—All right, all right, acquiesced the pastor. Every man has the right to form his own friendships, and I have no desire to impose my company upon you. I will just climb up the ladder, slip out the hatch, and make my way to another car.

—No, said Ulysses. This is the way you go.

For a moment, Pastor John hesitated. But when Ulysses made a move in his direction, he stepped toward the door.

Outside, the terrain did not look welcoming. Along the tracks was an embankment covered in a mix of gravel and scrub, while beyond that a dense and ancient wood. Who knew how far they were from the nearest town or road.

Sensing that Ulysses was now behind him, Pastor John looked back with an imploring expression, but the Negro didn't meet his gaze. He too was watching the trees flash by, watching them without remorse.

—Ulysses, he pled once more.

—With my help or without it, Pastor.

—All right, all right, Pastor John replied, while mustering up a tone of righteous indignation. I will jump. But before I do so, the least you can do is allow me a moment of prayer.

Almost imperceptibly, Ulysses shrugged.

—Psalm Twenty-Three would be appropriate, said Pastor John in a cutting manner. Yes, I should think that Psalm Twenty-Three would do very nicely.

Placing his palms together and closing his eyes, the pastor began:

—*The Lord is my shepherd; I shall not want. He maketh me to lie down in green pastures: he leadeth me beside the still waters. He restoreth my soul: he leadeth me in the paths of righteousness for his name's sake.*

The pastor began reciting the psalm slowly and quietly, in a tone of humility. But when he reached the fourth verse his voice began to rise with that sense of inner strength that is known only to the soldiers of the Lord.

—*Yea*, he intoned with an uplifted hand, as if he were waving the Good Book over the heads of his congregants. *Though I walk through the valley of the shadow of death, I will fear no evil: for thou art with me! Thy rod and thy staff they comfort me!*

There were only two verses left in the Psalm, but no two verses could be more apt. With Pastor John in full feather, having built up his oratory to an appropriate pitch, the line *Thou preparest a table before me in the presence of mine enemies* was sure to sting Ulysses to the very marrow. And he would all but tremble when Pastor John concluded: *Surely goodness and mercy shall follow me all the days of my life: and I will dwell in the house of the Lord for ever!*

But Pastor John never got the chance to ring this particular oratorical bell, for just as he was about to deliver the last two verses, Ulysses sent him sailing into the air.

Ulysses

WHEN ULYSSES TURNED FROM THE DOOR, he found the white boy looking up at him, his knapsack gripped in his arms.

Ulysses waved a hand at the dollars.

—Gather your things, son.

But the boy didn't make a move to do as he was told. He just kept staring back without a sign of trepidation.

He must be only eight or nine, thought Ulysses. Not much younger than my own boy would be by now.

—It's like you heard me tell the pastor, he continued more softly. I ride alone. That's the way it's been and that's the way it's going to stay. But in half an hour or so, there will be a steep grade and the train will slow. When we reach it, I will lower you into the grass and you won't come to harm. Do you understand?

But the boy kept on staring as if he hadn't heard a word, and Ulysses began to wonder if he was simple. But then he spoke.

—Were you in a war?

Ulysses was taken aback by the question.

—Yes, he said after a moment. I was in the war.

The boy took a step forward.

—Did you sail across a sea?

—All of us were overseas, replied Ulysses a little defensively.

The boy thought to himself, then took another step forward.

—Did you leave a wife and son behind?

Ulysses, who stepped back from no man, stepped back from the child. He stepped back so abruptly it would have appeared to an observer that the boy had touched a raw wire to the surface of his skin.

—Do we know each other? he asked, shaken.

—No. We don't know each other. But I think I know who you are named for.

—Everyone knows who I'm named for: Ulysses S. Grant, commander of the Union Army, the unwavering sword in Mr. Lincoln's hand.

—No, said the boy, shaking his head. No, it wasn't that Ulysses.

—I should think I would know.

The boy continued to shake his head, though not in a contrary way. He shook his head in the manner of patience and kinship.

—No, he said again. You must have been named for the *Great* Ulysses.

Ulysses looked at the boy with feelings of growing uncertainty, as one who has suddenly found himself in the presence of the unworldly.

For a moment the boy turned his gaze to the ceiling of the boxcar. When he looked back at Ulysses his eyes were opened wide as if he'd been struck by a notion.

—I can *show* you, he said.

Sitting down on the floor, he opened the flap of his knapsack and withdrew a large red book. He flipped to a page near the back and began to read:

> Sing to me, Oh Muse, of the great and wily wanderer
> Odysseus, or Ulysses by name
> One tall in stature and supple in mind
> Who having shown his courage on the field of battle
> Was doomed to travel this way and that
> From one strange land to the next . . .

It was Ulysses who took a step forward now.

—It's all here, said the boy, without looking up from his book. In ancient times, with utmost reluctance, the Great Ulysses left his wife and son and sailed across the sea to fight in the Trojan War. But once the Greeks were victorious, Ulysses set out for home in the company of his comrades, only to have his ship blown off course time and again.

The boy looked up.

—This must be who you were named for, Ulysses.

And though Ulysses had heard his name spoken ten thousand times before, to hear it spoken by this boy in this moment—in this boxcar somewhere west of where he was headed and east of where he had been—it was as if he were hearing it for the very first time.

The boy tilted the book so that Ulysses could see it more clearly. Then he shifted a little to his right, as one does when making room for another on a bench. And Ulysses found himself sitting beside the boy and listening to him read, as if the boy were the seasoned traveler hardened by war, and he, Ulysses, were the child.

In the minutes that followed, the boy—this Billy Watson—read of how the Great Ulysses, having trimmed his sails and trained his tiller homeward, angered the god Poseidon by blinding his one-eyed son, the Cyclops, and thus was cursed to wander unforgiving seas. He read of how Ulysses was given a bag by Aeolus, the Keeper of the Winds, to speed his progress, only to have his crewmen, who were suspicious that he was hiding gold, untie the bag, unleash the winds, and set Ulysses's ship a thousand leagues off course—at the very moment that the shores of his longed-for homeland had come into view.

And as Ulysses listened, for the first time in memory he wept. He wept for his namesake and his namesake's crew. He wept for Penelope and Telemachus. He wept for his own comrades-in-arms who had been slain on the field of battle, and for his own wife and son, whom he had left behind. But most of all, he wept for himself.

———

When Ulysses met Macie in the summer of 1939, they were alone in the world. In the depths of the Depression, they both had buried their parents, they both had left the states of their birth—she Alabama and he Tennessee—for the city of St. Louis. Upon arriving, they both had shifted from rooming house to rooming house and job to job without companions or kin. Such that by the time they chanced to be standing side by side at the bar near the back of the Starlight Ballroom—both more prone to listen than to dance—they had come to believe that a life of aloneness was all the heavens held in store for the likes of them.

With what joy they came to find otherwise. Talking to each other that night, how they laughed—as two who not only knew each other's foibles, but who had watched each other fashion them willfully out of their own dreams and vanities and foolhardy ways. And once he had worked up the courage to ask her to dance, she joined him on the dance floor in a manner never to be undone. Three months later, when he was hired as a lineman at the phone company making twenty dollars a week, they were married and moved into a two-room flat on Fourteenth Street, where from dawn till dusk, and a few hours more, their inseparable dance continued.

But then the troubles began overseas.

Ulysses had always imagined that, should the time come, he would answer the call of his country just as his father had in 1917. But when the Japs bombed Pearl Harbor in December of '41 and all the boys began converging on the recruitment office, Macie—who had waited in solitude for so many years—met his gaze with narrowed eyes and a slow-motion shake of the head, as much as to say: *Ulysses Dixon, don't you dare.*

As if the US government itself had been persuaded by Macie's unambiguous gaze, in early '42 it declared that all linemen with two years' experience were too essential to serve. So even as the war effort mounted, he and Macie woke in the same bed, ate breakfast at the same table, and went off to their jobs with the same lunch pails in hand. But with every day that passed, Ulysses's willingness to sidestep the conflict was being sorely tested.

It was tested by the speeches of FDR on the wireless as he assured the nation that through our shared resolve we would triumph over the forces of evil. Tested by the headlines in the papers. Tested by the neighborhood boys who were lying about their ages in order to join the fight. And most of all, it was tested by the men in their sixties who would look at him on his way to work with sideways glances, wondering what in the hell an able-bodied man was doing sitting on a trolley at eight in the morning while the rest of the world was at war. But whenever he happened to pass a new recruit in his newly issued uniform, there was Macie with her narrowed eyes to remind him of how long she had waited. So Ulysses swallowed his pride, and as the months ticked by, he rode the trolley with a downward gaze and burned his idle hours within the walls of their apartment.

Then in July of '43, Macie discovered that she was with child. As the weeks passed, no matter what the news from either front, she began to radiate an inner illumination that would not be denied. She started meeting Ulysses at his trolley stop, wearing a summer dress and a wide yellow hat, and she would hook her arm under his to stroll with him back to their apartment, nodding at friends and strangers alike. Then toward the end of November, just as she had begun to show, she persuaded him against his better judgment to put on his Sunday suit and take her to the Thanksgiving dance at the Hallelujah Hall.

As soon as Ulysses walked through the door, he knew he had made a terrible mistake. For everywhere he turned, he met the eye of a mother who had lost a son, a wife who had lost a husband, or a child who had lost a father, each individual gaze made all the more bitter by Macie's beatitude. Even worse was when he met the eyes of the other men his age. For when they saw him standing awkwardly at the edge of the dance floor, they came and shook his hand, their smiles tempered by their own manner of cowardice, their spirits relieved to find another able-bodied man to share in the brotherhood of shame.

That night when he and Macie returned to their flat, before they had even taken off their coats, Ulysses had announced his decision to enlist. Having prepared himself for the likelihood that Macie would grow angry or weep, he expressed his intentions in the manner of a foregone conclusion, a decision that broached no debate. But when he was finished with his talking, she didn't tremble or shed a tear. And when she responded, she didn't raise her voice.

—If you have to go to war, she said, then go to war. Take on Hitler and Tojo with one arm tied behind your back for all I care. But don't expect to find us here when you get back.

The next day, when he walked into the recruiting office, he feared that he'd be turned away as a man of forty-two, but ten days later he was at Camp Funston and ten months after that he was on his way to serve in the 92nd Infantry Division under the Fifth Army in the Italian campaign. All through those unforgiving days, despite the fact that he did not receive a single letter from his wife, he never imagined—or rather, never let himself imagine—that she and the child would not be waiting for him upon his return.

But when his train pulled into St. Louis on the twentieth of December 1945, they were not at the station. When he went to Fourteenth Street, they were not in the flat. And when he tracked down the landlord, and the neighbors, and her friends from work, the report was always the same: Two weeks after giving birth to a beautiful baby boy, Macie Dixon had packed up her things and left the city without leaving word of where she was headed.

Less than twenty-four hours after returning to St. Louis, Ulysses put his bag on his shoulder and walked back to Union Station. There, he boarded the very next train, unconcerned with where it was going. He rode that train as far is it went—to Atlanta, Georgia—and then without setting foot outside the station, he boarded the next train headed in a different direction and rode that one all the way to Santa Fe. That was more than eight years ago. He had been riding ever since—in the passenger cars while his money held out and in the boxcars once it was gone—back and forth across the nation, never allowing himself to spend a second night in any one spot before jumping the next train to wherever it was bound.

———·———

As the boy read on and the Great Ulysses went from landfall to landfall and trial to trial, Ulysses listened in silence, the tears falling from his eyes, unabashedly. He listened as his namesake faced the metamorphical spells of Circe, the ruthless seduction of the Sirens, and the closely knit perils of Scylla and Charybdis. But when the boy read of how Ulysses's hungry crew ignored the warnings of the seer, Tiresias, and slaughtered the sacred cattle of the sun god, Helios, prompting Zeus to besiege the hero once again with thunder and swells, Ulysses placed a hand across the pages of the young boy's book.

—Enough, he said.

The boy looked up in surprise.

—Don't you want to hear the end?

Ulysses was silent for a moment.

—There is no end, Billy. There is no end of travails for those who have angered the Almighty.

But Billy was shaking his head, once again in kinship.

—That isn't so, he said. Although the Great Ulysses angered Poseidon and Helios, he didn't wander without end. When did you set sail from your war in order to return to America?

Doubtful of what it could matter, Ulysses answered.

—On the fourteenth of November, 1945.

Gently pushing Ulysses's hand aside, the boy turned the page and pointed to a passage.

—Professor Abernathe tells us that the Great Ulysses returned to Ithaca and was reunited with his wife and son *after ten long years.*

The boy looked up.

—That means that you have almost come to the end of your

wanderings, and that you will be reunited with your family in less than two years' time.

Ulysses shook his head.

—Billy, I don't even know where they are.

—That's okay, the boy replied. If you knew where they were, then you wouldn't have to find them.

Then the boy looked down at his book and nodded his head in satisfaction that this is how it should be.

Was it possible? wondered Ulysses.

It was true that on the field of battle he had offended the teachings of His Lord, Jesus Christ, in every possible way, offended them to such a degree that it was hard to imagine crossing the threshold of a church in good conscience ever again. But all of the men whom he had fought alongside—as well as those he'd fought against—had offended the same teachings, broken the same covenants, and ignored the same commandments. So Ulysses had come to some peace with the sins of the battlefield, recognizing them as the sins of a generation. What Ulysses had not come to peace with, what weighed upon his conscience, was his betrayal of his wife. Theirs was a covenant too, and when he betrayed it, he betrayed it alone.

Even as he was standing in that poorly lit hallway of their old apartment house in full uniform, feeling less like a hero than a fool, he understood that the consequences of what he had done *should* be irrevocable. That is what had led him back to Union Station and into the life of a vagabond—a life destined to be lived without companionship or purpose.

But maybe the boy was right . . .

Maybe by placing his own sense of shame above the sanctity of their union, by so readily condemning himself to a life of solitude, he had betrayed his wife a second time. Had betrayed his wife and son.

As he was having this thought, the boy had closed his book and begun picking up the silver dollars, dusting them off with the cuff of his sleeve and returning them to their tin.

—Here, said Ulysses, let me help.

He too began picking up the coins, polishing them on his sleeve, and dropping them in the tin.

But when the boy was about to put the last coin away, he suddenly looked over Ulysses's shoulder as if he'd heard something. Quickly packing away the tin and his big red book, the boy tightened the straps on his knapsack and swung it on his back.

—What is it? asked Ulysses, a little startled by the boy's sudden movements.

—The train is slowing, he explained, rising to his feet. We must have reached the grade.

It took Ulysses a moment to understand what the boy was talking about.

—No, Billy, he said, following the boy to the door. You don't have to go. You should stay with me.

—Are you sure, Ulysses?

—I'm sure.

Billy nodded in acceptance, but as he gazed out the door at the brush flashing by, Ulysses could tell that he was taken with a fresh concern.

—What is it, son?

—Do you think that Pastor John was hurt when he jumped from the train?

—No more than he deserved.

Billy looked up at Ulysses.

—But he was a preacher.

—In that man's heart, said Ulysses, sliding the door shut, there is more treachery than preachery.

The two walked to the other end of the car with the intention of sitting back down, but as they were about to do so, Ulysses heard a scuffing behind him as if someone had carefully stepped off the ladder.

Without waiting to hear more, Ulysses spun about with his arms outstretched, inadvertently knocking Billy to the ground.

When Ulysses had heard the scuffing, it flashed through his mind that Pastor John had somehow reboarded the train and returned to confront him with vengeance in mind. But it wasn't Pastor John. It was a white youth with contusions and a determined look. In his right hand, he had the cinched bag of a thief. Dropping the bag, he took a step forward and assumed his own fighting stance, with his arms extended.

—I don't want to fight you, said the youth.

—No one wants to fight me, said Ulysses.

They both took a step forward.

Ulysses found himself wishing that he hadn't shut the boxcar door. If it were open, he could make a cleaner business of it. He would simply have to grab hold of the youth by the arms and cast him off the train. With the door closed he would have to either knock the youth unconscious or secure him in a grip and have Billy open the door. But he didn't want to put the boy anywhere within reach of the youth. So he would pick his moment. He would keep himself between Billy and the youth, draw a little closer, and then hit him on the bruised side of his face, where it was sure to be tender.

Behind him, Ulysses could hear Billy working his way onto his feet.

—Stay back, Billy, both he and the youth said at the very same time.

Then they looked at each other bewildered but unwilling to lower their arms.

Ulysses heard Billy taking a step to the side as if to see around him.

—Hey, Emmett.

With his arms still up and one eye on Ulysses, the youth took a step to his left.

—Are you all right, Billy?

—I'm all right.

—Do you know him? asked Ulysses.

—He's my brother, said Billy. Emmett, this is Ulysses. He fought in the war like the Great Ulysses and now must wander for ten years until he's reunited with his wife and son. But you needn't worry. We're not friends yet. We're just getting acquainted.

Duchess

LOOK AT ALL THE HOUSES, said Woolly in amazement. Have you ever seen so many houses?

—It's a lot of houses, I agreed.

Earlier that day, my taxi had come around the corner just in time for me to see Woolly emerging from a park. Across the street I could see where he'd left the Studebaker—in front of a fire hydrant with the passenger-side door open and the engine running. I could also see the cop standing at the back of the car with his ticket book in hand, jotting down the number of the license plate.

—Pull over, I told the cabby.

I don't know what Woolly said to the cop by way of explanation, but by the time I'd paid the cabby, the cop was putting away his ticket book and taking out his cuffs.

I approached wearing my best approximation of a small-town smile.

—What seems to be the trouble, officer?

(They love it when you call them officer.)

—Are you two together?

—In a manner of speaking. I work for his parents.

The cop and I both looked over at Woolly, who had wandered off to get a closer look at the fire hydrant.

When the cop gave me the rundown of Woolly's infractions, including the fact that he didn't seem to have his driver's license on him, I shook my head.

—You're preaching to the choir, officer. I kept telling them if they intended to bring him back home, they'd better hire someone to keep an eye on him. But what do I know? I'm just the groundskeeper.

The cop took another look at Woolly.

—Are you implying there's something wrong with him?

—Let's just say his receiver is tuned to a different frequency than yours and mine. He has a habit of wandering off, so when his mother woke up this morning and saw that her car was missing—again—she asked me to track him down.

—How did you know where to find him?

—He's got a thing about Abraham Lincoln.

The officer looked at me with a hint of skepticism. So I showed him.

—Mr. Martin, I called. Why did you come to the park?

Woolly thought about it for a moment, then smiled.

—To see the statue of President Lincoln.

Now the officer was looking at me with a hint of uncertainty. On the one hand he had his list of infractions and his oath to maintain law and order in the state of Illinois. But what was he supposed to do? Arrest some troubled kid who'd snuck out of the house in order to pay his respects to Honest Abe?

The cop looked from me to Woolly and back again. Then he straightened his shoulders and tugged at his belt, as cops are wont to do.

—All right, he said. Why don't you see him safely home.

—I intend to, officer.

—But a young man on his *frequency* should not be driving. Maybe it's time his family put the keys to the car on a higher shelf.

—I'll let them know.

Once the cop had driven off and we were back in the Studebaker, I gave Woolly a little talking to about the meaning of all for one and one for all.

—What happens if you get yourself arrested, Woolly? And your name ends up on the blotter? Before you know it, they'd have us both on a bus back to Salina. Then we'd never make it to the camp, and Billy wouldn't get to build his house in California.

—I'm sorry, Woolly said with a look of genuine contrition—and pupils as big as flying saucers.

—How many drops of your medicine did you take this morning?

. . .

—Four?

—How many bottles do you have left?

. . .

—One?

—One! Jesus, Woolly. That stuff isn't Coca-Cola. And who knows when we can get you some more. You'd better let me hold on to the last one for now.

Sheepishly, Woolly opened the glove compartment and handed over the little blue bottle. In return, I handed him the map of Indiana that I'd bought off the cabbie. He frowned when he saw it.

—I know. It's not a Phillips 66 map, but it's the best that I could do. While I'm driving, I need you to figure out how to get to 132 Rhododendron Road in South Bend.

—What's at 132 Rhododendron Road?

—An old friend.

———•———

Having reached South Bend around half past one, we were now in the middle of a brand-new subdivision of identical homes on identical lots, presumably inhabited by identical people. It almost made me long for the roads of Nebraska.

—It's like the labyrinth in Billy's book, said Woolly with a hint of awe. The one designed so ingeniously by Daedalus that no one who entered ever came out alive. . . .

—All the more reason, I pointed out sternly, for you to keep an eye on the street signs.

—Okay, okay. I got it, I got it.

After taking a quick glance at the map, Woolly leaned toward the windshield in order to give a little more attention to where we were going.

—Left on Tiger Lily Lane, he said. Right on Amaryllis Avenue . . . Wait, wait . . . There it is!

I took the turn onto Rhododendron Road. All the lawns were green and neatly mowed, but so far the rhododendron part was strictly aspirational. Who knows. Maybe it always would be.

I slowed down so that Woolly could keep an eye on the house numbers.

—124 . . . 126 . . . 128 . . . 130 . . . 132!

As I drove past the house, Woolly looked back over his shoulder.

—It was that one, he said.

I turned the corner at the next intersection and pulled the car over to the curb. Across the street an overfed pensioner in an undershirt was watering his grass with a hose. He looked like he could have used his own dousing.

—Isn't your friend at 132?

—He is. But I want to surprise him.

Having learned my lesson, when I got out of the car I took the keys with me rather than leaving them over the visor.

—I should only be a few minutes, I said. You stay put.

—I will, I will. But Duchess . . .

—Yeah, Woolly?

—I know we're trying to get the Studebaker back to Emmett as quickly as possible, but do you think we might be able to visit my sister Sarah in Hastings-on-Hudson before we head to the Adirondacks?

Most people make a habit of asking for things. At the drop of a hat, they'll ask you for a light or for the time. They'll ask you for a lift or a loan. For a hand or a handout. Some of them will even ask you for forgiveness. But Woolly Martin rarely asked for anything at all. So when he did ask for something, you knew it was something that mattered.

—Woolly, I said, if you can get us back out of this labyrinth alive, we can visit anyone you like.

Ten minutes later, I was standing in a kitchen with a rolling pin in my hand wondering if it would do the trick. Given its shape and heft, it certainly felt better than a two-by-four. But it struck me as an implement better used for comic effect—like by a hausfrau who's chasing her hapless husband around the kitchen table.

Putting the rolling pin back in its drawer, I opened another. This one was filled with a clutter of smaller implements, like vegetable peelers and measuring spoons. The next had the larger and flimsier tools like spatulas and whisks. Tucked under a ladle I found a meat tenderizer. Being careful not to jangle the other items, I removed it from the drawer and found it to have a nice wooden handle and a rough smacking surface, but it was a little on the delicate side, fashioned more for flattening a cutlet than for pounding a side of beef.

On the counter beside the sink were all the usual modern conveniences—a can opener, a toaster, a *three*-button blender, each perfectly engineered if your desire was to open or toast or blend someone. In the cabinets above the counter, I found enough canned food for a bomb shelter. Front and center were at least ten cans of Campbell's soup. But there were also cans of beef stew, chili, and franks and beans. Which seemed to suggest that the only appliance the Ackerlys really needed was the can opener.

I couldn't help but remark on the similarity between the food in Ackerly's cabinet and the menu at Salina. We had always chalked up the prevalence of this sort of cuisine to its institutional utility, but maybe it was an expression of the warden's personal tastes. For a moment I was tempted to use the can of franks and beans in the interests of poetic justice. But if you hit someone with a can, I figured you might do as much damage to your fingers as you did to his skull.

Closing the cabinet, I put my hands on my hips like Sally would have. She'd know where to look, I thought. Trying to see the situation through her eyes, I reviewed the kitchen from corner to corner. And what did I find sitting right there on the stovetop but a skillet as black as Batman's cape. Picking it up, I weighed it in my hand, admiring its design and durability. With a gentle taper and curved edges, the handle fit so securely in your palm you could probably deliver two hundred pounds of force without losing your grip. And the bottom of the pan had a sweet spot so wide and flat you could clean someone's clock with your eyes closed.

Yep, the cast-iron skillet was perfect in just about every respect, despite the fact that there was nothing modern or convenient about it. As a matter of fact, this very pan could have been a hundred years old. It could have been used by Ackerly's great-grandmother on the wagon train and handed down until it had fried porkchops for four generations of Ackerly men. With a tip of the hat to the westward pioneers, I picked up the pan and carried it into the living room.

It was a lovely little room with a television in the spot where the fireplace should have been. The drapes, a chair, and the couch were upholstered in a matching floral print. In all likelihood, Mrs. Ackerly wore a dress cut from the same fabric, so that if she sat on the couch quietly enough, her husband wouldn't know she was there.

Ackerly was still right where I had found him—stretched out on his BarcaLounger, sound asleep.

You could tell from the smile on his face that he loved that lounger. During his tenure at Salina, whenever Ackerly was dispensing strokes of the switch, he must have been dreaming about the day when he could own a lounger like this one in which to fall asleep at two in the afternoon. In fact, after all those years of anticipation, he was probably *still* dreaming about sleeping in a BarcaLounger, even though that's exactly what he was doing.

—To sleep, perchance to dream, I quoted quietly while raising the skillet over his head.

But something on the side table caught my eye. It was a recent photograph of Ackerly standing between two young boys, each with the Ackerly beak and brow. The boys were wearing Little League uniforms and Ackerly was wearing a matching cap, suggesting that he had come to a game to cheer his grandsons on. Naturally, he had a big, fat smile on his face, but the boys were smiling too, like they were glad to know that Grandpa had been in the stands. I felt a surge of tender feelings for the old man in a manner that made my hands sweat. But if the Bible tells us that the sons shall not have to bear the iniquity of the fathers, then it stands to reason that the fathers should not get to bear the innocence of the sons.

So I hit him.

When I made contact, his body gave a jolt, like a shot of electricity had gone through it. Then he slumped a little lower in the chair and his khaki pants grew dark at the groin as his bladder relaxed.

I gave an appreciative nod at the skillet, thinking here was an object that had been carefully designed for one purpose, yet was perfectly suited to another. An added benefit of using the skillet—versus the meat tenderizer, or the toaster, or the can of franks and beans—was that when it made contact, it emitted a harmonious *clong*. It was like the toll of a church bell calling the devoted to prayer. In fact, the sound was so satisfying, I was tempted to hit him again.

But I had taken the time to do my arithmetic with care, and I was pretty confident that Ackerly's debt to me would be satisfied with one solid whack on the crown. To hit him a second time would just put me in *his* debt. So I returned the skillet to the stovetop and slipped out the kitchen door, thinking: *One down, two to go.*

Emmett

REALIZING THAT HE HAD *been frittering away not only the fortune his father had left him, but the more valuable treasure of time, the young Arabian sold what few possessions he had left, joined the ranks of a merchant vessel, and set sail into the great unknown . . .*

Here we go again, thought Emmett.

That afternoon—while Emmett had been laying out the bread and ham and cheese that he'd secured from the Pullman car—Billy had asked Ulysses if he wanted to hear another story about someone who had traveled the seas. When Ulysses said that he would, Billy took out his big red book, sat at the black man's side, and began reading of Jason and the Argonauts.

In that story, the young Jason, who is the rightful king of Thessaly, is told by his usurping uncle that the throne is his to reclaim if he can sail to the kingdom of Colchis and return with the Golden Fleece.

In the company of fifty adventurers—including Theseus and Hercules in the years before their fame—Jason sets course for Colchis with the winds at his back. In the untold days that follow, he and his band travel from trial to trial, variously facing a colossus made of bronze, the winged harpies, and the *spartoi*—a battalion of warriors who spring from the soil fully armed when the teeth of a dragon have been sown. With the help of the sorceress Medea, Jason and his Argonauts eventually overcome their adversaries, secure the Fleece, and make their way safely back to Thessaly.

So enthralled was Billy with the telling of the tale and Ulysses with the hearing of it, when Emmett handed them the sandwiches that he'd made on their behalf, they hardly seemed to notice they were eating them.

As he sat on the other side of the boxcar eating his own sandwich, Emmett found himself mulling over Billy's book.

For the life of him, Emmett could not understand why this so-called professor had chosen to mix Galileo Galilei, Leonardo da Vinci, and Thomas Alva Edison—three of the greatest minds of the scientific age—with the likes of Hercules, Theseus, and Jason. Galileo, da Vinci, and Edison were not heroes of legend. These were men of flesh and blood who had the rare ability to witness natural phenomena without superstition or prejudice. They were men of industry who with patience and precision studied the inner workings of the world and, having done so, turned what knowledge they'd gained in solitude toward practical discoveries in the service of mankind.

What good could possibly come from mixing the lives of these men with stories of mythical heroes setting sail on fabled waters to battle fantastical beasts? By tossing them together, it seemed to Emmett, Abernathe was encouraging a boy to believe that the great scientific discoverers were not exactly real and the heroes of legend not exactly imagined. That shoulder to shoulder they traveled through the realms of the known and unknown making the most of their intelligence and courage, yes, but also of sorcery and enchantment and the occasional intervention of the gods.

Wasn't it hard enough in the course of life to distinguish between fact and fancy, between what one witnessed and what one wanted? Wasn't it the challenge of making this very distinction that had left their father, after twenty years of toil, bankrupt and bereft?

And now, as the day was drawing to a close, Billy and Ulysses had turned their attention to Sinbad, a hero who set sail seven different times on seven different adventures.

—I'm going to bed, Emmett announced.

—Okay, the two responded.

Then, so as not to disturb his brother, Billy lowered his voice, and Ulysses lowered his head, the two looking more like conspirators than strangers.

As Emmett lay down, trying not to listen to the murmured saga of the Arabian sailor, he understood perfectly well that when Ulysses had happened upon their boxcar it had been a stroke of extraordinary luck; but it had been humbling too.

After Billy had made introductions, in his excited way he had re-counted everything that had happened from the moment of Pastor John's appearance to his timely departure from the train. When Emmett expressed his gratitude to Ulysses, the stranger had dismissed the thanks as unnecessary. But the first chance he got—when Billy was retrieving his book from his backpack—Ulysses had taken Emmett aside and given him a thorough schooling. *How could he be such a fool as to leave his brother alone like that? Just because a boxcar has four walls and a ceiling doesn't make it safe, not remotely so. And make no mistake: The pastor wasn't simply going to give Billy the back of his hand. He had every intention of throwing him from the train.*

When Ulysses had turned back to Billy and sat down at his side, ready to hear about Jason, Emmett had felt the sting of the reprimand burning on his cheeks. He felt the heat of indignation too, indignation that this man whom he had only just met should take the liberty of scolding him as a parent scolds a child. But at the same time, Emmett understood that his taking umbrage at being treated like a child was childish in itself. Just as he knew that it was childish to feel resentment that Billy and Ulysses hadn't lingered over their sandwiches, or to feel jealous over their sudden confederacy.

Trying to calm the roiling waters of his own temperament, Emmett turned his attention away from the events of the day toward the chal-lenges that lay ahead.

When they had all been seated together at the kitchen table in Morgen, Duchess had said that before going to the Adirondacks, he and Woolly were going to stop in Manhattan to see his father.

From Duchess's stories it was clear that Mr. Hewett rarely had a steady address. But on Townhouse's last day in Salina, Duchess had encouraged Townhouse to look him up in the city—by contacting one of his father's booking agencies. *Even if a has-been is on the run from creditors, wanted by the cops, and living under an assumed name,* Duchess had said with a wink, *he'll always leave word of where he can be found with the agencies. And in New York City, all the biggest bookers of has-beens have offices in the same building at the bottom of Times Square.*

The only problem was that Emmett couldn't remember the name of the building.

He was fairly certain it began with an *S.* As he lay there, he tried to jog his memory by going through the alphabet and systematically sounding out all the possible combinations of the first three letters of the building's name. Beginning with Sa, he would say to himself: Sab, sac, sad, saf, sag, and so on. Then it was the combinations flowing from Sc and Se and Sh.

Maybe it was the sound of Billy whispering, or his own murmuring of alphabetical triplets. Or maybe it was the warm, wooden smell of the boxcar after its long day in the sun. Whatever the cause, instead of recalling the name of a building at the bottom of Times Square, Emmett was suddenly nine years old in the attic of his house with the hatch pulled up, building a fort with his parents' old trunks—the ones that once had traveled to Paris and Venice and Rome and that hadn't traveled anywhere since—which in turn brought memories of his mother wondering where he could have gotten to and the sound of her voice calling out his name as she went from room to room to room.

SIX

—.—

Duchess

WHEN I KNOCKED ON THE DOOR of room 42, I heard a groan and a labored movement on the bedsprings as if the sound of my rapping had woken him from a deep sleep. Given it was nearly noon, that was right on schedule. After a moment, I could hear him put his hungover feet on the floor. I could hear him look around the room as he tried to get his bearings, taking in the cracked plaster of the ceiling and the peeling wallpaper with a hint of bewilderment, as if he couldn't quite grasp what he was doing in a room like this, couldn't quite believe it, even after all these years.

Ah, yes, I could almost hear him say.

Ever so politely, I knocked again.

Another groan—this time a groan of effort—then the release of the bedsprings as he rose to his feet and began moving slowly toward the door.

—Coming, a muffled voice called.

As I waited, I found myself genuinely curious as to how he would look. Barely two years had gone by, but at his age with his lifestyle, two years could do a lot of damage.

But when the door creaked open, it wasn't my old man.

—Yes?

Somewhere in his seventies, room 42's occupant had a genteel bearing and the accent to go with it. At one time, he could have been the master of an estate, or served the man who was.

—Is there something I can do for you, young man? he asked, as I glanced over his shoulder.

—I was looking for someone who used to live here. My father, actually.

—Oh, I see. . . .

His shaggy eyebrows drooped a little, as if he were actually sorry to have been the cause of a stranger's disappointment. Then his eyebrows rose again.

—Perhaps he left a forwarding address downstairs?

—More likely an unpaid bill, but I'll ask on my way out. Thanks.

He nodded in sympathy. But when I turned to go, he called me back.

—Young man. By any chance, was your father an actor?

—He was known to call himself one.

—Then wait a moment. I believe he may have left something behind.

As the old gent shuffled his way to the bureau, I scanned the room, curious as to his weakness. At the Sunshine Hotel, for every room there was a weakness, and for every weakness an artifact bearing witness. Like an empty bottle that has rolled under the bed, or a feathered deck of cards on the nightstand, or a bright pink kimono on a hook. Some evidence of that one desire so delectable, so insatiable that it overshadowed all others, eclipsing even the desires for a home, a family, or a sense of human dignity.

Given how slow the old man moved I had plenty of time to look, and the room was only ten by ten, but if evidence of his weakness was present, for the life of me I couldn't spot it.

—Here we are, he said.

Shuffling back, he handed me what he'd rummaged from the bureau's bottom drawer.

It was a black leather case about twelve inches square and three inches tall with a small, brass clasp—like a larger version of what might hold a double strand of pearls. The similarity wasn't a coincidence, I suppose. Because at the knee-high height of my father's fame, when he was a leading man in a small Shakespearean troupe performing to half-filled houses, he had six of these cases and they were his prized possessions.

Though the gold embossing on this one was chipped and faint, you could still make out the O of *Othello*. Throwing the clasp, I opened the lid. Inside were four objects resting snuggly in velvet-lined indentations: a goatee, a golden earring, a small jar of blackface, and a dagger.

Like the case, the dagger had been custom made. The golden hilt, which had been fashioned to fit perfectly in my old man's grasp, was adorned with three large jewels in a row: one ruby, one sapphire, one emerald. The stainless steel blade had been forged, tempered, and burnished by a master craftsman in Pittsburgh, allowing my father in act three to cut a wedge from an apple and stick the dagger upright into the surface of a table, where it would remain ominously as he nursed his suspicions of Desdemona's infidelity.

But while the steel of the blade was the real McCoy, the hilt was gilded brass and the jewels were paste. And if you pressed the sapphire with your thumb, it would release a catch, so that when my old man stabbed himself in the gut at the end of act five, the blade would retract into the hilt. As the ladies in the loge gasped, he would take his own sweet time staggering back and forth in front of the footlights before finally giving up his ghost. Which is to say, the dagger was as much a gimmick as he was.

When the set of six cases was still complete, each had its own label embossed in gold: *Othello, Hamlet, Henry, Lear, Macbeth,* and—I kid you not—*Romeo.* Each case had its own velvet-lined indentations holding its own dramatic accessories. For Macbeth these included a bottle of fake blood with which to smear his hands; for Lear a long gray beard; for Romeo a vial of poison, and a small jar of blush that could no more obscure the ravages of time on my old man's face than the crown could obscure the deformities of Richard III.

Over the years, the collection of my father's cases had slowly diminished. One had been stolen, another misplaced, another sold. Hamlet was lost in a game of five-card stud in Cincinnati, appropriately to a pair of kings. But it was not a coincidence that Othello was the last of the six, for it was the one my old man prized most. This was not simply because he had received some of his best reviews for his performance as the Moor, but because on several occasions the jar of blackface had secured him a timely exit. Sporting the uniform of a bellhop and the face of Al Jolson, he would carry his own luggage off the elevator and through the lobby, right past the debt collectors, or angry husbands, or whoever happened to be waiting among the potted palms. To have left the Othello case behind, my old man must have been in quite a hurry. . . .

—Yes, I said while closing the lid, this is my father's. If you don't mind my asking, how long have you been in the room?

—Oh, not long.

—It would be a great help if you could remember more precisely.

—Let's see. Wednesday, Tuesday, Monday . . . Since Monday, I believe. Yes. It was Monday.

In other words, my old man had pulled up stakes the day after we left Salina—having received, no doubt, a worrisome call from a worried warden.

—I do hope you find him.

—Of that I can assure you. Anyway, sorry for the bother.

—It wasn't a bother at all, the old gent replied, gesturing toward his bed. I was only reading.

Ah, I thought, seeing the corner of the book poking out from the folds of his sheets. I should have known. The poor old chap, he suffers from the most dangerous addiction of all.

As I was headed back toward the stairs, I noticed a slice of light on the hallway floor, suggesting that the door to room 49 was ajar.

After hesitating, I passed the stairwell and continued down the hall. When I reached the room, I stopped and listened. Hearing no sounds within, I nudged the door with a knuckle. Through the gap, I could see that the bed was empty and unmade. Guessing the occupant was in the bathroom at the other end of the hall, I opened the door the rest of the way.

When my old man and I first came to the Sunshine Hotel in 1948, room 49 was the best one in the house. Not only did it have two windows at the back of the building, where it was quiet, in the center of the ceiling was a Victorian light fixture with a fan—the only such amenity in the whole hotel. Now all that hung from the ceiling was a bare bulb on a wire.

In the corner, the little wooden desk was still there. It was another amenity that added to the value of the room in the eyes of the tenants, despite the fact that no one had written a letter in the Sunshine Hotel in over thirty years. The desk chair was there too, looking as old and upright as the gentleman down the hall.

It may have been the saddest room that I had ever seen.

—————

Down in the lobby I made sure that Woolly was still waiting in one of the chairs by the window. Then I went to the front desk, where a fat man with a thin moustache was listening to the ball game on the radio.

—Any rooms available?

—For the night or by the hour? he asked, after glancing at Woolly with a knowing look.

It never ceased to amaze me how a guy working in a place like this could still imagine that he knows anything at all. He was lucky I didn't have a frying pan.

—*Two* rooms, I said. For the night.

—Four bucks in advance. Another two bits if you want towels.

—We'll take the towels.

Removing Emmett's envelope from my pocket, I thumbed slowly through the stack of twenties. That wiped the smirk off his face faster than the frying pan would have. Finding the change that I'd received at the HoJo's, I took out a five and put it on the counter.

—We've got two nice rooms on the third floor, he said, suddenly sounding like a man of service. And my name's Bernie. If there's anything you want while you're here—booze, broads, breakfast—don't hesitate to ask.

—I don't think we'll be needing any of that, but you might be able to help me in another way.

I took another two bucks from the envelope.

—Sure, he said, with a lick of the lips.

—I'm looking for someone who was staying here until recently.

—Which someone?

—The someone in room 42.

—You mean Harry Hewett?

—None other.

—He checked out earlier this week.

—So I gather. Did he say where he was headed?

Bernie struggled to think for a moment, and I do mean struggled, but to no avail. I began to put the bills back from whence they came.

—Wait a second, he said. Wait a second. I don't know where Harry went. But there's a guy who used to live here who was very tight with him. If anyone would know where Harry is now, he would.

—What's his name?

—FitzWilliams.

—Fitzy FitzWilliams?

—That's the guy.

—Bernie, if you tell me where I can find Fitzy FitzWilliams, I'll give you a fin. If you'll loan me your radio for the night, I'll make it two.

—.—

Back in the 1930s when my father first became friends with Patrick "Fitzy" FitzWilliams, Fitzy was a third-rate performer on vaudeville's secondary circuit. A reciter of verses, he was generally shoved out onstage in between acts in order to keep the audience in their seats with a few choice stanzas in the patriotic or pornographic vein, sometimes both.

But Fitzy was a genuine man of letters and his first love was the poetry of Walt Whitman. Realizing in 1941 that the fiftieth anniversary of the poet's death was right around the corner, he decided to grow a beard and buy a floppy hat in the hope of convincing stage managers to let him honor the anniversary by bringing the words of the poet to life.

Now, there are all manner of beards. There's the Errol Flynn and the Fu Manchu, the Sigmund Freud and the good old Amish underneck. But as luck would have it, Fitzy's beard came in as white and woolly as Whitman's, so with the floppy hat on his head and his milky blue eyes, he was every bit the song of himself. And when he premiered his impersonation at a low-budget theater in Brooklyn Heights— singing of the immigrants continually landing, of the ploughmen ploughing and the miners mining, of the mechanics toiling away in the numberless factories—the working-class crowd gave Fitzy the first standing ovation of his life.

In a matter of weeks, every institution from Washington, DC, to Portland, Maine, that had planned on marking the anniversary of Whitman's death wanted Fitzy. He was traveling the Northeast Corridor in first-class cars, reciting in Grange halls, liberty halls, libraries, and historical societies, making more money in six months than Whitman made in his life.

Then in November 1942, when he returned to Manhattan for an encore performance at the New-York Historical Society, one Florence Skinner happened to be in attendance. Mrs. Skinner was a prominent socialite who prided herself on giving the most talked-about parties in town. That year she was planning to open the Christmas season with a glamorous affair on the first Thursday in December. When she saw Fitzy, it struck her like a bolt of lightning that with his big white beard and soft blue eyes, he would be the perfect Santa Claus.

Sure enough, a few weeks later when Fitzy appeared at her party with his bowl full of jelly and rattled off *The Night Before Christmas*, the crowd brimmed over with the joys of the season. The Irish in Fitzy tended to make him thirsty for a dram whenever he had to be on his feet, a fact that proved something of a liability in the theater world. But the Irish in him also made his cheeks go red when he drank, which turned out to be an asset at Mrs. Skinner's soirée because it provided the perfect polish to his Old Saint Nick.

The day after Mrs. Skinner's, the phone on the desk of Ned Mosely—Fitzy's booking agent—rang from dawn till dusk. The Van Whozens, Van Whyzens, and Van Whatsits were all planning holiday parties and they all just *had* to have Fitzy. Mosely may have been a third-rate agent, but he knew a golden goose when he was sitting on one. With only three weeks left until Christmas, he priced access to Fitzy on an accelerating scale. It was three hundred dollars for an appearance on the tenth of December and fifty bucks more for every day that followed. So if you wanted him to come down your chimney on Christmas Eve, it would cost an even grand. But if you threw in an extra fifty, the children were allowed to tug on his beard just to put their pesky suspicions to rest.

Needless to say, when it came to celebrating the birth of Jesus in this circle, money was no object. Fitzy was often booked for three appearances on a single night. Walt Whitman was sent to the showers, and Fitzy went ho-ho-ho-ing all the way to the bank.

Fitzy's stature as the uptown Santa grew from year to year, such that by the end of the war—despite working only for the month of December—he lived in a Fifth Avenue apartment, wore three-piece suits, and carried a cane that was topped with the silver head of a reindeer. What's more, it turned out that there was a whole class of young socialites whose pulse would quicken whenever they saw Saint Nick. So it wasn't particularly surprising to Fitzy when after performing at a Park Avenue party, the shapely daughter of an industrialist asked if she could call on him a few nights hence.

When she appeared at Fitzy's apartment, she was wearing a dress that was as provocative as it was elegant. But it turned out that romance was not on her mind. Declining a drink, she explained that she was a member of the Greenwich Village Progressive Society and that they were planning a large event for the first of May. When she had seen Fitzy's performance, it had occurred to her that with his big white beard, he would be the perfect man to open the gathering by reciting a few passages from the works of Karl Marx.

No doubt Fitzy was taken by the young woman's allure, swayed by her flattery, and influenced by the promise of a significant fee. But he was also an artist through and through, and he was game to take on the challenge of bringing the old philosopher to life.

When the first of May rolled around and Fitzy was standing backstage, it felt like any other night on the boards. That is, until he peeked from behind the curtain. For not only was the room packed to capacity, it was filled with hardworking men and women. Here were the plumbers and welders and longshoremen, the seamstresses and housemaids who in that dingy hall in Brooklyn Heights all those years ago had given Fitzy his first standing ovation. With a deep sense of gratitude and a surge of populist affection, Fitzy stepped through the gap in the curtain, assumed his place on the podium, and gave the performance of his life.

His monologue was drawn straight from *The Communist Manifesto*, and as he spoke he had that audience stirred to the soul. So much so, when he reached his fiery conclusion, they would have leapt to their feet and broken into thunderous applause—had not every door of the auditorium suddenly burst open to admit a small battalion of police officers blowing whistles and wielding billy clubs under the pretext of a fire code violation.

On the following morning, the headline in the *Daily News* read:

PARK AVENUE SANTA DOUBLES
AS COMMIE PROVOCATEUR

And that was the end of the high life for Fitzy FitzWilliams.

Having tripped over the end of his own beard, Fitzy tumbled down the stairs of good fortune. The Irish whiskey that had once put the jovial blush in his yuletide cheeks assumed command over his general welfare by emptying his coffers and severing his connections to clean clothes and polite society. By 1949, Fitzy was reciting dirty limericks on the subways with his hat in his hand and living in room 43 of the Sunshine Hotel—right across the hall from me and my old man.

I was looking forward to seeing him.

Emmett

I N THE LATE AFTERNOON as the train began to slow, Ulysses raised his head briefly out of the hatch, then came back down the ladder.

—This is where we get off, he said.

After helping Billy put on his backpack, Emmett took a step toward the door by which he and his brother had entered, but Ulysses gestured to the other side of the car.

—This way.

Emmett had imagined that they would be disembarking into a sprawling freight yard—like the one in Lewis, only larger—situated somewhere on the outskirts of the city, with the skyline marking the horizon. He imagined they would need to slip from the car with caution in order to make their way past railwaymen and security guards. But when Ulysses slid the door open, there was no sign of a freight yard, no sign of other trains or other people. Instead, what filled the doorway was the city itself. They appeared to be on a narrow stretch of track suspended three stories above the streets, with commercial buildings rising around them and taller buildings in the distance.

—Where are we? Emmett asked as Ulysses jumped to the ground.

—It's the West Side Elevated. A freight track.

Ulysses raised a hand to help Billy down, leaving Emmett to help himself.

—And the camp you mentioned?

—Not far.

Ulysses began walking in the narrow space between the train and the guardrail at the elevated's edge.

—Watch the ties, he warned without turning back.

For all the celebration of the New York City skyline in poetry and song, as Emmett walked he barely paid it notice. In his youth, he had never dreamed of coming to Manhattan. He hadn't read the books or watched the movies with an envious eye. He had come to New York for one reason and one reason alone—to reclaim his car. Now that they were here, Emmett's attention could turn to finding Duchess by finding his father.

When he'd awoken that morning, the first word on his lips had been *Statler*, as if his mind had continued sorting through the alphabetical combinations in his sleep. That's where Duchess had said the booking agencies were: the Statler Building. As soon as they arrived in the city, Emmett figured, he and Billy would go straight to Times Square to obtain Mr. Hewett's address.

When Emmett had explained his intentions to Ulysses, Ulysses frowned. He pointed out that they wouldn't be arriving in New York until five o'clock, so by the time he made it to Times Square, the agencies would be closed. It made more sense for Emmett to wait until morning. Ulysses said that he would take Emmett and Billy to a camp where they could sleep safely for the night; and on the following day he would watch over Billy while Emmett went uptown.

Ulysses had a way of saying what you should do as if it were a foregone conclusion, a trait that quickly got under Emmett's skin. But Emmett couldn't argue with the reasoning. If they arrived at five o'clock, it would be too late to go in search of the office. And when Emmett went to Times Square in the morning, it would be much more efficient if he could go alone.

On the elevated, Ulysses was walking with a long and purposeful stride, as if he were the one who had urgent business in the city.

While trying to catch up, Emmett checked to see where they were going. Earlier that afternoon, the train had shed two thirds of its freight cars, but there were still seventy cars between theirs and the locomotive. As he looked ahead, all Emmett could see was the same narrow gap between the boxcars and the guardrail receding into the distance.

—How do we get down from here? he asked Ulysses.

—We don't.

—Are you saying the camp is up here on the tracks?

—That's what I'm saying.

—But where?

Ulysses stopped and turned to Emmett.

—Did I say I was going to take you there?

—Yes.

—Then why don't you let me do so.

Ulysses let his gaze linger on Emmett for a second to make sure that his point had been made, then he looked over Emmett's shoulder.

—Where's your brother?

Turning, Emmett was startled to find that Billy wasn't there. So distracted had he been by his own thoughts and by trying to keep up with Ulysses, he had lost his awareness of his brother's whereabouts.

Seeing the expression on Emmett's face, Ulysses's own expression turned to one of consternation. Saying something curt under his breath, Ulysses brushed past Emmett and began walking back the way they'd come as Emmett tried to catch up, the color rising to his cheeks.

They found Billy right where they had left him—beside the boxcar in which they had ridden. Because if Emmett was not enraptured by the sight of New York, the same could not be said of Billy. When they had disembarked, he had taken two steps toward the railing, climbed on top of an old wooden crate, and looked out into the cityscape, mesmerized by its scale and verticality.

—Billy . . . , said Emmett.

Billy looked up at his brother, clearly no more aware of their separation than Emmett had been.

—Isn't it just like you imagined, Emmett?

—Billy, we've got to keep moving.

Billy looked up at Ulysses.

—Which one is the Empire State Building, Ulysses?

—The Empire State Building?

Ulysses said this with an impatience that sprang more from habit than urgency. But upon hearing his own voice, he softened his tone and pointed uptown.

—It's the one with the spire. But your brother's right. We've got to move along. And you need to keep closer. If at any time you can't reach out and touch one of the two of us, then you're not close enough. Understand?

—I understand.

—All right then. Let's go.

As the three resumed walking over the uneven ground, Emmett noticed that for the third time the train rolled forward for a few seconds, then stopped. He was wondering why it would do that, when Billy took his hand and looked up with a smile.

—That was the answer, he said.

—The answer to what, Billy?

—The Empire State Building. It's the tallest building in the world.

After they had walked past half of the boxcars, Emmett saw that some fifty yards ahead the elevated angled to the left. Due to a trick in perspective, just beyond the bend an eight-story building seemed to be rising straight from the tracks. But when they got closer, Emmett could see that it hadn't been a trick of perspective, after all. The building actually rose directly over the tracks—because the rails ran right through the middle of it. On the wall above the opening was a large yellow sign reading:

Private Property
No Admittance

Fifteen feet short, Ulysses signaled for them to stop.

From where they were standing, they could hear the sounds of activity up ahead on the other side of the train: the sliding of freight-car doors, the squeaking of dollies, and the shouting of men.

—That's where we're going, said Ulysses in a lowered voice.

—Through the building? whispered Emmett.

—It's the only way to get where we're headed.

Ulysses explained that at the moment there were five boxcars in the bay. Once the crew finished unloading them, the train would roll forward so that the crew could unload the next five. That's when they would go. And as long as they stayed behind the boxcar and moved at the same pace as the train, no one was going to see them.

This struck Emmett as a bad idea. He wanted to express his concern to Ulysses and explore whether there was an alternative route, but from farther up the tracks came a release of steam and the train began to move.

—Here we go, said Ulysses.

He led them into the building, walking in the narrow space between the boxcar and the wall at the exact same pace as the train. Half of the way through, the train suddenly stopped and they stopped with it. The sounds of the warehouse activity were louder now and Emmett could see the rapid movements of the laborers expressed by the shadows that flitted between the boxcars. Billy looked up as if intending to ask a question, but Emmett held a finger to his lips. Eventually, there was another release of steam and the train began to roll again. Being careful to move at the same speed as the car, the three emerged on the other side of the building unnoticed.

Once outside, Ulysses picked up his pace in order to put some distance between them and the warehouse. As before, they were walking in the narrow gap between the boxcars and the guardrail. But when they finally passed the locomotive, a great vista opened on their right.

Anticipating Billy's sense of wonder, this time Ulysses stopped.

—The Hudson, he said, gesturing toward the river.

After giving Billy a moment to appreciate the ocean liners, tugboats, and barges, Ulysses made eye contact with Emmett, then continued on. Understanding the point, Emmett took his brother by the hand.

—Look how many ships there are, Billy said.

—Come on, said Emmett. You can look at them while we walk.

As Billy followed along, Emmett could hear him counting the vessels under his breath.

After they had walked a bit, the way forward was blocked by a tall wire fence that transected the elevated from guardrail to guardrail. Stepping into the middle of the tracks, Ulysses took hold of a section of the fence that had been cut and pulled it back so that Emmett and Billy could pass through. On the other side, the rails continued receding southward, but they were overgrown with weeds and grass.

—What happened to this stretch of the line? asked Emmett.

—They don't use it no more.

—Why?

—Things get used and then they don't, said Ulysses in his impatient way.

A few minutes later, Emmett could finally see where they were headed. On a siding that abutted the abandoned tracks was a makeshift encampment with a scattering of tents and lean-tos. As they drew closer, he could see the smoke rising from two separate fires and the rangy silhouettes of men in motion.

Ulysses led them to the closer of the two fires, where two white tramps sat on a railroad tie eating from tin plates and a clean-shaven black man stirred the contents of a cast-iron pot. When the black man saw Ulysses, he smiled.

—Well, look who we have here.

—Hey, Stew, said Ulysses.

But the cook's expression of welcome transitioned to one of surprise when Emmett and Billy emerged from behind.

—They're with me, explained Ulysses.

—*Traveling* with you? asked Stew.

—Didn't I just say so?

—I guess you did. . . .

—There space over by your hut?

—I believe there is.

—I'll go see. In the meantime, why don't you fix us something to eat.

—The boys too?

—The boys too.

It seemed to Emmett that Stew was about to express surprise again, then thought better of it. The tramps who had stopped eating looked on with interest when Ulysses drew open a pouch that had been in his pocket. It took a moment for Emmett to realize that Ulysses intended to pay for his and his brother's meal.

—Wait, Emmett said. Let us pay for you, Ulysses.

Removing the five-dollar bill that Parker had stuffed in his shirt pocket, Emmett took a few steps forward and held it out to Stew. As he did so, he realized it wasn't a five-dollar bill. It was a fifty.

Stew and Ulysses both stared at the bill for a moment, then Stew looked to Ulysses, who in turn looked to Emmett.

—Put that away, he said sternly.

Feeling the color rising to his face again, Emmett returned the money to his pocket. Only once he had done so did Ulysses turn back to Stew and pay for the three meals. Then he addressed Billy and Emmett together in his presumptive fashion.

—I'm going to claim us some ground. You two sit and have something to eat. I'll be back in a minute.

As Emmett watched Ulysses walk off, he was disinclined to sit or to eat. But Billy already had a plate of chili and cornbread in his lap and Stew was fixing another.

—It's as good as Sally's, Billy said.

Telling himself it was the polite thing to do, Emmett accepted the plate.

With the first bite he realized how hungry he was. It had been some hours since they had eaten the last of the food from the Pullman car. And Billy was right. The chili was as good as Sally's. Maybe better. From the smokiness, you could tell that Stew used a good deal of bacon, and the beef seemed of surprisingly good quality. When Stew offered to bring a second helping, Emmett didn't object.

As Emmett waited for the return of his plate, he cautiously studied the two tramps who were sitting on the other side of the fire. Given their worn clothing and unshaven faces, it was hard to tell how old they were, though Emmett suspected they were younger than they appeared.

The tall, thin one on the left was not paying Emmett or his brother any heed, almost purposefully. But the one on the right, who was smiling in their direction, suddenly waved.

Billy waved back.

—Welcome, weary travelers, he called across the fire. From where do you hail?

—Nebraska, Billy called back.

—Nebraskee! replied the tramp. Plenty's the time I've been to Nebraskee. What brings you to the Big Apple?

—We've come to get Emmett's car, said Billy. So we can drive to California.

At the mention of the car, the tall tramp who'd been ignoring them looked up with sudden interest.

Emmett put a hand on his brother's knee.

—We're just passing through, he said.

—Then you've come to the right spot, said the smiling one. There's no better place in the world for passing through.

—Then why can't you seem to pass through it, said the tall one.

The smiling man turned to his neighbor with a frown, but before he could respond, the tall one looked at Billy.

—You've come for your car, you say?

Emmett was about to interject, but Ulysses was suddenly standing at the edge of the fire, looking down at the tall man's plate.

—Looks like you're done with your supper, he said.

The two tramps both looked up at Ulysses.

—I'm done when I say I'm done, said the tall one.

Then he tossed his plate on the ground.

—Now I'm done.

When the tall one got up, the smiling man winked at Billy and rose as well.

Ulysses watched the two of them walk away, then he sat on the tie where they'd been sitting and stared across the fire at Emmett, pointedly.

—I know, said Emmett. I know.

Woolly

I F IT HAD BEEN up to Woolly, they wouldn't have spent the night in
Manhattan. They wouldn't even have driven through it. They would
have gone straight to his sister's house in Hastings-on-Hudson, and
from there to the Adirondacks.

The problem with Manhattan, from Woolly's point of view, the
problem with Manhattan was that it was so terribly permanent. What
with its towers made of granite and all the miles of pavement stretching as far as the eye can see. Why, every single day, millions of people
went pounding along the sidewalks and across the marble-floored lob-
bies without even putting a dent in them. To make matters worse,
Manhattan was absotively filled with expectations. There were so many
expectations, they had to build the buildings eighty stories high so they
would have enough room to stack them one on top of the other.

But Duchess wanted to see his father, so they took the Lincoln
Highway to the Lincoln Tunnel, and the Lincoln Tunnel under the
Hudson River, and now here they were.

If they were going to be in Manhattan, thought Woolly as he
propped up his pillow, at least this was the way to do it. Because
once they emerged from the Lincoln Tunnel, Duchess had not taken
a left and headed uptown. Instead, he had taken a right and driven
all the way down to the Bowery, a street on which Woolly had

never been, to visit his father at a little hotel, of which Woolly had never heard. And then, while Woolly was sitting in the lobby looking out at all the activity in the street, he happened to see a fellow walking by with a stack of newspapers—a fellow in a baggy coat and floppy hat.

—The Birdman! exclaimed Woolly to the window. What an extraordinary coincidence!

Leaping from his chair, he rapped on the glass. Only to discover when the fellow turned about that he wasn't the Birdman, after all. But having been rapped at, the fellow entered the lobby with his stack of papers and made a beeline for Woolly's chair.

If Duchess was, as he liked to say, allergic to books, Woolly had a related affliction. He was allergic to the daily news. In New York City, things were happening all the time. Things that you were expected not only to be knowledgeable about, but on which you were expected to have an opinion that you could articulate at a moment's notice. In fact, so many things were happening at such a rapid pace, they couldn't come close to fitting them all in a single newspaper. New York had the *Times*, of course, the paper of record, but in addition, it had the *Post*, the *Daily News*, the *Herald Tribune*, the *Journal-American*, the *World-Telegram*, and the *Mirror*. And those were just the ones that Woolly could think of off the top of his head.

Each of these enterprises had a battalion of men covering beats, questioning sources, hunting down leads, and writing copy until well after supper. Each ran presses in the middle of the night and rushed off delivery trucks in every conceivable direction so that the news of the day would be on your doorstep when you woke at the crack of dawn in order to catch the 6:42.

The very thought of it sent chills down Woolly's spine. So, as the baggy-coated fellow approached with his stack of newspapers, Woolly was ready to send him on his way.

But as it turned out, the baggy-coated fellow wasn't selling today's newspapers. He was selling yesterday's newspapers. And the day before yesterday's. And the day before that!

—It's three cents for yesterday's *Times*, he explained, two cents for two days ago, a penny for three days ago, or a nickel for all three.

Well, that's a different kettle of fish altogether, thought Woolly. News that was one, two, and three days old didn't arrive with anywhere near the same sense of urgency as the news of the day. In fact, you could hardly call it news. And you didn't have to receive an A in Mr. Kehlenbeck's math class to know that getting three papers for a nickel was a bargain. But, alas, Woolly didn't have any money.

Or did he . . . ?

For the first time since putting on Mr. Watson's pants, Woolly put his hands in Mr. Watson's pockets. And would you believe, would you actually believe that out of the right-hand pocket came some rumpled bills.

—I'll take all three, said Woolly, with enthusiasm.

When the fellow handed Woolly the papers, Woolly handed him a dollar, adding magnanimously that he could keep the change. And though the fellow was pleased as could be, Woolly was fairly certain that he had gotten the better part of the deal.

Suffice it to say, when evening arrived and Duchess was running around Manhattan in search of his father, and Woolly was lying on his bed with his pillow propped and the radio on, having taken two extra drops of medicine from the extra bottle he'd put in Emmett's book bag, he turned his attention to the newspaper of three days past.

And what a difference three days made. Not only did the news seem much less pressing, if you chose your headlines carefully, the stories often had a touch of the fantastic. Like this one from Sunday's front page:

ATOM SUBMARINE
PROTOTYPE SIMULATES
A DIVE TO EUROPE

This story went on to explain how the first atomic submarine had completed the equivalent of a voyage across the Atlantic—while somewhere in the middle of the Idaho desert! The whole premise struck Woolly as incredible as something you'd find in Billy's big red book.

And then there was this one from the front page of two days past.

CIVIL DEFENSE TEST
IS AT 10 A.M. TODAY

Normally, *defense* and *test* were just the sort of words that made Woolly uneasy and generally prompted him to skip an article altogether. But in the two-day-old *Times*, the article went on to explain that in the course of this test, a fleet of imaginary enemy planes would be dropping imaginary atomic bombs on fifty-four cities, causing imaginary devastation all across America. In New York City alone, three different imaginary bombs were to drop, one of which was to land imaginarily at the intersection of Fifty-Seventh Street and Fifth Avenue—right in front of Tiffany's, of all places. As part of the test, when the warning alarm sounded, all normal activities in the fifty-four cities were to be suspended for ten minutes.

—All normal activities suspended for ten minutes, read Woolly out loud. Can you imagine?

Somewhat breathlessly, Woolly turned to yesterday's paper in order to see what had happened. And there on the front page—above the fold, as they say—was a photograph of Times Square with two police officers looking up the length of Broadway and not another living soul in sight. No one gazing in the window of the tobacconist. No one coming out of the Criterion Theatre or going into the Astor Hotel. No one ringing a cash register or dialing a telephone. Not one single person hustling, or bustling, or hailing a cab.

What a strange and beautiful sight, thought Woolly. The city of New York silent, motionless, and virtually uninhabited, sitting perfectly idle, without the hum of a single expectation for the very first time since its founding.

Duchess

A FTER GETTING WOOLLY SETTLED in his room with a few drops of medicine and the radio tuned to a commercial, I made my way to a dive called the Anchor on West Forty-Fifth Street in Hell's Kitchen. With dim lighting and indifferent clientele, it was just the sort of place my old man liked—a spot where a has-been could sit at the bar and rail against life's iniquities without fear of interruption.

According to Bernie, Fitzy and my old man were in the habit of meeting here every night around eight o'clock and drinking for as long as their money held out. Sure enough, at 7:59 the door swung open and in shuffled Fitzy, right on cue.

You could tell he was a regular from the way that everyone ignored him. All things considered, he hadn't aged so badly. His hair was a little thinner and his nose a little redder, but you could still see a bit of the Old Saint Nick hiding under the surface, if you squinted hard enough.

Walking right past me, he squeezed between two stools, spread some nickels on the bar, and ordered a shot of whiskey—in a highball glass.

A shot looks so measly in a highball glass, it struck me as an odd request for Fitzy to make. But when he lifted the drink from the bar, I could see his fingers trembling ever so slightly. No doubt he had learned the hard way that when a shot is served in a shot glass it's a lot easier to spill.

With his whiskey safely in hand, Fitzy retreated to a table in the corner with two seats. It was clearly the spot where he and my father were in the habit of drinking, because once he got comfortable, Fitzy raised his glass to the empty chair. He must be the last living soul on earth, I thought, who would raise a glass to Harry Hewett. As he began to move the whiskey to his lips, I joined him.

—Hello, Fitzy.

Fitzy froze for a moment and stared over the top of the glass. Then for what must have been the first time in his life, he put his glass back on the table without having taken a drink.

—Hey, Duchess, he said. I almost didn't recognize you. You've gotten so much bigger.

—It's all the manual labor. You should try it some time.

Fitzy looked down at his drink, then at the bartender, then at the door to the street. When he had run out of places to look, he looked back at me.

—Well, it's nice to see you, Duchess. What brings you to town?

—Oh, this and that. I need to see a friend up in Harlem tomorrow, but I'm also looking for my old man. He and I have got a little unfinished business, as it were. Unfortunately, he checked out of the Sunshine Hotel in such a hurry, he forgot to leave me word of where he was going. But I figured if anyone in the city of New York would know where Harry was, it would be his old pal Fitzy.

Fitzy was shaking his head before I finished speaking.

—No, he said. I don't know where your father is, Duchess. I haven't seen him in weeks.

Then he looked at his untouched drink with a downcast expression.

—Where are my manners, I said. Let me buy you a drink.

—Oh, that's okay. I still have this one.

—That little thing? It hardly does you justice.

Getting up, I went to the bar and asked the bartender for a bottle of whatever Fitzy was drinking. When I came back, I pulled the cork and filled his glass to the brim.

—That's more like it, I said as he looked down at the whiskey without a smile.

What a cruel irony, I thought to myself. I mean, here was the very thing that Fitzy had been dreaming of for half his life. Prayed for even. A highball glass filled to the top with whiskey—and at someone else's expense, no less. But now that it was sitting there in front of him, he wasn't so sure that he wanted it.

—Go on, I encouraged. There's no need to stand on ceremony.

Almost reluctantly, he raised the glass and tipped it in my direction. The gesture wasn't quite as heartfelt as the one he'd shown my old man's empty chair, but I expressed my gratitude nonetheless.

This time, when the glass made it to his lips he took a healthy swallow, like he was making up for the drink he hadn't taken before. Then, setting the glass down, he looked at me and waited. Because that's what has-beens do: They wait.

When it comes to waiting, has-beens have had plenty of practice. Like when they were waiting for their big break, or for their number to come in. Once it became clear that those things weren't going to happen, they started waiting for other things. Like for the bars to open, or the welfare check to arrive. Before too long, they were waiting to see what it would be like to sleep in a park, or to take the last two puffs from a discarded cigarette. They were waiting to see what new indignity they could become accustomed to while they were waiting to be forgotten by those they once held dear. But most of all, they waited for the end.

—Where is he, Fitzy?

Fitzy shook his head more at himself than at me.

—Like I said, Duchess, I haven't seen him in weeks. I swear to it.

—Normally, I'd be inclined to believe any word that fell from your lips. Particularly when you *swore* to it.

That one made him wince.

—It's just that when I sat down, you didn't seem so surprised to see me. Now, why would that be?

—I don't know, Duchess. Maybe I was surprised on the inside?

I laughed out loud.

—Maybe you were at that. Though, you know what I think? I think you weren't surprised because my old man told you I might be coming around. But in order for him to have done that, he must have spoken to you in the last few days. In fact, it probably happened while you were sitting right here.

I tapped the table with a finger.

—And if he told you he was hightailing it out of town, he must have told you where he was headed. After all, you two are as thick as thieves.

At the word *thieves*, Fitzy winced again. Then he looked even more downcast, if such a thing could be imagined.

—I'm sorry, he said softly.

—What's that?

I leaned a little forward, like I couldn't quite hear him, and he looked up with what appeared to be a genuine pang of regret.

—I'm so sorry, Duchess, he said. I'm sorry I put those things about you in that statement. Sorry that I signed it.

For a guy who didn't want to talk, suddenly you couldn't stop him.

—I had been drinking the night before, you see. And I get real uneasy around police, but especially when they're asking me questions. Questions about what I might have seen or heard, even though my sight and hearing weren't what they used to be. Or my memory either. Then when the officers began to express some frustration, your father took me aside and tried to help refresh my memory. . . .

As Fitzy went on, I picked up the bottle of whiskey and gave it a gander. In the middle of the label was a big green shamrock. It made me smile to see it. I mean, what luck did a glass of whiskey ever bring anyone. And Irish whiskey at that.

As I sat there feeling the weight of the bottle in my hand, it suddenly occurred to me that here was another fine example of something that had been carefully crafted for one purpose, yet was perfectly suited to another. Hundreds of years ago, the whiskey bottle had been designed to have a body that was big enough for holding, and a neck that was narrow enough for pouring. But if you happened to invert the bottle, taking hold of the neck, suddenly it's as if it had been designed to hit a blighter over the head. In a way, the whiskey bottle was sort of like a pencil with an eraser—with one end used for saying things, and the other for taking them back.

Fitzy must have been reading my mind because he was suddenly very quiet. And from the expression on his face, I could see that he had become frightened. His face had grown pale and the tremor in his fingers had gotten noticeably worse.

It may well have been the first time in my life that someone had become frightened of me. In a way, I couldn't believe it. Because I hadn't the slightest intention of hurting Fitzy. What would be the point? When it came to hurting Fitzy, he had the whole concession.

But under the circumstances, I figured his trepidation could be used to my advantage. So when he asked if we could just call it water under the bridge, I made a show of slowly setting the bottle down on the table.

—Would that I could, I mused. Would that I could turn back the clock and allow you to undo what you have done, Patrick FitzWilliams. But alas, my friend, the water isn't under the bridge. It isn't over the dam, for that matter. Rather, it is all around us. In fact, it is right here in this very room.

He gave me such a look of woe that I almost felt sorry for him.

—Whatever the reasons you did what you did, Fitzy, I think we can agree that you owe me one. If you tell me where my old man is, we'll call it even. But if you don't, I'll have to use my imagination to think of some other way for the two of us to settle up.

Sally

I FOUND MY FATHER OUT on the north corner fixing a stretch of fence with Bobby and Miguel, their horses standing idly by and a few hundred head of cattle grazing on the range behind them.

Turning off the road onto the shoulder, I skidded to a stop right where they were working and climbed from the cab as they shielded their eyes from the dust.

Always the comedian, Bobby made an elaborate show of coughing while my father shook his head.

—Sally, he said, you keep driving that truck over rough road like that and it's going to give out on you.

—I imagine I know by now what Betty can handle and what she can't.

—All I can say is that when the transmission falls out, don't expect me to replace it.

—Don't you worry about that. Because if I know what to expect from my truck, I know even better what to expect from you.

He was silent for a moment, and I suspect he was trying to decide if he should send the boys on their way.

—All right, he said, as if he were coming to an understanding with himself. You've barreled out here for a reason. I can see that plain enough. You might as well tell me what it is.

I opened the passenger-side door, took out the FOR SALE sign that was lying on the seat, and held it up so he could get a good long look at it.

—I found this in the trash.

He nodded.

—That's where I put it.

—And where, if you don't mind my asking, did it come from?

—The Watson place.

—Why would you take down the FOR SALE sign from the Watson place?

—Because it's no longer for sale.

—And how would you happen to know that?

—Because I bought it.

He said this in a curt and definitive manner, trying to show that he'd been about as patient as he intended to be, that he didn't have time for this sort of talk, that he and the boys had work to do, and that the moment had come for me to get in my truck and head back to the house, where, surely, I should be in the middle of making supper by now. But he was talking to the wrong person if he thought he knew something about patience that I didn't know.

For a moment, I bided my time. Without taking a step, I looked off in the distance in a thoughtful fashion, then I turned my gaze right back upon him.

—The speed with which you bought the place . . . It makes one wonder just how long you've been lying in wait to do so.

Bobby pushed the dust on the ground with the tip of his boot and Miguel looked back at the cattle while my father scratched the back of his neck.

—Boys, he said after a moment, I suspect you've got some work to do.

—Yes, sir, Mr. Ransom.

They mounted their horses and rode off toward the herd in the unhurried fashion of men at work. My father didn't turn to watch them go, but he waited for the sound of their hooves to recede before he spoke again.

—Sally, he said, using his I'm-going-to-say-this-once-and-only-once voice, there's been no lying and there's been no waiting. Charlie defaulted on his mortgage, the bank foreclosed, they put it up for sale, and I bought it. That's all there is to it. It didn't come as a surprise to anyone at the bank, it won't come as a surprise to anyone in the county, and it shouldn't come as a surprise to you. Because that's what ranchers do. When the opportunity presents itself and the price is right, a rancher will add to his land, contiguously.

—*Contiguously*, I said, impressed.

—Yes, he replied. Contiguously.

We stared at each other.

—So, in all those years that Mr. Watson struggled with the farm, you were too busy to lend a hand. But the moment the opportunity *presented itself*, your appointment book was clear. Is that about it? It sure sounds like lying and waiting to me.

For the first time, he raised his voice.

—Damn it, Sally. What did you expect me to do? Drive over there and take up his plow? Plant his seeds and harvest his crops? You cannot live another man's life for him. If a man has got the least bit of pride, he wouldn't want you to. And Charlie Watson may not have been a very good farmer, but he was a proud man. Prouder than most.

I gave the distance another thoughtful look.

—It is interesting, though, isn't it, how even as the bank was getting ready to put the property on the market, you were sitting on the porch step, telling the son of the owner that maybe it was time for him to pick up stakes and make a fresh start somewhere else.

He studied me for a moment.

—Is that what this is about? You and Emmett?

—Don't try to change the subject.

He shook his head again, like he had when I'd first arrived.

—He was never going to stay, Sally. Any more than his mother was. You watched it yourself. As soon as he could, he took a job in town.

And what did he do with his first bit of savings? He bought himself a car. Not a truck or a tractor, Sally. A car. Though I have no doubt that Emmett grieved deeply for the loss of his father, I suspect he was *relieved* by the loss of the farm.

—Don't talk to me about Emmett Watson like you know him so well. You don't know the first thing that's going through his mind.

—Maybe. But after fifty-five years in Nebraska, I think I can tell a stayer from a goer.

—Is that so, I said. Then tell me, Mr. Ransom: Which am I?

You should have seen his face when I said that. For a moment he went all white. Then, just as quickly, he went red.

—I know it's not easy for a young girl to lose her mother. In some ways it's harder on her than it is on the husband who's lost his wife. Because a father is not equipped to raise a young girl in the manner she should be raised. But that is especially so when the girl in question is contrary by nature.

Here he gave me a good long look, just in case it wasn't perfectly clear that he was talking about me.

—Many has been the night that I have knelt at the side of my bed and prayed to your mother, asking for guidance on how best to respond to your willfulness. And in all these years, your mother—God rest her soul—has not answered me once. So I have had to rely on my memories of how she cared for you. Though you were only twelve when she died, you were plenty contrary already. And when I would express my concern about that, your mother would tell me to be patient. Ed, she would say, our youngest is strong in spirit, and that should stand her in good stead when she becomes a woman. What we need to do is give her a little time and space.

It was his turn to look off in the distance for a moment.

—Well, I trusted your mother's counsel then and I trust it now. And that's why I have indulged you. I have indulged you in your manner and your habits; indulged you in your temper and your tongue.

But Sally, so help me God, I have come to see that I may have done you a terrible disservice. For by giving you full rein, I have allowed you to become a willful young woman, one who is accustomed to nursing her furies and speaking her mind, and who is, in all likelihood, unsuited to matrimony.

Oh, he enjoyed delivering that little speech. Standing there with his legs apart and his feet planted firmly on the ground, he acted as if he could draw his strength straight from the land because he owned it.

Then his expression softened and he gave me a look of sympathy that served only to infuriate.

Tossing the sign at his feet, I turned and climbed in the cab of my truck. Putting her in gear, I revved the engine, then drove down the road at seventy miles an hour, kicking up every piece of gravel, taking every divot, so that the chassis shook and the doors and windows rattled. Swerving into the entrance of the ranch, I aimed her at the front door and skidded to a stop with five feet to spare.

It was only as the dust blew past that I noticed a man with a hat sitting on our porch. And it was only when he rose and stepped into the light that I could see it was the sheriff.

Ulysses

As Ulysses watched the Watson boys retreat from the campfire in order to get ready for bed, Stew came to his side.

—They moving on tomorrow?

—No, said Ulysses. The older boy's got some business to see to uptown. He should be back in the afternoon and they'll be spending the night.

—All right then. I'll keep their bedding in place.

—You can keep mine too.

Stew turned a little sharply in order to look at Ulysses.

—You staying another night?

Ulysses looked back at Stew.

—That's what I just said, didn't I?

—That's what you said.

—There a problem with that?

—Nope, said Stew. No problem by me. Just that I seem to remember someone saying at some point that he never spent two nights in a row in the same place.

—Well then, said Ulysses, come Friday, he will have.

Stew nodded his head.

—I left some coffee on the fire, he said after a moment. I guess I'll go see to it.

—Sounds like a good idea, said Ulysses.

After watching Stew return to the campfire, Ulysses found himself scanning the lights of the city all the way from Battery Park to the George Washington Bridge—lights that held no enticement for him and promised no comfort.

But Billy had told him about the understanding he had with his brother, and it struck Ulysses as a reasonable one. He would stay two nights on the island of Manhattan. Come tomorrow, he and the boy would pass time as acquaintances, so the next day they could part company as friends.

FIVE

Woolly

A S THEY PULLED INTO his sister's driveway, Woolly could see that no one was home.

Woolly could always tell when a house was empty just by looking at the windows. Sometimes when he looked at the windows, he could hear all the activity inside the house, like the sounds of footsteps running up and down the stairs or celery stalks being chopped in the kitchen. Sometimes, he could hear the silence of two people sitting alone in different rooms. And sometimes, like now, from the way the windows looked back, he could tell that no one was home.

When Woolly turned off the engine, Duchess whistled.

—How many people did you say live here?

—Just my sister and her husband, Woolly replied. Although my sister's expecting.

—Expecting what? Quintuplets?

Woolly and Duchess got out of the Studebaker.

—Should we knock? asked Duchess.

—They won't be here.

—Will you be able to get in?

—They like to keep the front door locked, but they often leave the door in the garage open.

Woolly followed Duchess to one of the garage doors and watched as he pulled it up with a rattle.

Inside, the first two bays were empty. The first bay must have been where his sister parked, thought Woolly, because the oil spot on the concrete had the shape of a great big balloon—just like the one in Billy's book. The oil spot in the second bay, on the other hand, looked like one of those little storm clouds that hang over the head of a character in the funny papers when he's in a bad mood.

Duchess whistled again.

—What is that, he said, pointing to the fourth bay.

—A Cadillac convertible.

—Your brother-in-law's?

—No, said Woolly a little apologetically. It's mine.

—Yours!

Duchess spun on Woolly with an expression of such exaggerated surprise it made Woolly smile. Duchess didn't get surprised very often, so it always made Woolly smile when it happened. Woolly followed Duchess as he crossed the garage to have a better look.

—Where'd you get it?

—I inherited it, I guess. From my father.

Duchess gave Woolly a solemn acknowledgment. Then he walked the length of the car, running his hand along the long black hood and admiring the whitewall tires.

Woolly was glad that Duchess hadn't walked all the way around the car, because on the other side were the dents in the door from when Woolly had bumped into a lamppost.

"Dennis" had been very, very upset when Woolly had arrived with the dents one Saturday evening. Woolly knew that "Dennis" had been very, very upset because that's exactly how upset he'd said he was.

Just look at what you've done, he said to Woolly, while glaring at the damage.

Dennis, said his sister, interceding. *It isn't your car. It's Woolly's.*

Which was probably something that Woolly should have said: *It isn't your car, "Dennis." It's mine.* But Woolly hadn't thought to say it. At least, he hadn't thought to say it until after Sarah had said it already. Sarah always knew the right thing to say before Woolly did. When Woolly was in the middle of a conversation at boarding school or at a party in New York, he often thought to himself how much easier the conversation would be going if Sarah were there to say the right things on his behalf.

But the evening he had arrived with the dents in the door and Sarah had said to "Dennis" that the car wasn't his, it was Woolly's, this had only seemed to make "Dennis" more upset.

That it is his car is precisely my point. (Woolly's brother-in-law always made his points precisely. Even when he was very, very upset, he was very, very precise.) *When a young man is fortunate enough to be given something of great value from his own father, he should treat it with respect. And if he doesn't know how to treat it with respect, then he doesn't deserve to have it at all.*

Oh, Dennis, said Sarah. *It's not a Manet, for God's sake. It's a machine.*

Machines are the foundation of everything this family has, said "Dennis."

And everything it hasn't, said Sarah.

There she goes again, thought Woolly with a smile.

—May I? asked Duchess, gesturing to the car.

—What's that? Oh, yes. Of course, of course.

Duchess reached for the handle of the driver's door, hesitated, then took a step to his right and opened the door to the back.

—After you, he said with a flourish.

Woolly slid into the back seat and Duchess slid in after him. After closing the door, Duchess gave a sigh of appreciation.

—Forget the Studebaker, he said. This is how Emmett should arrive in Hollywood.

—Billy and Emmett are going to San Francisco, Woolly pointed out.

—Either way. This is how they should make the trip to California.

—If Billy and Emmett would like to make the trip to California in the Cadillac, they're welcome to do so.

—On the level?

—Nothing would make me happier, assured Woolly. The only problem is that the Cadillac is much older than the Studebaker, so it probably wouldn't get them to California anywhere near as quickly.

—Maybe so, said Duchess. But in a car like this, what's the rush.

As it turned out, the door inside the garage was locked, so Woolly and Duchess went back outside, and Woolly took a seat on the front step beside the flowerpots as Duchess removed the bags from the trunk.

—It could take me a few hours, said Duchess. Are you sure you're going to be all right?

—Most definitely, said Woolly. I'll just wait here until my sister comes back. I'm sure she won't be long.

Woolly watched as Duchess got in the Studebaker and backed out of the driveway with a wave. Once alone, Woolly retrieved the extra bottle of medicine from the book bag, unscrewed the eyedropper, and squeezed a few extra drops onto the tip of his tongue. Then he took a moment to admire the enthusiasm of the sunshine.

—There is nothing more enthusiastic than sunshine, he said to himself. And no one more reliable than grass.

At the word *reliable*, Woolly suddenly thought of his sister Sarah, who was another paragon of reliability. Putting the bottle in his pocket, he stood, lifted, and looked—and, sure enough, waiting patiently under the flowerpot was the key to his sister's house. All keys look alike, of course, but Woolly could tell that this one was the key to his sister's house because it turned in the lock.

Opening the door, Woolly stepped inside and paused.

—Hallo? he called. Hallo, hallo?

Just to be certain, Woolly gave a fourth hallo into the hallway that led to the kitchen, and another up the stairs. Then he waited to see if anyone would answer.

As he waited and listened, he happened to look down at the little table at the bottom of the staircase where a telephone sat. Shiny, smooth, and black, it looked like a younger cousin of the Cadillac. One thing about it that wasn't shiny, smooth, and black was the little rectangle of paper in the middle of the dial on which the phone number of the house had been written in a delicate hand—so that the phone would know exactly who it was, thought Woolly.

When no one answered Woolly's hallo, he stepped into the large, sunlit room on his left.

—This is the living room, he said, as if he were giving himself a tour.

Not much had changed in the room since he had been there last. His grandfather's grandfather clock was still by the window unwound. The piano was still in the corner unplayed. And the books still sat on their shelves unread.

One thing different was that there was now a giant oriental fan in front of the fireplace, as if the fireplace were shy of its appearance. Woolly wondered if it was there all the time, or if his sister removed it in winter so that they could build a fire. But if she did remove it, where did she put it? It seemed so delicate and awkward. Perhaps it could be folded up like a normal fan, thought Woolly, and tucked away in a drawer.

Satisfied with this notion, Woolly took a moment to wind the clock, then exited the living room and continued with his tour.

—This is the dining room, he said, where you will have dinner on birthdays and holidays. . . . Here is the only door in the house that doesn't have a doorknob and that swings back and forth. . . . And this is the kitchen. . . . And this is the back hallway. . . . And here is "Dennis's" office, in which no one is supposed to go.

Working his way through the rooms in this manner, Woolly completed a circuit such that he was right back at the foot of the stairs.

—And this is the staircase, he said as he ascended it. This is the hall. This is my sister and "Dennis's" room. This is the bathroom. And here . . .

Woolly stopped before a door that was slightly ajar. Easing it open, he entered a room that both was and wasn't what he expected.

For while his bed was still there, it had been moved to the center of the room and was covered with a great big piece of canvas. The canvas, which was a dingy white, had been splattered with hundreds of blue and gray driplets—like one of those paintings at the Museum of Modern Art. The closet, where Woolly's dress shirts and jackets had hung, was utterly empty. Not even a hanger had been left behind, or the box of mothballs that used to hide in the shadows of the upper shelf.

Three of the room's four walls were still white, but one of them— the one where the ladder was standing—was now blue. A bright friendly blue, like the blue of Emmett's car.

Woolly couldn't take issue with the fact that his closet was empty or that his bed was under a tarp because the room both was and wasn't his. When his mother had remarried and moved to Palm Beach, Sarah had let him use this room. She had let him use it over the Thanksgiving and Easter vacations, and for those weeks when he had left one boarding school and had yet to go to the next. Even though Sarah had encouraged him to think of the room as his own, he had always known that it wasn't meant to be a forever room, at least not for him. It was meant to be a forever room for somebody else.

From the lumpy shape of the tarp, Woolly could tell that some boxes had been stacked on the bed before it had been covered—giving it the appearance of a very little barge.

Checking first to make sure that none of the driplets on the tarp were wet, Woolly folded it back. On the bed were four cardboard boxes with his name written on them.

Woolly paused for a moment to marvel at the handwriting. For even though his name had been written in letters two inches tall with a big black marker, you could still tell it was his sister's handwriting—the very same handwriting that had been used to write the tiny little numbers on the tiny little rectangle in the telephone dial. Isn't that interesting, thought Woolly, that a person's handwriting is the same no matter how big or small.

Reaching out to open the box that was nearest, Woolly hesitated. He suddenly remembered the troubling theory of Schrödinger's Cat, which had been described by Professor Freely in physics class. In this theory, a physicist named Schrödinger had posited (that was the word that Professor Freely used: *posited*) that there was a cat with some poison in a box in a state of benign uncertainty. But once you opened the box, then the cat would either be purring or poisoned. So it was with a touch of caution that any man should venture to open a box, even if it was one that had his name on it. Or perhaps, especially if it had his name on it.

Steeling his nerves, Woolly opened the lid and breathed a sigh of relief. Inside were all the clothes that had been in the bureau that was and wasn't his. In the box below, Woolly found all of the things that had been on top of the bureau. Like the old cigar box, and the bottle of aftershave that he had been given for Christmas and never used, and the runner-up's trophy from the tennis club with the little golden man who would be serving a tennis ball for all eternity. And at the very bottom of the box was the dark blue dictionary that Woolly's mother had conferred upon him when he was headed off to boarding school for the very first time.

Woolly took the dictionary out and felt its reassuring heft in his hands. How he had loved this dictionary—because its purpose was to tell you exactly what a word meant. Pick a word, turn to the appropriate page, and there was the word's meaning. And if there was a word in the definition you didn't recognize, you could look up that word to find out exactly what *it* meant.

When his mother had given him the dictionary, it had been part of a set—tucked in a slipcase alongside a matching thesaurus. And as much as Woolly had loved the dictionary, he had loathed the thesaurus. Just the thought of it gave him the heebie-jeebies. Because the whole purpose of it seemed to be the opposite of the dictionary's. Instead of telling you exactly what a word meant, it took a word and gave you ten other words that could be used in its place.

How was one to communicate an idea to another person if when one had something to say, one could choose from ten different words for every word in a sentence? The number of potential variations boggled the mind. So much so that shortly after arriving at St. Paul's, Woolly had gone to his math teacher, Mr. Kehlenbeck, and asked him if one had a sentence with ten words and each word could be substituted with ten other words, then how many sentences could there be? And without a moment's hesitation, Mr. Kehlenbeck had gone to the chalkboard, scratched out a formula, and done a few quick calculations to prove incontrovertibly that the answer to Woolly's question was ten billion. Well, when confronted with a revelation like that, how was one to even begin writing an answer to an essay question during end-of-term exams?

Nonetheless, when Woolly left St. Paul's to attend St. Mark's, he had dutifully carried the thesaurus with him and set it down on his desk, where it remained snugly in its case, smirking at him with its tens of thousands of words that could be substituted one for the other. For the next year, it taunted, teased, and goaded him until finally, one evening shortly before Thanksgiving break, Woolly had taken the thesaurus from its case, carried it down to the football field, doused it with some gasoline that he'd discovered in the crew coach's launch, and set the dastardly thing on fire.

In retrospect, it probably would have been peaches and cream if Woolly had thought to set the thesaurus on fire on the fifty-yard line. But for some reason Woolly couldn't quite remember, he had put the book in the end zone, and when he'd thrown the match, the flames had quickly followed a trail of gas that had been sloshed on the grass, engulfed the gas can, and triggered an explosion that set the goalpost on fire.

Backing up to the twenty-yard line, Woolly had watched at first in shock and then amazement as the fire made its way up the center support, then moved simultaneously along the two shoulders and up the posts until the whole thing was in flames. Suddenly, it didn't look like a goalpost at all. It looked like a fiery spirit raising its arms to the sky in a state of exultation. And it was very, very beautiful.

When they called Woolly before the disciplinary committee, it was Woolly's intention to explain that all he had wanted was to free himself from the tyranny of the thesaurus so that he could do a better job in his exams. But before he was given a chance to speak, the Dean of Students, who was presiding over the hearing, said that Woolly was there to answer for the *fire* he had set on the football field. A moment later, Mr. Harrington, the faculty representative, referred to it as a *blaze*. Then Dunkie Dunkle, the student council president (who also happened to be captain of the football team), referred to it as a *conflagration*. And Woolly knew right then and there that no matter what he had to say, they were all going to take the side of the thesaurus.

As Woolly placed his dictionary back in the box, he heard the tentative creak of a footstep in the hall, and when he turned, he found his sister standing in the doorway—with a baseball bat in her hands.

—————

—I'm sorry about the room, said Sarah.

Woolly and his sister were sitting in the kitchen at the little table in the nook across from the sink. Sarah had already apologized for greeting Woolly with a baseball bat after finding the front door wide open. Now she was apologizing for taking away the room that was and wasn't his. Sarah was the only one in Woolly's family who said she was sorry and meant it. The only problem, it seemed to Woolly, was that she often said she was sorry when she hadn't the slightest reason to be so. Like now.

—No, no, said Woolly. There's no need to apologize on my account. I think it's wonderful that it's going to be the baby's room.

—We thought we might move your things to the room by the back stairs. You would have much more privacy there, and it would be easier for you to come and go as you please.

—Yes, said Woolly in agreement. By the back stairs would be dandy.

Woolly nodded twice with a smile and then looked down at the table.

After giving Woolly a hug upstairs, Sarah had asked if he was hungry and offered to make him a sandwich. So that's what was in front of him now—a grilled cheese sandwich cut into two triangles, one pointing up and one pointing down. As he looked at the triangles, Woolly could tell that his sister was looking at him.

—Woolly, she said after a moment. What are you doing here?

Woolly looked up.

—Oh, I don't know, he said with a smile. Gadding about, I suppose. Traveling hither and yon. You see, my friend Duchess and I each got a leave of absence from Salina and we decided to take a little trip and see some friends and family.

—Woolly . . .

Sarah gave a sigh that was so delicate, Woolly could hardly hear it.

—I got a call from Mom on Monday—after she got a call from the warden. So I know you don't have a leave of absence.

Woolly looked back down at his sandwich.

—But I phoned the warden so that I could speak to him myself. He told me that you have been an exemplary member of the community. And seeing as you only have five months left on your sentence, he said if you were to come right back of your own accord, he would do his best to limit the repercussions. Can I call him, Woolly? Can I call and tell him that you are on your way back?

Woolly turned his plate around so that the grilled cheese triangle pointing up was now pointing down, and the grilled cheese triangle pointing down was now pointing up. The warden called Mom who called Sarah who called the warden, thought Woolly. Then he broke into a smile.

—Do you remember? he asked. Do you remember when we would play telephone? All of us together in the great room at the camp?

For a moment, Sarah looked at Woolly with an expression that seemed so sorrowfully sad. But it was only for a moment. Then she broke into a smile of her own.

—I remember.

Sitting up in his chair, Woolly began remembering for the both of them, because while he wasn't any good at rememorizing, he was very good at remembering.

—As the youngest, I always got to go first, he said. And I would lean against your ear and hide my mouth behind my hand so that no one else could hear me, and I would whisper: *The captains were playing cribbage on their ketches.* Then you would turn to Kaitlin and whisper to her, and Kaitlin would whisper to Dad, and Dad would whisper to cousin Penelope, and cousin Penelope would whisper to Aunt Ruthie, and so it would go—all the way around the circle until it reached Mother. Then Mother would say: *The Comptons ate their cabbage in the kitchen.*

At the recollection of their mother's inevitable befuddlement, the brother and sister broke into laughter that was almost as loud as the laughter they had laughed all those years ago.

Then they were quiet.

—How is she? Woolly asked, looking down at his sandwich. How is Mom?

—She's well, said Sarah. When she called, she was on her way to Italy.

—With Richard.

—He is her husband, Woolly.

—Yes, yes, Woolly agreed. Of course, of course, of course. For richer or for poorer. In sickness and in health. And till death do them part—but not for one minute longer.

—Woolly . . . It wasn't a minute.

—I know, I know.

—It was four years after father died. And with you at school and Kaitlin and me married, she was all by herself.

—I know, he said again.

—You don't have to like Richard, Woolly, but you can't begrudge your mother the comforts of companionship.

Woolly looked at his sister, thinking: *You can't begrudge your mother the comforts of companionship.* And he wondered, if he had whispered that sentence to Sarah, and she had whispered it to Kaitlin, and Kaitlin had whispered it to his father, and so on all the way around the ring, when it finally reached his mother, what would the sentence have become?

Duchess

With the cowboy at the courthouse and Old Testament Ackerly, the balancing of accounts had been pretty straightforward. They were in the manner of one minus one, or five minus five. But when it came to Townhouse, the math was a little more complicated.

There was no question I owed him for the *Hondo* fiasco. I didn't make it rain that night, and I sure as hell didn't intend to bum a ride from a cop, but that didn't change the fact that had I just slogged my way home through the potato fields, Townhouse could have eaten his popcorn, seen the feature, and slipped back into the barracks undetected.

To his credit, Townhouse didn't make a big deal of it, even after Ackerly got out the switch. And when I tried to apologize, he just shrugged it off—like a guy who's come to expect that he's going to get a beating every now and then whether he deserves it or not. Still, I could tell he wasn't thrilled with the turn of events, any more than I would have been were the positions reversed. So in exchange for his taking the beating, I knew I owed him something.

What made the math complicated was the Tommy Ladue business. The son of an Okie who hadn't had enough sense to leave Oklahoma back in the thirties, Tommy Ladue was the sort of guy who looked like he was wearing overalls even when he wasn't.

When Townhouse joined us in Bunkhouse Four as Emmett's bunkmate, Tommy was none too pleased. As an Oklahoman, he said, he was of a mind that the Negroes should be housed in their own barracks and eat at their own tables in the company of their own kind. To look at the picture of Tommy's family in front of their farmhouse, you might wonder what the Ladues of Oklahoma were trying so hard to keep the black folks from, but that didn't seem to occur to Tommy.

That first night, as Townhouse was stowing his newly issued clothes in his footlocker, Tommy came over to set a few things straight. He explained that while Townhouse could come and go to his bed, he was not welcome in the western half of the bunkhouse. In the bathroom, which had four sinks, he was only to use the one that was farthest from the door. And as to eye contact, he'd best keep that to a minimum.

Townhouse looked like someone who could take care of himself, but Emmett had no patience with that sort of talk. He told Tommy that an inmate was an inmate, a sink was a sink, and Townhouse could move as freely through the barracks as the rest of us. If Tommy had been two inches taller, twenty pounds heavier, and twice as coura-geous, he might have taken a swing at Emmett. Instead, he went back to the western half of the bunkhouse in order to nurse his grievance.

Life on a work farm is designed to dull your wits. They wake you at dawn, work you till dusk, give you half an hour to eat, half an hour to settle down, and then it's out with the lights. Like one of those blindered horses in Central Park, you're not supposed to see anything other than the next two steps in front of you. But if you're a kid who's been raised in the company of traveling entertainers, which is to say small-time grifters and petty thieves, you never let yourself get *that* unobservant.

Case in point: I had noticed how Tommy had been cozying up to Bo Finlay, the like-minded guard from Macon, Georgia; I had over-heard them casting aspersions upon the darker races as well as the white men who favored them; one night behind the kitchen, I had seen Bo slipping two narrow blue boxes into Tommy's hands; and at two in the morning, I had watched as Tommy tiptoed across the bunkhouse in order to stow them inside Townhouse's footlocker.

So, I wasn't particularly surprised when during the morning review, Old Testament Ackerly—in the company of Bo and two other guards—announced that someone had been stealing from the pantry; I wasn't surprised when he walked straight up to Townhouse and ordered him to unpack his things onto his freshly made bed; and I certainly wasn't surprised when all that came out of Townhouse's footlocker were his clothes.

The ones who were surprised were Bo and Tommy—so surprised, they didn't have the good sense not to look at each other.

In a hilarious show of poor self-restraint, Bo actually brushed Townhouse aside and flipped his mattress over in order to see what was hiding underneath.

—Enough of that, said the warden, looking none too happy.

That's when I piped up.

—Warden Ackerly? I says, says I. If the pantry has been pilfered, and some scoundrel has impugned our honor by claiming that the culprit resides in Bunkhouse Four, I am of the opinion that you should search every one of our footlockers. For that is the only way to restore our good name.

—We'll decide what to do, said Bo.

—*I'll* decide what to do, said Ackerly. Open 'em up.

At Ackerly's command, the guards began moving from bunk to bunk, emptying each and every footlocker. And lo and behold, what did they find at the bottom of Tommy Ladue's but a brand-new box of Oreos.

—What can you tell us about this, said Ackerly to Tommy, while holding up the damning dessert.

A wise young man might have stood his ground and declared that he had never seen that light-blue box. A wily one might even have asserted with the confidence of the technically honest: *I did not put those cookies in my locker.* Because, after all, he hadn't. But without skipping a beat, Tommy looked from the warden to Bo and sputtered:

—If I was the one who took the Oreos, then where's the *other* box!

God bless him.

Later that night, while Tommy was sweating it out in the penalty shed and Bo was muttering into his mirror, all the boys in Bunkhouse Four gathered around to ask me what the hell had happened. And I told them. I told them how I'd seen Tommy cozying up to Bo, and the suspicious exchange behind the kitchen, and the late-night planting of evidence.

—But how did the cookies get from Townhouse's locker into Tommy's? asked some helpful half-wit, right on cue.

By way of response, I took a look at my fingernails.

—Let's just say they didn't walk there themselves.

The boys all had a good laugh over that one.

Then the never-to-be-underestimated Woolly Martin asked the pertinent question.

—If Bo gave Tommy two boxes of cookies and one of the boxes ended up in Tommy's locker, then what happened to the other box?

On the wall in the middle of the barracks was a big green board painted with all the rules and regulations we were meant to abide by. Reaching behind it, I retrieved the narrow blue box and produced it with a flourish.

—Voilà!

Then we all had a gay old time, passing around the cookies and laughing about Tommy's sputtering and the flipping of the mattress by Bo.

But once the laughter subsided, Townhouse shook his head and observed that I had taken quite a chance. At that, all of them looked at me with a touch of curiosity. Why did I do it, they were suddenly wondering. Why did I take the risk of pissing off Tommy and Bo for a barrackmate I hardly knew? And a black one at that.

In the silence that followed, I rested a hand on the hilt of my sword and looked from visage to visage.

—Took a chance? I said. No chance was taken here today, my friends. The chance was *given*. Each one of us has come from disparate parts to serve our disparate sentences for the commission of disparate crimes. But faced with a shared tribulation, we are given an opportunity—a rare and precious opportunity—to be men of one accord. Let us not shirk before what Fortune has laid at our feet. Let us take it up like a banner and march into the breach, such that many years from now, when we look back, we will be able to say that though we were condemned to days of drudgery, we faced them undaunted and shoulder to shoulder. We few, we happy few, we band of brothers.

Oh, you should have seen them!

They were rapt, I tell you, hanging on every syllable. And when I hit them with the old *band of brothers*, they let out a rousing cheer. If my father had been there, he would have been proud, if he weren't so inclined to be jealous.

After all the backs had been slapped and the boys had returned to their bunks with smiles on their faces and cookies in their stomachs, Townhouse approached.

—I owe you, he said.

And he was right. He did.

Even if we were a band of brothers.

But all these months later, the question remained: How *much* did he owe me? If Ackerly had found those cookies in Townhouse's footlocker, Townhouse would have been the one sweating in the penalty shed instead of Tommy, and for four nights instead of two. It was a credit to my account all right, but as credits go, I knew it wasn't enough to offset the eight strokes of the switch that Townhouse had received on his back.

That's what I was mulling over when I left Woolly at his sister's house in Hastings-on-Hudson, and what I kept mulling over all the way to Harlem.

—.—

At some point, Townhouse had told me that he lived on 126th Street, which seemed straightforward enough. But I had to drive the length of it six times before I found him.

He was sitting at the top of a brownstone's stoop, his boys assembled around him. Pulling over to the curb across the street, I watched through the windshield. On the step below Townhouse sat a big fat fella with a smile on his face, then a fair-skinned black with freckles, and on the bottom step, two kids in their early teens. I guess it was arranged like a little platoon, with the captain at the top, then his first lieutenant, his second lieutenant, and two foot soldiers. But the order could have been reversed, with Townhouse on the bottom step, and he still would have towered over the rest of them. It made you wonder what they had done with themselves while he was in Kansas. They'd probably bitten their nails and counted the days until his release. Now with Townhouse back in charge, they could exhibit a studied indifference, advertising to any who passed that they cared as little about their futures as they did about the weather.

When I crossed the street and approached, the young teens rose and took a step toward me, as if they were going to ask me for the password.

Looking over their heads, I addressed Townhouse with a smile.

—So, is this one of those dangerous street gangs I keep hearing about?

When Townhouse realized it was me, he looked almost as surprised as Emmett had.

—Jesus Christ, he said.

—You know this cracker? asked the freckle-faced one.

Townhouse and I both ignored him.

—What are you doing here, Duchess?

—I came to see you.

—About what?

—Come on down and I'll explain.

—Townhouse don't come off the stoop for no one, said freckles.

—Shut up, Maurice, said Townhouse.

I looked at Maurice with a feeling of sympathy. All he had wanted was to be a dutiful soldier. What he didn't understand was that when he says something like *Townhouse don't come off the stoop for no one*, a man like Townhouse has no choice but to do exactly that. Because while he may not take instructions from the likes of me, he doesn't take instructions from his second lieutenant either.

Townhouse rose to his feet and the boys made way for him like the Red Sea making way for Moses. When he got to the sidewalk, I told him how good it was to see him, but he just shook his head.

—You AWOL?

—In a manner of speaking. Woolly and I are passing through on our way to his family's place upstate.

—Woolly's with you?

—He is. And I know he'd love to see you. We're going to the Circus tomorrow night for the six o'clock show. Why don't you come along?

—The Circus isn't my sort of thing, Duchess, but give Woolly my regards just the same.

—I'll do so.

—All right then, Townhouse said after a moment. What's so important that you had to come to Harlem just to see me.

I gave him the shrug of the penitent.

—It's the *Hondo* fiasco.

Townhouse looked at me like he had no idea what I was talking about.

—You know. The John Wayne picture that we went to see on that rainy night back in Salina. I feel bad because of the beating you took.

At the word *beating*, Townhouse's boys dropped any semblance of indifference. It was like a jolt of electricity had gone right up the stoop. The big fella must have been too insulated to feel the full force of the charge because he just shifted in place, but Maurice came to his feet.

—A beating? asked the big fella with a smile.

I could see that Townhouse wanted to tell the big fella to shut up too, but he kept his eyes on me.

—Maybe I took a beating and maybe I didn't, Duchess. Either way, I don't see as it would be any cause of concern for you.

—You're your own man, Townhouse. I'd be the first to say so. But let's face it: You wouldn't have had to take this beating that you did or didn't take, if I hadn't hitched the ride from the cop.

This sent another jolt of electricity up the stoop.

Townhouse took a deep breath and gazed down the street almost wistfully, like he was looking back on simpler times. But he didn't contradict me. Because there was nothing to contradict. I was the one who baked the lasagna and he was the one who cleaned up the kitchen. It was as simple as that.

—What now? he asked after a moment. Don't tell me you came all this way to apologize.

I laughed.

—No, I don't put much stake in apologies. They always seem a day late and a dollar short. What I had in mind is something more concrete. Like a settling of accounts.

—A settling of accounts.

—Exactly.

—And how is that supposed to work?

—If it were only a matter of the movie, it could have been a switch for a switch. Eight minus eight and we'd be done. The problem is that you still owe me for the Oreo incident.

—The Oreo incident? said the big fella with an even bigger smile.

—It may not be worth the same as a switching, I continued, but it should count for something. Rather than an eight minus eight sort of situation, what we have here is more of an eight minus five. So I figure if you take three swings at me, that should make us even.

All the boys on the stoop were looking at me with varying degrees of disbelief. An act of honor has a way of doing that to the common man.

—You want to have a fight, said Townhouse.

—No, I said with a wave of the hand. Not a *fight*. A fight would imply that I'd try to hit you back. What I'm going to do is stand here and let you hit me, uncontested.

—You're going to *let* me hit you.

—Three times, I emphasized.

—What the fuck? said Maurice, his disbelief having transitioned into some form of hostility.

But the big fella, he was trembling with soundless laughter. After a moment, Townhouse turned to him.

—What do you make of this, Otis?

Wiping the tears from his eyes, Otis shook his head.

—I don't know, T. On the one hand, it seems pretty crazy. But on the other, if a white boy comes all the way from Kansas to ask you for a beating, I think you gotta give it to him.

As Otis began laughing again in his silent way, Townhouse just shook his head. He was disinclined to do it. I could tell. And if it were just the two of us, he probably would have sent me on my way, unsatisfied. But Maurice was staring at me now with a look of borrowed indignation.

—If you won't hit him, I will, he said.

There he goes again, I thought. Maurice just didn't seem to understand the chain of command. To make matters worse, when he volunteered to hit me, he did so with just enough bravado to imply that maybe the reason Townhouse was stalling was because he wasn't up to the task.

Townhouse turned to Maurice very slowly.

—Maurice, he said, just because you're my cousin doesn't mean I'm not willing to shut you the fuck up.

That put so much color into Maurice's face that his freckles almost disappeared. Then he was the one gazing down the street wishing it was simpler times.

It made me feel a little sorry for him, watching him get humiliated like that in front of the rest of us. But I also could tell that through his injudiciousness, he had raised Townhouse's temperature, which was just as well.

Sticking my chin out toward Townhouse, I pointed to it.

—Just give me a pop, T. What've you got to lose?

When I called him T, Townhouse grimaced like I knew he would.

Showing disrespect toward Townhouse was the last thing I wanted to do, but the challenge before me was to get him to take that first swing. Once he took the first one, I knew the rest would come easy. Because even if he didn't gripe about the switching, I'm sure he still carried a bit of a grudge.

—Come on, I said, intending to call him T one more time.

Before I got the chance, he delivered. The punch landed right where it was supposed to, but it only knocked me a few steps back, like he hadn't put everything into it.

—There you go, I said encouragingly. That's a pretty good one. But this time, why don't you give it some of the old Joe Louis.

And that's what he did. I mean, I didn't even see it coming. One second I'm standing there egging him on, and the next second I'm lying on the sidewalk aware of that strange aroma that you only smell when your skull has been rattled.

Planting both hands on the concrete, I pushed myself off the ground, rose to my feet, and went back to the hitting spot—just like Emmett.

The young teens were practically jumping up and down.

—Give it to him, Townhouse, they shouted.

—He asked for it, muttered Maurice.

—Mother Mary, said Otis in sustained disbelief.

Though all four spoke at once, I could hear each of them as clearly as if they'd spoken alone. But Townhouse couldn't. He couldn't hear any of them at all because he wasn't on 126th Street. He was back at Salina. Back in that moment that he'd sworn he'd never think about again: taking Ackerly's beating as the rest of us watched. It was the fire of justice that was burning through Townhouse now. The fire of justice that appeases the injured spirit and sets the record straight.

The third blow was an uppercut that put me flat on the pavement.

It was a thing of beauty, I tell you.

Townhouse took two steps back, heaving a little from the exertion, the sweat running down his forehead. Then he took another step back like he needed to, like he was worried that if he were any closer, he would hit me again and again, and might not be able to stop.

I gave him the friendly wave of one crying uncle. Then being careful to take my time so the blood wouldn't rush from my head, I got back on my feet.

—That's the stuff, I said with a smile, after spitting some blood on the sidewalk.

—Now we're square, said Townhouse.

—Now we're square, I agreed, and I stuck out my hand.

Townhouse stared at it for a moment. Then he took it in a firm grip and looked me eye to eye—like we were the presidents of two nations who had just signed an armistice after generations of discord.

At that moment, we were both towering over the boys, and they knew it. You could tell from the expressions of respect on the faces of Otis and the teens, and the expression of dejection on the face of Maurice.

I felt bad for him. Not man enough to be a man, or child enough to be a child, not black enough to be black, or white enough to be white, Maurice just couldn't seem to find his place in the world. It made me want to tussle his hair and assure him that one day everything was going to be all right. But it was time to move along.

Letting go of Townhouse's hand, I gave him a tip of the hat.

—See you round, pardner, I said.

—Sure, said Townhouse.

I'd felt pretty good when I settled the scores with the cowboy and Ackerly, knowing that I was playing some small role in balancing the scales of justice. But those feelings were nothing compared to the satisfaction I felt after letting Townhouse settle his score with me.

Sister Agnes had always said that good deeds can be habit forming. And I guess she was right, because having given Sally's jam to the kids at St. Nick's, as I was about to leave Townhouse's stoop I found myself turning back.

—Hey, Maurice, I called.

He looked up with the same expression of dejection, but with a touch of uncertainty too.

—See that baby-blue Studebaker over there?

—Yeah?

—She's all yours.

Then I tossed him the keys.

I would have loved to see the look on his face when he caught them. But I had already turned away and was striding down the middle of 126th Street with the sun at my back, thinking: *Harrison Hewett, here I come.*

Emmett

A T QUARTER TO EIGHT in the evening, Emmett was sitting in a run-down saloon at the edge of Manhattan with a glass of beer and a photograph of Harrison Hewett on the bar in front of him.

Taking a drink, Emmett studied the picture with interest. It showed the profile of a handsome forty-year-old man looking off in the distance. Duchess had never said exactly how old his father was, but from his stories one got the sense that Mr. Hewett's career dated back to the early 1920s. And hadn't Sister Agnes guessed that he was about fifty when he'd brought Duchess to the orphanage in 1944? That would make Mr. Hewett about sixty now—and this photograph about twenty years out of date. It also meant the photograph might well have been taken before Duchess was born.

Because the photograph was so old and the actor so young, Emmett had no problem seeing the family resemblance. In Duchess's words, his father had the nose, chin, and appetites of John Barrymore. If Duchess hadn't quite inherited his father's appetites, he had definitely inherited the nose and chin. Duchess's coloring was lighter, but perhaps that came from his mother, whoever she was.

However good-looking Mr. Hewett had been, Emmett couldn't help picture him with a certain distaste as the man of fifty who drove off in a convertible with a lovely young girl in the passenger seat, having just abandoned his eight-year-old son.

Sister Agnes had been right when she observed that Emmett was angry at Duchess for taking his car. And Emmett knew that she was also right when she observed that what Duchess needed more than anything else was a friend who, upon occasion, could save him from his own misguided intentions. Whether Emmett was up to the task remained to be seen. Either way, he would have to find Duchess first.

—— · ——

When Emmett had woken at seven that morning, Stew was already up and about.

Seeing Emmett, he pointed to an overturned crate where there was a bowl, a pot of hot water, soap, a razor, and towel. Stripping to the waist, Emmett bathed his upper body and shaved. Then having eaten a breakfast of ham and eggs—at his own expense—and received assurances from Ulysses that Billy would be watched over, he followed Stew's directions through a gap in some fencing and down a caged metal staircase, which led from the tracks down to Thirteenth Street. Shortly after eight, he was standing on the corner of Tenth Avenue looking eastward, feeling like he had a jump on the day.

But Emmett underestimated every aspect of what was to follow. He underestimated how long it would take to walk to Seventh Avenue. He underestimated how difficult it would be to find the entrance to the subway, passing it twice. He underestimated how disorienting the station would be once he got inside—with its network of gangways and staircases, and its bustling, purposeful crowd.

After being spun around by the current of commuters, Emmett found the token booth, he found a map of the subway system, he identified the Seventh Avenue line and determined there were five stops to Forty-Second Street, each step in the process posing its own challenges, its own frustrations, its own causes for humility.

As Emmett came down the steps to the platform, a train was beginning to board. Quickly, he joined the crowd that was pressing its way into the car. When the doors closed and Emmett found himself tucked shoulder-to-shoulder with some and face-to-face with others, he had the disorienting feeling of being at once self-conscious and ignored. Everyone on board seemed to have chosen some fixed point at which to stare with precision and disinterest. Following suit, Emmett trained his gaze on an advertisement for Lucky Strike cigarettes and began counting stops.

At the first two, it seemed to Emmett that people were getting off and on in equal number. But at the third stop, people mostly got off. And at the fourth, so many people got off that Emmett found himself in a nearly empty car. Leaning over to look through the narrow window onto the platform, he saw with a touch of unease that the station was Wall Street. When he had studied the map at Fourteenth Street, he hadn't paid much attention to the names of the intervening stops, seeing no need to do so, but he was fairly certain that Wall Street wasn't among them.

And wasn't Wall Street in lower Manhattan . . . ?

Stepping quickly to a map that was posted on the subway car's wall, Emmett ran a finger down the length of the Seventh Avenue line. Finding the Wall Street stop revealed that in his haste he had boarded an express train headed south rather than a local headed north. By the time he realized this, the doors had already closed. A second look at the map told Emmett that in another minute, the train would be somewhere under the East River on its way to Brooklyn.

Taking one of the now-empty seats, Emmett closed his eyes. Once again, he was headed in the wrong direction by a factor of a hundred and eighty degrees, but this time he had no one to blame but himself. At every step, there had been someone he could have asked for assistance, someone who could have eased his way by directing him to the right staircase, the right platform, the right train. Yet he had refused to ask a soul. With a grim self-awareness, Emmett remembered how

critical he had been of his father's reluctance to ask the more experienced farmers around him for advice—as if to do so would somehow
leave him unmanned. Self-reliance as folly, Emmett had thought.

As he rode from Brooklyn back to Manhattan, Emmett was determined not to make the same mistake twice. When he arrived at the
station at Times Square, he asked the man in the token booth which
exit would lead him downtown; on the corner of Forty-Second Street,
he asked the man in the newsstand where he could find the Statler
Building; and when he reached the Statler Building, he asked the uni-
formed man at the front desk which of the agencies in the building
were the biggest.

By the time Emmett arrived at the Tristar Talent Agency on the thirteenth floor, there were already eight people gathered in the small
waiting room—four men with dogs, two with cats, a woman with a
monkey on a leash, and a man in a three-piece suit and bowler hat
who had an exotic bird on his shoulder. He was talking to the middle-
aged receptionist. When he finished, Emmett approached the desk.

—Yes? the receptionist asked, as if she were already bored with
whatever Emmett had to say.

—I'm here to see Mr. Lehmberg.

She took a pencil from a holder and held it over a pad.

—Name?

—Emmett Watson.

The pencil scratched.

—Animal?

—I'm sorry?

She looked up from the pad and spoke with exaggerated patience.

—What sort of animal have you got?

—I don't have an animal.

—If there's no animal in your act, then you're in the wrong place.

—I don't have an act, explained Emmett. I need to speak to Mr. Lehmberg on a different matter.

—It's one thing at a time in this office, sonny. You want to talk to Mr. Lehmberg on a different matter, you'll have to come back on a different day.

—It shouldn't take more than a minute . . .

—Why don't you take a seat, Mac, said a man with a bulldog at his feet.

—I may not need to see Mr. Lehmberg at all, persisted Emmett. You might be able to help me.

The receptionist looked up at Emmett with an expression of serious doubt.

—I'm looking for someone who might have been one of Mr. Lehmberg's clients. A performer. I'm just trying to track down his address.

As Emmett completed his explanation, the receptionist's face darkened.

—Do I look like a phone book?

—No, ma'am.

As several of the performers behind Emmett laughed, he felt the color rising to his cheeks.

Stabbing her pencil back into its holder, the receptionist picked up the phone and dialed a number.

Imagining she might be calling Mr. Lehmberg, after all, Emmett remained at the desk. But when the call went through, the receptionist began talking to a woman named Gladys about what had happened on a television show the night before. Avoiding eye contact with the waiting performers, Emmett turned and headed back into the hallway—just in time to see the doors to the elevator closing.

But before they shut completely, the tip of an umbrella jutted through the gap. A moment later, the doors reopened to reveal the man with the bowler hat and the bird on his shoulder.

—Thank you, said Emmett.

—Not at all, said the man.

It hadn't looked like rain that morning, so Emmett guessed the umbrella was somehow part of the act. Looking up from the umbrella, Emmett realized the gentleman was staring at him expectantly.

—Lobby? he asked.

—Oh, I'm sorry. No.

Fumbling a little, Emmett removed from his pocket the list that the deskman downstairs had given him.

—Fifth floor, please.

—Ah.

The gentleman pressed the corresponding button. Then reaching into his pocket he produced a peanut, which he handed to the bird on his shoulder. Standing on one claw, the bird took the peanut with the other.

—Thank you, Mr. Morton, it squawked.

—My pleasure, Mr. Winslow.

As Emmett watched the bird shell the peanut with a startling facility, Mr. Morton noted his interest.

—An African grey, he said with a smile. One of the most intelligent of all our feathered friends. Mr. Winslow here, for example, has a vocabulary of one hundred and sixty-two words.

—One hundred and sixty-three, squawked the bird.

—Is that so, Mr. Winslow. And what was the hundred and sixty-third word?

—ASPCA.

The gentleman coughed in embarrassment.

—That is not a word, Mr. Winslow. It is an acronym.

—Acronym, squawked the bird. One hundred and sixty-four!

Only when the gentleman smiled at Emmett a little sadly did Emmett realize this little exchange was part of the act too.

Having reached the fifth floor, the elevator came to a stop and its doors opened. With a word of thanks, Emmett stepped off and the doors began to close. But once again, Mr. Morton stuck the tip of his umbrella in the gap. This time when the doors reopened, he got off the elevator, joining Emmett in the hall.

—I don't wish to intrude, young man, but I couldn't help hearing your inquiry back in Mr. Lehmberg's office. By any chance, are you now headed to McGinley & Co.?

—I am, said Emmett in surprise.

—May I offer you a piece of friendly advice?

—His advice is nice and worth the price.

When Mr. Morton gave the bird a hangdog expression, Emmett laughed out loud. It was the first time that he had laughed out loud in a good long while.

—I'd appreciate any advice you're willing to give, Mr. Morton.

The gentleman smiled and pointed his umbrella down the hallway, which was lined with identical doors.

—When you go into Mr. McGinley's office, you will not find his receptionist, Miss Cravitts, any more helpful than you found Mrs. Burk. The ladies who manage the desks in this building are naturally reticent, disinclined you might even say, to be helpful. This may seem ungenerous, but you have to understand that they are besieged from morning to night by artists of all persuasions who are trying to talk their way into a meeting. In the Statler Building, the Cravittses and Burks are all that stand between a semblance of order and the Colosseum. But if these ladies must be reasonably stern with performers, they have to be all the more so with those who come seeking names and addresses. . . .

Mr. Morton set the point of his umbrella down on the floor and leaned on the handle.

—In this building, for every performer an agent represents, there are at least five creditors in hot pursuit. There are outraged audience members, ex-wives, and cheated restaurateurs. There is only one person for whom the gatekeepers show the slightest courtesy, and that is the man who holds the purse strings—whether he be hiring for a Broadway show or bar mitzvah. So, if you're going into Mr. McGinley's office, may I suggest you introduce yourself as a producer.

As Emmett considered this advice, the gentleman studied him discreetly.

—I can see from your expression that the notion of misrepresenting yourself goes against the grain. But you should take heart, young man, that within the walls of the Statler Building, he who misrepresents himself well, represents himself best.

—Thank you, said Emmett.

Mr. Morton nodded. But then he raised a finger with an additional thought.

—This performer you're looking for. . . . Do you know his specialty?

—He's an actor.

—Hmm.

—Is something wrong?

Mr. Morton gestured vaguely.

—It's your appearance. Your age and attire. Let us just say that your image clashes with what one might expect from a theatrical producer.

Mr. Morton studied Emmett a little more brazenly, then smiled.

—May I suggest that you present yourself as the son of a rodeo owner.

—The man I'm looking for is a Shakespearean actor . . .

Mr. Morton laughed.

—Even better, he said.

And when he began to laugh again, his parrot laughed with him.

When Emmett paid his visit to the offices of McGinley & Co., he took care to do exactly as Mr. Morton had advised at every step, and he was not disappointed. When he entered the waiting room, which was crowded with young mothers and redheaded boys, the receptionist met him with the same expression of impatience that he'd been given at Tristar Talent. But as soon as he explained that he was the son of a touring rodeo operator looking to hire a performer, her expression brightened.

Standing and straightening her skirt, she ushered Emmett into a second waiting room, one that was smaller but with better chairs, a water cooler, and no other people. Ten minutes later, Emmett was shown into Mr. McGinley's office, where he was greeted with the warmth of an old acquaintance and offered a drink.

—So, said Mr. McGinley, resuming his seat behind his desk, Alice tells me you're looking for a man for your rodeo!

Emmett had been skeptical when Mr. Morton observed that the hunt for a Shakespearean actor to cast in a rodeo was *even better*. When he explained himself to Mr. McGinley, he did so with some hesitation. But as soon as he was finished speaking, Mr. McGinley slapped his hands together in satisfaction.

—A nice twist, if I do say so myself! There's no shortage of performers complaining that they've been pigeonholed into this, or pigeonholed into that. But time and again, the mistake that producers actually make is not pigeonholing their actors; it's pigeonholing their *audiences*. This group only wants this, they'll tell you, while that group only wants that. When, in all likelihood, what your theatrical devotee is hungry for is a little more horseplay, while what your fan of the rodeo craves is a little more *savoir faire*!

Mr. McGinley broke into a wide grin. Then suddenly serious, he put a hand on a pile of files that were stacked on his desk.

—Rest assured, Mr. Watson, that your troubles are behind you. For not only do I have an army of fine Shakespearean actors at my disposal, four of them can ride horses and two of them can shoot!

—Thank you, Mr. McGinley. But I am looking for a *particular* Shakespearean.

Mr. McGinley leaned forward with enthusiasm.

—Particular in what way? British? Classically trained? A tragedian?

—I'm looking for a monologist whom my father saw perform some years ago and has never forgotten. A monologist by the name of Harrison Hewett.

Mr. McGinley patted his desk three times, quietly.

—Hewett?

—That's right.

Patting the desk one last time, Mr. McGinley pressed the button on his intercom.

—Alice? Bring me the file on . . . Harrison Hewett.

A few moments later Alice entered and handed a folder to Mr. McGinley that could not have held more than a single sheet of paper. After taking a quick look inside, Mr. McGinley laid it on his desk.

—Harrison Hewett is an excellent choice, Mr. Watson. I can see why your father has never forgotten him. And he's a man who thrives on artistic challenges, so I am certain he would leap at the chance to perform in your revue. But by way of clarification, I should note that we represent Mr. Hewett on a cooperative basis. . . .

By Mr. Morton's estimation, the chances were better than fifty percent that Mr. McGinley would say exactly this.

—If an agent states that he represents a performer on a cooperative basis, explained Mr. Morton, this means that he does not represent the performer at all. But not to worry. The agents in the Statler Building are in universal agreement that to get a bird in the hand, they would happily pay ten percent to the bush. As a result, they all maintain active lists of the performers who work with their competitors, so that, for the appropriate commission, they can send an interested party up or down the stairs.

In Emmett's case, it was a trip up to a Mr. Cohen on the eleventh floor. As Mr. McGinley had called in advance, Emmett was greeted at the door and whisked straight into another interior waiting room. Ten minutes later, he was shown into Mr. Cohen's office, where he was

greeted warmly and offered another drink. Again, the idea of introducing a Shakespearean actor into a rodeo was celebrated for its ingenuity. But this time, when the button on the intercom was pressed
and a folder brought in, it was almost two inches thick—stuffed with
yellowed news clippings and playbills and a stack of outdated head-
shots, one of which was given to Emmett.

Once Mr. Cohen had assured Emmett that Mr. Hewett (who was
a close personal friend of Will Rogers) would be thrilled by this opportunity, he asked how Emmett might be reached.

Following Mr. Morton's instructions, Emmett explained that since
he was leaving the city on the following morning, he needed to hammer out any details right then and there. This sent the office into a
flurry of activity as terms were agreed to and contracts written up.

—If they actually prepare contracts, Emmett had asked Mr. Morton, should I agree to sign them?

—Sign anything they put in front of you, my boy! Make sure the
agent signs them too. Then insist upon receiving two executed copies
for your files. For once an agent has your signature, he would give you
the keys to his own mother's house.

The address that Mr. Cohen gave Emmett for Harrison Hewett led
him to a dingy hotel on a dingy street in downtown Manhattan. From
the well-mannered man who answered the door of room 42, Emmett
learned to his disappointment that Mr. Hewett was no longer a resident,
but he also learned that Mr. Hewett's son had been there the previous
morning and had apparently checked into the hotel for the night.

—Perhaps he's still here, said the gentleman.

In the lobby, the clerk with the pencil-thin moustache said sure,
sure, he knew who Emmett was talking about. Harry Hewett's kid.
He showed up asking about his old man's whereabouts, then booked
two rooms for the night. But he wasn't there no more. He and his
daydreaming pal had left around noon.

—With my fucking radio, added the clerk.

—Did he happen to say where he was going?

—He might have.

—Might have? asked Emmett.

The clerk leaned back in his chair.

—When I helped your friend find his father, he gave me ten bucks . . .

According to the clerk, Emmett would be able to find Duchess's father by speaking to a friend of his who drank at a West Side saloon every night after eight. With time to spare, Emmett walked up Broadway until he found a coffee shop that was busy, clean, and well lit. Sitting at the counter, he ordered the special and a piece of pie. He finished his meal with three cups of coffee, and a cigarette that he bummed from his waitress—an Irish woman named Maureen, who, despite being ten times busier than Mrs. Burk, had ten times her grace.

The information from the hotel clerk sent Emmett back to Times Square, which in the hour before dusk was already incandescent with brightly lit signs announcing cigarettes, cars, appliances, hotels, and theaters. The sheer scale and garishness of it all made Emmett disinclined to buy a single thing that was being advertised.

Emmett returned to the newsstand on the corner of Forty-Second Street, where he found the same newsman from earlier in the day. This time the newsman pointed to the northern end of the square, where a giant sign for Canadian Club whiskey was shining ten stories above the street.

—See that sign? Just beyond it, take a left onto Forty-Fifth and keep walking till you've run out of Manhattan.

Over the course of the day, Emmett had grown accustomed to being ignored. He'd been ignored by the commuters on the subway train, by the pedestrians on the sidewalks and the performers in the waiting rooms, chalking it up to the inimicality of city life. So he was a little surprised to discover that once he was beyond Eighth Avenue, he wasn't ignored anymore.

On the corner of Ninth Avenue, he was eyed by a beat cop in the middle of his rounds. On Tenth Avenue he was approached by one young man offering to sell him drugs and another offering to sell him his company. As he approached Eleventh, he was beckoned by an old black beggar, whom he avoided by quickening his pace, only to run right into an old white beggar a few steps later.

Having found the anonymity of the morning somewhat off-putting, Emmett would have welcomed it now. He felt he understood why the people of New York walked with that purposeful urgency. It was a dissuasive signal to the vagrants and drifters and the rest of the fallen.

Just before the river, he found the Anchor—the bar the clerk had told him about. Given its name and location, Emmett had imagined it would be a spot that catered to sailors or members of the merchant marine. If it ever had, the association had lapsed long ago. For inside there wasn't a man you might call seaworthy. To Emmett's eye, they all looked one step above the old beggars he'd dodged in the street.

Having learned from Mr. Morton how reluctant the agents were to share whereabouts, Emmett was worried that the bartender might be equally tight-lipped; or perhaps like the clerk at the Sunshine Hotel, he would expect to be handsomely reimbursed. But when Emmett explained that he was looking for a man named FitzWilliams, the bartender said that he'd come to the right place. So Emmett had taken a seat at the bar and ordered the beer.

—·—

When the door of the Anchor opened shortly after eight and a man in his sixties entered, the bartender gave Emmett the nod. From his stool, Emmett watched as the old man made his way slowly to the bar, picked up a glass and half-empty bottle of whiskey, and retreated to a table in the corner.

As FitzWilliams poured himself a drink, Emmett recalled the stories that Duchess had told of his rise and fall. It wasn't easy to imagine that this thin, shuffling, forlorn-looking man had once been paid handsomely to play the part of Santa Claus. Leaving some money on the bar, Emmett approached the old performer's table.

—Excuse me. Are you Mr. FitzWilliams?

When Emmett said the word *mister*, FitzWilliams looked up with a touch of surprise.

—Yes, he admitted after a moment. I am Mr. FitzWilliams.

Taking the empty chair, Emmett explained that he was a friend of Duchess's.

—I gather he may have come here last night to speak with you.

The old performer nodded, as if now he understood, as if he should have known.

—Yes, he said in a tone that verged on an admission. He was here. He was trying to find his father because of a little unfinished business between them. But Harry had left town, and Duchess didn't know where he'd gone, so he came to see Fitzy.

FitzWilliams offered Emmett a half-hearted smile.

—I'm an old friend of the family's, you see.

Returning the smile, Emmett asked FitzWilliams if he had told Duchess where Mr. Hewett had gone.

—I did, the old performer said, nodding his head at first, then shaking it. I told him where Harry went. To the Olympic Hotel in Syracuse. And that's where Duchess will go, I suppose. After he sees his friend.

—Which friend is that?

—Oh, Duchess didn't say. But it was . . . It was in Harlem.

—Harlem?

—Yes. Isn't that funny?

—No, it makes perfect sense. Thank you, Mr. FitzWilliams. You've been very helpful.

When Emmett pushed back his chair, FitzWilliams looked up in surprise.

—You're not going, are you? Surely, as two old friends of the Hewetts, we should have a drink in their honor?

Having learned what he had come to learn, and certain that Billy would be wondering where he was by now, Emmett had no desire to remain at the Anchor.

But having initially looked like he didn't want to be disturbed, the old performer suddenly looked like he didn't want to be alone. So Emmett got another glass from the bartender and returned to the table.

After FitzWilliams had poured their whiskeys, he raised his glass.

—To Harry and Duchess.

—To Harry and Duchess, echoed Emmett.

When they both had taken a drink and set down their glasses, FitzWilliams smiled a little sadly, as if moved by a bittersweet memory.

—Do you know why they call him that? Duchess, I mean.

—I think he told me it was because he was born in Dutchess County.

—No, said FitzWilliams, with a shake of the head and his half-hearted smile. That wasn't it. He was born here in Manhattan. I remember the night.

Before continuing, FitzWilliams took another drink, almost as if he needed to.

—His mother, Delphine, was a beautiful young Parisienne and a singer of love songs in the manner of Piaf. In the years before Duchess was born, she performed at all the great supper clubs. At El Morocco and the Stork Club and the Rainbow Room. I'm sure she would have become quite famous, at least in New York, if it weren't for becoming so sick. It was tuberculosis, I think. But I really can't remember. Isn't that terrible? A beautiful woman like that, a friend, dies in the prime of her life, and I can't even remember from what.

Shaking his head in self-condemnation, FitzWilliams raised his glass, but set it back down without taking a drink, as if he sensed that to have done so would have been an insult to her memory.

The story of Mrs. Hewett's death caught Emmett a little off guard. For in the few times that Duchess had mentioned his mother, he had always spoken as if she had abandoned them.

—At any rate, FitzWilliams continued, Delphine doted on her little boy. When there was money, she would quietly hide some from Harry so that she could buy him new clothes. Cute little outfits like those, what do you call them . . . lederhosen! She would dress him up in his finery, letting his hair grow down to his shoulders. But when she became bedridden and she would send him downstairs into the taverns to bring Harry home, Harry would . . .

FitzWilliams shook his head.

—Well, you know Harry. After a few drinks, it's hard to tell where Shakespeare ends and Harry begins. So when the boy would come through the door, Harry would stand up from his stool, make an elaborate flourish, and say, *Ladies and Gentlemen, I present to you, the Duchess of Alba.* And the next time it would be *the Duchess of Kent,* or *the Duchess of Tripoli.* Pretty soon some of the others began calling the boy Duchess. Then we all called him Duchess. Every last one of us. To the point where no one could even remember his given name.

FitzWilliams raised his glass again, this time taking a good, long drink. When he set the glass down, Emmett was startled to see that the old performer had begun to cry—letting the tears roll down his cheeks without bothering to wipe them away.

FitzWilliams gestured to the bottle.

—He gave me that, you know. Duchess, I mean. Despite everything. Despite all of it, last night he came here and bought me a brand-new bottle of my favorite whiskey. Just like that.

FitzWilliams took a deep breath.

—He was sent away to a work camp in Kansas, you know. At the age of sixteen.

—Yes, said Emmett. That's where we met.

—Ah. I see. But in all your time together, did he ever tell you . . . did he ever tell you how he came to be there?

—No, said Emmett. He never did.

Then after taking the liberty of pouring a little more of the old man's whiskey into both of their glasses, Emmett waited.

Ulysses

THOUGH THE BOY HAD already read the story once from beginning to end, Ulysses asked him to read it again.

Shortly after ten—with the sun having set, the moon yet to rise, and the others retreating to their tents—Billy had taken out his book and asked if Ulysses would like to hear the story of Ishmael, a young sailor who joined a one-legged captain on his hunt for a great white whale. Though Ulysses had never heard the story of Ishmael, he had no doubt it would be a good one. Each of the boy's stories had been good. But when Billy had offered to read this new adventure, with a touch of embarrassment Ulysses had asked if he would read the story of his namesake instead.

The boy hadn't hesitated. By the waning light of Stew's fire, he had turned to the back of his book and illuminated the page with his flashlight beam—a circle of light within a circle of light within a sea of darkness.

As Billy began, Ulysses felt a moment of worry that having read the story once before, the boy might paraphrase or skip over passages, but Billy seemed to understand that if the story was worth reading again, it was worth reading word for word.

Yes, the boy read the story exactly as he had in the boxcar, but Ulysses didn't hear it the same way. For this time, he knew what was to come. He knew now to look forward to some parts and dread others—to look forward to how Ulysses bested the Cyclops by hiding his men under the pelts of sheep, and to dread the moment when the covetous crew unleashed the winds of Aeolus, setting their captain's ship off course at the very moment that his homeland had come into view.

When the story was over, and Billy had closed his book and switched off his light, and Ulysses had taken up Stew's shovel to cover the embers, Billy asked if he would tell a story.

Ulysses looked down with a smile.

—I don't have any storybooks, Billy.

—You don't have to tell a story from a book, Billy replied. You could tell a story from yourself. Like one from the war overseas. Do you have any of those?

Ulysses turned the shovel in his hand.

Did he have any stories from the war? Of course, he did. More than he cared to remember. For his stories had not been softened by the mists of time or brightened by the tropes of a poet. They remained vivid and severe. So vivid and severe that whenever one happened to surface in his mind, Ulysses would bury it—just as he had been about to bury the embers of this fire. If Ulysses couldn't stomach the sharing of the memories with himself, he certainly wasn't going to share them with an eight-year-old boy.

But Billy's request was a fair one. Generously, he had opened the pages of his book and told the stories of Sinbad and Jason and Achilles, and of Ulysses's namesake twice. He had certainly earned a telling in return. So setting the shovel aside, Ulysses threw another log on the fire and resumed his seat on the railroad tie.

—I have a story for you, he said. A story about my own encounter with the king of the winds.

—When you were sailing across the wine-dark sea?

—No, said Ulysses. When I was walking across the dry and dusty land.

The story began on a rural road in Iowa in the summer of 1952.

A few days before, Ulysses had boarded a train in Utah, intending to travel over the Rockies and across the plains to Chicago. But halfway through Iowa, the boxcar in which he was traveling was shunted onto a siding in order to wait for a different locomotive, which was scheduled to arrive who knew when. Forty miles away was the junction in Des Moines, where he could easily catch another train headed east, or one headed north toward the Lakes, or south to New Orleans. With that in mind, Ulysses had disembarked and begun working his way across the countryside on foot.

He had walked about ten miles down an old dirt road when he began to sense that something was amiss.

The first sign was the birds. Or rather, the absence of them. When you're traveling back and forth across the country, Ulysses explained, the one great constant is the companionship of birds. On your way from Miami to Seattle or Boston to San Diego, the landscape is always changing. But wherever you go, the birds are there. The pigeons or buzzards, condors or cardinals, blue jays or blackbirds. Living on the road, you wake to the sound of their singing at dawn, and you lay yourself down to their chatter at dusk.

And yet . . .

As Ulysses walked along this rural road, there wasn't a bird to be seen, not circling over the fields or perched upon the telephone wires.

The second sign was the caravan of cars. While throughout the morning Ulysses had been passed by the occasional pickup or sedan moving along at forty miles an hour, suddenly he saw an assortment of fifteen cars, including a black limousine, speeding in his direction. The vehicles were driving so fast, he had to step off the shoulder in order to shield himself from the gravel that was kicked up by their tires.

After watching them race past, Ulysses turned back to look in the direction from which they'd come. That's when he saw that the sky in the east was turning from blue to green. Which in that part of the country, as Billy well knew, could only mean one thing.

Behind Ulysses was nothing but knee-high corn for as far as the eye could see, but half a mile ahead was a farmhouse. With the sky growing darker by the minute, Ulysses began to run.

As he drew closer, Ulysses could see that the farmhouse had already been battened down, its doors and shutters closed. He could see the owner securing the barn, then dashing to the hatch of his shelter, where his wife and children waited. And when the farmer reached his family, Ulysses could see the young boy pointing in his direction.

As the four looked his way, Ulysses slowed from a run to a walk with his hands at his side.

The farmer instructed his wife and children to go into the shelter— first the wife so that she could help the children, then the daughter, and then the little boy, who continued to look at Ulysses right up until the moment he disappeared from sight.

Ulysses expected the father to follow his family down the ladder, but leaning over to say one last thing, he closed the hatch, turned toward Ulysses, and waited for his approach. Maybe there was no lock on the shelter's hatch, thought Ulysses, and the farmer figured if there was going to be a confrontation then better to have it now, while still aboveground. Or maybe he felt if one man intends to refuse harbor to another, he should do so face-to-face.

As a sign of respect, Ulysses came to a stop six paces away, close enough to be heard, but far enough to pose no threat.

The two men studied each other as the wind began to lift the dust around their feet.

—I'm not from around these parts, Ulysses said after a moment. I'm just a Christian working my way to Des Moines so I can catch a train.

The farmer nodded. He nodded in a manner that said he believed Ulysses was a Christian and that he was on his way to catch a train, but that under the circumstances neither of those things mattered.

—I don't know you, he said simply.

—No, you don't, agreed Ulysses.

For a moment, Ulysses considered helping the man come to know him—by telling him his name, telling him that he'd been raised in Tennessee and that he was a veteran, that he'd once had a wife and child of his own. But even as these thoughts passed through Ulysses's mind, he knew that the telling of them wouldn't matter either. And he knew it without resentment.

For were the positions reversed, were Ulysses about to climb down into a shelter, a windowless space beneath the ground that he had dug with his own hands for the safety of his family, and were a six-foot-tall white man suddenly to appear, he wouldn't have welcomed him either. He would have sent him on his way.

After all, what was a man in the prime of his life doing crossing the country on foot with nothing but a canvas bag slung over his shoulder? A man like that must have made certain choices. He had chosen to abandon his family, his township, his church, in pursuit of something different. In pursuit of a life unhindered, unanswered, and alone. Well, if that's what he had worked so hard to become, then why in a moment like this should he expect to be treated as anything different?

—I understand, said Ulysses, though the man had not explained himself.

The farmer looked at Ulysses for a moment, then turning to his right, he pointed to a thin white spire rising from a grove of trees.

—The Unitarian church is a little less than a mile. It's got a basement. And you've got a good chance of making it, if you run.

—Thank you, said Ulysses.

As they stood facing each other, Ulysses knew that the farmer had been right. Any chance he had of making it to the church in time was predicated on his going as quickly as he could. But Ulysses had no intention of breaking into a run in front of another man, however good his advice. It was a matter of dignity.

After waiting, the farmer seemed to understand this, and with a shake of the head that laid no blame on anyone, including himself, he opened his hatch and joined his family.

With a glance at the steeple, Ulysses could tell that the shortest route to the church was directly across the fields rather than by way of the road, so that's the way he went, running as the crow would fly. It didn't take long for him to realize that this was a mistake. Though the corn was only a foot and a half high and the farmer's rows were wide and well kept, the ground itself was soft and uneven, making for cumbersome work. Given all the fields he'd slogged across in Italy, he should have known better. But it seemed too late to switch back to the road now, so with his eye on the steeple he pressed ahead as best he could.

When he was halfway to the church, the twister appeared in the distance at two o'clock, a dark black finger reaching down from the sky—the inversion of the steeple both in color and intent.

With every step now, Ulysses's progress was slowing. There was so much debris kicking up from the ground that he had to advance with a hand in front of his face to protect his eyes. Then he was holding up both hands with his gaze partly averted, as he stumbled onward toward the upward and downward spires.

Through the gaps in his fingers and the veil of the unsettled dust, Ulysses became aware of rectangular shadows rising from the ground around him, shadows that looked at once orderly and in disarray. Dropping his hands for a second, he realized he had entered a graveyard and he could hear the bell in the steeple beginning to toll, as if rung by an invisible hand. He couldn't have been more than fifty yards from the church.

But in all likelihood, it was fifty yards too far.

For the twister was turning counterclockwise and its winds were pushing Ulysses away from his goal rather than toward it. As hail began raining down upon him, he prepared for one final push. *I can make it,* he told himself. Then running with all his might, he began closing the distance between himself and the sanctuary—only to stumble over a low-lying gravestone and come crashing to the ground with the bitter resignation of the abandoned.

—Abandoned by who? asked Billy, with his book gripped in his lap and his eyes open wide.

Ulysses smiled.

—I don't know, Billy. By fortune, by fate, by my own good sense. But mostly by God.

The boy began shaking his head.

—You don't mean that, Ulysses. You don't mean that you were abandoned by God.

—But that's exactly what I mean, Billy. If I learned anything in the war, it's that the point of utter abandonment—that moment at which you realize no one will be coming to your aid, not even your Maker— is the very moment in which you may discover the strength required to carry on. The Good Lord does not call you to your feet with hymns from the cherubim and Gabriel blowing his horn. He calls you to your feet by making you feel alone and forgotten. For only when you have seen that you are *truly* forsaken will you embrace the fact that what happens next rests in your hands, and your hands alone.

Lying on the ground of that graveyard, feeling the old abandonment and knowing it for what it was, Ulysses reached up and took hold of the top of the nearest gravestone. As he hoisted himself upward, he realized the stone he was pushing on was not weathered or worn. Even through the maelstrom of dust and debris he could see it had the dark gray luminescence of a stone that had just been planted. Rising to his full height, Ulysses found himself looking over the shoulders of the marker down into a freshly dug grave, at the bottom of which was the shiny black top of a casket.

This is where the caravan of cars had been coming from, realized Ulysses. They must have been right in the middle of the interment when they received warning of the tornado's approach. The reverend must have hurried through whatever verses would suffice to commit the soul of the deceased to Heaven, and then everyone had dashed for their cars.

From the look of the coffin, it must have been for a man of some wealth. For this was no pine box. It was polished mahogany with handles of solid brass. On the lid of the coffin was a matching brass plaque with the dead man's name: Noah Benjamin Elias.

Sliding down into the narrow gap between the coffin and the wall of the grave, Ulysses bent over to unscrew the clasps and open the coffin's lid. Inside was Mr. Elias lying in state, dressed in a three-piece suit with his hands crossed neatly on his chest. His shoes were as black and shiny as his coffin, and curving across his vest was the thin gold chain of a watch. Though only about five foot six, Mr. Elias must have weighed over two hundred pounds—having dined in a manner suited to his station.

What was the nature of Mr. Elias's earthly success? Was he the owner of a bank or lumberyard? Was he a man of grit and determination, or of greed and deceit? Whichever he was, he was no longer. And all that mattered to Ulysses was that this man who was only five foot six had had a big enough sense of himself to be buried in a coffin that was six feet long.

Reaching down, Ulysses took hold of Elias by the lapels, just as you would when you intended to shake some sense into someone. Pulling him up out of the coffin, Ulysses hoisted him into a standing position so that they were almost face-to-face. Ulysses could see now that the mortician had applied rouge on the dead man's cheeks and scented him with gardenia, giving him the unsettling semblance of a harlot. Bending his knees in order to get under the weight of the cadaver, Ulysses raised him up out of his resting place and dumped him at the side of the grave.

Taking one last look at the great black finger that was swaying left and right as it bore down upon him, Ulysses lay back in the pleated white silk that lined the empty coffin, reached up a hand, and—

Pastor John

W HEN THE VENGEANCE OF the Lord is visited upon us, it does not rain down from the heavens like a shower of meteors trailing fire. It does not strike like a bolt of lightning accompanied by claps of thunder. It does not gather like a tidal wave far out at sea and come crashing down upon the shores. No. When the vengeance of the Lord is visited upon us, it begins as a breath in the desert.

Gentle and undaunting, this little expiration turns three times above the hardened ground, quietly stirring the dust and the scent of the sagebrush. But as it turns three times more, and three times again, this little whirlwind grows to the size of a man and begins to move. Spiraling across the land it gains in velocity and volume, growing to the size of a colossus, swaying and sweeping up into its vortex all that lays within its path—first the sand and stones, the shrubs and varmints, and then the works of men. Until at long last, towering a hundred feet tall and moving at a hundred miles an hour, swirling and spinning, turning and twisting, it comes inexorably for the sinner.

Thus concluded the thoughts of Pastor John as he stepped from the darkness and swung his oaken staff in order to smite the Negro called Ulysses on the crown of his head.

—·—

Left for dead. That's what Pastor John had been. With the tendons of his right knee torn, the skin of his cheeks abraded, his right eye swollen shut, he lay among the bushes and brambles preparing to deliver his own absolution. But at the very moment of his demise, the Lord had found him by the side of the tracks and breathed new life into his limbs. Lifting him up from the gravel and scrub, He had carried him to the edge of a cool running stream, where his thirst was slaked, his wounds washed, and into his hands delivered the branch of an ancient oak to be used as a staff.

In the hours that followed, not once did Pastor John wonder where he was going, how he would get there, or to what end—for he could feel the Spirit of the Lord working through him, making of him Its instrument. From the riverbank, It led him back through the woods to a siding where ten empty boxcars had been left unattended. Once he was safely inside, It brought forth a locomotive that hitched the cars and carried him eastward to the city of New York.

When Pastor John disembarked in the great railyard situated between Pennsylvania Station and the Hudson River, the Spirit shielded him from the eyes of the railway guards and led him not into the crowded streets but up onto the tracks of an elevated line. With his weight on his staff in order to spare his knee, Pastor John moved along the elevated, casting his shadow down upon the avenues. Once the sun had set, the Spirit led him onward—through an empty warehouse, through a gap in a fence, through the high and scraggly grass, through the darkness itself, until in the distance he could see a campfire shining like a star.

Drawing closer, Pastor John saw that in His infinite wisdom the Good Lord had lit the fire not only to guide him, but to illuminate the faces of the Negro and the boy—even as it made Pastor John's presence invisible to them. In the shadows outside the circle of the fire, Pastor John stopped and listened as the boy finished a story and asked if the Negro would tell one of his own.

Oh, how John had laughed to hear Ulysses rattle on about his frightful tornado. For that little twister was nothing compared to the widening gyre which is the vengeance of the Lord. Did he seriously think that he could throw a pastor from a moving train without fear of retribution? That his actions would somehow escape the eyes of the Divine and the hand of judgment?

The Lord God is all-seeing and all-knowing, Pastor John said without speaking. *He has paid witness to your misdeeds, Ulysses. He has paid witness to your arrogance and trespass. And He has brought me here to deliver His reprisal!*

With such fury did the Spirit of the Lord breathe into the limbs of Pastor John, when he brought his oaken staff down upon the Negro's head, the force of the blow snapped the staff in two.

When Ulysses slumped to the ground and Pastor John stepped into the light, the boy, complicit with the Negro at every step, stretched out his hands in the silent horror of the damned.

—May I join you by your fire? asked the pastor with a loud and hearty laugh.

His staff truncated, Pastor John was forced to limp toward the boy, but this didn't worry him. For he knew the boy would go nowhere and say nothing. Rather, he would withdraw into himself like a snail into its shell. Sure enough, when Pastor John pulled him up by the collar of his shirt, he could see that the boy had clenched his eyes closed and begun his incantation.

—There is no Emmett here, said the pastor. No one is coming to your aid, William Watson.

Then with the boy's collar fast in his grip, Pastor John raised the broken staff and prepared to deliver that lesson which Ulysses had interrupted two days before. To deliver it with interest!

But just when the staff was poised to fall, the boy opened his eyes.

—I am truly forsaken, he said with a mysterious gusto.

Then he kicked the pastor in his injured knee.

With an animal howl, Pastor John let loose the boy's shirt and dropped his staff. Hopping in place with tears of pain falling from his one good eye, Pastor John became more committed in his intent to teach the boy a lesson he wouldn't soon forget. But even as he thrust his hands outward, he could see through his tears that the boy was gone.

Eager to pursue, Pastor John looked frantically about for something to replace his broken staff.

—Aha! he shouted.

For there on the ground was a shovel. Picking it up, Pastor John stuck the blade into the dirt, leaned on the handle, and began moving slowly toward the darkness into which the boy had disappeared.

After a few steps, he could just make out the silhouettes of an encampment: a small pile of firewood covered with a tarp, a makeshift washstand, a line of three empty bedrolls, and a tent.

—William, he called softly. Where are you, William?

—What's going on out there, came a voice from inside the tent.

Holding his breath, Pastor John took a step to the side and waited as a stocky Negro emerged. Not seeing the pastor, he walked a few feet forward and stopped.

—Ulysses? he asked.

When Pastor John hit him with the flat of the shovel, he fell to the ground with a groan.

Off to his left Pastor John could hear other voices now. The voices of two men who may have heard the commotion.

—Forget the boy, he said to himself.

Using the shovel as his crutch, he hobbled as quickly as he could back to the campfire and made his way to where the boy had been sitting. There on the ground were the book and flashlight. But where was that damnable rucksack?

Pastor John looked back in the direction from which he had just come. Could it have been by the bedrolls? No. Where the book and the flashlight were, the rucksack was sure to be. Leaning over carefully, Pastor John dropped the shovel, picked up the flashlight, and switched it on. With a hop, he trained the beam onto the back side of the railroad ties and began moving from right to left.

There it is!

Sitting down on a tie with his injured leg stretched before him, Pastor John retrieved the rucksack and set it in his lap. Even as he did so, he could hear the music within.

With growing excitement, he undid the straps and began withdrawing items and tossing them aside. Two shirts. A pair of pants. A washcloth. At the very bottom he found the tin. Liberating it from the bag, he gave it a celebratory shake.

Tomorrow morning, he would pay a visit to the Jews on Forty-Seventh Street. In the afternoon, he would go to a department store for a new set of clothes. And tomorrow night, he would check into a fine hotel, where he would take a long, hot bath and send out for oysters, a bottle of wine, perhaps even some female companionship. But now, it was time to leave. Returning the flashlight and tin to the rucksack, he cinched its straps and hooked it over his shoulder. Ready at last to be on his way, Pastor John leaned to his left in order to pick up the shovel, only to find that it was no longer where he had—

Ulysses

FIRST THERE WAS DARKNESS without recognition. Then slowly, an awareness of it. An awareness that it wasn't the darkness of space—cold, vast, and remote. It was a darkness that was close and warm, a darkness that was covering him, embracing him in the manner of a velvet shroud.

Creeping from the corners of his memory came the realization that he was still in the fat man's coffin. He could feel along his shoulders the smooth, pleated silk of the lining and, behind that, the sturdiness of the mahogany frame.

He wanted to raise the lid, but how much time had passed? Was the tornado gone? Holding his breath, he listened. He listened through the pleated silk and polished mahogany and heard nothing. Not the sound of the wind whistling, or of hail falling on the coffin lid, or of the church bell swinging on its hook unattended. In order to be certain, he decided to open the coffin a crack. Turning his palms upward, he pressed at the lid, but the lid wouldn't budge.

Was it possible that he had become weakened with hunger and fatigue? Surely, not that much time had passed. Or had it? Suddenly, it occurred to him with a touch of horror that in the aftermath of the storm, while he was unconscious, someone might have happened upon the open grave and shoveled the mound of topsoil onto the coffin, finishing the job.

He would have to try again. After rolling his shoulders and flexing his fingers in order to restore the circulation to his limbs, he drew a breath, put his palms again against the inner surface of the lid, and pushed with all his might as the sweat that formed on his brow ran in droplets into his eyes. Slowly, the lid began to open, and cooler air rushed into the coffin. With a sense of relief, Ulysses gathered his strength and pushed the lid all the way back, expecting to be gazing up into the afternoon sky.

But it wasn't the afternoon.

It looked to be the middle of the night.

Raising a hand gently in the air, he saw that his skin reflected a flickering light. Listening, he heard the long, hollow horn of a ship and the laughter of a gull, as if he were somewhere at sea. But then, coming from a short distance, he heard a voice. The voice of a boy declaring his forsakenness. The voice of Billy Watson.

And suddenly, Ulysses knew where he was.

An instant later, he heard a grown man howling in anger or in pain. And though Ulysses didn't yet understand what had happened to himself, he knew what he must do.

Having rolled onto his side, with a great sluggish effort he raised himself onto his knees. Wiping the sweat from his eyes, he discovered by the light of the fire that it was blood, not sweat. Someone had hit him on the head.

Rising to his feet, Ulysses looked around the fire for Billy and for the man who had howled, but no one was there. He wanted to call out for Billy, but understood that to do so would signal to an unknown enemy that he had regained consciousness.

He needed to get away from the fire, outside of the circle of light. Under the veil of darkness, he would be able to gather his wits and strength, find Billy, and then begin the process of hunting his adversary down.

Stepping over one of the railroad ties, he walked five paces into the darkness and took his bearings. There was the river, he thought, turning on his feet; there was the Empire State Building; and there was their encampment. As he looked in the direction of Stew's tent he thought he saw movement. Quietly, almost too softly to hear, came the voice of a man calling Billy, calling him by his given name. The man's voice may have been almost too soft to hear, but it wasn't too soft to recognize.

While remaining in the darkness, Ulysses began circumventing the fire moving carefully, quietly, inevitably toward the preacher.

Ulysses stopped short when he heard Stew call his name. A moment later he heard the clang of metal and the thud of a body falling to the ground. Feeling a flash of anger with himself for being too cautious, Ulysses prepared to charge into the encampment when he saw a silhouette emerge from the darkness, moving unevenly.

It was the preacher using Stew's shovel as a crutch. Dropping the shovel on the ground, he picked up the boy's flashlight, switched it on, and began searching for something.

Keeping an eye on the preacher, Ulysses crept to the edge of the fire, reached over a railroad tie, and retrieved the shovel. When the preacher gave an exclamation of discovery, Ulysses stepped back into the darkness and watched as he picked up Billy's knapsack and sat with it in his lap.

In an excited voice, the preacher began talking to himself about hotels and oysters and female companionship while withdrawing Billy's belongings and tossing them on the ground—until he found the tin of dollars. At the same time, Ulysses began moving forward until he was directly behind the preacher. And when the preacher, having slung the knapsack over his shoulder, leaned to his left, Ulysses brought the shovel down.

With the preacher now lying in a heap at his feet, Ulysses felt himself heaving. Given his own injury, the effort to subdue the preacher had taken all his immediate strength. Worried that he might even faint, Ulysses stabbed the shovel into the ground and leaned on its hilt as he looked down to make certain the preacher was unmoving.

—Is he dead?

It was Billy, standing at his side looking down at the preacher too.

—No, said Ulysses.

Astoundingly, the boy seemed relieved.

—Are you all right? asked Billy.

—Yes, said Ulysses. Are you?

Billy nodded.

—I did like you said, Ulysses. When Pastor John told me that I was alone, I imagined that I had been forsaken by everyone, including my Maker. Then I kicked him and hid beneath the firewood tarp.

Ulysses smiled.

—You did well, Billy.

—What the hell is going on?

Billy and Ulysses looked up to find Stew standing behind them with a butcher knife in hand.

—You're bleeding too, Billy said with concern.

Stew had been hit on the side of the head so the blood had run down from his ear onto the shoulder of his undershirt.

Ulysses was suddenly feeling better now, more clearheaded and sure of foot.

—Billy, he said, why don't you go over there and fetch us the basin of water and some towels.

Sticking his knife through his belt, Stew came alongside Ulysses and looked at the ground.

—Who is it?

—A man of ill intent, said Ulysses.

Stew shifted his gaze to Ulysses's head.

—You better let me take a look at that.

—I've had worse.

—We've all had worse.

—I'll be all right.

—I know, I know, said Stew with a shake of the head. You're a big, big man.

Billy arrived with the basin and towels. The two men cleaned their faces and then gingerly dabbed at their wounds. When they were done, Ulysses sat Billy down beside him on one of the railroad ties.

—Billy, he began, we've had quite a bit of excitement tonight.

Billy nodded in agreement.

—Yes, we have, Ulysses. Emmett will hardly believe it.

—Well, that's just what I wanted to talk to you about. What with your brother trying to find his car and having to get you to California before the Fourth of July, he's got a lot on his mind. Maybe it's for the best if we keep what happened here tonight between us. At least for now.

Billy was nodding.

—It's probably for the best, he said. Emmett has a lot on his mind.

Ulysses patted Billy on the knee.

—One day, he said, you will tell him. You will tell him and your children too, about how you bested the preacher, just like one of the heroes in your book.

When Ulysses saw that Billy understood, he got up in order to speak with Stew.

—Can you take the boy back to your tent? Maybe give him something to eat?

—All right. But what are you going to do?

—I'm going to see to the preacher.

Billy, who had been listening behind Ulysses's back, stepped around him with a look of concern.

—What does that mean, Ulysses? What does that mean that you're going to see to the preacher?

Ulysses and Stew looked from the boy to each other and back again.

—We can't leave him here, explained Ulysses. He's going to come to just like I did. And whatever villainy had been on his mind before I crowned him is going to be there still. Only more so.

Billy was looking up at Ulysses with a furrowed brow.

—So, continued Ulysses, I'm going to take him down the stairs and drop him—

—At the police station?

—That's right, Billy. I'm going to drop him at the police station.

Billy nodded to indicate that this was the right thing to do. Then Stew turned to Ulysses.

—You know the stairs that go down to Gansevoort?

—I do.

—Someone's bent back the fencing there. It'll be an easier route, given what you'll be carrying.

Thanking Stew, Ulysses waited for Billy to gather his things, for Stew to put out the fire, and for the two to go back to Stew's tent before he turned his attention to the preacher.

Taking him under the armpits, Ulysses raised him up and draped him over his shoulders. The preacher wasn't heavier than Ulysses had expected, but he was gangly, making him an awkward burden. Shifting the body back and forth by increments, Ulysses tried to center it before he began walking in short, steady strides.

When he reached the staircase, if Ulysses had stopped to think, he might have rolled the preacher down the steps to preserve his own strength. But he was moving now, and he had the preacher's weight evenly distributed across his shoulders, and he was worried that if he stopped he might lose his balance or his momentum. And he would need them both. Because from the bottom of the stairs, it was a good two hundred yards to the river.

Duchess

WOOLLY'S SISTER CAME INTO the kitchen like a ghost. Appearing in the doorway in her long white robe and crossing the unlit room without a sound, it was like her feet didn't touch the floor. But if she was a ghost, she wasn't the harrowing sort—one of those that howl and moan and send shivers down your spine. She was the forlorn sort. The kind of ghost who wanders the halls of an empty house for generations, in search of something or someone that no one else can even remember. A visitation, I think they call it.

Yeah, that's it.

A visitation.

Without switching on the light, she filled the kettle and turned on the burner. From the cabinet she took out a mug and a tea bag and set them on the counter. From the pocket of her robe, she took out a little brown bottle and set it beside the mug. Then she went back to the sink and stood there looking out the window.

You got the sense that she was good at looking out the window—like maybe she'd gotten a lot of practice. She didn't fidget or tap her feet. In fact, she was so good at it, so good at getting lost in her thoughts, that when the kettle whistled it seemed to catch her by surprise, as if she couldn't remember having turned it on in the first place. Slowly, almost reluctantly, she left her spot at the window, poured the water, picked up the mug in one hand and the little brown bottle in the other, and turned toward the table.

—Trouble sleeping? I asked.

Caught off guard, she didn't cry out or drop her tea. She just gave the same little expression of surprise that she had given when the kettle whistled.

—I didn't see you there, she said, slipping the little brown bottle back in the pocket of her robe.

She hadn't answered my question about whether she had trouble sleeping, but she didn't need to. Every aspect of the way she moved in the dark—crossing the room, filling the pot, lighting the stove—suggested this was something of a routine. It wouldn't have surprised me in the least to learn that every other night she came down to the kitchen at two in the morning while her husband slept soundly, none the wiser.

Gesturing back toward the stove, she asked if I'd like some tea. I pointed to the glass in front of me.

—I found a little whiskey in the living room. I hope you don't mind.

She smiled softly.

—Of course not.

After taking the seat opposite mine, she trained her gaze on my left eye.

—How does it feel?

—Much better, thanks.

I had left Harlem in such high spirits that when I got back to Woolly's sister's house, I'd completely forgotten the beating I'd taken. When she answered the door and gasped, I practically gasped back.

But once Woolly had made the introductions and I had explained the spill I'd taken in the train station, she got a cute little first aid kit out of her medicine cabinet, sat me here at the kitchen table, cleaned the blood off my lip, and gave me a bag of frozen peas to hold over my eye. I would have preferred using a raw steak like a heavyweight champ, but beggars can't be choosers.

—Would you like another aspirin? she asked.

—No, I'll be all right.

We were both quiet for a moment as I took a sip of her husband's whiskey and she took a sip of her tea.

—You're Woolly's bunkmate . . . ?

—That's right.

—So, was it your father who was on the stage?

—He was under it as often as he was on it, I said with a smile. But yeah, that's my old man. He started out as a Shakespearean and ended up doing vaudeville.

She smiled at the word *vaudeville*.

—Woolly has written to me about some of the performers your father worked with. The escape artists and magicians . . . He was quite taken with them.

—Your brother loves a good bedtime story.

—Yes, he does, doesn't he.

She looked across the table as if she wanted to ask me something, but then shifted her gaze to her tea.

—What? I prompted.

—It was a personal question.

—Those are the best kind.

She studied me for a moment, trying to gauge whether or not I was being sincere. She must have decided I was.

—How did you end up at Salina, Duchess?

—Oh, that's a long one.

—I've barely started my tea. . . .

So, having poured myself another finger of whiskey, I recounted my little comedy, thinking: Maybe everyone in Woolly's family liked a good bedtime tale.

It was in the spring of 1952, just a few weeks after my sixteenth birthday, and we were living in room 42 at the Sunshine Hotel, with pops on the bedsprings and me on the floor.

At the time, my old man was what he liked to call *betwixt and between*, which just meant that having gotten fired from one job, he had yet to find the next job to get fired from. He was spending his days with his old pal, Fitzy, who was living across the hall. In the early afternoons, they would shuffle off to scour around the park benches, fruit carts, newsstands, and any other spots where someone was likely to drop a nickel and not bother to pick it back up. Then they would head down into the subways and sing sentimental songs with their hats in their hands. Men who knew their audience, they would perform "Danny Boy" for the Irish on the Third Avenue line and "Ave Maria" for the Italians at Spring Street station, crying their eyes out like they meant every word. They even had a Yiddish number about the days in the shtetl that they'd roll out when they were on the platform of the Canal Street stop. Then in the evenings—after giving me two bits and sending me off to a double feature—they would take their hard-earned pay to a dive on Elizabeth Street and drink every last penny of it.

Since the two of them didn't get up until noon, when I woke in the morning I would wander the hotel looking for something to eat or someone to talk to. At that hour, it was pretty slim pickings, but there were a handful of early risers, and the best of them, without a doubt, was Marceline Maupassant.

Back in the twenties, Marceline had been one of the most famous clowns in Europe, performing for sold-out runs in Paris and Berlin, complete with standing ovations and lines of women waiting at the backstage door. To be sure, Marceline was no ordinary clown. He wasn't a guy who painted his face and tromped around in oversize shoes honking a horn. He was the real McCoy. A poet and a dancer. A man who observed the world closely and felt things deeply—like Chaplin and Keaton.

One of his greatest bits was as a panhandler on a bustling city street. When the curtain came up, there he would be, navigating a crowd of metropolitans. With a little bow, he would try to get the attention of two men arguing over headlines by the newsstand; with a doff of his crooked hat, he would try to address a nanny whose mind was on the colicky baby in her care. Whether with a doff or a bow, everyone he tried to engage would go on about their business as if he weren't even there. Then when Marceline was about to approach a shy young woman with a downcast expression, a nearsighted scholar would bump into him, knocking his hat from his head.

Off in pursuit of the hat Marceline would go. But each time he was about to grab it, a distracted pedestrian would send it skidding in the other direction. After making several attempts at retrieval, to his utter dismay Marceline would realize that a rotund police officer was about to step on the hat unawares. With no other choice, Marceline would raise a hand in the air, snap his fingers—and everyone would be frozen in place. Everyone, that is, except Marceline.

Now the magic would happen.

For a few minutes, Marceline would glide about the stage, skating in between the immobile pedestrians with a delicate smile, as if he hadn't a care in the world. Then taking a long-stemmed rose from the flower vendor, he would present it shyly to the downcast young woman. He would interject a point or two to the men who were arguing by the newsstand. He would make faces for the baby in the pram. He would laugh and comment and counsel, all without making a sound.

But as Marceline was about to make another circuit through the crowd, he would hear a delicate chiming. Stopping at center stage, he would reach into his shabby vest and remove a solid gold pocket watch, clearly a vestige from another time in his life. Popping the lid, he would regard the hour and realize with a doleful look that his little game had gone on long enough. Putting the watch away, he would carefully take his crooked hat from under the fat policeman's foot—which had been hovering in the air for all this time, a feat of gymnastics in itself. Brushing it off, he would place it on his head, face the audience, snap his fingers, and all the activities of his fellow men would resume.

It was an act worth seeing more than once. Because the first time you saw the show, when Marceline snapped his fingers at the end, it would seem like the world had gone right back to the way it was. But the second or third time you saw it, you might begin to realize that the world wasn't *exactly* the way it was. As the shy young woman is walking away, she smiles to discover the long-stemmed rose in her hands. The two men debating by the newsstand pause in their arguments, suddenly less sure of their positions. The nanny who was trying so diligently to appease her crying charge is startled to find him giggling. If you went to see Marceline's performance more than once, all of this you might notice in the seconds before the curtain came down.

In the fall of 1929, at the height of his fame in Europe, Marceline was lured to New York by the promise of a six-figure contract for a six-month residency at the Hippodrome. With all the enthusiasm of an artist, he packed his bags for an extended stay in the Land of the Free. But as it so happened, the very moment that he was boarding his steamship in Bremen, the stock market on Wall Street had begun its precipitous plunge.

By the time he disembarked on the West Side piers, his American producers had been ruined, the Hippodrome was closed, and his contract was canceled. A telegram waiting for him at his hotel from his bankers in Paris informed him that he too had lost everything in the crash, leaving not even enough for a safe passage home. And when he knocked on the doors of other producers, he discovered that despite his fame in Europe, virtually no one in America knew who he was.

Now what had been knocked from Marceline's head was his self-esteem. And every time he leaned over to pick it back up, a passing pedestrian would kick it out of reach. Off in pursuit of it he went, from one sorry spot to the next, until at long last he found himself performing pantomimes on street corners and living in the Sunshine Hotel—right down the hall, in room 49.

Naturally enough, Marceline became a drinker. But not in the fashion of Fitzy and my old man. He wouldn't go to some dive where he could relive old glories and air old complaints. In the evenings, he'd buy a bottle of cheap red wine and drink it alone in his room with the door closed, refilling his glass in a smooth, elaborate motion, as if it were part of the act.

But in the mornings, he would leave his door ajar. And when I gave it a tap, he would welcome me with a doff of the hat that he no longer owned. Sometimes, if he had a little money on hand, he would send me out for milk, flour, and eggs and cook us tiny little crepes on the bottom of an electric iron. And as we ate our breakfast sitting on his floor, rather than talk about his past he would ask about my future—about all the places I would go, and all the things I would do. It was a grand old way to start the day.

Then one morning when I went down the hall, his door wasn't ajar. And when I tapped, there wasn't an answer. Placing an ear against the wood, I heard the slightest creaking, like someone turning on the bedsprings. Worried he might be sick, I opened the door a crack.

—Mr. Marceline? I said.

When he didn't reply, I opened the door the rest of the way, only to find that the bed hadn't been slept in, the desk chair was toppled over in the middle of the room, and Marceline was hanging from the ceiling fan.

The creaking, you see, hadn't come from the bedsprings. It had come from the weight of his body turning slowly back and forth.

When I woke my father and brought him to the room, he simply nodded his head as if it were what he had expected all along. Then he sent me down to the front desk to have them call the authorities.

Half an hour later there were three policemen in the room—two patrolmen and a detective taking statements from me and my father and the neighboring tenants who'd come poking their heads through the door.

—Was he robbed? one of the tenants asked.

By way of response, a patrolman gestured to Marceline's desk, where the contents of his pockets had been laid out, including a five-dollar bill and some change.

—Then where's the watch?

—What watch? asked the detective.

Everyone began talking at once—explaining about the solid gold pocket watch that had been so central to the old clown's act that he had never been willing to part with it, not even when he was broke.

After looking at the patrolmen, who shook their heads, the detective looked at my father. Then my father looked at me.

—Now, Duchess, he said, placing an arm over my shoulder, this is very important. I'm going to ask you a question, and I want you to tell me the truth. When you found Marceline, did you see his watch?

Silently, I shook my head.

—Maybe you found it on the floor, he suggested helpfully. And you picked it up, so it wouldn't get broken.

—No, I said with another shake of the head. I never saw his watch.

Patting me on the shoulder almost sympathetically, my father turned to the detective and gave the shrug of one who's tried his best.

—Search them, said the detective.

Imagine my surprise when the patrolman asked me to turn out my pockets and there, among the gum wrappers, was a golden watch on a long, golden chain.

Imagine my surprise, I say, because I was surprised. Stunned. Astounded even. For all of two seconds.

After that, it was plain as day what had happened. My old man had sent me downstairs to the front desk so that he could frisk the body. And when the watch was mentioned by the meddlesome neighbor, my father had draped his arm over my shoulder and given his little speech so that he could slip it into my pocket before he was patted down.

—Oh, Duchess, he said with such disappointment.

Within the hour, I was at the police station. As a minor committing his first offense, I was a good candidate for being released into my father's care. But given the value of the old clown's watch, the crime wasn't petty theft. It was grand larceny. To make matters worse, there had been reports of a few other thefts at the Sunshine Hotel, and Fitzy claimed in a sworn statement that he had seen me coming out of one or two rooms in which I didn't belong. As if that weren't enough, the people from child services discovered—to my father's utter shock—that I hadn't been to school in five years. When I appeared before the juvenile judge, my father was forced to admit that as a hardworking widower he was not in a position to protect me from the malevolent influences of the Bowery. For my own good, all agreed, I should be placed in a juvenile reform program until the age of eighteen.

When the judge delivered his decision, my father asked if he could offer a few words of advice to his wayward son before I was carted away. The judge acquiesced, probably assuming that my father would take me aside and be quick about it. Instead, my old man stuck his thumbs under his suspenders, puffed out his chest, and addressed the judge, the bailiff, the peanut gallery, and the stenographer. Especially the stenographer!

—As we part, my son, he said to one and all, my blessing goes with thee. But in my absence carry with you these few precepts: Be thou familiar, but by no means vulgar. Give every man thy ear, but few thy voice. Take each man's censure, but reserve thy judgment. And this above all: to thine own self be true. For then it must follow, as night follows day, that thou cannot be false to any man. Farewell, my son, he concluded. Farewell.

And as they led me from the room, he actually shed a tear, the old fox.

—How terrible, said Sarah.

And I could see from her face that she meant it. Her expression had suggestions of sympathy, indignation, and protectiveness. You could just tell that whether or not she became happy in her own life, she was bound to be a wonderful mother.

—It's okay, I said, trying to ease her distress. Salina wasn't all that bad. I got three meals a day and a mattress. And if I hadn't gone there, I never would have met your brother.

When I followed Sarah to the sink to clean my empty glass, she thanked me and smiled in her generous way. Then she wished me good night and turned to go.

—Sister Sarah, I said.

When she turned back, she raised her eyebrows in inquiry. Then she watched with that same muted surprise as I reached into the pocket of her robe and removed the little brown bottle.

—Trust me, I said. These won't do you any good.

And when she walked out of the kitchen, I stuck the bottle in the bottom of the spice rack, feeling like I'd done my second good deed of the day.

FOUR

Woolly

O N FRIDAY AT HALF PAST ONE, Woolly was standing in his absolute
favorite spot in the store. And that was really saying something!
Because at FAO Schwarz, there were so many wonderful spots to stand
in. Why, to get to this spot, he had to pass through the collection of
giant stuffed animals—including the tiger with the hypnotizing eyes,
and the life-size giraffe whose head nearly hit the ceiling. He had to
pass through motorsports, where two boys were racing little Ferraris
around a figure-eight track. And at the top of the escalator, he had to
pass through the magic set area where a magician was making the jack
of diamonds disappear. But even with all of that to see, there was
nowhere in the store that made Woolly quite as happy as the big glass
case with the dollhouse furniture.

Twenty feet long with eight glass shelves, it was even bigger than
the trophy case in the gym at St. George's, and it was filled from
bottom to top and side to side with perfect little replicas. On the left
side of the case was a whole section dedicated to Chippendale
furniture—with Chippendale highboys and Chippendale desks and a
dining-room set with twelve Chippendale chairs neatly arranged
around a Chippendale table. The table was just like the one that his
family used to have in the dining room of their brownstone on Eighty-
Sixth Street. Naturally, they didn't eat at the Chippendale every day.
It was reserved for special occasions like birthdays and holidays, when
they would set the table with the best china and light all the candles

in the candelabra. At least, that is, until Woolly's father died; and his mother remarried, moved to Palm Beach, and donated the table to the Women's Exchange.

Boy, had his sister Kaitlin gotten mad about that!

How could you, she had said to their mother (or sort of shouted) when the moving men appeared to pick up the set. *That was Great-grandma's!*

Oh, Kaitlin, replied his mother. *What could you possibly want with a table like that? Some fusty old thing that seats a dozen people. No one even* gives *dinner parties anymore. Isn't that right, Woolly.*

At the time, Woolly hadn't known whether people gave dinner parties or not. He still didn't know. So he hadn't said anything. But his sister had said something. She had said it to him as the moving men carried the Chippendale out the door.

Take a good hard look, Woolly, she said. *Because you'll never see a table like that again.*

So he had taken a good hard look.

But as it turned out, Kaitlin had been wrong. For Woolly had seen a table like that again. He had seen it right here in the display case at FAO Schwarz.

The furniture in the display case was arranged chronologically. So as you moved from left to right you could travel all the way from the Court of Versailles to a living room in a modern-day apartment, with a phonograph, and a cocktail table, and a pair of Mies van der Rohe chairs.

Woolly understood that Mr. Chippendale and Mr. van der Rohe were held in the highest esteem for the designs of their chairs. But it seemed to him that the men who made these perfect little replicas deserved at least as much esteem, if not more. For to make a Chippendale or van der Rohe chair in such tiny dimensions surely had to be harder than to make one you could sit on.

But Woolly's favorite part of the case was all the way over to the right, where there was a series of kitchens. At the top there was what

was called the Prairie Kitchen, with a simple wooden table and a butter churn and a cast-iron frying pan on a cast-iron stove. Next came
the Victorian Kitchen. You could tell this was the sort of kitchen in
which a cook did the cooking because there was no table or chairs at
which to sit and eat your supper. Instead, there was a long, wooden
island over which hung six copper pots in descending order of size.
And finally, there was the Kitchen of Today, with all the wonders of
the modern era. In addition to a bright white stove and a bright white
refrigerator, there was a table for four with a red Formica top and four
chrome chairs with red vinyl seats. There was a KitchenAid mixer,
and a toaster with a little black lever and two little pieces of toast.
And in the cabinet over the counter, you could see all the little boxes
of cereal and the tiny cans of soup.

—I knew I'd find you here.

Woolly turned to discover his sister standing at his side.

—How did you know? he asked in surprise.

—How did I know! repeated Sarah with a laugh.

And Woolly laughed too. Because, of course, of course, he knew
exactly how she knew.

When they were younger, every December Grandma Wolcott would
take them to FAO Schwarz so that they could each pick out their own
Christmas present. One year, as the family was getting ready to leave
with all of their coats buttoned and all of the big red bags filled to the
limit, they realized that in the midst of the holiday bustle, young Woolly
had somehow gone missing. Members of the family were dispatched to
every floor, calling out his name, until Sarah finally found him here.

—How old were we then?

She shook her head.

—I don't know. It was the year before Grandma died, so I suppose
I was fourteen and you were seven.

Woolly shook his head.

—That was so hard. Wasn't it?

—What was so hard?

—Choosing a Christmas present—from here of all places!

Woolly waved his arms about in order to encompass all of the giraffes, Ferraris, and magic sets in the building.

—Yes, she said. It was very hard to choose. But especially for you.

Woolly nodded.

—And then after, he said, after we had picked out our presents and Grandma had sent the bags home with the driver, she would take us to the Plaza for tea. Do you remember?

—I remember.

—We would sit in that big room with the palm trees. And they would bring those towers with the little watercress and cucumber and salmon sandwiches on the lower levels, and the little lemon tarts and chocolate eclairs on top. And Grandma would make us eat our sandwiches before we ate the cakes.

—*You have to climb your way to heaven.*

Woolly laughed.

—Yes, that was it. That's what Grandma used to say.

As Woolly and Sarah came off the escalator onto the ground floor, Woolly was explaining his brand-new notion that the dollhouse-chair makers deserved just as much regard, if not more, than Mr. Chippendale and Mr. van der Rohe. But as they were approaching the front door, someone was shouting urgently behind them.

—Excuse me! Excuse me, sir!

When Woolly and his sister looked back to see the source of the commotion, they discovered that a man with a very managerial appearance was chasing after them with a hand in the air.

—Just a moment, sir, the man called as he worked his way definitively in Woolly's direction.

Intending to wear an expression of comic surprise, Woolly turned to his sister. But she was still watching the man approach with a slight hint of dread. A slight but heartbreaking hint.

Reaching them, the man paused to catch his breath, then addressed Woolly.

—I apologize most sincerely for the shouting. But you've forgotten your bear.

Woolly's eyes opened wide.

—The bear!

He turned to his sister, who looked at once mystified and relieved.

—I'd forgotten the bear, he said with a smile.

A young woman who had been trailing after the manager now appeared, holding a panda that was almost as big as she was.

—Thank you both, said Woolly, taking the bear in his arms. Thank you ten times over.

As the two employees returned to their stations, Sarah turned to Woolly.

—You bought a giant panda?

—It's for the baby!

—Woolly, she said with a smile and a shake of the head.

—I considered the grizzly and polar bears, Woolly explained, but they both seemed a little too fierce.

By way of illustration, Woolly would have liked to raise his claws and bare his teeth, but his arms were too full of the panda.

His arms were so full of the panda that he couldn't get through the revolving door. So the man in the bright red uniform, who always stands guard at the entrance of FAO Schwarz, leapt into action.

—Allow me, he said gallantly.

Then he opened the unrevolving door to let the brother, sister, and bear onto the little terrace that separated the store from Fifth Avenue.

It was a beautiful day, with the sun shining down on all the horse carriages and hot-dog carts lined along the edge of Central Park.

—Come sit with me a moment, said Sarah, in a manner that suggested a serious conversation was coming.

A little reluctantly, Woolly followed his sister to a bench and sat down, placing the panda between them. But Sarah lifted the panda and put it to her side so that there was nothing between them.

—Woolly, she said, there's something I want to ask you.

As she looked at him, Woolly could see in her face an expression of concern, but also an expression of uncertainty, as if suddenly she wasn't sure that she wanted to ask him whatever it was that she had wanted to ask, after all.

Reaching out, Woolly laid his hand on her forearm.

—You don't have to ask me something, Sarah. You don't have to ask me anything.

Looking at her, Woolly could see the feeling of concern continuing to struggle with the feeling of uncertainty. So he did his best to reassure.

—Questions can be so tricky, he said, like forks in the road. You can be having such a nice conversation and someone will raise a question, and the next thing you know you're headed off in a whole new direction. In all probability, this new road will lead you to places that are perfectly agreeable, but sometimes you just want to go in the direction you were already headed.

They were both silent for a second. Then Woolly squeezed his sister's arm from the excitement of an additional thought.

—Have you ever noticed, he said, have you ever noticed how so many questions begin with the letter *W*?

He counted them off on his fingers.

—Who. What. Why. When. Where. Which.

He could see his sister's concern and uncertainty lifting for a moment as she smiled at this fascinating little fact.

—Isn't that interesting? he continued. I mean, how do you think that happened? All those centuries ago when words were first being coined, what was it about the sound of the *W* that made the word coiners use it for all of the questions? As opposed to, say, the *T* or the *P*? It makes you feel sort of sorry for *W*, doesn't it? I mean, it's a pretty big burden to carry. Especially since half the time when someone asks you a question with a *W*, they aren't really asking you a question. They're making a statement in disguise. Like, like . . .

Woolly adopted the posture and tone of their mother.

—*When are you going to grow up!* And *Why would you do such a thing!* And *What in God's name were you thinking!*

Sarah laughed, and it was good to see her do so. Because she was a great laugher. She was the absotively best laugher Woolly had ever known.

—All right, Woolly. I'm not going to ask you a question.

Now she was the one who reached out a hand to take a forearm.

—Instead, I want you to make me a promise. I want you to promise me that after your visit, you'll go back.

Woolly wanted to look down at his feet, but he could feel her fingers on his forearm. And he could see in her face that though her concern remained, the expression of uncertainty was gone.

—I promise, he said. I promise . . . that I'll go back.

Then she squeezed his forearm just as he had squeezed hers, and looking like a great weight had been lifted from her shoulders, she leaned back on the bench, so he did the same. And as they sat there beside the panda, they found themselves looking across Fifth Avenue— right at the Plaza Hotel.

With a big smile, Woolly stood and turned to his sister.

—We should go have tea, he said. For old times' sake.

—Woolly, Sarah said with a slump of the shoulders. It's after two o'clock. I still need to pick up my dress at Bergdorf's, have my hair done, and get back to the apartment so I can change in time to meet Dennis at Le Pavillon.

—Oh, blah, blah, blah, said Woolly.

Sarah opened her mouth to make another point, but Woolly picked up the panda and waggled it back and forth in front of his sister.

—Oh blah, blah, blah, he said in a panda's voice.

—All right, said Sarah with a laugh. For old times' sake, let's have tea at the Plaza.

Duchess

ON FRIDAY AT HALF PAST ONE, I was standing in front of the hutch in Woolly's sister's dining room admiring the orderly arrangement of her china. Like the Watsons, she had place settings that were worthy of being handed down, and perhaps already had been. But here were no teetering towers of coffee cups, no thin layer of dust. Sister Sarah's china was arranged in perfectly aligned vertical stacks, and each plate had a little circle of felt to protect its surface from the plate above it. On a shelf under the china was a long black case that contained an equally orderly arrangement of the family silver.

Locking the hutch's lower cabinet, I put the key back where I'd found it: in the tureen that was on display in the middle of the middle shelf. The lady of the house clearly had a nice sense of symmetry, which was no less laudable for being easy to decipher.

Wandering down the hall from the dining room, I satisfied myself that I had visited every room on the ground floor, then headed up the back stairs.

———•———

Over breakfast, Sarah had explained that she and Dennis would be spending the weekend at their apartment in the city because they had dinner engagements on both nights. When she added that she needed to head in before noon in order to run a few errands, and Woolly suggested that he come along to keep her company, Sarah looked at me.

—Would that be all right? she asked. If Woolly joined me in the city for a few hours?

—I don't see why not.

So it was settled. Woolly would drive in with Sarah, and I would come later in the Caddy to pick him up on our way to the Circus. When I asked Woolly where we should meet, naturally he suggested the statue of Abraham Lincoln in Union Square. Shortly after eleven, they pulled out of the driveway and headed for the city, leaving me with the run of the house.

For starters, I went into the living room. Pouring myself a finger of scotch, I put Sinatra on the hi-fi and kicked up my feet. The record was one I'd never heard before, but Ol' Blue Eyes was in fine form, singing an assortment of lightly swinging love songs with full orchestration including "I Get a Kick Out of You" and "They Can't Take That Away from Me."

On the cover of the album, two pairs of sweethearts were out for a stroll, while Sinatra leaned against a lamppost by himself. Dressed in a dark gray suit with a tilted fedora on his head, Sinatra was holding a cigarette so loosely between two fingers it looked like he might drop it. Just seeing the picture made you want to smoke, and wear a hat, and lean on lampposts all by your lonesome.

For a moment, I wondered whether Woolly's brother-in-law had bought the record. But only for a moment. Because, of course, it must have been Sarah.

Cuing up the record for a second time, I poured myself a second whiskey and meandered down the hall. According to Woolly, his brother-in-law was something of a Wall Street wunderkind, though you wouldn't have known it from his office. There was no ticker tape, or whatever they used nowadays to tell them what to buy and sell. There were no ledgers or calculators or slide rules. In their place was ample evidence of the sporting life.

On a shelf right across from the desk—where Dennis could easily see it—was a stuffed fish mounted on a post, forever turning its mouth toward the hook. On the shelf above the fish was a recent photo of four men having just finished a round of golf. Luckily it was in color, so you could take note of all the clothes you would never want to wear. Scanning the faces of the golfers, I picked out the one who seemed particularly smug and figured that was Dennis. To the left of the shelves was another photograph hanging above two empty J hooks that jutted from the wall. This photo was of a college baseball team with a two-foot trophy on the grass.

What there wasn't was a picture of Woolly's sister. Not on the wall, not on a shelf, not on the wunderkind's desk.

After rinsing out my whiskey glass in the kitchen, I found what I guess you'd call a pantry. But it wasn't like the one at St. Nick's, stacked from floor to ceiling with bags of flour and cans of tomatoes. This one had a little copper sink with a copper counter, and vases in every imaginable color and size, so that Sarah could perfectly display every bouquet of flowers that Dennis would never bring her. On the brighter side, Dennis had made sure that the pantry had a specially designed cabinet in which to store a few hundred bottles of wine.

From the kitchen I proceeded to the dining room, where I surveyed the china and silver, as previously reported; I stopped in the living room to recork the whiskey and switch off the phonograph, then headed upstairs.

Skipping over the room where Woolly and I had spent the night, I poked my head into another guest room, then what looked like a sewing room, before coming upon a bedroom that was being painted.

In the middle of the room, someone had pulled the protective tarp off the boxes that were stacked on the bed, exposing them to the hazards of the light blue paint. This didn't seem the sort of thing that Woolly's sister would do, so I took the initiative of putting the tarp back in place. And what did I discover leaning against the bedframe but a Louisville Slugger.

That must have been what was resting on those J hooks in Dennis's office, I thought to myself. He had probably hit a home run fifteen years ago, and he had hung the bat on the wall so he could be reminded of the fact whenever he wasn't looking at his fish. But for some strange reason, someone had brought it here.

Picking it up and weighing it in my hands, I shook my head in disbelief. Why hadn't I thought of it before?

In shape and principle, a Louisville Slugger couldn't be that different from the clubs our ancestors used to subdue wildcats and wolves. And yet, somehow it seems as sleek and modern as a Maserati. The gentle tapering of the shaft that ensures a perfect distribution of weight. . . . The lip at the base that catches the heel of the hand to maximize the strength of the swing without allowing the bat to slip from your grasp. . . . Carved, sanded, and polished with the same devotion that's brought to the crafting of violins and ships, a Louisville Slugger is simultaneously a thing of beauty and a thing of purpose.

In fact, I challenge you to name a more perfect example of form following function than when Joltin' Joe, having rested the barrel of a bat on his shoulder, suddenly sets his body in motion in order to greet the projectile that's headed toward him at ninety miles an hour and send it hurtling back in the opposite direction with a satisfying crack.

Yep, I thought to myself. You can forget your two-by-fours, your frying pans, and your whiskey bottles. When it comes to dispensing justice, all you need is a good old American baseball bat.

Walking down the hall with a whistle on my lips, I used the tip of the bat to push open the door of the master suite.

It was a lovely, light-filled room in which there was not only a bed, but a chaise longue, a high-back chair with a footstool, and a matching pair of his and her bureaus. There was also a matching pair of his and her closets. In the one on the left was a long line of dresses. Most of them were as bright and elegant as their owner, although tucked in the corner were a few skimpy numbers that I was almost too shy to look at, and she was certainly too shy to wear.

In the second closet were shelves with neatly folded oxford shirts and a hanging pole with a collection of three-piece suits progressing from tan to gray to blue to black. On a shelf above the suits was a row of fedoras arranged in a similar progression.

The clothes make the man, or so the saying goes. But all you have to do is look at a row of fedoras to know what a bunch of baloney that is. Gather together a group of men of every gradation—from the powerhouse to the putz—have them toss their fedoras in a pile, and you'll spend a lifetime trying to figure out whose was whose. Because it's the man who makes the fedora, not versa vice. I mean, wouldn't you rather wear the hat worn by Frank Sinatra than the one worn by Sergeant Joe Friday? I should hope so.

In all, I figured that Dennis had about ten fedoras, twenty-five suits, and forty shirts, for mixing and matching. I didn't bother calculating all the potential combinations of outfits. It was plain enough to the naked eye that were one to go missing, no one would even notice.

Emmett

O<small>N</small> F<small>RIDAY AT HALF PAST ONE,</small> Emmett was approaching a brownstone on 126th Street.

—Here we go again, said the fair-skinned black youth who was leaning on the railing at the top of the stoop.

When the fair-skinned one spoke, the big one who was sitting on the bottom step looked up at Emmett with an expression of welcome surprise.

—You here for a beating too? he asked.

As he began to shake with a noiseless laughter, the door to the building opened and out came Townhouse.

—Well, well, he said with a smile. If it isn't Mr. Emmett Watson.

—Hey, Townhouse.

Townhouse paused for a moment to stare at the fair-skinned one, who was partially blocking his way. When he begrudgingly stepped aside, Townhouse came down the stoop and took Emmett's hand.

—It's good to see you.

—It's good to see you too.

—I gather they let you out a few months early.

—Because of my father.

Townhouse nodded in an expression of sympathy.

The fair-skinned one was watching the interaction with a sour expression.

—Who's this then? he asked.

—A friend, Townhouse replied without looking back.

—That Salina must have been one friendly place.

This time Townhouse did look back.

—Shut up, Maurice.

For a moment, Maurice returned Townhouse's stare, then he looked up the street in his sour way while the jovial one shook his head.

—Come on, Townhouse said to Emmett. Let's take a walk.

As the two went down the street together, Townhouse didn't say anything. Emmett could tell that he was waiting to gain some distance from the others. So Emmett didn't say anything either until they had turned the corner.

—You don't seem that surprised to see me.

—I'm not. Duchess was here yesterday.

Emmett nodded.

—When I heard he'd gone to Harlem, I figured he was coming to see you. What did he want?

—He wanted me to hit him.

Emmett stopped and turned to Townhouse, so Townhouse stopped and turned too. For a moment, they stood eye to eye without speaking— two young men of different race and upbringing, but of similar casts of mind.

—He wanted you to hit him?

Townhouse responded in a lowered voice, as if he were speaking in confidence, though no one was within earshot.

—That's what he wanted, Emmett. He'd gotten some idea in his head that he owed me something—because of the switching I took from Ackerly—and if I gave him a few pops we'd be even.

—What'd you do?

—I hit him.

Emmett looked at his friend with a touch of surprise.

—He didn't give me much of a choice. He said he'd come all the way uptown to settle the score, and he made it clear he wasn't leaving until it was settled. Then when I hit him, he insisted I hit him again. Twice. He took all three in the face without even raising his fists, at the foot of the stoop where we were standing a minute ago, right in front of the boys.

Emmett looked away from Townhouse, considering. It wasn't lost on him that five days before he had taken a similar beating to settle a score of his own. Emmett wasn't prone to superstitions. He didn't favor four-leaf clovers or fear black cats. But the notion of Duchess taking three punches in front of a gathering of witnesses gave him a strange sense of foreboding. But that didn't alter what needed to be done.

Emmett looked back at Townhouse.

—Did he say where he was staying?

—No.

—Did he say where he was going?

Townhouse paused for a moment, then shook his head.

—He didn't. But listen, Emmett, if you're set on finding Duchess, you should know that you're not the only one looking for him.

—What do you mean?

—Two cops were here last night.

—Because he and Woolly skipped?

—Maybe. They didn't say. But they were definitely more interested in Duchess than Woolly. And I got the sense there might be more to it than hunting down a couple of kids who've gone over the fence.

—Thanks for letting me know.

—Sure. But before you go, I've got something you're going to want to see.

Townhouse led Emmett eight blocks away to a street that seemed more Hispanic than black—with a bodega and three men playing dominoes out on the sidewalk as a Latin dance number played on a radio. At the end of the block, Townhouse came to a stop across the street from a body shop.

Emmett turned to him.

—Is that *the* body shop?

—That's it.

The shop in question was owned by a man named Gonzalez, who had moved to New York from southern California after the war, with his wife and two sons—twins who were known in the neighborhood as Paco and Pico. From the time the boys were fourteen, Gonzalez had them working in the shop after school—cleaning tools, sweeping floors, and taking out the trash—so they would gain some understanding of what it took to earn an honest dollar. Paco and Pico got the understanding all right. And when at the age of seventeen they were given the responsibility of closing up on weekends, they got into a little business of their own.

Most of the cars in the shop were there because of a loose fender or a dent in a door, but otherwise in good working order. So on Saturday nights, the brothers began renting out the cars in the shop to the boys in the neighborhood for a few bucks an hour. When Townhouse was sixteen, he asked out a girl by the name of Clarise, who happened to be the best-looking girl in the eleventh grade. When she said yes, Townhouse borrowed five bucks from his brother and rented a car from the twins.

His plan was to pack a little picnic and drive Clarise over to Grant's Tomb, where they could park under the elm trees and gaze out on the Hudson. But as luck would have it, the only car the twins had available that night was a Buick Skylark convertible with chrome finishes. The car looked so good, it would have been a crime to get a girl like Clarise in the front seat and spend the evening watching barges being pushed up the river. Instead, Townhouse lowered the top, turned up the radio, and drove his date up and down 125th Street.

—You should have seen us, Townhouse had said one night at Salina as they lay on their bunks in the dark. I was wearing my Easter Sunday suit, which was almost as blue as the car, and she was in a bright yellow dress that was cut so low in the back you could see half her spine. That Skylark could have gone from zero to sixty in four seconds, but I was driving at twenty miles an hour so we could wave at everyone we recognized, and half the people we didn't. Down 125th we'd go, cruising past all the finely dressed folk out in front of the Hotel Theresa and the Apollo and Showman's Jazz Club; and when we got to Broadway, I'd turn her around and drive all the way back. Every time we made the circuit, Clarise would slide a little closer, until there was no more closer to slide.

In the end it was Clarise who suggested they go to Grant's Tomb to park under the elms, and that's where they were, making the most of the shadows, when the flashlights of two patrolmen shone into the car.

It turned out that the owner of the Skylark was one of those finely dressed folk in front of the Apollo Theater. Given all the waving that Townhouse and Clarise had been doing, it didn't take long for the cops to find them in the park. After untangling the young couple, one of the cops drove Clarise home in the Skylark while the other drove Townhouse to the station in the back of the black-and-white.

As a minor who had never been in trouble, Townhouse might have gotten off with a stern talking-to had he given up the twins. But Townhouse was no squealer. When the officers asked him how he happened to be behind the wheel of a car he didn't own, Townhouse said that he'd snuck into Mr. Gonzalez's office, slipped the key off the hook, and driven the car off the lot when no one was looking. So instead of the stern talking-to, Townhouse got twelve months in Salina.

—Come on, he said.

Crossing the street, the two passed the office where Mr. Gonzalez was talking on the phone and entered the repair area. In the first bay was a Chevy with its rear caved in, while in the second was a Road-master with a buckled hood, as if the two cars had been on opposite ends of the same collision. Somewhere out of sight, a radio was playing a dance number that to Emmett's ear could have been the same one he'd heard when they had passed the domino players, though he knew it probably wasn't.

—Paco! Pico! Townhouse called above the music.

The brothers emerged from behind the Chevy, dressed in dirty jumpsuits, cleaning their hands on rags.

If Paco and Pico were twins, you wouldn't have guessed so from a glance—the former being tall, thin, and shaggy, the latter stocky and close-cropped. It was only when they broke out into big white-toothed smiles that you could see the family resemblance.

—This is the friend I was telling you about, said Townhouse.

Turning to Emmett, the brothers offered him the same toothy grin. Then Paco gestured with his head toward the far end of the garage.

—It's over here.

Emmett and Townhouse followed the brothers past the Roadmaster to the last bay, where a car was under a tarp. Together, the brothers pulled back the cover to reveal a powder-blue Studebaker.

—That's my car, said Emmett in surprise.

—No kidding, said Townhouse.

—How'd it end up here?

—Duchess left it.

—Is it running all right?

—More or less, said Paco.

Emmett shook his head. There was just no making sense of what, when, or where Duchess chose to do what he did. But as long as the car was back in Emmett's possession and in good working order, he didn't need to make sense of Duchess's choices.

Doing a quick circuit, Emmett was pleased to find that there were no more dents in the car than when he had bought it. But when he opened the trunk, the kit bag wasn't there. More importantly, when he pulled back the piece of felt that covered the spare, he discovered that the envelope wasn't there either.

—Everything all right? asked Townhouse.

—Yeah, said Emmett, closing the trunk with a quiet click.

Walking toward the front of the car, Emmett glanced through the driver's window, then turned to Paco.

—Have you got the keys?

But Paco turned to Townhouse.

—We've got them, said Townhouse. But there's something else you need to know.

Before Townhouse could explain, an angry shout came from the other side of the garage.

—What the fuck is this!

Emmett assumed it must be Mr. Gonzalez, annoyed that his sons weren't at work, but when he turned he saw the one called Maurice marching toward them.

—What the fuck is this, Maurice repeated, though more slowly, punching every other word.

After muttering to Emmett that this was his cousin, Townhouse waited for Maurice to reach them before he deigned to reply.

—What the fuck is what, Maurice?

—Otis said you were going to hand over the keys, and I couldn't believe it.

—Well, now you can.

—But it's *my* car.

—There's nothing yours about it.

Maurice looked at Townhouse with an expression of amazement.

—You were right there when that nutjob gave me the keys.

—Maurice, said Townhouse, you've been climbing my tree all week and I've had just about enough of it. So, why don't you mind your own business before I mind it for you.

Clamping his teeth shut, Maurice stared at Townhouse for a moment, then he turned and marched away.

Townhouse shook his head. As a final slight to his cousin, he adopted the expression of one who was trying to remember the important shit he'd been saying before he was so needlessly interrupted.

—You were gonna tell him about the car, Paco prompted.

With a nod of remembrance, Townhouse turned back to Emmett.

—When I told the cops last night that I hadn't seen Duchess, they must not have believed me. Because this morning they were back, asking questions up and down the block. Like whether anyone had seen a couple of white boys hanging out on my stoop, or driving around the neighborhood—in a light-blue Studebaker . . .

Emmett closed his eyes.

—That's right, said Townhouse. Whatever trouble Duchess has gotten himself into, it looks like he was in your car when he got into it. And if your car was involved, the cops will eventually get around to thinking that you're involved too. That's one of the reasons I stashed it here instead of leaving it on the street. But the other reason is that when it comes to paint jobs, the Gonzalez brothers are artistes. Ain't that right, boys?

—*Los Picassos*, replied Pico, speaking for the first time.

—After *we're* through with her, said Paco, even her own mother wouldn't recognize her.

The two brothers began laughing, but stopped when they saw that neither Emmett nor Townhouse had joined in.

—How long would it take? asked Emmett.

The brothers looked at each other, then Paco shrugged.

—If we get started tomorrow and make good headway, we could have her ready by . . . Monday morning?

—*Sí*, said Pico nodding in agreement. *El lunes*.

Another delay, thought Emmett. But since the envelope was missing, he couldn't leave New York until he found Duchess anyway. And

Townhouse was right about the car. If the police were actively looking for a light-blue Studebaker, there was no point in driving one.

—Monday morning it is, said Emmett. And thanks to you both.

Outside the garage, Townhouse offered to walk Emmett back to the subway, but Emmett wanted to know something first.

—When we were at your stoop and I asked where Duchess was going, you hesitated—like someone who knows something that he doesn't want to admit to knowing. If Duchess told you where he was headed, I need you to tell me.

Townhouse blew some air.

—Look, he said, I know you like Duchess, Emmett. So do I. He's a loyal friend in his own crazy way, and he's one of the most entertaining shit slingers whom I've ever had the pleasure to meet. But he is also like one of those guys who are born with no peripheral vision. He can see everything that's right in front of him, see it more clearly than most, but the second that something is pushed an inch to the left or right, he doesn't even know it's there. And that can lead to all kinds of trouble. For him, and for anyone within spitting distance. All I'm saying, Emmett, is now that you've got your car, maybe you should let Duchess be.

—Nothing would make me happier than to let Duchess be, said Emmett, but it's not so simple. Four days ago, just as Billy and I were about to head to California, he took off with Woolly in the Studebaker, which was problem enough. But before my father died, he put an envelope with three thousand dollars in the trunk of the car. It was there when Duchess drove off, and now it's gone.

—Shit, said Townhouse.

Emmett nodded.

—Don't get me wrong: I am glad to have the car back. But I *need* that money.

—All right, Townhouse said, nodding his head in concession. I don't know where Duchess is staying. But before he left yesterday, he was trying to convince me to join him and Woolly at the Circus.

—The circus?

—That's right. In Red Hook. On Conover Street right near the river. Duchess said he was going to be there tonight for the six o'clock show.

As the two walked from the body shop to the subway station, Townhouse went the long way around in order to point out landmarks. Not the landmarks of Harlem, but the landmarks of their conversations. Places that had come up in the course of their time together, mentioned as they worked side by side in the fields or lay on their bunks at night. Like the apartment building on Lenox Avenue where his grandfather had kept pigeons on the roof, the same roof where he and his brother had been allowed to sleep on hot summer nights. And the high school where Townhouse had been a star shortstop. And on 125th Street, Emmett got a glimpse of that lively stretch of road on which Townhouse and Clarise had driven back and forth on their ill-fated Saturday night.

In leaving Nebraska, Emmett had little to regret. He didn't regret leaving behind their home or their possessions. He didn't regret leaving behind his father's dreams or his father's grave. And when he had driven those first few miles of the Lincoln Highway, he had savored the sensation of putting distance between himself and his hometown, even if he was headed in the wrong direction.

But as they walked through Harlem and Townhouse pointed out the landmarks of his youth, Emmett wished that he could return to Morgen, if only for a day, in the company of his friend, so that he could point out the landmarks of his life, the landmarks of the stories that he had told to pass the time. Like the airplanes that he had so painstakingly assembled and that still hung over Billy's bed; and the two-story house on Madison, the first that he'd helped build in Mr. Schulte's employ; and the wide, unforgiving land that may have bested his father, but which never lost its beauty in his eyes. And yes, he would show Townhouse the fairgrounds too, just as Townhouse without shame or hesitation had shown him the lively stretch of road that had led to his undoing.

When they reached the subway station, Townhouse followed Emmett inside and stayed with him right up until the turnstiles. Before they parted, almost as an afterthought, he asked if Emmett wanted him to come along that night—when he went looking for Duchess.

—That's all right, replied Emmett. I don't imagine he'll give me any trouble.

—No, he won't, agreed Townhouse. At least, not as intended.

After a moment, Townhouse shook his head and smiled.

—Duchess gets some crazy ideas into his head, but he was right about one thing.

—What's that? asked Emmett.

—I did feel much better after hitting him.

Sally

HALF THE TIME WHEN you could use the help of a man, he's nowhere to be found. He's off seeing to one thing or another that could just as easily be seen to tomorrow as seen to today and that just happens to be five steps out of earshot. But as soon as you need him to be somewhere else, you can't push him out the door.

Like my father at this very minute.

Here it is Friday at half past twelve, and he's cutting his chicken fried steak like he was some kind of surgeon and the life of his patient depended upon every placement of the knife. And when he has finally cleaned his plate and had two cups of coffee, for once in a blue moon he asks for a third.

—I'll have to brew another pot, I warn.

—I've got time, he says.

So I dump the spent grinds in the trash, rinse out the percolator, fill it back up, set it on the stove, and wait for it to simmer, thinking how nice it must be in this relentless world to have so much time at your bidding.

—·—

For as long as I can remember, my father has gone into town on Friday afternoon to run his errands. As soon as he's through with lunch, he'll climb in his truck with a purposeful look and head off to the hardware store, the feedstore, and the pharmacy. Then around seven o'clock—just in time for supper—he'll pull into the driveway with a tube of toothpaste, ten bushels of oats, and a brand-new pair of pliers.

How on God's green earth, you may rightly wonder, does a man turn twenty minutes of errands into a five-hour excursion? Well, that's an easy one: by yakking. Certainly, he's yakking with Mr. Wurtele at the hardware store, Mr. Horchow at the feedstore, and Mr. Danziger at the pharmacy. But the yakking isn't limited to the proprietors. For on Friday afternoons, in each of these establishments an assembly of seasoned errand runners convenes to forecast the weather, the harvest, and the national elections.

By my estimation, a solid hour is spent prognosticating at each one of the stores, but apparently three hours isn't enough. Because after predicting the outcomes of all the day's unknowables, the assembly of elders will retire to McCafferty's Tavern, where they can opine for two hours more in the company of bottles of beer.

My father is nothing if not a creature of habit so, as I say, this has been going on for as long as I remember. Then suddenly about six months ago, when my father finished his lunch and pushed back his chair, rather than heading straight out the door to his truck, he went upstairs to change into a clean white shirt.

It didn't take long for me to figure that a woman had somehow worked her way into my father's routine. Especially since she was partial to perfume, and I'm the one who has to wash his clothes. But the questions remained: Who was this woman? And where on earth did he meet her?

She wasn't someone in the congregation, I was pretty sure of that. Because on Sunday mornings when we filed out of the service onto the little patch of grass in front of the chapel, there wasn't a woman—married or unmarried—who gave him a measured greeting or an awkward glance. And it wasn't Esther who keeps the books at the feedstore, because she wouldn't've recognized a bottle of perfume if it fell from the heavens and hit her on the head. I might have thought it was one of the women who are known, upon occasion, to stop in at McCafferty's, but once my father started changing his shirt, he stopped coming home with the smell of beer on his breath.

Well, if he didn't meet her at church, the stores, or the bar, I just couldn't figure it. So I had no choice but to follow him.

On the first Friday in March, I made a pot of chili so I wouldn't have to worry about cooking dinner. After serving my father lunch, I watched out of the corner of my eye as he went out the door in his clean white shirt, climbed in his truck, and pulled out of the drive. Once he was half a mile down the road, I grabbed a wide-brimmed hat from the closet, hopped into Betty, and set off on my own.

Just like always, he made his first stop at the hardware store, where he did a bit of business and whiled away an hour in the company of like-minded men. Next it was off to the feedstore and then the pharmacy, where there was a little more business and a lot more whiling. At each of these stops a few women made an appearance in order to do a little business of their own, but if he exchanged more than a word with them, it wasn't so's you'd notice.

But then at five o'clock, when he came out of the pharmacy and climbed in his truck, he didn't head down Jefferson on his way to McCafferty's. Instead, after passing the library, he took a right on Cypress, a left on Adams, and pulled over across from the little white house with blue shutters. After sitting for a minute, he got out of his truck, crossed the street, and rapped on the screen door.

He didn't have to wait more than a minute for his rap to be answered. And standing there in the doorframe was Alice Thompson.

By my reckoning, Alice couldn't have been more than twenty-eight years old. She was three grades ahead of my sister in school and a Methodist, so I didn't have cause to know her very well. But I knew what everyone else knew: that she had graduated from Kansas State and then married a fellow from Topeka who got himself killed in Korea. A widow without children, Alice had returned to Morgen in the fall of '53 and taken a job as a teller at the Savings and Loan.

That's where it must have happened. While going to the bank was not a part of my father's Friday routine, he did stop in every other Thursday in order to pick up the payroll for the boys. One week he must have ended up at her window and been taken by her mournful look. The following week I could just imagine him carefully picking his place in line so that he'd end up at her window instead of Ed Fowler's, and then doing his damnedest to make a little conversation while she was trying to count the cash.

As I was sitting in Betty staring at the house, maybe you'd imagine that I was unsettled, or angry, or indignant that my father should be casting off memories of my mother in order to romance a woman who was half his age. Well, imagine all you like. It won't cost you nothing, and it'll cost me less. But later that night, after I'd served the chili, cleaned the kitchen, and switched off the lights, I knelt at the side of my bed, clasped my hands together, and prayed. *Dear Lord*, I said, *please give my father the wisdom to be gracious, the heart to be generous, and the courage to ask for this woman's hand in holy matrimony—so that someone else can do his cooking and cleaning for a change.*

Every night for the next four weeks, I made a similar prayer.

But then on the first Friday in April, my father didn't come home at seven in time for supper. He didn't come home while I was cleaning up the kitchen or climbing into bed. It was nearly midnight when I heard him pull into the drive. Parting the curtains, I saw his truck parked at a forty-five-degree angle with the headlights still on as he weaved his way to the door. I heard him walk past the supper I'd left out for him and stumble up the stairs.

They say the Lord answers all prayers, it's just that sometimes he answers no. And I guess he answered no to mine. Because the following morning, when I took his shirt from the hamper, what it smelled of was whiskey instead of perfume.

—·—

Finally, at quarter till two my father found the bottom of his coffee cup and pushed back his chair.

—Well, I guess I'd best get going, he said, and I didn't argue.

Once he'd climbed in his truck and pulled out of the drive, I looked at the clock and saw that I had just over forty-five minutes to spare. So I did the dishes, straightened up the kitchen, and set the table. By then it was two twenty. Taking off my apron, I mopped my brow and sat on the bottom step of the stairs, where there was always a nice little breeze in the afternoon, and from where I'd have no trouble hearing the phone when it rang in my father's office.

And that's where I sat for the next half an hour.

Standing up, I straightened out my skirt and returned to the kitchen. With my hands on my hips, I looked it over. It was neat as a pin: the chairs tucked in; the counter wiped; the dishes neatly stacked in their cabinets. So I set about making a chicken pot pie. When that was done, I cleaned the kitchen again. Then, even though it wasn't Saturday, I took the vacuum from the closet and vacuumed the rugs in the living room and den. I was about to carry the vacuum upstairs to see to the bedrooms when it occurred to me that with all the racket a vacuum makes, I might not be able to hear the phone from upstairs. So I put the vacuum back in the closet.

For a moment I stood there just staring at it, all curled up on the closet floor, wondering to myself which of the two of us was designed to serve the other. Then slamming the door shut, I went in my father's office, sat in his chair, took out his phone book, and looked up the number for Father Colmore.

Emmett

WHEN THEY EMERGED FROM the station at Carroll Street, Emmett knew he had made a mistake in bringing his brother.

His instincts had told him that he shouldn't do it. Townhouse hadn't been able to remember the exact address of the circus, so it was probably going to take some legwork to find it. Once Emmett was inside, he was going to have to find Duchess in the crowd. And once he found Duchess, there was the possibility, however remote, that Duchess wouldn't hand over the envelope without raising some sort of nonsense. All in all, it would have been smarter to leave Billy in the care of Ulysses, where he'd be safe. But how do you tell an eight-year-old boy who has wanted to go to the circus all his life that you intend to go to one without him? So at five o'clock, they descended the steel staircase from the tracks and headed for the subway together.

Initially, Emmett took some comfort from the fact that he knew the right station to go to, knew the right platform, knew the right train, having already made the journey to Brooklyn once, albeit in error. But the day before, when he had switched from the Brooklyn-bound train to the Manhattan-bound train, he had never left the station. So it was only when they came out of the Carroll Street stop that Emmett got a sense of how rough this part of Brooklyn was. And as they worked their way through Gowanus into Red Hook, it only seemed to get worse. The landscape soon became dominated by long, windowless warehouses abutted by the occasional flophouse or bar. It hardly seemed the neighborhood for a circus, unless they had raised a tent on the wharf. But as the river came into view, there was no sign of a tent, no flags, no marquees.

Emmett was about to turn back when Billy pointed across the street to a nondescript building with a small, brightly lit window.

It turned out to be a ticket booth occupied by a man in his seventies.

—Is this the circus? Emmett asked.

—The early show's started, the old man said, but it's two bucks a head just the same.

When Emmett paid, the old man slid the tickets across the counter with the indifference of one who's been sliding tickets across a counter all his life.

Emmett was relieved to find the lobby more in keeping with his expectations. The floor was covered in a dark, red carpet and the walls painted with figures of acrobats and elephants and an open-jawed lion. There was also a concession stand selling popcorn and beer, and a large easel advertising the main event: THE ASTOUNDING SUTTER SISTERS OF SAN ANTONIO, TEXXXAS!

As Emmett gave their tickets to the usherette in the blue uniform, he asked where they should sit.

—Anywhere you like.

Then after giving Billy a wink, she opened the door and told them to enjoy the show.

Inside it was like a small, indoor rodeo with a dirt floor surrounded by an oval bulwark and twenty rows of stadium seating. By Emmett's estimate, the hall was only a quarter full, but with the lighting trained on the oval, the faces of the audience members weren't easy to make out.

As the brothers sat on one of the benches, the lights dimmed and a spotlight illuminated the ringmaster. In keeping with tradition, he was dressed like a master of the hunt, with leather riding boots, a bright red jacket, and top hat. Only when he began to speak did Emmett realize he was actually a woman wearing a false moustache.

—And now, she announced through a red megaphone, returning from the East where she mesmerized the Raja of India and danced for the King of Siam, the Circus is proud to present the one, the only, Delilah!

With an extension of the ringmaster's hand, the spotlight shot across the oval to a gate in the bulwark through which an enormous woman in a pink tutu came riding the tricycle of a child.

As the audience erupted into laughter and bawdy cheers, two seals with old-fashioned police helmets strapped to their heads appeared and began to bark. Off Delilah went, pedaling frantically around the oval as the seals gave chase and the crowd egged them on. Once the seals had successfully corralled Delilah back through the gate, they turned and acknowledged the audience's appreciation by bobbing their heads and clapping their fins.

Next, two cowgirls rode into the ring—one dressed in white leather with a white hat on the back of a white horse, the other all in black.

—The Astounding Sutter Sisters, called the ringmaster through her megaphone as they trotted around the arena waving their hats to the cheers of the crowd.

After circling the arena once, the sisters began performing a series of stunts. Riding at a reasonable speed, they swung themselves from one side of their saddles to the other in perfect synchronicity. Then, while riding at a faster clip, the Sutter in black leapt from her horse to her sister's and back again.

Pointing at the arena, Billy looked up at his brother with an expression of amazement.

—Did you see that?

—I did, said Emmett with a smile.

But when Billy turned his attention back to the action, Emmett turned his to the audience. For the sisters' act, the lights in the arena had been raised, making it easier for Emmett to search the faces of the crowd. Having completed a first pass to no avail, Emmett looked to his immediate left and began working his way around the oval more systematically, looking from row to row and aisle to aisle. Emmett still couldn't find Duchess, but he noted with a touch of surprise that most of the audience members were men.

—Look! Billy exclaimed, pointing at the sisters, who were now standing on the backs of their horses as they rode side by side.

—Yes, said Emmett. They're very good.

—No, said Billy. Not the riders. Over there in the audience. It's Woolly.

Following the direction of Billy's finger, Emmett looked across the arena, and there in the eighth row was Woolly, sitting by himself. Emmett had been so focused on finding Duchess, it hadn't occurred to him to look for Woolly.

—Good job, Billy. Come on.

Following the wide center aisle, Emmett and Billy circumnavigated the arena to where Woolly sat with a bag of popcorn in his lap and a smile on his face.

—Woolly! called Billy as he ran the final steps.

At the sound of his name, Woolly looked up.

—*Mirabile dictu!* Out of nowhere, here come Emmett and Billy Watson. What serendipity! What a turn of events! Have a seat, have a seat.

Though there was plenty of space for the brothers to sit, Woolly slid along the bench to make more room.

—Isn't it a great show? asked Billy while removing his backpack.

—It is, agreed Woolly. It most certainly definitely is.

—Look, said Billy, pointing to the middle of the arena, where four clowns had driven four small cars.

Moving behind his brother, Emmett took the empty seat on Woolly's right.

—Where's Duchess?

—What's that? asked Woolly, without taking his eyes off the sisters, who were now jumping over the cars and scattering the clowns.

Emmett leaned closer.

—Where's Duchess, Woolly?

Woolly looked up as if he hadn't the faintest idea. Then he remembered.

—He's in the living room! He went to see some friends in the living room.

—Where's that?

Woolly pointed to the end of the oval.

—Up the steps and through the blue door.

—I'm going to get him. In the meantime, can you keep an eye on Billy?

—Of course, said Woolly.

Emmett held Woolly's gaze for a moment to stress the importance of what he'd just asked. Woolly turned to Billy.

—Emmett's going to go get Duchess, Billy. So you and I have to keep an eye on each other. Okay?

—Okay, Woolly.

Woolly turned back to Emmett.

—See?

—All right, said Emmett with a smile. Just don't go anywhere.

Woolly gestured to the arena.

—Why would we?

Climbing behind Woolly, Emmett made his way around the center aisle to the steps at the top of the oval.

Emmett wasn't one for circuses. He wasn't one for magic shows or rodeos. He hadn't even liked going to the football games at his high school, which were attended by nearly everyone in town. He'd simply never taken to the idea of sitting in a crowd to watch someone do something more interesting than what you were doing yourself. So when he began climbing the steps and he heard the double crack of toy pistols and a cheer from the crowd, he didn't bother looking back. And when he opened the blue door at the top of the steps and two more cracks of the pistol were followed by even louder cheers, he didn't look back then either.

If he had looked back, what Emmett would have seen was the Sutter sisters riding in opposite directions with their six-shooters drawn. As the two passed each other, he would have seen them take aim and shoot the hats from each other's heads. As the two passed a second time, he would have seen them shoot the shirts off their backs—revealing bare midriffs and lacy bras, one black, one white. And if he had waited just a few minutes more before stepping through the door, he would have seen the Sutter sisters firing their pistols in rapid succession until both of them were galloping on the backs of their horses as naked as Lady Godiva.

When the door at the top of the steps swung shut behind him, Emmett found himself at the end of a long, narrow hallway on either side of which were six doors, all of them closed. As Emmett walked its length, the muffled cheers of the crowd began to recede and he could hear a piece of classical music being played on a piano. It was coming from behind the door at the end of the hallway—a door that was illustrated with the large insignia of a bell like the one that was used by the phone company. When he put his hand on the knob, the classical piece slowed and then seamlessly transitioned into a saloon-style rag.

Opening the door, Emmett stood on the threshold of a large, luxurious lounge. Composed of at least four separate sitting areas, the room had couches and chairs upholstered in rich, dark fabrics. On the side tables were lamps with tasseled shades, and on the walls were oil paintings of ships. Stretched out on two facing couches, wearing nothing but delicate shifts, were a redhead and brunette, both smoking pungent cigarettes. While at the back of the room, near an elaborately carved bar, a blonde in a silk wrap leaned against the piano, tapping her fingers in time to the music.

Almost every element of the scene took Emmett by surprise: the plush furniture, the oil paintings, the scantily clad women. But nothing took him by more surprise than the fact that the person playing the piano was Duchess—wearing a crisp white shirt and a fedora tilted back on his head.

When the blonde at the piano looked to see who had come through the door, Duchess followed her gaze. Seeing Emmett, he ran his fingers once down the length of the keyboard, pounded a final chord, and leapt to his feet with a generous grin.

—Emmett!

The three women looked at Duchess.

—Do you know him? asked the blonde in an almost childlike voice.

—This is the guy I was telling you about!

The three women all turned their gazes back on Emmett.

—You mean the one from North Dakota?

—Nebraska, corrected the brunette.

The redhead lazily pointed her cigarette at Emmett with an expression of sudden understanding.

—The one who loaned you the car.

—Exactly, said Duchess.

The women all smiled at Emmett in recognition of his generosity. Striding across the room, Duchess took Emmett by the arms.

—I can't believe you're here. Just this morning, Woolly and I were lamenting your absence and counting the days until we'd see you again. But wait! Where are my manners?

Slipping an arm over Emmett's shoulder, Duchess led him toward the women.

—Let me introduce you to my three fairy godmothers. Here on my left, we have Helen. The second one in history to launch a thousand ships.

—Charmed, the redhead said to Emmett, extending her hand.

As Emmett reached to take it, he realized that her shift was so diaphanous, the dark circles around her nipples were visible through the fabric. Feeling the color rising to his cheeks, he averted his gaze.

—By the piano we have Charity. I don't think I have to tell you how she got her name. And here on my right is Bernadette.

Emmett was relieved when Bernadette, who was dressed exactly like Helen, didn't bother to extend her hand.

—That's quite a belt buckle, she said with a smile.

—It's nice to meet you, Emmett said to the women a little awkwardly.

Duchess turned to face him with a grin.

—This is so great, he said.

—Yeah, said Emmett, without much enthusiasm. Listen, Duchess, if I could have a word. Alone . . .

—Sure thing.

Duchess led Emmett away from the women, but rather than take him back into the hallway, where they would have privacy, he took him to a corner of the lounge about fifteen feet away.

Duchess studied Emmett's face for a moment.

—You're mad, he said. I can tell.

Emmett barely knew where to begin.

—Duchess, he found himself saying, I did not *lend* you my car.

—You're right, replied Duchess, holding up both hands in surrender. You're absolutely right. It would have been much more accurate for me to say I borrowed it. But like I told Billy back at St. Nick's, we were only using it to run that errand upstate. We would have had it back in Morgen before you knew it.

—Whether you took it for a year or a day doesn't change the fact that it's *my* car—with my money in it.

Duchess looked at Emmett like he didn't understand him for a second.

—Oh, you mean the envelope that was in the trunk. You don't have to worry about that, Emmett.

—Then you have it?

—Sure. But not on me. This is the big city, after all. I left it at Woolly's sister's place, along with your kit bag, where they'd be safe and sound.

—Then let's go get them. And on the way, you can tell me all about the cops.

—What cops?

—I saw Townhouse, and he says the cops came around this morning, asking about my car.

—I can't imagine why they would be, said Duchess, looking genuinely stupefied. That is, unless . . .

—Unless what?

Duchess was nodding his head now.

—On the way here, when I wasn't looking, Woolly parked in front of a fire hydrant. Next thing I knew, there was a patrolman asking him for the driver's license he didn't have. What with Woolly being Woolly, I convinced the cop not to write him a ticket. But he might have put a description of the car in the system.

—Great, said Emmett.

Duchess nodded soberly, but then suddenly snapped his fingers.

—You know what, Emmett? It doesn't matter.

—And why is that?

—Yesterday, I made the trade of the century. Maybe not as good as Manhattan for a string of beads, but pretty damn close. In exchange for one scuffed-up Studebaker hardtop, I landed you a 1941 Cadillac convertible in mint condition. There couldn't be more than a thousand miles on her, and the provenance is impeccable.

—I don't need your Cadillac, Duchess, wherever it came from. Townhouse gave me back the Studebaker. It's getting a new coat of paint and I'm picking it up on Monday.

—You know what, said Duchess, with a finger in the air. That's even better. Now we'll have the Studebaker *and* the Caddy. After we go to the Adirondacks, we can caravan to California.

—Oooh, said Charity from across the room. A caravan!

Before Emmett could dispel anybody's ideas about a caravan to California, a door behind the piano opened and in lumbered the woman who had ridden the tricycle, though now in a giant terrycloth robe.

—Well, well, she said in a raspy voice. Who do we have here?

—It's Emmett, said Duchess. The one I told you about.

She looked at Emmett with narrowed eyes.

—The one with the trust?

—No. The one I borrowed the car from.

—You're right, she said with a touch of disappointment. He does look like Gary Cooper.

—I wouldn't mind being cooped up with him, said Charity.

Everyone but Emmett laughed, and no one louder than the big woman.

As Emmett felt the color rising to his cheeks again, Duchess put a hand on his shoulder.

—Emmett Watson, let me introduce you to the sprightliest lifter of spirits in the city of New York: Ma Belle.

Ma Belle laughed again.

—You're even worse than your father.

When everyone was quiet for a moment, Emmett took hold of Duchess by the elbow.

—It's been nice to meet you all, he said, but Duchess and I need to be going.

—Not so soon, said Charity with a frown.

—I'm afraid we have some people waiting, explained Emmett.

Then he pressed his fingers into the soft spots of Duchess's joint.

—Ow, said Duchess freeing his elbow. If you were in such a hurry, why didn't you say so? Just give me a minute to talk with Ma Belle and Charity. Then we can go.

Patting Emmett on the back, Duchess went over to confer with the two women.

—So, said the redhead, you're off to Tinseltown.

—What's that? asked Emmett.

—Duchess tells us you're all going to Hollywood.

Before Emmett could process this news, Duchess turned and slapped his hands.

—Well, ladies, it's been divine. But the time has come for me and Emmett to hit the road.

—If you must, said Ma Belle. But you can't leave without having a drink.

Duchess looked from Emmett to Ma Belle.

—I don't think we have time, Ma.

—Poppycock, she said. Everyone's got time for a drink. And besides, you can't head off to California without letting us toast to your good fortune. It's just not done. Isn't that right, ladies?

—Yes, a toast! the ladies agreed.

Giving Emmett a shrug of resignation, Duchess went to the bar, popped the cork from a bottle of champagne that was waiting on ice, filled six glasses, and handed them around.

—I don't want any champagne, Emmett said quietly when Duchess reached him.

—It's rude not to join in a toast on your behalf, Emmett. And bad luck to boot.

Emmett closed his eyes for a moment, then took the glass.

—First, Ma Belle said, I'd like to thank our friend Duchess for bringing us these lovely bottles of bubbly.

—Hear, hear! cheered the ladies, as Duchess took a bow at every point of the compass.

—It is always bittersweet to lose the company of good friends, continued Ma Belle. But we take heart from the fact that our loss is Hollywood's gain. In closing, I would like to offer you a few lines from that great Irish poet William Butler Yeats: Through the teeth and over the gums, look out stomach here she comes.

Then Ma Belle emptied her glass at a throw.

The ladies all laughed and emptied theirs. Having little choice, Emmett did the same.

—There, said Duchess with a smile. Was that so bad?

As Charity excused herself from the room, Duchess began going from one woman to the next in order to express a farewell in a predictably wordy fashion.

Given the spirit of the moment, Emmett was trying his best to maintain his composure, but he had nearly run out of patience. To make matters worse, what with all the bodies and cushions and tassels, the room had grown overly warm, and the sweet smell of the women's cigarettes off-putting.

—Duchess, he said.

—All right, Emmett. I'm just saying my last goodbyes. Why don't you wait in the hallway, and I'll be right with you.

Setting down his glass, Emmett gladly retreated into the hallway to wait.

While the cooler air did provide Emmett some relief, the hallway suddenly seemed like it was longer and narrower than it had been before. And that there were more doors too. More doors on his left and more on his right. And though he was looking straight ahead, the arrangement of the doors began to give him a sense of vertigo, as if the axis of the building was being tipped and he might fall the length of the hallway and break through the door at the opposite end.

It must be the champagne, thought Emmett.

Shaking his head, he turned and looked back into the living room, only to see that Duchess was now sitting on the edge of the redhead's couch, refilling her glass.

—Christ, he said under his breath.

Emmett began walking back toward the living room, prepared, if necessary, to grab Duchess by the scruff of the neck. But before he had taken two steps, Ma Belle appeared on the threshold and began walking in his direction. Given her girth, there was barely enough room for her to fit in the hallway, and certainly not enough room for her to get past Emmett.

—Come on, she said with an impatient wave of the hand. Clear the way.

As she barreled toward him, Emmett, who was backing up, realized that the door to one of the rooms was open, so he stepped inside to let her pass.

But when she came in line with Emmett, rather than continuing down the hall, she paused and shoved him with a fleshy hand. As he stumbled back into the room, she pulled the door shut and Emmett heard the unmistakable sound of a key turning in a lock. Bounding forward, Emmett grabbed the knob and tried the door. When it wouldn't open, he began banging on it.

—Open the door! he shouted.

As he was repeating his demand, he was struck by the memory of a woman shouting the same thing at him through a closed door somewhere else. Then from behind Emmett came the voice of a different woman. A voice that was softer and more inviting.

—What's the rush, Nebraska?

Turning, Emmett discovered the one called Charity lying on her side on a luxurious bed, patting the covers with a delicate hand. Looking around, Emmett saw that there were no windows in the room, only more paintings of ships, including a large one over a bureau that depicted a schooner in full sail leaning into a high wind. The silk wrap that Charity had been wearing was now draped across the back of an arm chair, and she was in a peach-colored negligee with ivory trim.

—Duchess thought you might be a little nervous, she said in a voice that didn't sound so childlike anymore. But you don't need to be nervous. Not in this room. Not with me.

Emmett began to turn toward the door, but she said *not that way, this way,* so he turned back.

—Come over here, she said, and lie down beside me. Because I want to ask you some things. Or I can tell you some things. Or we don't have to talk at all.

Emmett felt himself taking a step in her direction, a difficult step, his foot landing on the floorboards with a slow and heavy tread. Then he was standing at the edge of the bed with its dark red covers, and she had taken his hand in hers. Looking down, he could see that she was holding it with the palm turned up, as a gypsy would. Emmett wondered, for a second, with a touch of fascination, if she was about to tell his fortune. Instead, she laid his hand against her breast.

Slowly, he drew it away from the smooth, cool silk.

—I've got to get out of here, he said. You need to help me get out of here.

She gave him a little pout, as if he had hurt her feelings. And he felt bad that he had hurt her feelings. He felt so bad that he was inclined to reach out and assure her. Instead, he turned once more toward the door. But this time when he turned, he turned and turned and turned.

Duchess

WAS IN HIGH SPIRITS. That's my excuse.

All day, I had been hopscotching from one pleasant surprise to the next. First, I'd been given the run of Woolly's sister's house and ended up with a fine set of threads; I'd had a nice visit with Ma Belle and the girls; against all odds, Emmett had shown up, giving me the chance (with Charity's help) to perform my third good deed in as many days; and now, here I was sitting behind the wheel of a 1941 Cadillac heading into Manhattan with the top down. The only wrench in the works was that Woolly and I had ended up with Billy in tow.

When Emmett had shown up at Ma Belle's, it hadn't occurred to me for one second that he had brought along his brother, so I was a little surprised to find him at Woolly's side. Don't get me wrong. Billy was a sweet kid as far as kids go. But he was also something of a know-it-all. And if know-it-alls are prone to get under your skin, no know-it-all gets under your skin like a young know-it-all.

We hadn't even been together for an hour and he had already corrected me three times. First, it was to point out that the Sutter sisters hadn't been shooting each other with real guns—like I was the one who needed an introduction to the elements of stagecraft! Next, it was to point out that a seal is a mammal, not some kind of fish, because it has warm blood and a backbone and yatata, yatata, yatata. Then as we were driving onto the Brooklyn Bridge with the skyline stretching before us in all its glory, and I happened to ask in my elevated state whether anyone could think of a single example in the history of mankind of a river crossing that felt more transformative, rather than quietly appreciating the poetry of the moment and the spirit of the remark, the kid—who's sitting in the back seat like a little millionaire—felt the necessity of chiming in.

—I can think of an example, says he.

—The question was rhetorical, says I.

But now he's got Woolly intrigued.

—What's your example, Billy?

—The crossing of the Delaware by George Washington. On Christmas night in 1776, General Washington crossed the river's icy waters to sneak up on the Hessians. Catching them unawares, Washington's troops routed the enemy and captured one thousand prisoners. The event was memorialized in a famous painting by Emanuel Leutze.

—I think I've seen that painting! exclaimed Woolly. Isn't Washington standing in the bow of a rowboat?

—Nobody stands in the bow of a rowboat, I pointed out.

—In Emanuel Leutze's painting, Washington is standing in the bow of a rowboat, said Billy. I can show you a picture, if you'd like. It's in Professor Abernathe's book.

—Of course, it is.

—That's a good one, said Woolly, who was always up for a bit of history.

As it was Friday night, there was some traffic and we ended up coming to a stop at the top of the bridge—which provided us with the perfect opportunity to appreciate the view in silence.

—I know another one, said Billy.

Woolly turned toward the back seat with a smile.

—Which one, Billy?

—When Caesar crossed the Rubicon.

—What happened that time?

You could almost hear the kid sitting up in his seat.

—In 49 B.C. when Caesar was the governor of Gaul, the Senate, which had become wary of his ambitions, recalled him to the capital, instructing him to leave his troops at the banks of the Rubicon. Instead, Caesar marched his soldiers across the river into Italy and led them straight to Rome, where he soon seized power and launched the Imperial Era. That's where the expression *crossing the Rubicon* comes from. It means passing a point of no return.

—Another good one, said Woolly.

—Then there was Ulysses, who crossed the river Styx. . . .

—I think we get the idea, I said.

But Woolly wasn't finished.

—What about Moses? he asked. Didn't he cross a river?

—That was the Red Sea, said Billy. It was when he was—

No doubt the kid had intended to give us chapter and verse on Moses, but for once, he interrupted himself.

—Look! he said, pointing in the distance. The Empire State Building!

All three of us turned our attention to the skyscraper in question, and that's when the idea hit me. Like a little bolt of lightning, it zapped me on the top of the head and sent a tingling sensation up and down my spine.

—Isn't that where his office is? I asked, peeking at Billy in the rearview mirror.

—Whose office? asked Woolly.

—Professor Abercrombie's.

—You mean Professor Abernathe's?

—Exactly. How does it go, Billy? *I write to you from the junction of Thirty-Fourth Street and Fifth Avenue on the isle of Manhattan.* . . .

—Yes, said Billy, his eyes opening wide. That's how it goes.

—Then why don't we pay him a visit.

Out of the corner of my eye, I could see that Woolly was disconcerted by my suggestion. But Billy wasn't.

—We can pay him a visit? he asked.

—I don't see why not.

—Duchess . . . , said Woolly.

I ignored him.

—What's that he calls you in the introduction, Billy? *Dear Reader?* What author wouldn't want to receive a visit from one of his dear readers? I mean, writers must work twice as hard as actors, right? But they don't get any standing ovations, or curtain calls, or people waiting outside the backstage door. Besides, if Professor *Abernathe* didn't want to receive visits from his readers, why would he have put his address on the first page of his book?

—He probably wouldn't be there at this hour, countered Woolly.

—Maybe he's working late, I countered right back.

As the traffic began to move again, I pulled into the right lane in order to take the uptown exit, thinking to myself that if the lobby wasn't open, we were going to climb that building like King Kong.

Having headed west on Thirty-Fifth Street, I took the left onto Fifth Avenue and pulled over right in front of the building's entrance. A second later, one of the doormen was on me.

—You can't park there, buddy.

—We're just going to be a minute, I said, slipping him a five. In the meantime, maybe you and President Lincoln can get to know each other.

Now, instead of telling me where I couldn't park, he was opening Woolly's door and ushering us into the building with a tip of the hat. Capitalism, they call it.

As we entered the lobby, Billy had a look of anxious excitement. He just couldn't believe where we were and what we were about to do. In his wildest dreams, he hadn't imagined it. Woolly, on the other hand, looked at me with a frown that was decidedly out of character.

—What? I said.

Before he could answer, Billy was tugging at my sleeve.

—How will we find him, Duchess?

—You know where to find him, Billy.

—I do?

—You read it to me yourself.

Billy's eyes opened wide.

—On the fifty-fifth floor.

—Exactly.

With a smile I gestured to the elevator bank.

—Are we taking the elevator?

—We're certainly not taking the stairs.

We boarded one of the express cars.

—I've never been in an elevator, Billy said to the operator.

—Enjoy the ride, the operator replied.

Then he pulled the lever and sent us shooting up into the building.

Normally, Woolly would have been humming a ditty on a ride like this, but I was the one who was doing the humming tonight. And Billy, he was quietly counting the floors as we passed them. You could tell by the movement of his lips.

—Fifty-one, he mouthed. Fifty-two, fifty-three, fifty-four.

At the fifty-fifth floor, the operator opened the doors and we disembarked. When we proceeded from the elevator bank into the hallway, we found rows of doors stretching to our left and right.

—What do we do now? asked Billy.

I pointed to the nearest door.

—We'll start there and work our way around the floor until we find him.

—Clockwise? Billy asked.

—Anywise you like.

So we set about going from door to door—clockwise—and Billy would read out the names that were etched on the little brass plaques, just like he'd called out the floors on the elevator, only this time out loud. It was quite a parade of paper pushers. In addition to attorneys and accountants, there were brokers of real estate, insurance, and stocks. Not from the big firms, you understand. These were the shops operated by the guys who couldn't make it in the big firms. The guys who resoled their shoes, and read the funny pages while waiting for the phone to ring.

The first twenty shingles Billy read in a punchy, upbeat manner, like each one was a pleasant little surprise. The next twenty he read with a little less enthusiasm. After those, his delivery began to flag. You could almost hear the thumb of reality beginning to press down on that spot in the soul from which youthful enthusiasm springs. Reality was almost certainly going to leave its mark on Billy Watson tonight. And that mark was likely to stay with him for the rest of his life as a helpful reminder that while the heroes in storybooks are usually figments of the imagination, most of the men who write about them are figments of the imagination too.

When we turned the fourth corner, we could see the last stretch of doors leading up to the spot where we'd begun. Slower and slower Billy moved, softer and softer he spoke, until finally, in front of the second-to-last door, he came to a stop and said nothing at all. He must have read out fifty little plaques by then, and though I was standing behind him, I could tell from his posture that he'd simply had enough.

After a moment, he looked up at Woolly with what must have been an expression of disappointment on his face, because Woolly suddenly had an expression of sympathy on his. Then Billy turned to look at me. Only his expression wasn't of disappointment. It was of wide-eyed amazement.

Turning back to the little brass plaque, he extended a finger and read the inscription out loud.

—Office of Professor Abacus Abernathe, MLA, PhD.

Turning to Woolly with my own expression of amazement, I

realized that the sympathy on his face hadn't been meant for Billy; it had been meant for me. Because once again, the feet I had pulled the rug out from under were my own. After spending a few days with this kid, you'd think I might have known better. But like I said: I blame the high spirits.

Well, when circumstances conspire to spoil your carefully laid plans with an unexpected reversal, the best thing you can do is take credit as quickly as possible.

—What'd I tell you, kid.

Billy gave me a smile, but then he looked at the doorknob with a touch of apprehension, as if he weren't sure he had the gumption to turn it.

—Allow me! exclaimed Woolly.

Stepping forward, Woolly turned the knob and opened the door. Inside, we found ourselves in a small reception area with a desk, coffee table, and a few chairs. The room would have been dark but for a faint light that shone through the open transom over an interior door.

—I guess you were right, Woolly, I said with an audible sigh. Looks like nobody's home.

But Woolly raised a finger to his lips.

—Shhh. Did you hear that?

We all looked up when Woolly pointed at the transom.

—There it is again, he whispered.

—There's what? I whispered back.

—The scratching of a pen, said Billy.

—The scratching of a pen, said Woolly with a smile.

Billy and I followed Woolly as he tiptoed across the reception area and gently turned the second knob. Behind this door was a much bigger room. It was a long rectangle lined from floor to ceiling with books and furnished with a standing globe, a couch, two high-back chairs, and a large wooden desk, behind which sat a little old man writing in a little old ledger by the light of a green-shaded lamp.

Wearing a wrinkled seersucker suit, he had thinning white hair and a pair of reading glasses perched on the tip of his nose. In other words, he looked so much the part of a professor, you had to figure that all the books on the shelves were for show.

At the sound of our entry, the old man looked up from his work without a hint of surprise or dismay.

—May I help you?

After the three of us had taken a few steps, Woolly nudged Billy one step more.

—Ask him, he encouraged.

Billy cleared his throat.

—Are you Professor Abacus Abernathe?

After moving his reading glasses to the top of his head, the old man tilted the shade of his lamp so that he could get a better look at the three of us. Though mostly, he trained his gaze on Billy, having understood in the instant that the boy was the reason we were there.

—I am Abacus Abernathe, he replied. What can I do for you?

Although there seemed to be no end to the things that Billy knew, apparently what he did not know was what Abacus Abernathe could do for him. Because rather than give an answer, Billy looked back at Woolly with an unsure expression. So Woolly spoke on his behalf.

—We're sorry to interrupt you, Professor, but this is Billy Watson from Morgen, Nebraska, who's just arrived in New York City for the very first time. He is only eight years old but he has read your *Compendium* of adventurers twenty-four times.

Having listened to Woolly with interest, the professor shifted his gaze back to Billy.

—Is that so, young man?

—It is so, said Billy. Except that I have read it twenty-five times.

—Well, said the professor, if you have read my book twenty-five times and have come all the way from Nebraska to New York City to tell me so, then the least I can do is offer you a chair.

With an open hand, he invited Billy to take one of the high-back chairs in front of his desk. For Woolly and me, he gestured to the couch by the bookcase.

Let me say right now that it was a very nice couch. It was upholstered with dark brown leather, pinpointed with shiny brass rivets, and almost as big as a car. But if three people who come into a room accept a fourth person's offer of a seat, then no one's going anywhere anytime soon. It's human nature. Having taken all the trouble of making themselves comfortable, people are going to feel the need to chew the fat for at least half an hour. In fact, if they run out of things to say after twenty minutes, they'll start making them up just to be polite. So when the professor offered us the seats, I opened my mouth with every intention of observing that it was getting quite late and our car was at the curb. But before I could get a word out, Billy was climbing onto the high-back chair and Woolly was settling into the couch.

—Now tell me, Billy, said the professor—once we were all irreparably ensconced—what brings you to New York?

As conversations go, it was a classic opener. It was the sort of question that any New Yorker would ask a visitor with a reasonable expectation of a one- or two-sentence reply. Like *I'm here to see my aunt,* or *We have tickets for a show.* But this was Billy Watson, so instead of one or two sentences, what the professor got was the whole megillah.

Billy started back in 1946, on the summer night that his mother walked out on them. He explained about Emmett's doing the hitch at Salina and his father dying of cancer and the brothers' plan to follow the trail of a bunch of postcards so that they could find their mother at a fireworks display in San Francisco on the Fourth of July. He even explained about the escapade and how since Woolly and I had borrowed the Studebaker, he and Emmett had to hitch a ride to New York on the Sunset East.

—Well, well, well, said the professor, who hadn't missed a word. And you say that you traveled to the city by freight train?

—That's where I began your book for the twenty-fifth time, said Billy.

—In the boxcar?

—There wasn't a window, but I had my army surplus flashlight.

—How fortuitous.

—When we decided to go to California and make a fresh start, Emmett agreed with you that we should only carry what we could fit in a kit bag. So I put everything I need in my backpack.

Having leaned back in his chair with a smile, the professor suddenly leaned forward again.

—You wouldn't happen to have the *Compendium* in your backpack now?

—Yes, said Billy. That's just where I have it.

—Then, perhaps I could inscribe it for you?

—That would be terrific! exclaimed Woolly.

At the professor's encouragement, Billy slid off the high-back chair, took off his backpack, undid the straps, and removed the big red book.

—Bring it here, said the professor with a wave of the hand. Bring it over here.

When Billy came around the desk, the professor took the book and held it under his light in order to appreciate the wear and tear.

—There are few things more beautiful to an author's eye, he confessed to Billy, than a well-read copy of one of his books.

Setting the book down, the professor took up his pen and opened to the title page.

—It was a gift, I see.

—From Miss Matthiessen, said Billy. She's the librarian at the Morgen Public Library.

—A gift from a librarian, no less, the professor said with added satisfaction.

Having written in Billy's book at some length, the professor applied his signature with a great big theatrical flourish—since when it comes to New York City, even the old guys who write compendiums perform for the back row. Before returning the book, the professor flitted once through the pages as if to make sure they were all there. Then letting out a little expression of surprise, he looked at Billy.

—I see that you haven't filled in any of the *You* chapter. Now, why is that?

—Because I want to start *in medias res*, explained Billy. And I'm not sure yet where the middle is.

It sounded like a kooky answer to me, but it left the professor beaming.

—Billy Watson, he said, as a seasoned historian and professional teller of tales, I think I can say with confidence that you have already been through enough adventures to warrant the beginning of your chapter! However . . .

Here, the professor opened one of his desk drawers and took out a black ledger just like the one that he'd been working in when we arrived.

—Should the eight pages in your *Compendium* prove insufficient for recording your story in its entirety—as I am almost certain they will—you can continue in the pages of this journal. And should you run out of pages in it, drop me a line, and I shall happily send you another.

Then, after handing over the two books, the professor shook Billy's hand and said what an honor it had been to meet him. And that, as they say, should have been that.

But after Billy had carefully put away his books, cinched the straps on his backpack, and taken the first few steps toward the exit, he suddenly stopped, turned, and faced the professor with a furrowed brow—which with Billy Watson could only mean one thing: more questions.

—I think we've taken up enough of the professor's time, I said, laying a hand on Billy's shoulder.

—That's all right, said Abernathe. What is it, Billy?

Billy looked at the floor for a second, then up at the professor.

—Do you think heroes return?

—You mean like Napoleon returning to Paris, and Marco Polo returning to Venice . . . ?

—No, said Billy shaking his head. I don't mean returning to a place. I mean returning in time.

The professor was quiet for a moment.

—Why do you ask that, Billy?

This go-round, the old scrivener definitely got more than he bargained for. Because without taking a seat, Billy launched into a story that was longer and wilder than the first one. While he was on the Sunset East, he explained, and Emmett had gone looking for food, a pastor who'd invited himself into Billy's boxcar tried to take Billy's collection of silver dollars with the intention of tossing Billy from the train. In the nick of time, a big black guy dropped through the hatch, and it ended up being the pastor who got the old heave-ho.

But apparently, the pastor, the silver dollars, and the last-minute rescue weren't even the point of the story. The point was that the black guy, whose name was Ulysses, had left behind a wife and son when he crossed the Atlantic to fight in the war and had been wandering the country on freight trains ever since.

Now, when an eight-year-old boy is spinning a yarn like this one— with black men dropping through ceilings and pastors being thrown from trains—you might think it would test the limits of someone's willingness to suspend his disbelief. Especially a professor's. But it didn't test Abernathe's in the least.

As Billy told his story, the good professor resumed his seat in slow motion, carefully lowering himself into his chair, then gently leaning back, as if he didn't want a sudden sound or movement to interrupt the boy's story, or his own attention to it.

—He thought he was named Ulysses for Ulysses S. Grant, said Billy, but I explained to him that he must be named for the Great Ulysses. And that having already wandered for over eight years without his wife and son, he was sure to be reunited with them once his ten years of wandering were complete. But if heroes don't return in time, Billy concluded with a touch of concern, then maybe I shouldn't have said that to him.

When Billy stopped speaking, the professor closed his eyes for a moment. Not like Emmett does when he's trying to hold in his exasperation, but like a lover of music who has just heard the ending of his favorite concerto. When he opened his eyes again, he looked from Billy to the books along his walls and back again.

—I have no doubt that heroes return in time, he said to Billy. And I think you were perfectly right to tell him what you did. But I . . .

Now it was the professor who looked at Billy with hesitation, and Billy who encouraged the professor to continue.

—I was just wondering, if this man called Ulysses is still here in New York?

—Yes, said Billy. He is here in New York.

The professor sat for a moment, as if working up the courage to ask a second question of this eight-year-old.

—I know it is late, he said at last, and you and your friends have other places to be, and I have no grounds on which to ask for this favor, but is there any chance that you might be willing to bring me to him?

Woolly

I T WAS ON A TRIP TO GREECE with his mother in 1946, while standing at the foot of the Parthenon, that Woolly first gained an inkling of the List—that itemization of all the places that one was supposed to see. *There it is*, she had said, while fanning herself with her map when they had reached the dusty summit overlooking Athens. *The Parthenon in all its glory*. In addition to the Parthenon, as Woolly was soon to learn, there were the Piazza San Marco in Venice and the Louvre in Paris and the Uffizi in Florence. There were the Sistine Chapel and Notre Dame and Westminster Abbey.

It was something of a mystery to Woolly where the List came from. It seemed to have been compiled by various scholars and eminent historians long before he was born. No one had ever quite explained to Woolly *why* one needed to see all the places on the List, but there was no mistaking the importance of doing so. For his elders would inevitably praise him if he had seen one, frown at him if he expressed disinterest in one, and chastise him in no uncertain terms if he happened to be in the vicinity of one and failed to pay it a visit.

Suffice it to say, when it came to seeing the items on the List, Woolly Wolcott Martin was Johnny-on-the-spot! Whenever he traveled, he took special care to obtain the appropriate guidebooks and secure the services of the appropriate drivers to get him to the appropriate sights at the appropriate times. *To the Colosseum, signore, and step on it!* he would say, and off they would zip through the crooked streets of Rome with all the urgency of policemen in pursuit of a gang of thieves.

Whenever Woolly arrived at one of the places on the List, he always had the same threefold response. First was a sense of awe. For these were not your run-of-the-mill stopping spots. They were big and elaborate and fashioned from all sorts of impressive materials like marble and mahogany and lapis lazuli. Second was a sense of gratitude toward his forebears since they had gone to all the trouble of handing down this itemization from one generation to the next. But third and most important was a sense of relief—a relief that having dropped his bags at his hotel and dashed across the city in the back of a taxi, Woolly could check one more item off the List.

But having considered himself a diligent checker-offer since the age of twelve, earlier that evening when they were driving to the circus, Woolly had something of an epiphany. While the List had been handed down with consistency and care by five generations of Wolcotts— which is to say, Manhattanites—for some strange reason it did not include a single sight in the city of New York. And though Woolly had dutifully visited Buckingham Palace, La Scala, and the Eiffel Tower, he had never, ever, not even once driven across the Brooklyn Bridge.

Growing up on the Upper East Side, Woolly had had no need to cross it. To get to the Adirondacks, or Long Island, or any of those good old boarding schools up in New England, you would travel by way of the Queensborough or Triborough bridges. So after Duchess had driven them down Broadway and circled round City Hall, it was with a palpable sense of excitement that Woolly realized they were suddenly approaching the Brooklyn Bridge with every intention of driving across it.

How truly majestic was its architecture, thought Woolly. How inspiring the cathedral-like buttresses and the cables that soared through the air. What a feat of engineering, especially since it had been built back in eighteen something-something, and ever since had supported the movement of multitudes from one side of the river to the other and back again, every single day. Surely, the Brooklyn Bridge deserved to be on the List. It certainly had as much business being there as the Eiffel Tower, which was made from similar materials at a similar time but which didn't take anybody anywhere.

It must have been an undersight, decided Woolly.

Like his sister Kaitlin and the oil paintings.

When his family had visited the Louvre and the Uffizi, Kaitlin had expressed the highest admiration for all those paintings lined along the walls in their gilded frames. As they walked from gallery to gallery, she was always giving Woolly the shush and pointing with insistence at some portrait or landscape that he was supposed to be quietly admiring. But the funny thing of it was that their townhouse on Eighty-Sixth Street had been chock-full of portraits and landscapes in gilded frames. As had been their grandmother's. And yet, in all those years of growing up, not once had he seen his sister stop in front of one of them in order to contemplate its majesty. That's why Woolly called it an undersight. Because Kaitlin didn't notice those oil paintings even though they were right under her nose. That must have been why the Manhattanites who'd handed down the List had failed to include any of the sights of New York. Which, come to think of it, made Woolly wonder what else they had forgotten.

And then.

And then!

Just two hours later, when they were driving over the Brooklyn Bridge for a second time in one night, Billy stopped speaking midsentence in order to point in the distance.

—Look! he exclaimed. The Empire State Building!

Well, that definitely belongs on the List, thought Woolly. It was the tallest building in the world. It was so tall, in fact, a plane had actually crashed into the top of it once. And yet, even though it was located right there in the middle of Manhattan, Woolly had never, ever, not even once set foot inside.

As such, when Duchess suggested they go there in order to pay a visit to Professor Abernathe, you might have expected Woolly to feel the same excitement that he'd felt when he realized they'd be driving over the Brooklyn Bridge. But what he felt was a pang of anxiety—a pang that stemmed not from the thought of riding a teeny little elevator up into the stratosphere, but from the tone of Duchess's voice. Because Woolly had heard that tone before. He had heard it from three headmasters and two Episcopal ministers and a brother-in-law named "Dennis." It was the tone that people used when they were about to set you straight.

Now and then, it seemed to Woolly, in the course of your everyday life, you are likely to be blessed with a notion. Say, for instance, it's the middle of August and you're drifting in your rowboat in the middle of the lake with the dragonflies skimming the water, when suddenly the thought occurs to you: Why doesn't summer vacation last until the twenty-first of September? After all, the *season* doesn't come to its conclusion on Labor Day weekend. The season of summer lasts until the autumnal equinox—just as surely as the season of spring lasts until the summer solstice. And look at how carefree everyone feels in the middle of summer vacation. Not only the children, but the grown-ups too, who take such pleasure in having a tennis game at ten, a swim at noon, and a gin and tonic at six o'clock on the dot. It stands to reason that if we all agreed to let summer vacation last until the equinox, the world would be a much happier place.

Well, when you have a notion like this, you have to be *very* careful in choosing whom you share it with. Because if certain people get wind of your notion—people like your headmaster or your minister or your brother-in-law "Dennis"—they are likely to feel it's their moral responsibility to sit you down and set you straight. Having gestured for you to take the big chair in front of their desk, they will explain not only how misguided your notion is, but how much better a person you're bound to be once you recognize this fact for yourself. And that was the tone that Duchess was using on Billy—the one that preceded the dispelling of an illusion.

You can just imagine the satisfaction that Woolly felt, the jubilation even, when after elevating all the way up to the fifty-fifth floor, trudging down all the corridors, and squinting at every little plaque, with only two more plaques to go, they came upon the one that read: Professor Abacus Abernathe, AbC, PhD, LMNOP.

Poor Duchess, thought Woolly with a smile of sympathy. Maybe he's the one who will be learning a lesson tonight.

As soon as they entered the professor's inner sanctum, Woolly could see that he was a sensitive man, a genial man. And even though he had a high-back chair in front of a big oak desk, Woolly could tell that he was not the sort who would want to sit you down and set you straight. What's more, he was not the sort to hurry you along because time was money, or of the essence, or a stitch in nine, or what have you.

When you are asked a question—even a question that on the surface seems relatively simple and straightforward—you may have to go quite a ways back in order to provide all the little details that will be necessary for someone to make sense of your answer. Despite this, there are many inquisitors who, as soon as you start providing these essential details, will start to make a face. They'll fidget in their seat. Then they'll do their best to hurry you along by pressing you to leap from point A to point Z while skipping all the letters in between. But not Professor Abernathe. When he asked Billy a deceptively simple question and Billy went all the way back to the cradle in order to give a comprehensive reply, the professor leaned back in his chair and listened with the attentiveness of Solomon.

So when Woolly and Billy and Duchess finally rose to take their leave, having visited two of the city's world-famous sites in a single night (Check! Check!), and proven the irrefutable existence of Professor Abacus Abernathe, you might have thought that the night could not get any better.

And you'd be wrong.

Thirty minutes later, they were all in the Cadillac—the professor included—driving down Ninth Avenue to the West Side Elevated, another place of which Woolly had never heard.

—You take that next right, said Billy.

As instructed, Duchess took the right onto a cobblestone street lined with trucks and meatpacking facilities. Woolly could tell they were meatpacking facilities because on one loading dock, two men in long white coats were carrying sides of beef off a truck while over another was a large neon sign in the shape of a steer.

A moment later, Billy told Duchess to take another right and then a left and then he pointed to some wire caging rising from the street.

—There, he said.

When Duchess pulled over, he didn't turn off the engine. On this little stretch, there were no more meatpackers and no more neon signs. Instead, there was an empty lot in which was parked a car without its wheels. At the end of the block, a lone silhouette, stocky and short, passed under a streetlamp, then disappeared into the shadows.

—Are you sure this is it? Duchess asked.

—I'm sure this is it, said Billy while slipping on his backpack.

Then just like that, he was out of the car and walking toward the caging.

Woolly turned to Professor Abernathe in order to raise his eyebrows in surprise, but Professor Abernathe was already on his way to catch up with Billy. So Woolly leapt from the car in order to catch up with the professor, leaving Duchess to catch up with him.

Inside the caging was a staircase of steel that disappeared overhead.

Now it was the professor who looked to Woolly with his eyebrows raised, though more in excitement than surprise.

Reaching out, Billy took hold of a patch of the fencing and began pulling it back.

—Here, said Woolly. Allow me, allow me.

Extending his fingers through the mesh, Woolly pulled so that everyone could slip through. Then up the stairs they went, going round and round, their eight feet clanging on the old metal treads. When they reached the top, Woolly pulled back another bit of fencing so that everyone could slip out.

Oh, what amazement did Woolly feel when he emerged from the caging into the open air. To the south, you could see the towers of Wall Street, while to the north, the towers of Midtown. And if you looked very carefully to the south-southwest, you could just make out the Statue of Liberty—another New York City landmark that surely belonged on the List and to which Woolly had never been.

—Never been, yet! Woolly pronounced in defiance to no one but himself.

But what was amazing about the elevated tracks wasn't the view of Wall Street or Midtown or even the great big summer sun that was setting over the Hudson. What was amazing was the flora.

While they had been in Professor Abernathe's office, Billy had explained that they would be going to a segment of elevated railroad that had stopped being used three years before. But to Woolly's eye, it looked like it had been abandoned for decades. Everywhere you turned there were wildflowers and shrubs, and the grass between the railroad ties had grown almost as high as their knees.

In just three years, thought Woolly. Why, that's less time than it takes to go to boarding school, or to get a college degree. It's less time than a presidential term, or the span between Olympics.

Only two days before, Woolly had remarked to himself how terribly permanent Manhattan remained, despite being marched upon by millions of people every day. But apparently, it wasn't the marching of the millions that was going to bring the city to its end. It was their absence. For here was a glimpse of a New York left to itself. Here was a patch of the city upon which people had turned their backs for just a moment and up through the gravel had come the shrubs and ivy and grass. And if this is what it was like after just a few years of disuse, thought Woolly, imagine what it will be like after a few decades.

As Woolly looked up from the flora in order to share his observation with his friends, he realized that they had pressed ahead without him, working their way toward a campfire in the distance.

—Wait up, he called. Wait up!

As Woolly rejoined his party, Billy was introducing the professor to a tall black man, the one named Ulysses. Though the two men had never met, both had learned something of the other from Billy, and when they shook hands, it struck Woolly that they did so with solemnity, a great and enviable solemnity.

—Please, said Ulysses, as he gestured to the railroad ties around the fire much as the professor had gestured to the couch and chair in his office.

When they had taken their seats, everyone was silent for a moment as the fire crackled and sparked, and it seemed to Woolly that he and Billy and Duchess were young warriors who had been given the privilege of witnessing the meeting between two tribal chiefs. But in the end, it was Billy who spoke first, encouraging Ulysses to tell his tale.

After nodding at Billy, Ulysses turned his eyes to the professor and began. First, he explained how he and a woman named Macie, both alone in the world, had met in a dance hall in St. Louis, fallen in love, and been joined in holy matrimony. He explained how, when the war began, Macie had kept him close to her side as his able-bodied neighbors joined the fray, and how she had tightened her grip once she was radiant with child. He explained how despite her warnings, he had enlisted, fought in Europe, and returned some years later to find that— good as her word—she and the boy had disappeared without a trace. Finally, he described how he had returned to Union Station that day, boarded the first train to anywhere, and been riding the rails ever since. And it was one of the saddest stories that Woolly had ever heard.

For a moment no one spoke. Even Duchess, who was always eager to follow someone else's story with a story of his own, kept his silence, sensing, perhaps, as Woolly did, that something of great consequence was unfolding right before their eyes.

After a few minutes, as if he had needed the moment of silence in order to gather himself, Ulysses continued.

—I am of the opinion, Professor, that everything of value in this life must be earned. That it *should* be earned. Because those who are given something of value without having to earn it are bound to squander it. I believe that one should earn respect. One should earn trust. One should earn the love of a woman, and the right to call oneself a man. And one should also earn the right to hope. At one time I had a wellspring of hope—a wellspring that I had not earned. And not knowing what it was worth, on the day I left my wife and child, I squandered it. So over these last eight and a half years, I have learned to live without hope, just as surely as Cain lived without it once he entered the land of Nod.

To live without hope, said Woolly to himself as he nodded his head and wiped the tears from his eyes. To live without hope in the land of Nod.

—That is, said Ulysses, until I met this boy.

Without taking his gaze from the professor, Ulysses put a hand on Billy's shoulder.

—When Billy said that as one named Ulysses, I might be destined to see my wife and child again, I felt a stirring within me. And when he read to me from your book, I felt it even more strongly. So much more strongly, that I dared to wonder if, after all these years of traveling the country alone, I might finally have earned the right to hope again.

As Ulysses said this, Woolly sat up straighter. Earlier that day, he had tried to give his sister Sarah some sense of how a statement disguised as a question could be an ugly sort of thing. But beside the campfire, when Ulysses said to Professor Abernathe, *I might finally have earned the right to hope again,* Woolly understood that here was a question disguised as a statement. And Woolly found it to be beautiful.

Professor Abernathe seemed to understand this as well. For after a moment of silence, he offered an answer. And as the professor spoke, Ulysses listened with the same deference that the professor had shown to him.

—My life, such as it is, Mr. Ulysses, has been the opposite of yours in many respects. I have never been to war. I have not traveled this country. In fact, for most of the last thirty years, I have remained on the island of Manhattan. And for most of the last ten, I have remained in that.

Turning, the professor pointed to the Empire State Building.

—There I have sat in a room surrounded by books, as insulated from the sounds of crickets and seagulls as from the reach of violence and compassion. If you are right, as I suspect you are—that what is valuable must be earned or it's bound to be squandered—then surely, I am among the squanderers. One who has lived his life in the third person and the past tense. So let me start by acknowledging that anything I say to you, I say with the utmost humility.

Ceremoniously, the professor bowed his head to Ulysses.

—But having confessed that I have lived my life through books, I can at least report that I have done so with conviction. Which is to say, Mr. Ulysses, that I have read a great deal. I have read thousands of books, many of them more than once. I have read histories and novels, scientific tracts and volumes of poetry. And from all of these pages upon pages, one thing I have learned is that there is just enough variety in human experience for every single person in a city the size of New York to feel with assurance that their experience is unique. And this is a wonderful thing. Because to aspire, to fall in love, to stumble as we do and yet soldier on, at some level we must believe that what we are going through has never been experienced quite as *we* have experienced it.

The professor turned his gaze from Ulysses so that he could make eye contact with everyone in the circle, including Woolly. But returning his gaze to Ulysses, the professor raised a finger in the air.

—However, he continued, having observed that there is enough variety in human experience to sustain our sense of individuality in a locus as vast as New York, I strongly suspect that there is only *just* enough variety to do so. For were it in our power to gather up all the personal stories that have been experienced in different cities and townships around the world and across time, I haven't the slightest doubt that doppelgängers would abound. Men whose lives—despite the variation here and there—were just as our own in every material respect. Men who have loved when we loved, wept when we wept, accomplished what we have accomplished and failed as we have failed, men who have argued and reasoned and laughed exactly as we.

The professor looked around again.

—Impossible, you say?

Though no one had said a word.

—It is one of the most basic principles of infinity that it must, by definition, encompass not only one of everything, but everything's duplicate, as well as its triplicate. In fact, to imagine that there are additional versions of ourselves scattered across human history is substantially less outlandish than to imagine that there are none.

The professor turned his gaze back to Ulysses.

—So, do I think it is possible that your life could be an echo of the life of the Great Ulysses, and that after ten years you could be reunited with your wife and son? I am certain of it.

Ulysses had taken in what the professor had said with the greatest gravity. Now he stood, and the professor stood, and the two clasped hands, each seeming to have found an unexpected solace from the other. But when the two men let their hands drop and Ulysses turned, the professor took him by the arm and drew him back.

—But there is something you need to know, Mr. Ulysses. Something that I didn't put in Billy's book. In the midst of his travels, when the Great Ulysses visited the underworld and met the ghost of Tiresias, the old soothsayer told him that he was destined to wander the seas until he had appeased the gods through an act of tribute.

Had Woolly been in Ulysses's position, upon hearing this additional piece of news, he would have felt a great sense of defeat. But Ulysses didn't seem to. Instead, he nodded his head at the professor, as if this was just as it should be.

—What act of tribute?

—What Tiresias tells Ulysses is that he must take up an oar and carry it into the countryside until he has reached a land so unfamiliar with the ways of the sea that a man in the road will stop to ask: *What is that you carry upon your shoulder?* At that spot, the Great Ulysses was to plant the oar in the ground in Poseidon's honor, and thenceforth he would be free.

—An oar . . . , said Ulysses.

—Yes, said the professor excitedly, in the case of the Great Ulysses, an oar. But in your case, it would be something different. Something pertinent to *your* story, to your years of wandering. Something . . .

The professor began looking about.

—Something like that!

Bending over, Ulysses picked up the heavy piece of iron the professor had pointed to.

—A spike, he said.

—Yes, said the professor, a spike. You must carry that to the place where someone is so unfamiliar with the railways that they ask you what it is, and on that spot, you should hammer it into the ground.

—.—

When Woolly and Billy and Duchess were ready to leave, Professor Abernathe decided to stay behind in order to speak with Ulysses further. Then, just a few minutes after the three of them had gotten in the Cadillac, both Billy and Duchess had fallen asleep. So, as Woolly drove up the West Side Highway toward his sister's house, he had a moment to himself.

If Woolly were perfectly honest, most of the time he'd rather not have a moment to himself. Moments with other people, he found, were much more likely to be filled with laughter and surprises than moments with oneself. And moments with oneself were more likely to circle inward toward some thought that one didn't want to be having in the first place. But on this occasion, on this occasion that he found himself with a moment to himself, Woolly welcomed it.

Because it provided him with the opportunity to revisit the day. He began at FAO Schwarz, when he was standing in his favorite spot and his sister had suddenly appeared. Then it was across the street to the Plaza for old times' sake where they had tea with the panda and retold some of the grand old stories. Upon parting with his sister, finding it to be a lovely day, Woolly had walked all the way to Union Square so he could pay his respects to Abraham Lincoln. Then it was off to the circus, and over the Brooklyn Bridge, and up the Empire State Building where Professor Abernathe had bestowed upon Billy a book filled with blank pages in which to set down his adventures. Then Billy had taken them all to the overgrown elevated, where they had sat around the campfire and listened to the extraordinary exchange between Ulysses and the professor.

But after that, after all of the all of that, when it was finally time to go, and Ulysses had shaken Billy's hand and thanked him for his friendship, and Billy had wished Ulysses well on his quest to find his family, Billy had taken a pendant from around his neck.

—This, he said to Ulysses, is the medal of St. Christopher, the patron saint of travelers. It was given to me by Sister Agnes before our journey to New York, but I think that you should have it now.

And then, so that the medal could be hung around his neck, Ulysses knelt before Billy, just as the members of the Round Table had knelt before King Arthur in order to be knighted.

—When you put it, said Woolly to no one but himself, while wiping a tear from the corner of his eye, when you put it all together just like that, with the beginning at the beginning, the middle in the middle, and the end at the end, there is no denying that today was a one-of-a-kind kind of day.

THREE

—·—

Woolly

CORIANDER! SAID WOOLLY TO himself with enthusiasm.

For while Duchess was showing Billy how to *properly* stir a sauce, Woolly had set about alphabetizing the spice rack. And it didn't take long for him to discover just how many spices began with the letter C. In the entire rack there was only one that started with the letter *A*: Allspice, whatever that was. And Allspice was followed by just two spices that began with the letter *B*: Basil and Bay Leaves. But once Woolly moved on to spices that began with the letter C, well, it seemed there was no end to them! So far, there had been Cardamom, Cayenne, Chili Powder, Chives, Cinnamon, Cloves, Cumin, and now, Coriander.

It certainly made one wonder.

Perhaps, thought Woolly, perhaps it was like the matter of the *Ws* at the beginning of questions. At some point in ancient times, the letter C must have seemed particularly suitable to the naming of spices.

Or maybe it was at some *place* in ancient times. Some place where the letter C had more sway over the alphabet. All of a sudden Woolly seemed to remember from one of his history classes that many moons ago there had been something called the Spice Route—a long and arduous trail along which tradesmen traveled in order to bring the spices of the East to the kitchens of the West. He even remembered a map with an arrow that arced across the Gobi Desert and over the Himalayas until it touched down safely in Venice, or some such spot.

That the C spices originated on the other side of the globe struck Woolly as a clear possibility, since he didn't even know what half of them tasted like. He knew Cinnamon, of course. In fact, it was one of his favorite flavors. Not only was it used in the making of apple and pumpkin pie, it was the *sine qua non* of the cinnamon bun. But Cardamom, Cumin, and Coriander? These mysterious words struck Woolly as having a distinctly oriental ring.

—Aha! said Woolly, when he discovered the bottle of Curry hiding behind the Rosemary in the second-to-last row of the rack.

For Curry was most certainly definitely a flavor from the East.

Making some space, Woolly tucked the Curry beside the Cumin. Then he turned his attention to the very last row, running his fingers along the labels of the Oregano and the Sage and the—

—What in the world are *you* doing there? Woolly wondered to himself.

But before he could answer his own question, Duchess was asking another.

—Where did he go?

Looking up from the spice rack, Woolly discovered Duchess in the doorway with his hands on his hips and Billy nowhere to be seen.

—I turn my back for one minute and he abandons his post.

It was true, thought Woolly. Billy had left the kitchen despite having been put in charge of stirring the sauce.

—He hasn't gone back to that goddamn clock, has he? asked Duchess.

—Let me investigate.

Quietly, Woolly headed down the hallway and peeked into the living room, where, in fact, Billy had returned to the grandfather clock.

Earlier that morning, when Billy had asked when Emmett would arrive, Duchess had replied with a great deal of confidence that he would be there in time for supper—which was to be served at eight o'clock on the dot. Normally, this would have prompted Billy to take an occasional glance at his army surplus watch, but the watch had been broken by Emmett on the freight train. So he really had no choice but to pay an occasional visit to the living room instead, where the hands on the grandfather clock now indicated, rather unambiguously, that it was 7:42.

Woolly was tiptoeing back toward the kitchen in order to explain this to Duchess when the telephone rang.

—The phone! Woolly exclaimed to himself. Maybe it's Emmett.

Making a quick detour into his brother-in-law's office, Woolly zipped around the desk and picked up the receiver on the very third ring.

—Hello, hello! he said with a smile.

For a moment Woolly's friendly greeting was met with silence. Then a question was posed in what could only be described as a sharply pointed voice.

—Who is this? the woman on the other end of the line wanted to know. Is that you, Wallace?

Woolly hung up.

For a moment he stared at the phone. Then plucking the receiver out of its cradle, he dropped it on the desk.

What Woolly loved about the game of telephone was that a phrase coming out at the end of the line could be so very different from the phrase that had first gone in. It could be more mysterious. Or surprising. Or amusing. But when someone like his sister Kaitlin spoke into an *actual* telephone, it did not come out even slightly more mysterious or surprising or amusing. It came out just as sharply pointed as it was at the start.

On the desktop the receiver began buzzing like a mosquito in a bedroom in the middle of the night. Woolly swept the phone into one of the drawers and closed it as best he could, what with the cord sticking out.

—Who was that? asked Duchess, when Woolly returned to the kitchen.

—A wrong number.

Billy, who also must have been hoping it had been Emmett, turned to Duchess with a worried look.

—It is almost eight o'clock, he said.

—Is it? said Duchess, in a manner suggesting that one hour was much like the next.

—How's the sauce coming? Woolly asked, in hopes of changing the subject.

Duchess held the stirring spoon out to Billy.

—Why don't you give it a try.

After a moment, Billy took the spoon and dipped it in the pot.

—It looks pretty hot, Woolly cautioned.

Billy nodded and blew carefully. When he put the spoon in his mouth, Woolly and Duchess leaned forward in unison, eager to hear the verdict. What they heard instead was the ding-dong of the doorbell.

The three looked at one another. Then Duchess and Billy were off like a shot, the former down the hallway and the latter through the dining-room door.

Woolly smiled for a moment at the sight of it. But then he had a worrisome thought: What if this was another instance of Schrödinger's Cat? What if the ringing of the bell initiated two different potential realities such that if the door were opened by Billy, it would be Emmett who was standing on the stoop, while were it opened by Duchess, it would be a door-to-door salesman? In a state of scientific uncertainty and heightened anxiety, Woolly hurried down the hall.

Duchess

WHEN THE NEW BOYS would arrive at St. Nick's, Sister Agnes would put them to work.

If we are asked to apply ourselves to that which is before us, she would say, *we are less likely to fret over that which is not.* So when they showed up on the doorstep looking a little shell-shocked, a little shy, and generally on the verge of tears, she would send them to the dining room to put out the silverware for lunch. Once the tables were set, she'd send them to the chapel to lay out the hymnals in the pews. Once the hymnals were in place, there were towels to be collected, sheets to be folded, and leaves to be raked—until the new boys weren't the new boys anymore.

And that's what I did with the kid.

Why? Because breakfast wasn't even over before he was asking when his brother would arrive.

Personally, I didn't expect Emmett to show up before noon. Knowing Charity, I figured he would've had his hands full until two in the morning. Assuming he slept until eleven and lingered under the covers, he might make it to Hastings-on-Hudson by two in the afternoon. At the earliest. To be on the safe side, I told Billy he'd be here for dinner.

—What time is dinner?

—Eight o'clock.

—Eight o'clock on the dot? asked Woolly.

—On the dot, I confirmed.

Nodding, Billy excused himself politely, paid a visit to the clock in the living room, and returned with the news that it was 10:02.

The implication was plain enough. There were 598 minutes between now and his brother's promised arrival, and Billy intended to count every one of them. So as soon as Woolly started clearing the breakfast dishes, I asked Billy if he'd give me a hand.

First, I brought him to the linen closet, where we picked out a fine tablecloth and spread it across the dining-room table, taking care to ensure that it draped over the ends in equal measure. At the four places, we laid out linen napkins, each with a different flower embroidered on it. When we turned our attention to the hutch and Billy observed it was locked, I observed that keys were rarely far from their escutcheons, and reached my hand into the tureen.

—Voilà.

With the hutch's doors open, out came the fine china plates for the appetizer, main course, and dessert. Out came the crystal for the water and wine. Out came the two candelabra and the flat black case that held the family silver.

Having instructed Billy how to lay out the cutlery, I figured I'd have to tighten up his work once he was finished. But when it came to setting places, it turned out Billy was a natural. It looked like he had positioned each fork, knife, and spoon with his ruler and compass.

As we stood back to admire our work, he asked if tonight was going to be a special dinner.

—Exactly.

—Why is it a special dinner, Duchess?

—Because it's a reunion, Billy. A reunion of the Four Musketeers.

The kid broke out in a big smile over that one, but then his brow furrowed. With Billy Watson there was never more than a minute between the smile and the furrow.

—If it's a special dinner, what are we going to eat?

—An excellent question. At the request of one Woolly Martin, we are going to have a little something known as *Fettuccine Mio Amore*. And that, my friend, is as special as it gets.

After getting Billy to write out a shopping list of all the ingredients we would need, we were off to Arthur Avenue, driving at a speed of three hundred questions an hour.

—What's Arthur Avenue, Duchess?

—It's the main drag in the Italian section of the Bronx, Billy.

—What's an Italian section?

—It's where all the Italians live.

—Why do all the Italians live in one place?

—So they can mind each other's business.

What's a trattoria, Duchess?

What's a paisano?

What's an artichoke and pancetta and tiramisu?

When we returned a few hours later, it was too early to start cooking, so having confirmed that Billy's mathematics were up to snuff, I took him into Woolly's brother-in-law's office to do a little accounting.

Seating him at the desk with a pad and pencil, I lay down on the rug and rattled off all the expenses that Woolly and I had racked up since leaving St. Nick's. The six tanks of gas; the room and board at two Howard Johnson's; the beds and towels at the Sunshine Hotel; and the two meals at the diner on Second Avenue. To be on the safe side, I had him add an extra twenty for future outlays, then tally the whole list under the heading of Operational Expenses. Once we recovered Woolly's trust from the Adirondacks, these costs were to be reimbursed to Emmett before a single dollar was divvied.

In a separate column under the heading of Personal Expenses, I had Billy include the long-distance call to Salina; the ten bucks for Bernie at the Sunshine Hotel; the bottle of whiskey for Fitzy; the champagne and companionship at Ma Belle's; and the tip for the doorman at the Empire State Building. Since none of these outlays were essential to our shared endeavor, I figured they should come out of my end.

At the last second, I remembered the expenditures on Arthur Avenue. You could argue that they belonged under the Operational Expenses since we'd all be eating them together. But with an ah-what-the-hell, I told Billy to put them in my column. Tonight, dinner was on me.

Once Billy had all the numbers down and he'd double-checked his sums, I encouraged him to take out a fresh sheet of paper and transcribe the two tallies. At a suggestion like that, most kids would have wanted to know why after doing the job once, they had to do it all over again. But not Billy. With his instinctive preference for the neat and tidy, he took out a new piece of paper and began duplicating his work with the same precision that he had laid out the forks and knives.

When he was finished, Billy nodded his head three times, giving the tally his patented seal of approval. But then his brow furrowed.

—Shouldn't it have a title, Duchess?

—What did you have in mind?

Billy thought about it for a second while biting the end of his pencil. Then after writing it out in big capital letters, he read:

—The Escapade.

Now, how do you like that?

When the expense report was finished, it was after six o'clock—time to start cooking. After laying out the ingredients, I taught Billy everything that Lou, the chef at Leonello's, had taught to me. First, how to make a basic tomato sauce from canned tomatoes and a soffritto (*What's a soffritto, Duchess?*). Once that was on the stove, I showed him how to properly dice the bacon and properly slice the onion. Taking out a saucepan, I showed him how to properly sauté them together with the bay leaves. How to simmer them in white wine with oregano and pepper flakes. And finally, how to stir in one cup of the tomato sauce, and not a teaspoon more.

—The important thing now, I explained, is to keep an eye on it, Billy. I've got to go to the washroom, so I want you to stand right where you are and occasionally give it a stir. All right?

—All right, Duchess.

Handing Billy the spoon, I excused myself and headed for Dennis's office.

Having said that I didn't think Emmett would be here by two, I'd thought for sure that he'd be here by six. After quietly closing the door, I dialed Ma Belle. It took her twenty rings to answer, but after giving me an earful about the etiquette of calling someone while they're in the middle of their bath, she brought me up to speed.

—Uh oh, I said as I hung up the phone.

Having done one accounting with Billy, I found myself doing another on my own: With Emmett already a little peeved about the Studebaker, I had hoped to make it up to him by giving him the night with Charity; but clearly that hadn't gone as planned. How was I supposed to know that Woolly's medicine was so strong? Then to top it all off, I'd forgotten to leave an address. Yep, I thought to myself, there is a distinct possibility that when Emmett arrives, he'll be in a bad mood. Assuming, that is, that he can find us . . .

Returning to the kitchen, I discovered Woolly staring at the spice rack and no one tending the sauce. That's when things began to accelerate.

First, Woolly went off on reconnaissance.

Then the telephone rang and Billy reappeared.

Then Woolly returned with word of a wrong number, Billy announced it was nearly eight, and the doorbell rang.

Please, oh please, oh please, I said to myself as I dashed down the hall. With my heart in my mouth and Billy hot on my heels, I swung the door open—and there was Emmett in a clean set of clothes, looking only a little worse for wear.

Before anyone had a chance to speak, the clock in the living room began to chime the hour of eight.

Turning to Billy, I stuck out my arms and said:

—What'd I tell you, kid?

Emmett

A T THE START OF Emmett's junior year, the new math teacher, Mr. Nickerson, had presented Zeno's paradox. In ancient Greece, he'd said, a philosopher named Zeno argued that to get from point A to point B, one had to go halfway there first. But to get from the halfway mark to point B, one would have to cross half of that distance, then halfway again, and so on. And when you piled up all the halves of halves that would have to be crossed to get from one point to another, the only conclusion to be drawn was that it couldn't be done.

Mr. Nickerson had said this was a perfect example of paradoxical reasoning. Emmett had thought it a perfect example of why going to school could be a waste of time.

Just imagine, thought Emmett, all the mental energy that had been expended not only to formulate this paradox, but to pass it down through the ages, translating it from language to language so that it could be scratched on a chalkboard in the United States of America in 1952—five years after Chuck Yeager broke the sound barrier over the Mojave Desert.

Mr. Nickerson must have noticed Emmett's expression at the back of the classroom, because when the bell rang, he asked Emmett to stay.

—I just want to make sure you followed the argument this morning.

—I followed it, said Emmett.

—And what did you think?

Emmett looked out the window for a moment, unsure of whether he should share his point of view.

—Go ahead, encouraged Mr. Nickerson. I want to hear your take.

All right then, thought Emmett.

—It seemed to me a long and complicated way of proving something that my six-year-old brother could disprove in a matter of seconds with his own two feet.

But as Emmett said this, Mr. Nickerson didn't seem the least put out. Rather, he nodded his head with enthusiasm, as if Emmett was on the verge of making a discovery as important as Zeno's.

—What you're saying, Emmett, if I understand you, is that Zeno appears to have pursued his proof for argument's sake rather than for its practical value. And you're not alone in making that observation. In fact, we have a word for the practice, which is almost as old as Zeno: *Sophistry*. From the Greek *sophistes*—those teachers of philosophy and rhetoric who gave their students the skills to make arguments that could be clever or persuasive but which weren't necessarily grounded in reality.

Mr. Nickerson even wrote the word out on the chalkboard right below his diagram of the infinitely bisected journey from A to B.

Isn't that just perfect, thought Emmett. In addition to handing down the lessons of Zeno, scholars have handed down a specialized word, the sole purpose of which is to identify the practice of teaching nonsense as sense.

At least that's what Emmett had thought while standing in Mr. Nickerson's classroom. What he was thinking as he walked along a winding, tree-lined street in the town of Hastings-on-Hudson was maybe Zeno hadn't been so crazy after all.

—·—

That morning, Emmett had come to consciousness with a sensation of floating—like one who's being carried down a wide river on a warm summer day. Opening his eyes, he found himself under the covers of an unfamiliar bed. On the side table was a lamp with a red shade that cast the room in a rosy hue. But neither the bed nor the lamplight were soft enough to mollify the ache in his head.

Emitting a groan, Emmett made an effort to raise himself, but from across the room came the patter of bare feet, then a hand that gently pressed against his chest.

—You just lie there and be quiet.

Though she was now wearing a simple white blouse and her hair was pulled back, Emmett recognized his nurse as the young woman in the negligee who, the night before, had been lying where he was lying now.

Turning toward the hallway, Charity called out, *he's awake*, and a moment later Ma Belle, dressed in a giant floral housedress, was standing in the doorway.

—So he is, she said.

Emmett hoisted himself up again, this time with more success. But as he did so, the covers fell from his chest and he realized with a start that he was naked.

—My clothes, he said.

—You think I'd let them put you in one of my beds while dressed in those filthy things, said Ma Belle.

—Where are they . . . ?

—Waiting for you right there on the bureau. Now, why don't you get yourself out of bed and come have something to eat.

Ma Belle turned to Charity.

—Come on, honey. Your vigil here has ended.

When the two women closed the door, Emmett threw back the covers and rose carefully, feeling a little uneasy on his feet. Crossing to the bureau he was surprised to find his clothes freshly laundered and neatly folded in a pile, his belt coiled on top. As Emmett buttoned his shirt, he found himself staring at the painting he had noticed the night before. Only now he could see that the mast was at an angle not because the ship was leaning into a high wind, but because it was foundering against the rocks with some sailors hanging from the rigging, others scrambling into a dory, and the head of one bobbing in the high white wake on the verge of being either dashed upon the rocks or swept out to sea.

As Duchess never tired of saying: *Exactly*.

When Emmett exited the bedroom, he made a point of turning to his left without looking down the vertiginous succession of doors. In the lounge, he found Ma Belle in a high-back chair with Charity standing at her side. On the coffee table were a breakfast cake and coffee.

Dropping onto the couch, Emmett ran a hand over his eyes.

Ma Belle pointed to a pink rubber bag on a plate beside the coffee pot.

—There's an ice pack, if you're partial to them.

—No thanks.

Ma Belle nodded.

—I never understood the attraction myself. After a big night, I wouldn't want a bag of ice anywhere near me.

A big night, thought Emmett with a shake of the head.

—What happened?

—They gave you a mickey, said Charity with a mischievous smile.

Ma Belle scowled.

—It wasn't a mickey, Charity. And there was no *they*. It was just Duchess being Duchess.

—Duchess? said Emmett.

Ma Belle gestured at Charity.

—He wanted to give you a little present. In honor of finishing your time at that work farm. But he was worried you might get a case of the jitters—what with your being a Christian and a virgin.

—There's nothing wrong with being a Christian or a virgin, Charity said supportively.

—Well, I'm not so sure about that, said Ma Belle. Anyway, in order to set the mood, I was supposed to suggest a toast and Duchess was going to put a little something in your drink to help you relax. But the little something must have been stronger than he thought it was, because once we got you into Charity's room, you spun around twice and out went the lights. Isn't that right, honey?

—It's a good thing you landed in my lap, she said with a wink.

Both of them seemed to find this an amusing turn of events. It just made Emmett grind his teeth.

—Oh, don't get all angry on us now, said Ma Belle.

—If I'm angry, it's not with you.

—Well, don't get angry with Duchess either.

—He didn't mean no harm, said Charity. He just wanted you to have a good time.

—That's a fact, said Ma Belle. And at his own expense.

Emmett didn't bother pointing out that the intended good time, like the champagne the night before, had been paid for with his money.

—Even as a boy, said Charity, Duchess was always making sure that everybody else was having a good time.

—Anyway, continued Ma Belle, we're supposed to tell you that Duchess, your brother, and that other friend . . .

—Woolly, said Charity.

—Right, said Ma Belle. Woolly. They'll all be waiting for you at his sister's house. But first, you should have something to eat.

Emmett ran a hand over his eyes again.

—I'm not sure I'm hungry, he said.

Ma Belle frowned.

Leaning forward, Charity spoke a little under her breath.

—Ma Belle doesn't generally serve breakfast.

—You're damn right, I don't.

After accepting a cup of the coffee and a slice of the coffee cake in order to be polite, Emmett was reminded that half the time, manners are there for your own good. For as it turned out, the coffee and cake were just what he needed. So much so that he readily accepted the offer of seconds.

As he ate, Emmett asked how the ladies had come to know Duchess when he was a boy.

—His father worked here, said Charity.

—I thought he was an actor.

—He was an actor all right, said Ma Belle. And when he couldn't get any work onstage, he acted like a waiter or a maître d'. But for a few months after the war, he acted like our ringmaster. Harry could act like just about anything, I suppose. But most of the time, he acted like his own worst enemy.

—In what way?

—Harry's a charmer with a soft spot for the sauce. So while he could talk his way into a job in a matter of minutes, he could drink his way back out of it almost as quickly.

—But when he was working at the Circus, chipped in Charity, he would leave Duchess with us.

—He'd bring Duchess here? asked Emmett, a little shocked.

—That's right, said Ma Belle. At the time, he was probably about eleven years old. And while his father was downstairs, he'd work up here in the lounge. Taking hats and pouring drinks for the customers. He made good money too. Not that his father let him keep it.

Emmett looked around the room, trying to imagine Duchess at the age of eleven taking hats and pouring drinks in a house of ill repute.

—It wasn't like it is now, Ma Belle said, following his gaze. Back then on a Saturday night, the Circus was standing-room-only and we had ten girls working up here. And it wasn't just the boys from the Navy Yard. We had *society* people.

—Even the mayor came, Charity said.

—What happened?

Ma Belle shrugged.

—Times changed. The neighborhood changed. Tastes changed.

Then she looked around the room a little nostalgically.

—I thought it was the war that was going to put us out of business; but in the end, it was the suburbs.

Shortly before noon, Emmett was ready to take his leave. Receiving a peck on the cheek from Charity and a shake of the hand from Ma Belle, he thanked them for the clean clothes, for the breakfast, for their kindness.

—If you could just give me the address, I'll be on my way.

Ma Belle looked at Emmett.

—What address?

—The one for Woolly's sister.

—Why would I have that?

—Didn't Duchess leave it with you?

—He didn't leave it with me. How 'bout you, honey?

When Charity shook her head, Emmett closed his eyes.

—Why don't we check the phone directory, Charity suggested brightly.

Charity and Ma Belle both looked to Emmett.

—I don't know her married name.

—Well, I guess you're shit-out-of-luck.

—Ma, chided Charity.

—All right, all right. Let me think.

Ma Belle looked off for a moment.

—This friend of yours—Woolly. What's his story?

—He's from New York. . . .

—So we gathered. But what borough?

Emmett looked back without understanding.

—What *neighborhood*. Brooklyn? Queens? Manhattan?

—Manhattan.

—That's a start. Do you know where he went to school?

—He went to boarding school. St. George's . . . St. Paul's . . . St. Mark's . . .

—He's Catholic! said Charity.

Ma Belle rolled her eyes.

—Those aren't Catholic schools, honey. Those are WASP schools. Fancy ones at that. And having known more than my share of their alumni, I'd bet you a blue blazer that your friend Woolly is from the Upper East Side. But which one did he go to: St. George's, St. Paul's, or St. Mark's?

—All of them.

—All of them?

When Emmett explained that Woolly had been kicked out of two, Ma Belle shook with laughter.

—Ho, boy, she said at last. If you get thrown out of one of those schools, to get into another you need to come from a pretty old family. But to get thrown out of two and go to a third? You need to have arrived on the *Mayflower*! So what's this Woolly character's *real* name?

—Wallace Wolcott Martin.

—Of course, it is. Charity, why don't you go in my office and bring me the black book that's in my desk drawer.

When Charity returned from the room behind the piano, Emmett was expecting her to have a little address book. Instead, she was carrying a large black volume with a dark red title.

—The *Social Register*, explained Ma Belle. This is where everybody's listed.

—Everybody? asked Emmett.

—Not my everybody. When it comes to the *Social Register*, I've been on it, under it, behind and in front of it, but I've never been in it.

Because it was designed to list the *other* everybody. Here. Make room, Gary Cooper.

When Ma Belle dropped onto the couch at Emmett's side, he could feel the cushions sink a few inches closer to the floor. Glancing at the cover of the book, Emmett couldn't help but notice it was the 1951 edition.

—It's out of date, he said.

Ma Belle gave him a frown.

—You think it's easy to get ahold of one of these?

—He doesn't know, said Charity.

—No, I suppose not. Listen, if you were looking for some Polish or Italian friend whose grandparents landed on Ellis Island, then, first of all, there wouldn't be no book in which to look. But even if there was a book, the problem would be that those sort change their names and addresses like they change their clothes. That's why they came to America in the first place. To get out of the rut their ancestors put them in.

With a show of reverence, Ma Belle laid her hand on the book in her lap.

—But with this crowd, nothing ever changes. Not the names. Not the addresses. Not a single damn thing. And that's the whole point of who *they* are.

It took Ma Belle five minutes to find what she was looking for. As a young man, Woolly didn't have his own entry in the registry, but he was listed as one of the three children of Mrs. Richard Cobb, née Wolcott; widow of Thomas Martin; member of the Colony Club and the DAR; formerly of Manhattan, currently of Palm Beach. Her two daughters, Kaitlin and Sarah, were both married and listed with their husbands: Mr. & Mrs. Lewis Wilcox of Morristown, New Jersey, and Mr. & Mrs. Dennis Whitney of Hastings-on-Hudson, New York.

Duchess hadn't said which sister they were staying with.

—Either way, said Ma Belle, you've got to go back to Manhattan to catch the train. If I were you, I'd start with Sarah, since Hastings-on-Hudson is a shorter ride and has the added benefit of not being in New Jersey.

—·—

When Emmett left Ma Belle's, it was already half past twelve. In the interest of saving time, he hailed a cab, but when he instructed the driver to take him to the train station in Manhattan, the driver asked which one.

—There's more than one train station in Manhattan?

—There's two, pal: Penn Station and Grand Central. Which do you want?

—Which one is bigger?

—Both is bigger than the other.

Emmett had never heard of Grand Central, but he remembered the panhandler in Lewis saying that the Pennsylvania Railroad was the largest in the nation.

—Penn Station, he said.

When Emmett arrived, he figured he had chosen well because the façade of the station had marble columns that towered four stories over the avenue, and the interior was a vast expanse under a soaring glass ceiling with legions of travelers. But when he found the information booth, Emmett learned that there were no trains to Hastings-on-Hudson leaving from Penn. Those were on the Hudson River Line out of Grand Central. So instead of going to Sarah's house, Emmett boarded the 1:55 for Morristown, New Jersey.

When he arrived at the address that Ma Belle had given him, he asked the cabbie to wait while he went to knock on the door. The woman who answered said that yes, she was Kaitlin Wilcox, in a reasonably friendly manner. But as soon as Emmett asked whether her brother, Woolly, happened to be there, she grew almost angry.

—Suddenly, everyone wants to know if my brother is here. But why would he be? What's this all about? Are you in league with that girl? What are you two up to? Who are you?

As he made his way quickly toward the cab, Emmett could hear her shouting from the front door, demanding once more to know who he was.

So it was back to the Morristown depot, where Emmett took the 4:20 to Penn Station, then a cab to Grand Central, which, as it turned out, had its own marble columns, its own soaring ceiling, its own legions of travelers. There, he waited half an hour to board the 6:15 for Hastings-on-Hudson.

When Emmett arrived shortly after 7:00, he climbed into his fourth taxi of the day. But ten minutes into the ride, he saw the meter advance a nickel to $1.95, and it occurred to him that he might not have enough money for the fare. Opening his wallet, he confirmed that the various trains and taxis had left him with only two dollars.

—Can you pull over? he asked.

With a quizzical glance in the mirror, the cabbie pulled onto the shoulder of a tree-lined road. Holding up his wallet, Emmett explained that all he had left was what the meter was showing.

—If you're out of money, then you're out of the cab.

Nodding in understanding, Emmett handed the cabbie the two dollars, thanked him for the ride, and got out. Fortunately, before pulling away, the cabbie had the graciousness to roll down the passenger window and give Emmett directions: *About two miles up take a right onto Forest; another mile after that take a left onto Steeplechase Road.* When the cab pulled away, Emmett began to walk, his mind taken up with the scourge of infinitely bisected journeys.

America is three thousand miles wide, he thought to himself. Five days before, he and Billy had set out with the intention of driving fifteen hundred miles west to California. Instead, they had traveled fifteen hundred miles east to New York. Having arrived, Emmett had crisscrossed the city from Times Square to lower Manhattan and back. To Brooklyn and Harlem. And when, at long last, it seemed his destination was within reach, Emmett had taken three trains, four taxis, and now was on foot.

He could just imagine how Mr. Nickerson would have diagrammed it: with San Francisco on the left side of the chalkboard, Emmett's zigzagging progression on the right, and every leg of his journey growing shorter than the last. Only, the paradox that Emmett had to contend with wasn't Zeno's. It was the fast-talking, liberty-taking, plan-upending paradox known as Duchess.

But as exasperating as this was, Emmett understood that having to spend his afternoon shuttling back and forth was probably for the best. Because when he had walked out of Ma Belle's earlier that day burning with frustration, had Duchess been standing in the street, Emmett would have pounded him into the ground.

Instead, the train rides and taxi rides and this three-mile walk had given him the time not only to revisit all the causes for fury—the Studebaker, the envelope, the mickey—but the causes for temperance too. Like the promises he had made to Billy and Sister Agnes. And the advocacy of Ma Belle and Charity. But most of all, what gave Emmett pause, and called for some sense of measure, was the story that Fitzy FitzWilliams had told him over glasses of whiskey in that dead-end bar.

For almost a decade, Emmett had quietly nursed a sense of condemnation toward his father's follies—the single-minded commitment to an agrarian dream, the unwillingness to ask for help, and the starry-eyed idealism that sustained him, even as it cost him his farm and his wife. But for all his shortcomings, Charlie Watson had never come close to betraying Emmett in the manner that Harry Hewett had betrayed Duchess.

And for what?

A trinket.

A bauble stripped from the body of a clown.

The irony hidden in the old performer's story wasn't lost on Emmett for a second. It announced itself loud and clear—as a rebuke. For of all the boys whom Emmett had known at Salina, he would have ranked Duchess as one of the most likely to bend the rules or the truth in the service of his own convenience. But in the end, Duchess was the one who had been innocent. He was the one who had been sent to Salina having done nothing at all. While Townhouse and Woolly had stolen cars. And he, Emmett Watson, had ended another man's life.

What right did he have to demand of Duchess that he atone for his sins? What right did he have to demand it of anyone?

Within seconds of ringing the Whitneys' bell, Emmett could hear the sound of running inside. Then the door swung open.

At some level, Emmett must have been expecting Duchess to appear contrite, because he felt a sharp stab of annoyance to find him standing there smiling, looking almost victorious as he turned to Billy and extended his arms—just as he had in the doorway of the Watsons' barn—in order to say:

—What'd I tell you, kid?

With a big smile, Billy stepped around Duchess in order to give Emmett a hug. Then he began to gush.

—You're not going to believe what happened, Emmett! After we left the circus—while you were with your friends—Duchess drove us to the Empire State Building so that we could find Professor Abernathe's office. We rode the express elevator all the way to the fifty-fifth floor and not only did we find his office, we found Professor Abernathe! And he gave me one of his notebooks in case I ran out of blank pages. And when I told him about Ulysses—

—Hold on, said Emmett, smiling in spite of himself. I want to hear all about it, Billy. I really do. But first, I need to talk to Duchess alone for just a minute. Okay?

—Okay, Emmett, said Billy, sounding a little unsure of the idea.

—Why don't you come with me, said Woolly to Billy. I wanted to show you something anyway!

Emmett watched as Billy and Woolly climbed the stairs. Only when they had disappeared down the hall did he turn to face Duchess.

Emmett could see that Duchess had something to say. He had all the telltale signs: his weight on the balls of his feet, his hands ready to gesture, his expression eager and earnest. But he wasn't simply getting ready to speak. He was going to launch himself heart and soul into another explanation.

So before he could say a word, Emmett grabbed him by the collar and drew back his fist.

Woolly

IT WAS QUITE TRUE that in Woolly's experience, when somebody said they wanted to speak to someone else in private, it could be difficult to know what to do with yourself. But when Emmett asked to speak to Duchess, Woolly knew exactly what to do. In fact, he had been thinking about it ever since 7:42.

—Why don't you come with me, he said to Billy. I wanted to show you something anyway!

Leading Billy upstairs, Woolly took him to the bedroom that was and wasn't his.

—Come in, come in, he said.

When Billy stepped inside, Woolly closed the door—leaving it a few inches ajar so that they wouldn't be able to hear what Emmett had to say to Duchess, but they would be able to hear when Emmett was ready to call them back.

—Whose room is this?

—Once upon a time it was mine, said Woolly with a smile. But I gave it up so that the baby can be closer to my sister.

—And now you have the room by the back staircase.

—Which is much more sensible, said Woolly, what with all my comings and goings.

—I like the blue, Billy said. It's like the color of Emmett's car.

—That's just what I thought!

Once they had appreciated the hue of the blue, Woolly turned his attention to the covered pile in the middle of the room. Throwing back the tarp, he located the box he was looking for, opened the top, set aside the tennis trophy, and took out the cigar box.

—Here we go, he said.

Then since the bed was covered with Woolly's belongings, he and Billy sat on the floor.

—Is that a collection? Billy asked.

—It is, said Woolly. Though not like your silver dollars, or your bottle caps back in Nebraska. Because it's not a collection of different versions of the same thing. It's a collection of the same version of different things.

Opening the lid, Woolly tilted the box toward Billy.

—See? These are the sorts of things that one rarely uses, but that one should set safely aside so that one knows exactly where to find them when they're suddenly in need. For instance, this is where I keep my father's shirt studs and cuff links should I suddenly have to wear a tuxedo. And those are some French francs, should I happen to go to France. And that's the biggest piece of sea glass that I have ever found. But here . . .

Gently pushing aside his father's old wallet, Woolly removed a wristwatch from the bottom of the box and handed it to Billy.

—The dial is black, said Billy in surprise.

Woolly nodded.

—And the numbers are white. The very opposite of what you'd expect. It's called an officer's watch. They made them this way so that when an officer needed to look at the time on the field of battle, enemy snipers wouldn't be able to aim for the white of his dial.

—Was it your father's?

—No, said Woolly with a shake of the head. It was my grandfather's. He wore it in France during the First World War. But then he gave it to my mother's brother, Wallace. And then Uncle Wallace gave it to me as a Christmas present when I was younger than you. He's the Wallace that I was named after.

—Your name is Wallace, Woolly?

—Oh yes. Very much so.

—Is that why they call you Woolly? So that people won't get you and your uncle confused when you're together?

—No, said Woolly. Uncle Wallace died years ago. In a war, just like my father. Only, it wasn't in one of the world wars. It was in the Spanish Civil War.

—Why did your uncle fight in the Spanish Civil War?

Quickly wiping away a tear, Woolly shook his head.

—I'm not sure, Billy. My sister says that he had done so many things that were expected of him, he wanted to do one thing that no one expected at all.

They both looked at the watch, which Billy was holding gently in his hand.

—You see, said Woolly, it has a second hand too. Only, instead of it being a big second hand going around the big dial like the one on your watch, it's a tiny little second hand going around its own little dial. Seconds are very important to keep track of in wars, I should think.

—Yes, said Billy, I should think so too.

Then Billy held the watch out in order to return it.

—No, no, said Woolly. It's for you. I took it out of the box because I want you to have it.

Shaking his head, Billy said that such a watch was far too precious to be given away.

—But that's not so, countered Woolly excitedly. It's not a watch that's too precious to be given away. It's a watch that's too precious for keeping. It was handed down from my grandfather to my uncle, who handed it down to me. Now I am handing it down to you. And one day—many years from now—you can hand it down to someone else.

Perhaps Woolly hadn't put his point to perfection, but Billy seemed to understand. So Woolly told him to wind it up! But first, he explained the watch's only quirk—that once a day it should be wound *exactly* fourteen times.

—If you wind it only twelve times, said Woolly, by the end of the day, it will be running five minutes slow. Whereas, if you wind it sixteen times, it will be running five minutes fast. But if you wind it exactly fourteen times, then it will keep the time exactly.

After taking this in, Billy wound the watch exactly fourteen times while quietly counting to himself.

What Woolly did not tell Billy was that sometimes—like when he first arrived at St. Paul's—he would wind the watch sixteen times for six days in a row on porpoise so that he could be half an hour ahead of everybody else. While other times, he would wind it twelve times for six days in a row so that he could be half an hour behind. Either way—whether he wound it sixteen times or wound it twelve—it was a little like when Alice stepped through the looking glass, or the Pevensies through the wardrobe, only to find themselves in a world that was and wasn't theirs.

—Go ahead and put it on, said Woolly.

—You mean I can wear it now?

—Of course, said Woolly. Of course, of course, of course. That's the whole point!

So, without any help, Billy strapped it on his wrist.

—Doesn't that look fine, said Woolly.

And having said so, Woolly would have repeated himself for emphasis, but for the fact that from somewhere downstairs suddenly came a sound that was very much like a gunshot. Exchanging wide-eyed glances, Woolly and Billy leapt to their feet and dashed out the door.

Duchess

EMMETT WAS IN A bad mood all right. He was trying to hide it because that's the kind of guy he is. But I could tell just the same. Especially when he cut Billy off in the middle of his story, saying he wanted to speak to me alone.

Hell, if I were him, I'd want to speak to me alone too.

Another one of Sister Agnes's favorite sayings was *the wise man tattles on himself.* Her point, of course, was that if you did something wrong—whether it was behind the maintenance shed or in the dead of night—she was going to find out. After assembling the clues, she was going to deduce it from the comfort of her armchair like Sherlock Holmes. Or she'd discern it from your manner. Or hear it straight from the mouth of God. Whatever the source, she would come to know of your transgressions, of that there was no doubt. So in the interests of saving time, it was best to tattle on yourself. To admit you've overstepped, express contrition, and promise to make amends—ideally, before anyone else could get a word in edgewise. So the second Emmett and I were alone, I was ready.

As it turned out, Emmett had a different idea. An even better one. Because before I could get a word out of my mouth, he had grabbed me by the collar in order to lay one on me. I closed my eyes and waited for redemption.

But nothing happened.

Peeking out of my right eye, I saw that he was grinding his teeth, struggling with his own instincts.

—Go ahead, I told him. You'll feel better. I'll feel better!

But even as I tried to give him encouragement, I could feel the slackening in his grip. Then he shoved me back a foot or two. So I ended up getting to give my apology, after all.

—I am so sorry, I said.

Then, without taking a breath, I began ticking my missteps off on my fingers.

—I borrowed the Studebaker without asking; I stranded you in Lewis; I misjudged your interest in the Caddy; and on top of all that, I screwed up your night at Ma Belle's. What can I say? I showed poor judgment. But I'm going to make it up to you.

Emmett raised both hands in the air.

—I don't want you to make anything up to me, Duchess. I accept your apology. I just don't want to talk about it anymore.

—All right, I said. I appreciate your willingness to put this chapter behind us. But first things first . . .

Producing his envelope from my back pocket, I returned it with a touch of ceremony. He was visibly relieved to have it in hand. He may even have let out a sigh. But at the same time, I could tell he was weighing the contents.

—It's not all there, I admitted. But I've got something else for you.

From another pocket, I produced the accounting.

Emmett seemed a little perplexed when he took the paper in hand, but even more so once he'd had a look.

—Is this Billy's handwriting?

—It sure is. I'm telling you, Emmett, that kid's got a head for figures.

I stepped to Emmett's side and gestured loosely at the columns.

—It's all there. The necessary expenses like the gas and hotels, which will be reimbursed to you off the top. Then there's the more discretionary expenses, which will come out of my end—just as soon as we get to the Adirondacks.

Emmett looked up from the sheet with a hint of disbelief.

—Duchess, how many times do I have to tell you that I am not going to the Adirondacks. As soon as the Studebaker's ready, Billy and I are heading for California.

—I get it, I said. Since Billy wants to be there by the Fourth of July, it makes sense to get a move on. But you said your car won't be ready until Monday, right? And you must be starving. So tonight, let's have a nice meal, just the four of us. Then tomorrow, Woolly and I will take the Caddy to the camp and pick up the dough. We've got to make a quick stop in Syracuse to see my old man, but then we'll hit the high-way. We shouldn't be more than a few days behind you.

—Duchess . . . , said Emmett, with a woeful shake of the head.

He even looked a little defeated, which was out of character for such a can-do guy. Obviously, something about the plan didn't sit right with him. Or maybe there was some new complication I didn't know about. Before I got the chance to ask, we heard a small explosion coming from the street. Turning slowly, Emmett stared at the front door for a moment. Then he closed his eyes.

Sally

I F I WERE BLESSED one day to have a child, I would no sooner raise her to be an Episcopalian than I would to be a Catholic. The Episcopalians may be Protestant by designation, but you wouldn't know it from their services—what with all the vestments and English hymns. I guess they like to call it high church. I call it high and mighty.

But one thing you can count on from the Episcopal Church is that they'll keep their records straight. They're almost as insistent upon it as the Mormons. So, when Emmett didn't call as promised on Friday at 2:30, he left me little choice but to contact Father Colmore over at St. Luke's.

Once I got him on the line, I explained that I was trying to track down a member of the congregation of an Episcopal church in Manhattan, and did he have any ideas on how I might go about doing so. Without a second thought, he told me I should contact Reverend Hamilton Speers, the Rector of St. Bartholomew's. He even gave me the number.

This St. Bartholomew's must be some kind of church, I'll tell you that. Because when I called, instead of getting Reverend Speers, I reached a receptionist who asked me to hold (despite the fact it was a long-distance call); then she patched me through to an assistant rector, who, in turn, wanted to know why I needed to speak to the reverend. I explained that I was distantly related to a family in his congregation, that my father had died in the night, and while I needed to alert my

New York cousins to his passing, for the life of me I could not find my father's address book.

Now, in the strictest sense, this was not an honest claim. But while the Christian religion generally frowns upon the drinking of spirits, a sip of red wine is not only countenanced, it plays an essential role in the sacrament. And I figure that while the church generally frowns upon prevarication, a little white lying can be as Christian as the sip of Sunday wine, if performed in the service of the Lord.

What was the name of the family? The assistant wanted to know.

When I replied it was the family of Woolly Martin, he asked me to hold again. A few nickels later, Reverend Speers was on the line. First, he wanted to express his deepest sympathies for my loss, and his wishes that my father rest in peace. He went on to explain that Woolly's family, the Wolcotts, had been members of the St. Bartholomew's congregation since its founding in 1854, and that he had personally married four of them and baptized ten. No doubt he had buried a good deal more.

In a matter of minutes, I had the phone numbers and addresses of Woolly's mother, who was in Florida, and the two sisters, who were both married and living in the New York area. I tried the one called Kaitlin first.

The Wolcotts may have been members of St. Bartholomew's since its founding in 1854, but Kaitlin Wolcott Wilcox must not have paid much attention to the lessons. For when I said that I was trying to find her brother, she became wary. And when I said I'd heard he might be staying with her, she became outright unfriendly.

—My brother is in Kansas, she said. Why would he be here? Who told you that he would be here? Who is this?

And so forth.

Next I dialed Sarah. This time the phone rang and rang and rang.

When I finally hung up, I sat there for a moment, drumming my fingers on my father's desk.

In my father's office.

Under my father's roof.

Going into the kitchen, I retrieved my purse, counted out five dollars, and left them by the phone in order to cover the cost of the long-distance calls. Then I went to my room, took my suitcase from the back of my closet, and started to pack.

—.—

The journey from Morgen to New York took twenty hours spread over the course of a day and a half.

To some that may seem like an onerous bit of driving. But I don't believe that I'd had twenty hours of uninterrupted time to think in my entire life. And what I found myself thinking on, naturally enough I suppose, was the mystery of our will to move.

Every bit of evidence would suggest that the will to be moving is as old as mankind. Take the people in the Old Testament. They were always on the move. First, it's Adam and Eve moving out of Eden. Then it's Cain condemned to be a restless wanderer, Noah drifting on the waters of the Flood, and Moses leading the Israelites out of Egypt toward the Promised Land. Some of these figures were out of the Lord's favor and some of them were in it, but all of them were on the move. And as far as the New Testament goes, Our Lord Jesus Christ was what they call a peripatetic—someone who's *always* going from place to place—whether on foot, on the back of a donkey, or on the wings of angels.

But the proof of the will to move is hardly limited to the pages of the Good Book. Any child of ten can tell you that getting-up-and-going is topic number one in the record of man's endeavors. Take that big red book that Billy is always lugging around. It's got twenty-six stories in it that have come down through the ages and almost every one of them is about some man going somewhere. Napoleon heading off on his conquests, or King Arthur in search of the Holy Grail. Some of the men in the book are figures from history and some from fancy, but whether real or imagined, almost every one of them is on his way to someplace different from where he started.

So, if the will to move is as old as mankind and every child can tell you so, what happens to a man like my father? What switch is flicked in the hallway of his mind that takes the God-given will for motion and transforms it into the will for staying put?

It isn't due to a loss of vigor. For the transformation doesn't come when men like my father are growing old and infirm. It comes when they are hale, hearty, and at the peak of their vitality. If you asked them what brought about the change, they will cloak it in the language of virtue. They will tell you that the American Dream is to settle down, raise a family, and make an honest living. They'll speak with pride of their ties to the community through the church and the Rotary and the chamber of commerce, and all other manner of stay-puttery.

But maybe, I was thinking as I was driving over the Hudson River, just maybe the will to stay put stems not from a man's virtues but from his vices. After all, aren't gluttony, sloth, and greed all about staying put? Don't they amount to sitting deep in a chair where you can eat more, idle more, and want more? In a way, pride and envy are about staying put too. For just as pride is founded on what you've built up around you, envy is founded on what your neighbor has built across the street. A man's home may be his castle, but the moat, it seems to me, is just as good at keeping people in as it is at keeping people out.

I do believe that the Good Lord has a mission for each and every one of us—a mission that is forgiving of our weaknesses, tailored to our strengths, and designed with only us in mind. But maybe He doesn't come knocking on our door and present it to us all frosted like a cake. Maybe, just maybe what He requires of us, what He expects of us, what He hopes for us is that—like His only begotten Son—we will go out into the world and find it for ourselves.

As I climbed out of Betty, Emmett, Woolly, and Billy all came spilling out of the house. Billy and Woolly both had big smiles on their faces, while Emmett, per usual, was acting like smiles were a precious resource.

Woolly, who had obviously been raised right, wanted to know if I had any bags.

—How nice of you to ask, I replied without looking at Emmett. My suitcase is in the back of the truck. And Billy, there's a basket in the back seat, if you'd be so kind. But no peeking.

—We'll get everything, said Billy.

As Billy and Woolly carried my things inside, Emmett shook his head.

—Sally, he said with more than a hint of exasperation.

—Yes, Mr. Watson.

—*What* are you doing here?

—What am I doing here? Well, let me see. I didn't have much on the calendar that was particularly pressing. And I have always wanted to see the big city. And then there was that small matter of sitting around yesterday afternoon and waiting for the phone to ring.

That took him down a notch.

—I'm sorry, he said. The truth is I completely forgot about calling you. Since leaving Morgen, it's been one problem after another.

—We all do have our trials, I said.

—Fair enough. I won't bother with excuses. I should have called. But when I failed to, was it really necessary for you to drive all the way here?

—Maybe not. I suppose I could have crossed my fingers and hoped that you and Billy were all right. But I figured you'd want to know why the sheriff came to see me.

—The sheriff?

Before I could explain, Billy had his arm around my waist and was looking up at Emmett.

—Sally brought more cookies and preserves.

—I thought I told you no peeking, I said.

Then I tussled his hair, which clearly had not been washed since I'd seen him last.

—I know you said that, Sally. But you didn't mean it. Did you?

—No, I didn't mean it.

—Did you bring *strawberry* preserves? asked Woolly.

—I did. And raspberry too. Speaking of preserves, where's Duchess?

Everybody looked up a little surprised, as if they'd only just noticed that Duchess was missing. But at that very moment, he emerged from the front door wearing a shirt and tie under a clean white apron, saying:

—Dinner is served!

Woolly

O H, WHAT A NIGHT they were having!

To start things off, at the stroke of eight Duchess opened the front door to reveal Emmett on the doorstep, a cause for celebration in itself. Not fifteen minutes later—just after Woolly had presented his uncle's watch to Billy—there was a small explosion and who to their wondering eyes should appear, but Sally Ransom, having driven all the way from Nebraska. And before they had a chance to celebrate *that*, Duchess was standing in the doorway announcing that dinner was served.

—Right this way, he said, as they all went back inside.

But instead of heading to the kitchen, Duchess led them into the dining room, where the table had been set with china and crystal and the two candelabra, even though it wasn't a birthday or holiday.

—My, oh my, said Sally when she came through the door.

—Miss Ransom, why don't you sit here, said Duchess, pulling out her chair.

Then Duchess seated Billy next to Sally, Woolly across the table, and Emmett at the head. Duchess reserved the other end of the table for himself, the one that was closest to the kitchen door, through which he promptly disappeared. But even before the door had stopped swinging, he was back with a napkin over his arm and a bottle of wine in hand.

—You can't appreciate a good Italian dinner, he said, without a little *vino rosso*.

Circling the table, Duchess poured a glass for everyone, including Billy. Then having set the bottle down, he was through the kitchen door and back again, this time carrying four plates at the same time with one in each hand, and another balanced on the crook of each arm—the exact set of circumstances, thought Woolly, for which the swinging door had been designed!

After zipping once around the table in order to serve a plate to everyone else, Duchess disappeared and reappeared in order to serve one to himself. Only this time when he came through the door, his apron was gone and he was wearing a vest with all the buttons buttoned.

When Duchess resumed his seat, Sally and Emmett were staring at their plates.

—What in tarnation, said Sally.

—Stuffed artichokes, said Billy.

—I didn't make them, Duchess confessed. Billy and I picked them up earlier today on Arthur Avenue.

—That's the main drag in the Italian section of the Bronx, said Billy.

Emmett and Sally both looked from Duchess to Billy and back to their plates, no less perplexed.

—You scrape the meat off the leaves with your bottom teeth, explained Woolly.

—You what? said Sally.

—Like this!

In order to demonstrate, Woolly plucked one of the leaves, scraped it with his teeth, and dropped it on his plate.

Within a matter of minutes, everyone was having a grand old time plucking leaves, and sipping wine, and discussing with due admiration the very first person in the history of mankind who'd had the audacity to eat an artichoke.

When everyone had finished their appetizer, Sally straightened the napkin in her lap and asked what they were having next.

—*Fettuccine Mio Amore*, said Billy.

Emmett and Sally looked to Duchess for an elaboration, but since he was clearing plates, he asked Woolly to do the honors.

So Woolly told them the whole story. He told them of Leonello's—that restaurant at which no reservations were taken and no menus given. He told them of the jukebox and the mobsters and Marilyn Monroe. He told them of Leonello himself, who went from table to table greeting his customers and sending them drinks. And finally, he told them how when the waiter came to your table, he didn't even mention *Fettuccine Mio Amore*, because if you didn't know enough to ask for it, then you didn't deserve to eat it.

—I helped make it, said Billy. Duchess showed me how to properly slice an onion.

Sally was staring at Billy in a mild state of shock.

—Properly?!

—Yes, said Billy. Properly.

—And how, pray tell, is that?

Before Billy could explain, the door swung open and Duchess appeared with all five plates.

As he had been describing Leonello's, Woolly could see that Emmett and Sally were a little skeptical, and he couldn't blame them. For when it came to telling stories, Duchess was a bit of a Paul Bunyan, for whom the snow was always ten feet deep, and the river as wide as the sea. But after the very first bite, everyone at the table could set their doubts aside.

—Isn't this delicious, said Sally.

—I've got to hand it to you both, said Emmett. Then raising his glass, he added: To the chefs.

To which Woolly responded: Hear, hear!

And hear, hear said they all.

The dinner was so delicious that everyone asked for a second helping, and Duchess poured some more wine, and Emmett's eyes began to glitter as Sally's cheeks grew red, and the candle wax dribbled delightfully down the arms of the candelabra.

Then everyone was asking somebody else to tell something. First, it was Emmett asking Billy to tell about the visit to the Empire State Building. Then it was Sally asking Emmett to tell about the ride on the freight train. Then Woolly asking Duchess to tell about the magic tricks that he had seen on the stage. And finally, it was Billy asking Duchess if *he* knew any magic tricks.

—Over the years, I suppose I've learned a few.

—Will you do one for us?

Taking a sip of wine, Duchess thought for a moment, then said: Why not.

After pushing back his plate, Duchess took the corkscrew from the pocket of his vest, removed the cork, and set it on the table. Then picking up the wine bottle, he poured out the dregs, and forced the cork back inside—not simply into the neck where it usually resides, but all the way *through* the neck so that it dropped down to where the dregs had been.

—As you can see, he said, I have placed the cork in the bottle.

Then he passed the bottle around so that everyone in turn could confirm the bottle was made of solid glass and the cork was truly inside. Woolly even turned the bottle upside down and gave it a shake in order to prove what everyone knew in principle: that if it was hard to push a cork all the way into a bottle, it was impossible to shake it back out.

When the bottle had completed its circuit, Duchess rolled up his sleeves, held up his hands to show that they were empty, then asked Billy if he would be so kind as to give us a countdown.

To Woolly's great satisfaction, not only did Billy accept the task, he used the tiny little second hand in the dial of his new watch in order to execute it precisely.

Ten, he said as Duchess picked up the bottle and lowered it into his lap out of sight. *Nine . . . Eight . . .* , he said, as Duchess breathed and exhaled. *Seven . . . Six . . . Five . . .* , as Duchess began rolling his shoulders back and forth. *Four . . . Three . . . Two*, as his eyelids fell so low it looked like he had closed them altogether.

How long is ten seconds? thought Woolly as Billy's countdown took place. It is long enough to confirm that a heavyweight boxer has lost his bout. Long enough to announce the arrival of another new year. But it didn't seem anywhere near long enough to remove a cork from the bottom of a bottle. And yet, and yet, at the very moment that Billy said *One*, with one hand Duchess thumped the empty bottle on the table, and with the other set the cork upright at its side.

With a gasp, Sally looked at Billy and Emmett and Woolly. And Billy looked at Woolly and Sally and Emmett. And Emmett looked at Billy and Woolly and Sally. Which is to say that everybody looked at everybody. Except for Duchess, who stared straight ahead with the inscrutable smile of a sphinx.

Then everyone was talking all at once. Billy was pronouncing it magic. And Sally was saying, *I never!* And Woolly was saying, *Wonderful, wonderful, wonderful*. And Emmett, he wanted to see the bottle.

So Duchess passed the bottle around and everyone got to see that it was empty. Then Emmett suggested, rather skeptically, that there must have been two bottles and two corks, and Duchess had made the switch in his lap. So everyone looked under the table and Duchess turned around with his arms extended, but there was no second bottle to be found.

Now everyone was talking again, asking Duchess to show them how he did it. Duchess replied that a magician never reveals his secrets. But after a *proper* amount of pleading and prodding, he agreed to do so, nonetheless.

—What you do, he explained after returning the cork to the bottom of the bottle, is take your napkin, slide the folded corner into the bottle's neck like so, toss the cork until it lands in the trough of the fold, then gently withdraw.

Sure enough, as Duchess gently pulled, the folded napkin corner wrapped around the cork, drew it through the neck, and liberated it from the bottle with a satisfying pop.

—Let me try, said Billy and Sally at once.

—Let's all try! suggested Woolly.

Bounding from his chair, Woolly dashed through the kitchen into the pantry where "Dennis" stored his wine. Grabbing three bottles of *vino rosso*, he brought them into the kitchen, where Duchess pulled the corks so that Woolly could pour the contents down the drain.

Back in the dining room, Billy, Emmett, Sally, and Woolly each forced their own corks down into their own bottles and folded their own napkins as Duchess circled the table giving helpful instructions.

—Fold it a little more at the corner like this. . . . Toss the cork up a little more like that. . . . Get it to rest a little deeper in the trough. Now pull, but gently.

Pop, pop, pop went Sally's, and Emmett's, and Billy's corks.

Then everyone looked to Woolly, a circumstance which generally made Woolly want to get up and leave the room. But not after dining on artichokes and *Fettuccine Mio Amore* with four of his closest friends. Not tonight!

—Hold on, hold on, he said. I've got it, I've got it.

Biting the tip of his tongue, Woolly jostled and coaxed, then ever so, ever so gently he began to tug. And as he tugged, everyone around the table, even Duchess, held their breath until the moment that Woolly's cork went *pop* and they all erupted into a great round of hurrahs!

And that's when the swinging door swung and in walked "Dennis."

—My, oh my, said Woolly.

—What in God's name is going on here? "Dennis" demanded, using one of those *W* questions for which he expected no answer.

Then the swinging door swung again and there was Sarah with an expression of anticipatory concern.

Stepping abruptly forward, "Dennis" picked up the bottle that was in front of Woolly and looked around the table.

—Château Margaux '28! You drank four bottles of Château Margaux '28?!

—We only drank one bottle, said Billy.

—That's true, said Woolly. We poured the other three bottles down the drain.

But as soon as Woolly had said this, he realized he shouldn't have. Because "Dennis" was suddenly as red as his Château Margaux.

—You poured them out!

Sarah, who had been standing quietly behind her husband holding open the door, now stepped into the room. This is where she would say what needed to be said, thought Woolly, the very thing that he would later wish he'd had the presence of mind to say himself. But when she stepped around "Dennis" and had the chance to take in the scene in its entirety, she picked up the napkin from beside Woolly's plate, which, like all the others on the table, was stained with big red splotches of wine.

—Oh, Woolly, she said, ever so softly.

Ever so heartbreakingly softly.

Everyone was silent now. And for a moment, no one seemed to know where to look. Because they didn't quite want to look at each other, or the bottles, or the napkins. But when "Dennis" put the empty bottle of Château Margaux on the table, it was as if a spell had been broken, and they all looked directly at Woolly, especially "Dennis."

—Wallace Martin, he said, can I speak to you in private.

When Woolly followed his brother-in-law into the office, he could tell that a bad situation had just gotten worse. Because despite "Dennis" having made it perfectly clear that he did not like people going into his office when he wasn't there, here was his telephone stuffed in the desk drawer with the cord hanging out.

—Sit down, "Dennis" said as he returned the phone to its proper spot with a bang.

Then he looked at Woolly for a good long minute, which was something that the people sitting behind desks often seemed to do. Having insisted upon speaking to you without further delay, they sit there for a good long minute without saying a word. But even a good long minute comes to an end.

—I suppose you're wondering why your sister and I are here?

In fact, Woolly hadn't thought to wonder that at all. But now that "Dennis" mentioned it, it did seem worthy of wondering, since the two of them were supposed to be spending the night in the city.

Well, it turned out that on Friday afternoon, Kaitlin had received a phone call from a young woman asking if Woolly was at her house. Then earlier today, a young man had appeared on Kaitlin's doorstep with the very same question. Kaitlin couldn't understand why people would be asking if Woolly was there, when he was supposed to be completing his sentence in Salina. Naturally enough, she became concerned, so she decided to call her sister. But when she dialed Sarah's house and Woolly answered, not only had he hung up on her, he apparently had left the phone off the hook, because when Kaitlin kept calling back, all she got was a busy signal. This turn of events left Kaitlin little choice but to track Sarah and "Dennis" down—even though they were dining at the Wilsons.

When Woolly was a boy, punctuation had always struck him as something of an adversary—a hostile force that was committed to his defeat, whether through espionage, or by storming his beaches with overwhelming force. In seventh grade, when he had admitted this to the kind and patient Miss Penny, she explained that Woolly had it upside down. Punctuation, she said, was his ally, not his enemy. All those little marks—the period, the comma, the colon—were there to help him make sure that other people understood what he was trying to say. But apparently "Dennis" was so certain that what he had to say would be understood, he didn't need any punctuation at all.

—After giving our apologies to our hosts and driving all the way home to Hastings what do we find but a pickup truck blocking the driveway a mess in the kitchen strangers in the dining room drinking our wine and the table linens my God the table linens that your grandmother gave your sister now soiled beyond repair because you have treated them like you treat everything else like you treat everyone else which is to say without the slightest respect

"Dennis" studied Woolly for a moment, as if he were genuinely trying to understand him, trying to take the full measure of the man.

—At the age of fifteen your family sends you to one of the finest schools in the country and you get yourself thrown out for a reason I cant even remember then its off to St Marks where you get kicked out again for burning down a goalpost of all things and when no reputable school is willing to give you a second look your mother convinces St Georges to take you in by invoking the memory of your uncle Wallace who not only excelled there as a student but eventually served on its board of trustees and when you get thrown out of there and find yourself not in front of a disciplinary committee but in front of a judge what does your family do but lie about your age so that you wont be tried as an adult and hire a lawyer from Sullivan and Cromwell no less who convinces the judge to send you to some special reformatory in Kansas where you can grow vegetables for a year but apparently you dont even have the backbone to see that inconvenience through to its conclusion

"Dennis" stopped for the weighty pause.

As Woolly well knew, the weighty pause was an essential part of speaking to someone in private. It was the signal for both the speaker and the listener that what was coming next was of the utmost importance.

—I gather from Sarah that if you return to Salina they will let you complete your sentence in a matter of months so that you can apply to college and go on with your life but the one thing that has become abundantly clear Wallace is that you do not yet value an education and the best way for someone to learn the value of an education is to spend a few years doing a job which doesnt require one so with that in mind tomorrow I will be reaching out to a friend of mine at the stock exchange who is always looking for a few young men to serve as runners and maybe he will have a little more success than the rest of us in teaching you what it means to earn your keep

And right then Woolly knew for certain what he should have known the night before—as he stood in such high spirits among the wildflowers and the knee-high grass—that he was never going to visit the Statue of Liberty.

Emmett

WHEN MR. WHITNEY FINISHED speaking to Woolly, he had gone upstairs to his bedroom, followed a few minutes later by his wife. Saying he wanted to check on the progress of the stars, Woolly had gone out the front door, followed a few minutes later by Duchess, who wanted to make sure that he was all right. And Sally, she had gone upstairs in order to get Billy settled. Which left Emmett alone in the kitchen with the mess.

And Emmett was glad of it.

When Mr. Whitney had come through the dining-room door, Emmett's emotions had switched in the instant from merriment to shame. What had they been thinking, the five of them? Carousing in another man's house, drinking his wine and staining his wife's linens in pursuit of a childish game. Adding to the sting of embarrassment was the sudden memory of Parker and Packer in their Pullman car with their food thrown about and the half-empty bottle of gin on its side. How quickly Emmett had judged those two; condemned them for the spoiled and callous manner in which they treated their surroundings.

So Emmett did not begrudge Mr. Whitney his anger. He had every right to be angry. To be insulted. To be outraged. The surprise for Emmett had been in Mrs. Whitney's response, in how gracious she had been, telling them in her gentle way when Woolly and Mr. Whitney had left the room, that it was all right, that it was just some napkins and a few bottles of wine, insisting—without a suggestion of resentment—that they leave everything for the housekeeper, then telling them in which rooms they could sleep and in which closets they could find extra blankets and pillows and towels. Gracious was the only word for it. A graciousness that compounded the sense of Emmett's shame.

That's why he was glad to find himself alone, glad to have the chance to clear the dining-room table and set about cleaning the dishes as some small act of penance.

Emmett had just finished washing the plates and was moving on to the glasses when Sally returned.

—He's asleep, she said.

—Thanks.

Without saying another word, Sally took up a dish towel and began drying the plates as he washed the crystal; then she dried the crystal as he washed the pots. And it was a comfort to be doing this work, to be doing this work in Sally's company without either of them feeling the need to speak.

Emmett could tell that Sally was as ashamed as he was, and there was comfort in that too. Not the comfort of knowing that someone else was feeling a similar sting of rebuke. Rather, the comfort of knowing one's sense of right and wrong was shared by another, and thus was somehow more true.

TWO

—·—

Duchess

WHEN IT CAME TO vaudeville, it was all about the setup. That was as true for the comedians as it was for the jugglers and magicians. The members of the audience entered the theater with their own preferences, their own prejudices, their own sets of expectations. So, without the audience members realizing it, the performer needed to remove those and replace them with a new set of expectations—a set of expectations that he was in a better position to anticipate, manipulate, and ultimately satisfy.

Take Mandrake the Magnificent. Manny wasn't what you'd call a great magician. In the first half of his act, he'd produce a bouquet of flowers out of his sleeve, or colored ribbons out of his ears, or a nickel out of thin air—basically the stuff you'd see at a ten-year-old's birthday party. But like Kazantikis, what Manny lacked in the front of his act, he made up for in the finale.

One difference between Mandrake and most of his peers was that rather than having some leggy blonde at his side, he had a large white cockatoo named Lucinda. Many years before while traveling in the Amazon—Manny would explain to the audience—he had discovered a baby bird that had fallen from her nest to the forest floor. After nursing the chick back to health, he had raised her to adulthood and they had been together ever since. Over the course of the act,

Lucinda would perch on her gilded stand and assist by holding a set of keys in her claws or rapping three times on a deck of cards with her beak.

But when the act was winding up, Manny would announce that he was going to attempt a trick he had never performed before. A stage-hand would wheel out a pedestal on which sat a black enamel chest illustrated with a big red dragon. On a recent trip to the Orient, Manny would say, he had discovered the object in a flea market. The moment he saw it, he recognized it for what it was: a Mandarin's Box. Manny knew only a bit of Chinese, but the old man who was selling the curiosity not only confirmed Manny's suspicions, he went on to teach Manny the magic words that made it work.

Tonight, Manny would announce, *for the first time anywhere in the Americas, I will use the Mandarin's Box to make my trusted cockatoo vanish and reappear right before your eyes.*

Gently, Manny would place Lucinda in the chest and shut the doors. Closing his eyes, he would utter an incantation in a Chinese of his own invention, while tapping the chest with his wand. When he reopened the doors, the bird was gone.

After bowing for a round of applause, Manny would ask for silence, explaining that the spell to make the bird reappear was far more complicated than the one that made it vanish. Taking a deep breath, he would double up on his oriental mumbo jumbo, working it to a suitable pitch. Then opening his eyes, he would point his wand. Seemingly from nowhere, a ball of fire would explode and engulf the chest, prompting the audience to gasp and Manny to take two steps back. But once the smoke had cleared, there was the Mandarin's Box without so much as a scratch. Stepping forward, tentatively, Manny would open the doors of the chest . . . reach his hands inside . . . and withdraw a platter on which sat a perfectly roasted bird surrounded by all the fixings.

For a moment, the magician and audience would share the silence of the stunned. Then raising his gaze from the platter, Manny would look out into the theater and say: *Oops.*

How that would bring down the house.

So. Here's what happened on Sunday, the twentieth of June. . . .

Having woken at the crack of dawn, at Woolly's insistence we packed our bags, tiptoed down the back stairs, and slipped out the door without making a sound.

After putting the Caddy in neutral and rolling her out of the drive, we fired her up, put her in gear, and half an hour later were sailing up the Taconic State Parkway like Ali Baba on his magic carpet.

What cars were on the road all seemed to be headed in the opposite direction, so we were making good time, passing through Lagrangeville by seven o'clock and Albany by eight.

After being given the business by his brother-in-law, Woolly had tossed and turned for most of the night and woken up looking as low as I'd ever seen him, so when I saw a blue steeple on the horizon, I put on the blinker.

Being back in the bright orange booth seemed to lift his spirits. Though he didn't seem as interested in his place mat, he ate almost half of his pancakes and all of my bacon.

Not long after we passed Lake George, Woolly had me turn off the highway and we began winding our way through the great bucolic wilderness that makes up ninety percent of New York's landmass and none of its reputation. With the townships getting farther apart and the trees getting closer to the road, Woolly almost seemed himself, humming along with the commercials even though the radio wasn't on. It must have been about eleven when he sat up on the edge of his seat and pointed to a break in the woods.

—You take that next right.

Turning onto a dirt road, we began winding our way through a forest of the tallest trees that I had ever seen.

To be perfectly honest, when Woolly had first told me about the hundred and fifty grand that was stashed in a safe at the family's camp, I had my doubts. I just couldn't seem to picture all that money sitting in some log cabin in the woods. But when we emerged from the trees, rising before us was a house that looked like a hunting lodge owned by the Rockefellers.

When Woolly saw it, he breathed an even bigger sigh of relief than I did, as if he'd had his own doubts. Like maybe the whole place had been a figment of his imagination.

—Welcome home, I said.

And he gave me his first smile of the day.

When we got out of the car, I followed Woolly around to the front of the house and across the lawn to where a giant body of water shimmered in the sun.

—The lake, Woolly said.

With the trees coming right down to the shoreline, there wasn't another residence in sight.

—How many houses are on this lake? I asked.

—One . . . ? he asked back.

—Right, I said.

Then he began giving me the lay of the land.

—The dock, he said pointing to the dock.

And the boathouse, he said pointing to the boathouse. And the flagpole, he said pointing to the flagpole.

—The caretaker hasn't been here yet, he observed with another sigh of relief.

—How can you tell?

—Because the raft isn't on the lake and the rowboats aren't at the dock.

Turning, we took a moment to appreciate the house, which looked down over the water like it had been there since the beginning of America. And maybe it had.

—Perhaps we should get our things . . . ? Woolly suggested.

—Allow *me*!

Hopping to it like a bellboy at the Ritz, I skipped over to the car and opened the trunk. Setting aside the Louisville Slugger, I took out our book bags, then followed Woolly to the narrow end of the house, where two lines of white-painted stones led to a door.

On the top of the stoop were four overturned flowerpots. No doubt when the raft was on the lake and the rowboats at the dock, they would be planted with whatever sort of flower that WASPs found to be ornamental without being showy.

After peeking under three of the pots, Woolly retrieved a key and unlocked the door. Then showing a decidedly un-Woolly presence of mind, he put the key back where he'd found it before letting us inside.

First, we entered a little room in which cubbyholes, hooks, and baskets held an orderly arrangement of everything you'd need for the great outdoors: coats and hats, rods and reels, bows and arrows. In front of a glass cabinet showcasing four rifles were several large white chairs stacked one on top of the other, having been hauled in from their picturesque spots on the lawn.

—The mudroom, Woolly said.

As if mud had ever found its way onto the shoe of a Wolcott!

Over the gun cabinet there was a big green sign like the one in the barracks at Salina, painted with its own rules and regulations. Most everywhere else on the wall—hanging right up to the ceiling—were dark-red boards in the shape of chevrons with lists painted in white.

—The winners, Woolly explained.

—Of what?

—The tournaments we used to have on the Fourth of July.

Woolly pointed from one to another.

—Riflery, archery, the swim race, the canoe race, the twenty-yard dash.

As I gazed over the boards, Woolly must have thought I was looking for his name because he volunteered that it wasn't there.

—I'm not very good at winning, he confessed.

—It's overrated, I assured.

Exiting the mudroom, he led me down the hall, naming rooms as we went.

—The tearoom . . . the billiard room . . . the game closet . . .

Where the hallway ended, it opened into a large living area.

—We call this the great room, said Woolly.

And they weren't kidding. Like the lobby of a grand hotel, it had six different seating areas with couches and wing-back chairs and standing lamps. There was also a card table topped with baize, and a fireplace that looked like it belonged in a castle. Everything was in its proper place, except for the dark-green rocking chairs huddled by the outside doors.

Seeing them, Woolly seemed disappointed.

—What is it?

—Those really belong on the porch.

—No time like the present.

Setting our bags down and tossing my fedora on a chair, I helped Woolly shuttle the rockers onto the porch, being careful to arrange them, per his instructions, at equal intervals. Once they were all in place, Woolly asked if I wanted to see the rest of the house.

—Absotively, I said, which brought an even bigger smile. I want to see all of it, Woolly. But we can't forget the reason we're here. . . .

After looking at me with curiosity for a moment, Woolly put a finger of recognition in the air. Then he led me down the hallway on the other side of the great room and opened a door.

—My great-grandfather's study, he said.

As we had walked through the house, it seemed laughable I had ever doubted that money could be stashed here. Given the scale of the rooms and the quality of the furnishings, there could have been fifty grand stuffed under a mattress in the maid's room and another fifty lost among the cushions of the couches. But if the majesty of the house boosted my confidence, that was nothing compared to Great-grandpa's study. Here was a room of a man who knew not only how to make money, but how to keep it. Which, after all, are two different things entirely.

In some ways, it was like a small version of the great room, with the same wooden chairs, and red rugs, and another fireplace. But there was also a great big desk, bookcases, and one of those little sets of steps that the bookish use to reach the volumes on upper shelves. On one wall was a painting of a bunch of colonial fellows in tight pants and white wigs gathered around a desk. But over the fireplace was a portrait of a man in his late fifties with fair coloring and a handsome, decisive-looking face.

—Your great-grandfather? I asked.

—No, said Woolly. My grandfather.

In a way, I was relieved to hear it. Hanging a portrait of oneself over the fireplace in one's study didn't seem a very Wolcotty thing to do.

—It was painted at the time my grandfather took over for my great-grandfather at the paper company. When he died shortly thereafter, my great-grandfather had it moved here.

Looking from Woolly to the portrait I could see the family resemblance. Except for the decisive part, of course.

—What happened to the paper company? I asked.

—Uncle Wallace took over when Grandpa died. He was only twenty-five at the time and he ran it until he was about thirty, but then he died too.

I didn't bother observing that the head of the Wolcott paper company was a job to be avoided. I suspect Woolly knew that already.

Turning, Woolly walked over to the painting of the colonials and held out a hand.

—The presentation of the Declaration of Independence.

—No kidding.

—Oh yes, said Woolly. There's John Adams and Thomas Jefferson and Ben Franklin and John Hancock. They're all there.

—Which one's the Wolcott, I asked with a Puckish grin.

But taking another step forward, Woolly pointed to a small head at the back of the crowd.

—Oliver, he said. He also signed the Articles of Confederation and was the governor of Connecticut. Though that was seven generations ago.

We both nodded for a few seconds, in order to give old Ollie his due. Then reaching up, Woolly opened the painting like it was a cabinet door and, lo and behold, there was Great-grandpa's safe, looking like it had been fashioned from the metal of a battleship. With a nickel-plated handle and four little dials, it must have been a foot and a half square. If it was also a foot and a half deep, it would be big enough to hold the life savings of seventy generations of Hewetts. But for the solemnity of the moment, I would have whistled.

From Great-grandpa's perspective, the contents of the safe were probably an expression of the past. In this grand old house, behind this venerable old painting, were documents that had been signed decades before, jewelry that had been handed down from generation to generation, and cash that had been accumulated over several lifetimes. But in just a few moments, some of the safe's contents would have been transformed into a representation of the future.

Emmett's future. Woolly's future. My future.

—There it is, said Woolly.

—There it is, I agreed.

Then we both let out a sigh.

—Would you like to . . . ? I asked, gesturing at the dials.

—What's that? Oh, no. You go right ahead.

—All right, I said, trying to resist the temptation of rubbing my hands together. Just give me the combination, and I'll do the honors.

After a moment of silence, Woolly looked at me with an expression of genuine surprise.

—Combination? he asked.

Then I laughed. I laughed until my kidneys hurt and the tears poured out of my eyes.

Like I said: When it comes to vaudeville, it's all about the setup.

Emmett

THAT'S A FINE JOB, said Mrs. Whitney. I really can't thank you enough.

—It was my pleasure, said Emmett.

They were standing at the threshold of the baby's room looking at the walls, which Emmett had just finished painting.

—You must be hungry after all that work. Why don't you come down and I'll fix you a sandwich.

—I'd appreciate that, Mrs. Whitney. Just let me clean up.

—Of course, she said. But please. Call me Sarah.

That morning, Emmett had come downstairs to find that Duchess and Woolly were gone. Having woken in the early hours, they had driven off in the Cadillac, leaving only a note behind. Mr. Whitney was gone too, having headed back to their apartment in the city without taking time for breakfast. And Mrs. Whitney, she was standing in the kitchen dressed in dungarees, her hair pulled back in a kerchief.

—I promised I'd finally finish painting the baby's room, she explained with a look of embarrassment.

It didn't take much convincing for her to let Emmett take over the job.

With Mrs. Whitney's approval, Emmett moved the boxes of Woolly's belongings to the garage, stacking them in the spot where the

Cadillac had been. With some tools he found in the basement, he took apart the bed and stowed the pieces beside the boxes. When the room was empty, he finished taping the trim, laid the tarp across the floor, stirred the paint, and went to work.

When you had the job set up right—with the room clear and the trim taped and the floor protected—painting was peaceful work. It had a rhythm about it that allowed your thoughts to quiet down, or fall silent altogether. Eventually, all that you were aware of was the movement of the brush sweeping back and forth, turning the primed white wall to its new shade of blue.

When Sally saw what Emmett was doing, she nodded her head in approval.

—You want a hand?

—I've got it.

—You spilled some paint on the tarp over there by the window.

—Yep.

—All right, she said. Just so's you know.

Then Sally looked up and down the hallway with a bit of a frown, as if she were disappointed there wasn't another room that needed painting. She wasn't used to being idle, certainly not as an uninvited guest in another woman's home.

—Maybe I'll take Billy into town, she said. Find a soda fountain where we can have lunch.

—Sounds like a good idea, agreed Emmett, placing the brush on the rim of the can. Let me get you some money.

—I think I can afford to buy your brother a hamburger. Besides, the last thing Mrs. Whitney needs now is you tracking paint all through her house.

—·—

When Mrs. Whitney went downstairs to make the sandwiches, Emmett brought all the work materials down the back staircase (having checked his shoes twice to make sure there was no paint on the soles). In the garage, he cleaned the brushes, the paint tray, and his hands with turpentine. Then he joined Mrs. Whitney in the kitchen where a ham sandwich and glass of milk were waiting on the table.

When Emmett sat down, Mrs. Whitney took the chair opposite him with a cup of tea, but nothing to eat.

—I need to go into the city to join my husband, she said, but I gather from your brother that your car's in the shop and won't be ready until tomorrow.

—That's right, said Emmett.

—In that case, why don't you three stay the night. You can help yourself to what's in the refrigerator for dinner, and in the morning you can lock the door behind you when you go.

—That's very generous of you.

Emmett doubted that Mr. Whitney would have welcomed such an arrangement. If anything, he had probably communicated to his wife that he wanted them out of the house as soon as they awoke. Emmett felt his suspicion confirmed when Mrs. Whitney added, almost as an afterthought, that if the phone were to ring, they should leave it unanswered.

As Emmett ate, he noticed that in the middle of the table was a folded piece of paper standing upright between the salt and pepper shakers. Following his gaze, Mrs. Whitney acknowledged that it was Woolly's note.

When Emmett had first come down in the morning and Mrs. Whitney had told him that Woolly had gone, she had seemed almost relieved by his departure, but a little worried too. As she looked at the note, the same emotions returned to her face.

—Would you like to read it? she asked.

—I wouldn't presume.

—That's all right. I'm sure Woolly wouldn't mind.

Emmett's normal instinct would have been to demur a second time, but he sensed that Mrs. Whitney wanted him to read the note. Putting down his sandwich, he took it from its slot between the shakers.

Written in Woolly's hand and addressed to *Sis*, the note said that Woolly was sorry for muddling things up. Sorry about the napkins and the wine. Sorry about the phone in the drawer. Sorry to be leaving so early in the morning without having the chance to say a proper good-bye. But she shouldn't worry. Not for a minute. Not for a moment. Not for the blink of an eye. All would be well.

Cryptically, he concluded the note with the postscript: *The Comptons ate their cabbage in the kitchen!*

—Will it? Mrs. Whitney asked when Emmett set the note down on the table.

—I'm sorry?

—Will all be well?

—Yes, replied Emmett. I'm sure it will.

Mrs. Whitney nodded, but Emmett could see that this was less an expression of agreement with his reply than of gratitude for his reassurance. For a moment, she looked down into her tea, which must have been tepid by now.

—My brother wasn't always in trouble, she said. He was Woolly, of course, but things changed for him during the war. Somehow, when Father accepted his commission in the navy, it was Woolly who ended up at sea.

She smiled a little sadly at her own witticism. Then she asked if Emmett knew why her brother had been sent to Salina.

—He told us once that he had taken someone's car.

—Yes, she said with a bit of a laugh. That was it, more or less.

It happened when Woolly was at St. George's, his third boarding school in as many years.

—One spring day in the middle of classes, she explained, he decided to walk into town in search of an ice cream cone, of all things. When he arrived at the little shopping center a few miles from campus, he noticed there was a firetruck parked at the curb. Having looked around and found no signs of any firemen, he became convinced—in a way that only my brother can become convinced—that it must have been forgotten. Forgotten like—oh, I don't even know—like an umbrella on the back of a chair, or a book on the seat of a bus.

With a smile of affection, she shook her head, then continued.

—Eager to return the firetruck to its rightful owners, Woolly climbed behind the wheel and went looking for the station house. Around the town he drove with a fireman's hat on his head—as it was later reported—tooting the horn for any children he passed. After circling for God knows how long, he found a station house, parked the engine, and walked all the way back to campus.

The affectionate smile that Mrs. Whitney had been wearing began to fade now as her mind leapt forward to all that followed.

—As it turned out, the firetruck had been in the parking lot of the shopping center because several of the firemen were in the grocery store. And while Woolly was driving around, a call came in for a stable that was on fire. By the time the engine from a neighboring town arrived, the stable had burned to the ground. Thankfully, there were no people hurt. But the young stable hand who was on duty alone couldn't get all of the horses out of the building, and four of them died in the fire. The police tracked Woolly back to the school and that was that.

After a moment, Mrs. Whitney pointed to Emmett's plate in order to ask if he was finished. When he said that he was, she cleared it along with her cup to the sink.

She was trying not to imagine it, thought Emmett. Trying not to imagine those four horses trapped in their stalls, whinnying and rising on their hind legs as the flames grew closer. Trying not to imagine the unimaginable.

Though her back was now to Emmett, he could tell from the movement of her arm that she was wiping away tears. Deciding that he should leave her in peace, Emmett tucked Woolly's note back in its spot and quietly pushed back his chair.

—Do you know what I find so strange? Mrs. Whitney asked, still standing at the sink with her back to Emmett.

When he didn't respond, she turned, wearing a mournful smile.

—When we're young, so much time is spent teaching us the importance of keeping our vices in check. Our anger, our envy, our pride. But when I look around, it seems to me that so many of our lives end up being hampered by a virtue instead. If you take a trait that by all appearances is a merit—a trait that is praised by pastors and poets, a trait that we have come to admire in our friends and hope to foster in our children—and you give it to some poor soul in abundance, it will almost certainly prove an obstacle to their happiness. Just as someone can be too smart for their own good, there are those who are too patient for their own good, or too hardworking.

After shaking her head, Mrs. Whitney looked at the ceiling. When she looked down again, Emmett could see that another tear was making its way down her cheek.

—Those who are too confident . . . or too cautious . . . or too kind . . .

Emmett understood that what Mrs. Whitney was sharing with him was her effort to understand, to explain, to make some sense of the undoing of her bighearted brother. At the same time, Emmett suspected that tucked in Mrs. Whitney's list was an apology for her husband, who was either too smart, too confident, or too hardworking for his own good. Perhaps all three. But what Emmett found himself wondering was what virtue did Mrs. Whitney have too much of? The answer, his instincts told him, though he was almost reluctant to admit it, was probably forgiveness.

Woolly

AND THIS WAS MY favorite rocking chair, said Woolly to no one.
He was standing on the porch, a little while after Duchess had gone to the general store. Giving the chair a push, he listened to the thwapping of its rockers as it rocked back and forth, noting how each individual thwap came closer and closer together as the back and forths became smaller and smaller, until they stopped altogether.

Setting the chair in motion again, Woolly looked out at the lake. For the time being, it was so still you could see every cloud in the sky reflected on its surface. But in another hour or so, right around five o'clock, the afternoon breeze would begin to pick up and the surface would ripple and all the reflections would be swept away. Then the curtains in the windows would start to stir.

Sometimes, thought Woolly, sometimes at the end of summer when the hurricanes roamed the Atlantic, the afternoon breeze would grow so strong that the bedroom doors would all slam shut and the rocking chairs would rock themselves.

After giving one last push to his favorite chair, Woolly went back through the double doors into the great room.

—And this is the great room, he said, where we would play Parcheesi and complete jigsaw puzzles on rainy afternoons . . . And this is the hallway . . . And this is the kitchen, where Dorothy made fried chicken and her famous blueberry muffins. And that's the table where we ate when we were too young to dine in the dining room.

Removing from his pocket the note that he had written while sitting at his great-grandfather's desk, Woolly tucked it neatly between the salt and pepper shakers. Then he left the kitchen by means of the only door in the house that swung back and forth.

—And here is the dining room, he said, gesturing to the long table around which his cousins and aunts and uncles would gather. Once you were old enough to eat in here, he explained, you could sit in any seat you wanted as long as it wasn't the seat at the end of the table, because that's where Great-grandpa would sit. And there is the head of the moose.

Exiting the other dining-room door, Woolly reentered the great room, where, after admiring it from corner to corner, he picked up Emmett's book bag and began climbing the stairs, counting as he went.

—Two, four, six, eight, who do we appreciate.

At the top of the stairs, the hallway shot off in both directions, east and west, with bedroom doors on either side.

While there was nothing hanging on the wall to the south, on the wall to the north were photographs everywhere you looked. According to family legend, Woolly's grandmother had been the first person to hang a photograph in the upstairs hallway—a picture of her four young children, which she put right above the side table opposite the stairs. Soon after, a second and third photograph were hung to the left and right of the first photograph. Then a fourth and fifth were hung above and below. Over the years, photographs had been added leftward and rightward, upward and downward, until they radiated in every direction.

Setting down the book bag, Woolly approached the first photograph, then began looking at all the others in the order that they had been hung. There was the picture of Uncle Wallace as a little boy in his little sailor suit. And there the picture of his grandfather out on the dock with the tattoo of the schooner on his arm, getting ready to take his twelve o'clock swim. And there the picture of his father holding up his blue ribbon after winning the riflery contest on the Fourth of July in 1941.

—He always won the riflery contest, said Woolly, while brushing a tear from his cheek with the flat of his hand.

And there, one step farther from the side table, was the one of Woolly with his mother and father in the canoe.

This picture was taken—oh, Woolly didn't know for sure—but around the time that he was seven. Certainly before Pearl Harbor and the aircraft carrier. Before Richard and "Dennis." Before St. Paul's and St. Mark's and St. George's.

Before, before, before.

The funny thing about a picture, thought Woolly, the funny thing about a picture is that while it knows everything that's happened up until the moment it's been taken, it knows absotively nothing about what will happen next. And yet, once the picture has been framed and hung on a wall, what you see when you look at it closely are all the things that were *about* to happen. All the un-things. The things that were unanticipated. And unintended. And unreversible.

Wiping another tear from his cheek, Woolly removed the photograph from the wall and picked up the book bag.

As with the chairs around the dining-room table, there was one bedroom on the hallway that you weren't allowed to sleep in because it was Great-grandpa's. Everyone other than Great-grandpa would sleep in different bedrooms at different times depending on how old they were, or whether they were married, or how early or late in the summer they happened to arrive. Over the years, Woolly had slept in a number of these rooms. But for the longest time, or what seemed like the longest time, he and his cousin Freddy had slept in the second to last room on the left. So that's where Woolly went.

Stepping inside, Woolly set down the book bag and leaned the photograph of him and his parents on the bureau behind the pitcher and glasses. After looking at the pitcher for a moment, he carried it down the hall to the bathroom, filled it with water, and brought it back. Pouring water into one of the glasses, he picked it up and moved it to the bedside table. Then after opening a window, so that the breeze could find its way into the room after five, he began to unpack.

First, he took out the radio and placed it on the bureau beside the pitcher. Then he took out his dictionary and placed it beside the radio. Then he took out the cigar box, in which he kept his collection of the same version of different things, and placed it beside the dictionary. Then he took out his extra bottle of medicine and the little brown bottle that he'd found waiting for him in the spice rack and placed them on the bedside table beside the glass of water.

As he was taking off his shoes, Woolly heard the sound of a car pulling into the driveway—Duchess returning from the general store. Moving to the doorway, Woolly listened to the screen door in the mudroom open and close. Then footsteps passing through the great room. Then furniture being moved in the study. And finally, the sound of clanging.

It wasn't a dainty sort of clanging, like that of a cable car in San Francisco, thought Woolly. It was an emphatic clanging like that of a blacksmith who's beating a red-hot horseshoe on an anvil.

Or perhaps not a horseshoe . . . , thought Woolly with a pang.

Better that it was a blacksmith beating something else. Something like, something like, something like a sword. Yes, that was it. The clanging sounded like an ancient blacksmith hammering on the blade of Excalibur.

With that happier image in mind, Woolly closed the door, switched on the radio, and went to lie down on the bed on the left.

In the story of Goldilocks and the Three Bears, Goldilocks has to climb into three different beds before she finds the one that's just right for her. But Woolly didn't need to climb into three different beds, because he already knew that the one on the left would be just right for him. For as in his youth, it was neither too hard nor too soft, too long nor too short.

Propping up the pillows, Woolly polished off the extra bottle of his medicine and made himself comfortable. As he looked up at the ceiling, his thoughts returned to the jigsaw puzzles that they would complete on rainy days.

Wouldn't it have been wonderful, thought Woolly, if everybody's life was like a piece in a jigsaw puzzle. Then no one person's life would ever be an inconvenience to anyone else's. It would just fit snugly in its very own, specially designed spot, and in so doing, would enable the whole intricate picture to become complete.

As Woolly was having this wonderful notion, a commercial came to its end and the telecast of a mystery show began. Climbing back out of bed, Woolly turned the volume on the radio down to two and a half.

The important thing to understand about listening to a mystery show on the radio, Woolly well knew, is that all the parts designed to make you anxious—like the whispering of assassins, or the rustling of leaves, or the creaking of steps on a staircase—were relatively quiet. While the parts designed to set your mind at ease—like the sudden epiphany of the hero, or the peeling of his tires, or the crack of his pistol—were relatively loud. So if you turned the volume down to two and a half, you could barely hear the parts designed to make you anxious, while still getting to hear all the parts designed to set your mind at ease.

Returning to his bed, Woolly poured all the little pink pills from the little brown bottle onto the table. With the tip of his finger, he pushed them into the palm of his hand, saying, *One potato, two potato, three potato, four. Five potato, six potato, seven potato, more.* Then washing them down with a big drink of water, he made himself comfortable again.

With the pillows properly propped, the volume properly lowered, and the little pink pills properly swallowed, you might think that Woolly wouldn't know what to think about, what with Woolly being Woolly and prone to all the old Woolly ways.

But Woolly knew exactly what to think about. He had known that he would think about it almost as soon as it had happened.

—I'll start in front of the cabinet at FAO Schwarz, he said to himself with a smile. And my sister will come, and we'll have tea at the Plaza with the panda. And after Duchess meets me at the statue of Abraham Lincoln, he and I will attend the circus, where Billy and Emmett will suddenly reappear. Then we'll go over the Brooklyn Bridge and up the Empire State Building, where we'll meet Professor Abernathe. Then it's off to the grassy train tracks where, sitting by the fire, we'll hear the story of the two Ulysses and the ancient seer who explained how they could find their ways home again—how they could find their ways home, after ten long years.

But one mustn't rush, thought Woolly, as the window curtains stirred, and the grass began to sprout through the seams between the floorboards, and the ivy climbed the legs of the bureau. For a one-of-a-kind kind of day deserves to be relived at the slowest possible pace, with every moment, every twist, every turn of events remembered to the tiniest detail.

Abacus

MANY YEARS BEFORE, Abacus had come to the conclusion that the greatest of heroic stories have the shape of a diamond on its side. Beginning at a fine point, the life of the hero expands outward through youth as he begins to establish his strengths and fallibilities, his friendships and enmities. Proceeding into the world, he pursues exploits in grand company, accumulating honors and accolades. But at some untold moment, the two rays that define the outer limits of this widening world of hale companions and worthy adventures simultaneously turn a corner and begin to converge. The terrain our hero travels, the cast of characters he meets, the sense of purpose that has long propelled him forward all begin to narrow—to narrow toward that fixed and inexorable point that defines his fate.

Take the tale of Achilles.

In hopes of making her son invincible, the Nereid Thetis holds her newborn boy by the ankle and dips him into the river Styx. From that finite moment in time and pinch of the fingers, the story of Achilles begins. As a strapping young lad, he is educated in history, literature, and philosophy by the centaur Chiron. On the fields of sport, he gains in strength and agility. And with his comrade Patroclus, he forms the closest of bonds.

As a young man, Achilles ventures forth into the world, where he proceeds from one exploit to the next, vanquishing all manner of opponents until his reputation precedes him far and wide. Then, at the very height of his fame and the peak of his physical prowess, Achilles sets sail for Troy to join the likes of Agamemnon, Menelaus, Ulysses, and Ajax in the greatest battle ever fought by men.

But somewhere on this crossing, somewhere in the middle of the Aegean Sea, unbeknownst to Achilles, the widening rays of his life turn their corners and begin their relentless trajectory inward.

Ten long years, Achilles will remain on the fields of Troy. Over the course of that decade, the area of conflict will grow smaller as the battle lines draw ever closer to the walls of the besieged city. The once countless legions of Greek and Trojan soldiers will grow smaller, diminishing with every additional death. And in the tenth year, when Hector, prince of Troy, slays the beloved Patroclus, Achilles's world will grower smaller still.

From that moment, the enemy with all its battalions is reduced in Achilles's mind to the one person responsible for the death of his friend. The sprawling fields of battle are reduced to the few square feet between where he and Hector will stand. And the sense of purpose that at one time encompassed duty, honor, and glory is now reduced to the single burning desire for revenge.

So perhaps it is not surprising that just a matter of days after Achilles succeeds in killing Hector, a poison arrow lofting through the air pierces the one unprotected spot on Achilles's body—the ankle by which his mother had held him when she dipped him in the Styx. And in that very instant, all of his memories and dreams, all of his sensations and sentiments, all of his virtues and vices are extinguished like the flame of a candle that has been snuffed between a finger and a thumb.

Yes, for the longest time, Abacus had understood that the great heroic stories were like a diamond on its side. But of late, what had taken up his thoughts was the realization that it wasn't simply the lives of the renowned that conform to this geometry. For the lives of miners and stevedores conform to it too. The lives of waitresses and nursemaids conform to it. The lives of the ancillary and the anonymous, of the frivolous and the forgotten.

All lives.

His life.

His life too began at a point—on the fifth of May in 1890, when a boy named Sam was born in the bedroom of a small painted cottage on the island of Martha's Vineyard, the only offspring of an insurance adjuster and a seamstress.

Like any child, Sam's first years were spent in the warm circumference of his family. But one day at the age of seven, in the aftermath of a hurricane, Sam accompanied his father to a shipwreck that needed to be assessed on behalf of the insurers. Having journeyed all the way from Port-au-Prince, this vessel had run aground on a shoal off West Chop, and there it remained, its hull breached, its sails in tatters, its cargo of rum washing ashore with the waves.

From that moment, the walls of Sam's life began to branch outward. After every storm, he would insist upon going with his father to see the wrecks: the schooners, the frigates, the yachts. Whether blown upon the rocks or swamped by a turbulent tide, Sam did not simply see a ship in distress. He saw the world the ship embodied. He saw the ports of Amsterdam, Buenos Aires, and Singapore. He saw the spices and textiles and ceramics. He saw the sailors who hailed from every seafaring nation around the globe.

Sam's fascination with shipwrecks led him to fantastical stories of the sea, like those of Sinbad and Jason. The fantastical stories led him to histories of the great explorers, his worldview widening with the reading of each additional page. Eventually, Sam's ever-growing love of history and myth brought him to the ivy-covered halls of Harvard, and then to New York, where—having rechristened himself Abacus and declared himself a writer—he met musicians, architects, painters, financiers, as well as criminals and derelicts too. And finally, he met Polly, that wonder of wonders who brought him joy, companionship, a daughter, and a son.

What an extraordinary passage were those first years in Manhattan! When Abacus experienced firsthand the omnivalent, omnipresent, omnifarious widening that is life.

Or rather, that is the first half of life.

When did the change come? When did the outer limits of his world turn their corner and begin moving inexorably toward their terminal convergence?

Abacus had no idea.

Not long after his children had grown and moved on, perhaps. Certainly, before Polly died. Yes, it was likely at some point during those years when, without their knowing it, her time had begun to run out while he, in the so-called prime of life, went blithely on about his business.

The manner in which the convergence takes you by surprise, that is the cruelest part. And yet it's almost unavoidable. For at the moment when the turning begins, the two opposing rays of your life are so far from each other you could never discern the change in their trajectory. And in those first years, as the rays begin to angle inward, the world still seems so open, you have no reason to suspect its diminishment.

But one day, one day years after the convergence has begun, you cannot only sense the inward trajectory of the walls, you can begin to see the terminal point in the offing even as the terrain that remains before you begins to shrink at an accelerating pace.

In those golden years of his late twenties, shortly after arriving in New York, Abacus had made three great friends. Two men and a woman, they were the hardiest of companions, fellow adventurers of the mind and spirit. Side by side, they had navigated the waters of life with a reasonable diligence and their fair share of aplomb. But in just these last five years, the first had been stricken with blindness, the second with emphysema, and the third with dementia. How varied their lot, you might be tempted to observe: the loss of sight, of lung capacity, of cognition. When in reality, the three infirmities amount to the same sentence: the narrowing of life at the far tip of the diamond. Step by step, the stomping grounds of these friends had shrunk from the world itself, to their country, to their county, to their home, and finally to a single room where, blinded, breathless, forgetful, they are destined to end their days.

Though Abacus had no infirmities to speak of yet, his world too was shrinking. He too had watched as the outer limits of his life had narrowed from the world at large, to the island of Manhattan, to that book-lined office in which he awaited with a philosophical resignation the closing of the finger and thumb. And then this . . .

This!

This extraordinary turn of events.

A little boy from Nebraska appears at his doorstep with a gentle demeanor and a fantastical tale. A tale not from a leather-bound tome, mind you. Not from an epic poem written in an unspoken language. Not from an archive or athenaeum. But from life itself.

How easily we forget—we in the business of storytelling—that life was the point all along. A mother who has vanished, a father who has failed, a brother who is determined. A journey from the prairies into the city by means of a boxcar with a vagabond named Ulysses. Thence to a railroad track suspended over the city as surely as Valhalla is suspended in the clouds. And there, the boy, Ulysses, and he, having sat down by a campfire as ancient as the ways of man, began—

—It's time, said Ulysses.

—What's that? said Abacus. Time?

—If you're still coming.

—I'm coming! he said. Here I come!

Rising to his feet in a copse of woods twenty miles west of Kansas City, Abacus scrambled through the underbrush in the dark, tearing the pocket from his seersucker jacket. Breathlessly, he followed Ulysses through the break in the trees, up the embankment, and into the boxcar that was destined to take them who knows where.

Billy

E MMETT WAS ASLEEP. Billy could tell that Emmett was asleep because he was snoring. Emmett didn't snore as loudly as their father
used to snore, but he snored loudly enough that you could tell when
he was sleeping.

Quietly, Billy slipped out from under the covers and climbed down
onto the rug. Reaching under the bed, he found his backpack, opened
the upper flap, and removed his army surplus flashlight. Being careful
to point the beam at the rug—so he wouldn't wake his brother—Billy
switched the flashlight on. Then removing Professor Abernathe's *Compendium of Heroes, Adventurers, and Other Intrepid Travelers*, he turned
to chapter twenty-five and took up his pencil.

If Billy were going to start at the very beginning, he would go back
to the twelfth of December 1935, the day that Emmett was born. That
was two years after their father and mother had married in Boston and
moved to Nebraska. It was during the Depression, and Franklin Roosevelt was president, and Sally was almost one year old.

But Billy wasn't going to start at the very beginning. He was going
to start *in medias res*. The hard part, as Billy had explained to Emmett
in the train station in Lewis, was knowing where the middle was.

One idea that Billy had was to start on the Fourth of July 1946, when
he and Emmett and their mother and father went to Seward to watch
the fireworks display.

Billy was just a baby at the time, so he couldn't remember what the trip to Seward had been like. But one afternoon, Emmett had told him all about it. He had told Billy about their mother's love of fireworks, and the picnic basket in the attic, and the checkered cloth that they would spread on the lawn in the middle of Plum Creek Park. So Billy could use what Emmett had told him in order to describe the day exactly as it was.

But he also had the photograph.

Reaching into his backpack, Billy removed the envelope that was in the innermost pocket. Opening the flap, he slipped out the photograph and held it near the flashlight's beam. It was a picture of Emmett, Billy in a basinet, their mother, and the picnic basket all in a row on the checkered cloth. Their father must have been the one who took the picture because he wasn't in it. Everyone in the picture was smiling, and though Billy's father wasn't in the picture, Billy could tell that he must have been smiling too.

Billy had found the photograph together with the postcards from the Lincoln Highway in the metal box that was in the bottom drawer of their father's bureau.

But when Billy had put the postcards in the manila envelope so that he could show them to Emmett when Emmett returned home from Salina, he had put the photograph from Seward in a different envelope. He had put it in a different envelope because he knew that memories of the trip to Seward made his brother angry. Billy knew this because his brother had become angry when he had told Billy about the trip to Seward. And he had never told Billy about it again.

Billy had saved the picture because he knew that Emmett wouldn't always be angry with their mother. Once they had found her in San Francisco, and she had had the chance to tell them all the things that she had been thinking in the years that they had been apart, Emmett wouldn't be angry anymore. Then Billy would give him the picture, and he would be glad that Billy had kept it for him.

But it didn't make sense to start the story there, thought Billy, as he returned the picture to its envelope. Because on the Fourth of July 1946, their mother hadn't even left yet. So that night was closer to the beginning of the story than it was to the middle.

Another idea that Billy had was to start on the night that Emmett hit Jimmy Snyder.

Billy didn't need a photograph to remember that night because he had been there with Emmett and had been old enough to remember it himself.

It was on Saturday, October 4, 1952, the last night of the fair. Their father, who had gone with them to the fair the night before, decided to stay home on Saturday. So Emmett and Billy had driven there together in the Studebaker.

Some years, the temperature at the fair can feel like the beginning of fall, but that year, it felt like the end of summer. Billy remembered because as they drove to the fair they had their windows rolled down, and when they arrived, they decided to leave their jackets in the car.

They had left for the fair at five o'clock so that they could get something to eat, and go on some rides, and still have time to find seats near the front of the fiddling contest. Emmett and Billy both loved the fiddling contest, especially when they had seats near the front. But on that particular night, even though they had plenty of time to spare, they never did get to see the fiddlers.

It was while they were walking from the carousel to the stage that Jimmy Snyder began to say his mean things. At first, Emmett didn't seem to care what Jimmy was saying. Then he began to get angry, and Billy tried to pull him away, but Emmett wouldn't go. And when Jimmy tried to say one last mean thing about their father, Emmett punched him in the nose.

After Jimmy fell back and hit his head, Billy must have closed his eyes, because he didn't remember what the following minutes looked like. He only remembered how they sounded: with Jimmy's friends gasping, then calling for help, then shouting at Emmett as other people jostled around them. And then Emmett, who never once let go of Billy's hand, trying to explain what had happened to one person after another, until the ambulance arrived. And all the while, the calliope at the carousel playing its music and the rifles at the rifle range going *pop, pop, pop.*

But it didn't make sense to start the story there either, thought Billy. Because the night at the fair was before Emmett had been sent to Salina and learned his lesson. So it too belonged in the beginning.

To be *in medias res*, thought Billy, there should be just as many important things that have happened as important things that haven't happened yet. For Emmett, that meant that he should already have been to Seward to watch the fireworks; and their mother should already have followed the Lincoln Highway to San Francisco; and Emmett should already have stopped working on the farm in order to become a carpenter; and he should already have purchased the Studebaker with his savings; and he should already have grown angry at the fair and punched Jimmy Snyder in the nose and been sent to Salina and learned his lesson.

But the arrival of Duchess and Woolly in Nebraska, and the train ride to New York, and the search for the Studebaker, and the reunion with Sally, and the journey they were about to take from Times Square to the Palace of the Legion of Honor in order to find their mother on the Fourth of July, all of these things shouldn't have happened yet.

That's why Billy decided, as he leaned over chapter twenty-five with his pencil in hand, that the perfect place to start the story of Emmett's adventures was when he was driving home from Salina in the front seat of the warden's car.

ONE

—.—

Emmett

A T NINE IN THE MORNING, Emmett was walking alone from the train station at 125th Street into west Harlem.

Two hours earlier, Sally had come downstairs into the Whitneys' kitchen with the report that Billy was sound asleep.

—He's probably exhausted, said Emmett.

—I should think so, said Sally.

For a moment, Emmett thought Sally's remark was directed at him—a jab for exposing Billy to so many trials over the preceding days. But after looking at her expression, he could see that she was simply echoing his own sentiments: Billy was worn out.

So the two decided to let him sleep.

—Besides, said Sally. I'll need some time to wash the sheets and make the other beds.

In the meantime, Emmett would take the train to Harlem in order to pick up the Studebaker. Since Billy was set on beginning their journey in Times Square, Emmett suggested the three of them meet there at 10:30.

—All right, said Sally. But how will we find each other?

—Whoever gets there first can wait under the Canadian Club sign.

—And where might that be?

—Trust me, said Emmett. You won't have any trouble finding it.

.   .   .

When Emmett arrived at the body shop, Townhouse was waiting on the street.

—Your car's ready, he said after they'd shaken hands. You get your envelope back?

—I did.

—Good. Now you and Billy can head out to California. And not a moment too soon. . . .

Emmett looked at his friend.

—The cops came back last night, Townhouse continued. Only, it wasn't the patrolmen, it was two detectives. They asked me the same questions about Duchess, but this time they also asked about you. And they made it clear were I to hear from you or Duchess and not let them know, I'd be buying myself a heap of trouble. Because a car matching the description of your Studebaker was seen near the home of Old Testament Ackerly—on the same afternoon that someone put him in the hospital.

—The hospital?

Townhouse nodded.

—It seems a person or persons unknown went into Ackerly's house in Indiana and hit him on the head with a blunt object. They think he's going to be all right, but he hasn't come to yet. In the meantime, the boys in blue paid a visit to Duchess's old man at some flophouse downtown. He wasn't there, but Duchess had been. With another white youth and a light-blue car.

Emmett passed a hand over his mouth.

—Jesus.

—You said it. Look, as far as I'm concerned, whatever that motherfucker Ackerly got, he deserved. But for the time being, you should probably gain some distance from the city of New York. And while you're at it, gain some distance from Duchess too. Come on. The twins are inside.

Leading the way, Townhouse took Emmett through the repair bays to where the Gonzalez brothers and the one called Otis were waiting. With the Studebaker back under its tarp, Paco and Pico were wearing their big white smiles—two craftsmen eager to reveal their handiwork.

—All set? Townhouse asked.

—All set, said Paco.

—Then let's to it.

When the brothers pulled back the tarp, Townhouse, Emmett, and Otis were silent for a moment. Then Otis began shaking with laughter.

—Yellow? asked Emmett in disbelief.

The brothers looked from Emmett to each other, then back again.

—What's wrong with yellow? asked Paco, defensively.

—It is the color of a coward, said Otis with another laugh.

Pico began speaking rapidly to his brother in Spanish. When he finished, Paco turned to the others.

—He says it's not the yellow of a coward. It's the yellow of a hornet. But she don't only look like a hornet, she *sting* like one too.

Paco began gesturing to the car, a salesman highlighting a new model's features.

—In addition to the paint job, we took out your dents, polished your chrome, and flushed your transmission. But we also put some extra horsepower under the hood.

—Well, said Otis, at least the cops won't be able to recognize you now.

—And if they do, said Paco, they won't be able to catch you.

The Gonzalez brothers laughed with shared satisfaction.

Regretting his initial response, Emmett expressed his gratitude at some length, especially given the speed at which the brothers had done their work. But when he took the envelope of cash from his back pocket, they both shook their heads.

—This one's for Townhouse, said Paco. We owed him one.

. . .

As Emmett gave Townhouse a ride back to 126th Street, the two laughed about the Gonzalez brothers, about Emmett's car and its brand-new sting. By the time they pulled in front of the brownstone, they were quiet, but neither reached for a door handle.

—Why California? Townhouse asked after a moment.

For the first time aloud, Emmett described his plan for his father's money—the plan to buy a run-down house, repair it, and sell it in order to buy two houses more; and thus, the necessity of being in a state with a large and growing population.

—That's an Emmett Watson plan if ever I heard one, said Townhouse with a smile.

—What about you? asked Emmett. What are you going to do now?

—I don't know.

Townhouse looked out the passenger-side window at his stoop.

—My mother wants me to go back to school. She's got some pipe dream of me getting a scholarship and playing college ball, neither of which are going to happen. And pops, he wants to get me a job at the post office.

—He likes his, right?

—Oh, he doesn't like it, Emmett. He loves it.

Townhouse shook his head with a tempered smile.

—When you're a letter carrier, they give you a route, you know? The blocks that you have to lug your bag up and down every day—like some pack mule on a trail. But for my old man, it doesn't seem to feel like work. Because he knows everybody on his route and everybody knows him. The old ladies, the kids, the barbers, the grocers.

Townhouse shook his head again.

—One night about six years ago, he came home looking real low. Like we'd never seen him before. When Mom asked what was wrong, he burst into tears. We thought someone had died, or something. It turned out that after fifteen years, the powers that be had changed his route. They moved him six blocks south and four blocks east, and it nearly broke his heart.

—What happened? asked Emmett.

—He got up in the morning, trudged out the door, and by the end of the year, he'd fallen in love with that route too.

The two friends laughed together. Then Townhouse put a finger in the air.

—But he never forgot the first route. Every year on Memorial Day, when he's got the day off, he walks the old one. Saying hi to everybody who recognizes him, and half the people who don't. In his words, if you've got a job as a mailman, then the US government is paying you to make friends.

—When you put it that way, it doesn't sound so bad.

—Maybe so, agreed Townhouse. Maybe so. But as much as I love my father, I can't imagine living like that. Covering the same ground day after day, week after week, year after year.

—All right. If not college or the post office, then what?

—I've been thinking about the army.

—The army? asked Emmett in surprise.

—Yeah, the army, said Townhouse, almost as if he were trying out the sound of it on himself. Why not? There's no war right now. The pay's pretty good and it's all for keeps. And if you're lucky, maybe you get stationed overseas and see something of the world.

—You'd be back in a barracks, Emmett pointed out.

—I didn't mind that so much, said Townhouse.

—Falling in . . . following orders . . . wearing a uniform . . .

—That's just it, Emmett. As a black man, whether you end up carrying a mailbag, operating an elevator, pumping gas, or doing time, you're going to be wearing a uniform. So you might as well choose the one that suits you. I figure if I keep my head down, pay my dues, maybe I can climb the ranks. Become an officer. Get myself on the right end of a salute.

—I can see it, said Emmett.

—You know something? said Townhouse. So can I.

When Townhouse finally got out of the car, Emmett did too. Coming around the hood, Emmett met him on the sidewalk, where they shook hands with the silent affection of the kindred.

The week before, when Billy had laid out his postcards and explained to Emmett how they were going to find their mother by attending one of the largest Fourth of July celebrations in the state of California, Emmett had counted his brother's notion as fanciful at best. And yet, despite the fact that Emmett and Townhouse were two young men on the verge of heading out in different directions with no real assurance of where they would land, when Townhouse said at their parting, *I'll see you*, Emmett hadn't the slightest doubt that this was true.

—·—

—What in the Lord's name, said Sally.

—It's my car, said Emmett.

—That looks about as much like a car as one of these signs.

They were standing at the northern end of Times Square, where Emmett had parked the Studebaker right behind Betty.

Sally had good cause to compare his car to the signs around them because it was just as eye catching. So much so, it had begun to attract a small crowd of passersby. Reluctant to make eye contact with them, Emmett had no idea if they were pausing to snicker or admire.

—It's yellow! exclaimed Billy, as he returned from a nearby newsstand. Just like the yellow of corn.

—Actually, said Emmett, it's the yellow of a hornet.

—If you say so, said Sally.

Eager to change the subject, Emmett pointed at the bag in Billy's hand.

—What have you got there?

As Sally returned to her truck, Billy carefully slid what he had purchased out of the bag and handed it to Emmett. It was a postcard of Times Square. At the top of the picture, peeking out from behind the buildings, was a small patch of sky; and just like in the other cards in Billy's collection, it was an unblemished blue.

Standing at Emmett's side, Billy pointed from the postcard to the landmarks.

—You see? There's the Criterion Theatre. And Bond Clothiers. And the Camel cigarette sign. And the Canadian Club sign too.

Billy looked around in appreciation.

—The man at the newsstand says that at night the signs are lit up. Every last one of them. Can you imagine?

—It's quite something.

Billy's eyes opened wide.

—Have you been here when the signs are lit up?

—Briefly, Emmett admitted.

—Hey buddy, said a sailor with his arm over the shoulder of a brunette. How 'bout taking us for a ride?

Ignoring him, Emmett got down on his haunches to speak with his brother more closely.

—I know it's exciting to be here in Times Square, Billy. But we've got a long way to go.

—And we're just getting started.

—That's right. So why don't you take one last look around, we'll say our goodbyes to Sally, and then we'll hit the road.

—Okay, Emmett. I think that's a good idea. I'll take one last look around and then we'll hit the road. But we don't have to say goodbye to Sally.

—Why is that?

—Because of Betty.

—What's wrong with Betty?

—She's a goner, said Sally.

Emmett looked up to find Sally standing by the passenger-side door of his car with her suitcase in one hand and her basket in the other.

—She overheated twice on Sally's trip from Morgen, explained Billy. And there was a big cloud of steam and clanking noises when we arrived in Times Square. Then she conked out.

—I guess I asked a little more of her than she had to give, said Sally. But she got us as far as we needed to go, God bless her.

When Emmett stood back up, Sally looked from him to the Studebaker. After a moment, he stepped forward in order to open the back door on her behalf.

—We should all sit in front, said Billy.

—It might be a little crowded, said Emmett.

—It might be at that, said Sally.

Then putting her suitcase and basket onto the back seat, she closed the back door and opened the front.

—Why don't you slide in first, Billy, she said.

After Billy climbed in with his backpack, Sally climbed in after him. Then she looked straight ahead through the windshield with her hands in her lap.

—Thank you kindly, she said when Emmett closed the door.

By the time Emmett was in the driver's seat, Billy had unfolded his map. Looking up from it, he pointed through the window.

—Officer Williams—the second policeman I spoke to—said the official start of the Lincoln Highway is on the corner of Forty-Second Street and Broadway. From there, you take a right and head toward the river. He said that when the Lincoln Highway was first opened you had to ride a ferry across the Hudson, but now you can take the Lincoln Tunnel.

Gesturing to the map, Emmett explained to Sally that the Lincoln Highway was the first transcontinental road in America.

—You don't have to tell me, she said. I know all about it.

—That's right, said Billy. Sally knows all about it.

Emmett put the car in gear.

As they entered the Lincoln Tunnel, Billy explained to Sally's apparent dismay that they were going under the Hudson River—a river so deep that he had seen a flotilla of battleships sailing up it just a few nights before. Then for her benefit, he launched into a description of the elevated and Stew and the campfires, leaving Emmett to his own thoughts.

Now that they were in motion, what Emmett had imagined he would be thinking about, what he had looked forward to thinking about, was the road ahead. When the Gonzalez brothers had said that they put some extra horsepower under the hood, they weren't kidding. Emmett could feel it—and hear it—every time he put his foot to the accelerator. So if the highway between Philadelphia and Nebraska was reasonably empty, he figured they could average fifty miles an hour, maybe sixty. They could drop Sally in Morgen late the following afternoon, and be on their way, finally heading west, with the landscapes of Wyoming and Utah and Nevada stretching out before them. And at their terminus, the state of California with a population on its way to sixteen million.

But as they emerged from the Lincoln Tunnel, having put the city of New York behind them, what Emmett found himself thinking about rather than the road ahead was what Townhouse had said earlier that morning: that he should gain some distance from Duchess.

It was a sound piece of advice and one consistent with Emmett's own instincts. The only problem was that as long as the assault on Ackerly was an open matter, the police would be looking for Duchess *and* for him. And that was assuming that Ackerly recovered. Should Ackerly die without regaining consciousness, the authorities wouldn't rest until they had one of the two of them in custody.

Glancing to his right, Emmett saw that Billy had gone back to looking at his map while Sally was watching the road.

—Sally . . .

—Yes, Emmett?

—Why did Sheriff Petersen come to see you?

Billy looked up from his map.

—The sheriff came to see you, Sally?

—It was nothing, she assured the two of them. I would feel silly even discussing it.

—Two days ago, it struck you as important enough to drive halfway across the country, pointed out Emmett.

—That was two days ago.

—Sally.

—All right, all right. It was something to do with that bit of trouble you had with Jake Snyder.

—You mean when Jake hit him in town? asked Billy.

—He and I were just working something out, said Emmett.

—So I gather, said Sally. Anyhow. It seems that when you and Jake were working your somethings out, there was another fellow there, a friend of Jake's, and shortly afterward, he was hit on the head in the alley behind the Bijou. This fellow was hit so hard, he had to be taken to the hospital in an ambulance. Sheriff Petersen knows it wasn't you who did it because you were with him at the time. But then he heard talk of a young stranger being in town that day. And that's why he came to see me. To ask if you'd had some visitors.

Emmett looked at Sally.

—Naturally, I said no.

—You said no, Sally?

—Yes, Billy, I did. And that was a lie. But it was a *white* lie. Besides, the idea that one of your brother's friends was involved with that business behind the Bijou is nonsense. Woolly would walk a mile out of his way to avoid stepping on a caterpillar. And Duchess? Well, no one who can cook a dish like Fettuccine Whatsits and then serve it on a perfectly set table would ever hit another man in the head with a two-by-four.

And thus endeth the lesson, thought Emmett.

But he wasn't so sure. . . .

—Billy, on the morning when I went into town, were Duchess and Woolly with you?

—Yes, Emmett.

—The whole time?

Billy thought for a moment.

—Woolly was with me the whole whole time. And Duchess was with us for most of the whole time.

—When wasn't Duchess with you?

—When he went on his walk.

—How long did that last?

Billy thought again.

—As long as *The Count of Monte Cristo*, *Robin Hood*, *Theseus*, and *Zorro*. It's the next left, Emmett.

Seeing the Lincoln Highway marker, Emmett shifted to the other lane and took the turn.

As he drove toward Newark, Emmett could see in his mind's eye what must have happened back in Nebraska. Having been asked by Emmett to lie low, Duchess had gone into town anyway. (Of course, he had.) Once in town, he must have stumbled on Emmett's confrontation with Jake, and witnessed the whole sordid business. But if so, why would he have bothered to hit Jake's friend?

Thinking back on the tall stranger in the cowboy hat leaning against the Studebaker, Emmett remembered his lazy posture and smug expression; he remembered how he had egged Jake on during the fight; and finally, he remembered the first words that the stranger had said: *Seems like Jake's got some unfinished business with you, Watson.*

That's how he had put it, thought Emmett: *unfinished business.* And according to the old performer FitzWilliams, *unfinished business* is exactly what Duchess said he had with his father. . . .

Emmett pulled over and sat with his hands on the wheel.

Sally and Billy looked at him with curiosity.

—What is it, Emmett? asked Billy.

—I think we need to go find Duchess and Woolly.

Sally expressed surprise.

—But Mrs. Whitney said they were on their way to Salina.

—They're not on their way to Salina, said Emmett. They're on their way to the Wolcotts' house in the Adirondacks. The only problem is that I don't know where it is.

—I know where it is, said Billy.

—You do?

Looking down, Billy slid his fingertip slowly away from Newark, New Jersey, away from the Lincoln Highway, and up into the middle of northern New York, where someone had drawn a big red star.

Sally

WHEN WE WERE DRIVING through Why-would-anyone-on-God's-green-earth-live-here, New Jersey, and Emmett pulled over to announce that we needed to go to upstate New York in order to find Duchess and Woolly, I didn't say a word. Four hours later, when he pulled into a roadside motel that looked more like a place to drop off donations than to spend the night, I didn't say a word. And when in the motel's run-down little office, Emmett signed the register with Mr. Schulte's name, I didn't say a word then either.

However . . .

Once we'd found our accommodations and I'd sent Billy into the bathroom to take a bath, Emmett directed his attention right at me. Adopting a measure of gravity, he said he wasn't sure how long it would take for him to find Duchess and Woolly. It could take a few hours, maybe more. But once he returned, the three of us could have something to eat and get a good night's sleep, and if we were back on the road by seven in the morning, he guessed they could drop me off in Morgen on Wednesday night without going much out of their way.

And that's when my allotment of not saying a word was all used up.

—Don't you worry about going out of your way, I said.

—It's no problem, he assured.

—Well, whether it is or it isn't, doesn't make much difference. Because I have no intention of being dropped off in Morgen.

—All right, he said a little hesitantly. Then where do you want to be dropped off?

—San Francisco would do just fine.

For a moment Emmett looked at me. Then he closed his eyes.

—Just because you close your eyes, I said, doesn't mean that I'm not here, Emmett. Not by a long shot. As a matter of fact, when you close your eyes, not only am I here, Billy's here, this lovely motel's here, the whole wide world is here—right where you left it.

Emmett opened his eyes again.

—Sally, he said, I don't know what expectations I may have given you, or what expectations you may have come to on your own. . . .

What's this? I wondered. Expectations he may have given me? Expectations I may have come to on my own? I leaned a little closer to make sure I didn't miss a word.

— . . . But Billy and I have been through a good deal this year. What with losing dad and the farm . . .

—Keep going, I said. You've got my attention.

Emmett cleared his throat.

—It's just that . . . Given all we've been through . . . I think what Billy and I need right now . . . is to make a fresh start together. Just the two of us.

I stared at him a moment. Then I let out a little gasp.

—So that's it, I said. You think I'm inviting myself on the ride to San Francisco with the intention of becoming a part of your household.

He looked a little uncomfortable.

—I'm just saying, Sally. . . .

—Oh, I know what you're saying—because you just said it. It came through loud and clear, despite all the hemming and hawing. So let me be loud and clear right back. For the foreseeable future, Mr. Emmett Watson, the only household I intend to be a part of is mine. A household where all the cooking and cleaning that I'll be doing is for me. Cooking *my* breakfast, *my* lunch, *my* dinner. Cleaning *my* dishes.

Washing *my* clothes. Sweeping *my* floor. So don't you worry about me putting a damper on your fresh start. Last time I checked, there were plenty of fresh starts to go around.

As Emmett walked out the door and climbed into his bright yellow car, I thought to myself that there are surely a lot of big things in America. The Empire State Building and the Statue of Liberty are big. The Mississippi River and the Grand Canyon are big. The skies over the prairie are big. But there is nothing bigger than a man's opinion of himself.

With a shake of the head, I swung the door shut, then I knocked on the bathroom door to see how Billy was coming along.

—·—

Excepting his brother, I guess I know Billy Watson better than just about anybody. I know how he eats his chicken, peas, and mashed potatoes (starting with the chicken, moving on to the peas, and saving the potatoes for last). I know how he does his homework (sitting up straight at the kitchen table and using that little rubber eraser at the end of his pencil to remove any trace of a mistake). I know how he says his prayers (always remembering to include his father, his mother, his brother, and me). But I also know how he gets himself in trouble.

It was on the first Thursday in May.

I remember because I was in the middle of making lemon meringue pies for the church social when I received the call asking me to come on down to the schoolhouse.

I admit that when I walked into the principal's office, I was already a little miffed. I had just finished whipping the egg whites for the meringue when I received the call, so I had to turn off the oven and dump the egg whites in the sink. But when I opened the door and saw Billy sitting on a chair in front of Principal Huxley's desk staring at his shoes, I went red. I know for a fact that Billy Watson has never once in his life had cause to stare at his shoes. So if he's staring at his shoes, it's because someone has made him feel the need to do so, unjustly.

—All right, I said to Principal Huxley. You've got us here in front of you. What seems to be the trouble?

It turned out that shortly after lunch, the school had what they call a duck-and-cover drill. In the middle of class, while the children were receiving regular instruction, the school bell rang five times in a row, at which point the children were supposed to climb under their desks and put their hands over their heads. But apparently, when the bell had rung and Mrs. Cooper had reminded the children what to do, Billy had refused.

Billy does not refuse very often. But when he chooses to refuse, he does so with a capital *R*. And no matter how much cajoling, insisting, or reprimanding Miss Cooper resorted to, Billy simply would not join his classmates under their desks.

—I have tried to explain to William, explained Principal Huxley to me, that the purpose of the drill is to ensure his own safety; and that by refusing to participate, he not only puts himself at risk, he gives cause for disruption at the very moment when disruption could do its greatest harm to others.

The years had not been kind to Principal Huxley. His hair had grown scarce on the top of his head, and there was talk in town that Mrs. Huxley had a *friend* in Kansas City. So I suppose there was some call for sympathy. But I hadn't particularly liked Principal Huxley when I was a student at Morgen Elementary, and I saw little reason for liking him now.

I turned to Billy.

—Is this true?

Without looking up from his shoes, Billy nodded his head.

—Perhaps you could tell us why you refused to follow Miss Cooper's instructions, suggested the principal.

For the first time, Billy looked up at me.

—In the introduction to his *Compendium*, Professor Abernathe says that a hero never turns his back on danger. He says a hero always meets it face-to-face. But how is someone supposed to meet danger face-to-face, if he is under his desk with his hands over his head?

Plain speaking and common sense. In my book, there's just no substitute.

—Billy, I said, why don't you wait outside.

—Okay, Sally.

The principal and I both watched as Billy walked out of the office, still staring at his shoes. When the door closed, I turned to the principal so he could see me face-to-face.

—Principal Huxley, I said, while doing my best to maintain my good nature, are you telling me that just nine years after the United States of America defeated the forces of Fascism around the world, you are chastising an eight-year-old boy for his refusal to stick his head under his desk like an ostrich in the sand?

—Miss Ransom . . .

—I have never claimed to be a scientist, I continued. In fact, when I was at the high school, I received a C in physics and a B- in biology. But what little I learned in these subjects suggests to me that the top of a desk is as likely to protect a child from a nuclear explosion as the hairs combed over your head are to protect your scalp from the sun.

I know. It was not a Christian thing to say. But my feathers were up. And I only had another two hours in which to reheat my oven, finish making my pies, and deliver them to the church. So this was no time for serving soft-boiled eggs.

And wouldn't you know it: When I left the office five minutes later, Principal Huxley had agreed that to ensure the safety of the student body, one courageous soul by the name of Billy Watson would be appointed as the Duck-and-Cover Monitor. Henceforth, when the school bell rang five times in a row, rather than hide under his desk, Billy would go from room to room with a clipboard in hand in order to confirm the compliance of everybody else.

As I said, I know Billy better than just about anybody, including how he gets himself in trouble.

So I had no excuse to be surprised when after knocking on the bathroom door three times, I finally opened it to find the water in the bathtub running, the window open, and Billy gone.

Emmett

After driving a mile down the winding dirt road, Emmett began to suspect he had taken a wrong turn. The man at the filling station, who knew the Wolcotts by name, had told Emmett that he should continue along Route 28 for another eight and a half miles, then take a right onto the dirt road bordered by white cedars. Emmett had measured the distance on the odometer, and though he wasn't certain what white cedars looked like, the road he came upon was lined with evergreens, so he took the turn. But a mile later, there was still no sign of a residence. Luckily, the road wasn't wide enough for Emmett to turn around, so he drove onward and a few minutes later came upon a large timber house at the edge of a lake—beside which was parked Woolly's car.

Rolling to a stop behind the Cadillac, Emmett got out of the Studebaker and walked toward the lake. It was late in the afternoon and the water was so still its surface perfectly reflected the pine trees on the opposite shore and the disparate clouds overhead, giving the world an illusion of vertical symmetry. The only sign of movement was from a great blue heron that, having been disturbed by the closing of Emmett's car door, had taken flight from the shallows and now was gliding silently about two feet above the water.

To Emmett's left was a small building that appeared to be some kind of work shed, because resting nearby on a pair of sawhorses, awaiting repair, was an overturned dory with a breach in its bow.

To Emmett's right was the house overlooking the lawn, the lake, and the dock. Along its front was a grand porch with rocking chairs and a wide set of steps descending to the grass. There would be a main entrance at the top of those steps, Emmett knew, but on the other side of the Cadillac was a path bordered by painted stones that led to a stoop and an open door.

Climbing the steps, Emmett opened the screen and called inside.

—Woolly? Duchess?

Hearing nothing, he entered, letting the screen door slam behind him. He found himself in a muck room with an array of fishing rods, hiking boots, slickers, and skates. Everything in the room was neatly put away except for the Adirondack chairs that were stacked in the middle of the floor. Over a rifle cabinet hung a large hand-painted sign with a checklist entitled CLOSING THE HOUSE.

1. Remove firing pins
2. Stow canoes
3. Empty icebox
4. Take in rockers
5. Take out garbage
6. Make beds
7. Close flues
8. Lock windows
9. Lock doors
10. Go home

Leaving the muck room, Emmett entered a hallway, where he stopped, listened, and called again for Woolly and Duchess. Receiving no response, he proceeded to poke his head into various rooms. While the first two seemed untouched, in the third a cue and several balls had been left on the felt of the pool table, as if someone had stopped a game in midplay. At the hallway's end, Emmett stepped into a high-ceilinged living room with various arrangements of couches and chairs, and an open staircase that led to the second floor.

Emmett shook his head in appreciation. It was one of the finest rooms that he had ever seen. Much of the furniture was in the Arts and Crafts style, fashioned from cherry or oak, perfectly joined and discreetly detailed. Over the center of the room hung a large light fixture that, like the lamps, was shaded with mica, ensuring that the room would be cast in a warm glow once evening fell. The fireplace, the ceilings, the couches, the staircase had all been built larger than normal, but they were in proportion to each other and remained in harmony with a human scale, such that the room seemed at once cozy and generous.

It wasn't hard to understand why this house had maintained such a privileged position in Woolly's imagination. It would have maintained a privileged position in Emmett's, had he had the luxury of growing up in it.

Through a pair of open doors Emmett could see a dining room with a long oak table, and down the continuation of the hallway he could see doors leading to other rooms, including a kitchen at the end. But if Woolly and Duchess had been in one of those rooms, they would have heard him calling. So Emmett headed up the stairs.

At the top of the steps, the hallway led in both directions.

First, he checked the bedrooms to his right. Though they differed in terms of size and furnishings—some with double beds, some with single beds, one with a pair of bunks—they all shared a rough simplicity. In a house like this, Emmett understood, one wasn't meant to linger in one's bedroom. One was meant to join the family downstairs for breakfast at the long oak table, then spend the rest of the day out of doors. None of the rooms showed any sign of having been used the night before, so doubling back, Emmett headed for the other end of the hallway.

As Emmett walked, he glanced at the photographs on the wall, intending to give them only passing consideration. And yet he found himself slowing his pace, then stopping altogether in order to study them more closely.

Though the pictures varied in size, all were of people. Among them were portraits of groups and individuals, children and adults, some in motion, others at rest. Taken separately, there was nothing unusual about them. The faces and clothes were ordinary enough. But taken together, there was something profoundly enviable about this wall of photographs in their matching black frames. And it wasn't due to the prevalence of sunlight and carefree smiles. It was a matter of heritage.

Emmett's father had grown up in some version of this place. As he had written in his last letter, what had been handed down in his family from generation to generation were not simply stocks and bonds, but houses and paintings, furniture and boats. And when Emmett's father chose to tell anecdotes of his youth, there seemed no end to the cousins, uncles, and aunts gathered around the holiday table. But for some reason, for some reason that had never been fully explained, Emmett's father had left all of that behind when he moved to Nebraska. Left it behind without a trace.

Or almost without a trace.

There were the trunks in the attic with their exotic stickers from foreign hotels, and the picnic basket with its orderly arrangement of utensils, and the unused china in the hutch—remnants of the life that Emmett's father had relinquished in order to pursue his Emersonian ideal. Emmett shook his head, uncertain of whether his father's actions should give him cause for disappointment or admiration.

As usual with such puzzles of the heart, the answer was probably both.

Progressing down the hall, Emmett could tell from the quality of the photographs and the style of the clothing that the pictures were moving backward in time. Starting at some point in the 1940s, they receded through the thirties and the twenties all the way into the teens. But when Emmett passed the side table at the top of the stairs, the photographs reversed course and began advancing through the decades. It was when he had returned to the 1940s and was looking with curiosity at a blank space on the wall that Emmett heard the music—music coming faintly from somewhere down the hallway. Passing several of the rooms, he homed in on the sound until he stopped before the second-to-last door and listened.

It was Tony Bennett.

Tony Bennett singing that he would go from rags to riches, if you'd only say you care.

Emmett knocked.

—Woolly? Duchess?

When neither replied, he opened the door.

It was another simply furnished room, this one with two small single beds and a bureau. On one of the beds lay Woolly, his stocking feet extending beyond the end of the frame, his eyes closed, his hands crossed on his chest. On the bedside table were two empty medicine bottles and three pink pills.

With a terrible sense of foreboding, Emmett approached the bed. After saying Woolly's name, he shook him gently by the shoulder, finding him stiff to the touch.

—Oh, Woolly, he said, taking a seat on the opposite bed.

Feeling the onset of nausea, Emmett turned away from his friend's expressionless features and found himself staring at the bedside table. Having already recognized the little blue bottle as Woolly's so-called medicine, Emmett picked up the brown bottle. He had never heard of the medication printed on the label, but he saw that it had been pre-scribed to Sarah Whitney.

In just this way, thought Emmett, does misery beget misery. For as good as Woolly's sister was at forgiving, she would never be able to forgive herself for this. As he set the empty bottle back down, from the radio came a jazz number, swinging and discordant.

Rising from the bed, Emmett crossed to the radio and switched it off. On the bureau beside the radio was an old cigar box and a dictio-nary that could have come from anywhere, but leaning against the wall was a framed photograph that could only have come from the empty space in the hall.

It was a snapshot of Woolly as a boy sitting in a canoe between his mother and father. Woolly's parents—a handsome couple in their late thirties—each had a paddle resting across the gunwale, as if they were on the verge of setting out. From Woolly's expression, you could tell he was a little nervous, but he was laughing too, as if someone outside of the frame, someone on the dock, were making a face for his benefit.

Just a few days before—when they had been outside the orphanage waiting for Duchess—Billy had explained to Woolly about their mother and the fireworks in San Francisco, and Woolly, in turn, had explained to Billy about the Fourth of July celebrations his family would have here at the camp. It occurred to Emmett that this picture of Woolly sitting between his parents in the canoe could well have been taken on the very same day that Emmett had lain between his parents to watch the fireworks in Seward. And for perhaps the first time, Emmett had an inkling of why the journey west along the Lincoln Highway had become so important to his brother.

Gently, Emmett returned the photograph to its place on the bureau. Then after taking one more look at his friend, he went in search of a phone. But as he was heading down the hall, he heard a clanging coming from downstairs.

Duchess, he thought.

And the grief that had been welling up inside him was eclipsed by a feeling of fury.

Descending the stairs, Emmett moved quickly down the hallway in the direction of the kitchen, once again homing in on the source of a sound. Stepping through the first door on his left, he entered a room that looked like a gentleman's office, but in disarray—with books pulled from the bookcases, drawers withdrawn from the desk, and papers scattered on the floor. To Emmett's left, a framed painting jutted at a ninety-degree angle from the wall, while behind the painting stood Duchess, haplessly swinging an ax at the smooth gray surface of a safe.

—Come on, Duchess encouraged as he hit the safe again. Come on, baby.

—Duchess, called Emmett once.

Then again, more loudly.

Startled, Duchess checked his swing and looked back. But upon seeing Emmett, he broke into a smile.

—Emmett! Boy, am I glad to see you!

Emmett found Duchess's smile to be as discordant as the jazz number that had come on the radio in Woolly's room; and he felt the same urgent desire to switch it off. As Emmett moved toward Duchess, Duchess's expression transitioned from elation to concern.

—What is it? What's wrong?

—What's wrong? Emmett said, stopping in amazement. Haven't you been upstairs? Haven't you seen Woolly?

Suddenly understanding, Duchess set the ax down on a chair, then shook his head with a solemn expression.

—I saw him, Emmett. What can I say? It's terrible.

—But how . . . ? blurted Emmett. How could you *let* him?

—Let him? repeated Duchess in surprise. Do you seriously think if I had known what Woolly intended to do, I would have left him on his own? I've been keeping an eye on Woolly since the minute I met him. Not a week ago, I went so far as to take away the last bottle of his medicine. But he must have had another one stashed away. And don't ask me where he got hold of those pills.

With all his feelings of impotency and rage, Emmett wanted to blame Duchess. He wanted to blame him, badly. But he also understood that it wasn't Duchess's fault. And rising up within him, like bile in the throat, came the memory of his own assurance to Woolly's sister that all would be well.

—Did you call an ambulance, at least, Emmett asked after a moment, hearing his own voice falter.

Duchess shook his head with an expression of futility.

—By the time I found him, it was too late. He was already as cold as ice.

—All right, said Emmett. I'll call the police.

—The police . . . ? Why would you do that?

—We've got to tell somebody.

—Of course we do. And we will. But whether we do it now or later won't make any difference to Woolly. But it could make a big difference to us.

Ignoring Duchess, Emmett headed toward the telephone on the desk. When Duchess saw where Emmett was going, he scrambled in the same direction, but Emmett beat him to it.

Holding Duchess off with one hand, Emmett picked up the receiver with the other, only to find it silent—the service having yet to be restored for the season.

When Duchess realized the phone was dead, he relaxed his posture.

—Let's talk this through for a second.

—Come on, said Emmett, taking Duchess by the elbow. We'll drive to the station.

Steering Duchess out of the office, Emmett walked him down the hallway, barely listening as Duchess tried to make some sort of case for delay.

—It's terrible what's happened, Emmett. I'm the first to say so. But it's what Woolly chose for himself. For his own reasons. Reasons that we may never fully understand and that we have no real right to second-guess. What's important now is for us to keep in mind what Woolly would've wanted.

When they reached the screen door in the muck room, Duchess turned around in order to face Emmett.

—You should have been there when your brother talked about the house he wants to build in California. I've never seen Woolly so excited. He could just picture the two of you living there together. If we go to the cops now, I'm telling you, within the hour this place is going to be crawling with people, and we'll never get to finish what Woolly started.

With one hand, Emmett opened the screen door, with the other, he pushed Duchess down the steps.

After Duchess stumbled a few feet in the direction of the overturned dory, he suddenly spun around as if he'd had an idea.

—Hey! You see that boathouse? There's a workbench inside it with a whole selection of chisels and files and drills. They were of no use to me. But I bet you could get that safe open in a matter of minutes. After we liberate Woolly's trust, we can go find a telephone together. And once the ambulance is on its way, we can head for California, just like Woolly wanted.

—*We* are not going anywhere, Emmett said, his face growing flush. We are not going to San Francisco or Los Angeles or Tinseltown. My brother and I are going to California. *You* are going to Salina.

Duchess looked at Emmett in disbelief.

—Why on earth would I go to Salina, Emmett?

When Emmett didn't reply, Duchess shook his head and pointed to the ground.

—I am staying right here until I get that safe open. And if you don't want to stick around and help, that's your business. It's a free country. But I'm telling you, Emmett, as a friend: If you leave now, it's a decision you're going to regret. Because once you get to California, you'll realize that a couple of grand isn't going to get you very far. Then you'll wish you had your share of the trust.

Stepping forward, Emmett took Duchess by the collar just as he had at the Whitneys', only this time he used both hands, and he could feel the fabric tightening around Duchess's throat as he rotated his fists.

—Don't you get it? he said through his teeth. There is no trust. No inheritance. No money in the safe. It's a fairy tale. A fairy tale Woolly cooked up so you would take him home.

As if in disgust, Emmett shoved Duchess back.

Tripping over the stones that lined the pathway, Duchess fell on the grass.

—You're going to the cops, said Emmett, if I have to drag you to the station.

—But, Emmett, there *is* money in the safe.

Spinning around, Emmett discovered his brother standing in the doorway of the muck room.

—Billy! What are you doing here?

Before Billy could answer, his expression transitioned from one of instruction to one of alarm, prompting Emmett to turn back around— at the very moment that Duchess's arm went into motion.

The blow came hard enough to knock Emmett off his feet, but not hard enough to knock him unconscious. Feeling the coolness of blood on his brow, Emmett gathered his senses and rose onto all fours just in time to see Duchess push Billy into the house and slam the inner door.

Duchess

THE DAY BEFORE, after Woolly acknowledged that the notion of a combination had most certainly definitely slipped his mind, he wondered if I wanted to take a walk down to the dock.

—You go right ahead, I said. I think I'll take a moment to myself.

When Woolly went outside, I spent a few minutes in front of Great-grandpa's safe, staring at it with my hands on my hips. Then with a shake of the head, I went to work. First, I tried putting my ear against the metal and turning the dials to hear the clicks of the tumblers like they do in the movies—which worked about as well as anything else you try doing that you've seen in the movies.

Retrieving the Othello case from my book bag, I took out my old man's knife. My idea was to force the point of the blade into the seam between the door and the casing and wiggle it back and forth. But when I put my full weight behind the knife, what gave was the blade, snapping clean off at the hilt.

—Forged, tempered, and burnished by a master craftsman in Pittsburgh, my eye, I muttered.

Next, I went in search of some genuine tools. But after opening every kitchen drawer and rummaging through every closet, I proceeded to the mudroom, where I sifted through every cubbyhole and basket to no avail. For a moment, I considered shooting the safe with one of the rifles, but given my luck, I'd probably be hit by a ricochet.

So I went down to the dock, where Woolly was admiring the view.

—Hey, Woolly, I called from dry land. Do you know if there's a hardware store in the neighborhood?

—What's that? he asked turning around. A hardware store? I'm not sure. But there's a general store about five miles up the road.

—Perfect. I shouldn't be long. You need anything?

Woolly thought about it for a moment, then shook his head.

—I've got everything I need, he said with a Woolly sort of smile. I'm just going to wander around a bit and unpack my things. Then I thought I might take a little nap.

—Why not? I said. You've earned it.

Twenty minutes later, I was roaming the aisles of the general store thinking they must call it that because it generally has everything but what you're looking for. It was like someone had tipped a house on its side and shaken it until everything that wasn't nailed to the carpet came tumbling out the door: spatulas, oven mitts, and egg timers; sponges, brushes, and soaps; pencils, pads, and erasers; yo-yos and rubber balls. In a state of consumer exasperation, I finally asked the proprietor if he had any sledgehammers. The best he could do was a ball-peen hammer and a set of screwdrivers.

When I got back to the house, Woolly was already upstairs, so I returned to the office with my tools. I must have banged away on the face of that thing for about an hour with nothing to show for it but some chicken-scratched metal and a sweat-soaked shirt.

The next hour I spent searching the office for the combination. I figured a wily old moneymaker like Mr. Wolcott wouldn't be so careless as to leave the combination of his safe to the vicissitudes of memory. Especially considering that he lived into his nineties. He must have written it down somewhere.

Naturally enough, I started with his desk. First, I went through the drawers looking for a diary or address book where an important number might be logged on the final page. Then I pulled out the drawers and flipped them over to see if he had written it down on one of the undersides. I looked under the desk lamp and on the bottom of the bronze bust of Abraham Lincoln, despite the fact that it weighed about two hundred pounds. Next, I turned my attention to the books, flipping through their pages in search of a hidden scrap of paper. That endeavor lasted as long as it took me to realize that flipping through all the old man's books would take me the rest of my life.

That's when I decided to wake up Woolly—in order to ask him which of the bedrooms was his great-grandfather's.

Earlier, when Woolly had said he was going to take a little nap, I didn't think anything of it. As I mentioned, he hadn't gotten much sleep the night before, and then he'd woken me at dawn in order to make the hasty exit. So I figured a nap was exactly what he intended to take.

But the moment I opened the bedroom door, I knew what I was looking at. After all, I had stood on that threshold before. I recognized the suggestion of order—with Woolly's belongings lined up on the bureau and his shoes set side by side at the end of the bed. I recognized the stillness—set into relief by the delicate movement of the curtains and the murmur of a news broadcast on the radio. And I recognized the expression on Woolly's face—an expression that, like Marceline's, radiated neither happiness nor sorrow, but which did suggest some semblance of peace.

When Woolly's arm had fallen from his side, he must have been too far gone or too indifferent to bother lifting it up, because his fingers were brushing the floor, just like they had at the HoJo's. And just like then, I put his arm back where it belonged, this time crossing his hands on his chest.

At long last, I thought, the houses, cars, and Roosevelts had all come tumbling down.

—*The wonder is he hath endured so long.*

As I was leaving, I turned off the radio. But then I turned it on again, thinking that in the hours ahead, Woolly would probably appreciate having the occasional commercial to keep him company.

That night, I ate baked beans out of a can and washed them down with a warm Pepsi-Cola, the only things I could find in the kitchen to eat. So as not to crowd Woolly's ghost, I slept on a couch in the great room. And when I woke in the morning, I went right back to work.

In the hours that followed, I must have hit that safe one thousand times. I hit it with the hammer. I hit it with a croquet mallet. I even tried hitting it with the bust of Abe Lincoln, but I couldn't get a good enough grip.

Around four in the afternoon, I decided to pay a visit to the Caddy, in hopes of finding a tire iron. But as I was coming out of the house, I noticed that the rowboat overturned on a pair of sawhorses had a sizable hole in its bow. Figuring that someone had put it there to repair it, I went into the boathouse looking for an implement that might prove useful. Sure enough, behind all the paddles and canoes was a workbench with a slew of drawers. I must have spent half an hour going over every inch of it, but all it offered up was a new assortment of hand tools that weren't going to get me much further than the ones from the general store. Remembering that Woolly had mentioned an annual fireworks display at the camp, I tore the boathouse apart looking for explosives. Then, just as I was about to walk out in a state of moral defeat, I found an ax hanging between two pegs on the wall.

With the whistle of a lumberjack on my lips, I sauntered back to the old man's study, took up a position in front of the safe, and began to swing. I couldn't have made contact more than ten times when suddenly, out of the blue, Emmett Watson comes bursting through the door.

—Emmett! I exclaimed. Boy, am I glad to see you!

And I meant it. For if there was anyone I knew in this whole wide world who could find a way to get into that safe, it was Emmett.

Before I had a chance to explain the situation, the conversation got a little off course—if understandably so. For having arrived while I was in the boathouse and finding no one home, Emmett had gone upstairs and discovered Woolly.

He was clearly rattled by it. In all probability, he had never seen a dead body before, certainly not the body of a friend. So I really couldn't fault him for throwing some blame my way. That's what rattled people do. They point a finger. They point a finger at whoever's standing closest—and given the nature of how we congregate, that's more likely to be friend than foe.

I reminded Emmett that I was the one who'd been keeping an eye on Woolly for the last year and a half, and I could see that he was cooling down. But then he started talking a little crazy. Acting a little crazy.

First off, he wanted to call the cops. When he discovered that the phone was dead, he wanted to drive to the station—and he wanted to take me with him.

I tried talking some sense into him. But he was so tightly wound, he marched me down the hall, pushed me out the door, and knocked me to the ground, claiming that there was no money in the safe, that I was going to the police station, and that, if necessary, he was going to drag me there.

Given the state he was in, I have no doubt that's exactly what he would've done—no matter how deeply he would have regretted it later. In other words, he wasn't leaving me many options.

And fate seemed to agree. Because when Emmett knocked me down, I landed on the grass with my hand practically resting on one of those painted stones. And then out of nowhere, Billy pops up—just in time to draw Emmett's attention in the other direction.

The rock that I had my hand on was the size of a grapefruit. But I wasn't looking to do any serious damage to Emmett. I just needed to slow him down for a few minutes, so he could regain a little perspective before he did something he couldn't undo. Crawling a few feet out of my way, I picked up one that was no bigger than an apple.

Sure, it knocked him to the ground when I hit him with it. But that was more from the surprise than from the force of impact. I knew he'd be back in the swing of things before you knew it.

Figuring if anyone could talk some sense into Emmett, his brother could, I dashed up the steps, ushered Billy into the house, and locked the door behind us.

—Why did you hit Emmett? Billy cried, looking more rattled than his brother. Why did you hit him, Duchess? You shouldn't have hit him!

—You're absolutely right, I agreed, trying to settle him down. I shouldn't have done it. And I swear, I'll never do it again.

Leading him a few steps from the door, I took him by the shoulders and made a stab at talking to him man-to-man.

—Listen, Billy: There's been something of a snafu. The safe is here, just like Woolly said it would be. And I agree with you wholeheartedly that the money's inside of it, waiting to be claimed. But we don't have the combination. So what we need now is a little bit of time, some Yankee ingenuity, and plenty of teamwork.

As soon as I had taken Billy by the shoulders, he had closed his eyes. And before I was halfway through my speech, he was shaking his head and quietly repeating his brother's name.

—Are you worried about Emmett? I asked. Is that it? I promise there's no cause for concern. I barely hit him. In fact, he should be back on his feet any second now.

Even as I said this, we could hear the knob rattling behind us, then Emmett pounding on the door and shouting our names.

—There, I said leading the kid into the hallway. What'd I tell you?

When the pounding on the door stopped, I lowered my voice in order to speak in confidence.

—The fact of the matter, Billy, is that for reasons I can't go into at this moment, your brother wants to call the authorities. But I fear that if he does that, we'll never get in the safe, there'll be no divvying, and that house of yours—the one for you, and Emmett, and your mother—it'll never get built.

I thought I was making a pretty good case, but Billy just kept shaking his head with his eyes closed and saying Emmett's name.

—We're going to talk to Emmett, I assured him with a touch of frustration. We're going to talk with him all about it, Billy. But for the moment, it's just you and me.

And just like that, the kid stopped shaking his head.

Here we go, I thought. I must be getting through!

But then he opened his eyes and kicked me in the shin.

Isn't that priceless?

A moment later, there I was, hopping on one foot as he ran down the hallway.

—Jeezo peezo, I said, taking off after him.

But when I got to the great room, he was gone.

As God is my witness, even though the kid hadn't been out of my sight for more than thirty seconds, he had vanished into thin air—like Lucinda the cockatoo.

—Billy? I called out, looking behind one couch after another. Billy?

From somewhere different in the house, I heard another doorknob rattling.

—Billy! I called to the room at large, with a growing sense of urgency. I know the escapade hasn't been playing out exactly as we planned, but the important thing is that we stick together and see it through! You, your brother, and me! All for one and one for all!

That's when from the direction of the kitchen came the sound of breaking glass. A moment later Emmett would be in the house. Of that there was no doubt. Having no other choice, I made a beeline for the mudroom where, finding the rifle cabinet locked, I picked up a croquet ball and threw it through the glass.

Billy

AFTER THEY HAD CHECKED IN to room 14 at the White Peaks Motel on Route 28, and Billy had taken off his backpack, Emmett said he was heading out to find Woolly and Duchess.

—In the meantime, he told Billy, it's probably for the best if you stay here.

—Besides, said Sally, when was the last time you took a bath, young man? I wouldn't be surprised if it was back in Nebraska.

—That's true, said Billy nodding. The last time I took a bath was back in Nebraska.

As Emmett began talking quietly to Sally, Billy put his backpack back on his back and headed toward the bathroom.

—Do you really need that thing in there with you? Sally asked.

—I need it, said Billy with his hand on the doorknob, because it's where my clean clothes are.

—All right. But don't forget to wash behind your ears.

—I won't.

When Emmett and Sally went back to talking, Billy went into the bathroom, closed the door, and turned on the bathtub faucets. But he didn't take off his dirty clothes. He didn't take off his dirty clothes because he wasn't going to take a bath. That had been a white lie. Like the one that Sally had told Sheriff Petersen.

After double-checking to make sure that the drain was open so that the tub wouldn't overflow, Billy tightened the straps on his backpack, climbed on top of the toilet, pushed up the sash, and slipped out the window, leaving no one the wiser.

Billy knew that his brother and Sally might only be talking for a few minutes, so he had to run as fast as he could around the motel to where the Studebaker was parked. He ran so fast, when he climbed into the trunk and lowered the lid, he could hear his heart beating in his chest.

When Duchess had told Billy how he and Woolly had hidden in the trunk of the warden's car, Billy had asked how they had gotten out again. Duchess had explained that he had brought along a spoon in order to pop the latch. So before climbing into the Studebaker's trunk, Billy had taken his jackknife out of his backpack. Then he had also taken out his flashlight because it was going to be dark in the trunk once the lid was closed. Billy wasn't afraid of the dark. But Duchess had said how difficult it had been to pop the latch without being able to see it. *We came this close*, Duchess said holding his thumb and finger an inch apart, *to riding all the way back to Salina without even getting a glimpse of Nebraska.*

Switching on his flashlight, Billy took a quick look at Woolly's watch to check the time. It was 3:30. Then he switched off the flashlight and waited. A few minutes later, he heard the car door open and close, the engine start, and they were on their way.

———◆———

Back in the motel room, when Emmett had told Billy that it was probably for the best if he stayed behind, Billy hadn't been surprised.

Emmett often thought it was for the best that Billy remain behind while he was going someplace else. Like when he went into the courthouse in Morgen in order to be sentenced by Judge Schomer. *I think it's for the best*, he'd said to Billy, *that you wait out here with Sally.* Or when they were at the depot in Lewis and Emmett had gone to find out about the freight trains to New York. Or when they were on the West Side Elevated and he had gone looking for Duchess's father.

In the third paragraph of the introduction to his *Compendium of Heroes, Adventurers, and Other Intrepid Travelers*, Professor Abernathe says the hero often leaves his friends and family behind when setting out on an exploit. He leaves his friends and family behind because he is concerned about exposing them to peril, and because he has the courage to face the unknown by himself. That's why Emmett often thought it best for Billy to remain behind.

But Emmett didn't know about Xenos.

In chapter twenty-four of his *Compendium*, Professor Abernathe says: *As long as there have been great men who have accomplished great things, there have been storytellers eager to recount their exploits. But whether it was Hercules or Theseus, Caesar or Alexander, what feats these men accomplished, what victories they achieved, what adversities they overcame would never have been possible without the contributions of Xenos.*

Although Xenos sounds like it might be the name of a figure from history—like Xerxes or Xenophon—Xenos is not the name of a person at all. *Xenos* is a word from ancient Greek that means foreigner and stranger, guest and friend. Or more simply, the Other. As Professor Abernathe says: *Xenos is the one on the periphery in the unassuming garb whom you hardly notice. Throughout history, he has appeared in many guises: as a watchman or attendant, a messenger or page, a shopkeeper, waiter, or vagabond. Though usually unnamed, for the most part unknown, and too often forgotten, Xenos always shows up at just the right time in just the right place in order to play his essential role in the course of events.*

That's why when Emmett had suggested it was for the best that Billy stay behind while he went in search of Woolly and Duchess, Billy had no choice but to sneak out the window and hide in the trunk.

—·—

Thirteen minutes after they had left the motel, the Studebaker came to a stop and the driver's door opened and closed.

Billy was about to pop the latch of the trunk when he smelled the fumes of gasoline. They must be at a filling station, he thought, and Emmett is asking for directions. Though Woolly had put a big red star on Billy's map to show the location of his family's house, the map was drawn at too big a scale to include the local roads. So while Emmett knew he had reached the vicinity of Woolly's house, he didn't know exactly where it was.

Listening carefully, Billy heard his brother call out thanks to someone. Then the door opened and closed and they were driving again. Twelve minutes later, the Studebaker took a turn and began moving slower and slower until it rolled to a stop. Then the engine went off, and the driver's door opened and closed again.

This time Billy decided he would wait at least five minutes before trying to pop the latch. Training his flashlight beam on Woolly's watch, he saw that it was now 4:02. At 4:07 he heard his brother calling out for Woolly and Duchess, followed by a screen door's slam. Emmett had probably gone inside the house, thought Billy, but he waited another two minutes. When it was 4:09, he popped the latch and climbed out. He put his jackknife and flashlight back in his backpack, his backpack back on his back, and quietly closed the trunk.

The house was bigger than just about any house that Billy had ever seen. At its near end was the screen door that Emmett must have gone through. Quietly, Billy climbed the steps of the stoop, peeked through the screen, and let himself inside, being sure not to let the door slam behind him.

The first room he entered was a storage area with all sorts of things that you would use outside, like boots and raincoats, skates and rifles. On the wall were the ten rules for *Closing the House*. Billy could tell the list was written in the order in which you were supposed to do things, but he wondered about the last item, the one that said *Go home*. After a moment, Billy decided it must have been put there in jest.

Poking his head out of the storage room, Billy could see his brother at the end of the hallway, staring at the ceiling of a large room. Emmett would do that sometimes—stop and stare at a room in order to understand how it had been built. After a moment, Emmett climbed a set of stairs. When Billy could hear his brother's footsteps overhead, he snuck down the hallway and into the large room.

As soon as he saw the fireplace big enough for everyone to gather around, Billy knew exactly where he was. Through the windows he could see the porch with the overhanging roof, under which you could sit on rainy afternoons and on top of which you could lie on warm summer nights. Upstairs there would be enough rooms for friends and family to visit for the holidays. And there in the corner was the special spot for the Christmas tree.

Behind the staircase was a room with a long table and chairs. That must be the dining room, thought Billy, where Woolly gave the Gettysburg Address.

Crossing the large room and entering the opposite hallway, Billy poked his head into the first room that he passed. It was the study, right where Woolly had drawn it. While the large room had been neat and tidy, the study was not. It was a mess, with books and papers scattered about and a bust of Abraham Lincoln lying on the floor under a painting of the signing of the Declaration of Independence. On a chair near the bust were a hammer and some screwdrivers, and there were scratches all across the front of the safe.

Woolly and Duchess must have been trying to get into the safe with the hammer and screwdrivers, thought Billy, but it wasn't going to work. A safe was made of steel and designed to be impenetrable. If you could open a safe with a hammer and screwdrivers, then it wouldn't be a safe.

The door of the safe had four dials, each of which showed the numbers zero through nine. That meant there were ten thousand different possible combinations. Duchess and Woolly would have been better off trying all ten thousand by starting with 0000 and working their way up to 9999, thought Billy. That would have taken less time than trying to break in with the hammer and screwdrivers. Even better, though, would be to guess the combination that Woolly's great-grandfather had chosen.

It took Billy six tries.

Once the door of the safe was open, it reminded Billy of the box at the bottom of his father's bureau, in that there were important papers inside—just a lot more of them. But under the shelf with all of the important papers, Billy counted fifteen stacks of fifty-dollar bills. Billy remembered that Woolly's great-grandfather had put a hundred and fifty thousand dollars in his safe. That meant that each stack was made up of ten thousand dollars. Stacks of ten thousand dollars, thought Billy, in a safe with ten thousand possible combinations. Closing the door of the safe, Billy turned away, but then turned back again in order to spin the dials.

Leaving the study, Billy continued down the hallway and went into the kitchen. It was neat and tidy except for an empty soda pop bottle and a can of beans that had a spoon sticking straight up out of it like the stick on a candy apple. The only other sign that someone had been in the kitchen was the envelope tucked between the salt and pepper shakers on the table. The envelope, which said *To Be Opened in the Event of My Absence*, had been left there by Woolly. Billy could tell it had been left by Woolly because the handwriting on the envelope matched the handwriting on Woolly's drawing of the house.

As Billy was putting the envelope back between the salt and pepper shakers, he heard the sound of metal hitting metal. Tiptoeing down the hallway and peeking through the door of the study, he saw Duchess swinging an ax at the safe.

He was about to explain to Duchess about the ten thousand

combinations when he heard his brother's footsteps thumping down the stairs. Running back down the hallway, Billy slipped back into the kitchen and out of sight.

Once Emmett was inside the study, Billy couldn't hear what his brother was saying, but he could tell that he was angry from the tone of his voice. After a moment, Billy heard what sounded like a scuffle, then Emmett emerged from the study holding Duchess by the elbow. As Emmett marched him down the hallway, Duchess was speaking quickly about something that Woolly had chosen for himself for his own reasons. Then Emmett marched Duchess into the storage room.

Following quickly but quietly down the hallway, Billy peeked around the doorframe of the storage room in time to hear Duchess tell Emmett why they shouldn't go to the cops. Then Emmett pushed Duchess out the door.

In chapter one of the *Compendium of Heroes, Adventurers, and Other Intrepid Travelers*—after the part when Professor Abernathe explains how many of the greatest adventure stories start *in medias res*—he goes on to explain the tragic flaws of classical heroes. *All classical heroes,* he says, *however strong or wise or courageous they may be, have some flaw in their character which leads to their undoing.* For Achilles the fatal flaw had been anger. When he was angry, Achilles could not contain himself. Even though it had been foretold that he might die during the Trojan War, once his friend Patroclus was killed, Achilles returned to the battlefield blinded by a black and murderous rage. And that's when he was struck by the poisonous arrow.

Billy understood that his brother had the same flaw as Achilles. Emmett was not a reckless person. He rarely raised his voice or showed impatience. But when something happened to make him angry, the force of his fury could come to such a boil that it resulted in *an injudicious act with irreversible consequences.* According to Billy's father, that's what Judge Schomer had said Emmett was guilty of when he had hit Jimmy Snyder: *an injudicious act with irreversible consequences.*

Through the screen door, Billy could see that Emmett was coming to a boil right now. His face was growing red, and having taken Duchess by the shirt, he was shouting. He was shouting that there was no trust fund, no inheritance, no money in the safe. Then he shoved Duchess to the ground.

This must be it, thought Billy. This is the time and place at which I needed to be in order to play my essential role in the course of events. So Billy opened the screen door and told his brother that there *was* money in the safe.

But when Emmett turned around, Duchess hit him on the head with a stone and Emmett fell to the ground. He fell to the ground just as Jimmy Snyder had.

—Emmett! Billy shouted.

And Emmett must have heard Billy because he began to get up onto his knees. Then Duchess was suddenly at the doorway pushing Billy inside, locking the door, and talking quickly.

—Why did you hit Emmett? Billy said. Why did you hit him, Duchess? You shouldn't have hit him.

Duchess swore he wouldn't do it again, but then he went back to talking quickly. He was talking about something called a snafu. And then about the safe. And Woolly. And the Yankees.

When Emmett began banging on the storage-room door, Duchess pushed Billy into the hallway, and when Emmett's banging stopped, Duchess started talking again, this time about the authorities and the house in California.

And suddenly, Billy felt like he had been here before. The tightness of Duchess's grip and the urgency with which he was speaking made Billy feel like he was back on the West Side Elevated in the dark in the hands of Pastor John.

—We're going to talk to Emmett, said Duchess. We're going to talk with him all about it, Billy. But for the moment, it's just you and me.

Then Billy understood.

Emmett wasn't there. Ulysses wasn't there. Sally wasn't there. Once again, he was alone and forsaken. Forsaken by everyone, including his Maker. And whatever happened next rested only in his hands.

Opening his eyes, Billy kicked Duchess as hard as he could.

In the instant, Billy could feel Duchess's grip release. Then Billy was running down the hallway. He was running down the hallway to the hiding place under the stairs. He found the door with the tiny latch right where Woolly had said it was. The doorway was about half the size of a normal doorway and had a triangular top because it had been cut to fit under the staircase. But it was tall enough for Billy. Slipping inside, he pulled the door closed and held his breath.

A moment later he could hear Duchess calling his name.

Billy could tell that Duchess was only a few feet away, but he wouldn't be able to find Billy. As Woolly had said, no one ever thought to look in the hiding place under the stairs because it was right there in front of them.

Emmett

AFTER TRYING THE MUCK-ROOM door and finding it bolted, Emmett ran around the back of the house and tried the door that led into the dining room. When he found that door locked and then the kitchen door too, he was through trying doors. Removing his belt, he wrapped it around his right hand so that the buckle was on top of his knuckles. Then he smashed one of the panes of glass in the door. Using the metal surface of the buckle, he knocked away the remaining shards that jutted from the frame. Sticking his left hand through the cleared pane, he unlocked the door. The belt, he left wrapped around his fist, thinking it might come in handy right where it was.

As Emmett stepped into the kitchen, he saw Duchess's figure at the far end of the hallway turning a corner at a sprint and disappearing into the muck room—without Billy.

Emmett didn't run in pursuit. Understanding that Billy had broken free, he no longer felt a sense of peril. What he felt now was inevitability. No matter how fast Duchess ran, no matter where he ran to, it was inevitable that Emmett would have his hands upon him.

But as Emmett left the kitchen, he heard glass breaking. It wasn't the sound of a windowpane. It was a sheet of glass. A moment later, Duchess reappeared at the other end of the hallway holding one of the rifles.

That Duchess had a rifle didn't change anything for Emmett. Slowly, but unhesitantly, he began walking toward Duchess, and

Duchess walked toward him. When they were both about ten feet short of the staircase, they stopped, leaving twenty feet between them. Duchess was holding the rifle in one hand with the barrel pointing at the ground, his finger on the trigger. From the way he held the rifle, Emmett could tell that Duchess had held one before, but that didn't change anything either.

—Put down the rifle, he said.

—I can't do that, Emmett. Not until you calm down and start talking sense.

—Sense is what I've been talking, Duchess. For the first time in a week. Willing or unwilling, you're going to the police station.

Duchess looked genuinely frustrated.

—Because of Woolly?

—Not because of Woolly.

—Then why?

—Because the cops think you clobbered someone back in Morgen with a two-by-four, and then put Ackerly in the hospital.

Now Duchess looked dumbfounded.

—What are you talking about, Emmett? Why would I hit some guy in Morgen? I'd never been there in my life. And as to Ackerly, the list of people who'd like to put him in the hospital must be a thousand pages long.

—It really doesn't matter whether you did these things or not, Duchess. What matters is that the cops think you did them—and that I was somehow involved. As long as they're looking for you, they'll be looking for me. So you'll have to turn yourself in and sort it out with them.

Emmett took a step forward, but this time Duchess raised the rifle so that the barrel was pointing at his chest.

In the back of his mind, Emmett knew that he should be taking the threat from Duchess seriously. Like Townhouse had said, when Duchess was intent on something, everyone on the periphery was at risk. Whether his intentions now were focused on avoiding Salina, or obtaining the money from the safe, or seeing to the unfinished business with his father, in the heat of the moment Duchess was perfectly capable of doing something as stupid as pulling a trigger. And if Emmett got himself shot, what would happen to Billy?

But before Emmett could acknowledge the merits of this train of thought, before he had the chance to even hesitate, out of the corner of his eye he noticed a fedora on the cushion of a high-back chair, and the memory of Duchess sitting at the piano in Ma Belle's lounge with his hat tilted back on his head in that cocksure manner gave Emmett a new surge of anger that restored his sense of inevitability. Emmett would have Duchess in his hands, he would take him to the police, and soon enough, Duchess would be on his way back to Salina, or Topeka, or wherever they wanted to send him.

Emmett resumed walking, closing the gap between them.

—Emmett, said Duchess with an expression of anticipatory regret, I don't want to shoot you. But I will shoot you if you leave me no choice.

When they were three paces apart, Emmett stopped. It wasn't the threat of the rifle or the plea from Duchess that made him stop. It was the fact that ten feet beyond Duchess, Billy had appeared.

He must have been hiding somewhere behind the staircase. Now he was moving quietly into the open so that he could see what was happening. Emmett wanted to signal Billy that he should return to wherever he'd been hiding, to signal him without making Duchess aware.

But it was too late. Duchess had noted the change in Emmett's expression and glanced back to see what was behind him. When Duchess realized it was Billy, he took two steps to the side and rotated forty-five degrees so that he could still see Emmett while training the rifle's barrel on Billy.

—Stay there, Emmett said to his brother.

—That's right, Billy. Don't make a move. Then your brother won't make a move and I won't make a move, and we can talk this through together.

—Don't worry, said Billy to Emmett. He can't shoot me.

—Billy, you don't know what Duchess will or won't do.

—No, said Billy. I don't know what Duchess will or won't do. But I do know that he can't shoot me. Because he can't read.

—What? said Emmett and Duchess together, the one perplexed, the other offended.

—Who says I can't read? demanded Duchess.

—You did, explained Billy. First you said that small print gave you a headache. Then you said that reading in cars made you queasy. Then you said that you were allergic to books.

Billy turned to Emmett.

—He says it that way because he's too ashamed to admit that he can't read. Just like he's too ashamed to admit that he can't swim.

As Billy was talking, Emmett kept his attention on Duchess and he could see that Duchess was growing red. Maybe it was from shame, thought Emmett, but more likely from resentment.

—Billy, Emmett cautioned, whether or not Duchess can read doesn't make any difference right now. Why don't you just leave this to me.

But Billy was shaking his head.

—It does make a difference, Emmett. It makes a difference because Duchess doesn't know the rules for closing the house.

Emmett looked at his brother for a moment. Then he looked at Duchess—poor, misguided, illiterate Duchess. Taking the last three strides, Emmett put his hands on the rifle, and yanked it from Duchess's grip.

Duchess began talking a mile a minute about how he would never have pulled the trigger. Not against a Watson. Not in a million years.

But over Duchess's talking what Emmett heard was his brother saying a single word. Saying his name in the manner of a reminder.

—Emmett . . .

And Emmett understood. On the lawn of the county courthouse, Emmett had made the promise to his brother. A promise he intended to keep. So as Duchess rattled on about all the things he never would have done, Emmett counted to ten. And as he counted, he could feel the old heat subsiding, he could feel the anger seeping away, until he didn't feel angry at all. Then raising the butt of the rifle, he hit Duchess in the face, giving it everything he had.

—·—

—I think you should look at this now, insisted Billy.

After Duchess had hit the ground, Billy had gone to the kitchen. When he returned a moment later, Emmett told him to sit on the staircase and not move a muscle. Then taking Duchess under the armpits, he began dragging him through the living room. His plan was to drag him out of the muck room, down the stoop, and across the lawn to the Studebaker so that he could drive him to the closest police station and dump him at their door. He hadn't gotten more than two steps when Billy had spoken.

Looking up, Emmett could see that his brother was holding an envelope. Another letter from their father, Emmett thought with a touch of exasperation. Or another postcard from their mother. Or another map of America.

—I can look at it later, said Emmett.

—No, said Billy shaking his head. No. I think you should look at it now.

Dropping Duchess back on the floor, Emmett went over to his brother.

—It's from Woolly, said Billy. To be opened in the event of his absence.

A little stunned, Emmett looked at the inscription on the envelope.

—He is absent, isn't he? asked Billy.

Emmett hadn't quite decided how or whether he should tell his brother about Woolly. But from the way Billy said *absent*, it seemed like he already knew.

—Yes, said Emmett. He is.

Sitting on the steps beside Billy, Emmett opened the envelope. Inside was a handwritten note on a piece of Wallace Wolcott's stationery. Emmett didn't know if this Wallace Wolcott was Woolly's great-grandfather or his grandfather or his uncle. But it didn't matter whose stationery it was.

Dated the 20th of June 1954 and addressed *To Whom It May Concern*, the letter stated that the undersigned, being of sound mind and body, left one third of his one-hundred-and-fifty-thousand-dollar trust fund to Mr. Emmett Watson, one third to Mr. Duchess Hewett, and one third to Mr. William Watson—to do with as they pleased. It was signed *Most Sincereliest, Wallace Wolcott Martin*.

As Emmett closed the letter, he realized that his brother had read it over his shoulder.

—Was Woolly sick? he asked. Like Dad?

—Yes, said Emmett. He was sick.

—I thought he might be when he gave me his uncle's watch. Because it was a watch for handing down.

Billy thought for a moment.

—Is that why you told Duchess that Woolly wanted to be taken home?

—Yes, said Emmett. That's what I meant.

—I think you were right about that, said Billy, nodding in agreement. But you were wrong about the money in the safe.

Without waiting for Emmett to respond, Billy got up and walked down the hallway. Reluctantly, Emmett followed his brother back into Mr. Wolcott's office and over to the safe. By the bookshelves was a piece of furniture that looked like the first three steps of a staircase. Dragging it in front of the safe, Billy climbed the steps, rotated the four dials, turned the handle, and opened the door.

For a moment, Emmett was speechless.

—How do you know the combination, Billy? Did Woolly tell it to you?

—No. Woolly didn't tell it to me. But he told me how his great-grandfather loved the Fourth of July more than any other holiday. So the first combination I tried was 1776. Then I tried 7476 because that's one way of writing the Fourth of July. After that I tried 1732, the year that George Washington was born, but then I remembered that Woolly's great-grandfather said that while Washington, Jefferson, and Adams had the vision to found the Republic, it was Mr. Lincoln who had the courage to perfect it. So I tried 1809, the year that President Lincoln was born, and 1865, the year that he died. That's when I realized it must be 1119 because November 19 was the day of the Gettysburg Address. Here, he said, stepping down from the stairs, come take a look.

Pushing the stairs to the side, Emmett approached the safe, where, under a shelf of papers, thousands of brand-new fifty-dollar bills were neatly arranged in stacks.

Emmett ran a hand over his mouth.

One hundred and fifty thousand dollars, he thought. One hundred and fifty thousand dollars of old Mr. Wolcott's wealth had been handed down to Woolly, and now Woolly had handed it down to them. He had handed it down by means of a last will and testament that was duly signed and dated.

There could be no question of Woolly's intent. In that regard, Duchess had been quite right. It was Woolly's money and he knew exactly what he wanted to do with it. Having been found temperamentally unfit to use it himself, in his absence he wanted his friends to use it as they pleased.

But what would happen if Emmett finished dragging Duchess to the Studebaker and dumped him at the police station?

As much as Emmett hated to admit it, Duchess had been right about that too. Once Duchess was in the hands of the cops and it became clear that Woolly was dead, the wheels of Emmett's and Billy's future would grind to a halt. Police and investigators would descend upon the house, followed by family members and attorneys. Circumstances would be studied. Inventories taken. Intentions second-guessed. Endless questions asked. And any turns of good fortune would be viewed with the utmost suspicion.

In another few moments, Emmett would close the door to Mr. Wolcott's safe. That was a certainty. But once the door was closed, two different futures would be possible. In one, the contents of the safe would remain untouched. In the other, the space below the shelf would be empty.

—Woolly wanted the best for his friends, observed Billy.

—Yes, he did.

—For you and me, said Billy. And for Duchess too.

—— · ——

Once the decision was made, Emmett knew they would need to work quickly, putting things in order and leaving as few traces as possible.

After closing the door to the safe, Emmett gave Billy the task of cleaning up the office while he saw to the rest of the house.

First, having gathered up all the tools that Duchess had assembled—the hammer, screwdrivers, and ax—he carried them outside past the breached dory to the work shed.

Back inside, Emmett went to the kitchen. Certain that Woolly would never have eaten beans out of a can, Emmett put the empty can and Pepsi bottle in a paper bag to be carted out. Then he cleaned the spoon and returned it to the silverware drawer.

The broken pane of glass in the kitchen didn't worry him. The authorities would assume that Woolly had broken the pane in order to get inside the locked house. But the rifle cabinet was another matter. That would be more likely to raise questions. Serious questions. After returning the rifle to its place in the cabinet, Emmett removed the croquet ball. Then he repositioned the stack of Adirondack chairs to make it look like they had toppled over and crashed through the glass.

Now it was time to deal with Duchess.

Taking him under the arms again, Emmett dragged him down the hallway, out of the muck room, and onto the grass.

When Emmett and Billy had decided to take their share of the money and leave Duchess behind with his, Billy had made Emmett promise that he wouldn't hurt Duchess any more than he already had. But every minute that passed increased the risk that Duchess would regain consciousness and pose a whole new set of problems. Emmett had to put him somewhere that would slow him down for a few hours. Or at least long enough for Billy and Emmett to finish their work and be well on their way.

The trunk of the Cadillac? he wondered.

The problem with the trunk was that once Duchess regained consciousness, he would either be able to get out of it quickly or not at all, bad outcomes both.

The work shed?

No. There would be no way to secure its doors from the outside.

As Emmett was looking toward the shed, another idea presented itself, an interesting idea. But suddenly, at Emmett's feet Duchess emitted a groan.

—Shit, said Emmett to himself.

Looking down, he could see that Duchess was moving his head lightly from side to side, on the verge of coming to. As Duchess emitted another groan, Emmett looked back over his shoulder to make sure that Billy wasn't there. Then bending over, he lifted Duchess by the collar with his left hand and punched him in the face with his right.

With Duchess again at rest, Emmett dragged him in the direction of the shed.

Twenty minutes later, they were ready to go.

Unsurprisingly, Billy had done a perfect job of restoring the office. Every book was back on its shelf, every paper in its stack, every drawer in its slot. The only thing he hadn't replaced was the bust of Abraham Lincoln because it was too heavy. When Emmett picked it up and began looking around for a place to set it down, Billy crossed to the desk.

—Here, he said, placing a finger on the spot where the faintest outline of the sculpture's base could be seen.

As Billy waited by the kitchen door, Emmett locked the doors to the front porch and the muck room and then made a final swing through the house.

Returning to the bedroom upstairs, he stood in the doorway. His intention had been to leave everything exactly as he'd found it. But seeing the empty brown bottle, Emmett picked it up and put it in his pocket. Then he said one last goodbye to Wallace Woolly Martin.

As he was closing the door Emmett noticed his old book bag on a chair and realized that the one he had loaned Duchess must be somewhere in the house as well. After checking all the bedrooms, Emmett searched the living room and found it lying on the floor next to a couch where Duchess must have spent the night. Only as he was headed for the kitchen to join Billy did Emmett remember and retrieve the fedora from the high-back chair.

As they walked from the kitchen past the dock, Emmett showed Billy that Duchess was safe and sound. In the front seat of the Cadillac, he tossed Duchess's book bag and the hat. In the trunk of the Studebaker, he put two paper bags—one with the trash from the kitchen, the other with their share of Woolly's trust. As he was about to close the trunk, he was reminded that just nine days before, he had been standing in the same spot when he received his father's legacies:

the money, and the quote from Emerson, which was half excuse, half exhortation. Having come fifteen hundred miles in the wrong direction, on the verge of traveling three thousand more, Emmett believed that the power within him was new in nature, that no one but he could know what he was capable of, and that he had only just begun to know it himself.

Closing the trunk, he joined Billy in the front seat, turned the key, and pushed the starter.

—I had originally been thinking that we'd spend the night up here, Emmett said to his brother. What do you say we pick up Sally and hit the road, instead?

—That's a good idea, said Billy. Let's pick up Sally and hit the road.

As Emmett backed the car in an arc in order to face it toward the driveway, Billy was already studying his map—with a furrowed brow.

—What is it? asked Emmett.

Billy shook his head.

—This is the fastest route from where we are.

Placing his fingertip on Woolly's big red star, Billy moved it along various roads headed in a southwestern trajectory from the Wolcotts' to Saratoga Springs and Scranton, then westward to Pittsburgh, where they would finally rejoin the Lincoln Highway.

—What time is it? asked Emmett.

Looking at Woolly's watch, Billy said that it was one minute to five.

Emmett pointed to a different road on the map.

—If we went back the way we came, he said, we could start our journey in Times Square. And if we hurry, we could get there just as all the lights are coming on.

Billy looked up in his wide-eyed way.

—Could we, Emmett? Could we, really? But wouldn't that take us out of our way?

Emmett made a show of thinking for a second.

—A little out of our way, I suppose. But what day is it?

—It's the twenty-first of June.

Emmett put the Studebaker in gear.

—Then we've got thirteen days to make the crossing, if we mean to be in San Francisco by the Fourth of July.

Duchess

I RETURNED TO CONSCIOUSNESS WITH a sensation of drifting—like one who's sitting in a boat on a sunny afternoon. And as it turned out, that's exactly where I was: sitting in a boat on a sunny afternoon! Giving my head a shake in order to clear it, I put my hands on the gunwales and hoisted myself up.

The first thing I noted, I'll readily admit, was the natural beauty before me. Though I was never much of a country mouse—finding the great outdoors to be generally uncomfortable and occasionally inhospitable—there was something deeply satisfying about the scenery. What with the pine trees rising from the lakeshore, and the sunlight cascading from the sky, and the surface of the water stirred by a gentle breeze. One couldn't help but sigh at the majesty of it all.

But thanks to the ache in my keister, I was brought back to reality. Looking down, I could see that I was sitting on a pile of painted stones. Picking one of them up in order to consider it more closely, I realized that not only was there dried blood on my hand, there was dried blood all down the front of my shirt.

Then I remembered.

Emmett had hit me with the butt of the rifle!

He had burst through the door while I was trying to open the safe. We'd had a difference of opinions, something of a scuffle, and a bit of tit for tat. In the interest of theatrics, I had brandished a gun, waving it in the general direction of Billy. But having leapt to the wrong con-

clusion about my intentions, Emmett had grabbed the rifle and let me have it.

He may even have broken my nose, I thought. Which would explain why I was having so much trouble breathing through my nostrils.

As I reached up to give my injury a gingerly probe, I heard the engine of a car revving. Looking to my left, I saw the Studebaker, as yellow as a canary, backing up, idling, then roaring out of the Wolcotts' drive.

—Wait! I shouted.

But as I leaned to my side in order to call Emmett's name, the boat took a dip toward the water.

Lurching back, I carefully resumed my place in the center.

Okay, I thought to myself, Emmett knocked me out with the rifle. But then rather than taking me to the police station as threatened, he set me adrift in a rowboat without a paddle. Why would he do that?

Then my eyes narrowed.

Because little Mr. Know-It-All had told him I couldn't swim. That's why. And by setting me adrift on the lake, the Watson brothers figured they would have all the time they needed to get into the safe and claim Woolly's inheritance for themselves.

But even as I was having this ugly thought—a thought for which I will never be able to fully atone—I noticed the stacks of cash in the bow.

Emmett had gotten into the old man's safe, all right, just like I knew he would. But rather than stranding me empty-handed, he had left me with my rightful share.

It was my rightful share, wasn't it?

I mean, isn't that about what fifty thousand dollars would look like?

Naturally curious, I began moving toward the front of the boat in order to do a quick accounting. But as I did so, the shifting of my weight lowered the front of the boat and water began pouring in through a hole in the bow. Retreating quickly to my seat, the bow lifted, and the inrush stopped.

This wasn't just any rowboat, I realized, as water sloshed about my feet. This was the rowboat that was being repaired by the boathouse. And that's why Emmett had loaded the stones in the stern. To keep the compromised bow above the waterline.

The ingenuity of it, I thought with a smile. A boat with a hole and no oars in the middle of a lake. It was like a setup for Kazantikis. The only thing better would have been if Emmett had tied my hands behind my back. Or put me in cuffs.

—All right then, I said, feeling every bit up to the challenge.

By my estimate, I was a few hundred feet from shore. If I leaned back, stuck my hands in the water, and paddled gently, I should be able to make my way safely to solid ground.

Reaching my arms over the back of the boat turned out to be surprisingly awkward, and the water turned out to be surprisingly cold. In fact, every few minutes I had to interrupt my paddling in order to warm my fingers.

But just as I was beginning to make progress, a late afternoon breeze began picking up, such that every time I took a break from paddling, I would find myself drifting back toward the center of the lake.

To compensate, I started paddling a little faster and taking shorter breaks. But as if in response, the breeze blew harder. So much so, that one of the bills flitted off the top of its stack and landed about twenty feet away on the surface of the water. Then off flitted another. And another.

Paddling as fast as I could, I stopped taking breaks altogether. But the breeze kept blowing and the bills kept taking flight, fluttering over the side of the boat, fifty bucks at a crack.

Having no other choice, I stopped paddling, rose to my feet, and started creeping forward. When I took my second little step, the bow dipped an inch too far and water began flowing in. I took a step back and the inflow stopped.

There would be no doing this cautiously, I realized. I was going to have to make a grab for the cash, then retreat quickly back to the stern before too much water had entered the boat.

Steadying myself with my arms before me, I prepared for the lunge.

All it required was deftness. A quick motion combined with a gentle touch. Like when you're removing a cork from a bottle.

Exactly, I thought to myself. The whole endeavor shouldn't take more than ten seconds. But without Billy to assist, I'd have to do the count-down on my own.

At the word *Ten*, I took the first step forward and the boat rocked to the right. At *Nine* I compensated by stepping to the left and the boat lurched left. At *Eight*, what with all the rocking and lurching, I lost my balance and tumbled forward, landing right on top of the cash as water rushed in through the breach.

Reaching for the gunwale, I tried to push myself up, but my fingers were so numb from the paddling that I lost my grip and fell forward again—whacking my broken nose on the bow.

With a howl, I reflexively scrambled to my feet as the freezing water continued to rush in around my ankles. With all of my weight in the front of the boat and the stern rising up behind me, painted stones rolled toward my feet, the bow took another dip, and I went head over heels into the lake.

Kicking at the depths with my feet and slapping at the surface with my arms, I tried to take a deep breath of air, but took a deep breath of water instead. Coughing and thrashing, I felt my head go under and my body begin to sink. Looking up through the dappled surface, I could see the shadows of the bills floating on the water like autumn leaves. Then the boat drifted over me, casting a much larger shadow, a shadow that began to extend outward in every direction.

But just when it seemed as if the entire lake would be subsumed in darkness, a great curtain was raised and I found myself standing on a crowded street in a busy metropolis, except that everyone around me was someone I knew, and all of them were frozen in place.

Sitting together on a nearby bench were Woolly and Billy, smiling at the floor plan of the house in California. And there was Sally leaning over a pram in order to tuck in the blanket of the child in her care. And there by the flower cart was Sister Sarah looking wistful and forlorn. And right there, not more than fifty feet away, standing by the door of his bright yellow car, was Emmett, looking honorable and upright.

—Emmett, I called.

But even as I did so, I could hear the distant chiming of a clock. Only it wasn't a clock, and it wasn't distant. It was the gold watch that had been tucked in the pocket of my vest and that now was suddenly in my hand. Looking down at its face, I couldn't tell what time it was, but I knew that after another few chimes, the entire world would begin moving once again.

So taking off my crooked hat, I bowed to Sarah and Sally. I bowed to Woolly and Billy. I bowed to the one and only Emmett Watson.

And when the final chime sounded, I turned to them all in order to utter with my very last breath, *The rest is silence*, just as Hamlet had.

Or was that Iago?

I never could remember.

The Rise of socialist fiction
1880-1914

By the same author

Marxistische Literaturkritik in England (ed.)
Caudwell im Kontext
The Socialist Novel in Britain (ed.), Harvester Press and
    St. Martin's Press 1982
The Literature of Labour, Harvester Press and St. Martin's
    Press 1985

The Rise of socialist fiction 1880-1914

Editor
H. Gustav Klaus

Part-time Reader in English,
University of Osnabrück

THE HARVESTER PRESS · SUSSEX

ST. MARTIN'S PRESS · NEW YORK

First published in Great Britain in 1987 by
THE HARVESTER PRESS LIMITED
Publisher: John Spiers
16 Ship Street, Brighton, Sussex
and in the USA by
ST. MARTIN'S PRESS, INC.
175 Fifth Avenue, New York, NY 10010

British Library Cataloguing in Publication Data
The Rise of socialist fiction.
  1. Socialism in literature   2. English
  fiction—19th century—History and
  criticism   3. English fiction—20th
  century—History and criticism
  I. Klaus, H. Gustav
  823'.8'09358   PR830.S626
  ISBN 0-7108-1085-7

Library of Congress Cataloging-in-Publication Data
The Rise of socialist fiction, 1880-1914.
  Includes index.
  1. English fiction—History and criticism.
2. Socialism in literature.   3. Labor and laboring
classes in literature.   I. Klaus, H. Gustav, 1944-
PR830.S626R57   1987   823'.8'09358   87-9483
ISBN 0-312-00946-6

Typeset in 11/12 Palatino by
Just Words Phototypesetters, Ellen Street, Portslade, Sussex

Printed in Great Britain by
Mackays of Chatham Ltd

Contents

Notes on contributors

Kiernan Ryan is a Fellow and Lecturer in English at New Hall, Cambridge. He has published essays on Conrad, Lawrence, Renaissance narrative and marxist literary theory, and is the author of a forthcoming study of *Shakespeare*.

Brunhild de la Motte is an assistant lecturer at the Pädagogische Hochschule in Potsdam (GDR). She has published articles on modern British drama, and is presently working on a study of the conjunction of feminism and socialism in late nineteenth-century fiction.

Jack Mitchell is a Reader in English at the Humboldt University of Berlin (GDR). He has written many articles on socialist literature, and is the author of *Robert Tressell and the Ragged Trousered Philanthropists* (1969) and *The Essential Sean O'Casey* (1980).

H. Gustav Klaus has lectured in Australia, Britain, Denmark and Spain, and is at present part-time Reader in English at the University of Osnabrück (W. Germany). His books include *The Socialist Novel in Britain* (1982), *The Literature of Labour* (1985) and a forthcoming anthology of working-class stories, *Tramps, Workmates and Revolutionaries*.

J. M. Rignall is a Lecturer in English and Comparative Literary Studies at the University of Warwick. He has written extensively on nineteenth-century fiction.

Graham Holderness is Head of Drama at the Roehampton Institute, London. His books include *D. H. Lawrence: History, Ideology and Fiction* (1982) and *Shakespeare's History* (1985). He has also written articles on nineteenth-century fiction and on the mining novel.

Ingrid von Rosenberg teaches in the English Language Department of the University of Duisburg (W. Germany). Her books include *Der Weg nach oben: Englische Arbeiter-romane 1945-78* (1980) and a study, *Alan Sillitoe: Saturday Night and Sunday Morning* (1984).

Paul Salveson works in trade-union and adult education in the North-west of England. He has done much to revive an interest in the work of Allen Clarke. He is the present editor of *North West Labour History* and co-editor of *The Lancashire Scrapbook*.

Michael Wilding is Reader in English at the University of Sydney. His books include *Political Fictions* (1980) and *Dragon's Teeth: Literature in the English Revolution* (1987); the novels *Living Together* (1974), *Pacific Highway* (1982) and *The Paraguayan Experiment* (1985); and a collection of short stories, *The Man of Slow Feeling* (1985).

Ronald Paul works in adult education (at the Folkuni-versitet) in Gothenburg (Sweden). He is the author of *Fire in Our Hearts* (1982), a study of the portrayal of youth in English working-class literature.

Edmund and *Ruth Frow* are the founders of the Working-Class Movement Library in Manchester, which houses a unique collection of pamphlets, journals and books relating to the British labour movement. They have co-authored several books on the history of trade unionism, including *1868: Year of the Unions* (1968) and *Strikes: a Documentary History* (1971), both with Michael Katanka.

Introduction

> The validity of uniting knowledge and commitment is demonstrated through a dialectical practice which reconstructs that which has been suppressed out of the historical traces of its suppression.
>
> Jürgen Habermas[1]

This book continues the enquiry opened with *The Socialist Novel in Britain*. Like its predecessor, it is a collaborative effort, bringing together the research of scholars who work in many different contexts and countries, but who share a concern for a neglected literary tradition whose contours are at last visible in outline now that the veil of silence covering it is being lifted.[2]

One difference from the earlier project is that the present collection of essays, all specially commissioned for this volume, focuses on a clearly defined period. This allows not only ampler treatment of genres, authors and themes, but also the occasional contrasting analysis of working-class and middle-class attitudes to the same subject, and the probing into the relationship between socialist fiction and the mainstream. And it furnishes the space to look beyond the boundaries of English literature: by establishing the status of Zola's *Germinal*, and the impact of that remarkable text on a number of English novelists (see chapters 6 and 7); by introducing the prose of Australian-born Henry Lawson, whose powerful sketches and short stories enjoyed wide English distribution and recognition at the turn of the century and who came to live and write in

1

Britain for a couple of years (see the contribution by Michael Wilding); and, most importantly, by taking stock of the almost simultaneous international breakthrough of the socialist novel in the 1900s, in the works of Andersen Nexö, Maxim Gorky, Upton Sinclair and Robert Tressell (see the essay by Ronald Paul).

The main emphasis of the volume rests naturally on fiction from the British Isles. But here too there is a significant shift away from an exclusive concentration on the slum fiction of the metropolis, which has dominated most accounts of the late-Victorian 'social' novel. Margaret Harkness set three of her novels in the East End, but her *A Manchester Shirtmaker* and W. E. Tirebuck's *Dorrie* situated in Liverpool (both featured in Ingrid von Rosenberg's contribution) remind us that there is a similar, less well-known range of fiction exploring the working-class environment and poverty in the provincial cities.[3] What is more, Lancashire can claim an entire school òf working-class novelists of its own, growing out of a strong regional socialist culture and gathering round the once immensely popular figure of Allen Clarke. Their achievement has altogether passed out of the literary historians' sight, and Paul Salveson does much here to retrieve this unique moment in the history of English socialist literature.

To see the interest of this line of socialist narratives merely 'in the illumination it casts on the mainstream of English fiction',[4] as has been suggested, is to miss its essence, which is its radical otherness. This quality is embodied in a set of values often at odds with, and sometimes diametrically opposed to, most middle- and upper-class attitudes. But it can also be located in the re-working of many structural elements of the novel in the process of its critical appropriation by socialist practitioners. This difference extends to the channels of distribution (note, for example, how many of the works discussed here, starting with Shaw's *An Unsocial Socialist* and Morris's *Pilgrims of Hope*, were first and sometimes only serialised in the labour press), and often involved modes of reception quite different from the isolated act of reading.[5] As the British working class of this period led (in Standish Meacham's

phrase) 'a life apart',[6] so the socialist fiction of the time represents a world of its own, by which, of course, I am not implying that it was in any way autonomous or self-determined.

There is no need here to repeat the full argument for the use of the term 'socialist novel';[7] if it does nothing else, the present volume at least provides fresh evidence for the view that there is a substantial area of writing worthy of this name, and that it emerges conspicuously in our period. But it may require pointing out that, as socialism got under way in Britain in the 1880s and 1890s, a variety of rival notions and doctrines was being negotiated in the movement, including powerful strains of a Christian-inspired and ethically oriented socialism, which successfully infiltrated imaginative literature. The novels of William Edwards Tirebuck, analysed here from three different angles (see chapters 1, 4 and 7), are a case in point. Yet though we may be rightly sceptical of some of the more abstruse variants of this 'religion of socialism', it will not do to evaluate the socialist perspective of a particular work without a proper understanding of the cultural and ideological texture that shaped it. As Stephen Yeo has shown,[8] this exciting phase of practical socialism dedicated to brotherhood and sisterhood had strengths as well as weaknesses; and when it finally exhausted itself and gave way in the mid-1890s under the pressure both from outside forces (as new leisure industries and means of communication transformed recreational patterns) and from internal reorientations (towards parliamentary party politics), a whole lived culture vanished in its wake.

It is hardly incidental that the conjunction of feminism and socialism, examined here by Brunhild de la Motte, found its strongest fictional expression in those early years of the movement, when many issues were far from sealed. Feminist criticism (and publishing) has yet to rediscover its socialist mothers of the novel. So far the current vogue of reprints has bypassed the works of Clementina Black, Emma Brooke, Ethel Carnie, Gertrude Dix, Margaret Harkness, Constance Howell and others. Considering that even for specialists of the period most of the authors dealt

with in the following pages will be unfamiliar, this comes as no real surprise. During the thirty-year run of the academic journal *English Literature in Transition 1880-1920* only one or two forlorn articles have treated socialist narratives.[9] So much for the selective critical consensus which has assigned our authors to the graveyard of the justly forgotten.

I would suggest that a number of them deserve better, not only the above-mentioned women novelists, but also Allen Clarke and some of his fellow writers from Lancashire (such as Arthur Laycock and Fred Plant), Frank Harris, W. E. Tirebuck and the writers' duo D. F. E. Sykes and G. H. Walker. Where is that Library of Socialist Classics which will help to recirculate and reclaim their stories, romances and novels; facilitate additions to syllabus lists; enable irritated critics to fault our readings; give general readers a chance to judge for themselves on the merits and flaws of these works; and offer the historian and the socialist an imaginative insight into the aspirations and struggles of those forerunners 'who strove . . . not merely to rend the chains of the prisoners, but had to achieve the more difficult task of convincing them that they would be happier if they were free'?[10]

NOTES

1. Jürgen Habermas , *Technik und Wissenschaft als 'Ideologie'* (Frankfurt, 1968), p.164 (my translation—HGK).

2. Since 1982 there has also been Jeremy Hawthorn's valuable collection *The British Working-Class Novel in the Twentieth Century* (London, 1984) and my own *The Literature of Labour. Two Hundred Years of Working-Class Writing* (Brighton, 1985).

3. For a discussion of the Manchester-based fiction of this kind see T. Thomas, 'Representation of the Manchester working class in fiction, 1850-1900', in Alan J. Kidd and K. W. Roberts (eds.), *City, Class and Culture. Studies of Social Policy and Cultural Production in Victorian Manchester* (Manchester, 1985), pp.193-216.

4. P. J. Keating, *The Working Classes in Victorian Fiction* (London, 1979; first pub. 1971), p.245.
5. See Stephen Yeo, 'A new life: the religion of socialism in Britain 1883-1896', *History Workshop*, 4 (Autumn 1977), pp.5-56, for an account of the function of readings and songs in meetings, and of the spell-binding effect of declamations from *News from Nowhere* on audiences; and Peter Miles, 'The painter's Bible and the British workman. Robert Tressell's literary activism', in Hawthorn (ed.), *op. cit.*, pp.1-17, for an account of the uses made of *The Ragged Trousered Philanthropists*.
6. Standish Meacham, *A Life Apart. The English Working Class, 1890-1914* (London, 1977).
7. Cf. *The Socialist Novel in Britain* (Brighton, 1982), pp.1-3; and *The Literature of Labour*, *op. cit.*, pp.xi-xii, 107-9.
8. Yeo, *op. cit.*
9. See for example James G. Kennedy, 'Voynich, Bennett, and Tressell. Two alternatives for realism in the transition age', XIII (1970), pp.254-86; and Suzanne Rahn, 'The Story of the Amulet and the socialist Utopia', XXVIII (1985), pp.124-44, which deals with Edith Nesbit.
10. Mark Rutherford, *The Revolution in Tanner's Lane* (1887), ch. VIII. For a discussion of this novel see chapter 5 by J. M. Rignall.

Citizens of centuries to come: the ruling-class rebel in socialist fiction

KIERNAN RYAN

> The age is not yet ripe for my ideal. Meanwhile I live, a citizen of centuries to come.
>
> Schiller[1]

The conversion to socialism of men and women of the middle and upper classes was a crucial factor in the struggle to establish the movement in Britain in the closing decades of the nineteenth century. As Stanley Pierson has pointed out:

> The inner dynamic of socialism was supplied in large part by those adherents who had been loosened from conventional interests; a deep commitment to socialism presupposed, as Marx had recognised, a strong sense of social and cultural disinheritance. But such a condition was more characteristic of marginal members of the middle classes than it was of working class leaders.[2]

Certainly the early recruits tended to be people who were 'seeking to overcome a painful social and psychological condition' resulting from the fact that 'traditional institutions and value systems had ceased to provide any satisfactory orientation to life'.[3] For such people the commitment to socialism possessed a special intensity dictated by their drive to resolve the urgent inner conflict between their old selves and their emerging new identities. Hence it came about that 'the Socialist movement drew much of its initial vitality as well as its continuing force from individuals who were suffering from an acute

sense of self-division', from 'the social estrangements and the ontological anxieties of marginal individuals and their struggles to find a "new life" '.[4] And nowhere were these estrangements and anxieties more sharply felt than by those who had defected from the ruling classes, not only to help forge a juster socialist society, but to invest their lives with a feeling of purpose and worth, which their complicity in the injustice of capitalist society had hitherto denied them.

Such figures exercised an understandable hold over the imaginations of socialist novelists during this seminal period, not least because the authors no doubt found in them ways of voicing and probing versions of their own lived predicaments and political longings. This essay looks at several of the more interesting novels written on this theme between 1880 and 1914. All of them deal with men or women who have made, or are making, the lonely and difficult journey from the culpable security of a bourgeois or even aristocratic way of life to the rootless and thankless uncertainties of radical commitment in a world with little appetite for emancipation.

Between them the protagonists of these novels undergo conversion to a range of creeds and standpoints, reflecting the complex spectrum of secular and Christian variations on the socialist vision with which the dissident mind was obliged to wrestle around the turn of the century.[5] In most of the narratives, however, the representation of the convert's experience instils in us no sense of having arrived at some absolute conviction or conclusive solution. On the contrary, what come through are feelings of permanent dislocation and restlessness, an endless striving to surmount irresolvable contradictions, and the enduring ache of unrealised aspirations. Stranded in a social limbo between their own class and the proletariat, marooned in the gulf of time which persistently divides their utopian visions from historical reality, the central characters of these fictions inevitably tend to be isolated, awkwardly singular individuals, who resist easy or complete absorption into any of the prevalent political definitions.

But that recalcitrant individuality and visionary intran-

sigence, which at times makes these mavericks so impossible for the immediate practical purposes of a disciplined mass movement, is the source of their value to the socialist novelist as a means of keeping the spirit of creative dissatisfaction constantly alive. All the protagonists considered here are at some level variants of the wise fool or the holy fool, inspired eccentrics and prophetic misfits living as internal exiles in their own society, and thus ideally situated to be used by the author to subvert the ruling-class world from within by insistently exposing what it takes to be normal and desirable as outrageous and intolerable. Yet at the same time, without leading the novelist to relax the grip of his commitment, these figures can also serve to illuminate what is limited and questionable about the alternative ways of living and thinking, and so sustain a salutary awareness of the human need for more than the available manifestations of socialism can yet imagine or supply.

The fictional possibilities of the ruling-class recruit are already brilliantly exploited in the earliest and best-known of the novels I wish to bring into focus, George Bernard Shaw's *An Unsocial Socialist* (1884). The title-role belongs to the bizarre Sidney Trefusis, the scion of a wealthy, self-made manufacturer and an aristocratic mother. Trefusis' privileged education and inherited fortune have only succeeded in furnishing him with the intellectual and financial means to occupy his life 'partly in working out a scheme for the reorganisation of industry, and partly in attacking my own class, women and all' (p.208).[6] The novel's skeletal romantic plot provides, indeed, little more than a series of shameless pretexts for his virtuoso assaults on the social and sexual order of the day.

Trefusis is unapologetic about being a vociferous socialist while remaining an abundantly propertied capitalist. He is marvellously free of moralising guilt about the origins and advantages which have made him literally his own worst enemy, and has no illusions about the futility of seeking moral salvation by renouncing his wealth and power:

I was made a landlord and capitalist by the folly of the people; but they can unmake me if they will. Meanwhile I have absolutely no means of escape from my position except by giving away my slaves to fellows who will use them no better than I, and becoming a slave myself; which, if you please, you shall not catch me doing in a hurry. (p.77)

The explanation displays the disarmingly frank impudence of the clown, whose licence Trefusis adopts as a way of thriving on the radical contradictions in his situation and distancing himself ironically from the conflicting selves which he slips in and out of at will: 'I am just mad enough to be a mountebank . . . With my egotism, my charlatanry, my tongue, and my habit of having my own way, I am fit for no calling but that of saviour of mankind—just of the sort they like' (pp.106-7).

As that self-mocking allusion to messianic fantasies might suggest, Trefusis' protean fooling creates valuable opportunities to burlesque the stereotyped postures lying in wait to trap the otherwise progressive mind in bourgeois illusions. Thus Trefusis' attempt to conceal himself behind the ludicrous persona and stage-rustic's dialect of the 'sham labourer',[7] Jeff Smilash, humorously underlines the distance which separates the upper classes from the actual labouring man, and the absurdity of disaffected members of those classes trying to turn themselves into proletarians. Even more central to the novel is Shaw's sabotaging through Trefusis of 'the sham lover of middle-class romance'[8] as part of the wider endeavour to dismantle the dominant sexual ideology, a task Shaw considered indivisible from the undermining of capitalism.

This disjunctive framing of accustomed modes of perception expands to embrace a parodic guying of the romantic conventions of the novel itself, as when Trefusis and his female counterpart, Agatha, brazenly discuss their fictional fate as the hero and heroine about to wind up the plot through the inexorable device of their own marriage (pp.225-5). The novel's baring of its devices, in order to expose and unsettle the stultifying assumptions they would normally smuggle through unseen, culminates in

the remarkable 'Appendix' which Shaw added as an integral part of the text in the 1888 edition. The 'Appendix' purports to be a letter from the 'real' Trefusis to the author, whom he takes to task for his craven submission to the 'romantic system of morals' (p.257) which the largely female readership of novels dictates, and the consequent 'acceptance of the infatuation of a pair of lovers as the highest manifestation of the social instinct' (p.258). And Shaw's parting shot to himself in the guise of this fresh incarnation of Trefusis is: 'allow me to express my regret that you can find no better employment for your talents than the writing of novels' (p.262). The effect is to open to playful questioning not only the implications of the form but the authority of both the hero and Shaw himself.

In the complex, volatile figure of Trefusis, Shaw finds the perfect candidate for the part of 'incorrigible mountebank', licensed to scandalise his class with 'his terrible truth-telling'.[9] Even the bereaved and grieving parents of his own recently deceased young wife are not spared an acid reminder that 'plenty of people are starving and freezing today in order that we may have the means to die fashion-ably' (p.127). Trefusis' systematic violation of conventional expectations is what renders him an 'unsocial' socialist. But since indeed 'what is now called "society" ' is not 'society in any real sense' (p.258), to be unsocial is ines-capable for the truthful socialist, who appears callous and heartless only to those who define their humanity in terms of the hypocritical moralism and shallow sentimentality of class society.

Shaw's casting of the capitalist convert as clown equips him with an arresting means of arguing an angrily engaged point of view while flaunting the blatant inconsistencies and ambiguity of the position from which it is being argued. The bare-faced fictionality of Trefusis and the novel's reflexive profiling of its own devices hold us suffi-ciently detached and alert throughout to prevent an un-qualified acceptance of the perspectives it promotes. Instead the novel keeps these perspectives in solution, mindful of their own provisionality and thus reluctant to congeal into incontestable doctrine. In *An Unsocial Socialist*

Shaw turns the potentially tragic dilemma of a divided self into a wily and exuberant fighting virtue.

Grant Allen's *Philistia* (1884), on the other hand, revolves around an altogether more tormented experience of enlistment in the cause. Ernest Le Breton, an aristocratic but impecunious young intellectual, is undoubtedly cast in the mould of the holy fool rather than the wise fool, and the novel charts this socialist pilgrim's bleak progress to the understanding possessed by Shaw's more worldly-wise Trefusis from the start. It's the dismaying realisation that

> if he was going to live in the world at all, he must do so by making at least a partial sacrifice of political consistency. You may step out of your own century if you choose, yourself, but you can't get all the men and women with whom you come in contact to step out of it also just to please you.[10]   (II, 151)

Le Breton is obliged to learn that uncompromising idealism and selfless devotion to the socialist dream are not rewarded by a personal sense of moral absolution and political salvation. It is here that the irrepressible analogies between the socialist convert and the Christian convert are most prone to break down completely. The novel is centrally occupied, in fact, with the complicated relationships between contemporary socialist experience and the narratives of religion.[11] The title, *Philistia*, signifies the land of the uncivilised bourgeoisie, the class-divided England in which the socialist chosen people, the 'Children of Light' (p.1), find themselves in bondage, fighting to keep their faith alive. Through an external framework of chapter headings, such as 'The daughters of Canaan' and 'The Philistines triumph', as well as through a whole internal network of religious allusions, a mock-epic effect is created, whereby the heroic realm of biblical legend maintains a running ironic commentary on the incongruity of its imputed parallels with the social and political realities of upper-class Britain in the late nineteenth century. Built into the basic idea of the novel is a sympathetically critical endeavour to prise contemporary socialism away from the delusively providential and redemptive terms in which its

identification with religious experience, however involuntary, commonly led it to be perceived. Not to recognise the difference, as Ernest Le Breton discovers, can be soul-destroying, especially when one's confidence in the power of moral and religious sentiments over objective social forces is repeatedly proved extravagant.

Ernest looks to socialism to still above all the profound moral and existential anxieties which have seethed within him since he first understood himself to be nothing more than a useless parasite on the labour of the proletariat:

> The thing that troubles me is not so much how to reform the world at large as how to shape one's own individual course aright in the actual midst of it . . . The great difficulty I myself experience in this, is that I can't discover any adequate social justification for my own personal existence.   (I, 99)

As this might suggest, Ernest is the kind of intense and humourless ethical socialist who lacerates his conscience constantly. Like Shaw's Trefusis, he can be relied upon at every occasion, however innocuous, to remind everyone that 'others are dying of sheer want, and cold, and nakedness' (I, 84) while they themselves indulge in meaningless frivolity. Unlike Trefusis, however, Le Breton has no other acts up his sleeve, certainly none that would raise any laughs, and Allen does not disguise how insufferable such a remorselessly moralistic socialist can be, not least to other socialists. As the daughter of Ernest's political mentor, the emigré Max Schurz, remarks: living with Le Breton 'would be like living with an abstraction', and a woman 'might just as well marry Spinoza's Ethics or the Ten Commandments. He's a perfect model of a Socialist, and nothing else' (I, 199).

Yet it may be these very qualities which give such a man his special value to a militant young socialist movement. As Max Schurz points out to his daughter in defence of Ernest, as far as sheer selfless dedication to the good of others is concerned there is much to be said for the argument that 'the best socialists never come from the *bourgeoisie*, nor even from the proletariat; they come from

among the voluntarily *déclassés* aristocrats' (I, 200).

On the other hand, Le Breton's refusal to compromise his principles in the slightest, even where the most scrupulous would concede there to be no other option, loses him job after job as a teacher and then as a journalist, and brings himself, his wife and their baby to the point of penniless starvation. And only the secret offices of good friends with money and influence finally save this infuriating absolutist from himself, making it possible for him to end up the editor of an influential new Radical periodical, *The Social Reformer*, whose success restores his guttering health and solves all his family's financial problems.

Even this welcome change in his fortunes, however, leaves Ernest at heart no more contented than before, no less reluctant to come to terms with the world as it so far stubbornly remains. The harrowing disillusionments he has suffered have, indeed, brought him to fear that there may be 'no fitting feeling for a social reformer except brave despair' (III, 272). Yet nothing can quite kill the 'pure idealistic Utopian philanthropy' (III, 30) which drives him, and by the close of the novel it becomes hard to withhold an exasperated respect for a spirit so resolutely intolerant of things as they are that nothing short of escaping completely from the mire of history could satisfy his craving for innocence and integrity. The novel, at any rate, leaves him the last word:

> As things are constituted now, there seems only one life that's really worth living for an honest man, and that's a martyr's. A martyr's or else a worker's. And I, I greatly fear, have managed somehow to miss being either. The wind carries us this way and that, and when we would do that which is right, it drifts us away incontinently into that which is only profitable.
>
> (III, 287-8)

The exploratory complexity of both Shaw's and Allen's novels is highlighted by turning to Constance Howell's *A More Excellent Way* (1888). This is a narrower, far less troubled narrative, whose hero's conflicts and setbacks never gain enough weight to pose a real threat to his con-

victions. But it does furnish an illuminating chronicle of the intellectual and psychological process of conversion from complacent bourgeois into embattled advocate of socialism.

The subject of this chronicle is the unfortunately named Otho Hathaway, the Harrow-educated offspring of a colonial administrator and a covertly feminist, Free-thinking mother, who sows the first seeds of intellectual dissent in her adult son's mind and entrusts to him the task of taking her own ideas and struggle further. The catalytic event occurs, however, some time after his widowed mother's death, when Otho, now a footloose and finan-cially independent young man in his late twenties, and vaguely Radical in his sympathies, witnesses a march of the unemployed from a window at his friend's club. He is overcome by disgust and shame at the callous boorishness displayed towards the marchers by the upper-class yobs around him, and by the realisation that 'it is my own class that are the brutes' (p.118).[12] His first encounter with real, livid class-hatred leaves a searing impression on his mind and sets him on the road to discover its source and the solution: 'Nothing could be again as it had been. The condition of the masses was no longer an abstract thought to him . . . His political faiths were breaking up, and he could not rest until he had a new faith' (p.133).

His outrage at the spineless response of the Liberals, the Freethinkers and the Radicals to the rigged trial of the group of Socialists who had led the march makes plain to him in what direction he must look. He gives his bookseller a huge order and settles down to a crash course in Marx, Engels, Lassalle, Bebel, Gronlund, Kropotkin, Elisée Reclus, Hyndman, Morris and Belfort Bax. The theory of 'Collectivist Socialism' which emerges from these works is 'a revelation to him' (p.138). But the clinching shock is its moral bearing on himself as 'one of the idle classes who, by their very existence, are oppressors. It was he who helped to cause the degradation of the poor' (p.139). Stricken with guilt and indignation, Hathaway joins the National Socia-list Federation and embarks on a lifetime's work as a labour organiser and public speaker for the movement.

Meanwhile, on the romantic front, Hathaway's political development has brought him into increasingly acrimonious conflict with the expectations of his fiancée Evangeline and her family, who are desperately hoping that he will outgrow this faddish socialist nonsense once he assumes the burdens of respectable married life. Otho finds himself bewilderingly divided:

> He was leading two lives, with two different sets of companions, witnessing the most opposite scenes, and hearing the most opposed sentiments. And as the one life attracted him more and more, the other became repugnant to him. And yet he was of the middle class; by blood and education and tastes, he was bound to it; he could not throw in his lot with the members of the working class, for he did not belong to them'. (p.196)

To his middle-class friends, moreover, he scarcely appears to be inhabiting the same temporal dimension: ' "Mr Hathaway is so strange," thought Agnes Champneys; "he seems to stand aside, and view the present time as if he did not belong to it" ' (p.160).

Nowhere is this clearer than when Otho is genuinely surprised at the selfish and worthless Evangeline's refusal to sacrifice all in order to become the wife of an itinerant activist, living on a fraction of the income whose bulk Otho has given away to assuage his guilt. But such trustful naïveté is perhaps only to be expected from one who confidently predicts the arrival of 'a rationally-ordered community' (p.228) by the end of what he regards as this 'wonderful century' (p.253). It's not so much that Otho's prediction, certainly as far as Britain is concerned, has proved unduly optimistic, or that he may not ultimately be right to maintain that 'it must come right in the end. The solidarity of the working class is no forlorn hope. Socialism is a certain success' (pp.270-1). It's rather that the authority of his conviction suffers from not being plausibly tested by the sort of demoralising reversals which Allen's Ernest Le Breton is forced to survive.

Hathaway's unrewarding attempts to organise the hop-pickers in his area do cause him to reflect on the incon-

venient apathy and frequent rank conservatism of the working man. But his consternation at the fact that the workers 'do not stretch out their hands to welcome this thing which will be their salvation' (p.277) is swiftly eclipsed by his resolve simply to switch his theatre of operations and henceforth make it his mission 'to recommend socialism to the professional and upper classes' (p.262). The author allows herself to voice a mild qualm about Otho's 'great faith in his class' being 'more faith than it seemed they merited' (p.271), and gives his benignly sceptical uncle just enough room to wonder, 'Is that a clear view he has into the future, or is it a mirage?' (p.271). But even these few notes of quiet reservation are drowned out by the grand, self-inflating chord on which Hathaway is left to conclude the novel:

> If I were giving the workers my life in another way, if I were fighting by their side, shedding my blood, under the red flag, that would be a glorious death to die! And yet this must be better, because it is more useful. The time has not come yet to give my life for the people. I will give my life to the people.
> (p.278)

In Howell's novel the private world of love and the public realm of political commitment prove irreconcilable, and it is part of the protagonist's heroic sacrifice that he forgoes the former for the sake of the latter. In W. E. Tirebuck's *Miss Grace of All Souls'* (1895), by contrast, the heroine succeeds in uniting the personal and the political through a truly heroic marriage, which cuts across class divisions and convincingly prefigures the real human possibilities beyond them in a manner unparalleled by the other novels dealt with here.

Grace Waide is the daughter of the vicar of Beckerton, a Yorkshire mining village. When the narrative opens she is facing the prospect of an engagement to Harry Brookster, the son and heir of the local coal magnate. But she has begun to find herself drawn to the young miners' leader Sam Ockleshaw, whose family she regularly visits and has come to care deeply for. The injustice of the wretched

conditions under which they and the other mining families live and work becomes unbearable to her. And this in turn makes even more excruciating the contradiction between what the Christian gospel preaches and what the Church permits to proceed with its blessing. Her own tacit complicity in this hypocrisy compels her one day early on, as she leaves the Ockleshaws' home, to pledge to herself that 'henceforth she would be true to the logical interpretation of the Gospel according to the light of God in her soul, rather than according to the lights of man in treaty with the ways of the world' (p.39).[13]

The moment marks the beginning of an exhausting endeavour to swim against the tide of social expectation and some of the deepest currents of feeling within herself. The first open rebellion is her refusal of Harry Brookster's proposal, which brings her into violent conflict with her father, the Reverend Egerton Waide. She explains to him that she does not want to marry Brookster because her political sympathies are on the side of the workers whom he and his father exploit. Moreover, to take the part of the working class, she argues, is surely the only course for a true Christian, who should condemn the Church's collusion with 'land, property and wealth' as 'against both the spirit and the letter of the Church's own Scripture' (p.53). Her father, who has himself, she now perceives, 'become entangled in the world' (p.53) beyond redemption, is left 'staring at her as if she had become a stranger' (p.55), which is exactly what she has become. As she painfully sheds the 'false ideal of her father, of the Church, and of society' (p.97), everything she has been brought up to regard as normal and familiar appears now as alien and remote as if it belonged to some other age. Yet to slip the shackles of her old self altogether and forge a fresh identity is as yet beyond her. As Sam's mother Nance shrewdly observes: 'There's a some'ut, Sam, i' yon vicarage lassie's look as if her mind wor tryin' to get out i'to somebody else's, an couldn' ' (p.122).

When the appalling deprivation of the 'Coal War' hits Beckerton, Grace's relationship with Sam grows closer and deeper as they work tirelessly together to meet the needs

and maintain the morale of the strike-bound miners and their families. But once the battle has been won and the urgencies of the strike recede, family obligations and the returning pressures of convention conspire to push them apart again; and Grace needs all her resources to endure the isolation and despair which threaten to engulf her as the social and psychological barriers to the union they both inwardly desire—that 'plighted troth of the most daring kind' (p.305)—press in upon her mind:

> She was alone, estranged. The old anchorage had gone, and she wanted new. Nay, she had new anchorage already . . . and yet all the world seemed to push between, calling, 'You'll cast yourself away. You'll break your "father's" heart!'   (p.295)

But when Harry Brookster calls to try his luck with Grace again, a sudden rush of courage spurs her to reveal not only that her heart is elsewhere engaged, but that 'it is one of your own poorly-paid men, Harry' (p.323). And she proceeds to spell out to the dumbfounded Brookster the radically different social and sexual perspective she can now boldly profess:

> You will forget that I still look at things from the point of view of the equal value of all labour, including the labour of the master . . . I would be proud to be the means of lifting up one of that class—understand me—not to a better kind of work, but to a better kind of life in connection with that work, however so-called humble or so-called mean, than to simply repeat the old, old kind of marriage with one's so-called superior, and fail to reach any justifying motive either in love or life.   (p.320)

After this breakthrough, Grace feels 'quite equal to both the romance and the reality of her recent life' (p.349), and in the novel's closing scene it is she who goes alone to Sam's home to resolve the deadlock between them. As they walk out together in silent understanding, climbing over a stile into the open fields in an image charged with symbolic promise, the novel achieves a real sense of possible emancipation, a sense that new ground has been cleared within

the bounds of personal accomplishment, but with no illusions about the difficulty that remains of cultivating and extending that terrain.

The eponymous hero of James Adderley's strange little novel, *Stephen Remarx. The Story of a Venture in Ethics* (1893), desires even more passionately than Grace Waide to preach and to practise the socialist vision which he sees at the heart of Christ's gospel. But the path which he follows in pursuit of his ideal, leading him as it does to become 'like a second Baptist . . . a "Voice" solemn and alone, crying in the wilderness of London society' (p.65), is quite extraordinary.[14] The novel offers in effect an imaginary biography of a Christian Socialist saint and martyr (as his name itself intimates), complete with invented newspaper reports, letters and reconstructions from contemporaries' notebooks to lend the fantasy a flavour of historical authenticity.

Stephen is an orphaned aristocrat, the son of Lord Remarx of Balustrade Abbey. After Eton he goes on to Oxford, where he comes under the influence of a progressive don, Frederick Hope. It is Hope's advanced ideas on social and theological questions which prove decisive in bringing about Stephen's conversion and subsequent ordination as a radical Anglican priest who believes in Christ as 'the One True Liberator' (p.6) and in his own duty to preach, to the rich above all, 'a divine discontent' (p.19).

Stephen's first curacy, however, is in the working-class parish of Hoxton which, thanks to the neglect of its idle and self-centred vicar, has become 'a hotbed of Secularism' (p.22). He joins the radical clubs to 'show them that so far as their ideals go, they are the right and true ones, because they are the ideals of Christ', and that, essential as the economic demands of the labour movement are, 'something more was wanted than material improvement for the masses' (p.28). But he is brought up short one day by a socialist lecturer's unanswerable attack on 'these co-called Christian Socialists who talk about Christ, the poor working man, who had not where to lay his head, while they themselves, who claim to represent Him, have never been without a comfortable bed in their lives. Let them

show us what He was like, and then, perhaps, we may listen' (pp.36-7).

Stephen's attempt to respond to this challenge occupies the rest of the novel. The question of how far one can really understand and identify with the experience of a class which is not one's own is of course a thorny one for all ruling-class socialists, especially as it opens the moral authority of their socialism to serious question. For John Oxenham, one of the leaders of the great Dock Strike whom Stephen eventually converts, the answer is clear: 'Nobody can sympathise unless he has really experienced the sufferings of those whom he proposes to compassionate' (p.54). Convinced of the truth of this, Stephen astounds the wealthy congregation of his new West-End parish by announcing his foundation of a special religious community for those of them brave enough to take Christ's gospel literally and practise at last what they profess to believe. To the landlords, bankers, businessmen, lawyers and the like sitting stupefied before him he makes a heartfelt appeal that they surrender the sources of all their comfort and luxury 'to what is right and good' (p.108), since 'a man clothed in soft raiment and living in king's palaces cannot be a prophet' (p.110). The announcement of this utopian experiment in Christian Socialism, the 'venture in ethics' of the title, provokes outrage in upperclass circles and ridicule from the press, which derides the 'Remarkables' (as Stephen's followers become popularly known) as 'Lunatics, Jesuits, Jumpers, Vagabonds, and Anarchists' (p.128).

Needless to say, there is no stampede to join the tiny band of Remarkables and vow with them 'to keep Christ's law in the midst of this wicked world' (p.124). The testimonies of the few who do make the grade afford, however, excellent occasions for mordant satire on the consequences of actually living up to that vow. A reformed priest, who has been ostracised by his own family, confesses to having never understood till now 'why it might be necessary to hate one's father and mother' (p.133). While the converted stockbrokers are driven to despair by the fact that 'their life in the light of an earnest following of Christ appeared to be

made up of ghastly fictions and unreal bargaining' (p.134).

The community's blatant lack of success in securing 'the triumph of Religion over Belgravia' (p.132) leaves Stephen undismayed. Being publicly hated, mocked and spat upon simply confirms his confidence in their role as a necessary thorn in the overfed flesh of the ruling class. Besides, as he points out, 'it is against our rules to trouble ourselves about results. We must be content to go on until we die, even if nothing substantial seems to come of it' (p.127). And in fact Stephen's own death arrives with indecent haste in the shape of a stupid street accident triggered by the aggression of a couple of upper-class thugs, infuriated by the sight of 'that canting idiot, Remarx' (p.147).

Adderley's abrupt resort to a bathetic fantasy of martyrdom, with the dying Stephen explicitly identified on the final page with the saint whose name he bears, only underscores, of course, the wild futility of the whole utopian venture from any realistic political viewpoint. If the social revolution has to wait upon the voluntary moral reformation of the rich and powerful, it will be quite a wait. Yet in his very absurdity there remains something haunting about the yearning, unworldly Remarx, whose quixotic experiment retains its inseparable imaginative virtue as a measure of the still monstrous gap between the allegedly Christian values and the brutally unchristian realities of capitalist Britain.

Although caustically critical of religion, Wargrave Lincoln, the dour middle-class militant featured in Olive Birrell's *Love in a Mist* (1900), would agree with Stephen Remarx on the need for would-be socialists from the bourgeoisie and above to 'come down to the common level of humanity' because 'until you have been poor you do not know what sorrow is' (p.53).[15] He himself claims to have 'never understood how poor men feel until I had brought myself to actual starvation' (p.53). But this deliberate self-impoverishment in the interests of ideological integrity gets a much rougher ride from Birrell's all too plausible, starkly disillusioned perspective. Her novel is a scathing but bracing exposure of the human cost of a lifetime's dedication to a rigid misconception of what socialism

should mean.

Over the years Lincoln has given away almost all his money to the poor or lost it in nobly conceived but catastrophic co-operative projects. We learn that both his wife and his first son died as an indirect result of his calculated impoverishment and neglect of his family. The action of the novel discovers him living on the shabby verge of penury with his grown-up daughter Sibylla and his second little son Pippin, to whom Sibylla is devoted. It is no surprise that life with this nomadic father, so dispassionately egalitarian in his love of humanity at large that he can spare no special affection for his own children, has alienated Sibylla completely from his world. Indeed she has been driven into the arms of Keith Hamilton, a man who may be a bourgeois capitalist, but who is at least capable of elementary human kindness and emotional warmth. As Hamilton observes in outrage at Lincoln's 'strange obliquity of sight': 'Sibylla had been dragged out of her natural sphere, placed on the level of the people her father professed to pity, deprived of the very things he pronounced the birthright of each human being' (p.313). In tracing a young woman's rebellious marital return to the middle class from the clutches of a drab proletarian existence, artificially enforced by her father's abstract principles, the story of Sibylla entails a telling reversal of the route followed by Grace Waide in Tirebuck's novel.

At the heart of the book is Sibylla's unavoidable showdown with her father over her desire to leave and marry Hamilton. Reproved by him for lacking the sympathy with his cause which would have led her to consider such a marriage 'repulsive' (p.135), she replies, 'I have sympathised with you more than you think . . . only I see there are mistakes. We help the poor by lifting them up to our own level, not by sinking to theirs' (pp.136-7). In Lincoln's view, Sibylla's special love for Pippin and for Hamilton are symptoms of the bourgeois disease he is trying to cure: 'It is that inspired selfishness you call love which has wrecked our social progress' (p.139). For Sibylla, in contrast, her father will never achieve anything for 'the whole of humanity' (p.139) until he has learned how to love another

individual: 'You do not know that love is, and yet you hope to save the world' (p.144).

It is not long after Sibylla has left him that the truth of her words comes home. At the age of only fifty-one the physical and emotional strain of his unflagging fight for socialism finally takes its toll and his health collapses. Reviewing his life's labour, he perceives only 'a long history of disappointment' (p.237). He suffers agonies of remorse for his dead wife and his neglect of the children she entrusted to him. And in the end he succumbs to a terrible despair:

> During the greater part of his life he had been in love with an idea, and believed in it, worshipped it, sacrificed all the things men usually value to promote its growth. Now in these dark moments, when strength was fast slipping away, for the first time the chilliness of doubt invaded the sanctuary where it lay enshrined. Like Joan of Arc in her dungeon, he began to question the reality of his visions: 'It is true, it is true, I heard the voices!' He, too, had heard voices, and they had guided him, as it now appeared, straight to destruction.   (pp.244-5)

His dying hours do bring him reconciliation with his estranged daughter, who has come to understand and forgive this man who 'was never on speaking terms with the world' (p.314) and 'his fierce determination to carry out one great idea, regardless of the torture he inflicted on those who should have been dearer to him than the whole earth' (p.276). But the feeling that the 'one great idea' may well have been an illusion stays with Sibylla and with us until the last page of the novel, where only a determined intervention by the author herself has the power to reverse the current of dismay and transform Lincoln's tragedy by placing it in the wider and longer perspective to which the characters within the narrative are blind:

> It seemed to her that his sacrifice had failed of its purpose. He had vanished, and this dark old earth, which has witnessed the fall of so many monarchies, the destruction of such countless hopes and ambitions, rushed through immensity with her burden of human sorrow quite unchanged. Sibylla was mis-

taken, though. Her father's spirit still lived and energised, through herself, through Hudson, through many others who had caught the fire of his great enthusiasm, and added to it a power of loving he had never known.   (pp.326-7).

A similar process of isolation and disenchantment is undergone by the protagonist of the last novel I want to look at, *George Eastmont: Wanderer* (1905) by Margaret Harkness. But the experience is turned to more positive ends because of what Eastmont learns about himself and his relation to the socialist movement and to history. To a degree unmatched by the other novels, *George Eastmont* grasps and lays bare the ironic double-bind inherent in the predicament of the bourgeois socialist: the fact that the very individualism which fuels his rebellion against his own class and his single-minded drive for a different world is what keeps him in thrall to the divisive, alienating reality he seeks to escape, laying him wide open to disappointment and disillusionment every time the limits of his individual powers are inevitably exposed.

The problem emerges right from the start of Eastmont's conversion. Eastmont is a Sandhurst-educated soldier, whose 'baptism of fire' butchering 'poor savages' (p.12)[16] in Africa pitches him into a slough of self-loathing and brings on a nervous breakdown. While convalescing on his aristocratic grandfather's estate in Ireland, he reads by chance Adam Smith and from there runs rapidly through Ruskin, Kingsley, Maurice and more, until at last there is no resisting the seductive revelation which strikes him: 'A saviour of the masses was wanted, someone who would go amongst them and show them how to help themselves, rouse them out of their apathy and ignorance, and give them hope. Where was the man?' (p.15).

It takes bitter experience to teach young Eastmont the folly of casting himself in this glamorous, self-gratifying role. At first the sheer exhilaration of his success as a passionate speaker at mass rallies leads him to fantasise that 'possibly the chasm that now yawned between the masses and the classes might be closed by himself, who like the Roman of old would leap into the yawning cleft'

(p.21). But his attempt to bridge that chasm, by the calculated 'experiment' (p.23) of a theoretically desirable but loveless marriage with a woman of 'the People', is disastrous and ends with the wretched woman's death from an accidental overdose of the drugs she has taken to alleviate her misery. Eastmont's remorseful realisation of his callous stupidity marks the culmination of a series of incidents which have begun to undermine his previously unshakeable confidence not only in himself but in the political will and wisdom of the masses.

Thus by the opening of Part II of the novel he has lost faith in the ballot and the bullet alike, and is unsure of his direction. The messianic fantasies have given way to a more sober, if somewhat jaundiced assessment of what is needed and what is possible:

> It is useless to pretend that our ideas have taken hold of the masses . . . Our social system is a sham, a gross injustice, but it will go on until working men learn to help themselves. I want to understand working men in order to work with them. I wanted to be one of them once, now I am not so ambitious.
>
> (p.118)

His arrogant assumption that the workers are at present irremediably apathetic is proved howlingly wrong when the great Dock Strike breaks out as if from nowhere to 'upset all his calculations' (p.130) and teach him another timely lesson. But the fact that the workers reveal themselves to be not yet strong enough to clinch the victory without ruling-class allies soon has him brooding and searching again for a more satisfactory course of action in the aftermath of the strike. He has no faith in trade unionism, and refuses a job as an organiser because 'I will not bind myself to think as others think on any subject, I must be free to hold my own opinions' (p.165). His reply to the union man who urges that now is the time for them all to pull together is: 'The strongest man is he who stands alone' (p.167).

But he must pay a price for the luxury of that creed. 'Cut off from his own people, and also from the people for

whose sake he had given up his friends and relations' (p.168), henceforth 'he must go on by himself, and that meant isolation and loneliness' (p.169). Eastmont's stubborn self-sufficiency, combined with his frustration at the refusal of history and utopia to converge forthwith in a 'coup-de-théâtre' (p.175), threaten to lock him into a cynical dismissal of the whole labour movement as 'a thing that had now begun to pall on him' (p.183). But he swerves away from the edge of recantation to reaffirm that:

> He was a Socialist, although he did not see how to put his ideas into practice. Things were moving, he felt sure of that, only they did not move fast enough. He would never be a reactionary, but keep an open mind, and strike wherever a blow would be really effective. (p.189)

After a *Wanderjahr* spent in Australia, first as a clerk in a desolate labour-settlement and later as a newspaper editor grappling with the politics of the Land Question, he returns to found an experiment in communal ownership on the estate which his grandfather has left him in Ireland. With the prospect of this specific, practical and consciously provisional task he is, for the moment, as content with himself as such a man in such a plight can be. For he has come to terms not only with the compulsively nomadic loner whom his origins and history have conspired to turn him into, but with the limits of what any committed individual can expect to accomplish within the constraints of his moment in time:

> He must go on; only death could put a stop to this onward movement. Always on, and on, and by himself, to a goal he could not see, for he had long ago given up the hope of doing anything definite in the work he had set himself. He had learnt that he was only one with the rest. (p.238)

In somehow holding fast to his commitment despite himself, despite the evidence of the present, and despite the deep shadow of uncertainty cast by an unknown future, Eastmont has perhaps found a way of being heroic after all, from which those who still face the quandaries of these ruling-class rebels may have something to learn today.

NOTES

1. *Don Karlos,* ed Paul Böckmann (Stuttgart, 1974), lines 4432-4 (my translation).
2. Stanley Pierson, *British Socialists. The Journey from Fantasy to Politics* (Cambridge, Mass., and London, 1979), p.349.
3. *ibid.,* p.1.
4. *ibid.,* pp.2, 347.
5. For an invaluable survey of this spectrum, see Stanley Pierson, *Marxism and the Origins of British Socialism. The Struggle for a New Consciousness* (Ithaca and London, 1973).
6. George Bernard Shaw, *An Unsocial Socialist* (London, 1888). The most stimulating criticism on the novel is to be found in Alick West's superb study of Shaw, *A Good Man Fallen Among Fabians* (London, 1950), ch. II, and more recently in Eileen Sypher's ' Fabian anti-novel: Shaw's *An Unsocial Socialist',* in *Literature and History,* xi, 2 (Autumn 1985), pp.241-53.
7. Shaw quoted in Michael Holroyd's (unpaginated) Introduction to the Virago edition of *An Unsocial Socialist* (London, 1980).
8. Shaw, *ibid.*
9. Shaw, *ibid.*
10. Cecil Power [Grant Allen], *Philistia,* 3 vols (London, 1884).
11. For an excellent historical account of this whole question see Stephen Yeo, 'A new life: the religion of socialism in Britain, 1883-1896', in *History Workshop,* 4 (Autumn 1977), pp.5-56.
12. Constance Howell, *A More Excellent Way* (London, 1888). The novel is also discussed in Brunhild de la Motte's contribution to this volume and in P. J. Keating's *The Working Classes in Victorian Fiction* (London, 1971), pp.241-2.
13. William Edwards Tirebuck, *Miss Grace of All Souls'* (London, 1895). See also the accounts of Tirebuck and *Miss Grace* in the essays by H. Gustav Klaus and Ingrid von Rosenberg elsewhere in this volume.
14. James Adderley, *Stephen Remarx. The Story of a Venture in Ethics* (London, 1893).
15. Olive Birrell, *Love in a Mist* (London, 1900).
16. John Law [Margaret Harkness], *George Eastmont: Wanderer* (London, 1905). On the fiction of Margaret Harkness (excluding *George Eastmont)* see John Goode's fine essay, 'Margaret Harkness and the socialist novel', in H. Gustav Klaus (ed.), *The Socialist Novel in Britain* (London, 1982), pp.45-66.

· 2 ·

Radicalism—feminism—socialism: the case of the women novelists

BRUNHILD DE LA MOTTE

During the 1880s and 1890s the British book market saw a flood of novels dealing in one way or another with problems of the working class. The growing conflict of developing monopoly capitalism and the resulting polarisation of the classes led, on a sociological-ideological level, to a general politicisation of the working people and, on a moral level, to attempts by middle-class people to solve the conflict by concepts of humanist transcendence. Both, the political and the humanistic aspects were reflected in the literature of the period. Yet, whereas in the 1840s the general trend of the 'social-problem novels' by middle-class authors was a humanitarian concern for fellow citizens linked with the liberal hope to reduce the gap between the two classes by reforms, the perspective presented in the slum novels and Cockney-school novels of the 1890s indicated that a simplified solution in this direction was no longer possible. And when it was presented, as in Walter Besant's *All Sorts and Conditions of Men* (1882) or Robert Blatchford's *Julie* (1900?), the picture of the benevolent bourgeois or 'corrigeable' worker expressed a point of view that by the end of the century had become conservative. In contrast, the representation of working-class life by Arthur Morrison and George Gissing characterised poverty as a social evil and thus shook the confidence of the bourgeois reader in a 'unified' world; however, their novels were a curious mixture of pity and disgust as well as frustration.

There were, however, a number of novels that did not just present the problems of the working class but put them

in a political context and tried to communicate the spirit of socialism spreading at that time, that is they showed a solution to the problem of poverty and human degradation in the transformation of the social system. Not surprisingly, many of these novels came from writers who were born into the working class, for example, H. J. Bramsbury, Allen Clarke and W. E. Tirebuck. It is, however, a striking phenomenon that their voices were joined by middle-class women who unreservedly sided with the working class and with the struggle for socialism. I would name here Constance Howell with her novel *A More Excellent Way* (1888), Clementina Black with *An Agitator* (1894), the novels by Margaret Harkness, especially *Out of Work* (1888) and *George Eastmont: Wanderer* (1905), Emma Brooke's *Transition* (1895) and Gertrude Dix with her novel *The Image Breakers* (1900).[1] By showing problems and consequences of political actions in the form of a narrative, these novelists took part in the public discussion about socialism. Of importance is the fact that the fictional heroes of these novels, despite the difficulties they face, basically retain their socialist conviction and do not withdraw into isolation at the end. The awareness of social confrontation and the necessity of taking sides and assuming an active part in social change is, in varying degrees, a predominant feature of these novels. Throughout they are characterised by a conviction that the situation of the working class can only be changed by political action. Thus these novels stand, in ideological terms, as P. J. Keating says, 'completely apart from the mainstream of late-Victorian urban working-class fiction'.[2]

Examining more closely these socialist novels by women we are not surprised to find that in most of them the Woman Question—as it was then called—played a significant part. This fact suggests a connection between the specific problems women faced in Victorian society and their political commitment. That there is a connection is confirmed by the simultaneous occurrence of vigorous feminist novels by writers such as Sarah Grand, Olive Schreiner, Mona Caird and George Egerton.[3] Presenting the psychological torments and sufferings of women forced

into a gender role that made any development outside home and the family impossible and showing the devastating results of sexual ignorance, their novels are not just individual tragic stories—though this is the form all these writers chose as a contrast to the Victorian 'happy ending'— but point to the social sources of this situation. Attacking the patriarchal family and its attendant ideology, these novelists, by implication, threatened the bourgeois system which had incorporated patriarchy as one of its ideological pillars.

We find, then, during the 1880s and 1890s novels that criticise both class and gender role as two aspects of the bourgeois social system, that is, a combination of socialist commitment and feminist concern. This conjunction suggests that there is an objective factor at work which makes women more aware of the oppressed in society. And when we look at the novels written by women over the centuries we discover that not a few among them take sides with the underprivileged: for example, the anti-slavery novels of Aphra Behn (*Oroonoko*, 1688), Charlotte Tonna (*The System*, 1827), Harriet Beecher Stowe (*Uncle Tom's Cabin*, 1852) and Elizabeth Browning (*Aurora Leigh*, 1856); or the social novels of Maria Edgeworth (*The Absentee*, 1812) Elizabeth Gaskell (*Mary Barton*, 1848) and Charlotte Brontë. Numerous women in the past have presented with insight and partisanship the plight and, partially, the struggle of the oppressed—whether victims of class, race or sex discrimination.[4]

It is characteristic of the social status of women in class society that though divided by class they are linked by a common lack of rights. Although there clearly is a difference between a bourgeois woman and a proletarian, a white lady and a black slave, it is nevertheless true that, within her class and race, woman has a more inferior status than man. This situation is the result of private property either as material fact (in the property-owning classes) or as ideological orientation (in the oppressed classes) which forms the basis of man's dominance and causes the dependence of woman. It is this relationship of dominance and

submission that provokes some feminist sociologists to see women as a class. Others consider them in terms of a 'caste' since women very often accept their position and perpetuate it by adapting to it. Or women's status is compared with that of a minority because of their marginalised position in society and the impossibility of escaping from this identity. Gerda Lerner repudiates these positions, in my view, most convincingly:

> Women are not a minority in any sense. Women are a sex. They have experienced educational, legal, and economic discrimination, as have members of minority groups, but they unlike truly marginal groups, are distributed through every group and class in society . . . Women are more closely allied to men of their own group than they are to women of other classes and races. Finally, women have always indoctrinated their children of both sexes in the very values by which they themselves have been doctrinated to subordination . . . Yet woman's position, whether as a member of the oppressed lower classes or as a member of the ruling elite, was always different in essentials from that of the male of her group.[5]

For a working-class woman the sex difference expressed itself not through her absence from work but rather through the quality of the workplace and the character of her work. As against male workers, the majority of women did not work in factories but in sweatshops and as servants[6]—which meant that there was a big difference in wages. Moreover, even when a woman did the same work as a man under the same circumstances she got paid less, since her work—according to patriarchal ideology—was additional to the income of her husband or father. Again, woman's existence was seen only in relation to and dependent on man. A woman from the working class, too, was expected to marry—yet, for her, this meant additional (unpaid) labour at home. Furthermore, the numerous pregnancies that usually followed in many cases ruined her health since she was forced to continue to work despite her condition because of the poor wages in general. If she did not get married she risked the possibility of being seduced and left with an illegitimate child for which she alone was

responsible and which therefore shaped (and very often destroyed) her whole life, or she faced the harsh alternative of having to earn (extra) money by prostituting herself, thus, again, being dependent on men. All of this indicates that the situation of the working-class woman was in practice determined by her class *and* sex, which put her at a disadvantage in comparison with male workers. This situation was complicated even more by the rigid laws of capitalist exploitation which enforced competition between men and women on the labour market, for a woman would be hired at a lower wage—a fact for which women were blamed and which caused male workers to insist of gender roles, namely 'public' work for men and 'private' occupation for women in accordance with patriarchal ideology.

This contradictory situation illustrates the problematic nature of the interests of class and sex, namely that they are not automatically identical. Depending on the issue, working-class women could form alliances either with men from their own class to achieve class goals, or with women from other classes to fight for their rights as a sex, or, in fact, with both at the same time. In other words, although women like men are divided by class interests, they have a common interest in the achievement of equality. Therefore, women are not only linked with their own class but also across class lines to fight for legal, educational and political rights. By its very nature—since women's subordination is part of bourgeois ideology determined by private property *and* patriarchal ideology—this fight is ultimately a threat to bourgeois society and has therefore a potential link with the fight for socialism.[7] Moreover, there is an objective connection between the woman's cause and the socialist movement which was pointed out by Eleanor Marx and Edward Aveling: 'The truth is that she [woman], like the labour-classes, is in an oppressed condition; that her position, like theirs, is one of unjust and merciless degradation.' And they stressed that neither for women nor for the working class was a solution in sight unless the condition of society was changed, and that the emancipation both of women and of the working class needed to

be carried out by their own forces.[8]

With the growing integration of women into the work process during the course of the nineteenth century—and this was true for women from the working class who were forced to work outside the home as a result of the industrial revolution, as well as for women from the middle class who finding themselves without sufficient parent capital or husband had to support themselves by work—their politicisation increased. Middle-class women especially, who were forced to become active in the fight for opportunities to work, including the education necessary for that work, and who found themselves confronted with barriers and restrictions on the basis of sex in practically all the professions, became conscious of their suppression as women. It is this context that made them take an interest in the conditions of women from the working class. Due to their own involvement in work, this interest took less the form of charity activities, as was predominantly the case in the 1840s, than of active participation: women produced studies about the conditions in factories and sweatshops and enforced some basic health regulations; they fought against the 'white slave traffic' and the Contagious Diseases Acts, which in practice were mainly directed against working-class women. In a somewhat different category were women who rejected their class background and threw their lot in with working women by supporting strikes, helping to organise trade unions (most prominently Emma Patterson and Clementina Black) and by forming women's associations, of which the Women's Co-operative Guild was the most important.[9] Barbara Hutchins, a political activist of this period, describes the mutual stimulation of both the women's and the labour movement:

> As the women's movement draws towards the labour movement, as it is now so rapidly doing, it tends to lose the narrow individualism derived from the middle-class ideals of the last century. Mere freedom to compete is seen to be a small thing in comparison with opportunity to develop. The appeal for fuller opportunity is now stimulated less by the desire merely to do

the same things that men do, more by the perception that the whole social life must be impoverished until we get the women's point of view expressed and recognised in the functions of national life. On the other hand, the women Unionists, who have long been taxed with apathy and lack of interest in their trade organisations, are drawing from the women's movement a new inspiration and enthusiasm.[10]

But there was not only mutual stimulation but also a concern by activists with both socialist and feminist problems. Thus Annie Besant, member of the Social Democratic Federation (SDF) and the Fabian Society, was also active in the birth-control movement.

Without trying to argue that all feminists became socialists—the ideological divisions between bourgeois feminists, women conservatives and socialists were very often considerable when their class concerns rather than the general liberation of all women were stressed—it is legitimate to say that practically all leading women within the socialist movement (and it is from them and not from the rank-and-file members that we have the records) were feminists as well. This was an international phenomenon as becomes clear with Clara Zetkin in Germany, Eleanor Marx in England, Alexandra Kollontai in Russia, Anna Kuliscioff in Italy and Florence Kelley in the USA. Therefore, the conclusion seems justified that this conjunction is due to the dialectical relationship between the liberation of the working class and of women.[11]

However, although the Second International at its foundation congress in 1889 had adopted a paragraph in its programme stressing that the equality of women was to be a leading principle for all member parties, the conjunction of socialism and feminism was in practice not without its problems. On the one hand, women's issues were often underestimated because of a mechanistic understanding of Marxism resulting in reductionist attitudes about class as well as patriarchal views on gender among labour leaders; and, on the other hand, some women overestimated the immediate importance of their own problems in relation to the class struggle. However, as a whole, this conjunction

strengthened both the women's cause and the labour movement; for it meant that talented middle-class women supported a socialist perspective.

Given this background, the phenomenon that some of the most radical novels of the 1880s and 1890s were written by middle-class *women* who had become politicised, is hardly accidental. These authors combined their interests as women with the socialist perspective available through the political movements of the period, which meant that they identified with the fight of the working class rather than viewing it from a distance.

CONSTANCE HOWELL, *A MORE EXCELLENT WAY* (1888)

Constance Howell's novel begins with a feminist issue: a woman of thirty, married to an officer in India, feels isolated and lonely. The cause of this unhappiness is a very common one among women of middle- and upper-class background: she did not really know her husband before the marriage; for, within the conventions of bourgeois match-making, a woman did not have much of a chance of getting to know the man she was to marry, further than that he was good-looking, had excellent manners and a secure position in society. The result was that the woman was often literally trapped in marriage and found herself confronted with a husband whom she could not warm to; it often happened that they were totally different in character and disagreed on moral, educational and political issues. This conflict is a frequent subject of feminist novels of the period, for example in Sarah Grand's *The Heavenly Twins* (1893) and Mona Caird's *The Daughters of Danaus* (1894). Constance Howell develops it in a political way by pointing out that the gender role of women (being submissive, superficially educated, religious) serves to maintain bourgeois society. This point is made apparent in the novel by the heroine's insight into the political function of religion. Reading in her husband's library Agatha Hathaway begins to doubt her religious belief and finally renounces Chris-

tianity altogether. This decision brings her into conflict not just with her husband, who though himself an agnostic sees his public position threatened, but also with the norms of a society which has incorporated religion into its ideology. The kind of opposition Agatha faces makes clear that this religiosity is to be carried mainly by women, almost as a substitute for the education granted to (middle-class) men, and by the poor who are thus made to accept their place in society. By making this connection between women and the poor explicit, Howell indicates the potential link between the emancipation of women and that of the lower, the working class. Howell does not make her protagonist into an active feminist, but she allows her to see the unfair chances for women in personal and professional life. And when she talks about equality and the causes for the 'weak' female character she is strategically using the arguments of Mary Wollstonecraft and John Stuart Mill. Agatha sympathises with the people because she sees that they are indoctrinated with falsehood (Christianity). Since she has no contact with the people, her solidarity with them grows out of her general sense of justice, and it is this sense of justice that 'made her champion them as a class'.[12]

It is Agatha's son who, influenced by her, takes the next step and actively sides with the people in their fight against capitalist exploitation. In Otho Hathaway Howell creates a character who throughout the novel is a passionate, optimistic fighter for socialism, giving everything for the cause—his money, his profession, his private life. Coming from a middle-class background with the financial security, education and culture that go with it, he is converted into an atheist through his mother, and turned into a socialist through studying not just the conditions of the poor but through analysing the causes of poverty. As a converted socialist he gives speeches and lectures and tirelessly meets the prejudices and arguments of his rich relatives.

Howell uses an omniscient narrator who adopts temporarily the perspective of Agatha and Otho. We are thus shown the process of their conversion to atheism and

socialism. The context in which the conversions take place is skilfully established so as to show that learning the social facts involves an inner confict as well as, in the end, a conflict with one's own class. Agatha faces the problem that although she herself no longer believes in God, she is forced to have her son brought up as a Christian because according to the moral standards of her class a child would be taken away from its mother rather than denied a religious education. Howell's narrative strategy aims at the disclosure of the mechanism of bourgeois ideology whose proclaimed freedom proves to be a lie for women and the poor.

Otho's conversion to the cause of socialism happens as the result of experiencing the contrast between the 'mob' in the streets (the Trafalgar Square riots of 1886) and the contented, sneering members of his own class who watch the battle from a safe distance. In terms of narration we find a strategy similar to that described above: the basic conflict between the classes is named and then an analysis of the causes of this situation offered. This is supplemented by a summary of Otho's reading of socialist literature (including Marx, Lassalle, George) so that we have a political 'lecture' that at the same time functions as a report about Otho's learning process. At that stage of the novel, it is still the narrator who undertakes the political analysis, which includes a clear-sighted evaluation of the existing socialist groups of that period. But soon the narrator's comments are replaced by Otho's voice in the political process, that is, the political discussion now becomes part of the character's life. Otho gives his first speeches and, still predominantly moving in circles of his own class, has numerous discussions where he opposes the common arguments against socialism. These are the most successful parts of the novel because the arguments are sharp, witty and to the point— as no pamphlet could have been. By putting the socialist argument in the context of standard middle-class prejudice and tiresome clichés about the working class, Howell is able to show both the strength of socialist theory and the process of change in people coming to terms with it. Thus, through the confrontation of characters, the rational

argument is complemented by emotional involvement, which makes the reader's identification with the presented problem easier. But more than that, the drama of the arguments, the wit in rebuttal, the inanity of the bourgeois arguments about socialism give the novel an aesthetic dimension.

The novel is structured in such a way that, on the one hand, the disastrous economic consequences of capitalism for the masses are shown mainly through direct speech; on the other hand, the effect capitalism has on the individual is indicated through characterisation. Thus Mrs Fleming, a minor character in the novel, is described as follows:

> Mrs. Fleming, who kept the boarding-house, was a type of the woman whom a capitalistic system produces . . . The struggle for life had hardened and narrowed and spoilt her. Her whole being was absorbed in the effort to keep herself and her children in a certain station; and in her desperate fear they should fail and sink below it, all the evil of her nature was rampant against her fellows.[13]

The park keeper who stops Otho distributing leaflets is characterised as a conservative working man whose selfish contentment in his job blinds him to the interests of his class. Dr Hathaway, a freethinker sympathising with the poor, remains conservative for convention's sake in order to keep his position as a recognised medical man.

The novel ends with Otho's optimistic faith in an early victory of socialism, expressed in a tone that is almost unique in the literature of that period—without however giving the impression that the fight will be an easy one. Howell shows that the conversion of middle-class people to the socialist cause means a separation from friends, relatives and even lovers. (Otho has to give up the idea of a marriage with an apolitical girl from his class whom he passionately loves but who cannot understand his conviction and is unwilling to give up her way of life for it.) Howell makes no secret of the fact that a socialist activist like Otho is slandered by the upper class, scorned by the middle class which fears losing its position in the social

hierarchy, and misunderstood by a working class that is divided by the complacency of those who have jobs and the discontent of those who do not—in other words, who is opposed by the full impact of bourgeois ideology and working-class antagonism. Yet, in presenting Otho as a sympathetic character who analyses the reasons for these reactions by putting them into a wider political context, she makes this very contrast the basis of her social critique. Moreover, she creates a figure whose commitment and political knowledge anticipates many future heroes of socialist novels.

EMMA BROOKE, *TRANSITION* (1895)

Emma Brooke's work illustrates the interrelation of feminism and socialism in a remarkable way. Her first novel, *A Superfluous Woman* (1894), is a typical feminist work of the 1890s while her next novel, *Transition*, is clearly socialist-orientated. The first is a psychological study of an aristocratic woman who in accordance with the conventions of her class is reduced to meaningless activities illustrating merely a flamboyant life style. In her heroine Brooke demonstrates the ultimate connection between enforced passivity and a state of invalidism and neurasthenia. She has thus created a character which challenges a prevailing opinion in the nineteenth century that the fragile health of a 'lady' was a result of the weakness of the female sex. Brooke makes her heroine leave her family and seek experience outside her overprotected golden prison where she had withered away out of sheer boredom. In the countryside, as a helpmate to a farming couple, the young woman learns to appreciate the difficulties of poor people and their straightforwardness, recognising the contrast to the minor problems and deviousness of her own class. Leaving aside the oversimplification, we can see that Brooke offers a solution to the woman problem in the integration of women into the work process so that they are an active part of human development. Yet, with the further development of the plot, Brooke indicates that an

individual escape is no solution to a general problem.

Transition picks up the theme of women and society from an angle totally different from that of the previous novel. We are introduced to a highly intelligent Girton student who, after finishing her studies, plans to do research in Greek mythology. Instead, however, Honora is confronted with her father's decision not to live any longer on his income from the church, which means that she is forced to earn her own living by teaching—a fact she finds deeply humiliating since she had hoped to be able to ascend into the upper middle class. With Honora's reaction Brooke, though acknowledging the success of the women's movement in establishing the opportunity to study, points out the élitist consequences of bourgeois education. The character of this education becomes clear when the minister, who remembers the time of the Chartists, asks his daughter about them, and she has to plead ignorance except for the vague idea that they were 'demagogues'. Here father, however, stresses the justified demands of the Chartist movement which the Church had failed to support; he thus represents a group of Christians who towards the end of the century began to question the power of the official Church and sided with the working class.

With this constellation, two different class views are presented, involving the reader in the argument which is implicit in the statements of father and daughter. Brooke does not impose her position through the better argument of either character but through the practice of Honora's teaching career. In a London high school where because of her abilities she becomes headmistress after six months, she feels and is in fact isolated from the rest of the teachers because of her attitude towards this 'inferior' work. Only when she overcomes her prejudices with the help of her socialist colleague, Lucilla Dennison, does she begin to experience the pleasures of self-fulfilment through creative work and to appreciate the independence it offers her. Thus, after a conversation with her former Cambridge tutor, she realises her equality with him: 'I belong to myself now exactly as he belongs to himself! . . . I need not ask him, nor father, nor anyone.'[14]

The feminist theme is connected with the fight for socialism in the character of Lucilla, who 'never had pictured herself as the domestic companion of an unbroken and impossible happiness. In all her dreaming she went forward with a restless circle of fellow-workers, and waged warfare against a shameless world.[15] With the change of narration to Lucilla's perspective, the activities of the socialists are introduced. Brooke does not aim to show—as does Howell—the cause and process of people's conversion to socialism; she merely indicates it by presenting the socialists as coming from different social backgrounds (from self-educated journalist of lower-middle-class origin to civil servant and former Cambridge lecturer). She shows socialist leaders in their work with the masses and is able through language and atmosphere to capture their enthusiasm. Thus the speeches included in the novel are aimed not so much at converting characters in the novel (and by implication the reader), as at illustrating the commitment of the socialists to their cause and the satisfaction they gain from working for the good of the people. The identification with the working class becomes clear in the very conception of these characters, notably in Paul Sheridan, an International Labour Party (ILP) leader:

Sheridan's conversation was apt to be dotted with figures; he would use them to meet vague clever-sounding generalities, introducing them side by side with quotations from the poets. . .

In truth, the food for his imagination lay in the commonest things; he required no more than the every-day affairs of an every-day earth to set his heart a-working on its lifelong labour of divination. . .

It was that to his divining eye the commonest things told the deepest earth histories. The rhythm of his poetry had in it the fall of hammers, the hum of wheels, the ceaseless tramp of the workers' feet, the rattle of traffic, and the rush of steam. As the genius of the historian out of broken pottery and scattered shreds revives the palpitating life of the long-dead city, so he out of figures would extract the passionate realities and tragedies of present existence.

'Your truest poetry is found in statistics', he would say.[16]

Besides characterisation, Brooke uses irony in order to illustrate the moral superiority of the socialist idea. In the election campaign the Conservative and Liberal candidates are called Mr Tootle and Mr Bootle respectively, thus ridiculing the similarity of their programmes. In contrast, Sheridan—the first candidate put forward by the Socialists—offers a clear alternative. And while Tootle/Bootle hire an ignorant hand to put up their posters (which he does by placing them always next to each other), Sheridan's election work is characterised by an efficiency that originates from conviction and tremendous support by party members and working-class people, mainly women, who in fact very often did the leg work.

Yet, while presenting the power of the socialist idea, Brooke also indicates differences within the movement that threatened its strength: the conflicts between reformists and revolutionists, which is no other than that between a socialist and an anarchist position. This conflict is located in Lucilla who has a deep commitment to the socialist cause but is increasingly worried about the growing reformism of the party Sheridan represents. Her doubts and inner conflicts isolate her from her former friends and comrades, causing her to suffer; yet, for her the separation seems inevitable since while she dreams of a communist future she is convinced that reforms contradict this aim rather than bring it about. The study of Lucilla, with her conflict between conviction in the cause and anxiety about strategy, shows Brooke's ability of drawing characters and making the tension of longing and being, of idealism and pragmatism visible. Though she seems to give both positions, the socialist and the anarchist, equal room in the novel,[17] the apparent neutrality is resolved by the plot: Lucilla gets fully involved with the anarchists only to realise that their leader sees in her merely a psychosexual prop; disappointment, awareness of her delusion and her isolation lead to her death. Thus, by combining the political argument with problems of gender—setting true comradeship against sexual humiliation—Brooke shows the moral superiority of socialism, notwithstanding its contemporary weaknesses. She argues for tolerance in the

interest of unity and for the necessity of compromise in the struggle when she makes Lucilla say: 'My tremendous error was to dream that Truth is single.'[18]

What remains at the end, despite the heartache over personal losses, is the optimism of the socialist fight: Sheridan wins a seat for the Socialists; Honora, distanced from the cause throughout the novel, takes up Lucilla's place. It is this optimism, not just decoratively stated at the end but implied in the novel as a whole—by means of plot-construction, character-drawing and a passionate language full of metaphors—that makes the aesthetic quality of this narrative.

CLEMENTINA BLACK, *AN AGITATOR* (1894)

In her novel, *An Agitator*, Clementina Black combines problems of the socialist movement with questions of working-class leadership. Christopher Brand, of working-class origin and trained as an engineer, is introduced as a political activist who dedicates his life to the struggle of the working class. Being on his own (the premature death of his wife in childbed having been hastened by constant worries over his unemployment resulting from victimisation), he considers the working people of England his family, and Labour his party. He not only leads strikes and takes part in political debates, but also stands as a Labour candidate for Parliament. He becomes, however, the victim of an intrigue that loses him the newly-won seat and lands him in prison, which he eventually leaves with revived spirits and renewed conviction.

Yet, despite Brand's enthusiasm for the socialist cause and his uncompromising battling, he appears to be somewhat aloof from his class. Black offers an explanation for this distance in his biography: he is the illegitimate son of an aristocrat and a working-class woman. With this she also seems to indicate that Brand's abilities result from his 'aristocratic blood'. At the same time, she presents him with a deeply ingrained sense of class justice and makes him stand firmly with the working class on the occasion when

his father suddenly appears and tempts him with the prospect of a professional or political career under his protection. We have then a contradiction between the political–ideological physiognomy of a working-class leader and the uneasy biologist 'explanation' of his abilities to formulate and present socialist theory. This contradiction suggests that Black was aware of a problem for which she did not have a sufficient theoretical understanding: the working class itself does not produce theory—a fact that Lenin was to make clear later. Being conscious of this—not least through her practical work with workers—[19] and yet determined to create a positive working-class leader, Black gets around the problem by offering the biologist 'explanation'. While this is clearly not satisfactory, giving the novel an aesthetic flaw, the important point is that Black is tackling a problem of great relevance for working-class literature. She stresses in the character of Brand that it is not only education that makes a working-class leader, but a combination of knowledge plus the experience of everyday exploitation and the political conviction resulting from both. Moreover, as she shows with Brand's development from self-imposed isolation to a sense of comradeship with other workers, it is not through capable individual leadership but through the joint fight with the workers that the struggle can be won. To make this point by way of aesthetic presentation is an important merit of the novel and gives it its optimistic quality.

In this apparently personal story of the development of a political agitator other problems of the working-class movement are inserted. Thus the description of the atmosphere during a strike—the well-organised distribution of money, the problems with blacklegs, the discussions among the workers about an enforced compromise—is a moving tableau and an introduction into the practice of class struggle. Part of this struggle was the growing necessity to fight for social improvements through Parliament and therefore to put up independent candidates in an election—a fact Black works out with political clarity asserting that the Liberal Party, traditionally 'representing' the workers, can never be a workers' party owing to its

membership from among the property-owning class, and its politics. Also, the deviations and confusions within the socialist movement itself—an increasing problem in Britain during the 1890s—are ironically hinted at with the comment on the 'Russell Square Socialist Society':

> They are the middle-class wave of socialism . . . Socialism in the West End . . . is enthusiasm; in the East End it's revolt; in Bloomsbury it is business . . . The aim is to secure certain economic changes, one by one, without personal sacrifice. The methods are talking, lecturing, issuing pamphlets, joining Liberal and Radical Associations and blowing one another's trumpets . . .[20]

And with Mrs Pelham, the curate's wife, who supports the labour movement with commitment and intelligence yet cannot represent it in Parliament, Black raises the problem of the exclusion of women from public offices.

This enlargement of perspective functions as a sort of corrective to the concentration on an individual hero and points at the direction the socialist novel was to take with its further development. The novel is marked by the aesthetic weakness indicated above; yet, what I insist on is its importance in the historical context: picking up issues of the socialist struggle as a theme and presenting the movement in a positive light with a protagonist who retains his political faith despite the difficulties he faces, was a courageous effort by a woman who was surrounded by writers full of doubt and scepticism if not opposition and ridicule.

Common to all the novels briefly discussed here is their political radicalism. This radicalism is based, I would suggest, on the writer's experience of oppression as a woman and her politicisation during a time of the strengthening of the socialist movement which, in turn, led to a perception that her own problems were part of the problems of society as a whole and culminated, finally, in the conviction that a transformation of capitalism was necessary. Thus these middle-class women identified with the socialist movement because their own interests were

ultimately intertwined with it—which is a very different situation from that of a male writer like Gissing who for a time felt drawn to the working class but never really identified himself with the aims of its vanguard. It is the writer's identification with the subject presented that accounts for partisanship in a novel—a quality of particular importance for the socialist novel.

The fact, however, that the socialist novels by women of that period were as outspoken as the feminist novels were frank, suggests that the radicalism of these women writers was not only politically caused but sociologically determined. While men had various opportunities to express their ideas—in positions of authority in the state apparatus, in the academic world, law and political organisations—women, practically excluded from official public life, felt that writing afforded them one possibility of taking part in discussions on issues important to them as women. Novels, that is, were used by women as a medium for the representation of opinions that could not otherwise be expressed since they were denied positions of influence. Moreover, since they felt misrepresented by patriarchal ideology, they used literature to inform and instruct, to offer an alternative ideological perspective. To put it more generally, the didactic quality found in early socialist and feminist novels (as well as in Black literature) is caused by the fact that this literature is forced to work in a literary discourse which excludes the experience and world view of the oppressed class/sex/race. It is under these conditions that literature assumes the function of instructing, which means that the signified is more essential than the signifier. Therefore, we find, also in the novels discussed here, not so much an elaborated presentation of a perceived view but the attempt—through construction of plot, presentation of character and the use of argument and debate—to inform the reader, clarify doubts and win her/his understanding of the subject matter.

NOTES

1. It is surely no coincidence that practically all of these women were politically active: Clementina Black was for thirty-five years a leading organiser of the women's trade-union movement; Margaret Harkness was an active member of the SDF; Constance Howell is known to have supported campaigns against sweated work, and Gertude Dix was part of the socialist movement in Bristol.
2. P. J. Keating, *The Working Classes in Victorian Fiction* (London, 1979), p.239.
3. Sarah Grand is best known for *The Heavenly Twins* (1893), Olive Schreiner for *The Story of an African Farm* (1884), Mona Caird for *The Daughters of Danaus* (1894) and George Egerton for her short stories collected as *Keynotes* (1893) and *Discords* (1894).
4. This fact is confirmed by Joseph Kestner in his informative study *Protest and Reform. The British Social Narrative by Women, 1827-1867* (London, 1985) where he says about the period under investigation: 'Female social novelists were more aggressive than male novelists like Disraeli or Kingsley in their specificity. Particularly in showing inter-actions among women of different classes these novelists surpassed their male counterparts' (p.18).
5. Gerda Lerner, *The Majority Finds Its Past: Placing Women in History* (Oxford, 1981), pp.170-1.
6. See Patricia Branca, 'A new perspective on women's work: a comparative typology', *Journal of Social History*, IX (1975), pp.129-53. Though men also worked as servants they tended to be hired by the upper class whereas women did service for the middle class who paid less for more and harder work.
7. The need of women's emancipation as a prerequisite for social development was pointed out by people as diverse as Fourier, Marx and John Stuart Mill, which demonstrates that the woman question is not bound to a single class position though its effective solution is connected with the abolition of capitalism.
8. 'On the Woman Question', *Westminster Review*, VI (1885), p.211.
9. The Women's Co-operative Guild formed in 1883 was the first proletarian women's organisation with economic and educational concerns as well as political aims (enfranchise-

ment). See Jean Gaffin and David Thoms, *Caring and Sharing. The Centenary History of the Co-operative Women's Guild* (Manchester, 1983).

10. Barbara L. Hutchins, *Women in Modern Industry* (London, 1915), p.199.
11. For the complex relationship between the two movements see the stimulating study by Meredith Tax, *The Rising of the Women. Feminist Solidarity and Class Conflict, 1880-1917* (New York, 1980).
12. Constance Howell, *A More Excellent Way* (London, 1888), p.90.
13. *ibid.*, p.214.
14. Emma Brooke, *Transition* (London, 1895), p.140.
15. *ibid.*, p.77.
16. *ibid.*, p.168.
17. The socialist and anarchist positions in the book are increasingly represented by Sheridan and Lucilla respectively, and their long argument at the end of the novel is perhaps the most powerful and moving part of the book, as it is both politically and personally final.
18. Brooke, *op. cit.*, p.308.
19. Detailed information about Clementina Black's extensive trade-union work can be found in Liselotte Glage, *Clementina Black: A Study in Social History and Literature* (Heidelberg, 1981).
20. Clementina Black, *An Agitator* (London, 1894), p.53.

· 3 ·

Tendencies in narrative fiction in the London-based socialist press of the 1880s and 1890s

JACK MITCHELL

The history of modern, revolutionary-socialist and working-class narrative fiction in Britain begins with William Morris and 'H. J. Bramsbury', the first being one of the most famous men of letters of his age, the other a man (?) whose real identity remains a mystery. I refer to four works, three by Morris and one by Bramsbury, all published in serial form in *Commonweal* and *Justice*, the central organs of the Socialist League and the Social Democratic Federation respectively. Morris's tales appeared in *Commonweal*, of course. They were: 'The Pilgrims of Hope' (April 1885 to June 1886), 'A Dream of John Ball' (November 1886 to January 1887), and 'News from Nowhere' (January to October 1890). Bramsbury's novel appeared in *Justice* between June 1888 and April 1889. Its title—'A Working Class Tragedy'.

Thanks partly to Morris's tremendous influence, British socialists of the period were intensely aware of the importance of art and literature in propaganda work. Morris taught them how important it was to woo the imagination, the emotions, the moral-aesthetic sense, as well as the mind, away from the corrupted channels and models through which the bourgeoisie exercised its in-depth control. Many of them saw, perhaps more clearly than we do, so much more immersed as we are in the desperate day-to-day struggle, the need to inspire, to provide the 'gleam'. They grasped the necessity of creating a body and tradition of militant socialist and working-class literature which would be independent of bourgeois hegemony. Not

49

that they had a worked-out policy for the arts, or a theory. Morris's *theory*, which contained a tendency to view art as a florescence on healthy society rather than as an agent for helping to change society, did not always help them here. Sectarian though they were in many ways, some of them had moved beyond the tendency to be found in a good deal of Chartist criticism and fiction to reject the great tradition of bourgeois classical and critical realism as something alien to them. This was at least true of *Commonweal*, under Morris's guidance, from 1885 to 1889, where Dickens, Defoe and George Eliot, for instance, were recommended as great writers to learn from. Cobbett is criticised, but recommended for the poetry of his prose,[1] and, paradoxically, William Morris himself takes up the cudgels in defence of the truth of Zola's 'ugly realism' in the banned *Germinal*.[2]

Morris was not the only 'literary man' in the leading circles of the socialist movement. For such a small movement the proportion of this type of person was extremely high. By its very nature and the way it 'came to them' Socialism tended to attract people with an urge to express themselves in words. In the midst of a capitalism all too clearly entering upon its decadent imperialist stage, revolutionary socialism burst on them with the impact of an almost religious revelation. It stirred the imagination. Among the leading political workers who regularly contributed poetry or imaginative prose were, for instance, Tom Maguire, Edward Carpenter, Harry Quelch, Robert Blatchford, Bruce Glasier, James Connolly, R. B. Cunninghame Graham, Jim Connell.

Of course, in one sense this was symptomatic of an as yet undeveloped 'division of labour'. There were so few activists. Socialism at this stage was not a mass movement in any way comparable to Chartism, but a movement of a tiny minority. The Chartists had a far bigger reservoir to draw from. In criticising the severe limitations of socialist literature in the 1880s and 1890s we must keep in mind the narrowness of its base.

It was not just a matter of socialism attracting people of a literary bent. In their activities the socialist societies laid

tremendous weight on the word. The literature produced by these politician-writers was seen as an integral part of their main, almost their only activity—propaganda. They had no conception of a modern revolutionary party of the working class with its roots in the daily struggle of the masses. The societies (if not always the individual members!) saw themselves almost exclusively in the role of socialist 'evangelists' preaching the Word, tearing the blinkers from the workers' eyes, revealing the true nature of capitalist exploitation, preparing them ideologically to know 'what to do' when the System collapsed more or less spontaneously under its own inner contradictions. So all their energies and talents were poured into the Word; and of course they became very good at it—at explaining exploitation. How often do we express wonder at Robert Tressell's genius for this in *The Ragged Trousered Philanthropists*. But Tressell's genius did not arise immaculate from the waves. It is the finest flowering of a talent developed by the socialists in the course of the twenty preceding years, Something that once again goes to show how, in the case of working-class literary culture, no crisp and holy frontier can be drawn between the 'non-artistic' and the 'artistic' literary (or verbal) modes.

Clearly this situation was, in certain ways, a favourable one for the cultivation of imaginative writing as one important and respected sector of the word-front. As we shall see, however, the total context also contained negative pressures which hampered and circumscribed the development and adequate functioning of the new literature, preventing a major breakthrough to realism. This was particularly damaging in prose.

Of course, in the early years especially, the literary activists tended to express themselves in lyrical verse more than in the narrative fictional forms. It took some time for the socialists reluctantly to realise that the collapse of capitalism was not necessarily imminent, that the here and now was not just a purgatory pure and simple, soon to be passed through leaving no trace, but an on-going contradictory process in which the foreshadowings of future life and struggle were already present—an object worthy of

close scrutiny. But until this urge to scrutinise closely makes itself strongly felt there can be no firm foundation for the development of the realist narrative modes, which are *par excellence* the modes for getting to grips with the nitty-gritty of aesthetically unexplored terrain.

Morris was one of those who did at least realise that the revolution would be a long time a-coming, and that it was necessary to comb out the detested present for any glimmerings of Hope. Personally it went very much against the grain to do this, but with the courage and sense of responsibility so typical of the man, he set out to show the way.

This he attempted in his pioneering novel-in-verse 'The Pilgrims of Hope' (*Commonweal*, 1885-6).

Where might he find that gleam of hope for the future in his own time? The action shuttles between London and revolutionary Paris. A kind of socialist *Tale of Two Cities*. Feeling that the destiny of humanity is going to be forged in the modern city, the hero and his wife leave their country idyll to take up political work in London. At first the stupor of London deadens their hope, but the hero is 'born again' when he joins the communists. Forced down into the ranks of the proletariat, he works selflessly for the Cause despite losing the two things he treasures most—his pleasure in his work, and his wife's love, the latter to a well-off friend and comrade who supports them in time of need. All three go to Paris in 1871 to help in the defence of the Commune. There they are filled with the spirit of hope, for they have seen the future 'real, solid, and at hand'.[3] The hero's wife and friend are killed on the barricades. He is smuggled back to England, where he joins his young son in his native village, there to recuperate before plunging back into the struggle.

In the introduction ('The Message of the March Wind') Morris and his hero appear to be set on exchanging the outworn romance of the pastoral dream for a new, sober romance of the ugly urban fact and the revolutionary movement. But the story ultimately fails to fulfil this promise. Contemporary life as a whole is aesthetically distasteful to Morris and he is loath to look it steadily in the face *as an*

artist in search of beauty. (This was a difficult thing to demand of *any* socialist artist at this point in time, that is before the *first stirrings* of the mass historic initiatives which brought movement into the 'fen of stagnant waters' at the end of the eighties.)

The narrative continuously veers away, after slight contact with the outer world, into the author–hero's subjectivity. Outer reality is only interesting in so far as fleeting figments of it provide 'signs' to nourish the narrator's real preoccupation—his hope. English life provides him with no such signals, except for the everlasting hope embodied in nature, the tradition-rich English countryside. Revolutionary Paris does provide them. But it is not so much the actual, embattled Commune that interests him, rather it is his inner *dream* of the commune, which the Commune helps to feed. This dream comes between us and actual reality. For Morris it is the true reality. Wherever it is a matter of telling us how the future will relate to the Commune his verse comes temporarily to life. The 'real, solid, and at hand' never does.

Also part of this is the way in which that conventional theme of the contemporary bourgeois novel, the love-triangle, comes to overlay and emasculate the main drive of the political action. Certainly, the love-triangle is treated in a new way, from the point of view of a truly communist ethos, but the manner in which it gets between Morris and what should be his real story shows, I think, firstly how his own marital problems sneaked into the story, and secondly, that he felt the thinness of his narrative and introduced the tragic 'love interest' to stiffen and anchor it.

With this tenuous aesthetic relationship to contemporary reality there could be no question of Morris laying the basis here for a *realist* narrative exploration of present life and struggle. But the only way to win a wider working-class audience was through realism (see Tressell). How wide an audience did Morris intend to reach? The very lack of concreteness was perhaps an advantage as regards one of the aims Morris seems to have been pursuing. The story assumes certain allegorical or metaphorical overtones. It can also be read as an 'individualised' version of the

historical path followed by humanity from an (idealised) village community into the hell of urban capitalist exploitation and through to the first upsurge of modern revolt, with its striving towards the communist future. This is quite characteristic of the natural historicism and urge to wholeness which marked Morris's political vision. Seen from this angle the story is a 'disguised' version of a typical Socialist League lecture or tract on the historical development of society—but one composed for the amusement and edification of the more or less initiated. One of Morris's chief aims in writing was to warn and educate, encourage and inspire the small 'socialist band': the way will be fraught with setbacks; your generation might not see victory, but your lonely fight, modest though it appear, will be a living part of that true reality—the future. In this sense the Paris Commune becomes a heroic metaphor for the seemingly unheroic struggle of the socialists in Britain.

That Morris was not primarily aiming at a mass audience is clear from his choice of *verse* for this 'historical novel of the present'. Taking into account the general context discussed earlier, and also the whole complex problem of Morris's aesthetic relationship to his material, it was not unnatural that this first attempt at an extended narrative of the present from a revolutionary point of view should be in verse. On the one hand it indicates his underlying lyrical rather than epic, or objectivised, preoccupation. On the other hand it is a curiously shamefaced verse, for the most part, as if it felt it really ought to be prose. It moves in a stylistic limbo which corresponds to the vague setting the heroes move in. It has an evasive quality, helping to exalt material which Morris feels has, aesthetically, little to recommend it, and at the same time keeping this intransigent detail at arm's length.

He had done his best, but those seeking to 'conquer the present' would have to find their own more prosaic road. Morris was aware of his own unsuitedness for this job. He ends with the lines

And I cling to the love of the past and the love of the
  day to be,
And the present, it is but the building of the man to be
  strong in me.[4]

Four months after the conclusion of his first attempt to
body forth his dream of the commune he was back in the
columns of *Commonweal* with a new and more congenial
strategy. Taking his cue from the last lines of 'The Pilgrims
of Hope' he plunges into the past to find an image, this
time in his own beloved England of the Middle Ages.
Again he chooses a revolutionary situation—the Peasant
Revolt of 1381.

In the prose tale 'A Dream of John Ball' the socialist
narrator is transported back, in a dream, to an idealised
Kentish village at the point of coming-together and upsurge of the peasants under the inspiring words of John
Ball. The narrator experiences their *fellowship* (comradeship) and a victorious preliminary skirmish with the forces
of the lords. In a long concluding conversation with John
Ball he tells the latter how he and the peasants will be finally
vindicated in 'the change beyond the change'.

In contrast to 'The Pilgrims of Hope' there is a wealth of
concrete and loving detail here. Yet the image of society
which emerges has the static quality of pageantry, almost
of heraldry, where the brightness of the primary colours
screens a tangle of historical illogicalities. Morris sought to
achieve with his version of the Middle Ages what he could
not achieve with the stuff of the alienated present—give
real body to his vision of a fellowship in which the individual could flourish. But in order to do so he had to
distort, to stylise. The result is 'beautiful' but lacking in
intrinsic dynamism and so ultimately unconvincing. Indeed, the objective picture soon gives way to what it could
not embody—a discussion of future perspectives. So once
again it comes to a falling apart of the historically concrete
and the real vision, the ideal. So Morris's Middle Ages 'fail'
him too. Historical realism is not achieved.

These limitations are perhaps best put into perspective
by considering Morris's apparent intentions in writing.

His aim was surely to indicate that fellowship, something containing real qualities of the commune, had once been at home in this England that now seemed the mockery of these things, to show that English men and women had sacrificed themselves to defend this fellowship and expand it into the envisioned commune of all humanity, increasing their own fellowship in the process of struggle. What once was, albeit in a partial form, would come again, perfected and universalised through the dialectic of historical struggle. Fellowship, the commune, was the people's birthright, of which they had been robbed, not the pipe-dream of a few freaks and enthusiasts.

Clearly these aims do not preclude a wider readership, but the whole nature and emphasis of the story indicate that Morris was again mainly writing with the small band of the socialist fellowship in view. Again his intention was to sustain and inspire, to educate, but also to impress upon them the historic responsibility they bore as the executors of those who had fought the good fight in the past, the vital, tenuous link between the past and the future. Given this primary intention and readership, the revolutionary-romantic, stylised pageant-vision could fulfil its function quite effectively. But only historical realism could have captured a wider audience.

The way in which the two heroes, John Ball and the narrator, function is further evidence of the somewhat inward-turning tendency of the whole structure. In a sense they are a retreat on the heroes of 'The Pilgrims of Hope'. They take no direct part in the actual fighting, but, in accordance with the role assigned to themselves by the socialist societies in a popular upsurge, give 'the ideo-logical lead'. This is why John Ball and not, say, Wat Tyler, is the central figure. Ball plays the agitator's part at first hand, the narrator does so at one remove in that he gives the long historical perspective to Ball. The only real dyna-mism to be found in the story is contained in their *words*— in Ball's prophetic agitatory speech at the cross, and in the way the narrator leads Ball's mind and imagination into the distant future and the true realisation of their struggle.

The action-story is an induction leading into a disguised

version of a typical socialist excursion on the nature of capitalist exploitation, with a characteristic Morrisonian emphasis on its historical growth. Ball is a kind of 'alienating effect' here—the simple man whose naïveté serves as a sounding board for bringing out the social and historical paradoxes. Hence this conversation sets out not only to educate, but to educate the educators, providing an object lesson on how to relate to a simple audience.

Not that the socialist educator was expected to use the tortuous, at times almost incomprehensible pseudo-medieval no-language into which the style increasingly degenerates. Perhaps this was partly due to time pressure in meeting serialisation dead-lines (E. P. Thompson maintains that 'The Pilgrims of Hope' was written hastily in monthly instalments[5]), but basically, in the work under discussion as in its predecessor, the unsolved problem of style expresses firstly Morris's lack of real aesthetic-imaginative contact with the society he was portraying, and secondly the fact that he was primarily writing for a small circle of devotees. (Or does it indicate rather that he was not sure for whom he was, or ought to be, writing?)

Be that as it may, the limitations of Morris's attempts to get to artistic grips with actual, objective reality were clearly not only due to personal peculiarities but also to the isolation and sectarianism of the socialist sects, their 'contempt' for the present, for the day-to-day struggles of the masses to assert their humanity.

Morris's third serial in *Commonweal* did not follow immediately upon the second, but after an interval of three years. 'News from Nowhere' is by far the most considered of Morris's socialist narratives.

Now, in the free and uncluttered field of the far-off not-yet there can be no question of a falling apart of the historically concrete and the ideal. Here he can mould the 'historically concrete' to the exact specifications of his ideal. It is *his* historically concrete, his true reality realised, the product of his imagination in complete accordance with his ideal. Which does not mean with a dream, for his social ideal is 'scientific' in so far as it is a basically Marxist prognosis developed out of the revolutionary potential

already pushing through the dirt of the present. All the 'signs' given him in the course of his rich life-experience, especially in the socialist and labour movements, come together here, transmuted, fused and filled out by the synthesising power of his poetic imagination into a living totality. There is no need here to turn his back on the facts of life in order to sing in praise of mere signs of hope, of the future. The systematised and completed pattern of signs *is* the future, the hope realised, reality. Nothing else now exists to confuse, mar and separate.

Many things motivated Morris to produce his definitive image of true reality when he did, in 1890. No doubt his failure to achieve concreteness and wholeness in the two preceding serials set in the present and the past also urged him into the future dimension. But it was part of a long-term strategy too. 'News from Nowhere' is the most complete and mature statement of all the main strands in his thinking. There was a third thing however. The way in which victory was won by the 'hopeless mass' of rank-and-file workers in the fight for the Dockers' Tanner in 1889 had, surely, more than a little to do with the novel's timing and its triumph over all the limitations in Morris, limitations both of a purely personal kind and those reflecting the weaknesses of the socialist sects of the day. The sudden historic initiative of the masses in 1888 to 1889, which Engels called 'one of the greatest and most fruitful facts of this *fin de siècle*',[6] had demonstrated that the reawakened giant could indeed mould a new world according to its own best image. Morris goes out ahead, so to speak, and shows them this new world. The spirit of the Great Dock Strike, the new type of human relations (of *culture*) which it indicated, must have given added conviction to Morris's emphasis on the transformation of *the way people live together*.

The host of improbabilities in 'News from Nowhere' emerges more clearly with the passing of time, but so does the living core. A. L. Morton writes that the great polemical theme of the book is that 'Man has the power to transform his environment and in doing so, to transform himself.'[7] This is what the revolt of the non-skilled showed above

all—even the skilled artisans began at last to 'transform themselves' as a result. It is a universal theme embodied universally in the book and giving it a universal appeal. The narration is the product of 'scientific deduction' (from the present), the imagination, and a great love of humanity, all acting in unison. This appeal is universal also because it activates our thinking, our imagination and our emotions universally. Not only the working class of Morris's own day could recognise in 'News from Nowhere' all that was best, dynamic and forward-pointing in themselves. Succeeding generations, travelling towards the goal through all the contradictions and setbacks, recognise this core of *anticipatory realism* ever more clearly. The inspirational, activating intent, present in all Morris's political writing, but often narrowed in its appeal, reaches its final consummation here. In contrast to its two predecessors it possesses *the power to convert*.

One of the activating aspects of the work's realism is the way it encouraged, and encourages, people to look more closely at times present for the elusive signs of times to come. Thus it has helped to develop that positive, analytical curiosity about the present in all its ramifications which is a *sine qua non* of an artistic approach to contemporary life that is both socialist and realist. Anyone intimately acquainted with Tressell's *The Ragged Trousered Philanthropists* will agree that that great socialist realist novel of the here-and-now would not have been the same without 'News from Nowhere', the one socialist national classic that preceded it.

By the end of 1890 *Commonweal* had fallen hopelessly into the hands of the anarchists. But *Justice,* the rival journal run by the Social Democratic Federation, presumed to tread where the great man had preferred not to. In 1888 it began serialising a sustained narrative prose fiction called 'A Working Class Tragedy' by H. J. Bramsbury. The novel ran from June 1888 to April 1889. Its episodic, picaresque form points to its being written expressly for serialisation, possibly from one week to the next. This means it was probably composed during the rising wave of new mass

militancy which led up to the Great Dock Strike in August, four months after the serial had finished.

It is the hunted-man-who-returns type of picaresque tale, set in the present. Frank Wilson, a skilled mechanic, is framed and hounded because of his militancy. He flees to London from the provincial town in the south of England which is his home. In London the terrible experience of fighting for work at the docks, plus conversations with a socialist workmate, make him a socialist. He returns to his native town, incognito, to be near the local squire's daughter with whom he has fallen in love after rescuing her from distress in London. His efforts to set up a co-operative farm on the estate under her auspices are wrecked when she marries the son of the factory owner who has persecuted the hero. The latter is killed when he throws himself in front of a poacher's bullet aimed at the husband of his beloved.

As a whole this novel gives a thin and rather summary impression. Too much happens too quickly. Almost the only place where it dwells on detail is in describing miserable living conditions. Here it can well stand comparison with good naturalism. Similarity to the naturalists is also there in the high number of inevitable tragic fates, ending in death. William Morris was loath to describe such conditions because he could not as an artist *see in its own terms* the hidden and thwarted vitality which was there behind the degradation. Socialist writers like Bramsbury had no such qualms, but in a sense they justify Morris in themselves failing to get beyond naturalism at such points.

Yet, in its basic tendency 'A Working Class Tragedy' is a militantly anti-naturalist work. Far from narrowing the social scene down to a mere slice of life, it drives towards a new quality of social totality. With one exception, every significant aspect of life and character is encompassed—a differentiated portrait gallery of working-class and ruling-class types, the rural and the urban scene, legal and economic persecution, the misery of work and of unemployment, etc. In this way the author sets out to complete the image of capitalist society as an interlocking *system* of oppression, an image started but left incomplete by the

best of the bourgeois realists. Bramsbury demonstrates clearly that oppression is total and systematic because it is *class* determined. His method is the extensive (picaresque) mode of Fielding rather than the intensive mode of Dickens. (In Tressell there will be a final synthesis of the extensive and intensive dimension.)

Anti-naturalist, too, is the way the 'jungle law' operating in the labour market of the docks is shown as something *unnatural* and not in terms of social Darwinism.

The handling of the hero also runs directly counter to naturalism. Far from being a passive victim of circumstance he develops, through contact with socialist theory combined with what he learns from experience, from a traditional Radical into a class-conscious socialist. So instead of knuckling under to the death-trap in true naturalist style, he comes to grasp the only way in which it can be smashed. In this general trend of his development Frank Wilson is the prototype of a whole line of proletarian heroes in twentieth-century socialist literature. (Tressell's hero is fully 'made' when the action begins.)

The hunted-man picaresque mode was one already favoured by the Chartists writing novels for press serialisation.[8] 'A Working Class Tragedy' is in the tradition. So much can be made to happen in this kind of narrative. Among other things this is an advantage when one lacks an aesthetically intensive relationship to one's basic material. It is one sign that Bramsbury, like almost all the writers closely associated with the socialist sects, was not yet sufficiently moved by that curiosity about the feel and texture of the life described, which is so vital to the realist.

The picaresque hero-on-the-run is an isolated, flitting type who has no time to really cog in to life. In choosing this set-up the author seems to have rather wrongheadedly limited his opportunities for social typicalisation. In fact it is possible that this choice of hero to a certain extent reflects the isolation and 'distance' of the socialists themselves. Be that as it may, one must avoid too prescriptive an approach here. Having isolated his hero in this way the author turns this to negative advantage. For instance: it is quite true, and a real impoverishment of the book, that the *collective*

personality of the organised working class, with all its rebelliousness and solidarity, remains unportrayed (the key missing component in Bramsbury's totality); it is equally true that the traditional-type plot of personal intrigue, which involves members of the opposing classes in personal relationships, creates an image quite out of keeping with the impersonal nature of class relations, especially in modern monopoly capitalism (contrast Tressell here). But the point is, Bramsbury shows that in this very isolation lies the real working-class tragedy: 'Frank cursed the mischance that had precluded him from taking an active part in the movement.'[9] It is this isolation that leads him into the fatal partnership with the land-owner in the attempt to set up a co-operative farm, through which he goes down to tragic defeat, his great potential squandered.

Implicit, then, is the recognition that the only way to avoid tragedy is to integrate oneself into the collective movement of the working class.[10] And so, despite the fact that there is precious little sign of the coming revolt in the sections of the book set in the docks, Bramsbury indicates that the way forward lies in that direction only.

Was Bramsbury's aesthetic relationship to concrete working-class reality still relatively thin and one-sided because he was writing just too soon to experience the uplift of the New Unionism? Hard as it was to recognise the potentially revolutionising dynamism of the rank and file before 1888-9, a few writers did penetrate to it, notably the socialist poet Francis Adams in some of his *Songs of the Army of the Night* (first published in 1887).[11] But Adams was a 'loner'. His ties with the London leadership of the Social Democratic Federation were very tenuous, as was their theoretical influence on him. The London-based SDF was hardly less sectarian and isolated than the Socialist League, despite their policy of getting involved in (preferably) local elections and their admittance of a possible role for the trade unions, if only they would stop confusing the issue by fighting for 'palliatives' and get down to their proper job of overthrowing capitalism.

Despite the real anger at the suffering of working folk felt

by most members, the élitist policy emanating from the leader Hyndman and his circle resulted in crippling ambiguities on all questions relating to the real life and struggle of the workers. Thus, there was a strong tendency to 'wash one's hands of them' as a set of incorrigible dolts who refused to see at once the patent logic of the socialist propaganda. *They* were the real enemy: 'It is not the active worker in the cause nor the tools at his disposal [which are to blame], it is, and can only be, the material upon which the propagandist has to work.'[12] It was a pity one could not abolish them and replace them with a more amenable version of the working class.

What was the answer? 'The worse the condition of the people, the quicker they must recognise the need for a change, and since the crisis must come, let us rejoice at anything which tends to hasten its coming'.[13] Absolute impoverishment of the masses, then, increasing misery, was seen as the only really dynamic element driving towards radical social transformation. This was the only interesting and encouraging aspect of working-class life. Strikes in defence of living standards were therefore rather frowned upon, although given half-hearted support once they had 'broken out'.

Clearly this set of attitudes was hardly conducive to an all-sided narrative exploration of working-class life! There was no point of departure here for meeting Engels's contemporary demand that *realism* must also show 'The rebellious reaction of the working class against the oppressive medium which surrounds them, their attempts—convulsive, half-conscious or conscious—at recovering their status as human beings'.[14] All things considered, the wonder is that Bramsbury's novel achieved as much breadth and life as it did.

How did the workers' determined attempt at 'recovering their status as human beings' in 1888-9 modify this position? As far as the London-based SDF nucleus was concerned, not at all. With the exception of Engels the above quotations are all from the nineties. When the strike wave failed to precipitate a revolutionary situation *Justice* lost

interest. By 1898 the *Social Democrat* was proclaiming 'The end of the New Unionism'.[15]

Did this mean that the new stage in the development of the revolutionary historical personality of the working class found no reflection in advances towards realism in socialist literature, especially in the analytical prose genres? Yes, there were signs of a new, more complex and more confident approach to contemporary working-class life. This expressed itself indirectly in the poetry and in the prose parables of the Leeds-Irishman Tom Maguire, who was in the thick of the union struggle. His pieces were mainly published in provincial papers in the north (*Labour Leader, Labour Champion, Factory Times*).[16] Much more directly it appears in the lively novels of *Lancashire* working-class life by Charles Allen Clarke. Here at last is that inexhaustible curiosity about the lives of ordinary working-class men *and* women that leads straight into Tressell. But both these writers were active in the industrial north, far away from Hyndman and his doctrinaire sectarians.

Justice and, from 1897, also the *Social Democrat* certainly went on publishing pieces of imaginative prose with relative regularity, though there was never again (in our period) such a sustained and fruitful attempt as 'A Working Class Tragedy'. The following remarks are based on a close study of two sample periods taken from *Justice* (1895 and 1896) and the *Social Democrat* (1897 and 1898).

As one might expect from the narrowness of their approach, all the imaginative prose pieces published in these central socialist press organs were very short in the wind. Attempts at series rather than serials were now the rule. There were series of an essayistic type, for instance by the above-quoted H. W. Hobart who wrote on various aspects and 'illusions' of daily working-class life and character such as 'Home', 'Work', 'Drink', 'Borrowing', 'Bank Holiday', 'Leisure', etc.[17] Hobart was only one of those who specialised in scoffing at what he calls the B.W. (British Workman). In tune with the 'increasing misery' theory John Tamlyn tells the latter 'You'll have to be lowered. You'll have to come down!!!'[18] One can under-

stand how an average worker might think *Justice* was more against him than the *Daily Telegraph*. Of course, there was something here that leads into Tressell's satire on the 'ragged trousered philanthropists', but in the Hobart school it is unrelieved by Tressell's ability to present the 'habits and customs' of the working class as something contradictory, containing creative potential in an estranged form. Hobart reaches the depths of crass insensitivity around May Day 1895 when he jeers at the workers' traditional bank holiday behaviour and leisure activities— 'Leisure! The average British workman is as big a fool with his leisure as with everything else he has.'[19] This was around the same time as Allen Clarke was revelling in the vitality and inventiveness of the northern workers in their traditional holiday and leisure pursuits.[20]

Another type of series run by *Justice* at this time was short stories appearing under a common general heading indicating the direction to be taken. A series of this kind, written by 'Devilshoof' (Harry Quelch?), was published in 1895 and 1896, under the ominous title 'Creatures of Circumstance'. Pieces here included were 'The Agitator', 'The Self-Made Man', 'Orphans', 'A Gaol Bird', 'A Blackleg', etc.[21] Most of the titles indicate in themselves the 'increasing misery' tenor of the stories. In 1895 another series of a broadly similar nature was started (they ran partially parallel) called 'Types of the Day'. These were the work of 'Eugh Jay'. Despite their general depressive tendency they exhibit a real curiosity about circumstantial detail.[22] There is a hint of Tressell here.

In the sample years studied 'Eugh Jay's' paired stories 'Joe Buggins Learns the Fife' and 'Buggins Senior Joins the SDF'[23] are far and away the best of all the short stories. They are set in Birmingham (almost without exception the other stories printed are set in London).

Buggins senior, a gruff old cove who hasn't paid too much attention to his wild and motherless 'lad' Joe, comes home to a fiendish din. It's the 'lad' and some cronies playing the fife of all things. What's got into them? Joe mollifies and moves his Old 'Un with a competent rendering of the *Marseillaise* (old B. has joined the Socialists a

short time before). The latter is less pleased however, when he hears the lads have joined the band of the Labour Church, a politically suspect organisation to the sectarian Buggins senior. An inconclusive argument ensues, but young Joe knows one thing—it'll be him and not his dad that'll be playing the fife in the united Labour Day procession.

The second story goes back to Pa Buggins's joining the SDF, and the roles are reversed. Having joined, he is so full of the milk of human kindness he decides to take an unprecedented step—he invites the incredulous Joe to a pie shop for a feed. Joe thinks he's sickening for something and asks what's up.

> 'I'm blowed if I know exactly, but I think it must be because I joined the Socialists to-day.
> 'I joined the Socialists! repeated Joe. 'You! Well, strike, that takes the cake. Here, old 'un, you'd better join the Socialists every day', etc.[24]

This is diametrically opposed both to the naturalist and the 'Hobart' spirit. There is complete aesthetic confidence in one's material here. We are shown ordinary working people, old and young, rising above their sordid environment in their daily lives and pastimes, capable of creative enjoyment. Because these stories achieve the status of art they are fine propaganda for joining the socialist movement. It is subtly put forward as a step which humanises, which brings out the best in you, which heightens your appreciation of the bodily and spiritual joys of living, which socialises you and brings people closer together.

There is a *realist's* interest here in the characters and their speech for their own sake. They are shown in their contradictoriness and development. At the same time the stories remain openly didactic. In fact drawing the moral becomes part of the fun. The author works confidently in the grand discursive manner of the all-knowing and manipulating creator. There is something of the Sterne of *Tristram Shandy* here in these modest stories (an 'Irish' element that did *not* find a place in Tressell). He enters into discussions of his

own story with an assumed critical reader—a disarming distancing effect enabling him to 'sell' his moral while appearing to make fun of moralisers in a story within the story. (The author has interrupted his narrative just before Joe gets his feed in order to draw a moral-political lesson.)

'Is Joe ever going to get any dinner' [impatient reader]
'Certainly.'
But your impatience puts me in mind of a story told by old Batty the circus man. Hush, no profanity. I must tell you this. He had commissioned a recognised writer to write him a Christmas pantomime. The author put his whole soul into it, the fairy queen gave vent to moral sentiments of an austere intensity that would have qualified her for holding a leading position in the maw worm brigade of the London County Council. The comic man dealt with all the topics of the day with a stupendous ignorance and self-satisfied assurance that marked him out as fit, if not to be Prime Minister, at any rate to hold a high position in the Cabinet.

The pretty conceits of the heroine would (in the opinion of the author) have done credit to the Poet Laureate . . .

The effect was hardly satisfactory. Old Batty's face wore a bored nonchalant look; the bored air becoming heavier and heavier as the reader proceeded. Until at last, in the midst of one of the fairy queen's highest flights of virtue, he broke coarsely in with, 'Cut all that cackle and come to the horses.' And thou, thou unregenerate savage, would have me in the words of thy villain's slang, 'To cut all moral reflection and come to the grubbing stakes.'[25]

This is sophisticated sword-play in many directions at once! But perhaps a qualifying note to the Buggins stories is necessary. The basic process around which they are built is the *one* act recognised by the SDF as a valid one for a working man—joining their organisation.

The *Social Democrat*, started in 1897, also featured short stories—one in each monthly issue in its first years. Initially about half of these were definitely written by Harry Quelch, long-time editor of *Justice*. They never bear his name, but one can establish authorship through comparison with texts collected in a volume published in tribute to Quelch (*Literary Remains*).[26] Quelch was a self-

educated worker who became one of the most respected leaders of the SDF. He was not without literary talent. He had a good ear for working-class speech and those pieces where he uses a character-narrator (such as 'your-average-working-man' or a policeman)[27] to distance, relativise or add conviction to the scenes and attitudes portrayed, still retain a certain vigour. However, on the whole, his plots, conflicts and approach are quite characteristic of the type of story favoured by the London-based socialist press of the nineties. (There is circumstantial evidence that several of the unsigned or pseudonymous pieces in both the *Social Democrat* and *Justice* which cannot be traced back to *Literary Remains* are also by Quelch.)

All the stories in the *Social Democrat* seem to be set in London, though the degree of specification is so slight that usually one simply assumes this. The atmosphere is dark and claustrophobic. As with the stories in *Justice* one gets the impression that the author is intent on discouraging the workers from taking militant action, showing it as leading only to disaster and tragedy. This is a period when, although the employers were on the counter-attack, the new spirit was spreading and beginning to affect even the traditional skilled sections. The 'new' men and women of the new movement badly needed all the support, constructive criticism and inspiration they could get. The stories in *Justice* and the *Social Democrat*, including Quelch's, failed to provide this new spirit with a means of realist self-contemplation.

There is no portrayal of mass initiatives in organisation (which could have provided the much-needed narrative backbone for sustained work). The only form in which the collective personality of the workers appears is as an object of mockery (*Justice* is the worse offender here). Instead we are given individual 'fates'—people driven into isolation, defeat and death by the machinations of individual capitalists (there is no sign of the growing dominance of 'faceless' monopoly). These capitalists are often old-type self-made men who were initially the friends and mates of the hounded worker. But the latter is equally thrust down by lack of solidarity and betrayal on the part of his workmates

who turn on him after the defeat of strikes, strikes which they themselves had 'irresponsibly' instigated, which they had then asked him to lead, and which he had reluctantly led, out of a sense of solidarity. Women often feature as the worst offenders against gratitude and class loyalty. In a story like 'Companions in Misfortune' (three parts)[28] the line is that if you 'give a woman her head' the forces of official society will gang up with her and her 'legal rights' (!) to wring the man dry. This is so near the misogynist outpourings of Belfort Bax which mar the contemporary columns of the *Social Democrat* that one suspects he may actually have written this story (it is unsigned). Rank-and-file militancy of the kind that started the new unionism is depicted as a source of *dis*integration, the implication being that the workers should keep their heads down in face of the employers' counter-offensive. What this boils down to is a vulgarised naturalism in which the worker and his family are totally 'determined' by their alienated environment. In the few cases where the worker triumphs over circumstances it is through his becoming, by dint of ability, a capitalist himself (a socialist capitalist of course),[29] or through the support of his employer.[30]

Certainly, in these propaganda stories there is also something important that runs sharply counter to contemporary bourgeois English naturalism of the Gissing type— the attempt to show that the root of the misery lies not in man's inherent nature but in the inhuman system of capitalist exploitation. But even here the real enemy, as indicated above, is not kept firmly in the sights, and social typicality is so crudely and narrowly understood that the writers are continuously obliged to fall back on melodramatic 'extreme situations'. All this means that the actual fund of plots and situations is so circumscribed that cumulatively one gets the impression of merely reading variations on three or four basic stories. This makes the process of trying to establish possible authorship on the basis of analogy extremely problematic.

They were ineffective mass propaganda. But were they really aimed at a broad working-class readership? Both journals give a markedly inward-turning impression as a

whole. The stories seem aimed mainly at bolstering up the Hyndman leadership's view of the working class and of 'significant' social tendencies. They are a mirror in which the SDF contemplates with satisfaction its own isolation from the wellsprings of proletarian life and culture, its frustration at the 'thanklessness' of the workers, the view that since the workers will not listen to them the only thing that will bring matters to a head is the 'iron law' of increasing misery. The typical story is, in this sense, a piece of self-justification, a comforter, a piece of wish-fulfilment. Increasing misery is the theme of themes.

Of course there is another side to all this. Many of these tales contain elements which later find a place in the realist synthesis of *The Ragged Trousered Philanthropists*—such as the satire on the delusions of the workers, the lonely, often thankless fight of the isolated socialist, the actual descending spiral of social misery under maturing imperialism, even the use of melodramatic episodes, etc. Tressell emerges partly out of this background.

Then again, there are also occasional stories—in which the working class does not figure—which are worth reading in themselves. There is, for instance, Dan Baxter's excellent little fable 'The New-Shilling' in *Justice*.[31] The story is related by a newly-minted shilling, aware of its own beauty, believing it will be used as a brooch, and flabbergasted to find itself used instead as a mere counter to keep the rich rich and the poor poor. Socialist writers tended to be good at parables and fables: these kept the unruly stuff of actual living at arm's length while profiting from the relatively whole and systematic grasp of the workings of capitalist production relations, which the socialists possessed.

On the whole, however, anyone seeking inspiration, critical analysis and sheer literary enjoyment in the columns of *Justice* or the *Social Democrat* would find it first and foremost in the precise analytical prose of Theodore Rothstein in his exemplary political and historical articles,[32] or in the Whitmanesque sweep and passion of R. B. Cunninghame Graham in one of his anti-colonial essays.[33]

As far as imaginative prose from within the SDF was concerned, the situation at the turn of the century looked anything but promising. Yet five years later, Robert Tressell, a member of the SDF in the south-east of England, began work on our great socialist classic. In my essay in the predecessor to the present volume I tried to suggest some of the strategic developments that made this 'jump' possible.[34]

NOTES

1. *Commonweal*, 16 June 1888.
2. *Commonweal*, 25 August 1888.
3. 'The Pilgrims of Hope', in *Three Works by William Morris* (London and Berlin, 1968), p.168.
4. *ibid.*, p.178.
5. E. P. Thompson, *William Morris. Romantic to Revolutionary* (London, 1955), p.777.
6. *Marx and Engels on Britain* (Moscow, 1953), p.32.
7. In the *Morning Star*, 19 September 1968.
8. See Thomas Martin Wheeler, 'Sunshine and Shadow', *Northern Star* (1849-1850), and Ernest Jones, 'De Brassier; the history of a democratic movement', *Notes to the People* (1851-2).
9. 'A Working Class Tragedy', *Justice*, 2 February 1889.
10. The same theme is central to James Plunkett's *Strumpet City* (London, 1969).
11. See for instance 'In Trafalgar Square' and 'England in Egypt'.
12. H. W. Hobart, *Justice*, 7 September 1895.
13. William Sowdon, *Justice*, 25 May 1895.
14. Engels in his letter to Margaret Harkness ('John Law'), beginning of April 1888, in Marx-Engels, *Selected Correspondence* (Moscow, n.d.), p.479.
15. *Social Democrat*, March 1898.
16. Some of the best of these are collected in *Tom Maguire: a Remembrance* (Manchester, 1895).
17. *Justice*, 2 February, 9 February, 2 March, 9 March, 20 April, and 18 May 1895.
18. J. Tamlyn, *Justice*, 23 March 1895.

19. *Justice*, 18 May 1895.
20. See especially his *Lancashire Lasses and Lads*, published in 1906 (Manchester) but actually written ten years earlier. On Clarke see also chapter 8 by Paul Salveson.
21. *Justice*, 20 July, 3 August, 31 August, 30 November 1895; 11 April 1896.
22. See for instance 'The commercial hack', *Justice*, 23 November 1895.
23. *Justice*, 8 June, 6 July and 13 July 1895.
24. *Justice*, 13 July 1895.
25. *ibid*.
26. *Literary Remains* (London, 1914).
27. See 'Only—he was a socialist' and 'The dynamiter', *Social Democrat*, February and April 1897 respectively.
28. *Social Democrat*, September, October, November 1898.
29. See 'The rent of ability', *Social Democrat*, August 1898.
30. See 'The dynamiter', *Social Democrat*, April 1897.
31. *Justice*, 23 March 1895.
32. See for instance his 'Why is socialism in England at a discount?', *Social Democrat*, March and April 1898.
33. See 'Bloody niggers', *Social Democrat*, April 1897.
34. Jack Mitchell, 'Early harvest: three anti-capitalist novels published in 1914', in *The Socialist Novel in Britain. Towards the Recovery of a Tradition*, ed H. Gustav Klaus (Brighton, 1982).

· 4 ·

The strike novel in the 1890s

H. GUSTAV KLAUS

The strike fiction of the 1840s and 1850s has, under the rubric of 'industrial' or 'social (-problem)' novel, often been studied. Even a number of lesser works from the middle of the century, such as Camilla Toulmin's 'A Story of the Factories' or Fanny Mayne's *Jane Rutherford*, have recently found a sympathetic historian.[1] Scant attention has been paid, by contrast, to the strike novels of the end of the nineteenth century, just as the social fiction of this period has been generally neglected, except for an interest in the slum or Cockney novelists.[2]

One reason for this critical silence, and a major difference to the situation in early and mid-Victorian times, is no doubt the abstention of the leading novelists of the day from an engagement with the industrial scene in general and the strike issue in particular. Gissing was exceptional in his consistent grappling, in the 1880s, with the condition of the working class, but his proletarians are for the most part the casual poor of an industrially backward London, and he abandoned the treatment of working-class themes at precisely the moment when these downtrodden masses showed signs of awakening. Had he continued his imaginative investigation of London labour, or looked at the quite different working class of his native Yorkshire, Luke Ackroyd in *Thyrza* (1887) and John Hewett in *The Nether World* (1889) might have taken a different line of development, or found more confident and dignified successors. But this remains a matter for speculation.

Beyond mere conjecture there is meanwhile evidence of

73

various fictional representations of the theme of industrial conflict, and these narratives can claim at least as much interest as the works of Harriet Martineau or Charlotte Tonna who pioneered the treatment of the strike in English fiction in the early 1830s.[3] For some of the novels discussed below adopt, almost for the first time, an unequivocally working-class perspective in that they are written from a standpoint which is neither above nor outside that of the strikers portrayed. Given the archaic, almost pre-industrial character of the London economy, it is no surprise that the more militant and, at the same time, more rewarding of these novels should come from the industrial north rather than the metropolis.

Yet London led the way in other respects. It was here that the 'new unionism' of the low-paid and unskilled workers, who had hitherto been considered as unorganisable, celebrated its first triumphs, and from here the tide swept over to other parts of the country rousing the entire labour movement. In quick succession the matchgirls, the gas-workers and the dockers of the East End won major concessions from their employers, either through strikes or through the threat of action, aided in each case by prominent members of the new socialist groupings, which had likewise first taken root in London.

No labour struggle of these turbulent years captured the public mind so absorbingly as the great Dock Strike in the summer of 1889. That the waterside workers, who were generally regarded as synonymous with the helpless and demoralised 'residuum', should have the courage to challenge, hold out against and finally claim a sweeping victory over their bosses—all in a spirit of perfect order and discipline—was greeted enthusiastically not only by the labour movement but by large sections of the middle classes. Naturally the bourgeoisie had different motives for seeing the strike as a positive achievement. As two contemporary commentators put it: 'The effect of the organisation of dock labour—as of all classes of labour—will be to squeeze out the residium. The loafer, the cadger, the failure in the industrial race . . . will be no gainers by the change.'[4] Trade-union organisation is valued here as a more effective

instrument for the exertion of social control.

This sigh of relief from the middle classes is also audible in a novel by Emma Leslie, *The Seed She Sowed: A Tale of the Great Dock Strike* (1891), particularly when contrasted with one of her earlier works. In *How the Strike Began: A Story for Girls* (1888) a young girl in the domestic service of a cotton master is shown to be unwittingly contributing to the outbreak of a strike through her loose tongue. If Leslie's primary aim is to warn her juvenile readers of becoming a 'village gossip', she also seizes the opportunity to instil in them a distrust of strikes as a suitable means of solving industrial conflict. For though she is careful to share out the blame for what appears less a clash of antagonistic interests than a breakdown of mutual understanding on both sides, it would be difficult for an unguarded reader to resist the conclusion that strike action can only bring mischief.

Like the earlier work, *The Seed She Sowed* is written with a specific audience and an overtly didactic purpose in mind. Again we find a young working-class girl at the centre of the story. But there are also important differences. First, the cast and topography are now entirely working-class, whereas the former tale shifted not only between the factory owner's mansion and the working-class home but correspondingly revealed a narrator anxious to balance her sympathies between Capital and Labour. Second, Leslie fully endorses the demand for 'the full round orb of the docker's tanner',[5] whereas in *How the Strike Began* she expected the dye-factory workers to share their employer's losses in times of bad trade by consenting to wage reductions.

Three socially graded working-class families are depicted in *The Seed She Sowed*. Among these the Chaplins represent the once respectable section of the proletariat, which has become, under the conditions prevailing on the waterfront, increasingly derelict and depressed. Mr Chaplin is of visibly poor constitution and hence seldom picked out any more for a job. His wife, therefore, has to make up for the irregular income of the main breadwinner by taking on all kinds of domestic work. The fate of the

Chaplins illustrates the plight of the London dockers. In 1889 one of them was quoted as saying: 'Only a dock rat, that's what I've been called ever since I lost my place, and became a docker.'[6] Chaplin's words reiterate this loss of self-respect: 'Treat a man like a dog and you'll only get dog's work out of him.'[7] His growing bitterness in face of the casual nature of the work, the hideous system of the 'call-on', the short duration of an engagement and the starvation pay are all related with considerable sympathy. Were it not for the good influence of Winnie, their alert and unselfish daughter, the family would be doomed.

A step below the Chaplins, and fast approaching the status of *lumpenproletariat*, are Mr Brown and his daughter Annie: the father given to drink and generally of a vulgar and disorderly character; the girl good-natured but hot-tempered. On one occasion, when refused a respite from the demands for the rent, she flings a glass of beer at the landlord, for which she is promptly arrested and imprisoned.

At the upper end of the social scale we have the landlord's family. Rutter, once an ordinary docker himself, has, since his appointment as a foreman and subsequent rise to wealth, become the most hated man in the neighbourhood because of his intransigence over the rent.

Winnie's exemplary deed consists in presenting Annie, after the latter's release from prison, with a chance to start a new life in the country. This act soon bears fruit: Annie finds work in a rural pickle factory; and the prospect opening up to his daughter even reforms Brown, who now turns into a model strike leader, sober, disciplined and moderate. To crown it all, Annie repays the Chaplins by informing them of a vacant carpenter's post in her factory so that the worn-out docker can return to his former trade.

This conclusion echoes the contemporary discussions about the resettlement of the urban poor in rural areas. Though the docker's 'tanner' had been won, Leslie sees no future for the demoralised underemployed in the city. As a general remedy for chronic poverty, her proposal is about as helpful as the emigration schemes to the colonies earlier in the century—indeed there was talk of 'labour colonies' in

Britain in the 1880s.[8] But it provides Leslie with a fictional resolution, as emigration had furnished her mid-century predecessors with an escape route for their embattled characters.[9] Both devices amount to an implicit critique, not fully acknowledged in its consequences, of the inadequacies of the existing social order.

Leslie's immediate concern was, of course, to convey her simple-hearted philosophy that a beneficent attitude produces the most fruitful results. She demonstrates this on a personal level and expresses the hope that somehow the principle will also work in the social and economic sphere. But the trouble is that the two planes of action remain unconnected. The docks never enter her picture directly, and the whole Winnie–Annie plot with its happy end for the Chaplins is in fact conceivable independently of the strike issue. In other words, the Dock Strike only provides the background for the story, but is not its central theme.

One remarkable aspect of *The Seed She Sowed* is the lack of expiation for the death of Rutter, who has been found drowned in the dock. Though it is not stated explicitly that he met a violent death, there are strong hints of such a possibility. The mid-century novelists would not have missed the chance to track down the culprit and bring him to repent, while laying the blame at the door of the 'combinations' or outside agitators. It speaks volumes for the author's sympathetic treatment of the strikers that she does not follow this track. She still preaches the familiar virtues of moderation, endurance and self-denial, but instead of disarming and discrediting the strikers they are used to reassure and morally strengthen their wives and daughters:

> In this way women like Mrs. Chaplin and weak girls like Winnie saved London from riot and bloodshed, and gained for themselves a name of imperishable honour, setting the whole world an example of patient endurance and the divine might of doing the duty that lay nearest to them.[10]

It is a vast claim but entirely consistent with the domestic

focus of the tale.

Leslie's change of mind in such a short span of time is only explicable against the background of the upsurge of the 'new unionism' and its initially favourable reception by a significant part of middle-class opinion. Our next novel registers, among other things, the particular impact made on this public by Cardinal Manning's decisive intervention in the Dock Strike.

William Oakhurst's *The Universal Strike of 1899* (1891) draws its inspiration not only from the most dramatic labour conflict of the period, but also from the founding of the Second International in 1889. It considers the effects of a strike launched on a worldwide scale by the 'International Working Men's Society'.[11] Projected into the near future, it combines the narrative situation of a Utopia with the descriptive style of a reportage, but does not finally commit itself to either of these forms.

An intrusive narrator, who purports to be writing in 1909, is looking back at the stupendous seven days that shook the world in 1899. What fascinates and disturbs him (and the author alike) is the potential power wielded by the Paris-based 'Board' of the International. After secret deliberations this body issues the call for a simultaneous strike of the workers of all industrialised nations. The action immediately succeeds in paralysing Britain's economy, while provoking alarm and near-panic accompanied by occasional outbreaks of violence among the population. The anarchy prevailing on the first day is, however, checked by the establishment of a force of volunteers, recruited mainly from the middle class, who patrol the Clubland of the metropolis. These 'lovers of order' recall the 'Friends of Order' in William Morris's general strike and civil war chapter from *News from Nowhere*, of which there is more than one echo in *The Universal Strike of 1899*, and foreshadow the real historical Organisation for the Maintenance of Supplies in the General Strike of 1926. Incoming reports from Germany, France and Italy suggest similar, if more violent confrontations between the two sides; Russia is cut off.

The scenes of lawlessness and mob violence described here no longer reflect, of course, the atmosphere of the Dock Strike but reenact the traumatic experience of propertied London during the Trafalgar Square Riot of February 1886:

> London was an abomination of desolation, and there I was in the midst of it, cut off from all I cared about—without one atom of feeling in common with those around me, the noise of whose howling was occasionally varied by that of broken glass and the laughter that followed.[12]

That the disorderly elements 'around me', who have invaded the West End, include the strikers as well as 'the dregs of crime' corresponds to the undifferentiated view of the London proletariat prevalent among middle-class observers in the mid-1880s. In these years, as Gareth Stedman Jones has noted, 'propertied London came to regard the residuum as virtually co-extensive with the workforce in casualised industries, and the East End as an almost unalloyed centre of degeneration'.[13] Only as a result of the orderly and peaceful spectacle provided by the daily processions of the striking dockers in the City of London did more perceptive observers draw a line between the respectable working class and the casual poor.

Oakhurst, who writes in the aftermath of the strike, generally adheres to the latter view; the threat to civilisation has shifted in his novel, as will be seen, from the barbarians of the East End to a different degenerate race. But when the author relives the horror of real or imagined exposure to the 'scum' his tone becomes shrill with alarm and vindictiveness. His narrator cannot conceal the 'fiendish delight' he felt after he 'knocked one [aggressor] over at once with my stick and gave the other a merciless thrashing with my fists'.[14] The vicious sadism articulated in such sentences is the complement of the deep-seated fears noted above.

The 'universal' strike then takes an unexpected turn as hungry and freezing crowds implore their leaders to call it off. But for Richard King, the 'General Secretary of the

British Section of the International Working Men's
Society', it is a matter of honour to stick to the decision of
the Central 'Board'. Hurrying from one meeting to another,
exhorting the men to stay firm, he eventually suffers a
breakdown, and his death from exhaustion is accelerated
by a noble refusal to eat more than the starving rank and
file. Dying he quotes Browning's 'Pisgah-Sights':

> Over the ball of it,
>   Peering and prying,
> How I see all of it,
>   Life there outlying!
>
> Roughness and smoothness,
>   Shine and defilement,
> Grace and uncouthness:
>   One reconcilement—[15]

The idealised portrait of the working-class leader is
another instance of the altered approach of middle-class
novelists at the end of the century to the theme of industrial
conflict. Once a ruthless demagogue or impostor, he now
appears as the embodiment of integrity and self-abne-
gation. Similarly with the unions: if there is still something
dangerous about them, it is their unfortunate international
links, which are blamed for the unnecessary prolongation
of the strike. What is still upheld, however, as the
Browning quotation demonstrates, is the ideal of class
reconciliation. And it remains to a clergyman, the 'Canon
of St. Paul's Cathedral', to end the deadlock and bring
about a peaceful settlement of the dispute in a truly
Christian spirit.

The concern for national security is given added weight
in a chapter which has no real bearing on the course of the
strike but is clearly added as a warning. The day after the
return to work the Russian fleet is suddenly sighted in the
mouth of the Thames. The Tsar, it emerges, having quickly
dealt with his subservient subjects, is now trying to profit
from the situation. Recognising, however, a nation no
longer defenceless, the warships swiftly clap on all sail and
retreat. Had the strike entered its second week, as origi-

nally planned, 'the calamity that might have befallen Europe—and the world—surpasses imagination'.[16] This clever construction not only validates the Canon's intervention but at the same time serves to throw doubt on one of the foremost principles of the International, namely that 'Men must regard themselves as workers first, as Frenchman, Germans, Italians, English, after.'[17]

So obsessed is Oakhurst with his fears of the International that he overlooks, or chooses to ignore, the wild improbability at the heart of his narrative: how can one plan a strike of this dimension in secrecy and yet expect millions across the world to follow it? But the conspiratorial tactics imputed to the International are very much part of the author's alarmist attitude.

To the very end his view of the labour movement remains deeply ambivalent. On the one hand, he insists that a general strike is a terrible expedient which had better be buried for ever. On the other hand, 'I am inclined to think that life has been made appreciably easier by that awful week of 1899.'[18] Among the remarkable results of the strike he lists: a decline of abject poverty, a check to millionaires and monopolies, greatly improved industrial relations (watched over by arbitration boards with an equal representation of capital and labour) and, on the moral side, a lesson of mutual forbearance.

The two works discussed so far, though obviously inspired by the trade-union explosion of the late 1880s are not based on first-hand experience of an actual strike. For a much more faithful representation of an industrial conflict we have to wait until the appearance of Allen Clarke's *The Knobstick: A Story of Love and Labour* (1893). The title of this work immediately conveys two of its essential characteristics: a rootedness in a regional class culture, and a thoroughgoing identification with the labour movement. 'Knobstick' was a Lancashire term for what was elsewhere called a blackleg. Only someone writing from within the community portrayed in this novel could have used such a term as a matter of course. Charles Allen Clarke (1863-1935) was born into a large family of cotton-mill workers, and

though he himself left the mill at the age of fourteen to become first a pupil teacher, then a journalist, editor and writer, he never lost touch with his background.[19]

The distinguishing mark of Clarke's style is his effective use of local traditions and habits, and an effortless handling of the Lancashire dialect, often coupled with a down-to-earth and at times subversive brand of humour. Take this dialogue from the chapter 'A Lancashire Funeral':

'It's a bloomin cowd day', said the driver of the hearse, blowing his hands and holding them close to his rough red nose.
'It's a sneezer', returned the driver of the nearest mourning coach, 'it's nearly as cowd as a hepitaph. Is this affair a teetotal funeral?'
'I hopes not', said the hearse man, 'for if it is we'st be frozzen into coffins.'
'Ay', rejoined the other, 'it's time enoof to be teetotal when yo're a corpse. But for 't forestall bein a corpse afore yore time, keep takkin summit warm. Warmth is life, and cowd is deeth. I wish they'd bring summat t' sup—a nice hot glass of whiskey.'
'Ay, it's time they were shapin. I feel as if I'd geet a hiceberg on my stomach, and a snow-storm dancin in my bowels.'[20]

Earthly wisdom also hampers the progress of the Methodist preacher Twillman. When, after ranting in one of the foulest districts in the town and despairing at the scant response, he closes a fervent tirade with the words 'Oh, where will you spend eternity, my friends?', a half-drunken voice answers him: 'We corn't spend it in a worse place than this' (p.91).

Add the 'Lancashire Wedding' to the 'Lancashire Funeral', the figure of the tramp to that of the street preacher, the early morning round of the 'knocker-up' to the presence of the Irish, the dire poverty in the slums to the Whitsun seaside excursion, and a mosaic of Lancashire working-class life in the late nineteenth century takes shape, peopled not by downtrodden masses but by a living and multi-faceted community. To the spinners and engineers, who were among Clarke's first readers, these were all familiar sights and occurrences. But in presenting these

things in a new light or humorous guise, Clarke not only retained the interest of his readers but offered them fresh insights into their lives. This was possible because he 'never pandered to some lowest common denominator or insulted people's intelligence'.[21]

A case in point is his demonstration of how the strikers are doubly tricked by the Municipality of Spindleton. The damage caused during an anti-blackleg riot has to be paid

> 'out of the rates, so I hear,' said Belton, 'and that's what galls the men. They've to pay for the keep of these extra police and soldiers, and pay for the damage done to property out of their own pockets. That is wormwood to them; to have police and soldiers brought here to keep them down and protect their foes, the knobsticks, and then pay for it all out of their own pockets; that's where the rub comes in' (p.172)

In essence this argument prefigures the mordant attack on the Forty Thieves of the Mugsborough Council in *The Ragged Trousered Philanthropists*. But Clarke anticipates Tressell, with whom he shares his Irish origins, in more ways than one. Other common features include the satirical naming of the capitalists, the irony heaped on the representative of organised religion and the exemption of the socialist from idiomatic speech. Belton is, of course, a Londoner, but he does not speak Cockney either. Rather, as in a host of working-class novels to follow, his greater (self-) erudition and political awareness are seen to necessitate the use of Standard English as well as a solemn outlook. Both traits mark him off from Banks, the local trade-union leader.

As engineers, Belton and Banks are involved in their union's effort to redress a wage cut imposed during a trade depression. The resulting strike is the culminating point of the novel, which now gains substance from lively scenes of picket lines, demonstrations, assaults on blacklegs, clashes with police and the perversion of the law in the hands of the town magistrates. A real achievement is the centrally placed chapter 'The Great Strike Riot', which relates the 'welcome' reserved by the population for the knobsticks.

Though Clarke occasionally still uses the word 'mob' here, he effectively breaks with the abstract notion of a soulless rabble driven by criminal instincts, in depicting a body of real men, women and children engaged in a desperate common effort, to hold up the blackleg convoy. Throughout the assault on the bus and the counter-attack of the police, the adopted point of view is that of the pickets and their supporters.

An incident during the savage police charge, in which a child receives a fatal truncheon blow on the forehead, is also structurally important in that it links up with an earlier scene. When Belton had first arrived in Spindleton as a destitute tramp with a motherless child on his arms, he had been helped and cheered up on the wayside by a group of labourers. Now the roles are reversed: Belton carries the dying child into the wretched hovel of the Irish labourer, the father having been arrested after dragging the bludgeoning policeman off his horse. In this and other ways, as Mary Ashraf has shown, the idea of practical working-class solidarity is woven into the text.[22]

A weakness in the treatment of the strike, however, is the failure to lay bare its origins and illuminate the motivations of the men behind it. As it is, the strike comes almost out of the blue, casually introduced through a remark of Banks's at home: 'We're goin to strike, Jane' (p.71). When the idea is first mooted, Belton and Banks appear even set against it, though the reasons for their caution are not clear either. Nor is the progress or outcome of the strike, which is shown to have lasted for several months, set forth in any detail.

Another problem is the author's growing preoccupation with the intricacies of the plot, so that what had started as a social drama eventually gravitates towards melodrama and romance (as the subtitle suggests). Clarke had obviously intended to connect the two strands through the figure of the knobstick, Rugden, who is at the same time the seducer of Belton's wife. But the two interlocking love triangles command too much attention in themselves, and the only interesting side-aspect here is that the author associates depravity with brutal male chauvinism. This is true not

only of a miscreant such as Rugden but also of his fellow knobsticks, who, when hearing the story of how he treated Belton's wife, 'burst into loud laughter. Not one touch of sympathy for the woman. They regarded the whole tragedy as a screaming farce' (p.187).

The thoroughly negative portrayal of the strike-breakers is no doubt a reflection of the bitterness and anger aroused by their recruitment *en masse* from outside the town. But Clarke takes care to let his two most advanced-thinking characters assume a more understanding position: 'They may have left starvin wives and childer awhum, an may be decent enough, but poverty makes dastards of many good souls', remarks Banks. And Belton adds: 'As long as I shall live I shall always be on the side of the unfortunate, be they knobsticks or strikers. Both are to be pitied, and it's our accursed social system that's at the bottom of all the mischief, and that sets man against man' (pp.151-2).

Only an active Socialist could tackle this difficult subject so confidently and intelligently in the nineties, avoiding both the hysterical fear of 'mob' violence still rampant in *The Universal Strike of 1899* and the pitfalls of a fatalistic naturalism in the depiction of a poverty-stricken community. Clarke had become a member of the SDF in 1887, during the strike in his home town of Bolton that provided him with the material for *The Knobstick*. Probably still in the year of the book's publication he joined the newly-founded ILP, and in 1900 the two parties were to nominate him as joint candidate for the general election.

On the other hand, Clarke's socialism did not prevent him from occasionally wading deep into sentimentality and mysticism. The love-scenes of *The Knobstick* are difficult to stomach today. And an even greater impediment to a modern reception of the novel are the mystical bonds, based on a belief in spiritualism, that he establishes towards the end between some of the characters. His great *forte* remained the humorous sketch, and it is no coincidence that he is better remembered for the countless dialect pieces that he published under the pseudonym of Teddy Ashton. Yet when all is said and done *The Knobstick* remains a turning point in the history of English strike

fiction, and a contribution to working-class and socialist literature that no critical reassessment of the period can afford to overlook.

Like Clarke, W. E. Tirebuck (1854-1900) was attracted by the ethical socialism of the early ILP. He was, in fact, one of the contributors to the symposium *The New Party*, published in 1894 with essays by Robert Blatchford, Keir Hardie, Grant Allen and others. In his statement, 'On the verge of change', Tirebuck asserts the dignity and social value of work:

> Life depends upon Labour. That law alone elevates all necessary labour, however rough, however hard, above degradation. If it is no degradation to eat bread, it is no degradation to prepare the ground, and sow the seed, and reap the harvest . . . If it is no degradation to walk through clean streets, it is no degradation to brush them.[23]

From an emphasis on the primal necessity of labour Tirebuck goes on to proclaim the 'irrevocable inter-dependence of one kind of labour upon another'. By implication there is then no basic difference of value between manual and mental work. None of these propositions is exactly new, but in the face of constant denials of them, both theoretically and practically, Tirebuck felt that these simple truths needed hammering home through a joint effort of 'the priest, the politician, the poet, the scientist, and the artist'.[24]

Miss Grace of All Souls' (1895) is the poet's contribution to this end. It is on the basis of love and a mutual recognition of the principle that 'all necessary labour is co-equal'[25] that Grace Waide, a vicar's daughter, and Sam Ockleshaw, a miners' leader, enter a marriage of perfect understanding at the end of the novel. And their relationship is unlikely to end in the deadlock reached by the Morels in Lawrence's *Sons and Lovers*. Grace has proved during the 'Coal War' that she has freed herself from the shackles of a bourgeois upbringing. She has taken an unequivocal stand on the miners' side, alleviating their hardship wherever she could

and pleading their case before her unimpressed father and the mine-owners themselves, only to meet flat refusal and mild ridicule. 'Sentiment isn't business' (p.232), old Mr Brookster, the local coal magnate, reminds her as he gloats over the prospect of outwitting his competitors by means of this, to him not entirely unwelcome, industrial conflict. His son Harry, an MP, meanwhile exhibits an even uglier face of capitalism when told of some disturbances in the neighbourhood: 'I'm not afraid of the beastly fellows. By Jove, but they shall suffer for this. They'll be taught to— howl. They mean riots, do they? Dawbairn can soon get a few redcoats down; that will gallop them in their senses' (p.226).

In turning a cold shoulder to the approaches of Harry Brookster and marrying beneath her station, Grace wins the respect of the working people and baffles her own class. Not even the one other middle-class person who has sympathised with the miners can make sense of this choice. Mr Rew, her father's successor in the vicarage of All Souls, exemplifies the gap between compassionate feeling and practised social equality that Grace has closed. More doubts are cast on the future role of the newly appointed vicar when one bears in mind that in his early days Grace's father, the Reverend Egerton Waide, had also been 'on the side of the workers, the doers, the poor, the oppressed' (p.56), before he degenerated into a hypocrite and lackey of the ruling class, publicly preaching moderation to the miners, while inwardly fearing for his coal shares.

The picture of the industrial bourgeoisie and its auxiliary forces—a distorting press, a corrupt church, an oppressive military—is essential to Tirebuck's argument accounting as it does for Grace's final desertion of her class. But the chief interest of the novel lies in its contrasting re-creation of a mining community in time of strife.

It is with a view of a miner's home that *Miss Grace* opens (and closes). We see the inmates of the cottage, a three-generation family of miners, but we perceive them immediately as part of their neighbourhood as we catch a glimpse of Brookster's Yard, the miners' row, through the open cottage door. And through the window, illuminated

only for the fragment of a second by a flash of lightning, we see something else: the pit where Sam Ockleshaw is on night shift; and, in another instant, Beckerton Old Hall, the Brooksters' Estate. From the outset we are thus made aware of the two dominating influences in the life of a mining community, stretching right to the collier's hearth: the relations of ownership and dependency, further under-lined by the name of the miners' row and some scathing remarks of Ned Ockleshaw about the man who 'what they call "owns" coal' (p.3); and the pit itself with its harsh and dangerous work, epitomised in the final scene of the first chapter when the injured Sam is carried home under the eyes of the neighbours.

Tirebuck's presentation of the mining village combines typicality with graphic detail. 'Beckerton was another version of Barnsley; Barnsley another version of St. Helen's and Wigan. St. Helen's and Wigan had counterparts in the Wrexhams and Molds of North Wales; and North Wales had fighting counterparts in Gloucester and Warwick' (p.195). All these colliery districts belong to the Miners' Federation and are thus hit by the sixteen-week lock-out of 1893, which originated in the mine-owners' attempt to reduce the rates of wages by 25 per cent. Beckerton could be anywhere, but through the use of a specific dialect and the incorporation into the plot of the Featherstone incident, in which troops opened fire on the strikers, it is clearly located in Yorkshire.

The characterisation of the miners displays a similar combination of the representative and the individualised. For Grandfather Dan Ockleshaw, who has lived a quiet life governed by religious feelings and modest wishes, the present grim determination of the miners not to give in to the coal-owners' demand (later reduced in reality, though not in the novel, to 15 per cent) is presumptuous. 'There'll be mesters for men an' minds for muscles till doomsday!' (p.154) is his firm belief. Dan's attitude is contrasted with the militant spirit of his son Ned, whose fits of rage against ignominious social inequalities constantly lead him into trouble and eventually cost him his life. The limitations of this unerring, but also unreflecting class consciousness are

indicated by Ned's habit of seeing the whole conflict in personal terms, as a private feud between a clearly identifiable capitalist (Brookster) and an equally tangible group of workmen like himself. Finally, there is the youngest Ockleshaw, Sam, a working-class intellectual (whose early diet has included Cobbett's *Grammar*) with a sensitive nature and unfailing patience, fully dedicated to the cause of the miners and yet endowed, like Belton in *The Knobstick*, with a dim vision of socialism beyond the immediate struggle:

> 'I'm not after money *as* money, or we would be no better than those who in my opinion sin agen us, for it; but money means food, furniture, clothes; and these mean comfort; and comfort means better conditions of body and mind; and body and mind means morals. I've thought, and thought, and *thought*— and always come back to that.'   (p.165)

The attitudes of these three men can be taken to represent the historical march of the miners from subordination via militancy to socialism, but they also point to the divisions still existing within the contemporary mining population, temporarily forged together in a struggle for a great principle, a guaranteed living wage irrespective of profits.

These differences of outlook notwithstanding, we find, again as in Clarke,[26] several examples of unceremonious neighbourly help and active solidarity, suggestive of widely shared class values: when a miner is killed in a flooded pit and his wife as a consequence suffers a breakdown, the Ockleshaws look after their four children; when food parcels arrive in Brookster's Yard, Ned wastes no time in sharing his ration with his famished fellow-colliers. Traces of this class solidarity even survive in ex-miners such as Dick Ockleshaw, Sam's brother, now a soldier in the troops to be deployed in the coalfields, who prefers to go into hiding and to serve a month's hard labour for it rather than turn 'agen my owd mates' (p.284).[27]

Standing midway between Zola's *Germinal* (1885) and Lawrence's earliest short stories on mining life (1911), *Miss Grace* contains the first closely observed and sympathetic

view of a mining community in English fiction.²⁸ And this community, active and resourceful, suffering and yet stubbornly resisting, is the real protagonist of the novel, its collective hero. Not only the immorality of her own class but also the living humanity embodied by this community are at the root of Grace's conversion to the working-class cause.

One central aspect of the life of a mining community is not confronted squarely by Tirebuck: the work process underground. That this omission does not result from an unconscious neglect of the point of production is obvious from the author's programmatic statement quoted above, from the hazardous presence of the mine in the background of the story, and from a passage which shows the pit-bank girls at work. But Tirebuck had no first-hand knowledge of the various stages of coal-getting and made no pretence of covering up this lacuna.

For Zola, the minutely detailed descriptions of the pit, which appears at the same time as a voracious monster (le 'Voreux'), of the physical exertion involved in extracting and transporting the coal below ground, and of the human relations bred in this 'bestial' atmosphere, formed a major part of his project. In Tirebuck, or Lawrence, this 'underworld', though not its various consequences, is simply absent.²⁹

An account of the working conditions underground can, however, be found in another novel dealing with the lockout of 1893—Alfred H. Fletcher's *Lost in the Mine. A Tale of the Great Coal Strike* (1895). The author uses one of the two devices that will reappear time and again in twentieth-century mining fiction: the initiation into work of an outsider, a non-miner (as in Zola), through whose unaccustomed eyes we penetrate the obscurity of the mine:³⁰

Lights twinkled in every direction. Corves full of various kinds of coal came swinging along tiny sets of rails to the cage, where they were rapidly lifted aloft. There was a whizzing sensation in the air, and a giddiness in his brain as he stood uneasily upon his legs . . . The gloom was intense, and Jack

had great difficulty in following his guide. The ground seemed to oscillate under his feet, and to be as unstable as the surface of the sea during a stiff breeze. His confusion was 'worse confounded' because of the strangeness of his surroundings and the difficulty he experienced with his organs of vision.[31]

There can be little doubt that Fletcher, who appears to have been a Sheffield journalist, had observed pit-work and pit-villages from close quarters. His description of Mud-town, though it bears some fleeting resemblances to Dickens's uniform view of an industrial agglomeration in *Hard Times*, emphatically points to the 'many differences' among the miners and their families 'on close acquaintance' (p.52).

But despite close observation the narration always retains a sense of distance from its subject. It is not only that the (middle-class) reader is addressed in contorted, if well-meant explanations of the hazards of pit work. The external representation of the world of the miners is also strengthened through the weaving of the social and political content of the story into a curious tapestry of popular fictional forms ranging from mystery and melodrama to romance. Jack Harland, the new collier, is none other than the actual mine-owner, a gentleman compelled to take cover because he is unjustly suspected of having assassinated his father—an act in reality perpetrated by the mine-manager, who is also a Harland. With such a long-winded opening in the higher sphere of the gentry, it takes the author some sixty pages to arrive at the aforementioned description of the colliery town, and to descend at last into the depths of the mine.

In relating the origins and early progress of the strike Fletcher assumes at first a strictly neutral tone. He says of both sides in the industrial arena that 'the weapons with which they decided to fight were eminently fair and eminently British' (p.89). But then he introduces a presumably un-British element, a subversive organisation deceptively christened The Guild of Progress. Commanded by the immensely talented and idealistic, but also hopelessly fanatical, even 'Satanic', Dan Darrell, another gentleman-

turned-miner in search of a new identity (after the killing of his wife's lover), the Guild's ultimate aim is the overthrow of the existing social order. In one of several impassioned speeches Darrell addresses his followers thus:

> 'Awaken from your lethargy, men of Yorkshire! You are strong in number, and think that because of this your growl will suffice to subdue your tyrants instead of your deadly bite. Passive resistance leads to enslavement. 'Tis active rebellion, the outcome of indignation, which points the way to freedom . . .
>
> You may have to endure hardship, bodily pain, imprisonment, but fight on. Stab the coward Capital with the sword of the oppressed, and hew your way to victory over the corpse of a dishonoured past.'   (p.167)

If there ever was a sizeable body of revolutionaries at work attempting to turn the lock-out into a full-scale confrontation with state power,[32] it is doubtful that they would have been spurred on, in 1893, by this kind of Shelleyan rhetoric. But verisimilitude is not one of Fletcher's concerns. Aesthetic and structural considerations remain firmly subordinated in his novel to a 'demonstration' that whatever scenes of violence there were during the stoppage were the deeds of an initially marginal, but, as the situation deteriorated, increasingly dangerous band of political desperadoes. Hence the Guild is even blamed for having provoked the real historical Featherstone incident in which two men were killed and sixteen wounded when troops opened fire—an interpretation not only at odds with the true course of events,[33] but also diametrically opposed to Tirebuck's treatment of them.

Quite plainly then, where Clarke and Tirebuck had depicted a community in united action against employers, blacklegs and troops, Fletcher separates out the more intransigent of the strikers. He whitewashes the main body of the miners and their union only to discredit the pursuit of more far-reaching goals. There is, indeed, a systematic confusion of working-class militancy with sabotage, of the struggle for a political takeover with the 'madness for power' (p.220).[34] On a political level, this strategy con-

tinues the assessment made of the Dock Strike by the social explorers; only instead of 'the loafer, the cadger, the failure in the industrial race',[35] whom they were anxious to see squeezed out, it is now the 'extremist' (p.219), the 'Anarchist' (p.220), the 'agitator' (p.232), whose hold on the working class must be checked and eliminated.

Consequently, in *Lost in the Mine* the insurrectionary force has to be wiped out before 'the country breathed again more freely' (p.233). Darrell is killed by a bullet arriving mysteriously out of the dark, and in another echo of *Hard Times*, he is described as saying, as he dies: 'This is all—a mistake. But it is my Destiny!' (p.232), his last wish being that he be buried in a disused mine shaft. The novel's title can thus be taken to refer, if unintentionally, not only to the younger Harland's temporary submergence among the miners, but also to the disappearance from the industrial battlefield of the Anarchist.

Once this obstacle to an undivided sympathy for the miner's cause has been removed, Fletcher can record with deeply-felt compassion the distress of the starving, turnip-fed, typhoid-ridden mining families, whose morale nevertheless remains unbroken. Of course, the principal pole of identification for the reader remains the incognito figure of Jack Harland, whose constitution breaks first under the strain of deprivation and suffering. Yet in his unflagging support for the strike Jack is no exception to the rest of the miners. As one determined collier says: 'Aw doan't deny', . . . 'that sum on us will bite t'dust and goa under, but t'great army o' t' workmen will march on to victory' (p.242). As if he felt he had gone too far in his sympathetic treatment of the main body of the strikers, and in singling out two members of the upper middle class as villains of the story, Fletcher apologised, in his Preface, for the negative portrayal of the mine-manager, while predictably making no such amends for the blackening of the representative of the Guild of Progress.[36]

This survey of strike fiction during the first half of the 1890s has charted the differing responses of middle-class and working-class novelists to the union upsurge of the late

1880s[37] and the counter-offensive led by the employers around 1893. Perhaps the most significant aspect of the middle-class response is not—despite continued fears— the acceptance of trade unions and the strike weapon, or the shift from denunciation to idealisation in the portrayal of the (moderate) working-class leader, but the unwilling- ness of the major practitioners of the novel to engage with industrial confict at all. Class collision was, if at all, located elsewhere. When contrasted with the fictional interven- tions of Dickens, Gaskell and Eliot earlier in the century, this abstention appears as one more symptom of the novel's often-observed loss of public centrality towards the close of the century. In this respect Leslie, Oakhurst and Fletcher clearly fought a rearguard battle. And as often happens with insignificant descendants, their works, instead of inspiring others, quickly passed into oblivion, and are unlikely ever to be read again. This is not the case with Clarke and Tirebuck, whose novels were reprinted during the period covered by this book,[38] and who found a number of immediate followers. Chief amongst these are the writers of the 'Lancashire school', Arthur Laycock and Fred Plant, but also Ethel Carnie, who was not part of Allen Clarke's circle.[39]

Thus it is in the 1890s that the treatment of the strike is finally wrenched from the hands of middle-class novelists, whose domain it had been since early Victorian times, and given a distinct socialist slant. Strikes and lock-outs, while remaining 'exceptional moments' of working-class life, would henceforth be depicted not only as occasions of distress and tragedy (and no longer as acts of destruction and self-destruction), but also as ways of crystallising class consciousness and testing the values of humanity and soli- darity, and thereby furthering the working-class cause. As such the strike issue has entered twentieth-century socialist fiction as a recurring theme and a central concern.

NOTES

1. Jospeh Kestner, *Protest and Reform. The British Social Narrative by Women, 1827-1867* (London, 1985), pp.114-16, 177-82. For a more sceptical view of Fanny Mayne's novel see my *The Literature of Labour. Two Hundred Years of Working-Class Writing* (Brighton, 1985), pp.85-6.

2. A critical account of this area of writing can be found in P. J. Keating's *The Working Classes in Victorian Fiction* (London, 1971); see also his collection of *Working-Class Stories of the 1890s* (London, 1971).

3. Charlotte Elizabeth Tonna, *Combination (1832); Harriet Martineau, A Manchester Strike* (1832). For a discussion of both authors see Ivanka Kovačević, *Fact into Fiction. English Literature and the Industrial Scene* (Leicester, 1975), pp.211-23, 303-12. This book contains a complete reprint of *A Manchester Strike*. See also Catherine Gallagher, *The Industrial Reformation of English Fiction. Social Discourse and Narrative Form 1832-1867* (Chicago, 1985), pp.43-51, 55-61.

4. H. Llewellyn Smith and Vaughan Nash, *The Story of the Dockers' Strike* (London, n.d. [1889]), pp.164-5.

5. Coined by the union organiser John Burns, this was the ringing slogan of the struggle.

6. John Lovell, 'The new unionism and the Dock Strike of 1889' in David Rubinstein (ed.), *People for the People* (London, 1973), pp.154-5.

7. Emma Leslie, *The Seed She Sowed. A Tale of the Great Dock Strike* (London, 1891), p.19.

8. Cf. Gareth Stedman Jones, *Outcast London. A Study in the Relationship Between Classes in Victorian Society* (Harmondsworth, 1976; first pub. 1971), pp.302-8.

9. Mid-century industrial novels which use the emigration device include Frances Trollope, *Michael Armstrong, the Factory Boy* (1840); Elizabeth Gaskell, *Mary Barton* (1848); Charles Kingsley, *Alton Locke* (1850); and Fanny Mayne, *Jane Rutherford* (1854).

10. Leslie, *op. cit.*, p.137.

11. The misnaming of the International and its organs are among the minor confusions of this work.

12. William Oakhurst, *The Universal Strike of 1899* (London, 1891), p.34.

13. Stedman Jones, *op. cit.*, p.319.

14. Oakhurst, *op. cit.*, p.34.

15. *ibid.*, p.57. The quote is from Robert Browning's 'Pisgah-Sights I', which is included in his *Pacchiarotto* (1876). See *The Poetical Works of Robert Browning*, vol. XIV (London, 1889), p.49.

    For the popularity of the poem or at least its theme among Socialists of the day, see the following remark by Hugh Holmes Gore from the *Labour Prophet* of May 1895: 'We . . . sang them Pisgah-songs, we drew vivid pictures of the Promised Land, and enjoined them to hurry up and journey thither.' Quoted from Stephen Yeo, 'A new life: the religion of socialism in Britain 1883-1896', *History Workshop*, 4 (1977), p.45.

16. Oakhurst, *op. cit.*, p.34.

17. *ibid.*, p.6. The phrase is contained in a 'private and confidential' Manifesto. Note the contradiction in terms!

18. *ibid.*, p.86.

19. For further information about Clarke see chapter 8 by Paul Salveson.

20. C. Allen Clarke, *The Knobstick. A Story of Love and Labour* (Manchester, n.d. [1893]), pp.77-8. Subsequent page numbers given in the text are to this edition.

21. Paul Salveson, Preface to *Teddy Ashton's Lancashire Scrapbook* (Farnworth, 1985), p.1.

22. P. M. Ashraf, *Introduction to Working-Class Literature in Great Britain*, 2 vols, Part II: Prose (Berlin, 1979), p.156. This contains a full discussion of the novel.

23. William Tirebuck, 'On the verge of change' in Andrew Reid (ed.), *The New Party* (London, 1894), p.366.

24. *ibid.*, p.367.

25. William Edwards Tirebuck, *Miss Grace of All Souls'* (London, 1895), p.266. Subsequent page numbers given in the text are to this edition.

26. Another feature reminiscent of Clarke, emphasising the continuity and change of the labour movement, is the figure of 'a very old Chartist, with his long full grey hair, pass[ing] through dreamy resurrections of social strife.' *ibid.*, p.148.

    In all likelihood the two authors had knowledge of one another's work. Both were north of England authors, Clarke associated with Bolton and Blackpool, Tirebuck with Liverpool, though he spent his later years in Scotland and Wales. Clarke reprinted at least one of Tirebuck's short stories, 'Joe Clayton's Last Clogs', in his *Northern Weekly*, 1 February

1902.

27. This sub-strand of the plot may look contrived. But an incident during the Silesian weavers' uprising of 1844, which is the subject of Gerhart Hauptmann's famous naturalist play of the nineties, *The Weavers* (written 1892, first performed 1894), shows that Tirebuck's fiction is only catching up with real history. One of the soldiers deployed in Silesia was reported as having identified his own brother among the weavers killed, and as subsequently having thrown away his gun in despair; cf. *Kölnische Zeitung*, 18 June 1844, quoted from Hans Schwab-Felisch (ed.), Gerhart Hauptmann, *Die Weber. Dichtung und Wirklichkeit* (Frankfurt, 1974), pp.119-20.

28. Keating credits Tirebuck for having produced 'the most important industrial novel to be published in England since *Hard Times* almost exactly forty years earlier, and the most successful portrayal of industrial working-class life since *Mary Barton*'; *The Working Classes in Victorian Fiction*, p.235. For a reading of Tirebuck's novel, which differs from Keating's but also from my own, see chapter 7 by Ingrid von Rosenberg.

29. The term 'underworld' does not appear in Tirebuck but in H. G. Wells's tale *The Time Machine* from the same year (1895), where it refers to the subterranean work installations and habitations of the Morlocks, those repugnant spider- and monkey-like creatures that eat the refined upper-world species and threaten the Time Traveller, too.

Although this has to my knowledge never been established by Wells criticism, it is more than likely that the treatment of the Morlocks owes something to the action taken by the miners in the late summer of 1893. According to Wells's first biographer Geoffrey West, the fourth version of *The Time Machine*, which had a long and complex genesis, was written towards the end of 1893 (and published from March to June 1894 in the *National Observer*). The miners' lock-out lasted from July to November 1893.

Still according to West, this fourth version is 'the first recognisable casting of the familiar story. Certain incidents—such as . . . the descent to the underworld of the Morlocks (already thus named, though the Elois are still anonymous) are given practically as in the book,' Geoffrey West, *H. G. Wells* (London, 1930), Appendix, p.292.

So although the underworld appears to have existed

already in the second version, of which no draft has survived, it was only resumed and given its recognisable shape contemporaneously with, or in the immediate aftermath of, the lock-out. Certainly no social thinker of the time could have remained indifferent to this, the largest industrial dispute the country had ever seen.

Wells's beastly image of the underground toilers was not forgotten by the first British miner novelist. James C. Welsh's first novel was entitled *The Underworld* (1920), his second *The Morlocks* (1924). For a discussion of these works see H. Gustav Klaus, 'James C. Welsh. Major miner novelist', *Scottish Literary Journal*, XIII, 2 (1986), pp.54-75.

30. The other path, first chosen by James C. Welsh in 1920 (see preceding note), is the beginning of the working life of a boy, an empathetic description of the first day down the pit.

31. Alfred H. Fletcher, *Lost in the Mine. A Tale of the Great Coal Strike* (London, n.d. [1895]), p.60. Subsequent page numbers in the text are to this edition.

32. There is no historical evidence for this.

33. Cf. R. Page Arnot, *The Miners* (London, 1949), pp.236-41.

34. For an analysis of this confusion, see chapter 6 by Graham Holderness.

35. See note 4.

36. Fletcher was also the author of another strike novel, *The Clevelands of the Peak. A Derbyshire Romance* (Manchester, n.d. [1897]), which deals with union 'outrages' in the 1860s in the brickmakers' trade.

37. Clementina Black's *An Agitator* (1894) also opens with a view (of the last stage) of a strike, by wire-workers, another group of unskilled, low-paid and difficult-to-organise workers. However, its focus is on the subsequent political career of the strike leader, himself an engineer and the agitator of the title. For a discussion of this novel see chapter 2 by Brunhild de la Motte.

38. *The Knobstick*, repr. 1906; *Miss Grace of All Souls'*, repr. 1912. Oakhurst's work was admittedly also reprinted in 1911.

39. See the discussion of Laycock's *The Young Gaffer* (1898) and Plant's *The Conductor's Sweetheart* (1900-1) in chapter 8 by Paul Salveson; and of Carnie's *Miss Nobody* (1913) in chapter 11 by Edmund and Ruth Frow.

· 5 ·

Struggles of the past: brushing history against the grain

J. M. RIGNALL

Historicism, Walter Benjamin maintained, involves empathy with the victors in the struggles of history.[1] The historical novel, on the other hand, has, from *Waverley* onwards, commonly exploited the romantic potential of the lost cause. Yet the Jacobite rebellions that Scott focuses on, with their colourful trappings of highland clans, aristocratic intrigues and exiled royalty, allow a fictional treatment that is in the end quite compatible with an historicist perspective. The defeated Jacobites are given their romantic due of heroism and nobility while, at the same time, Scotland's future is shown to belong quite properly to the Union with England, the constitutional Hanoverian monarchy and the values of bourgeois society. The victors are shown to have history on their side and their success, however painful its price, is seen as necessary, inevitable and, on balance, welcome. It is this endorsement of the winning side that is markedly absent from the historical novels of the late nineteenth and early twentieth century that I shall discuss here: William Hale White ('Mark Rutherford'), *The Revolution in Tanner's Lane* (1887); E. L. Voynich, *The Gadfly* (1897); D. F. E. Sykes and Geo. Henry Walker, *Ben o' Bill's, the Luddite: A Yorkshire Tale* (1898); and James Haslam, *The Handloom Weaver's Daughter* (1904). Taking as their subject less romantic acts of rebellion against economic and political power than did Scott, they re-create history from the perspective of the dispossessed and defeated. Even if that defeat may be seen as only one lost battle in a continuing struggle, it is not written off as

the necessary and inevitable price of progress. In different ways all these novels adapt the conventions of historical fiction to perform what Benjamin saw as the proper task of a materialist historiography, 'to brush history against the grain'.[2]

Formally and ideologically these are very disparate works and they cannot conveniently be marshalled into a coherent alternative tradition of historical fiction with a clear set of common characteristics and a shared socialist outlook. Indeed, of these authors only Haslam was definitely a socialist.[3] However, in presenting history from the perspective of the oppressed they all deal openly and explicitly with violence, both of oppression and insurrection, and confront the problems that it poses. In so doing they lay themselves open to the problematic nature of history, often at the expense of that formal unity which better-known novels aspire to and which one kind of critical orthodoxy likes to honour as organic. It is on the different ways in which these works maintain this openness and manipulate or resist conventional forms of closure that I shall concentrate here.

Ben o' Bill's, the Luddite is a first-person account of the Luddite activity in Yorkshire in 1812 which culminated in the unsuccessful attack on Rawfolds mill and the murder of the mill-owner Horsfall a few days later. The authors, two local historians, claim that their work is 'mostly true' and varies in no significant respect 'from the story as it was gleaned from the lips and in part from the papers of the narrator',[4] a survivor of the Luddite rising, one Benjamin Bamforth, the Ben o' Bill's of the title. Nevertheless, the work reads like a lively novel, creating a world and peopling it with characters, and, as E. P. Thompson has suggested, it succeeds better as an 'imaginative reconstruction of the way of life, folk wisdom, and dialect of the Luddite community' than as factual history.[5] As Thompson also points out, the authors follow closely the account of events given by their fellow historian and contemporary Frank Peel in *The Risings of the Luddites* (1880), and, given that Peel's work precedes theirs by several years, seem to

have leant heavily upon it. However, the fact that Peel makes no mention of a Benjamin Bamforth may not be conclusive evidence of invention but it does indicate how, by centring their activities on this entirely decent and sympathetic young man, Sykes and Walker have done more than merely reproduce Peel's history in a different form. If they lean on his account they none the less significantly change the emphasis. Seeking to present a sympathetic understanding of the Luddites' actions and motives and to counter the commonly held view that they were 'a set of idle, dissolute knaves and cut-throats the country was well rid of' (p. 1), the authors can be seen to be working against the grain of Peel's more critical history and also, of course, of Charlotte Brontë's middle-class view of Luddism in *Shirley*.

The apology for the Luddites involves setting them in the context of a whole community and a way of life, and rooting the violent insurrection in the collective experience of that community and the personal characters and relationships of its members. George Mellor, the leader of the attack on Rawfolds mill and one of the three men who were eventually hanged for the murder of Horsfall, is presented as a cousin of the narrator and given the human countenance that Peel's history denies him. Where Peel describes him in the language of melodrama—'his black heart full of impotent rage'; 'his dark, flinty heart'[6]—*Ben o' Bill's* views him through the affectionate but not uncritical eyes of his cousin as 'a right proper man . . . six feet by the stick and with shoulders well back and strong, firm hands that gripped you to make you tingle' and who 'had a temper if you like, but never bore malice' (p.54). Even when he commits the murder of Horsfall, a deed which the horrified narrator cannot condone, he is shown to be acting not out of villainy but from a combination of outrage at social conditions and personal animosity. The novel includes a scene, not mentioned by Peel, which establishes a motive for the murder in these terms. A hot-headed, compassionate man, Mellor is moved to violent anger by the sight of a starving cropper's wife by the side of the road clutching a dead baby to her breast; and that anger focuses on

Horsfall who happens to ride past. Confronting the mill-owner with what Mellor sees as the direct, tragic result of his introduction of new machinery—' "Look at thi work William Horsfall; look at thi work an' be glad" ' (p.168)—he receives a cut across the face with a horse-whip in return. Horsfall rides away swearing ' "Yo's none heard th' last of this" ' while Mellor leaves the scene with a similarly strong resolve: ' "But, as the Lord's above me, that blow shall cost William Horsfall dear" ' (p.169). The incident, melodramatic in outline but saved from staginess by being recounted in Mellor's own earthy vernacular, provides grounds for the murder that are at once intensely personal and, at the same time, social and historical.

Despite the melodramatic quality of this scene, *Ben o' Bill's* does not reproduce stereotypes of class conflict. Horsfall, 'brusque, and a little petulant, but not unkindly of heart' (p.39), is a masterful man but not a tyrannical exploiter; and he is shown to be as much part of the community as those he employs and on friendly terms with the narrator's family. What is achieved by his murder, which 'revolted the general mind' (p.271), is not a strengthening of support for the Luddite cause but rather a rending of the community which destroys the popular basis of Luddism. The murder is, of course, only the last link in a chain of violence that can be traced back to the war with France and the Napoleonic blockade which has destroyed the continental market for the weaving industry, but the novel does not offer that wider pattern of historical causality as a moral justification of the murder. This is not a work of historical or metaphysical determinism. When a coin is tossed by the Luddites to determine whether Horsfall's mill or Cartwright's Rawfolds mill should be attacked first—an incident that is also recorded by Peel—Mellor, knowing that his cousin the narrator is well disposed towards Horsfall, surreptitiously turns the coin in his hand so that Cartwright's is chosen:

> 'But I knew tha wanted tails, so I turned it i' my palm when I stooped o'er th' fire.'
> And yet men talk about fate.   (p.46)

It is neither fate nor historical necessity that determines the course of history in this work, but the actions and decisions of individuals in determinate conditions. And if Mellor is not excused, neither is Horsfall, for the narrator, having described the desperate state of the local economy in 1812 and the starvation visible in the pinched and haggard faces of the famished Huddersfield workmen, concludes that the mill-owners could and should have acted differently:

> Now I cannot for my part think such a time was fitting for bringing in machinery. I know full well that water power and steam power and improved machinery have been of untold good to the poor; but those who were to reap the first profit should to my thinking have bided their time. But Mr. Cartwright, of Rawfolds, Mr. Horsfall, of Ottiwells' and some others, seemed callous to the sufferings around them. (p.75)

The Luddite violence and the specific actions and conditions that provoked it are thus not presented as inevitable, but they do bring about a fundamental change, rending the pattern of life of a whole community. That traditional pattern is affectionately re-created early in the novel in the Christmas scene at which George Mellor first appears, announcing his arrival out of the darkness and the snow with a strong baritone rendering of 'Christians Awake'. The contrast between this first appearance 'with a great red muffler round his neck and his coat all flaked with snow . . . now stamping his feet and now kicking them against the door-post' (p.53), and his last is striking and poignant. As the narrator stands before the scaffold in York his eyes fail him:

> There was a haze before my sight. I did not see the bolt withdrawn; only as through a mist see the quivering, swaying form. A long drawn sign, that ended in a sob like one deep breath from a thousand hearts, proclaimed the end, and Mr. Webster and I made our way from that tragic scene. (p.320)

In the shift from vivid, sensuous detail to distanced, hazy outline there is registered not only the tragic loss of an individual life, but also, vigorously if crudely emphasised

by that 'one deep breadth from a thousand hearts', the passing of a vital culture.

In its treatment of an unsuccessful historical rebellion *Ben o' Bill's* follows in some respects the conventions established by Scott, corresponding quite closely to the classical form of the historical novel as Lukács defines it with reference to the Waverley novels.[7] The narrator is cast in the mould of the neutral Waverley hero, caught up in a violent struggle but not wholeheartedly committed to either side in the conflict. In contrast to the passionately radical Mellor he is a moderate, unpolitical figure with modest expectations of what life has to offer: 'to make fair goods, to sell them at a fair price, to live in peace with my neighbours, and in time to marry, such was the sum of my ambition' (p.69). Sceptical from the outset of any attempt to fight against the law of the land, he finds himself torn between compassion for the starving weavers and his law-abiding inclinations: although 'filled with an intense sorrow for the suffering I know to be rife around us . . . I shrank from violence of any kind and from the conflict with the law, of which I had a wholesome dread' (p.79). His participation in the frame-breaking is thus reluctant and ridden with anxiety, and his equivocal stance could be said to allow Sykes and Walker to give an inside account of the Luddite rising while maintaining a respectable distance from the violence involved. However, this is not in effect a timid concession to respectability and the ruling class, but, rather, a graphic means of defending the Luddites against charges of criminality, of showing how they were, like the narrator, decent law-abiding men driven to desperate measures by desperate conditions.

Ben Bamforth's contempt for the military pretensions of some of the Luddites—their practice of drilling with arms 'seemed to me to be poor fooling, then and always' (p.96)— does not prevent him from honouring his promise to Mellor by joining the attack on Rawfolds mill, serving as one of the hammer-men who try to beat down the doors. His subsequent fate follows very much the pattern of Scott's typical neutral hero. Wounded in the attack, he is carried off unconscious and remains passively dependent

on family and friends to hide him from discovery by the forces of the law. Like Scott's Waverley he requires some authorially directed good fortune, which includes the good offices of magistrates and aristocrats, to prevent him from sharing the fate of many of his colleagues. George Mellor goes to his historical end on the gallows while Ben Bamforth, again like Waverley, is allowed the happy ending of marriage and a secure future. The novel comes close, indeed, to presenting a complacently conventional conclusion which consigns historical suffering to the safely distant past and dispenses morally appropriate rewards and punishments. The Luddite traitor Benjamin Walker, who informs on Mellor and others out of a combination of greed, cowardice, and jealousy over a girl, makes his last appearance immediately before the narrator's marriage, reduced now, having squandered his reward, to begging for a crust of bread. But even though in Ben Bamforth's final attitude to the informer charity gets the better of anger, the last paragraph of the novel strikes a note not of reconciliation but of resolute rejection—rejection of the criminal reputation commonly assigned to the Luddites: 'But don't tell me the Luds were a bad lot—misguided, short-sighted, ignorant, if you like, but rogues, and idle, dissolute n'er-do-weels—No! and still no!' (p.339). That emphatic final negation marks the novel's resistance to conventional closure and its refusal to acquiesce in the victors' verdict on the victims of history.

Sykes' and Walker's use of a narrator who is a relatively uncommitted but percipient participant in the struggle roots the story in the life and language of the community and creates a consistent tone and perspective. James Haslam's *The Handloom Weaver's Daughter* is a more uneven work in which a loftily generalising authorial commentary and an action that tends towards the melodramatic are never entirely integrated. However, Haslam certainly knew the world about which he was writing. The son of a handloom weaver himself, he later became a journalist after starting as a factory-worker, and he drew on his childhood memories as well as the testimony of old hand-

loom weavers for his novel about 'the tragedy involved in the struggle of the last of these cellar-workers against the development of steam machinery and the spread of the factory system'.[8] Although this tragedy is cast in the form of melodrama, and personal engagement too often manifests itself as a sentimental evocation of the pre-industrial past, Haslam does hold to a clear and uncompromising understanding of history to offset the formal clumsiness of what seems to have been his only attempt at a novel.[9]

Set in the late 1860s and early 1870s the story is that of Titus Bonney, one of the last of the handloom weavers of the old school, and his daughter Nancy; and it traces the course of their ruin by a self-made mill-owner William Bailey and his son Albert. The expansion of Bailey senior's business puts Titus out of work and drives him from his home, which is razed to the ground to make room for Bailey's new powerloom mill and spinning factory. At the same time Nancy is seduced, abducted and then abandoned, pregnant and destitute, by the evil Albert. This conflict of classes is temporarily mitigated by the activity of the enlightened younger son Willie Bailey, whose reading of Ruskin 'had imbued his mind with a love for idealism in industry' (p.116). But his scheme for organising and supporting the remaining handloom weavers fails and, in the violence that erupts at the end of the novel, he is shot by Titus and his accomplices who mistake him for his brother. Titus, now demented, proceeds to burn down Bailey's new mill and dies himself in the fire. Nancy has to emigrate to America to work as an operative in a new spinning mill. The other principal working-class character, Nancy's one-time fiancé the mechanic John Blake, suffers less dramatically but is similarly a victim of social and historical forces. Having invented a device for improving the operation of a spinning mill, he is cheated out of the patent by his employer Bailey and the local mayor, sacked and forced in the end to take work in India. He returns none the wealthier to witness the degradation of Nancy and continue a life of honest labour without social advancement.

In bare outline this is crude enough, and in some of its

details its fails to rise above the lowest level of cliché. Albert Bailey, 'pressing his voluptuous lips to the chastely chiselled mouth of the trembling maiden' (p.90), is never more than the stock villain of melodrama. And the evocation of life before the industrial fall slips too often into a sentimental version of pastoral: once, we are told, the weavers

> flourished everywhere in the neighbourhood like the delicious wild flowers they so dearly loved. But as the weavers had been crushed by the advancing wheel of time, the flowers also had been maimed and broken by the jerry-builder; where once the daisy and the cowslip reared their modest, fragrant heads side by side, badly-paved and sombre-looking streets had been formed. (p.4)

Nevertheless, despite such banalities, the simple polarities of melodrama and sentimental hyperbole do play a positive part in creating a distinctive vision of history. They articulate a stark conception of the irreconcilable nature of the contending forces. Haslam refuses to entertain the possibility of that reconciliation of classes, and of the old and the new, that is consistently urged by, for instance, the great industrial novels of the middle of the nineteenth century. When Nancy believes herself to be on the brink of marriage to Albert Bailey she projects a role for her marriage that might have been devised by Disraeli or Gaskell, or, in terms of historical development, by Scott;

> Then she fell to dreaming. It seemed to her present state of mind as if by her prospective marriage with Albert Bailey the representatives of the two great industrial periods were being joined together—the old and the new. (p.76)

But as soon as it is advanced this version of history is rejected:

> Had she been in a more philosophic mood, as was sometimes her wont, she would have asked herself if it were possible for the old and the new order of things to become as one consistent whole. (p.76)

The clear implication is that it is not, that the union of the old order and the new is merely the wishful dream of innocence. The intensification of the melodramatic mode towards the end of the novel serves to drive home this uncompromising lesson. The death of the Ruskinite reformer and Titus's suicidal attack on the new mill symbolically spell out the impossibility of peacefully resolving the class conflict inherent in the advance of industrial capitalism. The 'ever-grinding wheel of progress' (p.11) demands the destruction of the old by the new; and that destruction is seen as a violation of a state of nature, of an original organic unity. It is for this reason that the relationship of the pre-industrial handloom weavers to their work is nostalgically defined in terms of a harmony with nature. In the handloom cellar of the Bonneys' cottage Nancy 'could always see the flowers, the flight of birds, and the fall of the rain or snow outside, which made her feel more in touch with nature, and helped to retain her passion for the earth' (p.67). By contrast, the factory-workers 'breathed poison in the mill and poison in the bedroom. They were compelled through shortness of money to load their stomachs with unwholesome food and their minds with spurious notions' (p.35). In this context the melodramatic violence of the ending can be seen as an intensified rendering of the violence being done to a whole harmonious way of life.

This stark and uncompromising historical vision may owe something to Marxist thought,[10] but *The Handloom Weaver's Daughter* is clearly not the work of a revolutionary socialist. Like *Ben o' Bill's* it distances itself firmly from the use of violence as a political weapon. Whatever moral or emotional justification there may be for the arson that Titus commits, it is in no way excused, but labelled as 'criminal destruction' (p.279). When the handloom weavers are driven to revolt they are shown as descending to the level of animals:

> The handloom weavers' pride and independence began to assert themselves guardlessly. All human sympathy seemed to have been lost in the increased excitations of their animal

feelings. Their minds seemed only moved by the spirit of revenge, by desperation. They appeared not as reasoning men and women. They seemed to display that savage instinct only, which must have mainly characterised human beings before they had evolved to an intellectual beginning.   (p.247)

The abhorrence expressed here would not be out of place in any middle-class novel of the nineteenth century. But, unlike such works, Haslam's novel does not end with reconciliation and a consoling conclusion. Its radicalism lies not in any advocacy of revolution but in its open-ended vision of history as a continuing struggle:

The criminal destruction of the extensive spinning mill was the last impressive act of the defeated handloom weavers in the great Industrial Revolution. The conflict has still been waged in other ways, by other industrial forces, and was never, perhaps, more fierce than it is today.   (p.279)

There is no certainty of progress towards socialism expressed here, but neither is there resignation or despair. And if there is at least one concession to conventional closure in the marriage of the surviving John Blake, the final sentence of the novel deploys a nice irony against any interpretation of this as a definitive resolution of the conflicts presented in the novel: John Blake and Lily Braithwaite 'married at the little chapel of Lupton Yard, where they continued to live, strive, and bear children in the approved fashion of a respectable working-class family' (p.280). The ironic 'approved' identifies this respectable existence as all that a working-class family is permitted, not all that it might properly aspire to. The defeat of the weavers has put no one definitively in their place.

The Revolution in Tanner's Lane is the only one of the novels discussed here that has already received considerable critical attention, and my reading of it will be necessarily selective, seeking to establish Hale White's view of popular political action and its relation to the historical process rather than examining in any detail his account of the decline of dissenting religion. The 'revolution' of the title

is, of course, ironic, since nothing like a revolution occurs in the novel, least of all in Tanner's Lane; and irony is the mode in which radical political action is presented in the novel. From the great, comically satirical, opening scene of Louis the Eighteenth arriving in London to meet the Prince Regent amidst popular patriotic rejoicing, the novel looks sceptically at the collective intelligence and capacity of the people:

> There was a great crowd in the street when he came out of the hotel, and immense applause; the mob crying out, 'God bless your Majesty!' as if they owed him all they had, and even their lives. It was very touching, people thought at the time, and so it was. Is there anything more touching than the waste of human loyalty and love? As we read the history of the Highlands or a story of Jacobite loyalty such as that of Cooper's Admiral Bluewater, dear to boys, we sadden that destiny should decree that in a world in which piety is not too plentiful it should run so pitifully to waste, and that men and women should weep hot tears and break their hearts over bran-stuffing and wax.[11]

The mention of Jacobite loyalty and the history of the Highlands provokes a comparison between this ironic view of popular monarchism and that to be found in so many historical novels and romances from Scott onwards. The kind of loyalty that Scott celebrates even while exposing its anachronism is seen here as merely pitiful waste, and this signals at the outset how Hale White is going to work against the grain of conventional historical fiction. Yet this disenchanted view of the people is scarcely compatible with a radical alternative to Scott's conservatism, and, indeed, Hale White alternates disconcertingly between contempt for an oppressive autocratic regime and disdain for popular attempts to challenge it:

> What is so lamentable in the history of those times is the undisciplined wildness and feebleness of the attempts made by the people to better themselves. Nothing is more saddening than the spectacle of a huge mass of humanity goaded, writhing, starving, and yet so ignorant that it cannot choose

capable leaders, cannot obey them if perchance it gets them, and does not even know how to name its wrongs.   (p.159)

In this perspective it is not the people, but the leaders whom they fail to heed, who become the principal objects of sympathy; and the novel's account of the march of the Blanketeers centres on the actions and fates of Major Maitland, Caillaud, and Zachariah Coleman. It might seem that the popular movement only proves worthy of respect in the persons of a few enlightened and atypical individuals. But it is noticeable that, in honouring the latter, Hale White slips unobtrusively from the individual back to the general again:

> To work hard for those who will thank us, to head a majority against oppressors, is a brave thing; but far more honour is due to the Maitlands, Caillauds, Colemans, and others of that stamp who strove for thirty years from the outbreak of the French revolution onwards not merely to rend the chains of the prisoners, but had to achieve the more difficult task of convincing them that they would be happier if they were free. These heroes are forgotten, or nearly so. Who remembers the poor creatures who met in the early mornings on the Lancashire moors or were shot by the yeomanry? They sleep in graves over which stands no tombstone, or probably their bodies have been carted away to make room for a railway which has been driven through their resting place.
>
> (pp.110-11)

The named individuals are elided into the nameless masses, the heroic leaders become 'the poor creatures', indistinguishable from those whom they lead, and all of them forgotten victims of history.

The contradictions in the novel's attitude to the Blanketeers and working-class political action in general have been seen as the characteristic waverings of a well-disposed liberal of the 1880s. In the best critical account of Hale White's fiction to date John Lucas argues that, in creating the persona of Mark Rutherford, Hale White has deliberately presented a narrator who exhibits the classical dilemma of the liberal conscience, and that the novel is in

part concerned to expose the limitations of such a figure and his point of view.[12] Leaving aside the difficulty of establishing the grounds for taking Mark Rutherford as the object of Hale White's irony, for seeing the contradictions as deliberately posed rather than honestly entertained by the author himself, this reading has the defect of making sense of the novel's inconsistencies solely in terms of the narrator's limitations. Lucas is right to view the march of the Blanketeers as an historical crisis that is difficult to make sense of, but to argue that it produces crises and contradictions only in a liberal attempt to account for it is to define the difficulty too narrowly. What Hale White seems to show is that it resists recuperation in terms of conventional history altogether. The Blanketeers are shown to be peculiarly difficult to get clearly into focus; they are at once touchingly naïve in their faith in the good will of government and the Prince Regent; unjustly suspicious of their leader; misled by their literal-minded belief in the word of the Bible and their own imagined role as outnumbered Israelites; ignorantly determined to proceed with the march despite all the arguments against it; altogether absurd and foolish, and yet 'less ridiculous than those who hung and sabred them, less ridiculous than the Crimean war and numberless dignified events in human history, the united achievements of the sovereigns and ministries of Europe' (p.184). Their contradictions and weaknesses make them impossible subjects for the kind of conventional historian who narrates 'the dignified events in human history'; but such offical historians, with their bland assumptions of what is important, are themselves absurdly deluded. However foolish the Blanketeers, those 'silly God-fearing souls', may be, they are in the end right, it is implied, to believe that 'their Master's time was not their time . . . and that when it pleased Him they would triumph' (p.186). The ultimate success that would make sense of their defeat is not available to the narrator, or to any person, and can only be conjectured:

> It was not yet God's time in 1817, but God's time was helped forward, as it generally is, by this anticipation of it. It is a

commonplace that a premature outbreak puts back the hands of the clock and is a blunder. Nine times out of ten this is untrue, and a revolt instantaneously quenched in blood is not merely the precursor, but the direct progenitor of success.

(pp.186-7)

In writing the alternative history of the oppressed and defeated Hale White cannot produce a coherent teleological narrative that bestows meaning on events in the light of their positive conclusion, for, in consigning the success of which the Blanketeers are the progenitor to a millennial future known only to God, he indicates that the ending which would resolve contradiction and redeem inadequacy is one that cannot yet be written. Thus the kind of organic unity which he so admired in Scott[13] is one that he has deliberately to eschew since it has no part in his project. Seen from the point of view of the defeated, history must inevitably be incoherent, tailing off into darkness and oblivion.

The prospect of being consigned to oblivion, together with the doubts thus raised about the meaningfulness of their actions, is one that the characters in the novel consciously face up to. When Zachariah visits Caillaud in the condemned cell the latter reflects on the fact that his own life and the march of the Blanketeers are certain to be forgotten:

'To be hung like a forger of bank-notes—not even to be shot— and then to be forgotten. Forgotten utterly! This does not happen to be one of those revolutions which men remember.'

'No! men will not remember,' said Pauline, with an elevation of voice and manner almost oratorical. 'Men will not remember, but there is a memory in the world which forgets nothing.' (p.226)

Pauline's answer appears to be endorsed, however tentatively, by the novel. The notion of a memory in the world which forgets nothing is more than a secular and sentimental substitute for God; it is a way of asserting that actions may have significant consequences despite the insignificance or obliteration of the individuals who perform

them. In rescuing from oblivion 'the poor creatures who met in the early mornings on the Lancashire moors or were shot by the yeomanry' (p.110) the novel affirms the existence of a memory which forgets nothing. And in the second half of the work there is one incident which echoes Caillaud's own violent action—keeping his memory alive by example, as it were—and demonstrates quite literally the ability of individuals to leave their mark. When the young Pauline, Zachariah's daughter, has the unwelcome attentions of Thomas Broad forced upon her, she turns on him both verbally and physically:

> 'I will be silent,' she cried—what a relief it was to him to hear her say that!—'but I will mark you,' and before he could comprehend what she was doing she had seized a little pair of scissors which lay near her, had caught his wrist, and had scored a deep cross on the back of the hand. The blood burst out, and she threw him a handkerchief.   (p.291)

This melodramatic action, a violent reaction to violence like Caillaud's shooting of the soldier who killed Major Maitland, stands out vividly in the prosaic account of domestic and provincial life which comprises the second half of the novel. And unlike the election-night riot, which repeats the popular uprising of the Blanketeers as tawdry farce, it cannot be seen as another ironic illustration of the way the forces of the first part of the novel have dwindled into mocking shadows. Decline there may be in the radical energy of the dissenting tradition, but some continuity remains in the figures of individuals. The younger Pauline retains the fiery spirit of her mother and grandfather, and in this scene she makes a mark whose long-term effects cannot be foreseen. The scar left on Thomas Broad's hand later causes his disgrace in Cowfold, frustrates his father's arbitrary and unjust exercise of power as the minister in Tanner's Lane, and most probably precipitates the latter's fatal illness. None of these consequences is exactly momentous, but Pauline's action leads at least to the thwarting of a petty tyrant and the defeat of injustice in the diminished sphere of Cowfold. What benefit she may derive from it,

however, is never established for she herself is lost to sight.
The laconic final sentences of the novel despatch her and
her father into oblivion: 'What became of Zachariah and
Pauline? At present I do not know' (p.388). They sink back,
at least temporarily, into unrecorded history and the novel
remains open-ended, but in a way that does not represent a
capitulation to hopelessness. The individuals themselves
may not be remembered but their lives have left a mark,
and in that respect 'there is a memory in the world which
forgets nothing' (p.226).

E. L. Voynich's flamboyant historical romance *The Gadfly*
is as far removed from the sober restraint of Hale White's
novel as her early life was from his quiet routine as an
official in the Admiralty. Born in 1864 the youngest
daughter of George Boole, professor of mathematics at
Queen's College, Cork, she studied music in Berlin, was
captivated by the idea of Russian revolution, became
friends with the Russian revolutionary Stepniak in exile in
London, lived and travelled in Russia in the late 1880s, and
worked for the Russian revolutionary movement, travelling for instance to Lvov to help arrange the passage of
illegal publications into Russia through the Galician
frontier.[14] It was through her association with Stepniak
that she met her husband Wilfred Voynich, a Lithuanian
who escaped to London in 1890 from political imprisonment in Siberia. *The Gadfly*, her first novel, published in
1897, was an immediate success, particularly in Russia
where it has continued to be a bestseller to the present
day.[15] Drawing on her knowledge of European revolutionaries it deals not with popular insurrections of the
English nineteenth century but with the Italian struggle for
independence from the Austrian empire in the 1830s and
1840s. Where the other novels are provincial, this is exotic;
where they aspire to realism, this is an unashamed
romance.

The terms of its popular appeal lie doubtless in its qualities as a romantic adventure story. It is dramatic, fast-
moving, far-fetched, always poised on the brink of outright absurdity, and yet undeniably compelling. At the

beginning of the novel Arthur Burton, the youngest son of an English merchant in Leghorn, is a student in the theological seminary in Pisa and idealistically involved in the underground Young Italy movement. Since both his parents are dead and his step-brothers unsympathetic, his one close relationship is with his father-confessor, canon Montanelli. When Montanelli leaves Pisa on his appointment as a bishop, Arthur accepts the new head of the seminary, father Cardi, as his confessor and reveals to him in confession the details of his political involvement. Shortly afterwards he is arrested along with other student revolutionaries. After refusing to betray his associates he is eventually released through the intercession of Montanelli. Cardi, it emerges, has betrayed the secrets of the confessional to the authorities; but, through a combination of misunderstanding and official rumour, Arthur is believed at first to have been the traitor. At the same time he learns from his family that he is in fact the illegitimate son of Montanelli, who once had an affair with his mother. This double revelation shatters his faith in Christianity, and, making it look as though he has drowned himself in the harbour at Leghorn, he stows away on a ship to South America. Thirteen years later, half-crippled by his experiences in South America and unrecognisable to his former associates, he reappears in Italy as the notorious radical and anti-clerical pamphleteer Felice Rivarez, the gadfly of the title. Neurotically scarred and physically debilitated by his humiliating time in South America he nevertheless enters energetically into the activities of the revolutionary underground, until on a final mission he is arrested in the very town where his father is now a cardinal. Montanelli has the power to save the prisoner whom at first he does not recognise. But when Arthur reveals his identity he insists that Montanelli choose between him and Christ, that he will only accept assistance from his father if the latter renounces Christianity, joins the revolutionaries, and publicly acknowledges him as his son. Unable to abjure his faith, Montanelli is forced to leave Arthur to his fate, a bloody and bungled execution by an unwilling firing-squad. Torn apart by grief and pain the cardinal

finally goes mad.

History is here cast in the form of a Freudian family romance. The passionate resentment felt by the gadfly towards his unfortunate father cannot be understood in terms of reason and logic. Conrad, who roundly disliked *The Gadfly*, made the point with amusing irony: 'Look at the logic: He found his mutton-chop very tough *therefore* he arose and cursed his aunt.'[16] The tirade that Arthur directs at Montanelli in their final meeting certainly goes beyond justice or reason:

> 'You say you love me,—your love has cost me dear enough! Do you think I can blot out everything, and turn back into Arthur at a few soft words— I, that have been dish-washer in filthy half-caste brothels and stable-boy to Creole farmers that were worse brutes than their own cattle? I, that have been zany in cap and bells for a strolling variety show—drudge and Jack-of-all-trades to the matadors in the bull-fighting ring: I, that have been slave to every black beast who cared to set his foot on my neck; I, that have been starved and spat upon and trampled under foot; I, that have begged for mouldy scraps and been refused because the dogs had the first right? Oh, what is the use of all this! How can I *tell* you what you have brought on me? And now—you love me! How much do you love me? Enough to give up your God for me?'[17]

The margin of emotional excess in this demand for an absolute, unconditional love points to an unresolved Oedipal conflict that is rooted in the unconscious; and this unconscious is both personal and political. The oppressive power of the father that is charged here with causing the social degradation of Arthur is not adequately represented by the humane and sensitive Montanelli; and, in any case, the exile in South America is in the first place self-chosen. But the indictment attains socially symbolic proportions, passing through the biological father to implicate the institution of the Catholic Church and, through the treacherous father-confessor Cardi, the imperial régime itself. The political law of the father has banished Arthur to the lowest level of human society, lower even than the 'Creole farmers' and 'black beasts', the brutalised victims

of European imperial exploitation. It is a whole social and political order that is under attack, and the revolutionary hero has to be seen as an Oedipal rebel in the widest sense, who suffers in his person the pain and humiliation of the socially and politically oppressed.

It is, then, through the socially symbolic ramifications of the Freudian family romance that the violent and often melodramatic emotions in the novel are brought into relation with historical reality. Melodrama and romance provide a means of articulating the violent nature of the struggle for political emancipation. There are, however, problems involved in this treatment of history in terms of an unresolved Oedipal conflict, since the charge of personal feeling that it generates is so powerful that it constantly threatens to overwhelm the wider social and political implications. In particular the individual suffering and attendant pathos of the revolutionary as hero of romance are so dominant that the cause for which he fights, and the people whose champion he ostensibly is, are effectively marginalised. Whilst soliciting unqualified compassion for the victimised gadfly himself, the novel is, indeed, curiously ambiguous in its treatment of the collective victims of oppression, those coolies, negroes and half-castes of whom Arthur speaks with such bitter hostility.[18] And in the scene where Montanelli goes mad while conducting a service in his cathedral, it is the people rather than the church itself that he turns on, accusing them of having robbed him of his son: 'You have killed him! You have killed him! And I suffered it, because I would not let you die' (p.249). In his demented, guilt-ridden outburst he acts out the passion of God the father, whilst Arthur is elided into the crucified Christ, whose sacrifice has been undertaken for an undeserving and ungrateful people;

'The price of your banquet is paid for you; come, then, and gorge yourselves, cannibals, bloodsuckers—carrion beasts that feed on the dead! See where the blood streams down from the altar, foaming and hot from my darling's heart—the blood that was shed for you!'   (p.250)

The logic and language of this tirade may be those of a crazed mind, but it illustrates the way in which the personal pathos of this Oedipal drama is created at the expense of sympathy for the generality of human beings.

If it remains problematic in this respect, the novel does achieve a form of radical openness in its conclusion. As Arnold Kettle has pointed out, where everything seems to be set for 'either a happy ending or a morally comforting one', Voynich refuses to satisfy the expectations she has raised.'[19] In his prison cell Arthur confronts Montanelli with a stark choice and insists on his commitment to violent revolutionary action: 'I am not a man; I am a knife. If you let me live, you sanction knives' (p.231). No possibility of compromise is offered in either the personal or the political struggle; and although *The Gadfly* reaches an emotional closure with death, grief and madness, the wider conflict that it has brought dramatically to life remains resolutely unresolved. The fiction registers the unfulfilled, but also undimmed, revolutionary aspirations of Voynich's own time; and this novel, like the other three, shows how history, seen from the perspective of its victims, is never a closed chapter.

NOTES

1. Walter Benjamin, *Illuminations*, translated by Harry Zohn (London, 1973), p.258.
2. *ibid.*, p.259.
3. See for example his ILP Penny Pamphlet, *Cotton and Competition: Striking Facts and Figures* (London, 1909).
4. D. F. E. Sykes and Geo. Henry Walker, *Ben o' Bill's, the Luddite: A Yorkshire Tale* (London and Huddersfield, n.d.) p.i. Further references to this edition are given in parentheses. Although the title page carries no date, the British Library catalogue records 1898.
5. Introduction to the fourth edition of Frank Peel, *The Risings of the Luddites* (London, 1968), p.x.
6. Peel, *Luddites*, pp.93, 95.

7. Georg Lukács, *The Historical Novel*, translated by Hannah and Stanley Mitchell (Harmondsworth, 1969), pp.29-69.

8. James Haslam, *The Handloom Weaver's Daughter* (London, 1904), p.vii. Further references to this edition are given in parentheses.

9. See P. M. Ashraf, *Introduction to Working-class Literature in Great Britain*, Part II: Prose (Berlin, 1979), p.130, who gives a brief sketch of Haslam's career.

10. As Ashraf claims, *op. cit.*, p.131.

11. Mark Rutherford, *The Revolution in Tanner's Lane* (London, 1971), p.7. Further references to this edition are given in parentheses. The novel was first published in 1887.

12. John Lucas, 'William Hale White and the problems of deliverance', in his *The Literature of Change* (Hassocks, 1977), pp.57-118.

13. W. Hale White, *Last Pages from a Journal* (London, 1915), p.274.

14. See Anne Fremantle, 'The Russian best seller: *The Gadfly*', *History Today*, XXV (1975), pp.629-37.

15. Fremantle, *op. cit.*, cites sales of 5 million copies in over 100 editions in 22 languages of the USSR.

16. Letter of 11 October 1897. *The Collected Letters of Joseph Conrad: Volume I; 1861-1897*, Frederick R. Karl and Laurence Davies (London, 1983), p.395.

17. E. L. Voynich, *The Gadfly* (St Albans, 1973), pp.228-9. Further references to this Mayflower paperback edition are given in parentheses. The novel was first published in 1897.

18. The political ambiquity of the gadfly's stance was more than matched by that of his probable historical model, Sigmund Rosenblum, who had an affair with Voynich in 1895 and in later life became a passionate anti-Bolshevist. As the British spy Sidney Reilly he was executed in the USSR in 1925 while his fictional counterpart lived on as a hero to the Soviet reading public. See Fremantle, *op. cit.*

19. Arnold Kettle, 'E. L. Voynich: a forgotten English novelist', *Essays in Criticism*, VII (1957), pp.163-74 (p.171). Another, more recent, sympathetic study of Voynich is James G. Kennedy, 'Voynich, Bennett, and Tressell: two alternatives for realism in the transition age', *English Literature in Transition 1880-1970*, XIII (1970), pp.254-86.

Anarchism and fiction

GRAHAM HOLDERNESS

It would be misleading to speak, at least in relation to British culture, of a fiction of anarchism in the same sense that there is a fiction of socialism.[1] The various traditions of socialist and communist philosophy and political practice that penetrated British society within the period in question reflected and helped to constitute a broad socialist movement incorporating mass working-class experience and exerting powerful political influence over the tendencies of historical development. Although socialist fiction inevitably operated in a cultural terrain peripheral to the dominant ideology, its practitioners were able to found a genre capable of producing, at a later stage, in the writings of Tressell and Grassic Gibbon and Lewis Jones, novels of such artistic power and political impact that they could hardly be ignored by bourgeois culture: texts which called forth from literary criticism strategies of negotiation designed to isolate them from the historical movement as 'classics' of artistic achievement.

Anarchism, as theoretical philosophy and as political practice, has never been within British society more than a fringe activity, based on tiny libertarian groups and isolated individual intellectuals: 'a chorus of voices', in George Woodcock's memorable phrase 'crying in the wilderness'.[2] Anarchism in Britain never gained the kind of mass following that could make it an important social force in, for example, Republican Spain:[3] although instances to the contrary can be found, the labour movement in Britain has exhibited little more sympathy towards

anarchism than the established order itself. It is perhaps surprising that there is a fiction of anarchism at all: yet it is possible to discover in British fiction both an engagement with anarchism in the work of 'major' writers like Henry James and Joseph Conrad, and a body of fictional writing, small but significant, expressing some degree of commitment to anarchist ideas. Furthermore, as I will attempt to demonstrate, for particular social and cultural reasons anarchism exerted over the minds of certain writers an influence disproportionate to its historical role in the development of British society.

To some degree the fiction exhibits a serious interest in and engagement with the salient points of anarchist philosophy: the outright rejection not only of capitalist society, but of all social systems *per se;* the opposing of collectivist forms of socialism as dogmatic and contrary to the true nature of freedom; the belief in the natural goodness and perfectibility of man; the emphasis on the freedom and sovereignty of the individual; and the vision of a libertarian society of voluntary co-operation and mutual assistance. On the other hand there is a much wider and stronger reflection in fiction of the forms of political violence espoused by some anarchist groups and individuals: the employment in their war against society of weapons of terrorism and assassination. At some time and in some place the entire vocabulary of political dissent—socialist, communist, radical, left—has been demonised by conservative and reactionary interests: but no political term has been so comprehensively and systematically smeared as anarchism. The deliberate equation anarchy = chaos deflects the force of all arguments against government, and turns the anarchist's own title back on him with a charge of wanton destructiveness. In British culture anarchy has always meant what it meant to Matthew Arnold: barbarism, the negation of culture and civilisation. The almost automatic association, in the later nineteenth century, by the press and by other writers as well as by politicians, of anarchism with political violence, individual assassination and terrorist operations, was drawn from a general European experience: but the equation was,

in British conditions, to say the least, misleading. All the terrorist attacks which shocked, outraged and frightened London in the 1880s and 1890s were the work of Fenian nationalists: as George Woodcock observes, 'the only victim of anarchist violence in England was a Frenchman named Marcel Bourdin, who in 1894 accidentally blew himself up in Greenwich Park with a home-made bomb . . .'[4]

The Victorian establishment—monarchy, government, church, press etc.—had a vested interest in maximising the association of radical politics with destructive violence, and in blurring the distinctions between gradualist constitutional socialism, the revolutionary collectivism of the marxist parties and the libertarianism of the anarchists. Much writing of the period addresses anarchism within an ideological structure derived from the 'social-problem' novels of the 1840s: and systematically confuses working-class militancy, trade-union organisations, political demonstrations, secret societies, sabotage, terrorism, assassination and pointless destructiveness.[5] The identification of anarchism with terrorism also led several writers to confuse anarchism with the Russian nihilists, who certainly employed terrorism but with the very un-anarchistic objective of establishing constitutional government.[6] I have restricted my attention here to novels which represent some form of serious engagement with the historical phenomenon of anarchism: even though in some cases (especially that of Henry James) the contours of history are hard to discern through the obfuscating ideological texture of the fiction. I have begun with a non-British novel, Zola's *Germinal* (1885), since that remarkable text seems to have established parameters within which other fictional explorers of anarchism were content to operate.

THE NOVEL OF ANARCHISM

Emile Zola (1840-1902)

Zola's treatment of anarchism is, as we might expect, much

more historically specific and politically informed than the corresponding visions of Conrad and James. Where many writers, including James, could or would not distinguish between socialism and anarchism, Zola carefully differentiates marxist and more evolutionary forms of socialism from the anarchists, referring explicitly to the 1872 Marx/Bakunin split in the International. Zola's anarchist Souvarine is defined specifically in terms of his hostility to properly socialist ideas:

> 'Your friend Karl Marx is still at the stage of wanting to leave things to natural evolution. No politics, no conspiracies, isn't that the idea? . . . Don't talk to me about evolution! Raise fires in the four corners of cities, mow people down, wipe everything out, and when nothing whatever is left of this rotten world perhaps a better will spring up.'[7]

A dissident scion of the Russian nobility, Souvarine has served a terrorist apprenticeship with the Nihilists or Social-Revolutionaries, fleeing to France after an unsuccessful attempt on the life of the Tsar. Among the miners of France he lives a modest existence, emulating a spartan simplicity of proletarian lifestyle; he echoes (with a rather un-anarchistic emphasis on hegemony) the destructive rhetoric of his master, Bakunin: ' "He is the only one who can deal the knock-out blow . . . the International under his command is bound to wipe out the old world" ' (p.236); and in true anarchist fashion he refuses to construct or act upon any systematic vision of future social development: ' "Any reasoning about the future is criminal, for it prevents pure destruction and holds up the march of the revolution" ' (p.237).[8]

On the other hand Zola's novel shares with other less politically conscious works some of the cruder and more popular conventions employed in the fictionalising of anarchism. Souvarine exemplifies a type of dual personality often used by portrayers of anarchists to link, in a contradictory fictional archetype, the apparently baffling combinations of idealism and violence, philosophical intellectualism and destructive determination, a quasi-

religious faith in the good of humanity with a willingness to destroy those institutions by which humanity lives.[9] Souvarine combines physical weakness with an 'insanely intrepid' heroism, effeminancy of appearance with incredible tenacity of will: 'On the fair, girlish face of Souvarine . . . appeared an expression of silent scorn, the crushing scorn of the man prepared to sacrifice his own life in obscurity without even the glory of a martyr's crown' (p.234).[10] The narrative constantly foregrounds Souvarine's pet rabbit, 'Poland', to symbolise a tenderness for the cause of liberty utterly at odds with the apocalyptic severity of his revolutionary faith.

In some ways Souvarine represents a type akin to the 'Professor' in Conrad's *The Secret Agent:* the strange phenomenon of an individual devoted to a social cause, yet ostensibly independent of all effective social relationships. Having witnessed his lover and fellow-conspirator hanged in Moscow, Souvarine embraces and achieves a complete autonomy of the will, devoid of reciprocal obligations and affectional bonds: 'He did not want any ties, whether of women or friends, and then he was free to do what he liked with his own blood and the blood of others' (pp.142-3). The image of the anarchist as a fanatical devotee to some chiliastic religion is a popular one, and can indeed be found reflected in the Bakunin/Nechayev pamphlet *Revolutionary Chatechism* (1866): 'The revolutionary is a man under vow. He ought to occupy himself with one exclusive interest, with one thought and one passion: the Revolution . . . he has only one aim, one science: destruction.'[11] 'I have no weakness left in my heart' vows Souvarine; 'Nothing at all: no family, no wife, no friends, nothing to make my hand falter on the day when I have to take other people's lives or give my own' (p.430).

There is little trace in Souvarine of any special philosophy of anarchism—nothing of mutuality, co-operation, freedom of association, workers' control—his anarchism is a purely *individual* belief, a personal religion of destruction, fabricated by the simple expedient of hiving-off Bakunin's apocalyptic rhetoric from his constructive vision of a libertarian society.

Souvarine's climactic act of sabotage, carefully planned and executed, is to destroy the mine, 'Le Voreux', by damaging the lining of the main shaft sufficiently to permit inundation by the floodwaters of the 'underground sea'. By juxtaposing narrative perspectives—that of the fanatical saboteur and that of the miners (including the central characters Etienne and Catherine) who become trapped in the flooded pit, Zola foregrounds and insists emphatically on the inescapable interdependence of people and institutions: the terrorist who (quite correctly, in Zola's view) sees certain social institutions as oppressive and obstructive of human freedom and progress, must in order to strike at them by violence somehow suppress his sympathy for those whose lives are inevitably bound up with the 'target' of his destructive energy. Souvarine is portrayed in this connection as a callous murderer: he watches the miners file towards the doomed pit, 'counting them as a butcher might count animals going into a slaughter-house' (p.437).

Zola's description of the act of sabotage itself is far more ambiguous in its implications:

> Then he worked like one possessed. The breath of the invisible elated him, and the black horror of this rain-swept cavern filled him with a frenzy of destruction. He attacked the lining at random, hitting wherever he could, using his brace and bit or his saw as though his one idea were to rip everything open there and then on top of him. He put into the task the sort of ferocity with which he might have driven a knife into the flesh of some living being whom he loathed. He would kill this foul beast in the end, this pit with the ever-open jaws that had swallowed down so much human flesh.   (p.434)

The atmosphere of terror and fascination combines a horror at Souvarine's determined destructiveness with an intense admiration for his heroic self-disregard. Such aesthetic disjunctures of tone arise from deep emotional contradictions in the text's ideological structure: at one level of the novel's discourse, which might be described as a 'fabulous' or 'mythic' dimension, Souvarine appears as an epic hero, a dragonslayer confronting the 'foul beast' in

its lair and destroying it in single combat. The mine itself has been transformed into such a mythological monster only by the operations of the author's imagination: quite contrary to his own theory of naturalism, Zola has converted 'Le Voreux' from a piece of productive machinery into a monstrous and fabulous devourer of human flesh. The intense moral hatred of the pit, and the fanatical will to see it demolished, emanate from the author's contradictory ideology, and are constructed by the particular metaphoric texture of the narrative. The bourgeois novelist thus finds himself in a strange kinship with the anarchistic terrorist: each represents the faculty of daring imagination capable of conceiving of an economic institution as an autonomous force hostile and alien to human aspirations, threatening and devouring, challenging the heroic individual to a murderous final combat. The extravagant surrealism and imaginative finality of the writer's vision correspond therefore to the totalising purity of the anarchist's social philosophy.

The closing vision of the novel is attributed, in narrative terms, to the departing Etienne, who has never been shown to share Souvarine's anarchist faith: but in Etienne's meditations, the mythic conception of 'Le Voreux' is extrapolated to a general vision of a society under threat, and the anarchist's destruction of the mine becomes a model for a general apocalyptic transformation of society:

> One morning, confident in their solidarity, millions of workers against a few thousand idlers, they would take over power and be the masters. Ah, then indeed truth and justice would awake! Then that crouching, sated god, that monstrous idol hidden away in his secret tabernacle, gorged with the flesh of poor creatures who never even saw him, would instantly perish. (p.498)

The novel closes with the imagery implicit in its title, of natural regeneration and springtime growth. The visionary revelation of social transformation is effected not spontaneously by natural evolution, but by the spontaneous

revolutionary activity of the working class. Metaphors of fertility, birth, germination, are combined with a language of destructive vengeance in a juxtaposition fundamental to the language of anarchism. Here, for example, is Shelley, giving poetic form to Godwin's anarchist philosophy:

> The earth's great age begins anew
> The golden years return,
> The earth doth like a snake renew
> Her winter weeds outworn:
> Heaven smiles, and faiths and empires gleam
>   Like wrecks in a dissolving dream.[12]

Here Bakunin:

> Let us therefore trust the eternal spirit which destroys and annihilates only because it is the unfathomable and eternal source of all life. The passion for destruction is a creative passion, too![13]

And here is Zola:

> Life was springing from her fertile womb, buds were bursting into leaf and the fields were quickening with fresh green grass . . . Men were springing up, a black avenging host was slowly germinating in the furrows, thrusting upwards for the harvests of future ages. And very soon, their germination would crack the earth asunder.   (pp.489-9)

Joseph Conrad (1857-1924)

> The subject of *The Secret Agent*—I mean the tale—came to me in the shape of a few words uttered by a friend in a casual conversation about anarchists or rather anarchist activities . . . I remember remarking on the criminal futility of the whole thing, doctrine, action, mentality; and on the contemptible aspect of the half-crazy pose as of a brazen cheat exploiting the poignant miseries and passionate credulities of a mankind always so tragically eager for self-destruction. That was what made for me its philosophical pretences so unpardonable. Presently . . . we recalled the already old story of the attempt to blow up Greenwich Observatory; a bloodstained inanity of so fatuous a kind that it was impos-

sible to fathom its origin by any reasonable or even unrea-
sonable process of thought . . . that outrage could not be laid
hold of mentally in any sort of way, so that one remained faced
by the fact of a man blown to bits for nothing even remotely
resembling an idea, anarchistic or other. As to the outer wall of
the Observatory, it did not show so much as the faintest
crack.[14]

The point of view expressed here about anarchism and its
links with terrorist activities is substantially that of the
contemporary government and of the conservative press:
simple, crude, unenlightened and containing all the elements of popular prejudice. Conrad takes terrorism as the
prerogative of the anarchist: though in fact all the
bombings in the metropolis in the last decade of the nineteenth century had Fenian nationalist origins. The argument that anarchism could have no philosophical or
ideological basis is a crude elision of a powerful and highly
intellectual body of political thought. The identification of
anarchism and terror seems to echo the outraged prejudices
of a society challenged by the widespread radical movements of the period, and anxious to pin as much blame as
possible on a political group already demonised into a
mythological nightmare: as an intellectual position, it
seems an unlikely basis for the ideological substratum of a
'great' novel. Even the central anecdote of the discussion,
the death of Marcel Bourdin in 1884, shows Conrad's own
'reasonable process of thought' comfortably aligned with
the headlines of contemporary newspapers like *The Times*
(which simply voiced what was probably a deliberate
fiction of the government). The whole notion of a plot to
blow up Greenwich Observatory was fabricated without
any circumstantial or substantiating evidence: Bourdin
was either delivering or hiding the explosive, and had no
designs at all on the First Meridian. The 'Author's Note'
speaks of another element in the tale's development:

the vision of an enormous town presented itself, of a
monstrous town more populous than some continents and in
its man-made might as if indifferent to heaven's frowns and
smiles; a cruel devourer of the world's light. There was room

enough there to place any story, depth enough for any passion, variety enough there for any setting, darkness enough to bury five millions of lives.

Slowly the dawning conviction of Mrs. Verloc's maternal passion grew up to a flame between me and that background, tingeing it with its secret ardour, and receiving from it in exchange some of its own sombre colouring.

We seem then to be confronted with a novel which is more about personal relationships and their social context—especially perhaps the institution of marriage, which is at once a personal connection and a social institution—than it is about anarchism. Verloc's profession of secret agent, and the bomb-blast itself, seem more like symbols of the duplicity and violence immanent in bourgeois marriage, of the domestic lives of those trapped and lonely people who inhabit that monstrous city, 'great devourer of the world's light'. How then do the private and public dimensions of the novel intersect? What is the nature of its political and social vision?

We can begin, as Conrad does, with Verloc. What exactly is Verloc's *secret?*

The door of the shop was the only means of entrance to the house in which Mr Verloc carried on his business of a seller of shady wares, exercised his vocation of a protector of society, and cultivated his domestic virtues.   (pp. 14-15)

The emphasis on domestic virtues is ironic but not misleading; Mr Verloc *is* in fact a protector of society—a police informer and the confidant of a reactionary foreign government which is concerned to 'protect society' in the form of defending the prominent political figures and crowned heads who were in practice anarchist targets. *Secrecy* seems necessary to preserve the general social fabric as well as particular social institutions (such as the Verloc marriage): for the larger unit, the social macrocosm, embassy intrigues, *agents provacateurs*, the secrecy and professional rivalry of the police; for the smaller, the domestic microcosm, the silence of Verloc about the true sources of his income, and the acceptance by Winnie of a barren, hollow,

conventional marriage.

The plot to bomb Greenwich Observatory, which ends in Stevie's death, is hatched and organised by Mr Vladimir, official of the Tsarist state, working through his paid informer: it is a rigged terrorist atrocity, an act of calculated provocation. The plot owes its *insanity* entirely to Mr Vladimir's bizarre conception of what a truly frightening terrorist attack should be: 'an act of destructive ferocity so absurd as to be incomprehensible'. Verloc perceives it very clearly as an insane project: the man who knows the anarchists seems to be of the opinion that this is simply not the sort of thing they would dream of doing. None of the novel's revolutionaries, indeed, seems remotely capable of such an act: Conrad presents them as utterly impotent and innocuous individuals, all apparently incapable of hurting a fly.

The exception is the Professor, who is potentially a serious threat to society. A peculiar mixture of physical inadequacy and enormous egoism, he measures his own value by the 'force of will' necessary to make himself into a walking bomb. Though he seems perhaps to menace himself more than anyone else, he has some of the qualities of the historical anarchist: Conrad gives him at least integrity and consistency; his explosive potentialities render him, in line with the anarchist policy of 'propaganda by deed', a 'true propagandist'; and his professed intention—'to destroy public faith in legality'—would be a motive recognisable to an anarchist terrorist.[15]

The professor's opposite number is Inspector Heat, the police officer investigating the Greenwich Park explosion. Conrad spins around Heat the same web of irony that surrounds his other characters: he is presented as foolish and concerned only with his own reputation, his own status in his department. He also, like everyone else in the novel, has his secrets, which lead him to misunderstand or deliberately distort the evidence before him (see pp.104-5). It is difficult to understand, given this degree of irony, Barbara Arnett Melchiori's suggestion that Conrad 'sides with Chief Inspector Heat'.[16] It is a combination of secret personal interests, rather than the amazing intelligence of

the British police so stunning to Mr Vladimir, that leads to the disclosure of the truth. The end-product of the investigation is, finally, nothing: Mr Vladimir is blackballed from an 'extremely exclusive club', and the police plan to prosecute the hireling Verloc as a foreign spy. Nothing much will change, either in the world of anarchism, in that of the public services, or in terms of the pernicious vitality of that 'monstrous town' within whose secret shadows all these events take place.

Conrad's comprehensive vision of a corrupt society, involving the institutions of marriage and private property, police and parliament, city and state, comes strikingly close to the vision of the anarchist. Yet any philosophical acknowledgement of such a relationship is implicitly denied, since even Conrad's marxists and anarchists are not permitted any genuine theory or political belief. Revolutionary philosophy in *The Secret Agent* is reduced to ineffectual vanity or mere destructiveness: all ideologies are dismissed or negated. Once the whole philosophical side of marxist and anarchist politics has been sheared away, the writer is forced into a position where the only kind of imaginative commitment he can make is to the Professor's dream of total annihilation. What can be done with a world like this, once it has been created; a world devoid of internal possibilities for redemption or improvement? There is only one final solution: destruction. The only people who can dream of destroying a world are the anarchist and the artist: the novelist who can unmake the world he has made at will. As this novel ends, the Professor's dream is realised: the whole murky, shadowy, corrupt and secretive world of the novel disappears: into the blank whiteness of the unprinted page—'a whitewashed wall with no writing on it'.

It is not for nothing that Conrad once professed himself a kind of anarchist:

Mankind is an evil animal. His wickedness must be controlled. Society exists to organise that wickedness. Therefore society is criminal. That's why I agree with the extreme

anarchist: 'I want *total destruction*. That's good; above all, it's *clear*'.[17]

THE ROMANCE OF ANARCHISM

Henry James (1843-1916)

W. H. Tilley demonstrated plausibly that Henry James drew his plot for *The Princess Casamassima* (1886) from an unsuccessful attempt on the part of two conspirators, Rupsch and Küchler, acting under the orders of an anarchist leader named Reinsdorf, to assassinate the German emperor William I at Niederwald on 28 September 1883.[18] The detail that seems to have attracted James to the story was the fact that at their trial one of the would-be assassins, the twenty-one-year-old Rupsch, claimed to have deliberately frustrated the attempt out of some misgiving or change of heart. From these circumstances—extensively reported in the British magazines and newspapers of late 1884—James derived his story of a young radical whose political commitment compels him to swear to a great European anarchist a mysterious oath to undertake at some future time some unspecified act of terrorism. With the oath Hyacinth Robinson's revolutionary zeal begins to wither, and the novel ends with his frustrating by suicide his own appointed task of assassination.[19]

The historical origin does not in practice confer on James's novel any very obvious specificity of historical presentation: James's interest in the story is so far from any particularity of political definition that I have categorised *The Princess Casamassima* as a romance rather than a novel of anarchism. The heart of the plot is a conventional 'moral-problem' dilemma: Hyacinth finds himself compelled to choose between a growing love of 'life' (represented by his increasing fascination with the slumming radical aristocrat-by-marriage, Princess Christina, and by brief trips to Paris and Venice); and the 'duty' which devolves to him by virtue of his revolutionary allegiance. In the 'Preface' James characterises Hyacinth as 'some individual sensitive

nature of fine mind, some small obscure intelligent creature'[20] whose social deprivation fills him with jealousy of
'all the ease of life of which he tastes so little'. That intelligible envy is figured (in James's metaphor) as a kind of
rabid dog which infects the subject with socialism: 'bitter,
under this exasperation, with an aggressive, vindictive,
destructive social faith' (p.18). The plot is made to turn on a
'change-of-heart' crisis: 'the deep dilemma of the disillusioned and repentant conspirator', whose 'militant
socialism' becomes 'out of all tune with his passion, at any
cost, for life itself, the life, whatever it be, that surrounds
him' (p.18). The ideological innocence, the naïve transparency of the novel's underlying ideas is quite alarming
when one considers James's 'status' in the literary
hierarchy: political radicalism springs from envy and is
incompatible with a love of life; 'love' and 'life' itself are
conceived as inseparably bound up with aristocratic
affiliation and with bourgeois culture.

The allusions to socialism and anarchism are positively
Gothic in their elusive and spectral mysteriousness:
though so acutely 'sensitive' to fine discriminations of
social nuance and emotional subtlety, James was as little
concerned as *The Times* to make any serious political
distinction between socialism, communism, anarchism
and terrorist violence. The 'militant socialism' of the novel
appears in the curiously unrecognisable form of a vast
international underground conspiracy dedicated in some
unspecified way to the destruction of civilisation as Henry
James knew it. Paul Muniment describes it:

> 'there's an immense underworld peopled with a thousand
> forms of revolutionary passion and devotion. The manner in
> which it's organised astonished me . . . In silence, in dark-
> ness, but under the feet of each one of us, the revolution lives
> and works. It's a wonderful, immeasurable trap, on the lid of
> which society performs its antics. When once the machinery is
> complete there'll be a great rehearsal.'   (pp.290-1)

The defensive convolutions of James's 'Preface' stand as a
sufficient acknowledgement of the fact that this immense

subterranean conspiracy corresponds to nothing other than the author's social paranoia:

> My vision of the aspects I more or less fortunately rendered was, exactly, my knowledge. If I made my appearances live, what was this but the utmost one could do with them? Let me at the same time not deny that, in answer to probable ironic relections on the full licence for sketchiness and vagueness and dimness taken indeed by my picture, I had to bethink myself in advance of a defence of my 'artistic position'. Shouldn't I find it in the happy contention that the value I wished most to render and the effect I wished most to produce were precisely those of our not knowing, of society's not knowing, but only guessing and suspecting and trying to ignore, what 'goes on' irreconcilably, subversively, beneath the vast smug surface?
> (p.22)

Hyacinth's mysterious vow of commitment derives directly from the political novels and romances of the 1840s (for example *Mary Barton* and *Sybil*) in which trade unions enjoin on their members, by arcane rituals and threats of violent reprisal, terrible oaths of obligation. The emotional reverberations of moral panic surrounding this motif can only derive from a deep-seated ideological terror of dissent: a profound anxiety at the very thought of ritualised commitment to something other than the established order—'He had taken a vow of blind obedience, the vow as of the Jesuit fathers to the head of their order' (p.294).

James's approach to the subject differs most strikingly from Zola's and Conrad's, not in his lack of interest in political and historical actuality, but in his relative incapacity to participate in the operations of the destructive imagination, or to recognise that link between artist and anarchist so evident in the other two writers. A passage of *The Princess Casamassima* may seem to echo exactly both *Germinal* and *The Secret Agent:*

> he seemed to see, immensely magnified, the monstrosity of the great ulcers and sores of London—the sick, eternal misery crying out in the darkness in vain, confronted with granaries and treasure-houses and palaces of delight where shameless

satiety kept guard. In such a mood as this he felt there was no
need to consider, to reason: the facts themselves were as imperative as the cry of the drowning . . . the day had come for a
forcible rectification of horrible iniquities.   (p.254)

Yet the narrative tone here is in fact ironic: the fanatic's
apocalyptic vision of outcast London is offered as in itself a
betrayal of the 'reason' and 'consideration' which should,
presumably, be applied to the understanding of social
problems and the manner of their solution. Denied any
access to the aesthetic power of the libertarian imagination, James's concluding artistic gesture is to occlude the
social dimension and contain the destructive energies of
anarchism within the melodramatic perimeters of individual self-sacrifice: 'Mr Robinson has shot himself
through the heart!' (p.537).

E. Douglas Fawcett (1866-19?)

E. Douglas Fawcett's *Hartmann the Anarchist: or the Doom of
the Great City* (1893), a futuristic romance in the manner of
Jules Verne and H. G. Wells, offers (perhaps with the
greater transparency of popular fiction) a more overt disclosure of the contradictions at the heart of contemporary
artistic responses to anarchism. Narrative devices and
manipulations of plot secure for the reader a voyeuristic
fantasy of anarchist violence, while the narrator is privileged to remain consistently aloof from anarchist activities,
and free to erect a barrier of moral diatribe between his own
bourgeois consciousness and the revolutionary terrorism
he witnesses and becomes involved in.

From the narrative perspective of an old man reminis-
cing in a quiet German retreat, Arthur Stanley offers a
detached retrospective of events supposed to have
occurred in 1920. His avowed narrative purpose is em-
pirical documentation: 'to weigh each event impartially in
the balance';[21] yet his story is one of reluctant participation
in an unsuccessful European revolution engineered by a
combination of anarchist terrorism and violent insurrection—he is drawn unintentionally into the political

action, and wastes no opportunity of reassuring the reader of the probity of his motives.

As in *Germinal* anarchism is defined politically in opposition to evolutionary socialism: the narrator is a 'labour advocate and socialist', and prospective parliamentary candidate for Stepney. His Socialism is explicitly defined as moderate and gradualist: 'I myself, though a socialist, was averse to barricades. "Not revolution, but evolution" was the watchword of my section' (p.5). Socialism is defined as the peaceful 'nationalisation of land and capital, of the means of production and distribution' (p.5). The spectre of independent political action by the working class is depicted in all the lurid colours of the Victorian reformist novel:

> How were the details of this vast change to be grappled with amid the throes of revolution? How deliberate with streets slippery with blood, the vilest passions unchained, stores, factories and workshops wrecked . . . what man or convention could beat out a workable constitution in the turmoil?
>
> (pp.5-6)

The narrator Arthur Stanley's social-democratic ideology is challenged by his friend Burnett,

> a man of the most advanced revolutionary opinions, in fact an apostle of what is generally known as anarchical communism. No law, no force, reference of all social energies to voluntary associations of individuals, were his substitutes for the all-regulating executive of the socialist. He made no secret of his intentions: he meant to wage war in every effective mode, violent or otherwise, against the existing social system.   (p.8)

Stanley characterises the anarchists, by comparison with the broad popular basis of the labour movement, as a 'handful of people, politically speaking of no account' (p.10); Burnett, in rejecting the possibility of a peaceful transition to socialism, invokes in a 'dark hint' an alternative source of political power, which might become available to such a dedicated minority group:

I detest both society as it is and society as you hope it will be.
Today the capitalist wolves and a slavish multitude; tomorrow
a corrupt officialism and the same slavish multitude, only with
new masters. But about our numbers, my friend, you think
that we must be politically impotent because we are relatively
few . . . But suppose, suppose, I say, our people had some
incalculable force . . .   (p.11)

That force is in fact already available in the hands of the
anarchist Hartmann, the Captain Nemo of the story, who
proposes to use it to destroy capitalist civilisation and
establish a system of 'supervised anarchy'. It is in fact a
flying machine, barbarically christened the *Attila*, with
which the anarchists are able to attack London from the air.
By drawing into fictional relationship anarchist terrorism
and the popular fantasy of the miraculous invention,
Fawcett was able to link in contradictory unity the intense
excitements and anxieties created by terrorist attacks, with
the ambivalent hopes and fears provoked by technological
advance. Even the inviolable morality of the narrator is
captivated by the excitements of the flying machine, which
combine aesthetic pleasures with a realisation of power—
'when to these purely artistic joys are added those of
power, when the roar of wondering cities rises upwards,
and you lean over the bulwarks serenely conscious of
superiority, you must be described as realising here on
earth one of the paradises of dreamland' (p.138). Equally
strong is his moral outrage of compassion at the vulnerability of the city and its people as that 'power' is exercised
destructively on London:

As we rode over the heart of the city—that sanctum of capital,
where the Bank of England, many other banks of scarcely less
brilliant fame, the Royal Exchange, Stock Exchange, where
credit companies, insurance offices, and discount houses in-
numerable lie herded—the bombs fell in a tempest, shattering
fabric after fabric, and uprooting their very foundations.
There was a constant roar of explosions, and the loss of life
must have been something terrible.   (p.151)

Terrorist attacks on London during the 1880s and 1890s

created an intense awareness of the vulnerability of a city to clandestine assault. Fawcett's fantasy extrapolates that anxiety to a futuristic fear of aerial bombardment, as Hartmann's craft unloads explosive bombs, boiling oil and blazing petrol on to the buildings and crowds below. The effect, for us, is sharply ironic: the fantasy of an illegal, dissident force wielding such weapons clashes against the known and familiar violence of constitutional governments—incendiary bombs on Hamburg and Dresden, nuclear explosions over Hiroshima and Nagasaki, napalm billowing over the forests of Cambodia and North Vietnam.

The dominant image of the novel, effectively foregrounded in a frontispiece illustration, is the fall of the Houses of Parliament under the assault of Hartmann's bombs. Inevitably writers who touched this topic were concerned to stress the inseparable nature of the state and its citizens, of institutions and the people whose lives are interrelated with them. There can be no such thing as a violent physical attack on an institution (which many writers could have understood or even condoned) which is not also an 'outrage' directed against innocent people. Where Zola focused on the identity of the mine and its workforce, so Souvarine could not destroy the one without damaging the other; Fawcett focuses on the interdependence of Parliament and people, as Westminster falls, 'bruising into jelly a legion of buried wretches' (p.15).

Hartmann's plot fails, and in the established context of anarchist atrocity the narrator heartily endorses the brutal repression—such as summary execution of suspected anarchists—entailed in a re-establishing of 'order'. The most curious feature of the book lies, not in its disclosure of contradictory responses, but in its absent conclusion. Hartmann's global ambition was to deal what Souvarine called the 'knock-out blow' to world capitalism.

His aim was to pierce the ventricle of the heart of civilisation, that heart which pumps the blood of capital everywhere, through the arteries of Russia, of Australia, of India . . . 'Paralyse this heart,' he has said, 'and you paralyse credit and

the mechanism of finance almost universally.'   (p.148)

But this objective recording of Hartmann's fanatical aspiration is completed by a striking conclusion: 'The result already known to history proves that he was right' (p.148). By means of some unspecified and undescribed social transition, the anarchist ideals and terrorist violence of Hartmann have in practice succeeded in destroying capitalism and clearing a path for the development of a socialist state. The narrator's final relapse into civilised domestic life and individual creativity (he retires from politics to take up the secluded domestic pleasures of marriage and 'literary studies') takes place on the basis of a quiet revolution effected in the aftermath of Hartmann's war. An eloquent silence thus articulates in the novel the desirability of that which is most feared.

ANARCHIST NOVELS

Olivia Rossetti (1873-19?)

'Isabel Meredith', pseudonymous authoress of *A Girl among the Anarchists*, (1903) was in fact Olivia Rossetti, daughter of William Michael of the pre-Raphaelite circle. With her sister Helen she began in 1895 to publish *The Torch: a Revolutionary Journal of Anarchist Communism*, a short-lived but impressive production, which published work by European anarchists such as Louise Michel, Malatesta and Zhukovsky, and managed to include writing by Zola himself. This youthful involvement with the cultural propaganda of anarchism is addressed retrospectively in the prose work in question.

    A Girl among the Anarchists does not employ the classic novel form, though it is certainly a work of fiction: it gives the appearance of a fictionalised memoir or semi-documentary *Bildungsroman*. In an interesting preface, Morley Roberts suggests that it is in fact an autobiographical 'testament of youth':

There is nothing whatever in *A Girl among the Anarchists* which is invented, the whole thing is an experience told very simply, but I think convincingly. Nevertheless as such a human document must seem incredible to the ordinary reader, I have no little pleasure in saying that I know what she has written to be true . . . I knew 'Kosinski' and still have an admiration for 'Nekrovitch'.[22]

Considered as such the novel is a useful historical document, an informed eye-witness account of the intellectual and political circle gathered around Kropotkin during his long residence in England from 1886, and of its links with the anarchist movement in Europe. None the less, despite these documentary pretensions, the work possesses a particular artistic form which in turn is the articulation of its ideological engagement with anarchist philosophy and political practice.

The book's design enacts a trajectory of disillusionment, as the narrator–heroine throws herself with enthusiasm into the anarchist movement and is ultimately expelled on a curve of chastened disenchantment. Its 'deep structure' could therefore be said to align with that of *The Princess Casamassima;* but the effective differences are substantial and instructive. Rossetti's narrative describes and enacts an actual engagement with anarchist ideas, which are articulated and debated in the text with clarity and understanding; and testifies to the actuality of radical political commitment on the cultural fringes of the labour movement during the 1890s. 'Isabel's' ultimate decision to turn her back on anarchism, though articulated, like Hyacinth Robinson's, as a decision in favour of 'life', is remote from the Jamesian revulsion against his own crude popular identification of anarchism with violence. It is not an abhorrence of terrorism that induces Isabel to leave the movement, but a confirmed dissatisfaction with anarchism as an effective political force, and with the anarchist philosophy as a satisfactory guide to individual living (pp.271 ff.).

The familiar paradox of idealism and violence is broached immediately in Roberts's 'Preface':

> Curiously enough I have found most Anarchists of the mildest
> dispositions . . . For it must be understood that the 'red wing'
> of the Anarchists is a very small section of the body of philo-
> sophers known as Anarchists. There is no doubt that those of
> the dynamite section are practically insane.   (p.vi)

Where the 'Preface' is defensively apologetic (though quite
clear about the repression of anarchism as a pretext for
illegitimate state violence) the text turns on a rather different version of that paradox: where Roberts reproduces the
conventional antithesis between innocuous idealism and
pernicious violence, Rossetti constantly poses anarchist
idealism, as morally heroic and politically powerful,
against the various kinds of selfishness, weakness, lazi-
ness and sordid calculation which are seen as drawing
people to the fringes of an anarchist group. Isabel is
initially attracted to the anarchist position for its lofty
idealism, which seems to shame the mundanity and petty
materialism of Social Democracy:

> Quite a new side of the problem—that of its moral bearings
> and abstract rights as opposed to the merely material right to
> daily bread which had first appealed to my sense of justice and
> humanity—now opened before me. The right to complete
> liberty of action, the conviction that morality is relative and
> personal and can never be imposed from without, that men are
> not responsible, or only very partially so, for their surround-
> ings, by which their actions are determined, and that conse-
> quently no man has the right to judge his fellow; such and
> similar doctrines which I heard frequently upheld, impressed
> me deeply. I was morally convinced of their truth, and conse-
> quently more than half an anarchist.   (p.17)

This structural opposition often relegates 'politics' to the
realm of the trivial and sordid: while true anarchism is
admired both for its moral purity and for the decisive
political will expressed in acts of terrorism. The Greenwich
Park explosion of 1892 which stands at the centre of *The
Secret Agent* is woven into the action of *A Girl among the
Anarchists*. But where the 'supremely intelligent' Conrad
followed *The Times* in suspecting and condemning some

insane project of destruction, Rossetti offers an interestingly different version: the dead anarchist is seen as a victim of his brother's treachery, and the brother subjected to an intense moral condemnation for the cowardice of denying any terrorist intention (pp.50-2). Isabel assists in procuring the escape of one 'Jean Matthieu', 'suspected of complicity in the Paris bomb explosions' (p.160).²³ Later in the novel an attempt is made to explain the psychological condition of the anarchist terrorist, by the case of Emile Henry, who was historically responsible for the bombing of the Café Terminus at the Gare St Lazare in 1894. The fanaticism of the terrorist is related to the fanaticism of the 'secular saint':

> Among the Anarchists, who may be said to represent the intellectual rather than the material side of the Socialist movement—there were many fanatics. This fanaticism showed itself in different ways—sometimes in the most admirable self-abnegation, in the sacrifice of wealth, position, and happiness; frequently in abnormal actions of other kinds, and most noticeably in deeds of violence.
>
> . . . Emile Henry, the dynamitard of the Café Terminus, belonged to the number of what I may call the theoretical dynamitard. His terrible acts were the outcome of long and earnest thought; they were born of his mental analysis of the social canker. He committed them not in moments of passion, but with all the *sang froid* of a man governed by reason. His defence when on trial was a masterpiece of logical deduction.
>
> (p.188)

The culminating action of the novel appears to be a fictionalisation of more than one incident in the history of Spanish anarchist terrorism: including the failed attempt on the life of Martínez Campos, Captain-General of Barcelona, in 1893, and the shooting of Antonio Canovas by an Italian anarchist Michele Angiolilli, in reprisal for the widespread repression and appalling tortures that followed the Barcelona bombing of June 1886. In the novel the Italian anarchist 'Giannoli' makes an unsuccessful attempt on the life of the Spanish Prime Minister in Madrid. The narrative presents this action not as a providentially

deflected atrocity, but as an unfortunately unsuccesful attempt to secure justice:

> This then was the deed he had been contemplating! . . . he would be garotted; I only hoped that he might not be tortured first. I gave a hasty glance at the other details given by the paper. A column was dedicated to the virtues of the prime-minister. He was . . . represented as the man who had saved Spain from ruin and disaster by his firm repression of the revolutionary parties: by which euphonious phrase the papers referred to the massacres of strikers which had taken place at Barcelona and Valladolid, and the wholesale arrest and imprisonment of Anarchists and Socialists in connection with a recent anti-clerical movement which had convulsed the Peninsula.   (p.291)

Olivia Rossetti's proximity to the *avant-garde* cultural circle which had its firm connections, through figures like William Morris, with the revolutionary socialist movement, render her interests in anarchism to some extent aesthetic-bohemian in nature; and her romantic adulation for political idealism and moral perfection is capable of projecting the very category of politics into the untouchable sordidness of a mean and petty present. Her intellectual grasp of political ideas enables her however to recognise, in an insight inaccessible to Conrad or James, that anarchist philosophy could be seen to embody enduring and imperative values, and that anarchist politics should be evaluated in the context of the legitimised violence and repression of the imperialist nation-states.

Frank Harris (1855-1931)

Frank Harris's *The Bomb* (1908) is distinguished by its consistent endorsement not only of anarchist philosophy and ideals, but even of acts of revolutionary terrorism—specifically the bomb which killed a number of policemen in Chicago in 1886. A workers' demonstration was fired on by police and several men killed. The following day, as the police moved in to break up a protest meeting, a bomb was thrown from a side-alley and casualties fell. A round-up of

anarchists followed, and eight local leaders, including August Spies and Albert Parsons, editors respectively of two of Chicago's five anarchist papers, were put on trial. The process was clearly a show trial, since no attempt was made to prove complicity in the bombing: the prosecution sought only to prove that the accused were anarchists and revolutionaries. A subsequent enquiry found that none of the accused had any part in the bombing: but four had already been executed.

The Bomb is thus a historical novel, weaving a fictional framework around documented facts, and presenting a vivid and open dramatisation of the anarchist point of view. The central incident of the bomb-throwing is used both to portray a legitimate resistance to intolerable economic, social and political conditions, particularly the aggressive brutality of the police, mobilised to break up peaceful demonstrations; and to disclose the machinery of injustice provoked into action to secure the judicial murder of Chicago labour leaders.

The true Chicago bomb-thrower was never discovered, and Harris's fiction supplies that absence by attributing the deed to his narrator–hero, Rudolph Schnaubelt. An expatriate German 'freethinker and republican', Schnaubelt arrives in the United States with lofty egalitarian ideals and a meritocratic confidence in the likelihood of personal success. But the experience of prolonged unemployment breeds bitter and vindictive thoughts:

> The humiliations filled me with rage, and this rage and fear fermented in me into bitterness which bred all-hating thoughts. When I saw rich men entering a restaurant, or driving in Central Park, I grew murderous . . . One conclusion settled itself in me; there was something rotten in a society which left good brains and willing hands without work.[24]

Harris describes effectively the misery of unemployment, with its burden of shame, humiliation and personal guilt. Among the workers Schnaubelt finds comradeship and the solidarity of 'human sympathy'; and gradually his feelings set in anger against the rich: 'It is only the poor who help

the poor. I have been down in the depths, and have brought back scarcely anything more certain than that. One does not learn much in hell except hate . . .' (p.27). Finding work at last, he enters the physically intolerable conditions of working on the foundations of the Brooklyn Bridge (pp.31-8); and from that baptism of fire emerges in full political consciousness to join the ranks of a 'proletariat ready for revolt'. Against that growing force Chicago arraigns its notoriously brutal police force: 'for the first time in America orderly meetings on vacant lots are dispersed with force, and thoughts are met with police bludgeons' (p.85).

As in *Hartmann the Anarchist*, the power of the organised working class is not deemed sufficient to resist the aggression of an incited state: and the force required is found in an anarchist saint, Louis Lingg. To Schnaubelt he is a saviour, a Redeemer: 'the greatest man that ever lived, I think . . . He had vitality enough in him to bring the dead to life, passion enough for a hundred men . . . he is the spring of all my growth' (pp.8-9). Lingg proposes that the movement should meet force with force: 'Violence must be met with violence' (p.97). His anarchism combines syndicalism with individualism: society should allow the individual as much freedom as possible by permitting economic control to rest with individuals. And it is as an individual that Lingg will strike at the heart of the bourgeoisie, with the aid of a powerful explosive device.

Schnaubelt throws the bomb, Lingg guides him to freedom, and is subsequently himself arrested. Sentenced to death, he offers as a defiance his theory of equal forces and of 'propaganda by deed':

> 'I believe in force just as you do. That is my justification. Force is the supreme arbiter in human affairs. You have clubbed unarmed strikers, shot them down in your streets, shot down their women and their children. So long as you do that, we who are Anarchists will use explosives against you.'   (p.268)

After reaching England Schnaubelt himself endures an attenuated existence, living vicariously in the events of

Chicago: the trial and subsequent death of Lingg in prison by his own explosives. His final purpose becomes that of telling Lingg's story and establishing his fame as an anarchist martyr:

> One thing is past doubt. Louis Lingg was a great man, and a born leader of men, who with happier chances might have been a great reformer, or a great statesman. When they talk of him as a murderer, it fills me with pity for them, for in Lingg, too, was the blood of the martyrs: he had the martyr's pity for men, the martyr's sympathy with suffering and destitution, the martyr's burning contempt for greed and meanness, the martyr's hope for the future, the martyr's belief in the ultimate perfectibility of man. (p.309)

Anarchist violence is seen both as the outcome of a fanatical logic, and as a resistance to conditions of repression so harsh as to justify among the workers extreme measures of self-defence. Both the theory of anarchism and the practice of political violence are explored in the historical context of capitalist crisis and class struggle, and in the psychological context of unemployment and individual impotence in the face of bourgeois power. Frank Harris's treatment of the anarchist theme is certainly drawn towards the more mystical and quasi-religious dimension of anarchist thought, but at the same time located into contexts calculated to render anarchism intelligible rather than merely terrifying as a political force.

CONCLUSION

It is therefore possible to speak, despite my initial reservations, of a fiction of anarchism within the apparatus of late-Victorian/Edwardian British culture: a body of writing spanning the whole spectrum of artistic and ideological perspectives, from the established canonical 'great' writers who found the subject worth exploring, to the writers considered towards the end of this essay, who articulated in fictional form an engaged and appreciative response to anarchist philosophy and politics. What it was that attrac-

ted writers to anarchism, beyond the sensational appeal of terrorist outrages and the melodramatic possibilities lurking in dark illegal conspiracies, should now be clear. Anarchism offered an analysis and condemnation of society which in its totalising purity resembled the comprehensive moral visions of the imaginative artist. Some of the foundations of anarchist philosophy—their faith in the innate goodness of man, their belief in the possibility of ultimate individual liberty—are in themselves imaginative conceptions, mythical rather than materialist in form, and were inevitably attractive to those who chose to explore society by means of the imagination. Finally the artist who hopes to assist or secure through his art political or social change, finds himself in close kinship with the individualist anarchist, who also seeks the transformation of society by application of the individual will. I have identified in the novel of anarchism a species of political fiction: the relationships may well consist in the fact that anarchism is itself a species of fictional (which is not, of course, the same thing as non-existent) politics.

NOTES

1. See Jeremy Hawthorn (ed.), *The British Working-Class Novel in the Twentieth Century* (London, 1984); and H. Gustav Klaus (ed.), *The Socialist Novel in Britain* (Brighton, 1982).
2. See George Woodcock, *Anarchism* (Harmondsworth, 1963), p.414, which is the best introduction to the subject. Also useful are James Joll, *The Anarchists* (London, 1964); and David Miller, *Anarchism* (London, 1984).
3. See Robert W. Kern, *Red Years, Black Years* (Philadelphia, 1978); and J. Romero Maura, 'The Spanish case' in David Apter and James Joll (eds.), *Anarchism Today* (London, 1971).
4. Woodcock, *op. cit.*, p.414.
5. See for example Edward Jenkins, *A Week of Passion, or the Dilemma of Mr George Barton the Younger* (London, 1884); and cf. my discussion of Henry James's *The Princess Casamassima* (1886), see p.134.

6. See for example Grant Allen, *For Maimie's Sake: a Tale of Love and Dynamite* (London, 1886); George Griffith, *The Angel of the Revolution: a Tale of the Coming Terror* (London, 1893); and, for a rather clearer analysis, Joseph Conrad's *Under Western Eyes* (London, 1911).

   For the role of true anarchism in Russian conditions, see Paul Avrich, *The Russian Anarchists* (Princeton, 1967).

7. Emile Zola, *Germinal*, translated by Leonard Tancock (Harmondsworth, 1954), p.144. Subsequent page references are to this edition and will be included in the text.

   For Marx and Bakunin, see Paul Thomas, *Karl Marx and the Anarchists* (London, 1980).

8. See Woodcock, *op. cit.*, p.21; and Daniel Guérin, *Anarchism* (New York, 1970), pp.41 ff.

9. See Woodcock, *op. cit.*, p.14; Morley Roberts, Preface to Isabel Meredith, *A Girl among the Anarchists* (London, 1903); and Barbara Arnett Melchiori, *Terrorism in the Late Victorian Novel* (London, 1985), pp.123, 137-8. The latter study came to hand in the middle of research for this essay: I found its assistance invaluable, though I disagree strongly with some of Melchiori's conclusions, especially on Zola (see p.148n.) and Conrad (see p.81).

10. The residual sexism of the antithesis made here should not obscure Zola's remarkable portraits of working-class women, especially that of Maheude.

11. Quoted in Woodcock, *op. cit.*, p.166.

12. P. B. Shelley, 'Hellas' (1822); see *The Poetical Works of Shelley*, ed Thomas Hutchinson (London, 1905, reset 1943), p.477.

13. Sam Dolgoff (ed.), *Bakunin on Anarchy* (London, 1973), p.57.

14. Joseph Conrad, 'Author's Note' (1920) to *The Secret Agent* (1907). This quotation is taken from the Penguin edition (Harmondsworth, 1963), pp.8-9. Subsequent page references are to this edition and will be included in the text.

15. Cf. Ulrike Meinhof's ambition to 'provoke by violence the latent fascism in the state'.

16. Melchiori, *op. cit.*, p.81.

17. Letter of February 1899; in C. T. Watts (ed.), *Joseph Conrad's Letter to R. B. Cunninghame Graham* (London, 1969), p.117. I have translated Conrad's French.

18. W. H. Tilley, *The Background of 'The Princess Casamassima'* (Gainesville, Florida, 1961).

19. An ending which resembles that of Oscar Wilde's play *Vera: or the Nihilists* (1882).
20. Henry James, *The Princess Casamassima* (Harmondsworth, 1977), p.8. Subsequent page references are to this edition and will be included in the text.
21. E. Douglas Fawcett, *Hartmann the Anarchist: or the Doom of the Great City* (London, 1893), p.1. Subsequent page references in the text.
22. Meredith, *op. cit.*, p.vi. Subsequent page references in the text.
23. See Woodcock, *op. cit.*, pp.287-94.
24. Frank Harris, *The Bomb* (London, 1908), p.22. Subsequent page references in the text.

· 7 ·

French naturalism and the English socialist novel: Margaret Harkness and William Edwards Tirebuck

INGRID VON ROSENBERG

DEFINITIONS

In France as well as in Germany or in Scandinavia there has never been much doubt about what 'naturalism' was; it has always been understood to be literature produced under the influence of scientific observation methods which were so conspicuously advanced in the last decades of the nineteenth century, a literature that approached society and the human psyche in a similar way as the sciences approached natural phenomena—hence the term 'naturalism'. Zola, for his part, made the point quite clear in his famous programmatic article 'Le roman expérimental' (1879). In Britain, on the other hand, a certain shyness could always be observed about using the term 'naturalism'. Both contemporary and later writers and critics preferred terms that hinted at the subject matter or setting like 'slum literature', 'social novel', 'novel of misery', etc., or used the confusing label 'realistic', which had already been applied in earlier literary contexts.[1] Whether this uncertainty originally sprang from the authors' wish to avoid the discrimination which French literature was meeting with in Britain or whether it simply mirrored the fact that the new way of writing in Britain did not stand in such sharp contrast to earlier traditions as in France, need not bother us here. What seems essential is to abandon evasive terms and to define the object of investigation clearly. By naturalistic literature I mean works that are obviously influenced by the new continental mode of writing, works that show

characteristic features such as a new precision in describing the details of a certain milieu, a preoccupation with the determining influence of social circumstances and heredity on people, and a new frankness in dealing with the dark sides of human existence, such as sickness, addiction and death, but also with human instincts, especially sexuality. The milieu described need not necessarily be a proletarian one; indeed, many continental writers turned in preference to bourgeois circles or rural communities rather than to the industrial proletariat, and even Zola set only three of his novels in working-class surroundings. But they were the works which by their subject and treatment inevitably appealed most to British writers with social or even socialist inclinations. As naturalism is not an ideology in itself, but merely a literary method bred under certain historical and epistemological conditions, it could be put to a variety of ideological uses, and this is what happened.

The term 'socialist novel' is not unproblematic either.[2] In order to cut a long discussion short I would like to describe socialist literature here simply as literature written from any kind of socialist viewpoint current at the time; and this, for the end of the century, means a large variety of diverse and not always stringent concepts. It would seem historically unfair, for instance, to demand compliance with the concept of socialist realism which was formulated only forty years later and within the context of a later development of socialist theory. Starting from these working definitions I shall look at the political convictions of the two authors to be considered here and examine to what extent and purpose they have used the new naturalistic writing techniques.

ZOLA AND HIS BRITISH DISCIPLES

The dramatic story of the reception of French naturalism in Britain is well known and need not be repeated here, but a few remarks may be apt.[3] Despite the hysterical public campaign against it, which culminated in the imprison-

ment of the publisher Vizetelly in 1889, British authors like
George Moore and George Gissing had from very early on
reacted with interest and admiration to the new mode of
writing. Two naturalistic subjects commanded particular
attention: the situation of the poorest levels of the proletariat, especially in the city slums; and the psychological
deprivation of middle-class women. In this essay I am not
concerned with the topic of female frustration; and I am not
going to discuss the work of the better known authors of
slum-fiction such as Gissing, Arthur Morrison or Richard
Whiteing, though particularly Gissing in *The Nether World*
(1889) and Morrison in *Tales of Mean Street* (1894) and *A
Child of the Jago* (1896) gave descriptions of life in the
London slums that in their clinically precise observation of
the appalling environment and in their grim insistence on
resultant phenomena like sickness, drink, violence and
prostitution come closer to Zola than those of any other
British writers. But their work has received quite a lot of
attention from critics already; and, more importantly, none
of them wrote from a socialist point of view. I want to focus
on the work of two writers with definite socialist inclinations who also followed in Zola's steps, though it should be
stated right from the beginning that they neither wrote
pure naturalism nor ever reached the literary mastership of
their great model.

In the case of Margaret Harkness we have two direct
hints in her novels that she actually had read and admired
Zola.[4] Tirebuck mentions Zola nowhere, but the traces of
his influence are unmistakeable, as will be shown presently. There was in any case no language problem, for
Vizetelly published translations of Zola's works in quick
succession, and some novels like *Germinal* (1885) came out
in England in the same year as in France.

Looking at the socialist literature of the 1880s and 1890s
one may be surprised to find only few British writers
making use of the new writing mode. John Goode has
pointed out that the two 'writers of substance' who identified themselves with socialism, namely Morris and Shaw,
'felt compelled to work in a different aesthetic frame from
that of a realist novel'.[5] Other writers of a lesser reputation

did choose the novel as their frame, but also abstained from realism. Examples are Constance Howell's *A More Excellent Way* (1888) and J. H. Clapperton's *Margaret Dunmore: or a Socialist Home* (1888). In the former novel the hero, well-to-do but socialist nevertheless, finds his special field of work in spreading the 'gospel' to his own class; in the latter the heroine inherits a big house which she converts into a 'socialist home' for a group of her middle-class friends.[6]

It seems to me that the scarcity of realism in socialist literature may have something to do with the situation of the working class as well as of the socialist movement at the time. Proletarian writers were rare, due to the modest general level of education and very limited leisure time. Novelists with socialist ideas came as a rule from, or were close to, the still large and dominant middle-class membership of the various socialist groups and fractions and may have felt too remote from the everyday experience of the workers, particularly the poorest levels, to write about them. Margaret Harkness and Tirebuck were, as journalists, in an exceptional position. But there may have been a further obstacle to the use of naturalism on a larger scale: the concept of determinism is not easy to reconcile with the socialist conviction of the possibility of change through the victims of society themselves. If the living conditions of the proletariat were depicted in their true dark colours, it would be difficult to create characters growing up in this milieu who were convincingly strong and educated enough to fight back or even lead the struggle. This dilemma has puzzled left-wing theoreticians ever since the emergence of naturalism, and some, like Georg Lukács and Bertolt Brecht, rejected naturalism altogether as a suitable literary technique to promote socialism.

That despite such theoretical difficulties, a socialist perspective could very well be combined with the naturalistic writing mode had, however, been proved by Zola, and perhaps in no other novel better than in *Germinal* (1885), the story of a strike in one of the northern French coalfields.

MARGARET HARKNESS (1854-192?)

Margaret Harkness was a clergyman's daughter.[7] Having trained and worked as a nurse for some years, she became a journalist, doing research on, and writing about, the slums in the East End of London. Through her contacts with leading personalities of the left she quickly assimilated socialist ideas which gave perspective to her observations, but she was never able to develop a well-founded and stable political stance.

Though Harkness's work covers a wide range of interests, her five socialist novels stand out as central. In the first four of these she made a marked use of naturalism, and it is worth noting that she did so almost as early as George Moore, who is commonly regarded as Zola's first British disciple: Harkness's first four novels were published between 1887 and 1890, at the peak of the British controversy over the new mode.

The reader of these novels is immediately struck by the cool accuracy of the many descriptions of streets and interiors, of living rooms, kitchens, prison cells, workhouses, hospitals and pubs in the poor quarters of the industrial centres of London and Manchester. Some of these descriptions would fit well into one of the social reports of the time, by, for instance, Charles Booth. Take this passage from *Out of Work* (1888):

> He was taken into a cell that measured eight feet by four feet, at the end of which was a small dark hole called the stone-pit. The cell was lighted by a jet of gas . . . Jos sat down on the low bedstead, and looked at the cell. It had no furniture whatsoever, except the mattress and the rug on which he was sitting. An icy wind swept through the stone-pit, so he went to see if a door would shut out the draught. But no door was there, only a large iron window, with bars across, through which flints must be thrown . . . Large blocks of granite lay in the stone-pit, also a hammer. There was no seat, and the floor of the place dipped in the middle, so it was difficult to stand upright.[8]

With equally dry precision social habits, bred in the

circumstances, are reported: the drinking; the violence among the men and also among the women; the drug-taking to dull the hunger; the crude entertainment in pubs, music halls and penny gaffs; the crime, even murder. But Harkness also tells of mutual help and tentative signs of solidarity: the down-and-outs in the doss-house in *Out of Work* share their last scraps of food, and an old tramp watches from afar over the steps of the lonely young widowed mother in *A Manchester Shirtmaker* (1890).

As to the intensity of such naturalistic descriptions I see a development in Harkness's work in the form of a wave: Whereas in her first novel *A City Girl* (1887) naturalism is still strongly mixed with romance, it becomes dominant in *Out of Work* (1888), *Captain Lobe* (1889) and *A Manchester Shirtmaker* (1890), but is absent from *George Eastmont: Wanderer*, published fifteen years later in 1905. The latter work resembles such earlier novels of ideas as Howell's *A More Excellent Way*, telling the story of Harkness's disappointment with socialism in the form of a *Bildungsroman* with a young upper-class idealist as the hero. The stages of his disillusionment are more marked by theoretical discussions and intellectual 'insights' than by living experience of working-class reality.[9] Thus it seems as if Harkness's use of naturalism was closely bound up with her socialist convictions, and, indeed, at the time when she was writing her slum novels her political commitment was strongest: in 1888 she supported Keir Hardie in an (unsuccessful) by-election campaign in Ayrshire, and in 1889 she was involved in the organisation of the great London dockers' strike. Yet her handling of naturalistic techniques was not equally skilful in her four slum novels, the weakest being *Captain Lobe*, possibly due to a first shadow of doubt. In the fourteenth chapter there is some sharp criticism of all socialist groups existing at the time, which foreshadows her later break with the movement. A nameless 'lady', a thinly disguised mouthpiece of the author, says: ' "They are so jealous. They cannot work together. They split into small parties, and spend their time quarrelling . . .!" '[10] When in this novel the reader witnesses street fights, family rows or drunken bouts, he does so through the eyes

of Salvation Army members, who are observers but not personally affected. As these scenes are not integrated into the plot, the novel is in danger of disintegrating into a loose series of unconnected tableaux seen from a distance.

The three other slum novels escape this danger as the naturalistic observations are to a large extent linked to the main characters, thereby forming constituents of the plot. So the violence in *A City Girl*, perpetrated by the heroine's brother, is directly aimed at her, and so is the cold indifference of the hospital nurses with whom Nelly has to leave her sick baby. In *A Manchester Shirtmaker* the heroine herself experiences the exploitation of sweat labour and kills her baby with drugs because she has no more food to give him.[11] And in *Out of Work* the reader is confronted directly with the growing hopelessness of the permanently unemployed through the hero's experience, though the general significance is underlined by the addition of a whole range of further sufferers.

The choice of a working-class hero or, more frequently, heroine also helped to strengthen the impact of Harkness's political message, notwithstanding a rather simple character psychology. As a complementary step she deliberately broke with a convention of the middle-class social novel, the angelic heroine. In *Out of Work* a pious young middle-class beauty makes her appearance in the person of Polly, the devoted Methodist, who is engaged to Jos, the jobless carpenter. But no unrealistic union between the classes through the medium of religion takes place. When Jos cannot find work and gradually sinks to the level of a tramp, Polly jilts him and marries her Methodist instructor, who has a safe and highly symbolic job at the Royal Mint. At the moment of final parting Jos unmasks not only Polly but a whole literary tradition when he calls her a 'little hypocrite', a judgement that keeps resounding in his memory.[12] Harkness skilfully juxtaposes the falling goddess of the past with the new working-class heroine in the person of Squirrel, a selfless little flower-girl, who becomes Jos's second love. When, in her weaker novel *Captain Lobe*, Harkness does make use of the conventional middle-class heroine, she does so only half-heartedly, for though Ruth

means well and does no harm, her parasitical nature is exposed in the end: 'She was one of those creatures who cannot stand alone, who must fall to the earth if they have nothing to keep them upright. "A poor sort of creature," Jane Hardy said, "not much better than a young curate." '[13]

However, not even in Harkness's three strongest novels was the use of naturalism complete, and it remains to look at the limitations, which need not necessarily be artistic weaknesses. First, even though she did not only describe deplorable social conditions but also their degrading effects on the psyche, she went the whole way only with her minor characters. With her central figures she took great pains not to let them sink morally too low. Nowhere do they take part in violence or serious crime; none has an innate flaw of character like so many of Zola's protagonists. Jos in *Out of Work* does give way to his inherited tendency to drink and behaves selfishly to the loving Squirrel, but he is shown as generous at the beginning when he buys medicine for a friend's sick child with his first earnings after a long period of unemployment; Mary, the shirt-maker, may kill her own child, but only after she has starved herself for the baby's sake. Neither of them can really be condemned, not even by the strict standards of Victorian morality, so obviously are they merely driven by circumstances. This is also true of Nelly, the city girl guilty of extra-marital sex. Presumably Harkness wanted to make her central figures sympathetic to the reader on behalf of her socialist conviction: it was important to show the plight of the proletariat and even the moral dangers they were in, but it would not do to show them beyond hope of redemption, given different circumstances.

Another limitation may be due to less conscious and less positive reasons. Harkness is, in marked contrast to French naturalists, very secretive about the description of sexual feelings, let alone activities. The seduction in *A City Girl*, for instance, takes place in the space of two lines.[14] Besides, Nelly does not seem drawn to Mr Grant so much by passion, but because by his well-groomed appearance, smart clothes and fine speech 'he became mixed up with the ideal, nameless lover who played so great a part in her

thoughts'.[15] He represents a brighter life to her, and there may be a faint echo of *Madame Bovary* here rather than of Zola. In Harkness's following books no more physical encounters happen at all: Jos in *Out of Work* has two platonic loves; the shirtmaker is a widow; and in *Captain Lobe* the seduction theme, though embarked upon, is dropped halfway, the heroine running away at the critical moment. Perhaps even more significant seems that, though Nelly, the city girl, is not condemned but pitied by the author, her physical surrender is, nevertheless, treated as a lapse and Nelly is, if not actually killed by the author, then at least punished by her child's death. This ambivalent treatment of physical love, still so much in conformity with official Victorian morals, may well have had something to do with a personal insecurity on the part of Margaret Harkness. Other new women writers, such as Olive Schreiner, had similar difficulties, and while George Moore, Grant Allen and 'George Egerton' (Mary Chavelita Dunne) were already breaking the taboos, the works of Schreiner, Sarah Grand and others bear witness to the same personal conflicts: theoretically they underlined a woman's right to sexual fulfilment in their books, but they dared not allow their heroines to enjoy it on the level of action.

But, as John Goode has pointed out, it is of some importance that Nelly—in contrast to so many other heroines of British naturalistic fiction such as Gissing's Thyrza, Moore's Kate, Hardy's Tess and also Tirebuck's Dorrie—is after all permitted to live on after her crisis. Though it may be slightly exaggerated to see in Nelly's endurance the vehicle of all the 'novel's political thrust', it can certainly be valued as a sign of budding feminism.[16] In George Moore's *Esther Waters* (1894), which was published seven years later, the feature is already much more pronounced: Esther does not merely survive, but is allowed to bring up her illegitimate son and even later to enter into a happy marriage with her former seducer.

It seems to me that the political message of the novel rests on the whole of the narrative fabric, that is Harkness's naturalistic picture of working-class life including the suffering as well as the brave endurance. Remembering

that Harkness's use of naturalism was most stringent while her socialist commitment was strongest, one may draw the conclusion that it was just the power of pictures of poverty and degradation that she trusted to win over readers to a new world-view. In other words: Harkness obviously held naturalism to be an effective literary technique to convey socialist ideas, even without incorporating theoretical arguments into the text. If this was so, one can understand why she did not follow Engels's advice, who in his famous letter concerning *A City Girl* had taken issue with Harkness's portrayal of the working-class characters as a purely passive mass. For though she may have made her characters more 'typical' in the later novels, she never depicted workers who were active in the labour movement. Instead she went on drawing her grim pictures of the downtrodden, proving her faith in naturalism's power of persuasion.

WILLIAM EDWARDS TIREBUCK (1854-1900)

Born in Liverpool in 'humble circumstances', Tirebuck left school at the age of eleven to work in various offices.[17] Early literary inclinations made him turn to journalism, but his journalistic career, during which he worked for some time for the *Yorkshire Post*, was short, and he soon retired to live first in Scotland, later in Wales, his mother's homeland. During those years of withdrawal he wrote twelve books including art criticism, short stories, various romantic novels and the three novels dealing with problems of social reality that are of interest in our context. Two biographical points seem relevant for his view of the world: on the one hand his biographer Hogben testifies to a certain 'unworldliness' in him, on the other hand Tirebuck contributed an article 'On the verge of change' to an anthology *The New Party* (1894) containing essays by members and sympathisers of the newly founded Independent Labour Party. These two forces, Christian beliefs and socialist views, were to leave their characteristic stamp on his work.

Tirebuck's second novel and the first to include natura-

listic traits, *Dorrie* (1891), can be read as proof that his socialism grew out of Christian convictions. Dorrie is a beautiful and buxom girl of seventeen. She keeps house with her less attractive, but pious and diligent sister Katherine (the pair are reminiscent of Hetty and Dinah in George Eliot's *Adam Bede*), and they have a lodger, the blind young lay preacher Nathaniel Brant, who spends his day quoting from the Bible on a street corner. Both girls are attracted by Nat who feels more drawn to Dorrie. But he suffers from pangs of conscience, for his feelings are more of the physical than of the spiritual kind. After some dramatic scenes Dorrie runs away to make a career in the theatre, while Nat meets a middle-class benefactor, Mr Franklin, the richest merchant in Liverpool, who not only takes him to Italy for an operation to restore his eyesight, but sets him up as a preacher with a house of his own in the village of his manor house. Some years later Nat who, though living with Katherine, has kept looking out for Dorrie, finally discovers her as a prostitute in a Liverpool brothel, mortally ill with syphilis. He takes her home, and together with Katherine nurses her in her last illness. At the very end a strange secret is revealed: Mr Franklin's wife, who has been unaccountably moody and ailing all through the action, confesses that she is Dorrie's illegitimate mother and had long ago left her child with a respectable working-class family. Mother and daughter die in a first and last embrace, while Nat and Katherine finally marry.

Naturalistic elements can be located in this novel not so much in faithful descriptions of Liverpool streets and places—though there are a few—as in the emphasis on the influence of heredity in Dorrie's story. In the end it is revealed that the vitality, restlessness and frivolity that had puzzled her sister and Nat so much, were in fact inherited from her mother, and so perhaps was her syphilis, though she may instead have contracted it from one of her lovers. Again and again the author stresses the influence of the past on Dorrie's behaviour: 'The fact was, though Dorrie herself did not know it, the greater part of her conflict was with the past, a past that insisted upon the present, a past that was at that moment moulding the possibilities of

her future.'[18]

Dorrie's craving for the theatre and indeed some of the adventures in her bohemian life may well owe something to specific novels by Zola or to George Moore's *A Mummer's Wife* (1885). Dorrie resembles Moore's Kate—although she is not an adulteress, but an unmarried girl—in using the theatrical world as a means of escape from the drab domestic life of a respectable working-class home and the boredom of sewing for her living. Moore, in his turn, was indebted mainly to *Thérèse Raquin* (1867) and *Nana* (1880).[19] Some of the scenes in *Dorrie* in their precise observation of setting as well as of human behaviour remind one indeed of scenes from *Nana*. When Dorrie, for instance, manages to advance to the office of a theatre director for an audition but is rejected because she cannot read properly, the vividly painted scene reflects social realities. But there are equally many fantastic incidents—not just at the end of the novel—which are more reminiscent of Dickens than of Zola and hamper the realism of the story. For example, her career begins with a wildly romantic kidnapping: a Bengali restaurant owner holds her captive after a meal and forces her to dance on the stage of his music hall.

Where Tirebuck, like Harkness, does not follow his French models is in the treatment of sexuality. Though Dorrie has her lovers and becomes a prostitute, there is no explicit sexual scene; everything happens backstage. Tirebuck, of course, conforms to British Victorian morality like most other writers of his time who deal with the popular subject of the 'fallen woman'. But, interestingly, in this novel his conformity is not as complete as later in *Miss Grace of All Souls'* (1895). There are a number of situations when Dorrie's vivacity and hunger for pleasure are not treated as sinful, but appear as nothing more wicked than a natural and even charming liveliness. Such is the impression of some scenes in the country when Dorrie is looking for Nat, who is staying with the Franklins, and gets involved in a village dance or plays with children in the woods. At such moments she suddenly seems superior to Nat with his religious scrupulousness and primness, and it is this slight, but noticeable deviation from conventional

morality that makes the novel interesting reading. To Rhoda, Mr Franklin's rather subdued daughter and Dorrie's half-sister (though neither know this), Dorrie even seems something of a heroine, and her secret thoughts have a surprisingly feminist touch:

> In both a remote and near way Dorrie's case seemed one of discontent like her own. Dorrie, Rhoda fancied, must have felt Brant rather serious, strict, and emphatic. *She* felt that he was so . . . Rhoda could quite believe that Dorrie had passed through something like her own cramped existence, only Dorrie had carried her ideas much further than she could—she had carried them out in fact.[20]

But, of course, this tone is only a subversive undercurrent, and in the end Dorrie, like so many other 'fallen women' in Victorian literature, is sentenced to death.

Yet Dorrie's story is only part of the plot; the reader actually loses sight of her in the middle of the novel to meet her again only near the end. It is Nat who dominates the scene, not just because his presence is the more continuous, but, more importantly, because his standpoint provides the transcendent perspective. Through him the religious perspective becomes the dominant message of the novel. His story, which, in contrast to Dorrie's punishment for her sins, is one of virtue rewarded, conveys the impression that religiousness is enough to overcome the differences between the classes. When Nat is first brought to Mr Franklin's office and is offered a position as a preacher in a Liverpool chapel, the author comments:

> There, in secret committee, sat four of the wealthiest men in the town . . . but in their midst was one of the poorest men in the town . . . And yet those five lives were warmly united by an unexpressed fellowship with a sixth—the mystical and yet assured fellowship of a spirit greater than theirs—the humbling and yet ennobling, the subduing and yet rousing fellowship of God. It was remarkable, it was beautiful, it was touching that they should meet as they did.[21]

It is striking that Tirebuck, though he accentuates the

contrast between the modest lifestyle of the sisters and the luxurious one of the Franklins, does not introduce any socialist ideas into this novel, particularly as in his first novel *Saint Margaret* (1888) there had been some discussion of political ideas. The hero, also a religious young man working in the mission hall of a Liverpool church, leaves the church out of disappointment that so little is done for the poor of the parish and joins the United Liberals in a small town. There he is disappointed, too—the leaders seem to him merely personally ambitious and the workers undisciplined and lazy—so that he returns to his church to renew his efforts there. Thus religion wins, but at least the question of a possible political path is raised.

In contrast to these two earlier novels *Miss Grace of All Souls'* deals with a historical event, the great lock-out of the miners in 1893, which affected large parts of the English and Welsh coalfields, particularly in the north and the Midlands. The reason for this choice of subject, unusual for Tirebuck, may well have been that, living in the north, he actually witnessed and was deeply impressed by what happened.

When Tirebuck set out to describe what he had experienced there was a literary model ready at hand, published and translated into English ten years earlier: Zola's *Germinal*. Though there are indeed some astonishing resemblances between the two novels, which suggest that Tirebuck very probably took Zola's work as a model, there are also marked differences. The most important similarity lies in the general message. Both authors describe the awakening of a group of miners, hitherto patient slaves of the coal-owners, to joint political action and self-confident class consciousness. The change is brought about under the pressure of a particularly ruthless attempt to curtail the already barely sufficient wages. In *Germinal* the strikers are—in accordance with historical events—in the end defeated, but their spirit is unbroken: the seed, the 'germ', is sown, as the title suggests. In Tirebuck's novel the miners are victorious in the material sense: the old wage is guaranteed. But more important seems the feeling of union and common strength that has grown among them and might

be tapped in future struggles. The message of hope then is very similar in both novels and may indeed be called socialist—at least at a first glance.

Though there are very few minute descriptions of the work process and no Zolaesque pictures of domestic interiors, Tirebuck obviously borrowed a whole range of structural elements from *Germinal*, which helped to provide *Miss Grace* with a more unitary form than the still half-romantic *Dorrie*. Zola had personalised his subject by placing a typical working-class family of three generations at the centre of his novel, which gave him the opportunity to explore the full range of working-class experience from the young to the old and including women as well as men. In *Miss Grace* we find in the Ockleshaws a family almost exactly matching the composition of the Maheus in *Germinal:* there is a grandfather, a father, a mother, one grown-up daughter and two half-adult sons; only the younger brothers and sisters are missing. The growth of political consciousness through the generations is similar in both stories, and even the incident of the father's death by army bullets returns in *Miss Grace*. In addition, both authors contrast their central working-class family with a middle-class counterpart representing the employers. But while Zola, in order to symbolise the split of power and profit characteristic of an advanced stage of capitalism, introduced the two families of a rentier and of a managing director, Tirebuck needed only one family to mirror the more old-fashioned power-structure of the British coal industry: the Brooksters are owners as well as managers of the Beckerton pits. Both authors highlight the contrast between the two milieux by juxtaposing, for example, the frugal meals in the miner's kitchen with the luxurious dinner parties of the bourgeoisie. In both novels there is an additional network of minor characters, particularly a wide range of further working-class figures. But while in *Germinal* one may truly speak of the first emergence of a collective working-class hero, this is prevented in *Miss Grace* by the peculiar choice of the central figure.[22]

Structural similarities of the kind described need not necessarily indicate a true kinship of spirit, and, indeed,

despite the similar political message the tone of the two novels is profoundly different. Zola's stance may perhaps be summed up as a blending of the sharp observation of the workers' appalling living conditions with hope for their own and humanity's future, based on a thorough study of socialist theory, the discussion of which is integrated into the framework of the novel. When Zola describes the miserable present he does not shrink from including also the distortions of character wrought by want and lack of education. He is very explicit about the envy and gossiping of the women, the ignorance and the violence of the men, and the raw, sometimes brutal sexual relationships between them. Political maturity is achieved at the end after many errors, disappointments and great efforts and only by very few people, perhaps only by Etienne, the strike leader, and Maheude, the widowed mother.

Tirebuck's novel, on the other hand, is tuned to a hopeful note right from the beginning. There is never any real doubt that the workers will win in the end, and this impression is generated not so much by the integration of a coherent socialist perspective as by the portrayal of the workers. They may be poor and approach the brink of starvation during the lock-out, yet they remain warm-hearted and good, their solidarity never wavering. Here is a typical assessment of their reaction: 'The dumb endurance of the men in this and in other ways, their good temper, their self-control, their self-respect, their respect for others, were among the most appealing traits of the whole struggle.'[23] The miners share their last slice of bread, and the women help by taking on heavy physical work or by sacrificing their food to husbands and children. Solidarity even spreads to other groups of workers: 'railway-men, gas-men, iron-workers, tool makers, mill and factory hands of Beckerton and district were out by thousands' (p.189). This ubiquitous goodness, though certainly based on many actual observations, seems slightly idealised, as no exceptions are allowed.

The tendency is intensified by a further deviation from Zola. In his treatment of sexual relations Tirebuck again avoids the frank dealing with physical love, so integral a

a part of Zola's picture of proletarian life. Physical feelings are mentioned even less than in *Dorrie*; everything is thoroughly romantic between the three couples heading for their happy ends, their stories being thus elevated to the lofty realms of romance. Perhaps scared by the scandal around Zola, but more likely himself still firmly adhering to Victorian morality, Tirebuck in this respect kept to the common course of Victorian writing.

His bonds with traditional nonconformist religion were indeed so strong that he seems to have based his socialism on Christian teachings. As mentioned before, Tirebuck was close to the ILP, a party in whose foundation the element of ethical socialism played an important part. Stanley Pierson has described it thus:

> Ethical Socialism was highly eclectic. Around the central Socialist goal of public ownership were gathered many of the diverse and often contradictory ideas which had entered the movement during the first decade. Spokesmen for Ethical Socialism might employ Marxist ideas of exploitation and the class struggle, or Fabian notions of rent and general enlightenment. But they were distinguished by their appeals to moral and religious sentiment and they promised a fundamental change in the quality of life.[24]

It seems significant that in *Miss Grace* there is little discussion of socialist ideas and that the little there is is frequently clad in Christian arguments. When Grace chides her father, the vicar who opportunistically sides with the coal-owners, she quotes the Bible: ' "While the many are working at the rods of the vine, the few are eating the grapes" ' (p.51). And she condemns her father's attitude: 'It was wrong—it was sinful—it was against both the spirit and the letter of the Church's own Scripture' (p.53). Not only the vicar's daughter, also the workers quote Christ in their support: ' "But our Saviour didn't say tak' twenty-five per cent off the poor to mak' them poorer, an' put twenty-five in the pockets o' the rich to mak' the rich richer" ' (p.154). It is in accordance with a basically Christian stance that within the scope of the novel not a complete reversal of the social order is envisaged as the

final goal, but merely a correction of all too obvious injustices. When Grace in the face of an impending riot confronts Brookster, she appeals to his sense of responsibility, revealing the author's belief in the possibility of a paternalistic organisation of society: ' "As the proprietor of Beckerton pits, Mr. Brookster, it is in your power to save at least four thousand men, women and children from want . . ." ' And she asks: ' "Why will not employers admit . . . that masters and men are, after all, one in their interdependence upon each other?" ' (p.234). The workers argue from a similar basis when Sam Ockleshaw, the most politically articulate among them, does not demand common ownership as the struggle's aim, but, apart from some vague hints about a share in the control of the pits, merely a fair part of the wealth produced by the workers: ' "The man that gets, should at least be paid his meat" ' (p.155).

That religion is a weak basis for socialism and prevents a development of socialist concepts becomes obvious when Tirebuck, as in *Dorrie*, lets piety and moral goodness function as forces able to bridge the gulf between the classes. Although, like Zola, he applies a fair amount of sarcasm to his portrayal of the political tricks and business deals of his entrepreneur family and their accomplices, including the vicar, he allows individuals to feel remorse and even to change sides: Dora, the Brookster daughter, becomes a friend to the miners by marrying the young curate Rew, who had helped the miners at Grace's side and intends to live by Grace's ideals. Grace, as the vicar's daughter also a member of the middle class, has been an ally of the miners all through the struggle, and in the end actually joins the working class by marrying Sam Ockleshaw. This symbolical union, to my mind, impairs the final political message of the novel by substituting a Christian dream of the brotherhood of man for the socialist perspective.

The eponymous heroine requires a few final remarks. Surprising as it may seem that Tirebuck should have linked his lock-out theme to the central figure of an angelic middle-class girl, he could and probably did draw on a literary tradition. In some of the industrial novels of the

1840s and 1850s the same device was employed to make working-class topics digestible for a bourgeois reading public used to love stories about pure middle-class heroines: Mrs Gaskell's Margaret Hale in *North and South* and Disraeli's Sybil can be seen in this way. Their treatment reflects a real social function of middle-class women in the nineteenth century where it had become one of the acknowledged duties of the 'angel in the house' to exercise charity: Women were expected to 'do good' by giving alms to the individual poor while their husbands were often exploiting the working class on a large scale. If the author of a socialist novel applies a literary device reflecting this middle-class division of labour, even if he does so without fully realising the implications, the danger of weakening the socialist message arises. What finally saves *Miss Grace* from this danger is the novel's emphasis on the life and struggle of the miners.

Looking back at Tirebuck's social novels one must say that none of them, not even *Miss Grace*, can be called a purely socialist novel, and, equally, none of them is consistently naturalistic—and for the same reasons. Tirebuck's two strong driving motives, his real sympathy with the working class and his trust in true religiousness to overcome social evils, were, though widely spread at his time, inherently at odds with each other. Tirebuck's piety and Christian morality allowed him to include socialist ideas only in so far as they were reconcilable with Christian convictions. They also prevented a more daring use of naturalism, particularly in the field of sexual relations, but also with regard to characterisation. That he introduced naturalistic writing techniques at all was a happy circumstance, for it prevented his 'unworldliness' from entirely having the upper hand and gave his portrayal of working-class people a more realistic profile.

William Edwards Tirebuck and Margaret Harkness worked as pioneers in the field of applying naturalistic techniques to the ends of socialist fiction, and, as may have become apparent, their achievements cannot be called perfect. Their approach was in many ways half-hearted, and the traces of past values were still marked. When in

1914, more than twenty years later, Robert Tressell and Patrick MacGill made their appearance on the literary stage and included in their first novels admirably written naturalistic descriptions of the living and working conditions of house-painters in Hastings and potato-pickers and navvies in Scotland, they had a double advantage: being working-class themselves, they could draw on personal experience; but they could draw on naturalism too as a literary tradition that had already become well established. Harkness and Tirebuck were among those who helped to form this tradition.

NOTES

1. Margaret Harkness's novels *A City Girl* and *A Manchester Shirtmaker* were published with the subtitle 'a realistic story'.
2. For a detailed discussion of the term see H. Gustav Klaus (ed.) Introduction to *The Socialist Novel in Britain* (Brighton, 1982), pp.1-2.
3. See William C. Frierson, 'The English controversy over realism in fiction 1885-1895, *PMLA*, 43 (1928), pp.533-50; William C. Frierson, *The English Novel in Transition 1885-1940* (New York, 1965); and Clarence R. Decker, *The Victorian Conscience* (New York, 1952).
4. John Law (Margaret Harkness), *Out of Work* (London, 1888), p.204: 'That place [a prison cell] needs a Zola to do it justice.' John Law (Margaret Harkness), *George Eastmont: Wanderer* (London, 1905), p.125: 'He had just returned from a visit to the mines of Scotland and there he had found *Germinal* better than any guide-book.'
5. John Goode, 'Margaret Harkness and the socialist novel' in Klaus (ed.) *The Socialist Novel in Britain*, pp.45-66 (p.46).
6. For a discussion of Constance Howell's *A More Excellent Way* see chapter 2 by Brunhild de la Motte.
7. For more details of Harkness's biography see Goode, *op. cit.*, and Beate Kaspar, *Margaret Harkness: A City Girl* (Tübingen, 1984).
8. Harkness, *Out of Work*, pp.181-3.

9. For a discussion of *George Eastmont: Wanderer* see chapter 1 by Kiernan Ryan.

10. John Law (Margaret Harkness), *In Darkest London* [first published 1889 under the title of *Captain Lobe*] (London, 1891), p.153.

11. For a recent discussion of *A Manchester Shirtmaker* see T. Thomas, 'Representation of the Manchester working class in fiction, 1850-1900', in Alan J. Kidd and K. W. Roberts (eds.), *City, Class and Culture. Studies of Social Policy and Cultural Production in Victorian Manchester* (Manchester, 1985), pp.210-12.

12. Harkness, *Out of Work*, pp.221-2, 227-8.

13. Harkness, *In Darkest London*, p.280.

14. John Law (Margaret Harkness), *A City Girl* (London, 1887), p.84.

15. *ibid.*, p.63.

16. Goode, *op. cit.*, p.56.

17. For more biographical details see Hall Caine, 'Memoir' in W. E. Tirebuck, *Twixt God and Mammon* (London, 1903), pp.V-XXIII; and John Hogben, Foreword to W. E. Tirebuck, *Poems* (London, 1912), pp.5-15.

18. William Edwards Tirebuck, *Dorrie* (London, 1891), p.207.

19. See M. Chaikin, 'George Moore's *A Mummer's Wife* and Zola', *Revue de Littérature Comparée*, 31 (1957), pp.85-8.

20. Tirebuck, *Dorrie*, p.353.

21. *ibid.*, p.53.

22. For a different view of the novel's hero see chapter 4 by H. Gustav Klaus.

23. William Edwards Tirebuck, *Miss Grace of All Souls'* (New York, 1895), p.191. Subsequent page numbers given in the text are to this edition.

24. Stanley Pierson, *British Socialists. The Journey from Fantasy to Politics* (Cambridge, Mass., 1979), pp.35-6.

· 8 ·

Allen Clarke and the Lancashire school of working-class novelists

PAUL SALVESON

It is common to regard Tressell's great work, *The Ragged Trousered Philanthropists*, as the only novel of any importance written by a working-class socialist before the First World War. The purpose of this article is to show that there did in fact exist both a cohesive group of working-class novelists in the years between 1890 and 1914, and that they possessed a mass readership. They were based in Lancashire, and much of their writing reflects a strong regional, as well as class awareness. The central figure in this group was Allen Clarke (1863-1935) the son of Bolton mill workers, born at the height of the Lancashire cotton famine. At the age of twelve, he too went to work in the mills as a half-timer. His job as a piecer was a typical occupation for a working-class lad of his age in a northern mill town in the 1870s. It was both dangerous and exhausting, involving piecing up broken threads on the spinning mules, and cleaning the machinery (often when it was in motion). Clarke's mill career was mercifully short, although those early experiences undoubtedly provided him with material for his later industrial novels. He spent some years as a pupil teacher, trying to 'educate' the half-time kids such as he had once been, and, like many other humane members of his profession, became increasingly frustrated with the job. He had been writing, encouraged by his father, for many years and he dreamed of becoming a professional writer. He left his job as a teacher and started with the *Bolton Evening News* as a clerk—hoping that this would be the first step on the ladder of a writing career.

The hoped-for promotion never came, and he resigned in 1890 to start his own paper, *The Labour Light*. It was an uneasy combination of lengthy trade-union reports and speeches of working-class figures, together with humorous sketches of working-class life, written in Lancashire dialect. These were the *Tum Fowt Sketches*, recording the comic doings of Bill and Bet Spriggs and their friends. Although at first these were used as largely non-political light relief, Clarke (under the pseudoynm of 'Teddy Ashton') later developed these sketches into sharp political satire.

By the time Clarke started *The Labour Light* he was a convinced socialist. He had joined the Bolton branch of the Social Democratic Federation (SDF) in 1887, at the time of the great Bolton Engineers' Lock-Out, which he later used as the basis for his novel, *The Knobstick* (1893). Clarke could not, however, be described as a marxist. His political views found a better expression in the 'ethical' socialism of the early Independent Labour Party (ILP), seeing socialism as much a moral issue as a class one. This did not, however, mean that Clarke was unconcerned about working-class issues—for he was very much a part of that class—but he could still write:

> I would do justice to everybody—to shopkeeper, merchant and capitalist. I want fair play and fair opportunity all round. But the cause of the workers has first claim because the workers have been most unjustly treated and neglected.[1]

Clarke joined the Independent Labour Party, and stood as joint ILP–SDF candidate in Rochdale at the 1900 General Election. He polled 902 votes in a contest which included his 'Election Address to Th' Rachda Folk'—written, irreverently, in Lancashire dialect. The election experience also marked a turning point in Clarke's politics. As the ILP moved towards an alliance with right-wing trade-union leaders, Clarke became increasingly interested in libertarian politics, particularly the ideas of Tolstoy, and then the syndicalists. In 1903 he launched the 'Daisy Colony Scheme' for a working-class 'co-operative colony' near

Blackpool, and following its demise[2] used his paper, *Teddy Ashton's Northern Weekly*, as a mouthpiece for libertarian socialist groups, such as the Industrial Union of Direct Actionists. In later years he was an enthusiastic supporter of the Russian Revolution, and maintained this support until his death in December 1935. Clarke was an essentially non-sectarian socialist, who had no time for parliamentary manoeuvres and compromise, and no stomach either for the increasingly bitter inter-party feuds between the ILP and the SDF, and later between the Labour Party and the Communists.

THE THEMES OF ALLEN CLARKE'S NOVELS

This political and biographical background is essential for the understanding of Clarke's novels, and to appreciate his wider aims as a writer. In 1893 he expressed these aims in an editorial letter to his readers:

> I want to do something for all who are downtrodden and oppressed . . . I want to sing you songs of hope and tell you tales of truth. I want to picture faithfully in verse and prose the lives of the workers in towns and cities . . . Yet not merely do I want to delineate the life of labour but by so doing to draw attention to wrongs and evils, and if possible get them righted and remedied.[3]

There is no doubt then, that Clarke saw himself as a working-class writer writing about, and for, a primarily working-class readership. The subject matter of the majority of his novels is based on working-class life, mostly in Lancashire. Many of these have a contemporary setting, although some of his novels, including the first—*The Lass at the Man and Scythe* (1889)—about the English Civil war, are historical. Few of these novels were ever published in book form. Most were serialised in his newspapers such as *Teddy Ashton's Northern Weekly*, *The Cotton Factory Times*, and later, *The Liverpool Weekly Post*.

It would be impossible to given a complete survey of Clarke's novels in the space of this article; what seems most

helpful in considering his role as a socialist novelist is to examine certain key themes in his work which show development in response to working-class struggles, and relate to the work of other members of the 'Lancashire school'.

The condition of Lancashire

This is the main theme which Clarke returns to constantly in his novels, as well as in his non-fiction (for example *The Effects of the Factory System*, 1899). It includes a strong historical awareness of how his native county was despoiled by industrial capitalism, and its independent-minded domestic workers, the handloom weavers, forced into highly regulated, large-scale factories. Allen Clarke described his sense of shock when he returned to Bolton after living for some years in Blackpool, the Lancashire holiday resort situated amidst the green pastures of the Fylde countryside:

> When I went back for a brief visit to the cotton town where I was born, I saw it as I never saw it when I dwelt therein. Living there, I had grown familiar with the ugliness, and familiarity oftener breeds toleration than contempt; I had accepted the drab streets, the smoky skies, the foul river, the mass of mills, the sickly worker, as inevitable and usual—nay, natural, and did not notice them in a probing, critical way.[4]

Much of Allen Clarke's writing is an attempt to 'shock' his own readers into a similar critical recognition of their surroundings—the men and women who had grown up like him in a dirty cotton town but who had not shared his good fortune to get out of it. He often does this by using the perceptions of an outsider, such as the middle-class socialist journalist Haddon Peer in *Driving* (1901). Peer is being shown round a mill in 'Drivenden' with some other friends, and he reflects on the drastic changes which Lancashire has undergone with the coming of industrial capitalism:

> What a marvellous transformation James Watt's steam engine, aided by the spinning and weaving inventions of Kay, Har-

greaves and Crompton had wrought in a hundred years; an agricultural and pasturing shire had been turned into a county of manufacture; Lancashire's wild moorland vales had become the smoky workshop of the world; and once sweet hillsides were now cinder-heaps and once-bright brooks were now stinking sewers.[5]

Clarke's historical sensibility frequently draws out the contrasts between pre-industrial and present-day Lancashire, suggesting that what exists is not 'normal' but a state of affairs engineered by men—and it was up to men, and women, to change it. Clarke is under no illusions that this will be easy, and seems at times almost to despair of the possibility. His pessimism is seen through the 'outsider' Harold in *Lancashire Lasses and Lads* (1906), where he observes the early morning trek by thousands of men, women and children to the mill:

They're all mad, every one; man, woman and child. They must be mad to crawl out of warm beds, and shudder to horrid work through the cold. If they weren't mad they wouldn't do it; they'd stop in bed. They're mad to live as they do; to slave as if their very lives depended on killing themselves by work.[6]

Haddon Peer and Harold are clearly uttering the perceptions of outside observers; one a socialist who sympathises with the people, the other a rich man's son who has become a de-classed cynic.

Driving deals with one particularly unpleasant side of this industry—the 'driving' policy adopted in the weaving sheds. The term becomes a metaphor for life under capitalism. The overseers were under pressure (that is, driven) by their managers to increase production in the weaving sheds; the managers themselves were 'driven' by the owners who were in turn subject to the pressure of share holders to maintain and increase dividends. This led to intolerable bullying of the mostly female weavers, and the 'slate' system, in which the weavers with the lowest production figures had their names publicly displayed on a slate in the shed—often to the derision of their workmates. The suicide of weavers suffering under this system became

almost commonplace, and the story is based on the real-life suicide of a young Darwen weaver who fell foul of the 'slate'. In the plot, Ann Draper is the young weaver, orphaned and friendless, who is bullied by the tackler, and eventually kills herself:

> She was in charge of four looms and she did her best with them. She worked the hardest in the weaving shed, and yet got the least pay. She did not care about the money; but she was tortured by the constant effort, under the 'driving' of the tackler, or overseer, to do more than it was possible for her to do, and she suffered under the sneers of those who ought to have pitied.[7]

Allen Clarke's second wife, Eliza, was a weaver from Chorley, and much of the sharp detail of his accounts of weaving was owed to her assistance. In *The Little Weaver* (1893), we get one of the most dramatic descriptions of a factory waking up to the day's toil that could be imagined—the mill becomes almost human, a slumbering giant yawning and stretching, then gaining speed and confidence. The scene is Maggie's first day at the mill; her young friend Jenny accompanies her into the weaving shed just before six o'clock when all is quiet:

> Then, slowly, at six o'clock precisely, there stole a huzzing murmur on the silence; the shafts began to revolve, the straps that chained the looms creaked, stretched and yawned, as if reluctant to begin their duty, and commenced to climb languidly up to the ceiling, quickening their speed with every turn; the huzzing murmur grew and grew; the weavers touched the levers of their looms one by one, and set them on. The murmur had now become a rattling roar; the sound swelled; the straps whizzed faster; the threads of the warp flowed into the loom like a slow broad stream, and the shuttle darted across them like a swallow, binding them together and making them into cloth; there was creaking and groaning of wheels; the hissing and spluttering of leather straps, as if the animal moaned painfully in its hide; the air grew warmer; the noise became deafening; you could not hear your own voice; and the weaving shed was in full swing.[8]

Clarke was fascinated, as well as repelled, by the factory system. He hated the driving system, the child labour, and the hours of monotonous, tiring work. Yet the sight of a weaving shed full of roaring looms, or spinning mules drawing backwards and forwards on the carriages, and still more the spectacle of a huge spinning mill lit up at night are recurring images in Clarke's writing. Dick Dickinson, the mill-owner's son who leaves to make a new and independent life in 'Spindleton', observes the mills lighting up early on a winter's morning:

> Lights began to show in the great factories of four or five stories, with their many windows. Soon they were all lit up looking like a vast illumination. 'Very pretty to look at from the outside, and at a distance on a black, frosty morning,' said Dick, 'but it's a different matter toiling inside them. My father's mills will be lit up now. I wouldn't like to be one of the poor wretches that salves for *him*, anyhow; I'm sure they're not allowed to work in any comfort.'[9]

Clarke was well aware that within the cotton industry, despite the increasingly de-skilled nature of the work, a strong sense of pride remained. In *Driving* the socialist Bertha Lindley is depicted as the most competent weaver in the shed, just as capable of repairing a mechanical fault on her looms as her more highly paid male tackler. Belton, in *The Knobstick*, proves himself to be one of the most skilled engineers in the factory where he commences work, and Clarke shows him admiring the human achievement which goes into modern technology, and what he sees as the ultimately religious nature of creativity:

> 'Great and wonderful is man', mused Belton, 'Who conceived and constructed the railway train! It is almost alive! It flies along of itself and carries its maker in its arms like a child! Mighty and sublime must be he who made the locomotive! Then how much more mighty and sublime must that power be which made him who made the locomotive! There must be a God!'[10]

Indeed Clarke's attitude towards machinery in novels like

The Knobstick and even *Driving* and *The Little Weaver*, is less severe than in his *Effects of the Factory System*, which reflects on modern factory production and advocates a return to craft industry and agriculture. Perhaps such a Utopian vision squared badly with the need to present a believable story which simply set the reader thinking about a future society, rather than advocating a programmatic remedy which would detract from the novel.

Trade unionism

Clarke's criticism of the factory system focused on the ill-treatment of women and young children. The most obvious form of redress would be through the trade union, but the unions in the cotton industry were dominated almost totally by men. The spinner's union was exclusively male, and waged strikes against attempts to use female labour in the spinning room. The mostly female weavers were less well-organised, and officials tended to be men; the young piecers had no organisation, and attempts to form piecers' unions were firmly resisted by the spinners— from whose wages the piecers were paid. In *The Red Flag* (1907) the central character, Jim Campbell, is forced to become a tramp after he is sacked for attempting to form a piecers' union—an actual struggle which Clarke, along with J. R. Clynes of Oldham, was directly involved in. He tells how he came to lose his job:

> The employers of the piecers are the operative spinners; and like most middle-men look after themselves. They have for themselves anything from two pounds to four pounds a week, while paying the piecers a paltry fifteen or sixteen shillings . . . Though terrible trade unionists themselves they objected to their piecers forming a trade union. They smashed our litle union up by intimidating the members and sacking the leading spirits. I was one . . . Not only was I dismissed by a trade unionist, instigated by a society of trade unionists, for no more offence than seeking to promulgate trade unionism, but I was so boycotted by the same noble army of trade unionists . . .[11]

Clarke is not being excessively harsh in his depiction of the spinners' conduct; as with most of his writing, he bases a fictional episode on a real event and there is little doubt that the spinners were classic examples of well-paid and highly organised trade unionists who practised a rigorous form of exclusiveness and had little or no interest in their less well-organised sisters and brothers in the card-rooms and weaving sheds. The piecers were expected to behave themselves until such time as they could get their own 'mules' when they could continue the tradition of underpaying their own piecers, as they had been underpaid and exploited themselves.

However, Clarke's characterisation of trade unionism is not confined to the conservative spinners. In *A Daughter of the Factory* (1898) one of the most sympathetic characters is Kate Marford, secretary of the 'Women's Trade Union Association', who is shown travelling the north of England organising the women workers. When she reaches 'Slagbourne' she addresses a small gathering including Rose, and plants the first seeds of political radicalism in Rose's mind:

> 'There is no help for the people,' said Miss Marford, 'but in brotherly and sisterly combination. You will never get better wages, my friends, nor better anything, till you join hands together and ask for it with the voice of the union.'[12]

Rose herself becomes Kate's closest ally, and a representative of the union in the weaving shed; she becomes one of the leading figures in a strike of the weavers and is described as 'singing the workers into insurrection' at a mass meeting chaired by Kate Marford.

Clarke's main criticism of trade unionism is against the established, conservative unionism of the skilled man. The organisation of women and young people is shown as a necessary and positive step forward to defend their interests. On its own, though, trade unionism is not enough. He criticised the attitude in which trade unionists on the one hand opposed their employer on the industrial front, yet often sent the same person to Parliament; only a

a generalised political challenge to capital would bring any real change.

Socialism

The Red Flag represents a departure from the style of the earlier novels in being much more directly a propagandistic work for socialism. The struggle for political change is not introduced implicitly but in a much more direct manner, the bulk of the novel being based on the very strong socialist movement of Burnley ('Brunborough') and north-east Lancashire, in the early 1900s. The earlier part of the novel, set in the tramps' lodging houses and workhouses, is intended to represent the most acute human effects of capitalism. Whilst some of the inmates of the lodgings are depraved, many of the tramps are shown as ordinary, once-respectable people who have fallen on hard times—such as Jim Campbell, the victimised piecer. A feature of the story is the representation of the social reformer, Mary Higgs, as 'Mrs Wilkinson'. In real life Mrs Higgs, a well-to-do member of the Oldham middle class, disguised herself as a tramp to establish the facts about tramp lodgings and workhouses. Clarke uses this story in the novel, with Mrs Wilkinson accompanied round the lodging houses by the young ex-weaver May—who falls in love with Jim Campbell when they meet in Brunborough at a Labour Church gathering. Jim is converted to socialism from his previous trade unionism by listening to a socialist speaker in the Burnley marketplace, his own tragic experiences fitting in to a pattern of exploitation:

> He saw his own life passing before him, his hard struggle for bread, his willingness to work and no opportunity to get it, he saw his starving wife and child, he realised that all the misery and the death of his darlings had been brought about by this foul, murderous, competitive capitalist system which the speaker was so tremendously denouncing. He felt a wild anger against the rulers and authorities and employers, his soul rose in revolt, and he shouted out in excitement. 'By God you're right!'[13]

Someone reading this in the 1980s might find it a little incredible—people do not suddenly 'become socialists' by listening to a speaker, however fine an orator. Yet it should be remembered that the 'new socialism' of the 1890s frequently took on the semblance of being almost a religious crusade—converts were made in hundreds at meetings such as the one Clarke describes. First-hand accounts[14] of socialist propaganda meetings testify to the enormous appeal of speakers such as Caroline Martyn, Katherine St John Conway, Keir Hardie and others, who were expressing many of the subconscious hopes and fears of their audiences. Jim was not totally ignorant of working-class ideals—as a victimised piecer who had suffered direct personal tragedies he would obviously be receptive to the socialist message, as would many other people. Jim is befriended by the local socialists and given temporary accommodation in the Socialist Club House by Joe Summerfield, the socialist lecturer whom he had earlier been listening to. As Joe closes the club and goes home, Jim is left sitting in the club room, by the fireside. Above the fireside is a huge red flag; as he relaxes almost into sleep he sees a vision of all the poor and oppressed—his own parents, then thousands more people joining in a great procession: . . .'men, thin, pale, stunted; women, weary, white, worn down; little children pitiful to see, with sickly famished faces . . .' As the vision proceeds, this mass of the oppressed raise the red flag which stands before him, and they begin to sing:

> Raise the Scarlet Standard High,
> Within its shade we live or die . . .

The vision alters, and he sees an army of ghosts—men, women and children who had died of hunger and disease, of men and women who had killed themselves in despair, and those who had died in the workhouse. The vision changes yet again, and he sees thousands of living men and women joining the procession led by the Red Flag, people of all classes who had realised the evil of the present system; and then he even sees 'the heavens above the

people in mystic motion . . . the stars marched with them'. And

> he saw a picture of the land of good fellowship, towards which the Red Flag was being borne—he saw industry and trade so arranged that there was food for all, shelter for all—no pauperism, no unemployed, no starvation . . . and land, not of human beings who allowed a few money-maniacs to make trouble for the rest, but a land where all that the co-operative nation produced was shared out equitably amongst all—and over this happy land of healthy men and fair women and joyous children, the Red Flag waved triumphantly.[15]

I think 'The Vision of the Red Flag' is one of the most moving pieces of imaginative socialist writing, combing a moral denunciation of capitalism, with a vision of the future, and a sense of the coming together of men and women from diverse social backgrounds to fight for a common cause. Clarke realises the vision is a long way from its final fruition, and as Jim Campbell throws himself into the socialist movement he finds that there are divisions and disagreements. The relative positions of the ILP, the SDF and the Labour Church are discussed; the merits of each are different compared to the observations of Haddon Peer in *Driving*, written in 1901. Seven years later the ILP had become more opportunist and was observed to be watering down its socialism through an alliance with the moderate trade unions. The SDF is shown as the uncompromising socialist organisation, with no criticism directed at its 'materialism'. The Labour Church is shown in the most positive light, expressing Clarke's own ethical socialist beliefs, without the corruption which the ILP's socialism had suffered.

In the Socialist Club Jim Campbell listens to arguments between the older, more experienced comrades, and the younger socialists who believe in violence. The main advocate of violence is Fordham, the villain of the story. Joe Summerfield argues strongly against Fordham's provocative suggestions, and afterwards warns that he is either a spy, or a lunatic. As the socialist movement was making

rapid strides through peaceful struggle, Summerfield suggests that the authorities may attempt to discredit the cause through stirring up violence:

> 'Socialism is growing rapidly, and they're beginning to fear that the day of the blood suckers and money grabbers is at an end. Just be careful of Fordham, and have nothing to do with his schemes of violence. Our weapon is the ballot box and no other.'[16]

Fordham is not, in fact, a paid provocateur—he is simply embittered and degraded, a casualty of the system. Clarke suggests that such bitterness can lead people into irresponsible acts which damage the movement, and carefully uses the SDF stalwart, Summerfield, to warn against it. The way forward is shown through Jim Campbell being nominated by the SDF for the Board of Guardian elections—the body responsible for the administering of poor relief. Such elections, as well as the School Board contests, were seen as an important testing ground for the socialist movement's rise to power, and many ILP and SDF victories were won in Lancashire in the 1890s and early 1900s. The novel ends on a further apocalyptic note. This time, it does not come in a dream, but through the description of a huge socialist meeting on the summit of Pendle Hill, on May Day. Jim and May are happily united in marriage, and they join the crowd of thousands of working men and women, as well as teachers, doctors, clerks and other professional men and women:

> Then from the vast crowd, amid the still of the high moorlands, rose the chorus:
>
> Then raise the scarlet standard high;
> Within its shade we'll live or die;
> Though cowards flinch and traitors sneer
> We'll keep the Red Flag flying here.[17]

The revolutionary heroine

Clarke had heroines in many of his novels, though in some

cases they tended to be appendages to the male working-class hero. In *The Knobstick* Lizzie Banks is shown as an attractive, but innocent and unformed character until her relationship with Harry Belton turns her into a fiery defender of working people's rights. In his slightly later novel, *Lancashire Lasses and Lads*, Hannah Heyes, the young weaver, plays a similarly subsidiary role to the main character, Dick Dickinson. A major development takes place in *A Daughter of the Factory*, serialised in *The Northern Weekly* during 1898, although there is a curious twist to the characterisation of Rose Hilton as the female revolutionary. Her background is not that of a conventional working-class girl; she is the daughter of a gypsy woman, tricked into marriage and then deserted by a rakish mill-owner's son. Rose's incendiary rhetoric is shown as a result of the genetic combination of the gypsy and the young aristocrat, leavened by the experience of working-class life when she is brought up as an orphan by an ordinary family of Lancashire workers. There remains throughout the novel a suggestion of social distance between Rose and her workmates, illustrated by the following exchange between Rose and her friend Susy, about working-class apathy:

> 'Susy,' said Rose, 'the working people are idiots.'
> 'You shouldn't talk like that Rose,' said Susy, 'You're one of them.'
> 'I know that. That's what makes me madder than ever.'[18]

But the reader knows what Rose doesn't—by birth she isn't one of the workers, hence the irony of the discussion. Rose is 'different' not because she has developed a strong political awareness—but rather because of her 'gypsy and aristocratic blood'. In his book on the Fylde countryside, *Windmill Land*,[19] Clarke makes a similar observation in relation to the once-common practice of landowners seducing the village maidens—suggesting that this mixture of the supposedly 'noble' blood of the landowners with that of the 'common people' would result in a new breed of radicals by genetic means. Clearly, this is a con-

siderable weakness in his writing as a socialist, if the only working-class leaders that can be found are the result of illicit sexual behaviour by members of the ruling class. Kate Marford, the union organiser, is apparently of more orthodox working-class parentage, but she, too, has had an unusual background; having lost her parents when a child, she was brought up by a progressive middle-class woman who instils advanced political ideas into her. She returns to her class as a propagandist but there is again the suggestion that revolutionary ideas only take root when imported from an 'outside' agency or by dubious genetic means.

The importance of *A Daughter of the Factory* is that it is a fellow working-class woman, Kate Marford, who exercises the key influence on Rose. After hearing her speak she begins to think about the world in a new way, about the exploitation of the working class and the immense contrast between the luxury of the rich and the degradation of the poor. The next time Kate Marford visits Slagbourne, Rose joins her on the platform, and makes an impulsive speech which takes the gathering by storm:

> 'We are not horses to be thrashed and sworn at, and spat upon and bullyragged out of all existence by little two-legged terrors in white slops, called tacklers and clothlookers . . . (Laughter). Ah you may laugh. I laugh too, but I feel I could cry. If I were an Irishman, I would say to you, "Now women, arise and be men!" (Laughter). But as the samples of men I daily come into contact with are not the kind for imitating, I will say "My sisters—be Women!" Join together—there is nothing like union—holy matrimony for instance (Laughter). But quite as good a union as holy matrimony—I nearly said better—is trade unionism. Wake up and pay your entrance fee.'[20]

Yet, ultimately Rose leaves her friends in the weaving shed. The 'happy end' of the story includes her marriage to Captain Lever—a politically progressive young officer who is able to give her the cultured life she inwardly craves for.

Clarke's women characters show significant developments over the period of his novel writing, from the early 1890s to the First World War. The early weaknesses of characters like Lizzie Banks are slowly overcome, at least so

far as their dependence on the male hero. The obsession with genetics in *A Daughter of the Factory* mars what would otherwise have been a superb portrayal of the development of the woman revolutionary.

A LANCASHIRE SCHOOL

The success of Clarke's own novels, and the availability of a sympathetic outlet in his *Northern Weekly* encouraged other working-class writers to attempt novels on contemporary political themes. The following group of writers were all active in the socialist movement of the 1890s and early 1900s.

Arthur Laycock (1869-1957)

Laycock was Blackpool's first Labour councillor, and active in the unemployed movement, ILP and Clarion Club. He was the son of the famous Lancashire dialect poet Samuel Laycock and perhaps personifies the transition within Lancashire working-class literature from advanced liberalism to socialism. He wrote three novels which survived in published form. *The Young Gaffer* (1898) was his earliest, followed by *Steve the Outlander* (1900) and *Warren of Manchester* (c. 1906). *The Young Gaffer* was serialised in the *Northern Weekly* during 1898, in the aftermath of the national Engineers' Strike and is clearly influenced by that struggle. It deals with the forced migration of workers from country to town, and the demoralising effects of this on working people. Although rural 'Sunny Bank' is only separated from industrial 'Blastone' by a mere half-mile, they seem worlds apart:

> It was distant about half a mile from the fringe of the grimy town of Blastone, and with its snug, white-washed cottages standing out in bold relief against the sombre background of the great white moor, formed a striking contrast to the sombre, sooted habitations in the valley below.[21]

The contrast between town and country, and the morally corrupting nature of the latter, was a familar theme of working-class writers of the Lancashire School. In *The Young Gaffer*, Dick Haskett's family moves to Blastone, where he is unable to find work. As a result he becomes dissolute, neglectful of his family, and embittered. In contrast to Dick, Bob Sanders—the skilled engineer and trade unionist—remains in Sunny Bank and becomes a leading figure in the Engineers' Strike. His son, Lincoln— or the 'Young Gaffer'—is a socialist and falls in love with Sally, Dick Haskett's eldest daughter. As the lock-out drags on, the men become more desperate and violence is threatened.

Bob Sanders's hope of a negotiated settlement to the dispute comes under challenge at a mass meeting, from the labourers' spokesman—Dick Haskett.

> 'Let's ha less talk an more feightin,' shouted the first speaker.
> 'No!' said Bob Sanders, in a firm, clear voice which excited attention from the throng.
> 'No. We'll have no feightin, chaps—no physical force; leave that to th'brutes.'
> 'Masters are brutes,' cried the other, 'an' they threaten us wi physical force—police an sowjers. An we'll feight em an aw!'
> 'Goo lad Dick!' shouted some of the men gathered about the man with the shrill voice.
> 'No,' again said Bob, 'Let's feight fair lads, feight fair an be reasonable. Let us reason wi th'masters an no—'
> 'Reason be hanged!' cried the first speaker savagely. 'Yo cannot reason wi brutes; that's what th'masters are. They care nowt that our kids are clemming . . .'[22]

Whilst Bob Sanders represents the 'respectable' artisans, the skilled workers in receipt of strike pay, Dick Haskett is the spokesman for the unskilled labourers, receiving no strike pay and forced to beg on the streets. Dick and his fellow-labourers turn to sporadic violence against 'the knobsticks', or strike-breakers, and falsely accuse the 'Young Gaffer' of aiding them.

The knobsticks themselves are shown to be figures of pity as much as scorn—they are capitalism's most pathetic

victims. One of them is arrested by the police for assault and he splutters out his own path to becoming a 'knob-stick':

> 'I'm sick o'the life I've been leadin lately. This is how I were fixed . . . I lost my job at Warrington through no fault of my own. Machines started doin the work that formerly I'd done. I were a steady, sober chap then, but I soon get to be th'other sort, for a chap gets every encouragement to become a "wastrel". Then th'lock out came on and there were no chance of a job at my trade or any other, nobbut knobstickin . . .'[23]

There are very close parallels with Allen Clarke's *The Knob-stick*, even down to the engineering industry setting, and being based on an actual struggle. In Laycock's novel the knobsticks are, however, socially determined, whilst Clarke's 'knobstick' character is shown simply as a moral reprobate. Laycock also brings out more striking diffe-rences within the strikers themselves—the contradiction between the skilled and the unskilled, and the differing tactics espoused by the two groups.

An important sub-plot is the 'Young Gaffer's' technical ingenuity and the issue of the social effects of technology. Lincoln is shown attending night schools and becoming an ingenious inventor; however, he is conscious of how most modern machinery simply displaces labour and creates the sort of characters typified by the knobstick.

The main representative of the employing class, Darnton, is shown not as a villain—unlike his partner, White—but as someone who is just as much subject to the sort of social forces Clarke depicted in *Driving*, as are his workers. When the strike is finally settled, Darnton pro-vides Lincoln with the necessary capital to set up a co-operative factory based on the advanced technology he has patented. Whilst Darnton obviously sympathises with Lincoln's idealism, he sees it as a potentially judicious business proposition. Lincoln, however, sees it as pro-viding the basis for 'the factory of the future' such as William Morris had described:

> Lincoln felt that at last he had work before him to which he could devote his best energies, whole-heartedly; work which would enable him to help his less gifted fellows. Heretofore he had often felt that prosperity for him, namely the success of his labour-saving inventions, meant ruin to other men. Under the new regime his inventions would be a blessing, not a curse, to the working man.[24]

Laycock's comments on the social effects of modern technology form an interesting contrast with those of Clarke's. Clarke, both in his novels and in *Effects of the Factory System*, dismisses the harnessing of modern technology to progressive uses, and instead calls for a return to an agriculturally based, labour intensive form of production. Laycock accepts the dehumanising effects of modern technology within capitalism, but shows that in a more advanced system of social relations of production, technology can be the asset, not the enemy, of the working class.

Whilst *The Young Gaffer* is rooted in industrial Lancashire, *Steve the Outlander* has an international dimension, providing a link between Lancashire and South Africa at the eve of the Boer War. The hero, Steve, emigrates to South Africa after he has been victimised in the spinning mill. The increasing tensions between the Boers and the non-Dutch whites are very skilfully developed, and the subsequent conflict is shown as a provocation by British imperial interests, aided by the greed of the 'outlanders'. There is a clear sympathy for the Boer people as well as for the Black African. The most negative character in the novel, Ralph Cartleigh—perhaps predictably a mill-owner's son— sails to South Africa in pursuit of Ella, the heroine, who is torn between her love for Steve and her self-interested attachment to Cartleigh. In South Africa Cartleigh catches up with Ella and, failing to persuade her to forget Steve, proceeds to assault her. He is also shown as viciously racist in his attitude towards the Blacks, depicting them as lazy, ignorant and dishonest—qualities which the author implies fit Cartleigh, rather than the Blacks. Laycock had first-hand experience of life in South

Africa, having worked there for a period in the 1890s. Whilst his sympathy for the Boers was thus based on personal observation, support for the Boer Republic was widespread amongst ILP members during the war and led to frequent attacks on them by 'jingoite' mobs.[25]

His last published novel, *Warren of Manchester* is less concerned with working-class life than his earlier two works. It is based on social life in Blackpool and the seaside town's close ties with the great commercial centre of Manchester and the cotton-manufacturing districts of Lancashire. The main characters tend to be of the middle class: boarding-house keepers, mill-owners fallen on hard times, dealers on the Manchester stock exchange. Blackpool's role as the working-class seaside resort *par excellence* is well shown, as a backdrop to the lives of the boarding-house keepers. Laycock describes Blackpool in August at the height of 'the season' and the thousands of holiday-makers:

> These strenuous toilers in workshop, factory, foundry and mine gave themselves up whole-heartedly to genuine enjoyment. The 'Wakes' week came but once a year, and one must merrily make the most of its fleeting hours. For a brief spell the clang of hammers, the roar of looms, the 'ping' of the coal pick in the coal seam were all forgotten, and the pleasant present remembered alone.[26]

Laycock lived in Blackpool for most of his life, and was well-attuned to the subtle differences in the resort—the north and central piers as social boundaries, dividing the 'better class' visitors off from the mass, and the distinctions between the mere 'day-trippers' and the families staying 'for the week'.

John Tamlyn (1859-1921)

The novels of John Tamlyn which were published in *The Northern Weekly*—*The Hermit of Cottondale* (1902) and *The Love of a Northern Farmer* (1903)—had both been rejected by established publishers because of their political content. According to Tamlyn himself[27] Heinemann's—

one of the largest British fiction publishers—were full of praise for the novel but refused to publish because 'it was unconventional and preached socialism'.

Tamlyn himself was highly unconventional. He left home as a boy and made a living as a sailor, parson, meat-pie salesman and mechanic. He departed from the SDF in Burnley, and left the ILP after a brief stay hoping to set up a new Christian socialist organisation. He was imprisoned during a free-speech campaign in Plymouth. *The Hermit of Cottondale* is the story of Madeline—a soldier's daughter, seduced by an aristocrat and left with a child. She travels to Lancashire where she has friends, and meets 'the hermit', Eli Harding, a socialist and a solitary tram-car conductor with intellectual tastes, living high on the moors above 'Cottondale'. Madeline attends a socialist meeting with the 'hermit', and is astounded at his remarkable oratorical power. Speaking on 'Socialism', the Glorious Gospels of Salvation', Harding sets out, in a lengthy passage, the essentials of Tamlyn's own brand of 'christian communism'. It is highly moralistic, and identifies the future society as one which will be attuned to 'Nature', not struggling against it under capitalism:

> 'Millionaires, aristocrats, brewer baronets, these are the noblemen which a competitive society likes to honour. Verily, this society knoweth its own. Survival of the fittest? Of course! For the thieves den, the best thief; for a profit-mongering society, the best bester. Nature is very just, awfully just! Run your society on the brute basis, and you shall reap the brute . . . So hurrah for the new socialism! The new basis! No trimming of that which is rotten at the root; the world for the workers, the means of production for social production—a common effort for a common ends.'[28]

Tamlyn uses the questions at the end of the speech as a means to counter anti-socialist arguments: would individual private property be confiscated? Would everyone, industrious or lazy be paid the same wage? Did competition not bring out the best in people? Would not socialism crush human liberty? Harding answers each point skilfully, and often humorously. Later, Harding is billed as the

socialist speaker in a debate with a local priest. He exposes the contradictions of orthodox Christianity, and returns to the theme of human degradation being caused by capitalism. The means to the higher end is socialism:

> The poor are withered by poverty; the rich are rotted by luxury. The only way out is a return to the simple principles of Jesus—Life not Things. And the way to this? Free access to the same means of life! And the best way to secure this? The Socialist way. Let all work, land, machinery, and all other common things be for the work of all.[29]

The characterisation of socialists as isolated, Christ-like figures of derision by both oppressors and oppressed, returns in *The Love of a Northern Farmer*. Again the hero lives in an isolated moorland cottage. Again, the hero— John Heath—rescues the main female character, Kate Venn, from disaster. Kate, however, is no weak-willed girl. Whilst John Heath teaches her how to milk cows, she tells how she takes after her father in her political views:

> 'My father was a farmer like you. Oh, but he was an awful man. He used to harangue the men in the village public house upon politics—Republicanism, Socialism, all things common. Down with the parsons, squires, and all tyranny. I'm a bit like my father. I'd like to make a holocaust of kings, priests and all those who lord it over others.' 'Why, you're a full blown anarchist,' said John Heath.[30]

John Heath argues with Kate, suggesting that change must come through peaceful means, by socialist education. Kate stays with John, helping on the farm, and singing for countless local progressive groups, including performances in aid of strike funds. The relationship between John and Kate matures into romantic love, and Kate becomes the politically dominant partner—encouraging John to take an active part in the struggle, constantly appearing herself as a singer at socialist and union meetings. Her reputation as a militant socialist spreads, and the local reactionaries shun her—she is refused service in local shops, and many of the parishioners at the church

where she sings urge the vicar to expel her. Yet her own strong-mindedness and socialist principles win out—even to the extent of persuading a reactionary coal-owner that socialism is the only answer for the future of humanity. Her powers of persuasion are such that the coal-owner wills her his coal-mines when he dies, and she proceeds to run them along 'enlightened' principles.

The story is an unlikely one, though it has considerable interest as a further example of a working-class male writer developing the character of the revolutionary woman, clearly more 'advanced' than the men around her. Tamlyn uses the novel to draw out what he sees as the crucial political issues—the moral basis of socialism, a belief that even the ruling class can be persuaded of the 'truths' of socialism, and the Christian basis of communism. *The Love of a Northern Farmer* appears to have been popular with *The Northern Weekly* readership, and in a short article Tamlyn mentions being asked many times by comrades at meetings he has addressed when it would appear in book form. He mentions the rejection of the script by Heinemann and offers to sell the copyright to anyone who wishes to publish it. He intends not to write any more novels, for, he says,

> in this age of exuberant patronage and appreciation of letters, I incline to the belief that a fish and chip business is more profitable . . . the following of literature entails too many doctor's bills, and I don't want to shorten my natural life, so I'll look out for a fish-and-chip shop.[31]

Tamlyn never got his fish-and-chip shop. He had to make do with selling half-penny meat pies on the streets of Burnley, and finally returned to Plymouth, where he was known as 'the communist parson'.

Fred Plant (1866-1925)

Tamlyn had little time for trade unionism. Where it does appear in his novels, it is usually in the context of a 'palliative' which stops the workers from identifying with the loftier aim of 'pure socialism'. The work of Fred Plant,

which appeared in *The Northern Weekly* at around the same time as Tamlyn's novels, is much more rounded in its treatment of the relationship between trade unionism and socialism. Plant himself was an ILP activist and one of Stockport's first labour councillors. He worked for a time with Allen Clarke on *The Northern Weekly* and wrote scores of fascinating short stories of Lancashire working-class life. He also contributed dialect sketches under the pseudonym of 'Harry o'th'Hills'.

One of Plant's most directly socialist novels was *The Conductor's Sweetheart*, subtitled *A Tale of the Great Tram Strike* (1900-1). It appeared in *The Northern Weekly* as a serial beginning on 17 November 1900—less than a week after the end of the Ashton-under-Lyne tram strike on which it is directly based. Whereas Clarke in *The Knobstick*, and Laycock in *The Young Gaffer*, use an actual strike as a backdrop to their stories, the strike in *The Conductor's Sweetheart* is much more central to the action and very closely modelled on the actual events.[32] As was invariably the case in all these novels, a romantic love story structures the novel. The hero is Arthur Walton, one of the strike-leaders, who eventually wins 'his girl', Florrie, from the clutches of a dishonest suitor.

The strike's build-up is developed carefully by Plant, describing the injustices felt by the tramway workers, and the arrogance of the employers who dismiss the men's grievances with contempt; the one exception is Councillor Rathlane, a radical, who sits on the tramway board. The strike begins, and blacklegs are imported to run the trams. As with both Clarke's and Laycock's depiction of blacklegs, they are figures of pity and derision. However, Joe Radburn, a militant spinner, who is on short-time, argues that there are always alternative means of employment for someone who wants a job:

'There's other ways o'makin a livin without turnin blackleg. What did my brother Bill do when he were out o'wark after th' railway strike? Sooner than start wark as a blackleg he went to be a 'bobby' an has done well ever sin.'[33]

Other men argue with Joe Radburn that police are frequently used to break strikes, with unnecessary violence,
although Joe sticks to his belief that his brother would
never side with a 'knobstick' against a decent trade
unionist. There is a bitter irony in Joe's sincere belief about
his brother; in one of the most memorable scenes in the
novel—and indeed of most other Lancashire novels of this
period—the police attack a peaceful demonstration of
strikers and their families:

> Policemen drew their batons and used them with terrific effect
> on those about them. A splash of blood fell on Joe Radburn's
> cheek and a young fellow went down with a groan . . . Joe
> turned when he heard the young man's cry, and gripping the
> policeman's wrist he roared 'Theau damned murderer! Tum
> Smith's done nowt wrung! He's one o'th' quietest lads i'
> Cottonly an theau's smashed his yead. Take that! . . . an that!'
> and Joe struck wildly but with revengeful force at the broad
> back of the policeman. The latter turned, with his blood-
> stained baton uplifted. Joe saw his face and his eyes rolled like
> a madman's. 'Oh my God—eaur Bill!' came from his lips in a
> long wail. 'Eaur Bill, an theau't a damned murderer yet!' and
> Joe's fist crashed into the face of the brother whom he had
> hitherto loved as himself.[34]

The violence of the police attack—based on a real incident
during the strike—is shown not as the action of a group of
reckless constables, but as a premeditated assault planned
by the police and the tramway employers. The police are
shown drilling baton charges each day, and playing card-
games with the blacklegs, as well as riding on the tramcars
that were manned by the blacklegs.

Plant shows the strike as a community struggle, as much
as a simple trade-unionism issue; the trams are boycotted
by the vast majority of the population, and women hiss and
boo the strike-breakers. The violence of the police is answered by the violence of a group of strikers who stone the
trams and attempt to derail them, assisted by other workers
such as Joe Radburn, the cotton spinner. George Goldthorpe, president of the local Trades Council, intervenes in
the struggle to advise against provocations which would

jeopardise public support:

> 'Let us have no fighting . . . every blow struck will tell against the strikers. We mustn't give our opponents the opportunity to say we resorted to rowdyism . . . If the strikers let the public see they are conducting this struggle in legitimate fashion, and not out-stepping the law, the sympathy of the general public will be ours! If we get it, victory will lie with the tramwaymen; if we lose it, the issue is doubtful.'[35]

Whilst Plant shows the violence directed at the blacklegs as justified, he uses Goldthorpe to argue that tactically it is vital to avoid violence to maintain public support, in the form of the boycott and support for the strike fund. Ultimately, the strike is settled in the men's favour after Board of Trade arbitration, and the intervention of Councillor Rathlane.

The whole course of the strike is superbly described by Plant who clearly had first-hand insight into trade-union negotiation and strike action: it is not the superficial account of an outsider, but of someone who knows the movement inside out and has a clear grasp of class issues. His understanding of the relationship between capital and the state, particularly the role of the police, is also notable. Plant shows the strike as an instance of the battle between capital and labour, in an industry of, as he terms it, 'public usefulness'. The character of Councillor Rathlane is crucial in the ending of the strike and suggestive that such industries performing a socially useful purpose should be municipalised, rather than left at the behest of a group of grasping and irresponsible bourgeois. It is also interesting that Plant links the struggle to the war in South Africa, showing the strike begining just as 'the final curtain of supremacy's tragedy was being lowered to the accompaniment of "Rule Britannia" '.[36]

Plant's other major work, *Tamsie—The Tale of a Hatting Town* (1899) also features an industrial dispute, in the hatting trade, based on the small town of Denton, near Stockport. *Tamsie* is more concerned with the everyday aspects of working-class life, than with the 'exceptional'

such as a big strike. Details of the hatting industry itself are matched with careful description of working-class domestic life. Plant suggests that in the ordinary course of things, working people are more interested in the destination of next year's factory outing, 'than a parliamentary election or passing glimpses of royalty'. Standish Meacham's suggestion of working people inhabiting 'a life apart' from bourgeois society is dramatically illustrated.[37]

THE SIGNIFICANCE OF THE LANCASHIRE SCHOOL OF WORKING-CLASS NOVELISTS

Arthur Laycock, Tamlyn and Plant form the three main figures, alongside Clarke, in the 'Lancashire school of working-class novelists'. They were united in their general political approach, based on Independent Labour Party-style ethical socialism—though Laycock and Plant were more sympathetic to the limited aims of trade unionism than either Clarke or Tamlyn. The most obvious element was a common outlet for their work—Clarke's *The Northern Weekly*. Without this it seems unlikely that the Lancashire school would ever have appeared at all, given its highly political content, and the strong regional thrust, through its use of dialect and depiction of local customs and culture. The national labour movement papers may have found them too localised, and book publishers too controversial (as we have direct evidence of with Tamlyn's work). It is also important to remember that the four writers were close friends. At *The Northern Weekly* picnics in the Lancashire countryside, most of the circle would usually be present, though Tamlyn was less given to the social life of the movement than the others, preferring the solitary life of the ascetic which he glorified in his novels.

There were other writers on the periphery of 'the Lancashire school', such as James Haslam who shared Clarke's childhood experience as a piecer in the Bolton mills, and was taken on the staff of *The Northern Weekly* in the 1890s. He contributed several short stories of working-class life, and his novel *The Handloom Weaver's Daughter* (1906) was

first serialised in the paper as *The Mill on the Moor* (1898).[38] Jospeh Whittaker, the Black Country ILP activist contributed many stories to *The Northern Weekly* which later appeared in collected form as *Tales of Tumble Fold* (1898). Peter Lee, the leading figure in the Rochdale ILP during the 1890s, was a friend of Clarke and contributed occasional dialect verse to his papers. His novel *Mystery O'Sunny Fowt* (1906) incorporates many of the central themes of 'the Lancashire school', such as the 'moral' rightness of socialism, the superiority of country living over the towns, and the cross-class appeal of socialist politics.

These writers, and novels, represent an unprecedented flowering of working-class socialist literature which has gone virtually unrecognised by socialists and students of literature today. It was a highly specific movement, well justifying the title of 'school'. The master was Allen Clarke—his pioneering working-class novels and short stories gave the necessary encouragement to other working-class people to write. The success of his paper, *The Northern Weekly*, in reaching a broad working-class readership in Lancashire provided the essential outlet for their work and the sort of readers they wanted. All the members of the 'school' were attempting to depict the life of the working class in Lancashire in a way which was realistic, but at the same time pointed the way to a socialist future. They tried to avoid being pedantic, and aimed to bring out the socialist message in a natural, common-sense way—as one amongst a number of points of view held by working-class people. The socialist hero or heroine is invariably the best worker, the most upright character, and loving comrade who proves by example that socialism is a qualitatively different way of life from the old, corrupting and immoral capitalist system. All the novels are strongly rooted in Lancashire and form an impressive literary image of the great Lancashire cotton industry and its people at the turn of the century. The use of Lancashire dialect in the dialogue between working-class characters, and also as an emblem of class difference, is used by all of the writers we have looked at.

Whilst this technique was also employed by middle-

class novelists throughout the nineteenth century, in the novels of Clarke and Plant particularly, dialect is used as a distinctive form of working-class speech which the reader of *The Northern Weekly* could directly identify with. The working-class readership was encouraged to see bits of themselves in the characters—the mill girl struggling for a better life, the piecer frustrated at his lack of prospects and of the joyful aspects of life—in features such as romantic love, the trips to the seaside or the humour (displayed particularly by Clarke and Plant). The response of the *Northern Weekly* readers to these novels is one of the most interesting aspects of the history of the Lancashire school. The regular letters to the editor, commenting on particular novels—both critically and positively—was a feature of the working-class serial which was particularly important. The reader was not distanced in any sense from the novel—it was about their town (or a fictionalised town which could be anywhere in south Lancashire), and was about people like them. They could write in to 'their' paper commenting on particular episodes, and at *The Northern Weekly* social events could chat with the author of the current serial, and make face-to-face comments. I doubt very much whether any form of working-class literature has had such close interaction between reader and writer as this, and there is no doubt that Clarke and his school found it a particularly healthy feature of writing for *The Northern Weekly*.[39]

Judging by the letters sent to *The Northern Weekly*, these novels did have a strong impact on the Lancashire working-class families who read them each week. Stories like *The Knobstick, The Hermit of Cottondale, The Young Gaffer* and *The Conductor's Sweetheart* may have planted a few seeds in the minds of their readers which began to challenge the ingrained conservatism of the Lancashire cotton workers—their attachment to the bourgeois parties, the half-time system, the inequality of women, and their indifference to the grimy surroundings they had to live it. There is no doubt that the Lancashire school of working-class novelists was very much a part of that strong regional socialist culture which blossomed in the 1890s, and created 'a new world within our hearts'.[40]

NOTES

1. *Teddy Ashton's Northern Weekly* (hereafter given as the *Northern Weekly*), 20 October 1900.
2. See Paul Salveson, 'Getting back to the land. The Daisy Colony experiment', *North West Labour History*, 10 (1984).
3. *The Bellman*, 15 September 1893.
4. Allen Clarke, *The Effects of the Factory System* (London, 1899), p.38.
5. *Northern Weekly*, 27 July 1901.
6. Allen Clarke, *Lancashire Lasses and Lads* (Manchester, 1906), p.11.
7. *Northern Weekly*, 6 July 1901.
8. *The Bolton Trotter*, 16 June 1893.
9. Clarke, *Lancashire Lasses and Lads*, p.11.
10. C. Allen Clarke, *The Knobstick. A Story of Love and Labour* (Manchester, 1893), p.108. For a discussion of this novel see chapter 4 by H. Gustav Klaus.
11. Allen Clarke, *The Red Flag* (London, 1907), p.19.
12. *Northern Weekly*, 14 May 1898.
13. Clarke, *The Red Flag*, p.76.
14. See Stephen Yeo, 'A new life: the religion of socialism in Britain 1883-1896', *History Workshop*, 4 (Autumn 1977).
15. Clarke, *The Red Flag*, p.89.
16. *ibid.*, p.107.
17. *ibid.*, p.106.
18. *Northern Weekly*, 21 May 1898.
19. Allen Clarke, *Windmill Land* (London, 1916), pp.36-8. Referring to the custom of 'maiden rent', that is the seduction of the tenant's daughter by the lord of the manor on her wedding night, Clarke comments:

    > Yet even that vile custom would bring about its own retribution, even by this wicked old custom was introduced into the peasantry some aristocratic blood, with its everloving instincts, its resentment of domination, with perhaps a touch of culture.

    For Clarke, this is not simply a genetic process—it is partly mystical. The sub-heading of the section quoted above is 'Karma', the eastern mystical philosophy of cause and effect.
20. *Northern Weekly*, 9 July 1898.
21. *ibid.*, 12 March 1898.
22. *ibid.*, 21 May 1898.

23. *ibid.*, 25 June 1898.
24. *ibid.*, 6 August 1898.
25. See R. Price, *An Imperial War and the British Working Class* (London, 1972).
26. Arthur Laycock, *Warren of Manchester* (London, n.d. [*c.* 1906]), p.97.
27. *Northern Weekly*, 16 May 1903.
28. *ibid.*, 31 May 1902.
29. *ibid.*, 12 July 1902.
30. *ibid.*, 20 December 1902.
31. *ibid.*, 16 May 1902.
32. See S. Carter, 'The ILP in Ashton-under-Lyne 1893 to 1900', *Bulletin of the North West Group for the Study of Labour History*, 4 (1976-7). The article relates events of the Tram Strike to the ILP locally.
33. *Northern Weekly*, 24 November 1900.
34. *ibid.*, 19 January 1901.
35. *ibid.*, 17 November 1900.
36. *ibid.*
37. Standish Meacham, *A Life Apart. The English Working Class, 1890-1914* (London, 1977).
38. For a discussion of James Haslam's novel, see chapter 5 by J. M. Rignall.
39. A photograph of one of the 'Northern Weekly Picnics' appears in Allen Clarke, *Moorlands and Memories*, third edn (Blackpool, 1924), p.134.
40. A longer version of this chapter is available for inspection at Bolton Reference Library. A number of Allen Clarke's works have been reprinted recently, including *Teddy Ashton's Lancashire Scrapbook. Selections from Allen Clarke* (Bolton, 1985), ed Paul Salveson; *The Effects of the Factory System* (Littleborough, 1985); *Moorlands and Memories* (Littleborough, 1986); *Windmill Land* (Littleborough, 1986). All these works contain introductions by the present writer and are available from G. Kelsall, 22 Church Street, Littleborough, Lancashire.

Henry Lawson's radical vision

MICHAEL WILDING

In March 1902 Edward Garnett wrote 'An Appreciation' of the work of Henry Lawson in *Academy and Literature*, reprinted in his *Friday Nights* (1922) as 'Henry Lawson and the Democracy':

> Nothing is more difficult to find in this generation than an English writer who identifies himself successfully with the life of the working democracy, a writer who does not stand aloof from and patronise the bulk of the people who labour with their hands. This no doubt is because nearly all our writers have a middle-class bias and training, and so either write down to or write up to their subject when it leads them outside their own class, and accordingly their valuations thereof are in general falsified . . .
> It is therefore an immense relief to the unsophisticated critic, after looking East and West and North and South for writers untainted by the ambition to be mentally genteel, to come across the small group of able democratic writers on the 'Sydney Bulletin', of whom Mr Lawson is the chief.[1]

Lawson's first collection of stories, *While the Billy Boils* (1896) received English distribution and *The Times* found it 'a little in Bret Harte's manner, crossed, perhaps, with that of Guy de Maupassant'.[2] His second collection, *On the Track and Over the Sliprails* (1900), was similarly well received. Francis Thompson wrote in the *Daily Chronicle* that it 'will sustain the reputation its author has already won as the best writer of Australian short stories and sketches the literary world knows'.[3] Encouraged by his

reception Lawson came to London in 1900. Blackwood's published a selction from the two previous prose volumes, *The Country I Come from* (1900), and a new collection *Joe Wilson and His Mates* (1901) and Methuen published a further collection *Children of the Bush* (1902). Lawson returned to Sydney in 1902 but his work was remembered. Will H. Ogilvie wrote of him in the *Scotsman*, 2 May 1914:

> He became a confirmed Socialist in his early manhood, setting a high value on the brotherhood of man, and seeing nothing but virtue in the attitude of Trade Unionism in its long war against capital. Against the blue sky of the infinite Bush spaces fluttered for him for ever the red flag of Revolt. The gipsy in his nature, and his deep-rooted and romantic sense of fair play, made him a ready convert to the camaraderie of the river roads; and his talent for verse-writing made him the accepted and much-loved spokesman of the brotherhood.[4]

Henry Lawson (1867-1922) was born on the Grenfell goldfield in New South Wales. His father was a Norwegian seaman who had jumped ship in Australia. His mother was the daughter of English immigrants. 'They were supposed to have come of English gipsies and were hop pickers in Kent,' Lawson wrote in his uncompleted autobiography.[5] His parents separated and Lawson worked with his father as a carpenter and painter, and then went to live with his mother in Sydney:

> I worked about in various private shops and did a bit of house-painting too. I knew what it was, when I was out of work for a few days in winter, to turn out shivering and be down at the Herald office at four o'clock on bitter mornings, and be one of the haggard group striking matches and running them down the wanted columns on the damp sheets posted outside. I knew what it was to tramp long distances and be one of the hopeless crowd of applicants. I knew what it was to drift about the streets in shabby and patched clothes and feel furtive and criminal-like. I knew all that before I wrote 'Faces in the Street'—before I was twenty.[6]

In 1887 the Mayor of Sydney called a public meeting to plan celebrations for Queen Victoria's jubilee. The meeting and

its immediate successors were taken over by republicans and freethinkers. 'Recent immigrants from the English working classes and the petty bourgeoisie touched with socialistic principles, aided by the old convict leaven, had humiliated the loyalists,' writes Manning Clark.[7] A Republican Union emerged, attracting British-born radicals such as Thomas Walker, George Black and John Norton as well as native radicals like J. D. Fitzgerald and Louisa Lawson.[8]

Republicanism was a very broad category. It could express or conceal a number of political attitudes. It could be both robber baron capitalist or socialist revolutionary. The first issue of *The Republican* appeared on 4 July 1887—independence day for the United States of America, a country that had broken free of British imperialism and become a dynamic, capitalist nation. Both capitalist and communist could use republicanism as a catch-cry. Much of the radical reputation of *The Bulletin*, established in 1880, derived from its republicanism. Disrespect for Queen Victoria, or Westminster, could be the assertiveness of the colonial businessman or the class hostility of the working person or unemployed. The displacement of class-aware radical activism from confronting the social and economic situation within Australia to inveighing against the imperial rule of Australia was one of the achievements of the *Bulletin*. Whereas anti-bourgeois or anti-capitalist sentiments were threatening the social order, the same feelings could be displaced into anti-monarchical or anti-imperialist expression and have a certain nationalist respectability.

The socialist direction of Lawson's republicanism was quite clear in the political ballads that he now published in *Bulletin:* 'The Song of the Outcasts' (12 May 1888), 'Faces in the Street' (28 July 1888) and 'The Hymn of the Socialists' (24 August 1889). 'Song of the Outcasts' was reprinted in the Brisbane *Worker,* and under the title 'The Army of the Rear' widely reprinted in the USA. 'The Hymn of the Socialists' was reprinted in William Morris's *Commonweal* (30 November 1889).[9]

The especial force of these ballads lay in their showing poverty and oppression existing in this new world just as they existed in the old. The dominant myth was that Aus-

tralia offered a new world free from those exploitations. 'The workingman's paradise', Henry Kingsley had called Australia in *The Recollections of Geoffrey Hamlyn* (1859). This mystification is confronted in 'The Song of the Outcasts':

> I looked upon the mass of poor, in filthy alleys pent;
> And on the rich men's Edens, that are built on grinding rent;
> I looked o'er London's miles of slums—I saw the horrors there,
> And swore to die a soldier of the Army of the Rear.[10]

And in case there was any remaining ambiguity that might claim these English conditions were not replicated in Australia, he opened 'Faces in the Street':

> They lie, the men who tell us in a loud decisive tone
> That want is here a stranger, and that misery's unknown;

the answer Lawson offers is unambiguous:

> But not until a city feels Red Revolution's feet
> Shall its sad people miss awhile the terrors of the street.[11]

The encouragement of nationalism of an Australian republican variety was a strategy that served to break down the powerful transnational working-class alliances that were being established, notably in the £31,000 collected in Australia and sent to support the London dockers. Lawson wrote:

> I have seen the stern-faced unionists of Sydney gather in thousands (forming a meeting that had to be divided into three portions) and stand for five long hours arranging plans of campaign and subscribing funds to carry them out, simply because a body of men, whom they had never seen and who were separated from them by fifteen thousand miles of sea, sought their assistance against a bitter wrong. I refer to the great dock laborers' strike.[12]

Lawson's first story, 'His Father's Mate' (*Bulletin*, 22 December 1888) has as its central incident the death of a

child helping his father on the gold workings. A subsidiary theme is the fate of the elder brother who got into trouble with the police and has disappeared. Drawing on a true incident told him by his grandfather[13] Lawson presents the tragedy as emblematic of the wretchedness of working-class life, with its limited choice of useless toil, death, or criminality. This same range of possibilities structures the group of stories he wrote about urban working-class conditions and child labour: 'A Visit of Condolence' (*Bulletin*, 23 April 1892), 'Jones's Alley' (*Worker*, Sydney, 1, 8, 15 June 1892), 'Arvie Aspinall's Alarm Clock' (*Bulletin*, 11 June 1892) and 'Two Boys at Grinder Bros.' (*Worker*, Sydney, 7 October 1893). Drawing on his own experiences working for a firm of coach-builders when he first arrived in Sydney, Lawson turns the experience of humiliation and exploitation into the weapons of political action. Bill, Arvie's young workmate, calls to find out why he's not at work, and is told he's dead. Talking to Arvie's mother he asks 'How old was Arvie?'

> 'Eleven.'
> 'I'm twelve—going on for thirteen. Arvie's father's dead, ain't he?'
> 'Yes.'
> 'So's mine. Died at his work, didn't he?'
> 'Yes.'
> 'So'd mine. Arvie told me his father died of something with his heart.'
> 'Yes.'
> 'So'd mine; ain't it rum? You scrub offices an' wash, don't yer?'
> 'Yes.'
> 'So does my mother. You find it pretty hard to get a livin', don't yer, these times?'[14]

The paralleling of shared experiences generalises the individual tragedy into a larger class oppression. These are not individual calamities resulting from individual failure, but the consequence of the social order. Lawson uses the same device of parallelism in Bill's dialogue with Arvie in 'Two Boys at Grinder Bros.'. This is the technique of socialist education, of awakening the oppressed to the nature of

their conditions, to the shared exploitations. These stories have generally been labelled Dickensian and sentimental by Lawson's commentators;[15] as if infant mortality, the exploitation of child labour, and slum life were somehow literary tropes and not all too common, everyday realities. That they were everyday realities was a provocation to political action. Lawson was developing a political consciousness that could work strategically, that could see in the individual suffering the basis for a shared sense of outrage. This was exactly William Lane's strategy in *The Workingman's Paradise* (1892), where the child born at the beginning of the novel dies at the beginning of part II, a victim of the poverty and unhygienic conditions of Sydney's slums. 'The Slaughter of the Innocents', Lane titled the chapter in which the child dies.[16] The dying child is not at all an easy sentimental trope but a directed, political symbol for Lawson, as for Lane. The death of Arvie Aspinall is the triggering or concluding incident for four stories: Lawson is not being wanton with death. Quite remarkably and significantly he does not give us a succession of deaths like a Jacobean dramatist or contemporary thriller writer. That he uses the one incident for a number of stories suggests a shocked reverence in its economy.

Arvie's work is described in the final section of the last story of the group, 'Two Boys at Grinder Bros.':

> Arvie was late out of the shop that evening. His boss was a sub-contractor for the coach-painting, and always tried to find twenty minutes' work for his boys just about five or ten minutes before the bell rang. He employed boys because they were cheap and he had a lot of rough work, and they could get under floors and 'bogies' with their pots and brushes, and do all the 'priming' and paint the trucks. His name was Collins, and the boys were called 'Collins' Babies'. It was a joke in the shop that he had a 'weaning' contract. The boys were all 'over fourteen', of course, because of the Education Act. Some were nine or ten—wages from five shillings to ten shillings. It didn't matter to Grinder Brothers so long as the contracts were completed and the dividends paid. Collins preached in the park every Sunday. But this has nothing to do with the story.[17]

These details are presented almost perfunctorily, as if to say: these are the normal conditions of urban exploitation, why make anything of it, how can you be surprised? The perfunctory presentation of Arvie's death that concludes the story is in part a necessary strategy since Lawson had already published the three other Arvie Aspinall–Jones's Alley stories, so the event cannot be given in any full-blown way. But this suited Lawson's skill in the oblique, the understated. The perfunctory account of exploitation and death, undramatised, flatly recorded, serves as an explosive conclusion to the earlier dialogue between Bill and Arvie, the development of a relationship, from persecution to comradeship and solidarity. The story opened with Bill calling out ' "Here comes Balmy Arvie" ' as he sat with 'five or six half-grown larrikins'.[18] But this first section ends with an expression of friendship, comradeship, mateship: 'Look here, Arvie!' he said in low, hurried tones, "Keep close to me goin' out tonight, 'n' if any of the other chaps touches yer or says anything to yer I'll hit 'em!" '[19] What provokes the solidarity is Bill's perception of a shared pattern of class exploitation in the experiences of their two families. He realises, silently but so clearly—such is Lawson's art—that these are no serendipitous coincidences, but the demonstration of their shared situation as workers, as proletarians. Nothing is spelled out—there is no generalising, no theory, no moral-drawing. The bare facts, presented in parallel, reveal the socio-political truth:

'I say, Arvie, what did yer father die of?'
'Heart disease. He dropped down dead at his work.'
Long, low intense whistle from Bill. He wrinkled his forehead and stared up at the beams as if he expected to see something unusual there. After a while he said, very impressively: 'So did mine.'
The coincidence hadn't done striking him yet; he wrestled with it for nearly a minute longer. Then he said:
'I suppose yer mother goes out washin'?'
'Yes.'
'N' cleans offices?'
'Yes.'
'So does mine . . .'[20]

The details of 'Collins' Babies' that seem so artlessly tacked on to the story are tacked on to take their true place. Lawson's theme is not restricted to presenting working-class conditions, the victims of exploitation. That is known, that is familiar. What Lawson is dealing with is the ending of divisions within the working classes. The bullying and teasing that make Arvie's life a misery, the factionalism of the oppressed in picking on someone else to oppress, is here brought to an end by Bill's promise of solidarity. The story shows how the lumpenproletarian, semi-criminal, wanton agression of the larrikins can none the less turn into supportive mateship. This is a socialist fable, and it was first published in the union paper the Sydney *Worker*. The larrikins don't suddenly become respectable bourgeois citizens. The action describes the transformation of random, divisive provocative aggression into shared mateship. The further political point is that it is too late. Arvie dies before he can return to work and appreciate this new mateship with Bill, this first experience of class solidarity. The Queensland shearers had been defeated in their 1891 strike by non-union working-class labour recruited from the huge pool of unemployed. The lack of solidarity amidst the exploited, divided amongst themselves, led to a larger class defeat. When the Australian Workers union risked strike action in 1894 in NSW, it was defeated.

Simultaneously with these stories of urban working conditions, Lawson was publishing his stories of conditions outside the towns. These were not seen as separate concerns, though Lawson is generally presented as a writer of up-country and outback materials. 'The Drover's Wife' (*Bulletin*, 23 July 1892) offers a vision of outback life and a tribute to the courage and resilience of the women in the bush. It tells simply of a woman's vigil to protect her children when a snake gets under the house. She waits all night, and past events are recalled, flood and fire, giving the story a mythic dimension. Out of these recurrent experiences of pioneering life Lawson extracts the representative. In part the snake and woman confrontation is of course Edenic, an Australian Genesis, which is why the

story has had such a powerful impact. But the Edenic is itself a political myth. When Adam delved and Eve span, who was then the gentleman? When the snake has been killed the dog 'shakes the snake as though he felt the original curse in common with mankind',[21] the curse of labour, and suffering in childbirth. Henry Kingsley's phrase that Australia was a workingman's paradise provides the social specificity for the archetypal reference. Lane's novel re-examines *The Workingman's Paradise* from a socialist perspective. Lawson is doing the same in brief.

The situation the woman is in is quite specifically established. She is alone because her husband is away working: the economic cause underlying the break-up of the family, the enforced separations. He is also set in a precise social category. He is an ex-squatter. The squatter who has lost his land either to the banks or through alcohol or both, is a recurrent figure in Lawson's work—'Middleton's Rouseabout', and 'Telling Mrs Baker' are characteristic. The situation is clearly related to current social reality. The archetypal quality of Lawson's work comes from its precise observation of social class particularity. It is not a mystifying, unplaced, never-never land pastoral with figures unlocated in history or class that Lawson creates.

Lawson like Lane was concerned with class co-operation. Socialist propaganda required getting the middle classes sympathetic to the rights of labour, and showing them they too were vulnerable to the destructive effects of capitalism. Consistently in his work he tries to break down divisions: to show the parallels of the city and the country working-class life; to show the destructive effects of the system on working and middle classes. 'The Big Brassingtons came down in the world and drifted to the city, as many smaller people do, more and more every year,' he writes in 'The House That Was Never Built'.[22] In the background is the process remarked in the *Communist Manifesto*: 'the lower strata of the middle class . . . sink gradually into the proletariat . . .'[23]

A recognition of the situation of women and a concerted effort to press for women's rights was part of the developing socialist consciousness of the union movement. The

isolation, the loneliness, the hardship are succinctly evoked. Here is the drover's true mate, his marriage mate, his wife, separated from him by the work situation. At the same time another sexual politics emerges, and the woman's clubbing the snake to death suggests a revenge on the phallic, a refusal of the procreative. The dryness of the outback has dried out the sexuality of its struggling pioneers and left only resentment, resentment at being brought to and left in such an isolated place. The eldest child, who tries to get out of bed when the snake is killed 'but his mother forces him back with a grip of iron', offers an Oedipal conclusion to the story:

> 'Mother, I won't never go drovin'; blast me if I do!'
> And she hugs him to her worn-out breast and kisses him; and they sit thus together while the sickly daylight breaks over the bush.[24]

With its absent drover, 'The Drover's Wife' poignantly presents the broken family, 'the practical absence of the family among the proletarians' as the *Communist Manifesto* puts it;[25] the drought, as well as a naturalistic portrayal of conditions, represents too the drought of sexual absence; and this in its turn issues in the destruction of the masculine, the killing of the snake and burning it. Yet even so, dawn still breaks, there is still a positive note. Edward Garnett wrote:

> If this artless sketch be taken as the summary of a woman's life, giving its significance in ten short pages, Maupassant has never done better. Lawson has re-treated this subject at length in the more detailed picture in 'Water them Geraniums'; I leave it to mothers of all ranks and stations in life to say how it affects them, and whether it has not universal application to the life of working women wherever the sun goes down. Art stands for much, but sincerity also stands for much in art, and the sincerity of Lawson's tales nearly always drives them home.[26]

Garnett was well aware that the artlessness was in itself the mark of Lawson's art. He hedges his bets on how great art it

is, or nearly is, yet recognises the genius in this work that was so unlike the English norm. In the same way Garnett encouraged those other outsider, marginal figures— Conrad, W. H. Hudson, D. H. Lawrence.

> Read 'The Union Buries its Dead' . . . if you care to see how the most casual, 'newspapery' and apparently artless art of this Australian writer carries with it a truer, finer, more delicate commentary on life than do the idealistic works in any of our genteel school of writers. It isn't great art, but it is near to great art; and, moreover, great art is not to be found every 'publishing season'.[27]

'The Union Buries Its Dead' (*Truth*, 16 April 1893) is another classic picture of bad times in the bush. It opens with a delicate suggestion of Maupassant, and then the Seine is quickly redefined as a billabong:

> While out boating one Sunday afternoon on a billabong across the river, we saw a young man on horseback driving some horses along the bank. He said it was a fine day, and asked if the water was deep there. The joker of our party said it was deep enough to drown him, and he laughed and rode further up. We didn't take much notice of him.
>
> Next day a funeral gathered at a corner pub and asked each other in to have a drink while waiting for the hearse. They passed away some of the time dancing jigs to a piano in the bar parlour. They passed away the rest of the time sky-larking and fighting.
>
> The defunct was a young union labourer, about twenty-five, who had been drowned the previous day while trying to swim some horses across a billabong of the Darling.[28]

Manning Clark captures the tone of the story: 'he was telling Australians that the bush barbarians had their own way of showing they knew just as well as the author of the book of Ecclesiastes what life was all about'.[29]

The story has a more specific socialist purpose than this, however.

He was almost a stranger in town, and the fact of his having been a union man accounted for the funeral. The police found some union papers in his swag, and called at the General Labourers' Union Office for information about him. That's how we knew.[30]

The unionism is part of the subject. The General Labourers Union (GLU) of Australia had been established two years earlier in February 1891. The Australian Shearers Union (ASU) had organised the New South Wales shearers, the GLU 'took up the work of organising the woolshed laborers'.[31] W. G. Spence, who was president of the ASU and secretary of the GLU, recalled:

A great deal of good work was done by the GLU. It made experiments in the shape of carrying out road work and sewerage contracts under co-operation, the Union finding the deposit, plant, etc., and the men dividing the result of their labor. The Union also engaged Mrs Summerfield to organise the women workers.[32]

The progressive socialist position was to create one big union of an alliance of all working people. But class society permeated the working classes as well as the middle classes. The distinctions between skilled labour and unskilled labour persisted, not only in pay differentials but in status and union organisation. Although it was proposed to amalgamate the Australian Shearers Union with the General Labourers Union in 1892 and again in 1893, a majority of the shearers voted against the proposal; in 1892, 5,862 were for, 5,997 against. In 1893 4,825 were for, 5,686 against. However the New South Wales branches gave a majority of 576 in favour, and its branches were allowed to amalgamate. 'Practically amalgamation was agreed to at the Conference of 1894, but the new constitution was only adopted at the special convention held in Albury in February, 1895.'[33] The amalgamated organisation was called the Australian Workers Union. In 1904 the Queensland and New South Wales AWUs amalgamated.

These class divisions within the working classes are part of Lawson's story:

The procession numbered fifteen, fourteen souls following the broken shell of a soul. Perhaps not one of the fourteen possessed a soul any more than the corpse did—but that doesn't matter.

Four or five of the funeral, who were boarders at the pub, borrowed a trap which the landlord used to carry passengers to and from the railway station. They were strangers to us who were on foot, and we to them. We were all strangers to the corpse.

A horseman, who looked like a drover just returned from a big trip, dropped into our dusty wake and followed us a few hundred yards, dragging his pack-horse behind him, but a friend made wild and demonstrative signals from a hotel verandah—hooking at the air in front with his right hand and jabbing his left thumb over his shoulder in the direction of the bar—so the drover hauled off and didn't catch up to us any more. He was a stranger to the entire show.[34]

The separations between those on horseback and those on foot are class separations. 'A barrier which became equally marked was the one separating those who worked on horseback from those who did not,' G. A. Wilkes has noted, and he offers representative evidence from the literature.[35] The horseman does not have solidarity with the labourers on foot. A sympathy, yes, but mateship and the society of alcohol draw him off. Similarly the shearers pay their alcoholic respects to the procession but do not join in.

On the way to the cemetery we passed three shearers sitting on the shady side of a fence. One was drunk—very drunk. The other two covered their right ears with their hats, out of respect for the departed—whoever he might have been—and one of them kicked the drunk and muttered something to him.[36]

What Lawson represents are the class divisions within the working classes; at the same time the solidarity of the labourers is stressed in their attending the funeral of the unknown man. So we have Lawson's characteristic bittersweet plangency, that celebration of the impulse towards

solidarity, and the notation of the forces opposed to solidarity.

The divisions between labour had been considerably broken down, but progress still had to be made, before the horsemen would continue to the funeral, and the shearers get off the fence and join in with the rouseabouts. Lawson remarked on the sense of superiority of the shearers that underlay the class divisions between shearers and labourers in 'A Word in Season' in *The Worker* (Sydney) in 1894:

> Get rid of the idea that the shearers are the only wronged men on earth and the squatters the only tyrants.
>
> Remember that the hardship of bush life at its worst is not a circumstance compared with what thousands of poor women in cities have to go through.
>
> Remember that there are bitterer struggles and grander battles fought by the poor of cities than ever in the country.
>
> Remember that the fathers, the heroes of modern Liberty, fought and threw away their lives on barricades in the streets of cities.[37]

The opening of Harte's 'Tennessee's Partner'—'I do not think that we ever knew his real name'—[38] and the disquisition on the names people went by is taken up by Lawson and rewritten with political implication. Apart from being the representative unknown outback worker, the dead man's anonymity carries suggestions of the necessarily pseudonymous nature of early radical activity. The Queensland shearers' strikes had meant that many union activists had changed their names to avoid arrest or to gain re-employment. Mitchell remarks in 'The Man Who Forgot' 'and as for a name, that's nothing. I don't know mine, and I've had eight.'[39] Lane edited *The Worker* and wrote *The Workingman's Paradise* under a pseudonym, John Miller. Lawson regularly used the names Joe Swallow, Cervus Wright, and Jack Cornstalk to sign political pieces. Larry Petrie, the Scots-born secretary of the General Labourers Union, had been christened George Frederick Augustus Howard Carlyle Petrie, he said, and as G. F. Howard he booked a passage on a non-union crewed ship and was

arrested for causing an explosion aboard, in July 1893.[40]

In July 1893 the first 220 members of the New Australia Co-operative Settlement Association under the chairmanship of William Lane sailed for Paraguay. Lawson wrote a poem in support, 'Something Better'.[41] But the movement was seen by many as a further weakening of socialism within Australia. A second batch sailed in December, but by then the first group had already been split and the movement destabilised. Lawson stood in as editor of the Sydney *Worker*, hoping to be given the permanent position, but someone else was appointed, and he went to New Zealand looking for work. The voyage steerage issued in the poem 'For'ard', published in the *New Zealand Mail*, the Sydney *Worker*, and Keir Hardie's *Labour Leader*.[42] On the offer of a position on the new *Daily Worker* Lawson returned to Sydney, only to find the paper had collapsed. The unions were once again under attack from the pastoralists in the attempt to cut wages and the consequent strikes and violence of 1894. At this period Lawson seems to have been close to Mary Cameron (later Mary Gilmore), who was living in a boarding house kept by William Lane's wife, Annie, preparatory to joining Lane's Colonia Cosme, the second communist settlement in Paraguay. The other radical centre Lawson frequented was McNamara's bookshop in Sydney, a library and centre for international radical journals and discussions. In 1896, with his first book of poems *In the Days When the World Was Wide* published, he married McNamara's step-daughter, Bertha.[43]

This radical world had been Lawson's milieu for ten years. But now radicalism was in retreat; the unions had been badly defeated, membership dropped disastrously. Collecting his contributions from the papers of those years for book publication, he had to endure considerable sub-editorial emendations. The texts collected in his books often lack the political specificity of the original magazine publication. But encouraged by the critical reception of these books in England, Lawson made plans to go there, and sailed in April 1900.[44] The attempt to launch himself on a literary career in London was part of Lawson's attempt

to take remedial action and halt his descent into the vortex of depression and alcoholism. The political movement to which he had committed himself and which had provided the rationale and aesthetic of his work was in disarray. So that attempt at positive thinking, launching off on the next stage of a literary career, was one shrouded in the context of pervasive pessimism. Turning from the political to the private he had only his increasingly unhappy marriage, and the memory of his parents' stormy and unhappy marriage to confront. The four long stories about Joe Wilson and his wife Mary, an archetypal (Joseph and Mary) pair of young settlers, show the destructive effects of economic hardship and the struggles of the life of the small settler in the bush on marital relationships. The theme is there not only in Joe's and Mary's marriage, but reinforced in the lives of the few neighbours. Far longer than those early *Bulletin* sketches, these stories aspire to a fully-fledged realism of recorded detail, rather than that earlier allusive impressionism. ' "Water them Geraniums" ' opens with an inventory of Joe Wilson's furniture and possessions. But this realism is something of an illusion. Just as Lawson had produced material aceptable to the *Bulletin's* rigid preconceptions—short, boiled down, spare—now he could simulate the more discursive mode of mainstream British magazine realism. Much of the force of these stories, however, lies on their margins. The effects are as oblique as ever. The glancing, the tangential, the implied, the allusive, are the tactics Lawson uses to capture his material. The ostensible direction or mode of the story is not the 'point': rather it is a strategy employed by Lawson in order to slip in the unacceptable—the material the editors and publishers would refuse if they thought that was the central concern. The innocence of Joe and Mary is a way of introducing the sexual threats that could not be written about in a direct way, at a time of repressive censorship of sexual materials in the printed word. The story tells of Joe's slow, bashful courting. There is a delicately idyllic episode where Joe helps Mary hang out clothes, a celebration of ordinary, daily activity at that time not ordinarily experienced by those who could afford servants. 'I took the line from Mary,

and accidentally touched her soft, plump little hand as I did so: it sent a thrill right through me.'[45] The idyll turns into embarrassment as Mary shoos Joe away so she can hang up unnamed things he is not allowed to see. The sexual implications in the sheet hanging are now drawn attention to; not exactly made explicit because they are unmentionable. But the unmentionable exerts its strong force of absence, appropriate for Joe's unfulfilled inexpressible sexual yearning. Later Joe's 'handkerchiefs and collars disappeared from the room and turned up washed and ironed and laid tidily on my table' and, 'I felt so full of hope and joy.' Then Jack tells him, 'I see you've made a new mash, Joe. I saw the half-caste cook tidying up your room this morning and taking your collars and things to the wash house, (p.25). Not only is there the simple humour of love's delusions, there is also the racial categorising which again marks an unbridgeable gulf for Joe. All the racist complex of attitudes is brought into play here. The issues are also class issues. Mary, as Jack describes her early on is

> a nice little girl in service at Black's . . . She's more like an adopted daughter, in fact, than a servant. She's a real good little girl, and good-looking into the bargain. I hear that young Black is sweet on her, but they say she won't have anything to do with him. (p.7)

She is described in terms that make her appear of marginal working-class status. Though 'in service' she is treated like a daughter. The station owner's son could be just wanting sexual diversion, or it could be marriage; it is left unclear. Joe's relationship with Mary would be upwardly mobile; with the half-caste cook, unnamed, downwardly mobile. Racial and national and class characteristics are recurrently indicated in this story. Mary's father had

> been an old mate of Black's, a younger son of a well-to-do English family (with blue blood in it, I believe) and sent out to Australia with a thousand pounds to make his way . . . They think they're hard done by . . . I wish I'd had a thousand pounds to start on!

Mary's mother was the daughter of a German immigrant.
(p.262)[46]

All these issues of sexuality and race and class are
brought into play in the fight Joe has with Romany. The
Romany, the gypsy, presents the classic sexual threat to the
Anglo-Celtic.

> He was a big shearer, a dark, handsome fellow, who looked
> like a gipsy: it was reckoned that there was foreign blood in
> him. He went by the name of Romany. He was supposed to be
> shook after Mary too. He had the nastiest temper and the best
> violin in the district.   (p.26)

It is the alter ego of Joe Wilson–Henry Lawson. Joe's 'I
reckon I was born for a poet by mistake' (p.3) incites the
identification of Joe with Lawson, while Lawson continually recurred to his foreign blood, to his Norwegian
father and his gypsy grandfather. The innocent naïve bush
poet Joe fights the sexual, gypsy, bohemian violinist
Romany; Romany represents that sexual, decadent,
bohemian milieu Lawson was trying, maybe not wholeheartedly, to escape.

In fighting Romany, of course, Joe is displacing the
aggression he feels for the jackaroo, who has turned up at
Black's and is interested in Mary. Romany manages to stir
up Joe's sexual anxiety about the jackaroo, but Joe cannot
fight the jackaroo directly. The class divisions prevent it.
Lawson shows how an inexpressible aggression to the
ruling class produces an expressed aggression to the scape-
goat racial minority, the gypsy. This is no mere metaphor.
The gypsies no less than the Jews were victims of the
extermination camps, and continue to be harried and
harrassed in England and Europe today. Out of a simple,
purportedly innocent, clean, positive love story, Lawson
produces an oblique sexual-political-radical exploration.

The socialist aspects of the *Joe Wilson* volume had been
subdued and implicit. The years of writing for the radical
press had ensured the development of Lawson's radical
vision, whether political themes were explicitly pro-

claimed or not. The verses 'The Never-Never Country' that conclude the volume, however, pay explicit tribute to 'Oh rebels to society!' and 'The communism perfected!' (p.333). In *Children of the Bush* the socialist and unionist is fore-grounded. *The Athenaeum* commented:

one finds it right and natural that a strong democratic note should ring through these pages. But it is rather a pity that the note should be quite as insistent as it is, that it should be aggressive, and that, on occasion, it should sound bitter.[47]

Here he collects stories about unionists, stories about the meaning of socialism.

'Lord Douglas' proclaims its political context with its opening:

The Imperial Hotel was rather an unfortunate name for an out-back town pub, for out-back is the stronghold of Australian democracy; it was the out-back vote and influence that brought about 'One Man One Vote', 'Payment of Members', and most of the democratic legislation of late years, and from out-back came the overwhelming vote in favour of Australian as against Imperial Federation.[48]

And the hotel is described in its place in outback politics.

The Imperial Hotel was patronised by the Pastoralists, the civil servants, the bank manager and clerks—all the scrub aristo-cracy; it was the headquarters of the *Pastoralists' Union* in Bourke; a barracks for blacklegs brought up from Sydney to take the place of Union shearers on strike; and the new Governor, on his inevitable visit to Bourke, was banqueted at the Imperial Hotel. The editor of the local 'Capitalistic rag' stayed there; the Pastoralists' member was elected mostly by dark ways and means devised at the Imperial Hotel, and one of its managers had stood as a dummy candidate to split the Labour vote; the management of the hotel was his reward.

(p.45)

The manager is representative of a recurrent type in Lawson—the immigrant with nothing known about his background. After his arrival in England Lawson

developed his presentation of this type with a new sense of English class differentials.

> Jack Mitchell reckoned, by the way he treated his *employés* and spoke to workmen, that he was the educated son of an English farmer—gone wrong and sent out to Australia. Someone called him 'Lord Douglas', and the nickname caught on.   (p.46)

The story details some of the confrontations between unionists and 'Lord Douglas' up until the manager disappears and is gaoled for embezzlement, but the focus is on his return from gaol, when some are in favour of boycotting him, kicking him out of town, tarring and feathering him. But Mitchell insists on passing round the hat to help the manager get back on his feet. And is proved right; the final paragraph notes he opened a shop 'and the *Sydney Worker*, *Truth*, and *Bulletin* and other democratic rags are on sale at his shop' (p.57). It is a straightforward parable of samaritan socialism, class collaboration, though this bare outline of its conscious socialist content does not do justice to the subtlety, irony, comedy and self-awareness of the writing. It is not a naïve fable. It concludes:

> He is scarcely yet regarded as a straight-out democrat. He was a gentleman once, Mitchell said, and the old blood was not to be trusted. But, last elections, Douglas worked quietly for Unionism, and gave the leaders certain hints, and put them up to various electioneering dodges which enabled them to return, in the face of Monopoly, a Labour member who is as likely to go straight as long as any other Labour member.
>
> (p.57)

In 'Barney Take Me Home Again' in *Children of the Bush* the destructive aspects of migration are examined. This has never been a recognised theme in English language culture in the way it has in modern Greek culture, the loss and tragedy implicit in having to leave one's homeland in order to find work. Later the narrator visits the Johnsons who have returned to London and Lawson records his appalled reaction to English working-class conditions.

It was a blind street, like the long, narrow yard of a jail, walled by dark houses, all alike. The next door but one to that at which I knocked to inquire was where the Johnsons lived; they lived in a four-storey house, or rather a narrow section of a four-storeyed terrace. I found later on that they paid the landlord, or nearly paid him, by letting lodgings. They lived in one room with the use of the parlour and the kitchen when the lodgers weren't using them, and the son shared a room with a lodger. The back windows looked out on the dead wall of a poorhouse of some kind, the front on rows of similar windows opposite—rows of the same sort of windows that run for miles and miles in London. In one a man sat smoking in his shirt-sleeves, from another a slavey leaned out watching a four-wheeler that had stopped next door, in a third a woman sat sewing, and in a fourth a women was ironing, with a glimpse of a bedstead behind her. And all outside was gloom and soot and slush.

(p.183)

And he remarks as much as the material conditions, the defeat of spirit. 'I would never have recognised the Johnsons' he said, 'I found Johnson an old man—old and grey before his time' (p.183):

When I left Johnson I felt less lonely in London, and rather humbled in spirit. He seemed so resigned—I had never seen such gentle sadness in a man's eyes, nor heard it in a man's voice. I could get back to Australia somehow and start life again, but Johnson's day had been dead for many years.

(p.185)

The fullest expression of Lawson's English experience is collected in *Triangles of Life*, a volume proposed and prepared in 1907 but not published until 1913. The 94-page title story offers a comparative study of Australia and England, a theme broached with 'Barney Take Me Home Again'. There it was the woman who could not adjust to the rawness of pioneering life, and the account of her dissatis-factions are the substance of the first part of the story. In 'Triangles of Life' it is the young man, Billy, who has developed the horrors and is shipped back to England. The first part set in Australia describes his collapse, and the other two parts deal with what happens to him on his

return. The story takes its title from old Higgins's meditations on an old elementary book of Euclid. ' "Life," he'd
say, after some preliminary shuffles, coughs, and grunts,
"is wot I call made up of triangles—ekal hatteral triangles.'
But this is given a political gloss by 'Brennan, the silent
semi-foreman' (a *Reynold's Newspaper* reader): ' "You're
right there, Higgins, and you and me and the rest of us in
hundreds of English villages are shoring up the props. And
they're comin' down, Higgins!'[49] 'The triangles' are also
one of the infamous punishments of Australia's convict
days, the frame to which convicts were bound, to be
flogged. And so Lawson assembles this ambitious three-
part story, the first part in the bush, the second part seemingly irrelevant, digressive observations on village life
near London, and then the third side in which Billy,
returned from Australia, settles down with Lizzie, who has
had a child and various liaisons in London. Bob, Billy's old
mate from Australia who had nursed him through the
horrors, returns to England and stays with them, and the
gossip within the village generates and creates the very
situation it fantasised, Billy breaking up with Lizzie who
goes to live with Bob. It is an examination of the com-
plexities of mateship and communality, of the failures of
communication and of misunderstandings. It shows the
alienation and isolation of the workingman's life in the
bush; and then it shows the repressive nature of English
life—class ridden, controlled by the expectations of class
roles monitored by gossips. And nobody wins. Bob
doesn't want Lizzie, and at the story's end Billy is sailing
out to Australia again on the *Gera*,' and Bob was aboard the
Karlsruhe, a fortnight ahead'[50] with Lizzie left in England.

In 'The Letters to Jack Cornstalk' (*Argosy*, October 1900,
January and February 1901) Lawson presents himself as an
'Australian' for his critical perspective on England, not a
vanguard socialist or a proletarian. It leads to a quasi-Mark
Twain bumptiousness, a cocksureness that now seems
more defensive than anything else. It is the tone of the
upstart colonial, the proletarian larrikin mutated into the
colonial tourist, modelled on the American. Yet the
blustering critique of St Pauls retains a socialist basis: its

'atmosphere suggestive of wide spaces' 'is one of the apparently useless lies of civilisation—but I suppose it's born of commercialism, like most other lies—a little branch line lie of commercialism'.[51] Something of the indictment of the university D.H. Lawrence delivers in *The Rainbow* is captured here. But in general the assertive note suggests that Lawson is not totally at ease with the tone. It isn't his tone, but a tone he is adopting, a persona, an image. As a foreigner in England he is treated as a gentleman, but he knows he is a proletarian. But he knows the risks of a proclaimed proletarianism or a proclaimed socialism. He mentions the absence of politics in the English village. His own lack of politics he does not mention. But it is indicated by mention of this other, parallel, absence. The inexpressible politics are displaced into nationalism. The 'colonial' was an acceptable caricature, a mask. The problem, however, is that masks like nationalism can suffocate their wearers. The necessity of subterfuge meant that inside the mask Lawson was with difficulty holding on to his real identity.

Alcohol can be seen as the response to the crisis of his art in which his political commitment became increasingly inexpressible. The climate of repression with the defeat of the unions by the mid-nineties had made revolutionary sentiments unacceptable in the press. Lawson's poetic vision of revolution mutated into a vision of war, enemy unspecified. It could be the class enemy; but it could be taken as a national enemy and the solidarity that of patriotism or race, not class. The left itself was fragmented. The parliamentary labour party had little appeal for Lawson. While the failure of Lane's New Australia enterprise, with Lane himself leaving it in 1899, afforded little hope of alternatives to the parliamentary model.

But turning to personal themes of domesticity and sexuality, Lawson soon found these equally inexpressible. The political put him in impossible conflict with society, an author dependent on acceptance by the commercial media. The domestic-sexual-familial put him in impossible conflict with his wife, and his mother. His mode of transparency, of exploration and recollection of inter-

relationships, allowed few disguises. His aesthetic was based on drawing from life, on a realism he identified with his socialist commitment. In *Triangles of Life* he goes as far as psychically he dared push himself in writing about the collapse of his marriage. It is there in two powerful stories, 'Drifting Apart' and 'A Child in the Dark of a Foreign Father'. The failing marriage in that latter story suggests too the marriage of his parents, and his own childhood resentments of his mother.

Lawson's work is comparatively unknown outside Australia today. Within Australia, his profile adorning the ten-dollar note, he has become a nationalist icon, and his specifically socialist vision has been obscured, though not forgotten. It is something his friend, English born Fred Broomfield, stressed in 1930:

> Lawson's name is refused a place on the scroll of Australian literature by the superfine critics, on the ground that he voiced the emotions of a class—the rank and file of 'My Army, O My Army'—rather than of a nation—or, at least, that is one of the reasons given, apart from the alleged rudeness and crudity of his verse-form. But what a class! What a toiling universe of sorrow-smitten men and women found an utterance through his verse! It has been said that Lawson, when a lad, was caught in the spell of socialism. That may be, but he never altered. In one of his poems written in later life he declared that he was 'too old to rat'.[52]

NOTES

1. Edward Garnett, *Friday Nights: Literary Criticism and Appreciations* (London, 1922), pp.181, 182.
2. Quoted in advertisements in Angus & Robertson publications: for example Henry Lawson, *When I Was King* (Sydney, 1905), appendix of announcements of other books, p.5. Emile Saillens compared Lawson to Gorky in *Mercure de France*, 1 October 1910; reprinted in Colin Roderick (ed.), *Henry Lawson Criticism 1894-1971* (Sydney, 1972), p.147.

3. Francis Thompson, *Daily Chronicle* (London) 29 March 1901, reprinted in Roderick (ed.), *Henry Lawson Criticism*, p.108.

4. *ibid.*, p.163.

5. Henry Lawson, *Autobiographical and Other Writings 1887-1922*, ed. Colin Roderick (*Collected Prose*, volume 2) (Sydney, 1972), p.193. This edition is subsequently quoted *CP*.

6. *CP*, pp.209-10.

7. Manning Clark, *Henry Lawson, The Man and the Legend* (Melbourne, 1985), p.36.

8. Thomas Walker, born Preston 1858, had arrived via San Francisco as a spiritualist lecturer. George Black, born Edinburgh 1854, was a sub-editor on the *Bulletin* and later edited the *Workman* and the *Worker* and wrote *The Labor Party in New South Wales* (Sydney, 1917). John Norton, born Brighton, 1858, became proprietor of *Truth* and is one of the subjects of Cyril Pearl, *Wild Men of Sydney* (London, 1958) and Michael Cannon, *That Damned Democrat: John Norton an Australian Populist, 1858-1916* (Melbourne, 1981). On Henry's mother, Louisa Lawson, see Brian Matthews, 'Dawn crusade' in Eric Fry (ed.), *Rebels and Radicals* (Sydney, 1983), pp.148-62.

9. Anne Cranny-Francis, 'Pacifying the socialist: the "reform" of Henry Lawson's "The Hymn of the Socialists",' *Australian Literary Studies*, 10 (1982), pp.511-15.

   On the influence of Morris in Australia see Bruce Mansfield, 'The socialism of William Morris: England and Australia', *Historical Studies Australia and New Zealand* (1956), pp.271-90.

10. Henry Lawson, *Collected Verse: Volume One: 1885-1900*, ed. Colin Roderick (Sydney, 1967), p.11. Subsequently quoted as *CV*.

11. *CV*, pp.15-17.

12. *CP*, p.17.

13. Colin Roderick, *Henry Lawson, Commentaries on his Prose Writings* (Sydney, 1985), p.5.

14. Henry Lawson, *While the Billy Boils* (Sydney, 1896) p.211. All quotations from this edition. An English edition from Simpkin, Marshall appeared in 1897, jointly with Angus & Robertson, Sydney. E.V. Lucas reviewed it enthusiastically in *The Academy*, 17 July 1897:

He shows us what living in the bush really means. By force of sketch, dialogue, story and yarn, he brings before us the Bohemians and wastrels of that vast island: their humour, their way of thought, their vocabulary, their comradeship. The result is a real book, a book in a hundred.

In 1903 Angus & Robertson published a joint edition with Humphrey Milford, Oxford University Press, London. In 1927 it was issued in two volumes in Jonathan Cape's 'Traveller's Library' (nos. 38 and 39), London. See George Mackaness, *An Annotated Bibliography of Henry Lawson* (Sydney, 1951), pp.14-16.

15. A.G. Stephens, *Bulletin*, 29 August 1896, reprinted in *A.G. Stephens: Selected Writings*, ed. Leon Cantrell (Sydney, 1977) p.225; Brian Kiernan (ed.), *The Essential Henry Lawson* (South Yarra, 1982), p.14; John Barnes, *Henry Lawson's Stories* (Melbourne, 1985), p.13.

16. 'John Miller' (William Lane), *The Workingman's Paradise: An Australian Labour Novel* (1892), facsimile reprint (Sydney, 1980).

   See Michael Wilding, 'William Lane's *The Workingman's Paradise*: pioneering socialist realism', in Stephen Knight and S.N. Mukherjee (eds.), *Words and Worlds: Studies in the Social Role of Verbal Culture* (Sydney, 1983) p.44.

17. Henry Lawson, *On the Track and Over the Sliprails* (Sydney, 1900), p.127.

18. *ibid.*, p.123.

19. *ibid.*, p.127.

20. *ibid.*, pp.125-6.

21. *While the Billy Boils*, p.138.

22. Henry Lawson, *Children of the Bush* (Sydney, 1910), p.167.

23. Karl Marx and Frederick Engels, *Manifesto of the Communist Party*, translated by Samuel Moore (1888) (Moscow, 1973), p.53.

24. *While the Billy Boils*, p.138. Xavier Pons offers the fullest psychoanalytical approach to Lawson in *Henry Lawson: l'homme et l'oeuvre* (Paris, 1980), and *Out of Eden: Henry Lawson's Life and Works—A Psychoanalytical View* (Sydney, 1984).

25. *Manifesto*, p.68.

26. *Friday Nights*, p.184.

27. *ibid.*, p.183.

28. *While the Billy Boils*, p.91.

29. Clark, *op.cit.*, p.78.
30. *While the Billy Boils*, p.91.
31. W. G. Spence, *History of the A.W.U.*, (Sydney, 1911), p.47.
32. *ibid.*, pp.47-8.
33. *ibid.*, p.80.
34. *While the Billy Boils*, p.92.
35. G. A. Wilkes, *The Stockyard and the Croquet Lawn: Literary Evidence for Australia's Cultural Development* (Melbourne, 1981), pp.43-4. 'There is not a horse in the book from title page to imprint—not one horse!' David Ferguson (1896) in Roderick, *Henry Lawson Criticism*, p.48.
36. *While the Billy Boils*, p.93.
37. *CP*, 2, p.28.
38. *The Complete Works of Bret Harte*, II (London, 1903) p.135.
39. *While the Billy Boils*, p.34.
40. Lawson quotes the ballad Mary Cameron wrote on Petrie in 'A Hero in Dingo Scrubs'; see Roderick, *Commentaries*, pp.206-9. Petrie later went to Lane's Paraguayan settlement: see Gavin Souter, *A Peculiar People: The Australians in Paraguay* (Sydney, 1968), pp.170-1, and E. H. Lane, *Dawn to Dusk: Reminiscences of a Rebel* (Brisbane, 1939).
41. *New Australia*, 24 March 1894; *CV*, 1, 256-7. On New Australia, see Lloyd Ross, *William Lane and the Australian Labor Movement* (Sydney, 1937) and Souter, *A Peculiar People*.
42. Anne Cranny-Francis, 'Henry Lawson and the labour leader', *Australian Literary Studies*, 11 (1983), p.266.
43. The standard biographies are Denton Prout, *Henry Lawson: The Grey Dreamer* (Adelaide, 1963) and Colin Roderick, *The Real Henry Lawson* (Adelaide, 1982).
44. John Barnes, 'Henry Lawson in London', *Quadrant*, July 1979, pp.22-35; 'Henry Lawson in England: The "high tide": a revaluation', *Quadrant*, June 1984, pp.28-43.
45. Henry Lawson, *Joe Wilson and His Mates* (Sydney, 1902), pp.17-18. Subsequent page numbers given in the text are to this edition.
46. Lawson's wife, Bertha Marie Louise Bredt, was the daughter of two German immigrants. 'Remember I was brought up in a German district', (*CP*, 2, p.227) he wrote in 1913.
47. *The Athenaeum*, no. 3907, 13 September 1902, p.347.
48. *Children of the Bush* (Sydney, 1910), p.44. Subsequent page numbers in the text are to this edition.

49. *Triangles of Life* (Melbourne, 1913), pp.36, 37.
50. *ibid.*, p.92. Lawson's wife and two children sailed from England to Australia on the Karlsruhe on 30 April 1902 and Lawson followed on the *Gera* on 21 May (Clark, *op.cit.*, 133).
51. *ibid.*, p.119.
52. Fred J. Broomfield, *Henry Lawson and His Critics* (Sydney, 1930), p.37. On Broomfield see Ann-Mari Jorden, 'Fred J. Broomfield', *Australian Literary Studies*, 9 (1980), 468. The poem quoted is 'The Old Unionist', *CV*, 3 (1969), pp.94-5.

Tressell in international perspective

RONALD PAUL

From 1905 to 1914 the international labour movement experienced one of its most decisive and conflicting periods of political crisis and organisational growth. The pivotal year of 1905 in Russia not only marked an important stage in the maturation of the Russian working class but its stormy events reverberated throughout the world accelerating the impending rupture between the reformist and revolutionary tendencies within socialism. At the same time, also in the wake of the first Russian revolution were written some of the greatest pioneering works of socialist fiction—Maxim Gorky's *Mother* (1907), Jack London's *The Iron Heel* (1907), Upton Sinclair's *The Jungle* (1906), Martin Andersen Nexö's *Pelle the Conqueror* (1906-10) and Robert Tressell's *The Ragged Trousered Philanthropists* (*c.* 1906-10, pub. 1914). Clearly, the almost simultaneous appearance of these landmark novels reflected a level of consciousness and confidence within the working class of being capable of putting its own specific stamp on both the political and literary spheres of class society.

However, the most immediate political consequence of the defeat of the 1905 revolution was a strengthening of the reformist leaderships of the labour movements. The use of the mass strike as a revolutionary weapon for social change was subsequently rejected by many labour leaders in favour of a further parliamentary accommodation to capitalism, which finally led to their total capitulation at the outbreak of the First World War in 1914. Although all of the above novelists were personally associated with the left

wing of the socialist movement—Gorky with the Bolsheviks, London and Sinclair with the Socialist Party of America, Nexö with the then radical Danish Social Democrats, while Tressell was an active member of the Social Democratic Federation—only London seems to have been sensitive to the reformist watershed and used his novel to polemicise against both the increasing bureaucratic control of the movement as well as its fatal underestimation of the virulence of capitalist reaction faced with a fundamental threat to the system.[1] In the other works, this crucial juncture of organisational consolidation and concomitant political retreat from revolutionary principles is only distantly registered in their more restricted and basic preoccupation with the effects of capitalist oppression on the lives of individual protagonists. Perhaps in an attempt to close ranks against a state of growing ideological confusion, these novels are all thematically defined by the lowest common denominator of working-class consciousness at a very early point in its formation—the fundamental need to unite and struggle for political and trade-union rights. Tressell, for instance, basing himself on his own experience of the building trade in a small town on the south coast of England, confronts the reader with a picture of a political backwater—'Mugsborough'—where the prime obstacle is not so much the power of the local capitalists as the reluctance of the workers themselves to recognise their own class interests. This lack of even a limited trade-union militancy causes Frank Owen, Tressell's socialist alter ego in the novel, to express feelings of bitterness and despair over the conservatism and indifference of his workmates:

> As Owen thought of his child's future there sprung up within him a feeling of hatred and fury against the majority of his fellow workmen.
> *They were the enemy*. Those who not only quietly submitted like so many cattle to the existing state of things, but defended it, and opposed and ridiculed any suggestion to alter it.
> *They were the real oppressors*—the men who spoke of themselves as 'The likes of us', who, having lived in poverty and

degradation all their lives considered that what had been good enough for them was good enough for their children they had been the cause of bringing into existence.

He hated and despised them because they calmly saw their children condemned to hard labour and poverty for life, and deliberately refused to make any effort to secure for them better conditions than those they had themselves.[2]

In his ideological battle against this reactionary spirit of inertia, Owen's only apparent support comes from a rich middle-class socialist—Barrington—who has gone slumming in the guise of a housepainter, which seems to further undermine the image of the working class as the active instrument of its own emancipation.

In all of the novels, the actual realisation of socialism is projected in a very long-term perspective, to be reached either via the ballot box or through the peaceful but effective expansion of the state-owned industrial sector. Once again, the exception to this is *The Iron Heel*. Although writing in the Utopian mode himself, London, nevertheless, exposes this reformist tactic in his novel and it is significant to note that it was the only one of the five works that was originally greeted with hostility by the socialist press reviewers who, according to Robert Barltrop, 'attacked it for its pessimism and its preoccupation with violence'.[3] However, Barltrop also notes that the novel's 'reputation as a socialist classic derives from its first half, in which the case against capitalism is expounded dramatically'[4]—and in politically more orthodox terms. In contrast, the final volume of Nexö's sequence of novels about Pelle—*The Dawn*—manifests perhaps the most idyllic co-operative illusions of transforming capitalism, something which compelled Nexö later in the 1930s to write a sequel—*Morten the Red*—in which he exposes Pelle's reformist betrayal and counterposes the revolutionary communist politics of Pelle's childhood friend, Morten.

Despite the uneasy and in most cases unresolved relationship between these novels and the critical ideological debate within the labour movement at the time, it was their intrinsically didactic aspect that gave them an immediate

popularity and lasting appeal. Obviously, the propaganda impact of socialist ideas realised in an imaginative fictional setting could be a compelling formative support to both sympathisers and activists alike. In the case of all five novels, the fusion of politics and literature came at opportune moments when the balance of class forces was being shifted and where a work of fiction could make a powerful and even decisive intervention. Thus, Lenin's famous characterisation of Gorky's novel could, in fact, be applied to each of them: 'It is a book of the utmost importance; many workers who have joined the revolutionary movement impulsively, without properly understanding why, will benefit from reading *Mother*. It is a very timely book.'[5] It is remarkable just how 'timely' the publication dates of these novels have been. Although the initial response to the appearance of Tressell's book in 1914 was quickly swamped by the jingoistic euphoria over the outbreak of the war, Grant Richards, its astute-minded publisher, while privately admitting the novel to being 'damnably subversive',[6] understood its political and market value when he reissued it in 1917. This cheaper second edition was published to cash in on the revolutionary fervour of strikes and the creation of workers' councils that occurred after the February insurrection in Russia. The novel's function as one of the most effective and appreciated texts in the ideological arsenal of the British labour movement continued to grow with each new, albeit heavily expurgated edition. When the mood of the population once again became radicalised by the defeat of fascism in 1945, Alan Sillitoe recalled that Tressell's book was reputed to have lain behind the Labour victory in the general election in Britain later that year.[7] Similarly, Gorky's novel, as Lenin had predicted, acted as an essential morale booster for the Russian masses, although perhaps more importantly as a much needed political antidote to the widespread defeatism among the intelligentsia who were abandoning the revolution after 1905. In the case of *Pelle the Conqueror*, although centred around the events of the general strike and lock-out of 1899, Nexö's monumental work represents in fact a literary tribute to the reformist

coming-of-age of the Danish Social Democratic Party which was shaping itself for its future role as benevolent administrator of the modern Danish state. With the same symbolic span as Lewis Grassic Gibbon's *A Scots Quair*, Nexö sought to portray the social transformation of the Danish peasantry into a concentrated and politically organised industrial class, first in the small-scale manufacturing community on the island of Bornholm and later in the great industrial centre of Copenhagen itself. This sweeping socio-economic transition is personified by the main character of Pelle as he moves from a farm labourer to a shoemaker and finally factory worker. Pelle's struggle to 'conquer' a place in the sun for himself is the mainspring for the novel's psychological tension between his own individual rise to consciousness and the strivings of the working class as a collective. Thus, Nexö's epic has become established as the archetypal *Bildungsroman* of the whole Danish labour movement.

In America, London and Sinclair were actively engaged both as writers and agitators for the socialist cause. Sinclair himself later admitted that he had been inspired by his reading of his fellow author's sociological account of slum life in the East End of London, *The People of the Abyss* (1903). The avowed purpose of the two writers was to utilise the novel form in order to rally support for the rising Socialist Party of America, though the subsequent appearance of their novels had rather disparate results. The effect produced by *The Jungle* was immediate and tangible, after which Sinclair was forced to admit that while aiming at the hearts and minds of his readers, he had mainly succeeded in hitting them physically in their bellies. His efforts in the radical muckraking tradition of American journalism to expose the horrific working conditions and pestilential filth of the Chicago meat-packing industry led to such a public outcry that a Pure Food and Drug Act was rushed through the Senate. In contrast, the significance of London's book, *The Iron Heel*, was not fully appreciated until much later, in the 1930s in fact, when the political validity of some of his fundamental predictions had become painfully obvious. At an early stage, London had

shown a profound understanding of the reactionary role of the labour bureaucracy in the eventual collapse of the American socialist movement. Furthermore, his dystopian image of a capitalist oligarchy whose overriding ethic was to maintain its position of power at whatever cost proved a fateful insight into the psychology of fascism:

> In roar of shell and shrapnel and in whine of machine guns will our answer be couched. We will grind you revolutionists down under our heel, and we shall walk upon your faces. The world is ours, we are its lords, and ours it shall remain.[8]

Despite their distinctive political and historical influence, there remain some crucial literary weaknesses which the majority of these novels share as works of art. One such obvious limitation, common to all propaganda fiction, is the danger of character oversimplification. It has been, for example, a recurring problematic in the socialist literary tradition to depict a fully developed working-class protagonist in a psychologically convincing way. Only in a few cases have authors succeeded in avoiding the distorted projection of heroically romanticised, larger-than-life characters set against a realistic context of social and class environment. This exaggerated, idealised and hardly credible heroic enlargement is most visibly expressed in Jack London's novel where the main figure—Ernest Everhard—epitomises both physically and intellectually the image of the working-class superman:

> the cloth bulged with his muscles . . . His neck was the neck of a prize-fighter, thick and strong. So this was the social philosopher and ex-horseshoer my father had discovered, was my thought. And he certainly looked it, with those bulging muscles and that bull throat. Immediately I classified him—a sort of prodigy . . .
> He was a natural aristocrat—and this in spite of the fact that he was in the camp of the non-aristocrats. He was a superman, a blond beast such as Nietzsche has described, and in addition he was aflame with democracy.[9]

The didactically constructed early scenes in the novel are

manipulated set-pieces in the form of dinner gatherings, lectures etc., whose sole function is to reveal Everhard's crushing intellectual superiority over the mealy-mouthed or apoplectic representatives of the bourgeoisie. This over-whelming predominance of such a magnified working-class hero has, of course, political as well as aesthetic implications for the novel. The assertive individualism is, for example, in sharp contrast to the qualities of collective strength which the novels seek to underscore. In *Pelle the Conqueror*, also, Pelle's autodidactic development is not only the almost exclusive emotional pole around which the interest of the story revolves, but his own embodiment of the struggle of the labour movement makes it impossible to distinguish the person from the cause he is leading. In the end, Nexö's novel of class conflict dissolves into a portrait of a charismatic leader at the head of an anonymous grey mass:

> Pelle walked in the front rank beside the standard-bearers. He looked straight on, over the heads of those out walking . . . He had only one thought in his mind: the tread of fifty thousand men behind him. He had experienced it in his dream as a child, heard it as a roar from outside when he laid his head against the pillow. It was the great people's migration and now he was leading the multitude into the country.[10]

In Everhard's as in Pelle's case the implicit conclusion seems to be that the fate of the movement succeeds or fails with them as individual leaders. This blurring of political and personal identification is also true of the characters of Jurgis in *The Jungle* and Pelagea Nilovna in *Mother*. A large part of Pelagea's motivation merely seems to stem from a need to receive personal endorsement for her son's political involvement. Moreover, their almost superhuman efforts against enormous odds lifts them to the level of romantic heroes which, in respect to Jurgis's fate is not only im-plausible but has the inverted effect of appearing almost comic. Several Russian Marxist critics, including Plekhanov, while recognising the propaganda value of Gorky's novel, were more sceptical of his handling of the

literary and aesthetic aspects and a debate developed on the 'typicality' and 'individualism' of his main characters. Gorky himself indirectly accepted the justice of this criticism through his constant revision of the work during his lifetime. Six different versions were published and a seventh was in preparation at his death. Gorky is, of course, rightly hailed as the father of Soviet socialist realism and it is a short step from his portrayal of Pelagea's son, Pavel, to the stainless steel bolshevik heroes in many of the proletarian novels of the 1930s. This magnified stereotyped image of working-class heroes did not cease, however, but continued to be uncritically reproduced in the novels that formed part of the vogue of working-class writing during the post-1945 period, where it was given an aggressively individualist, sexist and often careerist expression in the early novels of Alan Sillitoe, John Braine and David Storey.

Of all these internationally outstanding works of socialist fiction, the one that was most successful in negotiating this literary pitfall was *The Ragged Trousered Philanthropists*. Here the author achieves a consistently anti-heroic emphasis which is finely balanced against the genuinely collective portrait of class experience. It is true, of course, that Tressell's narrative is primarily concerned with the character of Frank Owen, an intellectual workingman who seems rather isolated within the group of house painters. However, although somewhat out on an ideological limb, Owen is a measure of the social and political breadth of the working-class milieu in which he is so firmly placed as a character. It is this very tangible sense of community and collective strength that makes the book more politically optimistic than it first appears. Much of the sympathy which Owen engenders as a character stems from his basic qualities of human solidarity as well as the very ineffectiveness of his role as socialist agitator. Paradoxically, this weakness in a propaganda novel turns out to be one of its greatest psychological strengths. It is significant that Tressell chose to underscore this aspect and to counterpose a healthy scepticism among the workers to Owen's intel-

lectualism and often abstract level of debate. Tressell took care to give the compulsory set-pieces of socialist agitation a much more realistic, natural and lively context by constantly injecting the deflating comments of the workers themselves, thus preventing any tendency in the novel to project Owen as the superior socialist hero. Owen's now classic lecture—'The Oblong'—delivered during one of the dinner breaks, on the causes of poverty and exploitation is given the following introduction, for example:

> 'One of the finest speakers I've ever 'eard!' remarked the man on the pail in a loud whisper to the chairman, who motioned him to be silent.
> Owen continued:
> 'In some of my previous lectures I have endeavoured to convince you that money is in itself of no value and of no real use whatever. In this I'm afraid I have been rather unsuccessful.'
> 'Not a bit of it, mate,' cried Crass, sarcastically. 'We all agree with it.'
> ' 'Ear, 'ear,' shouted Easton. 'If a bloke was to come in 'ere now and orfer to give me a quid—I'd refuse it!'
> 'So would I,' said Philpot.[11]

On a more personal level, Owen is doomed to a life of oppressive poverty and sickness, despite his obvious talents and craftsmanship as a painter. This physical frailty only serves to increase the novel's emotional persuasiveness and to fundamentally emphasise the complete lack of any possible individualist perspective. In terms of the underlying political conclusions, the negation of any personal solution to Owen's predicament, either through professional promotion or collaboration with the bosses, confirms the total interdependence of individual and class which informs Tressell's novel throughout. The outcome of Owen's fate is bound firmly and finally to that of his fellow house painters. There is, however, one concession which Tressell makes, clearly under the influence of Dickens, to the sentimental drama of the story by allowing Barrington, the middle-class socialist, to intervene at the end with his money and Christmas presents. At this point also, Barring-

ton has succeeded Owen as the didactic voice in the novel, and his Beano speech contains a comprehensive picture of the future realisation of socialism. Despite this, the figure of Barrington is never allowed to distract in any decisive way from the collective celebration of the stoical strength and vitality of the working-class community which, for all its ideological limitations and contradictions, Tressell sees as providing the basis for the new society.

Tressell's warm sense of human fraternity is rarely transmitted in the same positive and compassionate way by his contemporaries, the socialist writers mentioned above who, instead, tend to underscore the idealised image of a working-class hero with a similarly distorted over-emphasis on the brutalisation of the mass of workers. This latter aspect was clearly a lingering echo from the naturalist movement of the 1880s and 1890s which had, for instance, impelled English novelists such as George Gissing and Arthur Morrison to represent the population of London's slum underworld as brutish, demoralised and semi-criminal. In Jack London, perhaps the most aesthetically instinctive and autodidactic of all the great pioneer writers of socialist fiction, the working-class blond beasts are contrasted with the frightening abyss of a degenerate lumpen-proletariat which threatens to well up and swamp the rest of society. Moreover, this reactionary mass is shown as being not only easy prey to the repressive forces of capitalist state power but also as one of the biggest obstacles to the success of the revolution itself. In *The Iron Heel*, Everhard's facile intellectual victories in lectures and debates give way in the later climactic chapters of the book to the harrowing scenes of bloody massacre during the Chicago Commune where London, with brilliantly dramatic skill, envisages the premature rising of the slum dwellers, significantly described as 'The People of the Abyss'. Here, London's taut narrative style comes into its own as he evokes this 'roaring abysmal beast' with a fascination and vigour that is in total contrast to the wooden characterisation and simplistic psychology of the individual portraits of the leaders. However, despite the heroic

supportive rearguard actions of Everhard and his comrades, the blind explosion of these slum dwellers does not provide any progressive political impetus but acts instead as a reactionary provocation that only incites the iron heel of the oligarchy to drown the whole revolutionary movement in blood. To London, the jungle of the city seems only to spawn a demoralised subhuman mob of rampaging yahoos:

> men, women and children, in rags and tatters, dim ferocious intelligences with all the godlike blotted from their features and all the fiendlike stamped in, apes, and tigers, anaemic consumptives and great hairy beasts of burden, wan faces from which vampire society had sucked the juice of life, bloated forms swollen with physical grossness and corruption, withered hags and death's heads bearded like patriarchs, festering youth and festering age, faces of fiends, crooked, twisted, misshapen monsters blasted with the ravages of disease and all the horrors of innutrition—the refuse and the scum of life, a raging, screaming, screeching, demoniacal horde.[12]

The slums of Chicago are also seen as an epitome of a capitalist hell on earth in *The Jungle*, where the scenes of Jurgis's descent into the inferno of the meat-packing industry rival those of Dante's circles of torment. Moreover, the condition of urban brutalisation is rendered in exactly the same animal terms as Jack London uses— 'hideous, beastly faces, bloated and leprous with disease, laughing, shouting, screaming in all stages of drunkenness, barking like dogs, gibbering like apes, raving and tearing themselves in delirium'.[13] At the same time, Sinclair's symbolism of the slaughterhouse of class society is obviously meant to be extended even further to include the actual working masses themselves, as much passive victims of the system as the cattle and hogs trapped in the factory pens outside. In an attempt to broaden the political scope of the novel, Sinclair manipulates the calamitous fate of Jurgis and his family so as to scan the whole barbaric spectrum of social oppression by moving through and highlighting a totality of human experience from worker to

convict, capitalist to criminal. Unfortunately, such an ambitious literary sweep and didactic concern often stretches the credibility of the novel's coincidences of plot to the limit. This is especially the case when Jurgis meets up with the drunken son of the owner of the whole Chicago meat-packing industry who takes him to their palatial residence so that the reader may gain an ideologically salutary insight into how the decadent, top-hatted bourgeoisie really live.

A further recurring convention adopted by several of our novelists in order to increase the moral indignation of their readership was to portray the seduction or forced prostitution of a workingman's wife or girlfriend, usually by a representative of the capitalist class or one of their hangers-on. The prostitution of Jurgis's wife to a factory foreman is, for example, the incident that destroys his dream of making good in the new world. After his prison sentence for assaulting the man and his own wife's death from shame, he loses all sense of social and class orientation and gradually sinks into criminal demoralisation until saved after a decidedly revivalist enlightenment at a socialist meeting near the end of the book. In *Pelle the Conqueror*, almost exactly the same moral complication is reproduced when Ellen, Pelle's wife, faced with Pelle's neglect of their family during the great lock-out, goes streetwalking in order to keep the children in food.[14] This, and his subsequent imprisonment for attempted forgery, also causes a profound emotional crisis in Pelle which impels him away from the revolutionary heart of the labour movement. From this point onwards, there is a marked shift in thematic emphasis towards a more exclusively individual preoccupation which becomes even further restricted in the final volume of Nexö's work, where Pelle's now limited reformist efforts towards social emancipation begin to coincide fully with Ellen's petit bourgeois dreams of family bliss in a home of their own. Moreover, Nexö's psychological exploration of the tension between the personal and the political in the novel is fundamentally weakened by this romantically Utopian solution of Pelle's country cottage and shoemakers' co-operative. As the titles

indicate, the glowing pastoral vision of *Dawn* has by this time completely replaced the grim and sombre realism which characterises the earlier parts of *The Great Strike* when Pelle first arrives in Copenhagen and lives in a slum ghetto called 'The Ark'. However, even here, it is possible to discern an underlying romantic tone which takes the edge off the poverty and brutality and reveals Nexö's pervadingly idealistic theme of the basic human goodness of all his characters—slum dweller or shopkeeper, worker or capitalist—and, more politically, his overriding faith in their social-democratic potential.

A tangible feeling of the community and humanity of the oppressed is also prevalent both in Gorky and Tressell although their images of brutalisation are applied solely to representatives of the capitalist class. The single exception is in the opening scene in *Mother* where Gorky suggests a level of working-class brutishness which he then totally banishes from the heroic sphere of the story:

> Worn out as they were by hard work, the drink went quickly to their heads, and some uncountable irritation rankled in their breasts, demanding an outlet. And so they seized the slightest opportunity to relieve their painful feelings by flying at one another with bestial ferocity. Bloody fights were the result. Sometimes they ended in serious injuries and occasionally in killings.[15]

This significant distinction in artistic treatment is what makes Gorky and Tressell differ from the other novelists discussed here. Despite a similar need to criticise and expose the ideological limitations of the workers, both novelists seem to have made a conscious literary choice to portray their working-class characters as straightforwardly sympathetic as possible while representing the class enemy as the embodiment of all that is brutal and corrupt. These were the really 'useless men' in Gorky's eyes. In *Mother*, for example, Pelagea's lingering doubts and political misgivings are finally dispelled when she comes face to face at Pavel's trial with the actual physical representatives of law, order and religion. The comparison

between the parasitical duplicity of the court officials and the transparent honesty and nobility of her son and his comrades exorcises the last remnants of her instinctive class fear and respect for authority:

> The mother kept her eyes on the judges and noticed that their excitement increased as they talked together . . . the young men roused in the old judges the gnawing, vengeful fury of worn-out beasts who see fresh food before them and lack the strength to seize it. Beasts who are no longer capable of taking their fill of other creatures' strength, but only growl and whine on seeing a means of satiety escaping them.[16]

It is also when he deals with the local echelons of capitalism in Mugsborough that Tressell turns on the full force of his ironic satire in order to caricature the bosses as savages totally lacking any redeeming qualities. They are exposed, as Jack Mitchell points out, as a class of 'Yahoos, as human beasts of prey'.[17] At the same time, it is important to note that Tressell, like Jack London, is careful to show that these people do not act merely as individuals but are forced to behave according to their position within the economic system:

> They all hated and blamed Rushton. Yet if they had been in Rushton's place they would have been compelled to adopt the same methods, or become bankrupt: for it is obvious that the only way to compete successfully against other employers who are sweaters is to be a sweater yourself. Therefore no one who is an upholder of the present system can consistently blame any of these men. Blame the system.[18]

Such a conscious socio-economic connection between character and context represented an important advance on the radical bourgeois novel tradition—as exemplified by Dickens's *Hard Times* or Elizabeth Gaskell's *Mary Barton*—where the capitalist is often shown experiencing a change of heart at the end, which not only strains the psychological plausibility but seriously blunts the critical edge of such novels. Nevertheless, Tressell himself does include a number of other literary stereotypes. He uses, for example,

the same convention of a seduced workingman's wife to strengthen the moral force of his religious critique, when Ruth is made pregnant and then abandoned by the hypocritically pious foreman, Slyme. The sometimes quite virulent attacks on organised religion form, in fact, a manifest and integral part of Tressell's ideological preoccupations throughout the novel and reflect, perhaps, a lingering reaction against his own Irish Catholic upbringing.[19] Moreover, as in all the other cases mentioned, Tressell's inclusion of the fallen woman theme as a very emotive moral indictment of the system reveals the socialist novel at this stage, despite the avowed revolutionary politics in the public sphere, still upholding very traditional bourgeois family values in the home. In Gorky's *Mother*, there is an even clearer separation of the personal and the political, the ties of the family and the wider struggle, in Pavel's rejection of ever realising his love for Natasha, a comrade militant, as it would interfere with their work for the cause.

Most certainly, it was the whole context of oppression—the descriptions of poverty and the accompanying threat of degradation—that sustained the explicitly didactic function of these socialist novels. However, the object was not only to awaken the conscience of their readers but, more decisively, to transform an initial emotional response into a consciousness of the need for political involvement. Thus, the socialist novelists sought to fuse the pessimistic realism of the naturalist novel, which had depicted the poor as passive victims of cruel circumstances, with a more optimistic image of working-class heroes actively striving to break through such social and economic constraints. This uneasy transition was provided for by the other essential novel ingredient—the intellectual appeal of the ideas of socialism and the labour movement transmitted usually in the form of a speech, a polemic or lecture. Tressell's biographer, Fred Ball, states for instance that Tressell started writing a series of agitational pamphlets at first but soon found himself with the embryo of a novel on his hands.[20] Despite the artistic elaboration, a chapter such

as 'The Oblong' can still easily be extracted as a classic set-piece in this didactic category, dealing as it does with a very practical lesson in the theory of surplus value. Apart from this immediate agitational function, all of the novels seek to project the longer-term perspective of a total transformation of society. But here a somewhat surprising ideological displacement of the working class occurs. In an attempt to give the concept of socialism more authority and persuasiveness, both Tressell and Sinclair assign middle-class characters to present the vision of change. Similarly, they also draw heavily on the Utopian theories of Edward Bellamy's *Looking Backward* (1888), which envisage a peacefully expanding state sector.[21] In exactly the same conciliatory way, although more pragmatically, Pelle, in *The Dawn*, is shown trying to realise this co-operative dream, using the private capital backing of a middle-class philanthropist. Despite Pavel's crushing indictment of the system of private property during the court scene in Gorky's *Mother*, the immediate prospect for the militants in the novel is one of imprisonment and exile—a realistic appraisal of the state of revolutionary ebb in Russia at that time. In Jack London's case, his vision of bloody repression is even more total and devastating, while the actual achievement of socialism is relegated to a series of Utopian footnotes which counterpose a three-hundred-year history of violent struggle against oligarchic reaction.

The different emotional and intellectual strategies of the novels remain, in most cases, on a rather mechanical, contrived and hardly integrated level, once again illustrating the perennial problem of the socialist novel of successfully fusing fiction and politics. The sense of militant pathos which these novelists sought to engender was, obviously, based on the deadly seriousness of their unremitting exposé of working-class poverty and misery. The exception to this is Tressell who complements the emotive and ideological effect of his message with the disarmingly sarcastic and affectionate humour of his working-class house painters. It is this key use of the comic ironic tradition of Dickens and, further back, the morality plays, which endows his novel with such a uniquely popular and

appealing quality. As Tressell himself modestly expresses it in his preface to the book:

> 'The Philanthropists' is not a treatise or essay, but a novel. My main object was to write a readable story full of human interest and based on the happenings of everyday life, the subject of Socialism being treated incidentally . . . As far as I dared I let the characters express themselves in their own sort of language and consequently some passages may be considered objectionable. At the same time I believe that—because it is true—the book is not without its humorous side.[22]

Thus, Tressell is the only one of the socialist writers compared here who consciously and effectively employs a whole range of humour from the bitingly ironic to farcically satiric as an integral part of the narrative tone of his novel. It is this essential quality which lifts his work above the sombre political gravity and strained didacticism that dogs much of the writing in the other novels in discussion. Partly, it also goes to explain the genuine affection which his book has engendered over the years amongst a mass audience of working-class readers both in Britain and abroad. Activists in the British labour movement, for example, may often refer to the works of Jack London and Upton Sinclair as having played an influential role in their own early political formation, but Tressell's fictional characters have become endowed with that mythical essence that has secured them a place in the industrial folklore of the working class. As Brendan Behan recalled in his own fictional autobiography:

> It was our book at home, too, and when my mother was done telling us of the children of Lir and my father about Fionn MacCumhaill they'd come back by way of nineteen sixteen to the *Ragged Trousered Philanthropists* and on every job you'd hear painters using the names out of it for nicknames, calling their own apprentice 'The Walking Colour Shop' and, of course, every walking foreman was called Nimrod, even by painters who had never read the book, nor any other book, either.[23]

In the context of Tressell's comic narrative technique, it is significant to note that, although the title of his novel contains an ironic comment on the misplaced charity of the workers in donating the surplus profit of their labour to the capitalists, there is little or no sustained satire directed against the working-class characters within the story itself. Here, Tressell's personal and political sympathies are clearly and consistently manifest, while artistically he obviously did not want to confuse the issues of his message. On the contrary, as has been mentioned, it is his own socialist alter ego—Frank Owen—who bears the fraternal brunt of the workers' chaffing scepticism. Instead, the full force of Tressell's humour and satire is played upon the figures of the capitalists and their hangers-on—Rushton, Sweater, Slyme—all of whom, as their names suggest, are remorselessly caricatured. Tressell's exposure of these representatives of the class enemy is as ruthless and unequivocal as it is devastatingly comic. Perhaps nowhere else in the novel does he succeed better in didactically realising the personification of oppression than through this rogues' gallery of outrageous portraits in the great radical tradition of Bunyan and Dickens. One such example of the mythical proportions of Tressell's burlesque satire is the fate of the hugely overfed and spiritually inflated preacher, the Reverend Mr Belcher of the Shining Light Chapel, who is literally exploding with hot spicy air:

'Who is this last party what's dead?' asked Harlow after a pause.
'It's a parson what used to belong to the "Shining Light" Chapel. He'd been abroad for 'is 'ollerdays—to Monte Carlo. It seems 'e was ill before 'e went away, but the change did 'im a lot of good; in fact, 'e was quite recovered, and 'e was coming back again. But while 'e was standin' on the platform at Monte Carlo Station waitin' for the train, a porter runned into 'im with a barrer load o' luggage and 'e blowed up.'
'Blowed up?'
'Yes', repeated Philpot. 'Blowed up! Busted! Exploded! All into pieces. But they swep' 'em all up and put it in a corfin and it's to be planted this afternoon.'[24]

Tressell's novel, with its celebration of working-class humour and compelling narrative of resilience and defiance, stands as one of the most remarkable achievements of that fruitful convergence of socialist politics and literature which occurred at the beginning of the twentieth century. The social tension which the growth of the labour movement generated within capitalism provided the creative climate for a group of writers who sought to extend the function of critical realism through the active intervention of their works of fiction as weapons for socialist change. Whatever their artistic limitations, the novels of Maxim Gorky, Jack London, Upton Sinclair, Martin Andersen Nexö and Robert Tressell firmly and irreversibly launched the theme of working-class struggle into the mainstream of world literature.

NOTES

1. In 1915, a year before his death, London broke with the American Socialist Party because, as he wrote in his letter of resignation, 'of its lack of fire and fight, and its loss of emphasis on the class struggle'. Quoted in Robert Barltrop, *Jack London: the Man, the Writer, the Rebel* (London, 1976), p.163.
2. Robert Tressell, *The Ragged Trousered Philanthropists* (London, 1971), p.46.
3. Barltrop, *op. cit.*, pp.127-8.
4. *ibid.*, p.123.
5. Quoted in B. Bursov's Preface to Gorky's *Mother* (Moscow, 1983), pp.9-10.
6. Quoted in F. C. Ball, *One of the Damned* (London, 1979), p.167.
7. See Sillitoe's Introduction to the Panther edition (1965), p.7.
8. Jack London, *The Iron Heel* (London, 1975), p.63.
9. *ibid.*, pp.7-8.
10. Martin Andersen Nexö, *Pelle the Conqueror* (Stockholm, 1976), vol. 3, p.388. (My translation—RP).
11. Tressell, *op. cit.*, p.280.
12. London, *op. cit.*, p.207.

13. Upton Sinclair, *The Jungle* (Harmondsworth, 1974), p.277.
14. In his autobiographical novel from the same period, *Children of the Dead End* (1914), Patrick MacGill includes both the convention of the seduction and prostitution of Norah, a working-class girl, and the matriarchal figure of Gourock Ellen, a prostitute with a heart of gold.
15. Maxim Gorky, *Mother* (Moscow, 1983), p.19.
16. *ibid.*, p.444.
17. Jack Mitchell, *Robert Tressell and the Ragged Trousered Philanthropists* (London, 1969), p.73.
18. Tressell, *op. cit.*, p.217.
19. See Ball, *op. cit.*, pp.67-8.
20. *ibid.*, p.147.
21. Sinclair was later to use the proceeds from his novel, *The Jungle*, to open Helicon Hall, a Utopian co-operative-living venture in Englewood, N. J.
22. Tressell, *op. cit.*, p.12.
23. Brendan Behan, *Borstal Boy* (London, 1975), p.302.
24. Tressell, *op. cit.*, p.269.

Ethel Carnie: writer, feminist and socialist

EDMUND AND RUTH FROW

The years 1909 to 1915 were Ethel Carnie's apprenticeship. She learned, during that time, to express her inherent and instinctive loathing of the capitalist system in political and positive terms; she found that her expressive needs could not be met by writing poetry and she became aware of herself as a woman, consciously and conscientiously writing with women as the pivot of her stories. She became an active socialist demanding a change in the system as well as the participation of workers in the determination of their lives.

CHILDHOOD AND FIRST POEMS

Ethel Carnie was born in Oswaldtwistle on 1 January 1886. Her parents were both cotton weavers and by the time Ethel was six years old they had moved to the growing textile town of Great Harwood near Blackburn in search of work. There, she attended the British School for a few years where she showed promise in composition and often had her essays read out in class, but otherwise displayed no outstanding ability.

Ethel Carnie's father was a member of the Social Democratic Federation (SDF). Great Harwood is within easy distance of Burnley which had one of the strongest SDF branches in the country. There was a club house and a lively programme of social and political activity. In Blackburn there was an SDF branch and a branch of The

Independent Labour Party (ILP). They worked amicably together in a friendly relationship. Mr Carnie took his daughter to political meetings and helped her to clothe her instinctive socialist attitudes with scientific understanding. In one of Ethel Carnie's later stories, a little girl is portrayed as being late for work because she cannot get up in time because of raging toothache. As she finally manages to make her preparations and rushes out of the door, she says 'Damn!' in a loud voice. This causes the girl's father to laugh and explain to his wife that the girl had been at a meeting the night before to hear Dan Irving speak. 'She looked so funny and it sounded so queer to hear her say "damn" like that. An' she's goin' to be a rebel, an' aw'm glad.'[1] Dan Irving was for many years Secretary of the Burnley SDF. He contested Board of Guardian and Town Council Elections when Ethel was a teenager.

At the age of eleven Ethel went half-time as a reeler in the nearest cotton mill. The following year she was taught the art of winding. At thirteen her formal education ended and she went full-time to the mill. She continued to work as a winder until she was eighteen when she was promoted to become a warper and beamer. The indignities of factory life bit deep into her consciousness and although she respected and admired her fellow workers, she hated factory life.

While still a winder at St Lawrence Mill, Ethel started composing poetry at work. According to her own testimony: 'From a child I found myself expressing my thoughts in rhythmic forms, and deriving great pleasure from so doing, accompanied though it was with a sense of restraint—that I must do so.'[2] Her first writing was published in the two Blackburn weekly papers. Blackburn had a strong radical and poetic tradition. The earliest local paper, *The Blackburn Mail*, had, from its inception, a column devoted to poetry, a practice that was continued over the years. As one commentator said: 'Although Blackburn cannot claim to be a town of outstanding literary associations, it is fortunate in possessing a tradition of native poetry far outrivalling many of its larger contemporaries.'[3]

The poem that drew attention to Ethel Carnie's talent was called 'The Bookworm':

I own no grand baronial hall,
No pastures rich in waving corn;
Leave unto me my love for books,
And rank and wealth I laugh to scorn.

The world of books—how broad, how grand!
Within its volumes, dark and old,
What priceless gems of living thought
Their beauties to the mind unfold.[4]

When Ethel read this poem before Blackburn Authors' Society to which she had been invited, its members were astonished that a mill girl of nineteen should be capable of such verse. Mr Barnett of the Society encouraged her, and a small volume of her poetry was issued as *Rhymes from the Factory* in 1907. The first edition of 500 copies sold out within a month. A second edition of a thousand followed, and in her preface Ethel Carnie reported that enquiries had come from all parts of the country and even from abroad and that she had dealt with as many as forty orders in one day.[5]

The second edition was reviewed by Keighly Snowdon in *The Woman Worker*. Snowdon pointed out that Ethel Carnie's poems were not about factory life, but thought poems reflecting wide reading[6] and a warm concern for her fellow workers:

If death be equal, why not also life?
Why should the toil, the suffering and the strife
Fall but to some?[7]

Snowdon commented that Ethel Carnie 'comes in quietly and takes her place among the poets one loves', but he recognised that the poetry varied in quality and that much of it was unpolished: 'Schooled critics can point out many a fault in Ethel Carnie's verse. Most likely they will refuse for a long time to notice her.'[8] That was an understatement. They allowed her to sink without trace as so many

working-class authors have done.

At first, however, the review had dramatic con-sequences. Robert Blatchford, editor of *The Clarion* and one of the founding fathers of the Independent Labour Party, took advantage of a visit to Lancashire to call on the author. He wrote an account of his interview in *The Woman Worker*. Although his style is patronising and paternalistic, he was obviously impressed by the young worker poet. He called Ethel Carnie 'an inscrutable, inexplicable, impossible fairy' and added that

> The Lancashire fairy lives at Great Harwood! Great Harwood is a monstrous agglomeration of ugly factories, of ugly gasometers, of ugly houses—brick boxes with slate lids. There is neither grace nor beauty in Great Harwood. It is the last place in which one would expect to find a poet.[9]

Blatchford described Ethel Carnie as a small quiet young woman, with quiet grey eyes, a quiet smile, and a dimple in her chin.

> There is not a single spark of conceit in Ethel Carnie. She is as free from affectation as a seagull; she has as much common sense as a policeman; she dresses plainly, speaks with a down-right homely Lancashire accent; and is a real lady in the best sense of that ill-used word . . . There is no decorative copy to be made out of the Lancashire fairy. Her appearance is in no wise striking; she is not brilliant, nor eccentric; she does not say fine things about 'literature', nor about 'nature'; she never used the word 'art'.[10]

EDITING THE WOMAN WORKER

Following that interview, Ethel Carnie took the momen-tous decision to leave the factory and try to earn her living through her writing. Little is known about the arrange-ments which enabled her to do this. But it is quite clear that Blatchford had persuaded her to move to London to work for *The Clarion* and, especially, *The Woman Worker*. Probably in July 1909 she took over as editor of *The Woman*

Worker, whose original editor Mary Macarthur had given up the post in order to concentrate on trade-union work. From March until July of that year either Blatchford or one of the *Clarion* team may have written the editorials. There is no indication as to exactly when Ethel Carnie took over as editor. Blatchford indicated in the issue of 14 July 1909 that he was retiring. There was no editorial in the following issue, but that of 28 July 1909 contained a polemic against the 'yellow' press. For the next six months, the editorials and the tone of the journal bear Ethel Carnie's imprint. Reading between the lines, it can be assumed that she left Lancashire early in 1909 and spent some months learning the business of running a journal which she was unlikely to have experienced in Great Harwood. She was persuaded to write prose and fiction during that time and when she came to write the first editorial comment, her style had developed sufficiently to be recognisable. Her name did not appear as editor on the title page as Mary Macarthur's and Julia Dawson's had done. But the paper reflected her class consciousness and gained readers from her realistic approach. The editorial heading had claimed 31,000 circulation. Her influence probably accounted for the more likely figure of 26,500 in July and made her claim of an additional hundred in the issue of 8 September more plausible.

Reading her editorial comments indicates how her thinking developed over the six months. In her first editorial, she inveighs against the 'yellow press':

> It panders to the lowest tastes. It prostitutes itself in the cause of commercialism. Its gods are the trinity of £.s.d. . . . and its supreme justification is that it supplies what the great public desire. Yet if the public paused to think, even for a moment, they would realise that they were subsidising the people who insult them by placing such a low value upon their intelligence.

And she added: 'These papers treat women as puppets—as playthings—as mere adjuncts to man. The insolence of the whole thing!'[11]

The following week she presents the week's news as if it

were on a cinema screen. She makes her anti-war feelings clear in a comment on the war in Spain:

> Oh, it is a pretty business—this war of brothers. And all because men are living not in brotherhood but in anarchy. Because, under an iniquitous social system, life is a terrible struggle in which only a minority can hope to survive with advantage to themselves.[12]

A constantly recurring theme is the universal brotherhood of man. 'The greatest ideal which has ever been preached', she called it and suggested that Europe would only be prevented from invasion from the Far East by 'their conversion to the international ideal which recognises no distinction of class, or creed, or clime, but would have the men and women of the world live together in loving comradeship'.[13] Returning to the theme later in the month she said:

> There is, however, another factor today in the world-game. That factor cannot be ignored; It is the factor of the international spirit. Remember, today there is a great army throughout the world. The Red Army. The Army which recognises the red standard as their flag—first last and all the time.[14]

On the Budget, she assured Lord Rosebery, the Chancellor, that

> for every concession given by the exploiting classes we will demand two, that the wedge shall be driven up to the hilt, and that the women and men of this country will never rest satisfied until there is no hungry child crying for bread, no woman forced to sell her honour to keep her body alive, no man compelled to go cap in hand to a master for permission to maintain himself, which is the common right of humanity.[15]

She also charged Lord Grey, the Minister for Foreign Affairs, with having covered himself and his Government with infamy because he had refused to intervene in a Russian pogrom in which twenty-nine Jews were killed and over a thousand injured.

The topic which exercised her attention almost every week in one way or another was the position of women. 'The demand of "Equal Pay for Equal Work" is being gradually forced upon the attention of all thinking people', she asserted and added that 'neither men nor women can work out their salvation as sexes—they must march hand in hand to the conquest of the world.'[16] Calling attention to women in the news who had climbed a peak in the Himalayas, swum fifteen miles of the Thames, and traversed the continent of Africa, she said: 'And there are still men who persist in "chivalrously" regarding women as frail creatures, unfit even to vote.'[17] She also rejoiced at the University of London results in which girls had been exceptionally successful.[18] But she warned that

> the only thing woman has to fear is stagnation—the inter-change of ideas can only help her on her road to emancipation; for those of both sexes who would keep woman in her tra-ditional shackles, fear only one thing, and that is her intellectual development.[19]

Calling for juries to be composed of both sexes, she pointed out the unjust course taken by the Liberal Government who, instead of giving women the vote, imprisoned them for demanding it and then, having driven them to extreme measures, 'as though to complete an impossible and Gilbertian situation, they endeavour to forcibly feed them by the use of the stomach pump'.[20]

Throughout her editorials, Ethel Carnie drew attention to the technological changes taking place. She was obvi-ously greatly impressed by the cinema and referred to it on several occasions. She also reported on the developments in flying and forecast an exciting future for women who were willing to try their hands at the less conventional exploits.[21]

Unemployment and poverty were rarely far from her mind.

> If you women [she informed her readers] were in deadly earnest you could, by propaganda, compel legislators to legislate for those who need legislation—the exploited—

instead of bolstering up a wretched system which is rapidly making life intolerable and impossible. Concentrate, as I have said before in these columns, on a Right To Work Bill. Once get that through, and force the State to take the unemployed off the market, and it is the beginning of the end for our present anarchic and archaic system.[22]

Ethel's own literary output accelerated once she had entered the atmosphere of the literary circle around *The Clarion*. By November 1909 she had contributed poems, articles and stories to *Woman's World*, *The Red Letter*, *Horner's Weekly*, *English Illustrated Magazine*, *Woman*, *Co-operative News*, *The Millgate Monthly*, *The Clarion* as well as the two Blackburn weeklies, *The Weekly Telegraph* and *Blackburn Times*.[23] In addition, of course, she contributed to each issue of *The Woman Worker*.

Ethel Carnie's editorial comments indicate her increasing politicisation and feminism. She brought a thread of realism to the paper. During her six months it certainly adopted a 'left' approach to the situation, in spite of Blatchford's reiteration that '*The Woman Worker* is not a class paper, its aim is to unite women of all classes: to get women into line with men.'[24] Such chauvinism would not have accorded with the growing feminism and personal confidence of the young editor.

By the middle of December 1909 there was a hint that Ethel Carnie had not fulfilled Blatchford's expectations of how the paper should develop. In the editorial, mention was made of readers thinking that the editor had been too emphatic in her condemnation of the Liberal–Labour alliance.[25] In January 1910 the paper changed its name to *Women Folk*, its editor to Blatchford's daughter, Winifred, and its policy to a much less pronounced socialism. Winifred's first editorial set the tone: 'And I hope we shall represent, so far as in us lies, those various states and professions, well balanced and impartially.'[26] Then there was 'An Open Letter to MISS ETHEL' by Pa B (Robert Blatchford?). The letter was a typical rambling mixture of paternalistic advice and inconsequential information. But one sentence gives a clue to what had happened: 'Ethel,

they told me, had contracted an acute form of home sickness, and had floated out of their ken upon a tempestuous
and saline sea of tears.'[27] For reasons beyond our knowledge, Ethel Carnie left London, returned to Great
Harwood and resumed her work as a warper and beamer in
a cotton mill.

She tried to continue writing and almost every issue of
Woman Folk has a contribution from her. But getting up
even earlier than she needed to get to the mill and retiring
after midnight hardly made ideal conditions. In spite of
that she managed to publish a second volume of poetry,
Songs of a Factory Girl,[28] only a year after her return home. It
was dedicated to her mother and it is possible that her
floods of tears may have been occasioned by the news that
her father had died—but that is speculation. In an interview with a journalist from the *Blackburn Weekly Telegraph*,
Ethel told him that her return to the mill was not necessarily
for all time and that she might leave it again to work with
her pen instead of at a winding machine. 'And as for my
poetry', she continued, 'there is plenty of inspiration in a
room full of girls at a mill—all with different characters and
temperaments and experience.'[29] She commented on work
in a mill and said that it was

> a lamentable obstacle to the development of true womanly
> character. This is no matter of sentiment. It is unnatural; but in
> many cases it is necessary because the husband's wage is not
> sufficient to keep the home together. They have grit and cheer-
> fulness, and this quality keeps them superior to their con-
> ditions, but it is none the less true that the life of many a
> woman with a family, who has to work in the mill, is the life of
> a slave.[30]

She determined to escape once again. With her mother
she took a small shop in Ancoats, Manchester, where she
was in touch with students from the University. But living
in Ancoats did not suit her and she failed to establish
rapport with the students, so she turned to writing again.
She returned to London to work at Bebel House encouraging working women to express themselves in writing.
When that job folded she returned to Lancashire and tried

her hand at selling ribbons and laces on Blackburn Market. Meanwhile she continued writing. Regular articles and stories of hers appeared in *The Wheatsheaf* as well as *Woman Folk* and *The Clarion*.

THE STORIES

Ethel Carnie's stories reflect her powers of observation and her sympathy with the poor and exploited. They are seldom revolutionary in content nor didactic in tone. She seems content to mirror scenes as she saw them and leave the reader to draw conclusions. Her constant standby is the life of the textile workers. Illness and poverty occur frequently but how else could she have portrayed factory workers?

Hannah is a weaver who has to keep her mother. She obtains a good place in a new mill, but soon becomes ill. ' "Tha morn't go, Hannah", said Mrs Smith firmly. "Never mind t'looms. Life is o' moor consequence than brass." "But brass means life for sich as us", said Hannah, turning over.'[31]

In nearly all her fiction, Ethel Carnie presents women as the central characters. They are not always ideal models, but they are always human. In 'The Giver' Mary is left to fend for herself as she has watched her mother's household bits and pieces sold for a pittance. She lodges with a desperately poor family who, however, manage to maintain a cheerful exterior. Mary is determined to ensure that she will not be caught in the poverty trap. She saves and denies her better instincts to give. Her mother gives her advice: ' "If I had all the half-crowns I've given in my lifetime—aye I could ha' covered this quilt wi' 'em . . . Mary lass, stick to thy half-crowns." ' Mary does just that. She banks her coppers weekly and by the end of the first year has acquired a bank balance of twenty pounds. She continues to save and is eventually able to purchase a house and to buy a woman a bracelet that she admired only to find herself caught in a trap of generosity.

The thin edge of the wedge grew thicker. Soon she was no better off than the average worker, but the look of strain had gone from her eyes . . . She felt richer than she had done in the doorway of the bank . . . born a giver, she remained a giver, and giving is the soul of love, of life, of the progress of the world.[32]

'The Unbeliever' is interesting because it is not only one of the few stories of Ethel Carnie which has a male central character but also indicates her attitude towards religion. In the story, the woman believes in a supreme being and wants to marry a man who shares her creed. But the man she encounters turns out to be an atheist. When challenged on this account, he replies, however: ' "Unbeliever, Janet? Why there isn't a man, woman or child in the village that I don't believe in." ' Janet pursues the argument by telling him that her father said he had never seen him in church. While she is talking she pulls a flower to pieces for which he remonstrates with her.

"Don't, Janet!" he said, sharply. "What?" "Destroy that poor flower—you couldn't make one." She looked up eagerly. "That's what I can't understand about you, Fred," she began. "Look at the beauty of the earth—the stars, and the sun, and the violets coming back every spring, just to the time. You can see all the wonder of it, but you can't believe in a maker for it all!"

In the end she walks away from him and he is left with the dog who looks at him with adoring eyes.[33]   Since the atheist is portrayed as much the more sympathetic character, Carnie leaves no doubt as to where her own feelings lay.

She was extremely fond of children and often wrote about the fate of the little half-timers in the mill which she knew so well from her own bitter experience. In one story she looks at the situation of a woman who has acquired a ready-made family by marrying a widower with five children. 'Plain, homely Susan' has accepted the responsibility and made an immediate success of it. But her husband is killed in a pit accident less than a fortnight after

the wedding. Susan's uncle arrives to give her the benefit of his advice, which is to parcel the children out amongst the family. At this she gets furious.

> 'These children are my children, do you hear, and they are not going to be separated and given away amongst Stephen's relatives like so many pups of a litter. Besides, when I married Stephen I married him chiefly for the children's sake . . . I wouldn't leave Bobby for all the world. That child needs a mother's care . . . So here I stay.'

Uncle retired discomforted. Susan brought up the family with success and Bobby repaid her devotion by looking after her in her old age.[34]

To complete the picture mention must be made of Ethel Carnie's children's stories. Several were published by Mr Stead in his series *Books For Bairns* which were penny booklets for children. Others were published in *The Wheatsheaf* and *The Woman Worker*, and a collection came out in 1911 under the title of *The Lamp Girl*.[35]

MISS NOBODY

T. A. Jackson once remarked that

> any sort of proletarian novel by a proletarian is welcome, if only as an attempt . . . Even if the book is not, taken as a whole, a masterpiece, or anything like one, it is in much of its detail much better done and much more readable than many 'best sellers' from people of established reputations.[36]

Much the same can be said about Ethel Carnie's first novel *Miss Nobody*, which came out in 1913. It shows one of the strengths of Ethel Carnie's fiction—an insightful and sympathetic representation of working women.

Books written by men often portray women in relation to men; and their moral worth is evaluated by how they cope with these relationships. By placing the relationships centrally around a working woman, the stage is set for working women to relate to the novel. As one reviewer

stated: 'One welcomes in Miss Ethel Carnie a writer possessing an instinctive sympathy with her sisters, whether they work in mills or factories or in the thousands upon thousands of little homes of the industrial towns.'[37] In preference to the large canvas Carnie chose to portray the local scene and the ordinary women and men in it. However, her class consciousness was an integral part of the story. Miss Nobody[38] is Carrie, an orphan, who with her brother and sister is brought up in an orphanage. She is a cheerful and sensible person who accepts life as it comes. But she comments along the way on other people and events from a working-class point of view. She marries a farmer and has to adjust to life in the country where she finds a different set of values from those in the town to which she has been accustomed. She copes with a jealous sister-in-law, a dissolute brother and with leading a strike in a flax mill, with equal equanimity.

Mary Ashraf commented:

> In *Miss Nobody* socialism is, as it were, hovering just out of range of these little people, who have not yet arrived at any clear class consciousness . . . Ethel Carnie takes people as they are and shows their hopeful side, the positive values and power of growth in spite of crippling disadvantages of upbringing and environment.[39]

For a first novel, *Miss Nobody* certainly showed promise. It is written in a lively style directed at a general readership. It is not polished, but it has a verve and fluency which indicate a desire to communicate. The plot is possibly contrived, but at the level at which it is pitched, it does not seem outlandish. The dialogue is generally terse and suitable. She does occasionally labour and over-accentuate situations in her effort to make certain the reader understands. This is particularly so in her descriptions of life in the remote village where the farm is situated. The town scenes are true to life and more credible.

Some of her characters have endearing qualities: the girl in the Ardwick slum who has been bedridden much of her life and is able to have an operation to give her back the

power to walk only after Carrie inherits a small fortune from her unknown father; the man who gives Carrie a lift when having set out to walk back to the village she changes her mind when she is half way and turns back to Manchester, and who explains his action as his belief in Socialism; the joy of the poor village idiot, Peter, in listening to Hans Andersen's stories; and the washerwoman who imitates animal noises to keep the soap suds out of her mind.

The petty, ingrained village life is contrasted unfavourably with the warmth and friendliness of the Manchester slum. It is, perhaps, overdrawn. Surely no one would sit up half the night to spy on her neighbours as Jane Wilkins is portrayed as doing; and the picture of Sarah, the jealous sister-in-law who finds herself ousted by the young enthusiastic wife, is hardly convincing. Even less so is her eventual change of heart and reconciliation.

Although *Miss Nobody* has the faults of a first novel written by an unsophisticated, down-to-earth woman with a comparatively limited perception of life, it has a vigour and depth which gives promise for her future work. *Miss Nobody* was the only Carnie novel published before the First World War but it is more than possible that some of her other work was actually written or prepared in her apprenticeship period. In 1917 her most successful novel, *Helen of the Four Gates*, was published with a print run of 25,000, and was subsequently made into a film. *The House that Jill Built* came out in 1920 and was followed in the same year by *The Marriage of Elizabeth*. Four years later, *General Belinda* was published and her only overtly socialist novel, *This Slavery*, came out in 1925. Her last publication was *Eagles Crag* in 1931.

At the foot of a story in *The Wheatsheaf* in April 1915 was a note saying that Miss Ethel Carnie and Mr Alfred Holdsworth had been married at Burnley on Saturday 3 April.[40] Shortly after the wedding, Ethel marched with Alfred to the railway station to see him off on his journey to his military call-up. She carried the Red Flag.[41]

Ethel Carnie's apprenticeship as a writer, as a woman and as a socialist had ended. She graduated with a record of

work in the movement and a creditable collection of published work. She had the knowledge that she had satisfied a need for literature which class-conscious workers and especially women workers could recognise as the experiences of their own lives and struggles from the working-class point of view.

NOTES

1. 'Tissie Wakes up', *Women Folk*, vol. 4, no. 35 (2 March 1910), p.755.
2. Preface to *Rhymes from the Factory* by a Factory Girl (Blackburn, 1907).
3. G. C. Miller, *The Evolution of a Cotton Town* (Blackburn, 1951), p.228.
4. 'The Bookworm', *Rhymes from the Factory*, p.1.
5. *ibid.*
6. Among authors with whose work Ethel Carnie was familiar were: Hillaire Belloc, Charlotte Brontë, Thomas Carlyle, Edward Carpenter, Coleridge, Dante, Defoe, Dickens, Ebenezer Elliott, Emerson, Bret Harte, Victor Hugo, Jerome K. Jerome, Ernest Jones, Keats, Lamb, Meredith, Scott, Shelley, Swinburne, Thackeray and Wordsworth.
7. 'The Rich and the Poor', *Rhymes from the Factory*, p.22.
8. Keighly Snowdon, 'A Book of the Hour', *The Woman Worker*, vol. I (new series), no. 5 (3 July 1908), p.135.
9. Robert Blatchford, 'A Lancashire Fairy', *The Woman Worker*, vol. I, no. 6 (10 July 1908), p.155.
10. *ibid.*
11. 'The Editor's Chair', *The Woman Worker*, vol. IV, no. 4 (28 July 1909), p.84.
12. *ibid.*, no. 5 (4 August 1909), p.108.
13. *ibid.*, no. 6 (11 August 1909), p.132.
14. *ibid.*, no. 8 (25 August 1909), p.180.
15. *ibid.*, no. 11 (15 September 1909), p.252.
16. *ibid.*, no. 18 (3 November 1909), p.418.
17. *ibid.*, no. 7 (18 August 1909), p.156.
18. *ibid.*, no. 23 (8 December 1909), p.518.
19. *ibid.*, no. 20 (17 November 1909), p.458.
20. *ibid.*
21. *ibid.*, no. 17 (27 October 1909), p.296.

22.   *ibid.*, no. 16 (20 October 1909), p.372.
23.   PEM, 'A Factory Girl Poet', *Millgate Monthly*, V (November 1909), pp.70-2. PEM is Priscilla E. Moulder.
24.   Editorial, *The Woman Worker*, vol. III, no. 10 (10 March 1909), p.228.
25.   'The Editor's Chair', *The Woman Worker*, vol. IV, no. 24 (15 December 1909), p.538.
26.   'The Editor's Chair', *Women Folk*, vol. IV, no. 31 (2 February 1910), p.678.
27.   Pa B, 'An Open Letter To Miss Ethel', *ibid.*, p.685.
28.   Ethel Carnie, *Songs of a Factory Girl* (London, 1911).
29.   *Blackburn Weekly Telegraph*, 15 April 1911.
30.   *ibid.*
31.   'Weaver', *The Wheatsheaf* (October 1911), p.60.
32.   'The Giver', *The Wheatsheaf* (December 1913), p.101.
33.   'The Unbeliever', *The Woman Worker*, vol. II, no. 17 (28 April 1909), p.390.
34.   'His Family', *The Wheatsheaf* (October 1912), p.61.
35.   Ethel Carnie, *The Lamp Girl and Other Tales* (London, n.d.).
36.   T. A. Jackson in *The Sunday Worker*, 21 April 1929.
37.   'Miss Nobody and Its Author', *The Wheatsheaf* (November 1913). p.85.
38.   For a full assessment of *Miss Nobody* see P. M. Ashraf, *Introduction to Working-Class Literature in Great Britain*, Part II: Prose (Berlin, 1979), pp.178-86.
39.   *ibid.*, p.185.
40.   *The Wheatsheaf* (April 1915), p.173.
41.   Oral evidence from the late Bessie and Harold Dickenson of Nelson.

Chronological Table

The following tables provide a conspectus of the period, relating the fiction discussed in this book to principal events in the history of the British labour movement, and to mainstream English fiction. It should be clear that the lefthand section contains neither an exclusive nor a comprehensive list of socialist narratives.

	Fiction discussed in this book	Events in labour history	Some mainstream English Fiction
1880			Butler, *The Way of All Flesh* (in progress)
1881		(Social) Democratic Federation founded	James, *The Portrait of a Lady*
1882			
1883		SDF turning socialist Marx died	
1884	Allen, *Philistia* Shaw, *An Unsocial Socialist* (serialised)	Third Reform Act SDF split Socialist League founded Fabian Society founded *Justice* started	
1885	Zola, *Germinal* Morris, *The Pilgrims of Hope* (ser.)	*Commonweal* started	

	Fiction discussed in this book	Events in labour history	Some mainstream English fiction
1886	Morris, *A Dream of John Ball* (ser.) James, *The Princess Casamassima*	Trafalgar Square riot	Gissing, *Demos*
1887	Harkness, *A City Girl* Rutherford, *The Revolution in Tanner's Lane*	'Bloody Sunday'	
1888	Howell, *A More Excellent Way* Bramsbury, *A Working Class Tragedy* (ser.) Harkness, *Out of Work*		
1889	Leslie, *How the Strike Began* Harkness, *Captain Lobe*	Great Dock Strike Second International founded *Fabian Essays*	Gissing, *The Nether World*
1890	Morris, *News from Nowhere* (ser.) Harkness, *A Manchester Shirtmaker*		
1891	Tirebuck, *Dorrie* Leslie, *The Seed She Sowed* Oakhurst, *The Universal Strike of 1899*	*Clarion* appeared	Hardy, *Tess of the D'Urbervilles* Wilde, *The Picture of Dorian Grey*
1892			
1893	Clarke, *The Knobstick* Fawcett, *Harmann the Anarchist* Adderley, *Stephen Remarx*	ILP founded 'Coal War' Blatchford's *Merrie England*	
1894	Black, *The Agitator*		Moore, *Esther Waters*

	Fiction discussed in this book	Events in labour history	Some mainstream English fiction
1895	Tirebuck, *Miss Grace of All Souls'* Fletcher, *Lost in the Mine* Brooke, *Transition*	Engels died	Hardy, *Jude the Obscure* Wells, *The Time Machine*
1896	Lawson, *While the Billy Boils*	Morris died	Morrison, *A Child of the Iago*
1897	Voynich, *The Gadfly*	*Social Democrat* started	Maugham, *Liza of Lambeth* Stevenson, *Weir of Hermiston*
1898	Clarke, *The Daughter of the Factory* (ser.) Laycock, *The Young Gaffer* (ser.) Sykes and Walker, *Ben o' Bill's*		
1899	Plant, *Tamsie*	Boer War	Conrad, *Heart of Darkness* (ser.)
1900	Laycock, *Steve the Outlander* Plant, *The Conductor's Sweetheart* (ser.) Lawson, *On the Track and over the Sliprails* Birrel, *Love in a Mist*	Labour Representation Committee founded	
1901	Clarke, *Driving* (ser.) Lawson, *Joe Wilson and His Mates*	Taff Vale decision	Kipling, *Kim*
1902	Tamlyn, *The Hermit of Cottondale* (ser.) Lawson, *Children of the Bush*		James, *The Wings of the Dove*

	Fiction discussed in this book	Events in labour history	Some mainstream English fiction
1903	Rossetti, *A Girl among the Anarchists* Tamlyn, *The Love of a Northern Farmer* (ser.)	Women's Social and Political Union founded	
1904	Haslam, *The Handloom Weaver's Daughter*		Conrad, *Nostromo*
1905	Harkness, *George Eastmont: Wanderer*		Forster, *Where Angels Fear to Tread*
1906	Clarke, *Lancashire Lasses and Lads* Laycock, *Warren of Manchester* Tressell, *The Ragged Trousered Philanthropists* (in progress) Sinclair, *The Jungle* Andersen Nexö, *Pelle the Conqueror*	Labour Party founded 29 Labour MPs returned in general election	Galsworthy, *The Man of Property*
1907	Clarke, *The Red Flag* Conrad, *The Secret Agent* London, *The Iron Heel* Gorky, *Mother*		
1908	Harris, *The Bomb*		Bennett, *The Old Wives' Tale*
1909			Wells, *Tono-Bungay*
1910			Forster, *Howard's End*
1911		Seamen's and transport workers' strike *Daily Herald* started	

272

	Fiction discussed in this book	Events in labour history	Some mainstream English fiction
1912		Miners' strike	
1913	Carnie, *Miss Nobody*		Lawrence, *Sons and Lovers*
1914	Tressell, *The Ragged Trousered Philanthropists* (publ.)	Outbreak of war	Joyce, *Dubliners*

Index

Note: Only authors substantially discussed have their works listed.